Praise for
Robert Jordan and
The Wheel of Time®

"His huge, ambitious Wheel of Time series helped redefine the genre." —George R. R. Martin, internationally bestselling author of *A Game of Thrones*

"Anyone who's writing epic secondary world fantasy knows Robert Jordan isn't just a part of the landscape, he's a monolith within the landscape." —Patrick Rothfuss, internationally bestselling author of The Kingkiller Chronicle

"*The Eye of the World* was a turning point in my life. I read, I enjoyed. (Then continued on to write my larger fantasy novels.)" —Robin Hobb, *New York Times* bestselling author of The Farseer Trilogy

"Robert Jordan's work has been a formative influence and an inspiration for a generation of fantasy writers." —Brent Weeks, *New York Times* bestselling author of *The Way of Shadows*

"Jordan has come to dominate the world Tolkien began to reveal." —*The New York Times*

"One of fantasy's most acclaimed series." —*USA Today*

"Robert Jordan was a giant of fiction whose words helped a whole generation of fantasy writers, including myself, find our true voices. I thanked him then, but I didn't thank him enough." —Peter V. Brett, internationally bestselling author of The Demon Cycle

"[Robert Jordan's] impact on the place of fantasy in the culture is colossal. . . . He brought innumerable readers to

The Wheel of Time®

By Robert Jordan

New Spring: The Novel
The Eye of the World
The Great Hunt
The Dragon Reborn
The Shadow Rising
The Fires of Heaven
Lord of Chaos
A Crown of Swords
The Path of Daggers
Winter's Heart
Crossroads of Twilight
Knife of Dreams

By Robert Jordan and Brandon Sanderson

The Gathering Storm
Towers of Midnight
A Memory of Light

By Robert Jordan and Teresa Patterson

The World of Robert Jordan's The Wheel of Time

By Robert Jordan, Harriet McDougal, Alan Romanczuk, and Maria Simons

The Wheel of Time Companion

THE PATH
OF
DAGGERS

ROBERT JORDAN

A TOM DOHERTY ASSOCIATES BOOK
NEW YORK

This is a work of fiction. All of the characters, organizations, and events portrayed in this novel are either products of the author's imagination or are used fictitiously.

THE PATH OF DAGGERS

Copyright © 1998 by Bandersnatch Group, Inc.

Excerpt from *Winter's Heart* copyright © 2000 by Bandersnatch Group, Inc.

The phrase "The Wheel of Time" and the snake-wheel symbol are trademarks of Bandersnatch Group, Inc.

All rights reserved.

Maps by Ellisa Mitchell
Interior illustrations by Matthew C. Nielsen and Ellisa Mitchell

A Tor Book
Published by Tom Doherty Associates
120 Broadway
New York, NY 10271

www.tor-forge.com

Tor® is a registered trademark of Macmillan Publishing Group, LLC.

ISBN 978-1-250-25209-8

Our books may be purchased in bulk for promotional, educational, or business use. Please contact your local bookseller or the Macmillan Corporate and Premium Sales Department at 1-800-221-7945, extension 5442, or by e-mail at MacmillanSpecialMarkets@macmillan.com.

First Edition: October 1998
First Premium Mass Market Edition: March 2020

Printed in the United States of America

0 9 8 7 6 5 4 3 2 1

For Harriet
My light, my life, my heart,
forever

Contents

MAP. . . . . .xii–xiii

PROLOGUE: Deceptive Appearances 1

1   To Keep the Bargain. 31
2   Unweaving 53
3   A Pleasant Ride 72
4   A Quiet Place 85
5   The Breaking Storm 99
6   Threads 119
7   A Goatpen 143
8   A Simple Country Woman 160
9   Tangles 186
10 Changes 206
11 Questions and an Oath 229
12 New Alliances. 246
13 Floating Like Snow. 267
14 Message from the M'Hael 279
15 Stronger Than Written Law 293
16 Unexpected Absences. 310
17 Out on the Ice 331
18 A Peculiar Calling 346
19 The Law 357
20 Into Andor. 375
21 Answering the Summons 391
22 Gathering Clouds 406
23 Fog of War, Storm of Battle 420
24 A Time for Iron. 441
25 An Unwelcome Return. 473
26 The Extra Bit 484
27 The Bargain 503
28 Crimsonthorn 526
29 A Cup of Sleep 540
30 Beginnings 558
31 After 574

GLOSSARY 577

Who would sup with the mighty must climb the path of daggers.

—Anonymous notation found inked in the margin of a manuscript history (believed to date to the time of Artur Hawkwing) of the last days of the Tovan Conclaves

On the heights, all paths are paved with daggers.

—Old Seanchan saying

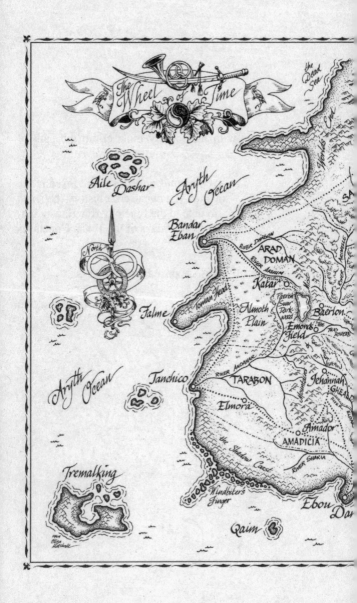

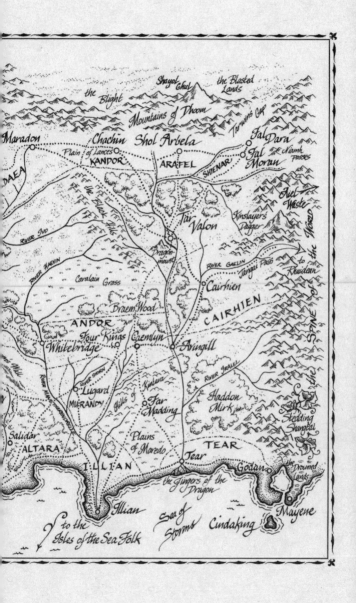

PROLOGUE

Deceptive Appearances

Ethenielle had seen mountains lower than these misnamed Black Hills, great lopsided heaps of half-buried boulders, webbed with steep twisting passes. A number of those passes would have given a goat pause. You could travel three days through drought-withered forests and brown-grassed meadows without seeing a single sign of human habitation, then suddenly find yourself within half a day of seven or eight tiny villages, all ignorant of the world. The Black Hills were a rugged place for farmers, away from the trade routes, and harsher now than usual. A gaunt leopard that should have vanished at the sight of men watched from a steep slope, not forty paces away, as she rode past with her armored escort. Westward, vultures wheeled patient circles like an omen. Not a cloud marred the blood-red sun, yet there were clouds of a sort. When the warm wind blew, it raised walls of dust.

With fifty of her best men at her heels, Ethenielle rode unconcernedly, and unhurriedly. Unlike her near-legendary ancestor Surasa, she had no illusion that the weather would heed her wishes just because she held the Throne of the Clouds, while as for haste. . . . Their carefully coded, closely guarded letters had agreed on the order of march, and that had been determined by each person's need to travel without attracting notice. Not an easy task. Some had thought it impossible.

Frowning, she considered the luck that had let her come this far without having to kill anyone, avoiding those flyspeck villages even when it meant days added to the journey. The few Ogier *stedding* presented no problem—Ogier paid little heed to what happened among humans, most times, and less than usual of late, it seemed—but the villages. . . . They were too small to hold eyes-and-ears for the White Tower, or for this fellow who claimed to be the Dragon Reborn—perhaps he was; she could not decide which way would be worse—too small, yet peddlers did pass through, eventually. Peddlers carried as much gossip as trade goods, and they spoke to people who spoke to other people, rumor flowing like an ever-branching river, through the Black Hills and into the world outside. With a few words, a single shepherd who had escaped notice could light a signal fire seen five hundred leagues off. The sort of signal fire that set woods and grasslands aflame. And cities, maybe. Nations.

"Did I make the right choice, Serailla?" Vexed at herself, Ethenielle grimaced. She might not be a girl any longer, but her few gray hairs hardly counted her old enough to let her mindless tongue flap in the breeze. The decision was made. It had been on her mind, though. Light's truth, she was not so unconcerned as she wanted to be.

Ethenielle's First Councilor heeled her dun mare closer to the Queen's sleek black gelding. Round face placid, dark eyes considering, Lady Serailla could have been a farmwife suddenly stuck into a noblewoman's riding dress, but the mind behind those plain, sweaty features was as sharp as any Aes Sedai's. "The other choices only carried different risks, not lesser," she said smoothly. Stout yet as graceful in her saddle as she was at dancing, Serailla was always smooth. Not oily, or false; just completely unflappable. "Whatever the truth, Majesty, the White Tower appears to be paralyzed as well as shattered. You could have sat watching the Blight while the world crumbled behind you. You could have if you were someone else."

The simple need to act. Was that what had brought her here? Well, if the White Tower would not or could not do what had to be done, then someone must. What good to guard the Blight if the world did crumble behind her?

Ethenielle looked to the slender man riding at her other side, white streaks at his temples giving him a supercilious air, the ornately sheathed Sword of Kirukan resting in the crook of one arm. It was called the Sword of Kirukan, at any rate, and the fabled warrior Queen of Aramaelle might have carried it. The blade was ancient, some said Power-wrought. The two-handed hilt lay toward her as tradition demanded, though she herself was not about to try using a sword like some fire-brained Saldaean. A queen was supposed to think, lead, and command, which no one could manage while trying to do what any soldier in her army could do better. "And you, Swordbearer?" she said. "Do you have any qualms at this late hour?"

Lord Baldhere twisted in his gold-worked saddle to glance back at the banners carried by horsemen behind them, cased in tooled leather and embroidered velvet. "I don't like hiding who I am, Majesty," he said fussily, straightening around. "The world will know us soon enough, and what we've done. Or tried to do. We'll end up dead or in the histories or both, so they might as well know what names to write." Baldhere had a biting tongue, and he affected to care more for music and his clothes than anything else—that well-cut blue coat was the third he had worn already today—but as with Serailla, appearances deceived. The Swordbearer to the Throne of the Clouds bore responsibilities much heavier than that sword in its jeweled scabbard. Since the death of her husband some twenty years ago, Baldhere had commanded the armies of Kandor for her in the field, and most of her soldiers would have followed him to Shayol Ghul itself. He was not counted among the great captains, but he knew when to fight and when not, as well as how to win.

"The meeting place must be just ahead," Serailla said suddenly, just as Ethenielle saw the scout Baldhere had sent forward, a sly fellow named Lomas who wore a foxhead crest on his helmet, rein in atop the peak of the pass ahead. With his lance slanted, he made the arm gesture for "assembly point in sight."

Baldhere swung his heavy-shouldered gelding and bellowed a command for the escort to halt—he could bellow, when he had a mind to—then spurred the bay to catch up to her and Serailla. It was to be a meeting between long-standing allies, but as they rode past Lomas, Baldhere gave the lean-faced man a curt order to "Watch and relay"; should anything go wrong, Lomas would signal the escort forward to bring their queen out.

Ethenielle sighed faintly when Serailla nodded approval at the command. Allies of long standing, yet the times bred suspicion like flies on a midden. What they were about stirred the heap and set the flies swirling. Too many rulers to the south had died or vanished in the last year for her to feel any comfort in wearing a crown. Too many lands had been smashed as thoroughly as an army of Trollocs could have achieved. Whoever he was, this al'Thor fellow had much to answer for. Much.

Beyond Lomas the pass opened into a shallow bowl almost too small to be named a valley, with trees too widely spaced to be called a thicket. Leatherleaf and blue fir and three-needle pine held to some green along with a few oaks, but the rest were sheathed in brown if not bare-branched. To the south, however, lay what had made this spot a good choice for meeting. A slender spire like a column of gleaming golden lace lay slanting and partly buried in the bare hillside, a good seventy paces of it showing above the treetops. Every child in the Black Hills old enough to run off leading strings knew of it, but there was not a village inside four days' travel, nor would anyone come within ten miles willingly. The stories of this place spoke of mad visions, of the dead walking, and death at touching the spire.

Ethenielle did not consider herself fanciful, yet she shivered slightly. Nianh said the spire was a fragment from the Age of Legends, and harmless. With luck, the Aes Sedai had no reason to recall that conversation of years ago. A pity the dead could not be made to walk, here. Legend said Kirukan had beheaded a false Dragon with her own hands, and borne two sons by another man who could channel. Or maybe the same one. She might have known how to go about their purpose and survive.

As expected, the first pair of those Ethenielle had come to meet was waiting, each with two attendants. Paitar Nachiman had many more creases in his long face than the stunningly handsome older man she had admired as a girl, not to mention too little hair and most of that gray. Fortunately he had relinquished the Arafellin fashion for braids and wore his hair cut short. But he sat his saddle straight-backed, his shoulders needed no padding in that embroidered green silk coat, and she knew he still could wield the sword at his hip with vigor and skill. Easar Togita, square-faced and his scalp shaved except for a white topknot, his plain coat the color of old bronze, was a head shorter than

the King of Arafel, and slighter, yet he made Paitar look
almost soft. Easar of Shienar did not scowl—if anything,
a touch of sadness seemed permanent in his eyes—but he
might have been made from the same metal as the long
sword on his back. She trusted both men—and hoped their
familial connections helped secure that trust. Alliances
by marriage had always bound the Borderlands together
as much as their war against the Blight did, and she had
a daughter wed to Easar's third son and a son to Paitar's
favorite granddaughter, as well as a brother and two sisters
married into their Houses.

Their companions appeared as different as their kings.
As always, Ishigari Terasian looked just risen from a stupor
after a drunken feast, as fat a man as she had ever seen in
a saddle; his fine red coat was rumpled, his eyes bleary, his
cheeks unshaven. By contrast, Kyril Shianri, tall and lean,
and nearly as elegant as Baldhere despite the dust and sweat
on his face, with silver bells on his boot tops and gloves as
well as fastened to his braids; he wore his usual expression
of dissatisfaction and had a way of always peering coolly
down his prominent nose at anyone but Paitar. Shianri really
was a fool in many ways—Arafellin kings rarely made
much pretense of listening to councilors, relying instead
on their queens—but he was more than he appeared at a
glance. Agelmar Jagad could have been a larger version of
Easar, a simple, plainly garbed man of steel and stone with
more weapons hung about him than Baldhere carried, sudden death waiting to be unleashed, while Alesune Chulin
was as slim as Serailla was stout, as pretty as Serailla was
plain, and as fiery as Serailla was calm. Alesune seemed
born to her fine, blue silks. It was well to remember that
judging Serailla by her surface was a mistake, too.

"Peace and the Light favor you, Ethenielle of Kandor,"
Easar said gruffly as Ethenielle reined in before them,
and at the same time Paitar intoned, "The Light embrace
you, Ethenielle of Kandor." Paitar still had a voice to make
women's hearts beat faster. And a wife who knew he was
hers to his bootsoles; Ethenielle doubted that Menuki had
ever had a jealous moment in her life, or cause for one.

She made her own greetings just as short, ending with a
direct "I hope you've come this far without detection."

Easar snorted and leaned on his cantle, eyeing her grimly.

A hard man, but eleven years widowed and still mourning. He had written poetry for his wife. There was always more than the surface. "If we've been seen, Ethenielle," he grumbled, "then we might as well turn back now."

"You speak of turning back already?" Between his tone and a flip of his tasseled reins, Shianri managed to combine disdain with barely enough civility to forestall a challenge. Even so, Agelmar studied him coldly, shifting in his saddle slightly, a man recalling where each of his weapons was placed. Old allies in many battles along the Blight, but those new suspicions swirled.

Alesune made her mount dance, a gray mare as tall as a warhorse. The thin white streaks in her long black hair suddenly seemed crests on a helmet, and her eyes made it easy to forget that Shienaran women neither trained with weapons nor fought duels. Her title was simply *shatayan* of the royal household, yet whoever believed any *shatayan*'s influence stopped at ordering the cooks and maids and victualers made a grave error. "Foolhardiness is not courage, Lord Shianri. We leave the Blight all but unguarded, and if we fail, maybe even if we succeed, some of us could find our heads on spikes. Perhaps all of us will. The White Tower may well see to it if this al'Thor does not."

"The Blight seems almost asleep," Terasian muttered, whiskers rasping as he rubbed his fleshy chin. "I've never seen it so quiet."

"The Shadow never sleeps," Jagad put in quietly, and Terasian nodded as if that, too, was something to consider. Agelmar was the best general of them all, one of the best to be found anywhere, but Terasian's place at Paitar's right hand had not come because he was a good drinking companion.

"What I've left behind can guard the Blight short of the Trolloc Wars coming again," Ethenielle said in a firm voice. "I trust you've all done as well. It hardly matters, though. Does anyone believe we truly can turn back now?" She made that last question dry, expecting no answer, but she received one.

"Turn back?" a young woman's high voice demanded behind her. Tenobia of Saldaea galloped into the gathering, drawing her white gelding up so that he reared flamboyantly. Thick lines of pearls marched down the dark gray sleeves of her narrow-skirted riding habit, while red-and-gold embroidery swirled thickly to emphasize the narrowness of her waist and the roundness of her bosom. Tall for a woman, she managed to be pretty if not beautiful despite a nose that was overbold at best. Large tilted eyes of a dark deep blue certainly helped, but so did a confidence in herself so strong that she seemed to glow with it. As expected, the Queen of Saldaea was accompanied only by Kalyan Ramsin, one of her numerous uncles, a scarred and grizzled man with the face of an eagle and thick mustaches that curved down around his mouth. Tenobia Kazadi tolerated the counsel of soldiers, but no one else. "I will not turn back," she went on fiercely, "whatever the rest of you do. I sent my *dear* Uncle Davram to bring me the head of the false Dragon Mazrim Taim, and now he and Taim *both* follow this al'Thor, if I can believe half what I hear. I have close to fifty thousand men behind me, and whatever you decide, *I* will not turn back until my uncle and al'Thor learn exactly who rules Saldaea."

Ethenielle exchanged glances with Serailla and Baldhere while Paitar and Easar began telling Tenobia that they also meant to keep on. Serailla gave her head the smallest shake, made the slightest shrug. Baldhere rolled his eyes openly. Ethenielle had not exactly hoped Tenobia might decide at the last to stay away, but the girl would surely make difficulties.

Saldaeans were a strange lot—Ethenielle had often wondered how her sister Einone managed so well married to yet another of Tenobia's uncles—yet Tenobia carried that strangeness to extremes. You expected showiness from any Saldaean, but Tenobia took delight in shocking Domani and making Altarans seem drab. Saldaean tempers were legendary; hers was wildfire in a high wind, and you could never tell what would provide the spark. Ethenielle did not even want to think of the difficulty in getting the woman to listen to reason when she did not want to; only Davram Bashere had ever been able to do that. And then there was the question of marriage.

Tenobia was still young, though years past the age she should have wed—marriage was a duty for any member of a ruling House, the more so for a ruler; alliances had to be made, an heir provided—yet Ethenielle had never considered the girl for any of her own sons. Tenobia's requirements for a husband were on a level with everything else about her. He must be able to face and slay a dozen Myrddraal at once. While playing the harp *and* composing poetry. He must be able to confound scholars while riding a horse down a sheer cliff. Or perhaps up it. Of course he would have to defer to her—she was a queen, after all—except that sometimes Tenobia would expect him to ignore whatever she said and toss her over his shoulder. The girl wanted *exactly* that! And the Light help him if he chose to toss when she wanted deference, or to defer when she wanted the other. She never said any of this right out, but any woman with wits who had heard her talk about men could piece it together in short order. Tenobia would die a maiden. Which meant her uncle Davram would succeed, if she left him alive after this, or else Davram's heir.

A word caught Ethenielle's ear and jerked her upright in her saddle. She should have been paying attention; too much was at stake. "Aes Sedai?" she said sharply. "What about Aes Sedai?" Save for Paitar's, their White Tower advisors had all left at news of the troubles in the Tower, her own Nianh and Easar's Aisling vanishing without a trace. If Aes Sedai had gained a hint of their plans. . . . Well, Aes Sedai always had plans of their own. Always. She would dislike discovering that she was putting her hands into two hornet's nests, not just one.

Paitar shrugged, looking a trifle embarrassed. That was no small trick for him; he, like Serailla, let nothing upset him. "You hardly expected me to leave Coladara behind, Ethenielle," he said in soothing tones, "even if I could have kept the preparations from her." She had not; his favorite sister was Aes Sedai, and Kiruna had given him a deep fondness for the Tower. Ethenielle had not expected it, but she had hoped. "Coladara had visitors," he continued. "Seven of them. Bringing them along seemed prudent, under the circumstances. Fortunately, they require little convincing. None, in truth."

"The Light illumine and preserve our souls," Ethenielle breathed, and heard near echos from Serailla and Baldhere. "Eight sisters, Paitar? Eight?" The White Tower surely knew every move they intended, now.

"And I have five more," Tenobia put in as if announcing

she had a new pair of slippers. "They found me just before I left Saldaea. By chance, I'm sure; they appeared as surprised as I was. Once they learned what I was doing—I still don't know how they did, but they did—once they learned, I was sure they'd go scurrying to find Memara." Her brows furrowed in a momentary glare. Elaida had miscalculated badly in sending a sister to try bullying Tenobia. "Instead," she finished, "Illeisien and the rest were more intent on secrecy than I."

"Even so," Ethenielle insisted. "Thirteen sisters. All that is needed is for one of them to find some way to send a message. A few lines. A soldier or a maid intimidated. Does any of you think you can stop them?"

"The dice are out of the cup," Paitar said simply. What was done, was done. Arafellin were almost as odd as Saldaeans, in Ethenielle's book.

"Farther south," Easar added, "it may be well to have thirteen Aes Sedai with us." That brought a silence while the implications hung in the air. No one wanted to voice them. This was far different from facing the Blight.

Tenobia gave a sudden, shocking laugh. Her gelding tried to dance, but she settled him. "I mean to press south as fast as I can, but I invite you all to dine with me in my camp tonight. You can speak with Illeisien and her friends, and see whether your judgment matches mine. Perhaps tomorrow night we can all gather in Paitar's camp and question his Coladara's friends." The suggestion was so sensible, so obviously necessary, that it brought instant agreement. And then Tenobia added, as if an afterthought, "My uncle Kalyan would be honored if you allowed him to sit beside you tonight, Ethenielle. He admires you greatly."

Ethenielle glanced toward Kalyan Ramsin—the fellow had sat his horse silently behind Tenobia, never speaking, hardly seeming to breathe—she merely glanced at him, and for an instant that grizzled eagle unhooded his eyes. For an instant, she saw something she had not seen since her Brys died, a man looking not at a queen, but at a woman. The shock of it was a blow taking her breath. Tenobia's eyes darted from her uncle to Ethenielle, her tiny smile quite satisfied.

Outrage flared in Ethenielle. That smile made it all clear as spring water, if Kalyan's eyes had not. This chit of a girl thought to marry off this fellow to *her*? This *child* presumed to . . . ? Suddenly, ruefulness replaced fury. She herself had been younger when she arranged her widowed sister Nazelle's wedding. A matter of state, yet Nazelle had come to love Lord Ismic despite all her protests in the beginning. Ethenielle had been arranging others' marriages for so long that she had never considered that her own would make a very strong tie. She looked at Kalyan again, a longer look. His leathery face was all proper respect once more, yet she saw his eyes as they had been. Any consort she chose would have to be a hard man, but she had always demanded a chance of love for her children's marriages, if not her siblings', and she would do no less for herself.

"Instead of wasting daylight on chatter," she said, more breathless than she could have wished, "let us do what we came for." The Light sear her soul, she was a woman grown, not a girl meeting a prospective suitor for the first time. "Well?" she demanded. This time, her tone was suitably firm.

All of their agreements had been made in those careful letters, and all of their plans would have to be modified as they moved south and circumstances changed. This meeting had only one real purpose, a simple and ancient ceremony of the Borderlands that had been recorded only seven times in all the years since the Breaking. A simple ceremony that would commit them beyond anything words could do, however strong. The rulers moved their horses closer while the others drew back.

Ethenielle hissed as her belt knife slashed across her left palm. Tenobia laughed at cutting hers. Paitar and Easar might as well have been plucking splinters. Four hands reached out and met, gripped, heart's blood mingling, dripping to the ground, soaking into the stony dirt. "We are one, to the death," Easar said, and they all spoke with him. "We are one, to the death." By blood and soil, they were committed. Now they had to find Rand al'Thor. And do what needed to be done. Whatever the price.

Once she was sure that Turanna could sit up on the cushion unaided, Verin rose and left the slumped White sister sipping water. Trying to sip, anyway. Turanna's teeth chattered on the silver cup, which was no surprise. The tent's entry-way stood low enough that Verin had to duck in order to put her head out. Weariness augered into her back when she bent. She had no fear of the woman shivering behind her in a coarse black woolen robe. Verin held the shield on her tight, and she doubted Turanna possessed enough strength in her legs at the moment to contemplate leaping on her from behind, even if such an incredible thought occurred to her. Whites just did not think that way. For that matter, in Turanna's condition, it was doubtful she would be able to channel a hair for several hours yet, even if she were not shielded.

The Aiel camp covered the hills that hid Cairhien, low earth-colored tents filling the space between the few trees left standing this close to the city. Faint clouds of dust hung in the air, but neither dust nor heat nor the glare of an angry sun bothered the Aiel at all. Bustle and purpose filled the camp to equal any city. Within her sight were men butchering game and patching tents, sharpening knives and making the soft boots they all wore, women cooking over open fires, baking, working small looms, looking after some of the few children in the camp. Everywhere white-robed *gai'shain* darted about carrying burdens, or stood beating rugs, or tended packhorses and mules. No hawkers or shopkeepers. Or carts and carriages, of course. A city? It was more like a thousand villages gathered in one spot, though men greatly outnumbered women and, except for the blacksmiths making their anvils ring, nearly every man not in white carried weapons. Most of the women did, as well.

The numbers certainly equaled one of the great cities', more than enough to envelop a few Aes Sedai prisoners completely, yet Verin saw a black-robed woman plodding away not fifty paces off, struggling to pull a waist-high pile of rocks behind her on a cowhide. The deep cowl hid her face, but no one in the camp except the captive sisters wore those black robes. A Wise One strolled along close to the hide, glowing with the Power as she shielded the prisoner, while a pair of Maidens flanked the sister, using switches to urge her on whenever she faltered. Verin wondered whether she had been meant to see. That very morning she had passed a wild-eyed Coiren Saeldain, sweat streaming down her face, with a Wise One and two tall Aielmen for

escort and a large basket heaped with sand bending her
back as she staggered up a slope. Yesterday it had been
Sarene Nemdahl. They had set her moving handfuls of
water from one hide bucket to another beside it, switched
her to move faster, then switched her for every drop spilled
when the water spilled because they were switching her to
move faster. Sarene had stolen a moment to ask Verin why,
though not as if she expected any answer. Verin certainly
had not been able to supply one before the Maidens drove
Sarene back to her useless labor.

She suppressed a sigh. For one thing, she could not truly
like seeing sisters treated so, whatever the reasons or need,
and for another, it was obvious that a fair number of the
Wise Ones wanted. . . . What? For her to know that being Aes Sedai counted for nothing here? Ridiculous. That
had been made abundantly clear days ago. Perhaps that she
could be put into a black robe, too? For the time she thought
she was safe from that, at least, but the Wise Ones hid a
number of secrets she had yet to puzzle out, the smallest
of them how their hierarchy worked. Very much the smallest, yet life and a whole skin lay wrapped inside that one.
Women who gave commands sometimes took them from
the very women they had been commanding earlier, and
then later it was turned about again, all without rhyme or
reason that she could see. No one ever ordered Sorilea,
though, and in that might lie safety. Of a sort.

She could not help a surge of satisfaction. Early this
morning in the Sun Palace, Sorilea had demanded to know
what shamed wetlanders most. Kiruna and the other sisters
did not understand; they made no real efforts to see what
was happening out here, perhaps fearing what they might
learn, fearing the strains knowledge might put on their
oaths. They still struggled to justify taking the path fate had
pushed them down, but Verin already had reasons for the
path she followed, and purpose. She also had a list in her
pouch, ready to hand to Sorilea when they were alone. No
need to let the others know. Some of the captives she had
never met, but she thought that for most women, that list
summed up the weaknesses Sorilea was seeking. Life was
going to grow much more difficult for the women in black.
And her own efforts would be aided no end, with luck.

Two great hulking Aielmen, each an axe handle wide

across the shoulders, sat right outside the tent, seemingly absorbed in a game of cat's cradle, but they had looked around immediately when her head appeared through the tentflaps. Coram had risen like a serpent uncoiling for all of his size, and Mendan waited only to tuck the string away. Had she been standing straight, her head barely would have reached the chest of either. She could have turned them both upside down and paddled them, of course. Had she dared. She had been tempted from time to time. They were her assigned guides, her protection against misunderstandings in the camp. And doubtless they reported everything she said or did. In some ways she would have preferred to have Tomas with her, but only some. Keeping secrets from your Warder was far more difficult than keeping them from strangers.

"Please tell Colinda that I'm done with Turanna Norill," she told Coram, "and ask her to send Katerine Alruddin to me." She wanted to deal first with the sisters who had no Warders. He nodded once before trotting off without speaking. These Aielmen were not much for civility.

Mendan settled into a crouch, watching her with startlingly blue eyes. One of them stayed with her no matter what she said. A strip of red cloth was tied around Mendan's temples and marked with the ancient symbol of Aes Sedai. Like the other men who wore that, like the Maidens, he seemed to be waiting for her to make a mistake. Well, they were not the first, and a great way from the most dangerous. Seventy-one years had passed since she had last made a serious mistake.

She gave Mendan a deliberately vague smile and started to pull back into the tent, when suddenly something caught her eye and held her like a vise. If the Aielman had tried to cut her throat right then, she might not have noticed.

Not far from where she stood stooped over in the mouth of the tent, nine or ten women knelt in a row, rolling the grindstones on flat stone handmills much like those on any isolated farms. Other women brought grain in baskets and took away the coarse flour. The nine or ten women knelt in dark skirts and pale blouses, folded scarves holding their hair back. One, noticeably shorter than the rest, the only one with hair that did not hang to her waist or below, wore not even a single necklace or bracelet. She glanced up, the resentment on her sun-pinkened face sharpening as she met Verin's gaze. Only for an instant, though, before she cringed hurriedly to her task.

Verin jerked back into the tent, her stomach roiling queasily. Irgain was Green Ajah. Or rather, had been Green, before Rand al'Thor stilled her. Being shielded dulled and fuzzed the bond to your Warder, but being stilled snapped it as surely as death. One of Irgain's two apparently had fallen over dead from the shock, and the other had died trying to kill thousands of Aiel without making any effort to escape. Very likely Irgain wished she also were dead. Stilled. Verin pressed both hands to her middle. She would *not* sick up. She had seen worse than a stilled woman. Much worse.

"There's no hope, is there?" Turanna muttered in a thick voice. She wept silently, staring into the silver cup in her trembling hands at something distant and horrifying. "No hope."

"There is always a way if you only look for it," Verin said, absently patting the woman's shoulder. "You must always look."

Her thoughts raced, and none touched Turanna. Irgain's stilling made her belly feel full of rancid grease, the Light knew. But what was the woman doing grinding grain? And dressed like the Aiel women! Had she been put to work just there so Verin could see? Foolish question; even with a *ta'veren* as strong as Rand al'Thor only a few miles away, there was some limit to the number of coincidences she would accept. Had she miscalculated? At worst, it could not be a large error. Only, small mistakes sometimes proved as fatal as large. How long could she hold out if Sorilea decided to break her? A distressingly short time, she suspected. In some ways, Sorilea was as hard as anyone she had ever met. And not a thing she could say that would stop it. A worry for another day. There was no point getting ahead of herself.

Kneeling, she put a little effort into comforting Turanna, but not too much. Soothing words that sounded as hollow to her as they did to Turanna, judging by the bleakness in her eyes. Nothing could change Turanna's circumstances except Turanna, and that had to come from within herself. The White sister just wept harder, making no sound as her shoulders shook, tears streaming down her face. The entry of two Wise Ones and a pair of young Aielmen who could not straighten up inside the tent was something of a relief. For Verin, anyway. She rose and curtsied smoothly, but none of them had any interest in her.

Daviena was a green-eyed woman with yellow-red hair, Losaine gray-eyed with dark hair that only showed glints of red in the sun, both head-and-shoulders taller than she, both wearing the expressions of women given a grimy task they wished on someone else. Neither could channel strongly enough to have any certainty of holding Turanna by herself, but they linked as though they had been forming circles all their lives, the light of *saidar* around one seeming to blend with that around the other despite the fact that they stood apart. Verin forced her face into a smile to keep from frowning. Where *had* they learned that? She would have wagered all she possessed that they had not known how only a few days ago.

Everything went quickly then, and smoothly. As the crouching men lifted Turanna to her feet by the arms, she let the silver cup fall. Empty, luckily for her. She did not struggle, which was just as well, considering that either could have carried her off under one arm like a sack of grain, but her mouth hung open, emitting a wordless keening. The Aiel paid no heed. Daviena, focusing the circle, assumed the shield, and Verin let go of the Source completely. None of them trusted her enough to let her hold *saidar* without a known reason, no matter what oaths she had sworn. Neither appeared to notice, but they surely would have had she held on. The men hauled Turanna away, her bare feet dragging across the layered carpets that floored the tent, and the Wise Ones followed them out. And that was that. What could be done with Turanna had been done.

Letting out a long breath, Verin sagged onto one of the bright, tasseled cushions. A fine golden ropework tray sat on the carpets next to her. Filling one of the mismatched silver cups from a pewter pitcher, she drank deeply. This was thirsty work, and tiring. Hours of daylight remained, yet she felt as if she had carried a heavy chest twenty miles. Over hills. The cup went back onto the tray, and she pulled the small, leather-bound notebook from behind her belt. It always took a little time for them to fetch those she asked for. A few moments to peruse her notes—and make some— would not be amiss.

There was no need for notes about the captives, but the sudden appearance of Cadsuane Melaidhrin, three days ago now, gave cause for concern. What *was* Cadsuane after? The woman's companions could be dismissed, but Cadsuane herself was a legend, and even the believable parts of the legend made her very dangerous indeed. Dangerous and unpredictable. She took a pen from the small wooden writing case she always carried, reached toward the stoppered ink bottle in its scabbard. And another Wise One entered the tent.

Verin scrambled to her feet so quickly that she dropped her notebook. Aeron could not channel at all, yet Verin made a much deeper curtsy for the graying woman than she had for Daviena and Losaine. At the bottom of her dip, she let go of her skirts to reach for her book, but Aeron's fingers reached it first. Verin straightened, calmly watching the taller woman thumb through the pages.

Sky blue eyes met hers. A winter sky. "Some pretty drawings and a great deal about plants and flowers," Aeron said coldly. "I see nothing concerning the questions you were sent to ask." She thrust the book at Verin more than handed it to her.

"Thank you, Wise One," Verin said meekly, tucking the book back safely behind her belt. She even added another curtsy for good measure, just as deep as the first. "I have the habit of noting down what I see." One day she would have to write out the cipher she used in her notebooks—a lifetime's worth of them filled cupboards and chests in her rooms above the White Tower library—one day, but she hoped not soon. "As for the . . . um . . . prisoners, so far they all say variations of the same thing. The *Car'a'carn* was to be housed in the Tower until the Last Battle. His . . . um . . . mistreatment . . . began because of an escape attempt. But you know that already, of course. Never fear, though; I'm sure I will learn more." All true, if not all of the truth; she had seen too many sisters die to risk sending others to the grave without a very good reason. The trouble was deciding what might cause that risk. The manner of young al'Thor's kidnapping, by an embassy supposedly treating with him, enraged the Aiel to the point of murder, yet what she called his "mistreatment" barely angered them at all as far as she could tell.

Gold and ivory bracelets clattered softly as Aeron adjusted her dark shawl. She peered down as though trying to read Verin's thoughts. Aeron seemed to stand high among the Wise Ones, and while Verin occasionally had seen a smile crease those dark-tanned cheeks, a warm and easy smile, it was never directed at an Aes Sedai. *We never suspected that* you *would be the ones to fail,* she had told Verin somewhat murkily. There had been nothing unclear in the rest of it, however. *Aes Sedai have no honor. Give me one hair of suspicion, and I will strap you till you cannot stand, with my own hands. Give me two hairs, and I will stake you out for the vultures and the ants.* Verin blinked up at her, trying to appear open. And meek; she must not forget meek. Docile, and compliant. She did not feel fear. In her time she had faced harder stares, from women—and men— without so much as Aeron's slim compunction about ending her life. But a good deal of effort had gone into being sent to ask those questions. She could not afford to waste it now. If only these Aiel let more show on their faces.

Abruptly she became aware that they were no longer alone in the tent. Two flaxen-haired Maidens had entered with a black-robed woman a hand shorter than either. They were half-holding her upright. At one side stood Tialin, a lanky redhead wearing a grim expression behind the light of *saidar*, shielding the black-robed prisoner. The sister's hair hung in sweat-soaked ringlets to her shoulders and strands that clung to her face, which bore so much dirt that Verin did not recognize her at first. High cheekbones, but not very high, a nose with just the hint of a hook to it, and the slightest tilt to the brown eyes. . . . Beldeine. Beldeine Nyram. She had instructed the girl in a few novice classes.

"If I may ask," she said carefully, "why was she brought? I asked for another." Beldeine had no Warder despite being Green—she had been raised to the shawl barely three years ago, and Greens were often especially choosy about their first—but if they started bringing whoever they selected, the next might have two or three Warders. She thought she could deal with two more today, but not if either had even one Warder. And she doubted they would give her a second chance at any of them.

"Katerine Alruddin escaped last night," Tialin nearly spat, and Verin gasped.

"You let her *escape*?" she burst out without thinking. Tiredness gave no excuse, but the words spilled from her tongue before she could stop them. "How could you be so foolish? She's Red! And neither a coward nor weak in the Power! The *Car'a'carn* could be in danger! Why were we not told of this when it happened?"

"It was not discovered until this morning," one of the Maidens growled. Her eyes could have been polished sapphires. "A Wise One and two *Cor Darei* were poisoned, and the *gai'shain* who brought them drink was found with his throat cut."

Aeron arched an eyebrow at the Maiden coldly. "Did she speak to you, Carahuin?" Both Maidens suddenly became engrossed in the task of keeping Beldeine on her feet. Aeron merely glanced at Tialin, but the red-haired Wise One lowered her gaze. Verin was the next recipient of those attentions. "Your concern for Rand al'Thor does you . . . honor," Aeron said grudgingly. "He will be guarded. You have no need to know more. Or so much." Abruptly her tone hardened. "But apprentices do not use that tone with Wise Ones, Verin Mathwin *Aes Sedai*." The last words were a sneer.

Smothering a sigh, Verin all but fell into another deep curtsy, a part of her wishing she were even as slim as she had been on arriving in the White Tower. She was not really constructed for all this bending and bobbing. "Forgive me, Wise One," she said humbly. Escaped! The circumstances made everything plain, to her if not to the Aiel. "Apprehension must have loosened my wits." A pity she had no way to make sure Katerine met with a fatal accident. "I will do my best to remember in the future." Not so much as the flicker of an eyelash told whether Aeron accepted that. "May I assume her shield, Wise One?"

Aeron nodded without looking at Tialin, and Verin quickly embraced the Source, taking up the shield Tialin released. It never ceased to amaze her that women who could not channel gave orders so freely to women who could. Tialin was not much weaker in the Power than Verin, yet she watched Aeron nearly as warily as the Maidens did, and when the Maidens hurried out of the tent at a gesture of

Aeron's hand, leaving Beldeine wavering where she stood, Tialin was only a step behind.

Aeron did not go, however, not immediately. "You will not speak of Katerine Alruddin to the *Car'a'carn*," she said. "He has enough to occupy his thoughts without giving him trifles to worry over."

"I will say nothing to him about her," Verin agreed quickly. Trifles? A Red with Katerine's strength was no trifle. Perhaps a note. It needed thought.

"Be certain to hold your tongue, Verin Mathwin, or you will use it to howl."

There seemed nothing to say to that, so Verin concentrated on meekness and docility, making yet another curtsy. Her knees wanted to groan.

Once Aeron departed, Verin allowed herself a sigh of relief. She had been afraid Aeron intended to remain. Gaining permission to be alone with the prisoners had required nearly as much effort as getting Sorilea and Amys to decide they needed to be questioned, and by someone intimate with the White Tower. If they ever learned they had been guided to that decision. . . . It was a worry for another day. She seemed to be piling up a great many of those.

"There's enough water to wash your face and hands, at least," she told Beldeine mildly. "And if you wish, I will Heal you." Every sister she had interviewed had carried at least a few welts. The Aiel did not beat the prisoners except for spilling water or balking at a task—the haughtiest words of defiance earned only scornful laughter, if that—but the black-robed women were herded like animals, a tap of the switch for go or turn or stop, and a harder tap if they did not obey quickly enough. Healing made other things easier, too.

Filthy, sweaty, wavering like a reed in the wind, Beldeine curled her lip. "I would rather bleed to death than be Healed by you!" she spat. "Maybe I should have expected to see you groveling to these wilders, these savages, but I never thought you would stoop to revealing Tower secrets! That ranks with treason, Verin! With rebellion!" She grunted contemptuously. "I suppose if you didn't shy at that, you'll stop at nothing! What else have you and the others taught them besides linking?"

Verin clicked her tongue irritably, not bothering to set the young woman straight. Her neck ached from looking up at Aiel—for that matter, even Beldeine stood a hand or more taller than she—her knees ached from curtsying, and entirely too many women who should know better had flung blind contempt and foolish pride at her today. Who should know better than an Aes Sedai that a sister had to wear many faces in the world? You could not always over-awe people, or bludgeon them, either. Besides, far better to behave as a novice than be punished like one, especially when it earned you only pain and humiliation. Even Kiruna had to see the sense of that eventually.

"Sit down before you fall down," she said, suiting her own words. "Let me guess what you've been doing to-day. By all that dirt, I'd say digging a hole. With your bare hands, or did they let you use a spoon? When they decide it's finished, they will just make you fill it again, you know. Now, let me see. Every part I can see of you is grubby, but that robe is clean, so I expect they had you digging in your skin. Are you sure you don't want Healing? Sunburn can be painful." She filled another cup with water and wafted it across the tent on a flow of Air to hover in front of Beldeine. "Your throat must be parched."

The young Green stared unsteadily at the cup for a moment; then suddenly her legs gave way and she collapsed onto a cushion with a bitter laugh. "They . . . *water* me frequently." She laughed again, though Verin could not see the joke. "As much as I want, so long as I swallow it all." Study-ing Verin angrily, she paused, then went on in a tight voice. "That dress looks very nice on you. They burned mine; I saw them. They stole everything except this." She touched the golden Great Serpent around her left forefinger, a bright golden gleam among the dirt. "I suppose they couldn't find quite enough nerve for that. I know what they're trying to do, Verin, and it won't work. Not with me, not with any of us!"

She was still on her guard. Verin set the cup down on the flowered carpet beside Beldeine, then took up her own and sipped before speaking. "Oh? What are they trying to do?"

This time, the other woman's laugh was brittle as well as harsh. "Break us, and you know it! Make us swear oaths to al'Thor, the way you did. Oh, Verin, how could you? Swearing fealty! And worse, to a *man*, to *him*! Even if you could bring yourself to rebel against the Amyrlin Seat, against the White Tower . . ." She made the two sound much the same. ". . . how could you do *that*!"

For a moment Verin wondered whether things would be better if the women now held in the Aiel camp had been caught up as she had been, a woodchip in the millrace of Rand al'Thor's *ta'veren* swirl, words pouring from her mouth before they had time to form in her brain. Not words she could never have said on her own—that was not how *ta'veren* affected you—but words she might possibly have said one time in a thousand under those circumstances, one time in ten thousand. No, the arguments had been long and hot over whether oaths given in that way had to be kept; and the arguments over how to keep them still continued. Much better as it was. Absently she fingered a hard shape inside her belt pouch, a small brooch, a translucent stone carved into what appeared to be a lily with too many petals. She never wore it, but it had not been out of her reach in nearly fifty years.

"You are *da'tsang*, Beldeine. You must have heard that." She did not need Beldeine's curt nod; telling the despised one was part of Aiel law, like pronouncing sentence. That much she knew, if very little more. "Your clothes, and anything else that would burn, were put to the fire because no Aiel would own anything that once belonged to a *da'tsang*. The rest was hacked to pieces or hammered into scrap, even the jewelry you had with you, and buried under a pit dug for a jakes."

"My . . . ? My horse?" Beldeine asked anxiously.

"They didn't kill the horses, but I don't know where yours is." Being ridden by someone in the city, probably, or perhaps given to an Asha'man. Telling her that might do more harm than good. Verin seemed to recall that Beldeine was one of those young women who had very deep feelings for horses. "They let you keep the ring to remind you of who you were, and increase your shame. I don't know whether they would let you swear to Master al'Thor if you begged. It would take something incredible on your part, I think."

"I won't! Never!" The words rang hollow, though, and Beldeine's shoulders slumped. She was shaken, but not sufficiently.

Verin put on a warm smile. A fellow had once told her that her smile made him think of his dear mother. She hoped he had not been lying about that, at least. He had tried to slide a dagger between her ribs a little later, and her smile had been the last thing he ever saw. "I can't think of the reason you would. No, I fear what you have to look forward to is useless labor. That's shaming, to them. Bone shaming. Of course, if they realize you don't see it that way. . . . Oh, my. I'll wager you didn't like digging without any clothes on, even with Maidens for guards, but think of, say, standing in a tent full of men that way?" Beldeine flinched. Verin prattled on; she had developed prattling to something of a Talent. "They'd only make you stand there, of course. *Da'tsang* aren't allowed to do anything useful unless there's great need, and an Aielman would as soon put his arm around a rotting carcass as. . . . Well, that's not a pleasant thought, is it? In any case, that's what you have to look forward to. I know you'll resist as long as you can, though I'm not sure what there is to resist. They won't try to get information out of you, or anything that people usually do with prisoners. But they won't let you go, not ever, until they're sure the shame is so deep in you there's nothing else left. Not if it takes the rest of your life."

Beldeine's lips moved soundlessly, but she might as well have spoken the words. *The rest of my life.* Shifting uncomfortably on her cushion, she grimaced. Sunburn or welts or simply the ache of unaccustomed work. "We will be rescued," she said finally. "The Amyrlin won't leave us. . . . We'll be rescued, or we'll— We *will* be rescued!" Snatching up the silver cup from beside her, she tilted her head back to gulp until it was empty, then thrust it out for more. Verin floated the pewter pitcher over and set it down so the young woman could pour for herself.

"Or you'll escape?" Verin said, and Beldeine's dirty hands jerked, splashing water down the sides of the cup. "Really, now. You have as much chance of that as you do of rescue. You're surrounded by an army of Aiel. And apparently al'Thor can call up a few hundred of those Asha'man whenever he wants, to hunt you down." The other woman shivered at that, and Verin nearly did. That little mess should have been stopped as soon as it started. "No, I fear you must make your own way, somehow. Deal with things as they are. You are quite alone in this. I know they don't let you speak to the others. Quite alone," she sighed. Wide eyes stared at her as they might have at a red adder. "There's no need to make it worse than it must be. Let me Heal you."

She barely waited for the other woman's pitiful nod before moving to kneel beside her and place hands on Beldeine's head. The young woman was almost as ready as she could be. Opening herself to more of *saidar*, Verin wove the flows of Healing, and the Green gasped and quivered. The half-filled cup dropped from her hands, and a flailing arm knocked the pitcher onto its side. Now she *was* as ready as she could be.

In the moments of confusion that gripped anyone after being Healed, while Beldeine still blinked and tried to come back to herself, Verin opened herself further, opened herself through the carved-flower *angreal* in her pouch. Not a very powerful *angreal*, but enough, and she needed every bit of the extra Power it gave her for this. The flows she began weaving bore no resemblance to Healing. Spirit predominated by far, but there was Wind and Water, Fire and Earth, the last of some difficulty for her, and even the skeins of Spirit had to be divided again and again, placed with an intricacy to boggle a weaver of fine carpets. Even if a Wise One poked her head into the tent, with the smallest of luck she would not possess the rare Talent needed to realize what Verin was doing. There would still be difficulties, perhaps painful difficulties one way and another, but she could live with anything short of true discovery.

"What . . . ?" Beldeine said drowsily. Her head would have lolled except for Verin's grip, and her eyelids were half-closed. "What are you . . . ? What is happening?"

"Nothing that will harm you," Verin told her reassuringly. The woman might die inside the year, or in ten, as a result of this, but the weave itself would not harm her. "I promise you, this is safe enough to use on an infant." Of course, that depended on what you did with it.

She needed to lay the flows in place thread by thread, but talking seemed to help rather than hinder. And too long a silence might rouse suspicion, if her twin guardians were listening. Her eyes darted frequently to the dangling doorflaps. She wanted some answers she had no intention of sharing, answers none of the women she questioned were likely to give freely even if they knew them. One of the smaller effects of this weave was to loosen the tongue and open the mind as well as any herb ever could, an effect that came on quickly.

Dropping her voice almost to a whisper, she continued. "The al'Thor boy seems to think he has supporters of some kind inside the White Tower, Beldeine. In secret, of course; they must be." Even a man with his ear pressed to the fabric of the tent should be able to hear only that they were talking. "Tell me anything you know about them."

"Supporters?" Beldeine murmured, attempting a frown that seemed beyond her ability. She stirred, though it hardly deserved the word agitation, feeble and uncoordinated. "For him? Among the sisters? It can't be. Except for those of you who. . . . How could you, Verin? Why didn't you fight it?"

Verin *tsked* vexedly. Not for the foolish suggestion that she should have fought a *ta'veren*. The boy seemed so certain. Why? She kept her voice low. "Do you have no suspicions, Beldeine? Did you hear no rumors before you left Tar Valon? No whispers? No one who hinted at approaching him differently? Tell me."

"No one. Who could . . . ? No one would. . . . I admired Kiruna so." There was a hint of loss in Beldeine's sleepy voice, and tears leaking from her eyes made tracks through the dirt. Only Verin's hands kept her sitting upright.

Verin continued to lay down the threads of her weaving, eyes flashing from her work to the doorflaps and back. She felt a little like sweating herself. Sorilea might decide she needed help with the questioning. She might bring out one of the sisters from the Sun Palace. Should any sister learn of this, stilling was a very real possibility. "So you were going to deliver him to Elaida neatly washed and well-behaved," she said in a slightly louder tone. The quiet had gone on too long. She did not want that pair outside reporting that she was whispering with the prisoners.

"I couldn't . . . speak out . . . against Galina's decision. She led . . . by the Amyrlin's command." Beldeine shifted again, weakly. Her voice was still dreamy, but it picked up an agitated edge. Her eyelids fluttered. "He had to . . . be made . . . to obey! He had to be! Shouldn't have been . . . treated so harshly. Like putting . . . him to . . . question. Wrong."

Verin snorted. Wrong? Disastrous was more like it. A disaster from the first. Now the man looked at any Aes Sedai almost the way Aeron did. And if they had succeeded in carrying him to Tar Valon? A *ta'veren* like Rand al'Thor actually inside the White Tower? A thought to make a stone tremble. However it had turned out, disaster would surely have been too mild a word. The price paid at Dumai's Wells was small enough, for avoiding that.

She went on asking questions in a tone that could be heard clearly by anyone listening outside. Asking questions she already had answers for, and avoiding those too dangerous to be answered. She paid little heed to the words coming out of her mouth or to Beldeine's replies. Mainly she concentrated on her weaving.

A great many things had captured her interest over the years, not all strictly approved of by the Tower. Almost every wilder who came to the White Tower for training—both true wilders, who really had begun teaching themselves, and girls who merely had started touching the Source because the spark born in them had quickened on its own; for some sisters, there was no real difference—nearly every one of those wilders had created at least one trick for herself, and those tricks almost invariably fell under one of two headings. A way to listen in on other people's conversations, or a way of making people do as they wanted.

The first, the Tower did not care much about. Even a wilder who had gained considerable control on her own quickly learned that as long as she wore novice white, she was not to so much as touch *saidar* without a sister or one of the Accepted standing over her. Which did tend to limit eavesdropping rather sharply. The other trick, however, smelled too akin to forbidden Compulsion. Oh, it was just a way to make Father give her dresses or trinkets he did not want to buy, or make Mother approve of young men she ordinarily ran off, things of that nature, but the Tower rooted the trick out most effectively. Many of the girls and women Verin had spoken to over the years could not make themselves form the weaves, much less use them, and a fair number could not even make themselves remember how. From bits and pieces and scraps of half-remembered weaves created by untrained girls for very limited purposes, Verin had reconstructed a thing forbidden by the Tower since its founding. In the beginning it had been simple curiosity on her part. *Curiosity,* she thought wryly, working at the weave on Beldeine, *has made me climb into more than one pickling kettle.* Usefulness came later.

"I suppose Elaida meant to keep him down in the open cells," she said conversationally. The grill-walled cells were intended for men who could channel, as well as initiates of the Tower under close arrest, wilders who had claimed to be Aes Sedai, and anyone else who must be both confined and blocked off from the Source. "Not a comfortable place for the Dragon Reborn. No privacy. Do you believe he is the Dragon Reborn, Beldeine?" This time she paused to listen.

"Yes." The word was a long hiss, and Beldeine rolled frightened eyes toward Verin's face. "Yes . . . but he must . . . be kept . . . safe. The world . . . must be . . . safe . . . from him."

Interesting. They had all said the world had to be kept safe from him; what was interesting was those who thought he needed protection, too. Some who had said that, surprised her.

To Verin's eyes, the weave she had made resembled nothing so much as a haphazard tangle of faintly glowing transparent threads all bundled around Beldeine's head, with four threads of Spirit trailing out of the mess. Two of those, opposite one another, she pulled, and the tangle collapsed slightly, falling inward, into something on the edge of order. Beldeine's eyes shot open wide, staring into the far distance.

In a firm, low voice, Verin gave her instructions. More like suggestions, though she phrased them as commands. Beldeine would have to find reasons within herself to obey; if she did not, then all this had been so much wasted effort.

With the final words, Verin pulled the other two threads of Spirit, and the tangle collapsed further. This time, though, it fell into what seemed perfect order, a pattern more precise, more complicated than the most intricate lace, and complete, tied off by the same action that began its shrinking. This time, it continued to fall inward on itself, inward around Beldeine's head. Those faintly glowing threads sank into her, vanished. Her eyes rolled back in her head, and she began to thrash, limbs quivering. Verin held her as gently as she could, but Beldeine's head still whipped from side to side, and her bare heels drummed on the carpets. Soon, only the most careful Delving would tell that anything had been done, and not even that would identify the weave. Verin had tested that carefully, and if she did say so herself, none surpassed her at Delving.

Of course the thing was not truly Compulsion as ancient texts described it. The weaving went with painful slowness, cobbled together as it was, and there was that need for a reason. It helped a great deal if the object of the weave was emotionally vulnerable, but trust was absolutely essential. Even catching someone by surprise did no good if they were suspicious. That fact cut down its usefulness with men considerably; *very* few men lacked suspicion around Aes Sedai.

Distrust aside, men were very bad subjects, unfortunately. She could not understand why. Most of those girls' weaves had been intended for their fathers or other men. Any strong personality might begin to question his own actions—or even forget doing them, which led to another set of problems—but all things being equal, men were much more likely to. Much more likely. Perhaps it was the suspicion again. Why, once a man had even remembered the weaves being woven on him, if not the instructions she had given him. Such a lot of bother *that* caused! Not something she would risk again.

At last Beldeine's convulsions lessened, stopped. She raised a filthy hand to her head. "What—? What happened?" she said, almost inaudibly. "Did I faint?" Forgetfulness was another good point about the weave, not unexpectedly. After all, Father must not remember that you somehow made him buy that expensive dress.

"The heat is very bad," Verin said, helping her to sit up again. "I have felt light-headed myself once or twice today." From weariness, not heat. Handling that much of *saidar* took it out of you, especially when you had already done it four times today. The *angreal* did nothing to buffer the effects once you stopped using it. She could have used a steadying hand herself. "I think that's about enough. If you're fainting, perhaps they'll find something for you to do out of the sun." The prospect did not seem to cheer Beldeine at all.

Rubbing the small of her back, Verin stuck her head

out of the tent. Coram and Mendan stopped their game of
cat's cradle once more; there was no sign that either had
listened, but she would not wager her life on it. She told
them that she was finished with Beldeine and, after a moment's thought, added that she needed another pitcher of
water since Beldeine had overturned hers. Both men's faces
darkened beneath their tans. That would be passed along
to the Wise One who came for Beldeine. It would serve as
something more to help her reach her decision.

The sun still had a long way to fall to the horizon, but the
ache in her back told her it was time to stop for the day. She
could still do one more sister, but if she did, by morning she
would feel it in every muscle. Her eyes fell on Irgain, now
with the women carrying baskets to the handmills. How
would her life have gone if she had not been so curious,
Verin wondered. For one thing, she would have married
Eadwin and remained in Far Madding instead of going to
the White Tower. She would be long dead, for another, and
the children she had never had, and her grandchildren, too.

With a sigh, she turned back to Coram. "When Mendan
returns, would you go tell Colinda that I would like to see
Irgain Fatamed?" The pain in her muscles tomorrow would
be a small penance for Beldeine's suffering over that spilled
water, but that was not why she did it, or even her curiosity,
really. She still had a task. Somehow, she had to keep young
Rand alive until it was time for him to die.

The room might have been in a grand palace, except that it
had neither windows nor doors. The fire on a golden marble
hearth gave no heat, and the flames did not consume the
logs. The man seated at a table with gilded legs, centered
on a silk carpet woven with glittering threads of gold and
silver, cared little for the trappings of this Age. They were
necessary to impress; no more. Not that he really needed
more than himself to overawe the stiffest pride. He called
himself Moridin, and surely no one had ever had more right
to name himself Death.

From time to time he idly stroked one of the two mindtraps that hung on plain silken cords around his neck. At
his touch, the blood-red crystal of the *cour'souvra* pulsed,
swirls moving in endless depths like the beating of a heart.

His real attention was on the game laid out before him on the table, thirty-three red pieces and thirty-three green arrayed across a playing surface of thirteen squares by thirteen. A re-creation of the early stages of a famous game. The most important piece, the Fisher, black-and-white like the playing surface, still waited in its starting place on the central square. A complex game, *sha'rah*, ancient long before the War of Power. *Sha'rah*, *tcheran*, and *no'ri*, the game now called simply "stones," each had adherents who claimed it encompassed all the subtleties of life, but Moridin had always favored *sha'rah*. Only nine people living even remembered the game. He had been a master of it. Much more complex than *tcheran* or *no'ri*. The first object was capture of the Fisher. Only then did the game truly begin.

A servant approached, a slim graceful young man clad all in white, impossibly handsome, bowing as he presented a crystal goblet on a silver tray. He smiled, but it did not touch his black eyes, eyes more lifeless than simply dead. Most men would have felt uncomfortable having that gaze on them. Moridin merely took the goblet and motioned the servant away. The vintners of this time produced some excellent wines. He did not drink, though.

The Fisher held his attention, baiting him. Several pieces had varying moves, but only the Fisher's attributes altered according to where it stood; on a white square, weak in attack yet agile and far-ranging in escape; on black, strong in attack but slow and vulnerable. When masters played, the Fisher changed sides many times before the end. The green-and-red goal-row that surrounded the playing surface could be threatened by any piece, but only the Fisher could move onto it. Not that he was safe, even there; the Fisher was never safe. When the Fisher was yours, you tried to move him to a square of your color behind your opponent's end of the board. That was victory, the easiest way, but not the only one. When your opponent held the Fisher, you attempted to leave him no choice for the Fisher but to move onto your color. Anywhere at all along the goal-row would do; holding the Fisher could be more dangerous than not. Of course, there was a third path to victory in *sha'rah*, if you took it before letting yourself be trapped. The game always degenerated in a bloody melee, then, victory coming only with complete annihilation of your enemy. He had tried that, once, in desperation, but the attempt had failed. Painfully.

Fury boiled suddenly in Moridin's head, and black flecks swam across his eyes as he seized the True Power. Ecstasy that amounted to pain thundered through him. His hand closed around the two mindtraps, and the True Power closed around the Fisher, snatching it into the air, a hair from crushing it to powder, crushing the powder out of existence. The goblet shattered in his hand. His grip bordered on crushing the *cour'souvra*. The *saa* were a blizzard of black, but they did not hinder his sight. The Fisher was always worked as a man, a bandage blinding his eyes and one hand pressed to his side, a few drops of blood dripping through his fingers. The reasons, like the source of the name, were lost in the mist of time. That troubled him sometimes, enraged him, what knowledge might be lost in the turnings of the Wheel, knowledge he needed, knowledge he had a right to. A right!

Slowly he set the Fisher back on the board. Slowly his fingers uncurled from around the *cour'souvra*. There was no need for destruction. Yet. Icy calm replaced rage in the blink of an eye. Blood and wine dripped from his gashed hand, unnoticed. Perhaps the Fisher did come from some dim remnant of a memory of Rand al'Thor, the shadow of a shadow. It did not matter. He realized he was laughing, and made no effort to stop. On the board, the Fisher stood waiting, but in the greater game, al'Thor moved already to his wishes. And soon, now. . . . It was very hard to lose a game when you played both sides of the board. Moridin laughed so hard that tears rolled down his face, but he was not aware of them.

CHAPTER

I

To Keep the Bargain

The Wheel of Time turns, and Ages come and pass, leaving memories that become legend. Legend fades to myth, and even myth is long forgotten when the Age that gave it birth comes again. In one Age, called the Third Age by some, an Age yet to come, an Age long past, a wind rose above the great mountainous island of Tremalking. The wind was not the beginning. There are neither beginnings nor endings to the turning of the Wheel of Time. But it was *a* beginning.

East the wind blew across Tremalking, where the fair-skinned Amayar farmed their fields, and made fine glass and porcelain, and followed the peace of the Water Way. The Amayar ignored the world beyond their scattered islands, for the Water Way taught that this world was only illusion, a mirrored reflection of belief, yet some watched the wind carry dust and deep summer heat where cold winter rains should be falling, and they remembered tales heard from the Atha'an Miere. Tales of the world beyond, and what prophecy said was to come. Some looked to a hill where a massive stone hand rose from the earth, holding a clear crystal sphere larger than many houses. The Amayar had their own prophecies, and some of those spoke of the hand and the sphere. And the end of illusions.

Onward the wind blew into the Sea of Storms, eastward beneath a searing sun in a sky abandoned by clouds, whipping the tops of green sea swells, battling winds from the south and westward winds, shearing and swirling as the waters below heaved. Not yet the storms of winter's heart, though winter should have been half gone, much less the greater storms of a dying summer, but winds and currents that could be used by ocean-faring folk to coast around the continent from World's End to Mayene and beyond, then back again. Eastward the wind howled, over rolling ocean where the great whales rose and sounded, and flying fish soared on outstretched fins two paces and more across, eastward, now whirling north, east and north, over small fleets of fishing ships dragging their nets in the shallower seas. Some of those fishermen stood gaping, hands idle on the lines, staring at a huge array of tall vessels and smaller that purposefully rode the wind's hard breath, shattering swells with bluff bows, slicing swells with narrow, their banner a golden hawk with talons clutching lightning, a multitude of streaming banners like portents of storm. East and north and on, and the wind reached the broad, ship-filled harbor of Ebou Dar, where hundreds of Sea Folk vessels rode as they did in many ports, awaiting word of the Coramoor, the Chosen One.

Across the harbor the wind roared, tossing small ships and large, across the city itself, gleaming white beneath the unfettered sun, spires and walls and color-ringed domes, streets and canals bustling with the storied southern industry. Around the shining domes and slender towers of the Tarasin Palace the wind swirled, carrying the tang of salt, lifting the flag of Altara, two golden leopards on a field of red and blue, and the banners of ruling House Mitsobar, the Sword and Anchor, green on white. Not yet the storm, but a harbinger of storms.

Skin prickled between Aviendha's shoulder blades as she strode ahead of her companions through palace hallways tiled in dozens of pleasing bright hues. A sense of being watched that she had last felt while still wed to the spear. *Imagination,* she told herself. *Imagination and knowing there are enemies about I cannot face!* Not so long ago that crawling sensation had meant someone might be intending to kill her. Death was nothing to fear—everyone died, today or on another—but she did not want to die like a rabbit kicking in a snare. She had *toh* to meet.

Servants scurried by close along the walls, bobbing bows and curtsies, dropping their eyes almost as if they understood the shame of the lives they lived, yet surely it could not be *them* that made her want to twist her shoulders. She had tried schooling herself to see servants, but even now, with the skin creeping on her back, her gaze slid around them. It had to be imagination, and nerves. This was a day for imagination and nerves.

Unlike the servants, rich silk tapestries snagged at her eye, and the gilded stand-lamps and ceiling lamps lining the corridors. Paper-thin porcelain in reds and yellows and greens and blues stood in wall niches and tall open-work cabinets alongside ornaments of gold and silver, ivory and crystal, scores upon scores of bowls and vases and caskets and statuettes. Only the most beautiful truly caught her gaze; whatever wetlanders thought, beauty held more worth than gold. There was much beauty here. She would not have minded taking her share of the fifth from this place.

Vexed with herself, she frowned. That was not an honorable thought beneath a roof that had offered her shade and water freely. Without ceremony, true, but also without debt or blood, steel or need. Yet better that than thinking about a small boy alone somewhere out in this corrupt city. Any city was corrupt—of that much she was certain, now, having seen some part of four—but Ebou Dar was the last where she would have let a child run loose. What she could not understand was why thoughts of Olver came unless she worked to avoid them. He was no part of the *toh* she had to Elayne, and to Rand al'Thor. A Shaido spear had taken his father, starvation and hardship his mother, yet had it been her own spear that took both, the boy was still a treekiller, Cairhienin. Why should she fret over a child from that blood? Why? She attempted to concentrate on the weave she was to make, but although she had practiced under Elayne's eye until she could have formed it sleeping, Olver's wide-mouthed face intruded. Birgitte worried about him even more than she, but Birgitte's breast held a strangely soft heart for small boys, especially ugly ones.

Sighing, Aviendha gave up trying to ignore her companions' conversation behind her, though irritation crackled through it like heat lightning. Even that was better than upsetting herself over a son of treekillers. Oathbreakers. A despised blood the world would be better off without. No concern or worry of hers. None. Mat Cauthon would find the boy in any case. He could find anything, it seemed. And listening settled her, somehow. The prickling faded away.

"I don't like it one bit!" Nynaeve was muttering, continuing an argument begun back in their rooms. "Not a bit, Lan, do you hear me?" She had announced her dislike at least twenty times already, but Nynaeve never surrendered just because she had lost. Short and dark-eyed, she strode fiercely, kicking her divided blue skirts, one hand rising to hover near her thick, waist-long braid, then thrust down firmly before rising again. Nynaeve kept a tight hold on anger and irritation when Lan was around. Or tried to. An inordinate pride filled her about marrying him. The close-fitting embroidered blue coat over her yellow-slashed silk riding dress hung open, showing far too much bosom in the wetlander way, just so she could display his heavy gold finger ring on a fine chain around her neck. "You have no right to promise to *take care* of me like that, Lan Mandragoran," she went on firmly. "I am not a porcelain figurine!"

He paced at her side, a man of proper size, towering head and shoulders and more above her, the eye-wrenching cloak of a Warder hanging down his back. His face seemed hacked from stone, and his gaze weighed the threat in every servant who passed, examined every crossing corridor and wall niche for hidden attackers. Readiness radiated from him, a lion on the brink of his charge. Aviendha had grown up around dangerous men, but never one to match *Aan'allein*. Had death been a man, she would have been him.

"You are Aes Sedai, and I am a Warder," he said in a deep, level voice. "Taking care of you is my duty." His tone softened, conflicting sharply with his angular face and bleak, never-changing eyes. "Besides, caring for you is my heart's desire, Nynaeve. You can ask or demand anything of me, but never to let you die without trying to save you. The day you die, I die."

That last he had not said before, not in Aviendha's hearing, and it hit Nynaeve like a blow to the stomach; her eyes started half out of her head, and her mouth worked soundlessly. She appeared to recover quickly, though, as always. Pretending to resettle her blue-plumed hat, a ridiculous thing like a strange bird roosting atop her head, she shot a glance at him from beneath the wide brim.

Aviendha had begun to suspect that the other woman often used silence and supposedly significant looks to cover ignorance. She suspected. Nynaeve knew little more about men,

about dealing with one man, than she did herself. Facing
them with knives and spears was much easier than loving
one. Much easier. How did women manage being married
to them? Aviendha had a desperate need to learn, and no
idea how. Married to *Aan'allein* only a day, Nynaeve had
changed much more than simply in trying to control her
temper. She seemed to flit from startlement to shock, however much she attempted to hide it. She fell into dreaminess
at odd moments, blushed at innocuous questions, and—she
denied this fiercely, even when Aviendha had seen her—she
giggled over nothing at all. There was no point in trying to
learn anything from Nynaeve.

"I suppose *you're* going to tell me about Warders and
Aes Sedai again, as well," Elayne said coolly to Birgitte.
"Well, you and I aren't married. I expect you to *guard*
my back, but I will *not* have you making promises about
me *behind* it." Elayne wore garments as inappropriate as
Nynaeve's, a gold-embroidered Ebou Dari riding dress of
green silk, suitably high-necked but with an oval opening
that bared the inner slopes of her breasts. Wetlanders spluttered at the mention of a sweat tent or being unclothed in
front of *gai'shain*, then walked about half-exposed where
any stranger could see. Aviendha did not really mind for
Nynaeve, but Elayne was her near-sister. And would be
more, she hoped.

The raised heels of Birgitte's boots made her almost a
hand taller than Nynaeve, if still shorter than Elayne or
Aviendha. In dark blue coat and wide green trousers, she
carried herself with much of the same warily confident
readiness as Lan, though it seemed more casual in her. A
leopard lying on a rock, and not nearly so lazy as she appeared. There was no arrow nocked in the bow Birgitte carried, but for all her stroll and smiles, she could have a shaft
out of the quiver at her waist before anyone could blink, and
be loosing her third before anybody else could have fitted a
second to bowstring.

She gave Elayne a wry grin and a shake of her head that
swung a golden braid as long and thick as Nynaeve's dark
one. "I promised to your face, not behind your back," she
said dryly. "When you've learned a little more, I won't have
to tell you about Warders and Aes Sedai." Elayne sniffed
and lifted her chin haughtily, busying herself with the ribbons

of her hat, which was covered with long green plumes and worse than Nynaeve's. "Perhaps a great deal more," Birgitte added. "You're tying another knot in that bow."

Had Elayne not been her near-sister, Aviendha would have laughed at the crimson that flooded her cheeks. Tripping someone who tried to walk too high was always fun, or watching it done, and even a short fall was worth a laugh. As it was, she leveled a firm stare at Birgitte, a promise that more might bring retribution. She liked the woman despite all her secrets, but the difference between a friend and a near-sister was a thing these wetlanders seemed unable to comprehend. Birgitte only smiled, glancing from her to Elayne, and murmured under her breath. Aviendha caught the word "kittens." Worse, it sounded *fond*. Everyone must have heard. Everyone!

"What's gotten into you, Aviendha?" Nynaeve demanded, prodding her shoulder with a stiff finger. "Do you intend to stand there blushing all day? We *are* in a hurry."

Only then did Aviendha realize by the heat in her face that she must be as red as Elayne. And standing still as stone besides, when they had need for haste. Cut by a word, like a girl newly wedded to the spear and unused to the banter among Maidens. She had almost twenty years, and she was behaving like a child playing with her first bow. That added flames to her cheeks. Which was why she all but leaped around the next turning and very nearly ran headlong into Teslyn Baradon.

Skidding awkwardly on red-and-green floor tiles, Aviendha half-fell backward, catching herself against Elayne and Nynaeve. This time she managed not to blush herself to fire, but she wanted to. She was shaming her near-sister as much as herself. Elayne always held her composure, no matter what. Luckily, Teslyn Baradon took the encounter little better.

The sharp-faced woman recoiled in surprise, gaping before she could stop herself, then shifting her narrow shoulders irritably. Gaunt cheeks and a narrow nose hid the ageless quality of the Red sister's features, and her red dress, brocaded in a blue that was nearly black, only made her appear bonier, yet she quickly gathered a clan roofmistress's self-possession, dark brown eyes as cool as deep shadows. They slid past Aviendha dismissively, ignoring Lan like a tool she had no use for, burned a brief moment at Birgitte. Most Aes Sedai disapproved of Birgitte being a Warder, though none could give a reason beyond sour mutters about tradition. Elayne and Nynaeve, however, the woman fixed by turns. Aviendha could have tracked yesterday's wind before reading anything on Teslyn Baradon's face now.

"I did already tell Merilille," she said in a thick Illianer accent, "but I may as well put your minds at rest, also. Whatever . . . mischief . . . you do be about, Joline and I will no interfere. I did see to that. Elaida may never learn of it, if you do have some care. Stop gaping at me like carp, children," she added with a grimace of distaste. "I be neither blind nor deaf. I do know of Sea Folk Windfinders in the palace, and secret meetings with Queen Tylin. And other things." That thin mouth tightened, and though her tone remained serene, her dark gaze flared with anger. "You will pay dearly yet for those other things, you and those who do allow you to play at being Aes Sedai, but I will look aside for now. Atonement can wait."

Nynaeve took a tight grip on her braid, back straight, head high, and her own eyes blazed. Under different circumstances Aviendha might have found some sympathy for the target of the tongue-lashing plainly about to erupt. Nynaeve's tongue carried more spines than a hair-needle *segade*, and sharper ones. Coldly, Aviendha considered this woman who thought she could look right through her. A Wise One did not stoop to thrashing someone with her fists, but she was still only an apprentice; perhaps it would not cost her *ji* if she just bruised this Teslyn Baradon a little. She opened her mouth to give the Red sister a chance to defend herself at the same instant Nynaeve opened hers, yet Elayne spoke first.

"What we are *about*, Teslyn," she said in a chill voice, "is none of your business." She, too, stood straight, her eyes blue ice; a chance ray of light from a high window caught her golden-red curls, seeming to set them afire. Right then, Elayne could have made a roof-mistress seem a goatherd with too much *oosquai* in her belly. It was a skill she honed well. She delivered each word with cold crystal dignity. "You have no right to interfere in anything we do, in anything that *any* sister does. No right whatsoever. So pull your nose out of our coats, you summer ham, and be glad we do not choose to take issue with *you* supporting a usurper on the Amyrlin Seat."

Perplexed, Aviendha glanced sideways at her near-sister. Pull her *nose* out of their *coats*? She and Elayne, at least, were not wearing coats. A summer ham? What did *that* mean? Wetlanders often said peculiar things, but the other women all looked as puzzled as she. Only Lan, staring at Elayne askance, appeared to understand, and he seemed . . . startled. And perhaps amused. It was difficult to tell; *Aan'allein* controlled his features well.

Teslyn Baradon sniffed, pinching her face even tighter. Aviendha was trying hard to call these people by only part of their names the way they themselves did—when she used a whole name, they thought she was upset!—but she could not begin to imagine being so intimate with Teslyn Baradon. "I will leave you foolish children to your *business*," the woman growled. "Be sure you do no get *your* noses caught in a worse crack than they already do be."

As she turned to go, gathering her skirts grandly, Nynaeve caught her arm. Wetlanders usually let emotion gild their faces, and Nynaeve's was the image of conflict, anger struggling to break through fixed determination. "Wait, Teslyn," she said reluctantly. "You and Joline may be in danger. I told Tylin, but I think she may be afraid to tell anyone else. Unwilling, anyway. It's nothing anybody really wants to talk about." She drew a long, deep breath, and if she was thinking of her own fears in the matter, she had cause. There was no shame in feeling fear, only in giving way to it, or letting it show. Aviendha felt a flutter in her own belly as Nynaeve went on. "Moghedien has been here in Ebou Dar. She might still be. And maybe another of the Forsaken, too. With a *gholam*, a kind of Shadowspawn the Power won't touch. It looks like a man, but it was made, and made to kill Aes Sedai. Steel doesn't seem to hurt it either, and it can squeeze through a mousehole. The Black Ajah is here, as well. And there's a storm coming, a bad storm. Only it isn't a storm, not weather. I can feel it; that's a skill I have, a Talent, maybe. There's danger headed for Ebou Dar, and trouble worse than any wind or rain or lightning."

"The Forsaken, a storm that is no a storm, *and* some Shadowspawn I did never hear of before," Teslyn Baradon said wryly. "Not to mention the Black Ajah. Light! The

Black Ajah! And the Dark One himself, perhaps?" Her twisted smile was razor thin. She plucked Nynaeve's hand from her sleeve contemptuously. "When you do be back in the White Tower where you belong, in white as you all truly belong, you will learn no to waste your hours with wild fancies. Or to carry your tales to sisters." Running her eyes over them, and once more skipping past Aviendha, she gave a loud sniff and marched off down the hallway so quickly that servants had to leap from her path.

"That woman has the nerve to . . . !" Nynaeve spluttered, glaring after the retreating woman and strangling her braid with both hands. "After I *made* myself . . . !" She almost choked on her spleen. "Well, I tried." And now regretted the attempt, by the sound.

"You did," Elayne agreed with a sharp nod, "and more than she deserves. Denying that we're Aes Sedai! I won't put up with that anymore! I won't!" Her voice had only seemed cold before; now it was cold, and grim.

"Can one like that be trusted?" Aviendha muttered. "Maybe we should be sure she cannot interfere." She examined her fist; Teslyn Baradon would see *that*. The woman deserved to be caught by the Shadowsouled, by Moghedien or another. Fools deserved whatever their foolishness brought.

Nynaeve appeared to consider the suggestion, but what she said was "If I didn't know better, I'd think she was ready to turn on Elaida." She clicked her tongue in exasperation.

"You can dizzy yourself trying to read the currents in Aes Sedai politics." Elayne did not say Nynaeve should know that by now, but her tone did. "Even a Red *might* be turning against Elaida, for some reason we can't begin to imagine. Or she could be trying to make us lower our guard, so she can somehow trick us into putting ourselves into Elaida's hands. Or—"

Lan coughed. "If any of the Forsaken are coming," he said in a voice like polished stone, "they could be here any moment. Or that *gholam* could. In either case, it would be best to be elsewhere."

"With Aes Sedai, always a little patience," Birgitte murmured as though quoting. "But the Windfinders don't seem to have any," she continued, "so you might do well to forget Teslyn and remember Renaile."

Elayne and Nynaeve turned stares on the Warders cold
enough to give ten Stone Dogs pause. Neither liked running from the Shadowsouled and this *gholam,* for all they
were the ones who had decided there was no choice. Certainly neither liked being reminded that they needed to run
to meet the Windfinders almost as much as to escape the
Forsaken. Aviendha would have studied those looks—Wise
Ones did with a glance or a few words what she had always
needed the threat of spear or fist for, only they usually did
it faster and with more success—she would have studied
Elayne and Nynaeve, except that their glares had no visible effect on the pair at all. Birgitte grinned and cut her
eyes toward Lan, who shrugged back at her with obvious
forbearance.

Elayne and Nynaeve gave over. Unhurriedly, and unnecessarily, straightening their skirts, they each took one
of Aviendha's arms before setting off again without so
much as a glance to see that the Warders followed. Not that
Elayne needed to, with the Warder bond. Or Nynaeve, if
not for the same reason; *Aan'allein's* bond might belong to
another, but his heart hung alongside his ring on that chain
around her neck. They made a great show of strolling casually, unwilling to let Birgitte and Lan think they had been
brought to hurry, yet the truth was, they did walk faster
than before.

As if to make up for that, they chatted with deliberate idleness, choosing the most frivolous subjects. Elayne
regretted not having a chance to truly see the Festival of
Birds, just yesterday, and never gave a blush for the scant
garments many people had worn. Nynaeve did not blush
either, but she quickly began talking about the Feast of Embers, to be held that night. Some of the servants claimed
there would be fireworks, supposedly made by a refugee
Illuminator. Several traveling shows had come to the city
with their strange animals and acrobats, which interested
both Elayne and Nynaeve, since they had spent some time
with such a show. They talked of seamstresses, and the va-
rieties of lace available in Ebou Dar, and the different qual-
ities of silk and linen that could be bought, and Aviendha
found herself responding with pleasure to comments on
how well her gray silk riding dress looked on her, and the
other garments given to her by Tylin Quintara, fine woolens

and silks, and the stockings and shifts to go with them, and jewelry. Elayne and Nynaeve also had received extravagant gifts. All together their presents filled a number of chests and bundles that had been carried down to the stables by servants, along with their saddlebags.

"Why are you scowling, Aviendha?" Elayne asked, giving her a pat on the arm and a smile. "Don't worry. You know the weave; you will do just fine."

Nynaeve leaned her head close and whispered, "I'll fix you a tea when I have a chance. I know several that will soothe your stomach. Or any woman's troubles." She patted Aviendha's arm, too.

They did not understand. No comforting words or teas would cure what ailed her. She was *enjoying* talk of *lace* and *embroidery*! She did not know whether to growl in disgust or wail in despair. She was growing soft. Never before in her life had she looked at a woman's dress except to think where it might be hiding a weapon, never to notice the color and cut, or think how it would look on her. It was past time to be away from this city, away from wetlander palaces. Soon she would start simpering. She had not seen Elayne or Nynaeve do that, but everyone knew wetlander women simpered, and it was obvious she had become as weak as any milk-water wetlander. Strolling arm-in-arm, chatting about *lace*! How was she to reach her belt knife if someone attacked them? A knife might be useless against the likeliest assailants, but she had had faith in steel long before she knew she could channel. Should anyone try to harm Elayne or Nynaeve—especially Elayne, but she had promised Mat Cauthon to protect them both as surely as Birgitte and *Aan'allein* had—should anyone try, she would plant steel in their hearts. Lace! As they walked, she wept inside at how soft she had become.

Huge, paired stable doors fronted three sides of the palace's largest stableyard, the doorways crowded by servants in green-and-white livery. Behind them in the white stone stables waited horses, saddled or loaded with wicker panniers. Seabirds wheeled and cried overhead, an unpleasant reminder of how much water lay nearby. Heat shimmered up from pale paving stones, but it was tension that thickened the air. Aviendha had seen blood spilled where there was less strain.

Renaile din Calon, in red and yellow silks, arms crossed
arrogantly beneath her breasts, stood before nineteen more
barefoot women with tattooed hands and brightly colored
blouses, most in trousers and long sashes just as brilliant.
Sweat glistening on dark faces did not lessen their grave
dignity. Some sniffed at lacy gold boxes, filled with heavy
scent, that hung about their necks. Five fat gold rings pierced
each of Renaile din Calon's ears, a chain from one dripping
medallions as it ran across her left cheek to a ring in her
nose. The three women close behind her each wore eight
earrings and slightly fewer bits of dangling gold. That was
how the Sea Folk marked rank among themselves, with the
women at least. All deferred to Renaile din Calon, Windfinder to the Mistress of the Ships to the Atha'an Miere, but
even the two apprentices at the rear, in dark trousers and
linen blouses instead of silk, added their own golden shim-
mers to the air. When Aviendha and the others appeared,
Renaile din Calon ostentatiously looked to the sun, past its
noon peak. Her eyebrows climbed as she directed her gaze
back to them, eyes black as her white-winged hair, a demanding stare of impatience so loud she might as well have
shouted.

Elayne and Nynaeve stopped short, dragging Aviendha
to an abrupt halt. They exchanged worried glances past her,
and deep sighs. She did not see how they were to escape.
Obligation bound her near-sister and Nynaeve hand and
foot, and they themselves had tied the knots tight.

"I'll see to the Knitting Circle," Nynaeve muttered under
her breath, and Elayne said, a little more stoutly, "I'll make
sure the sisters are ready."

Releasing her arms, they went in opposite directions,
holding their skirts up to step quickly and followed by
Birgitte and Lan. That left her facing Renaile din Calon's
gaze alone, the eagle stare of a woman who knew she held
the high ground and could not be dislodged. Fortunately,
the Windfinder to the Mistress of the Ships quickly turned
to her companions, so quickly that the ends of her long
yellow sash swung wide. The other Windfinders gathered
around her, intent on her quiet words. Hitting her even once
would surely ruin everything. Aviendha tried not to glare
at them, but as much she attempted to look elsewhere, her

eyes returned. No one had the right to catch her near-sister in a cleft stick. Nose rings! A good grip on that chain, and Renaile din Calon Blue Star would wear a very different expression.

Clustered together at one end of the stableyard, tiny Merilille Ceandevin and four more Aes Sedai also regarded the Windfinders, most with annoyance ill-concealed behind cool serenity. Even slender white-haired Vandene Namelle and her mirror-image first-sister Adeleas, who usually looked the most imperturbable of them all. Now and then one or another adjusted a thin linen dust-cloak or brushed at divided silk skirts. Sudden gusts did raise a little dust and stir the color-shifting cloaks of the five Warders just at their backs, yet clearly annoyance moved their hands. Only Sareitha, standing guard over a large white disc-shaped bundle, did not twitch, but she frowned. Merilille's . . . maid . . . Pol, scowled from behind them. The Aes Sedai heatedly disapproved of the bargain that had brought the Atha'an Miere from their ships and given them a right to stare at Aes Sedai with demanding impatience, but that bargain tied the sisters' tongues and choked them on their own irritation. Which they tried to hide; they might have succeeded with the wetlanders. The third group of women, in a tight knot at the opposite end of the yard, earned almost as much of their study.

Reanne Corly and the other ten survivors of the Kin's Knitting Circle stirred uneasily under that disapproving scrutiny, dabbing their sweaty faces with embroidered handkerchiefs, adjusting their broad, colorful straw hats, smoothing sober woolen skirts sewn up on one side to expose layers of petticoats as bright as the Sea Folk's garb. In part it was the stares of the Aes Sedai that had them shifting from foot to foot; fear of the Forsaken and the *gholam* added to it, and so did other things. The narrow, plunging necklines of those dresses should have been enough. Most of these women showed at least a few lines on their cheeks, yet they looked like girls caught with their hands full of stolen nutbread. All but stout Sumeko, fists planted on broad hips, who met the Aes Sedai stare for stare. A bright glow of *saidar* surrounded one of their number, Kirstian, who kept glancing over her shoulder. With a pale face perhaps ten years older than Nynaeve's, she appeared out of place among the others. That face grew whiter every time her black eyes met those of an Aes Sedai.

Nynaeve hurried to the women who led the Kin, her face beaming encouragement, and Reanne and the others smiled with visible relief. Marred a little, true, by the sidelong glances they directed at Lan; him they regarded as the wolf he resembled. Nynaeve, however, was the reason Sumeko did not wilt like the rest whenever an Aes Sedai glanced in her direction. She had vowed to teach those women that they possessed backbones, though Aviendha did not completely understand why. Nynaeve was Aes Sedai herself; no Wise One would ever tell anyone to stand up to Wise Ones.

However well that might be working with respect to the other Aes Sedai, even Sumeko wore a slightly fawning air for Nynaeve. The Knitting Circle found it strange, to say the least, that women as young as Elayne and Nynaeve gave orders to the other Aes Sedai and were obeyed. Aviendha herself found it peculiar; how could strength in the Power, something you were born with as surely as your eyes, weigh more heavily than the honor that years could bring? Yet the older Aes Sedai did obey, and for the Kinswomen, that was enough. Ieine, nearly as tall as Aviendha herself and almost as dark as the Sea Folk, returned Nynaeve's every glance with an obsequious smile, while Dimana, white streaking her bright red hair, ducked her head constantly under Nynaeve's eyes, and yellow-haired Sibella hid nervous giggles behind a hand. Despite their Ebou Dari garments, only Tamarla, lean and olive-skinned, was Altaran, and not even from the city.

They parted as soon as Nynaeve came close, revealing a woman on her knees, wrists bound behind her, a leather sack covering her head, and her fine clothes torn and dusty. She was as much the reason for their uneasiness as Meri-lille's frowns or the Forsaken. Perhaps more.

Tamarla dragged the hood off, leaving the woman's thin, bead-studded braids tangled; Ispan Shefar tried to rise, and managed to reach an awkward crouch before she staggered and sank back down, blinking and giggling foolishly. Sweat ran down her cheeks, and a few bruises from her capture marred her ageless features. She had been treated too gently for her crimes, to Aviendha's mind.

The herbs Nynaeve had forced down the woman's throat still fogged her wits as well as weakening her knees, but Kirstian held a shield on her with every shred of the Power she could summon. There was no chance the Shadowrunner might escape—even had she not been dosed, Kirstian was as strong in the Power as Reanne, stronger than most Aes Sedai Aviendha had met—yet even Sumeko plucked her skirts nervously and avoided looking at the kneeling woman.

"Surely the sisters should have her, now." Reanne's high-pitched voice carried, unsteady enough to belong to the Black sister Kirstian shielded. "Nynaeve Sedai, we . . . we should not be guar—uh—in charge of . . . an Aes Sedai."

"That's right," Sumeko put in quickly. And anxiously. "The Aes Sedai should have her, now." Sibella echoed her, and nods and murmurs of agreement rippled through the Kinswomen. They believed in their bones that they stood far below Aes Sedai; very likely they would have chosen guarding Trollocs over holding an Aes Sedai.

The disapproving stares from Merilille and the other sisters changed once Ispan Shefar's face was revealed. Sareitha Tomares, who had worn her brown-fringed shawl only a few years and still did not have the ageless appearance, glared with a disgust that should have flayed the Shadowrunner at fifty paces. Adeleas and Vandene, hands tightening on their skirts, appeared to struggle with hatred for the woman who had been their sister and betrayed them. Yet the stares they gave the Knitting Circle were not that much better. They, too, knew in their hearts that the Kin stood a very long way below them. There was much more to it than that, but the betrayer had been one of their own, and no one but they had the right to her. Aviendha agreed. A Maiden who betrayed her spear-sisters did not die quickly or unshamed.

Nynaeve pulled the sack back down over Ispan Shefar's head with some force. "You've done well so far, and you'll continue to do well," she told the Kinswomen firmly. "If she shows signs of coming round, pour some more of that mixture down her. It'll keep her giddy as a goat full of ale. Hold her nose, if she tries not to swallow. Even an Aes Sedai will swallow if you hold her nose and threaten to box her ears."

Reanne's jaw dropped and her eyes sprang wide, like most of her companions'. Sumeko nodded, but slowly, and goggled nearly as much as the others. When Kinswomen said Aes Sedai, they might have been naming the Creator. The thought of holding an Aes Sedai's nose, even a Shadowrunner's, painted their faces with horror.

By the popping eyes among the Aes Sedai, they liked the notion even less. Merilille opened her mouth, staring at Nynaeve, but just then Elayne reached her, and the Gray sister rounded on her instead, sparing barely a single disapproving frown for Birgitte. It was a measure of her agitation that her voice rose rather than dropping; normally Merilille was very discreet. "Elayne, you must speak to Nynaeve. Those women are confused and frightened out of their wits already. It won't help if she upsets them even more. If the Amyrlin Seat really does intend to allow them to go to the Tower," she shook her head slowly, trying to deny that, and perhaps a great deal else, "if she does mean to, they must have a clear picture of their places, and—"

"The Amyrlin does," Elayne cut her off. From Nynaeve, a firm tone was a fist shaken under your nose; from Elayne, it was calm certainty. "They will have their chance to try again, and if they fail, they still will not be sent away. No woman who can channel will be cut off from the Tower again. They will all be a part of the White Tower."

Fingering her belt knife idly, Aviendha wondered about that. Egwene, Elayne's Amyrlin Seat, said much the same. She was a friend, too, but she had wrapped her heart around being Aes Sedai. Aviendha herself did not want to be part of the White Tower. She very much doubted that Sorilea or any other Wise One did, either.

Merilille sighed and folded her hands, yet for all her outward acceptance, she still forgot to lower her voice. "As you say, Elayne. But about Ispan. We simply cannot allow—"

Elayne raised a hand sharply. Command replaced mere certainty. "Cease, Merilille. You have the Bowl of the Winds to watch. That is enough for anyone. It *will* be enough for you."

Merilille opened her mouth, then closed it again and bowed her head slightly in acquiescence. Under Elayne's steady gaze, the other Aes Sedai bent theirs, too. If some displayed reluctance, however small, not all did. Sareitha hurriedly picked up the disc-shaped bundle, wrapped in layers of white silk, that had been lying by her feet. Her arms barely went all the way around as she held the Bowl of the Winds to her bosom, smiling anxiously at Elayne as if to show that she really was keeping a close eye on it.

The Sea Folk women stared hungrily at the bundle, almost leaning forward. Aviendha would not have been surprised to see them leap across the stones to seize the Bowl. The Aes Sedai saw the same, plainly. Sareitha clutched the white parcel more tightly, and Merilille actually stepped between her and the Atha'an Miere. Smooth Aes Sedai faces tightened with the effort of remaining expressionless. They believed the Bowl should belong to them; *all* things that used or manipulated the One Power belonged to the White Tower in their eyes, no matter who happened to possess them at the moment. But there was the bargain.

"The sun moves, Aes Sedai," Renaile din Calon announced loudly, "and danger threatens. So you maintain. If you think to worm free in some fashion by delaying, think twice and again. Try to break the bargain, and by my father's heart, I will return to the ships at once. And claim the Bowl for redress. It was ours from the Breaking."

"You watch your tongue with Aes Sedai," Reanne barked, scandalized indignation from her blue straw hat to the stout shoes peeking from beneath her green-and-white petticoats.

Renaile din Calon's mouth curled into a sneer. "The jellyfish have tongues, it seems. A surprise they can use them, though, when no Aes Sedai gave permission."

In an instant the stableyard was full of shouted insults flying between Kin and Atha'an Miere, "wilder" and "spineless" and growing worse, strident cries that buried Merilille's attempts to hush Reanne and her companions on the one hand and soothe the Sea Folk on the other. Several Windfinders stopped fingering the daggers thrust behind their sashes and gripped hilts instead. The glow of *saidar* sprang up around first one then another of the brightly clad women. The Kinswomen looked startled, though it did not slow their tirade, but Sumeko embraced the Source, then Tamarla, then willowy, doe-eyed Chilares, and soon every one of them and every one of the Windfinders shone while words flew and tempers boiled.

Aviendha wanted to groan. Any moment blood would begin to flow. She would follow Elayne's lead, but her near-sister was glaring cold fury at Windfinders and Knitting Circle alike. Elayne had small patience with stupidity, in herself or others, and shouting insults when an enemy might be coming was the worst sort. Aviendha took a firm grip on her belt knife, then after a moment embraced *saidar*; life and joy filled her to near weeping. Wise Ones only used the Power when words had failed, but neither words nor steel would do here. She wished she had some idea of who to kill first.

"Enough!" Nynaeve's piercing shriek sliced the words short on every tongue. Astonished faces swiveled toward her. Her head swung dangerously, and she stabbed a finger at the Knitting Circle. "Stop behaving like children!" Although she had moderated her tone, it was by hairs. "Or do you mean to squabble until the Forsaken come to scoop up the Bowl *and* us? And you,"—the finger thrust at the Windfinders—"stop trying to wriggle out of your agreement! You won't get the Bowl until you've met every last word! Don't think you will!" Nynaeve swung round on the Aes Sedai. "And you . . . !" Met by cool surprise, her flow of words tapered off into a sour grunt. The Aes Sedai had not joined in the shouting except to try quieting it. None shone with the light of *saidar*.

That was not enough to calm Nynaeve completely, of course. She tugged fiercely at her hat, plainly still full of anger she wanted to loose. But the Kinswomen were staring at the paving stones in red-faced chagrin, and even the Windfinders appeared a little abashed—a little—muttering to themselves yet refusing quite to meet Nynaeve's glare. The glow winked out around one woman after another, until only Aviendha still held to the Source.

She gave a start as Elayne touched her arm. She *was* getting soft. Letting people sneak up on her, jumping at a touch.

"This crisis seems to be weathered," Elayne murmured. "Perhaps it's time to go before the next breaks out." A touch of color in her cheeks was the only sign that she had ever been angry. And a bit in Birgitte's; the two reflected one another in some ways since the bonding.

"Past time," Aviendha agreed. Much longer, and she would *be* a milk-hearted wetlander.

Every eye followed as she walked out into the open space in the center of the stableyard, to the spot she had studied and felt until she knew it with her eyelids closed. There was a joy in holding the Power, a joy in working *saidar*, that she could not have put into words. To contain *saidar*, to be contained by it, was to seem alive beyond any other time. A delusion, the Wise Ones said, as false and dangerous as a mirage of water in the Termool, yet it seemed more real than the paving stones beneath her feet. She fought the urge to draw more; already she held nearly as much as she could. Everyone crowded close as she began to weave the flows.

That there were things many Aes Sedai could not do still startled Aviendha, after all she had seen. Several of the Knitting Circle were strong enough, but only Sumeko and, surprisingly, Reanne openly studied what she was doing. Sumeko went so far as to shrug off the encouraging pats Nynaeve tried to give her—which earned a look of startled indignation from Nynaeve that Sumeko, her gaze fixed on Aviendha, never saw. All of the Windfinders had sufficient strength. They watched as hungrily as they had stared at the Bowl. The bargain gave them every right.

Aviendha focused, and the flows wove together, creating identity between this place and the place she and Elayne and Nynaeve had chosen on a map. She gestured as though opening tentflaps. That was no part of the weave Elayne had taught her, but it was almost all she could recall of what she herself had done, long before Egwene made her first gateway. The flows coalesced into a silvery, vertical slash that rotated and became an opening in the air, taller than a man and just as wide. Beyond lay a large clearing surrounded by trees twenty or thirty feet high, miles north of the city, on the far side of the river. Knee-high brown grass came right up to the gateway, swaying through in a small breeze; it had not truly turned, only seemed to. Some of those blades were sliced cleanly, though, some lengthwise. The edges of an opening gateway made a razor seem dull.

The gateway filled her with dissatisfaction. Elayne could make this weave with only a part of her strength, yet for some reason it required all but a fraction of Aviendha's. She was sure she could have woven a larger, as large as Elayne could, using the weaves she had made without thought while trying to escape Rand al'Thor what seemed a very long time ago, but no matter how often she tried, only scraps came back to her. She felt no envy—rather, she took pride in her near-sister's accomplishments—but her own failure made shame surge in her heart. Sorilea or Amys would be hard on her, if they knew that. About the shame. Too much pride, they would call it. Amys should understand; she had been a Maiden. There *was* shame in failing at what you should be able to do. If she had not had to hold the weave, she would have run away so no one could see her.

The departure had been carefully planned, and the whole stableyard sprang into motion as soon as the gateway opened fully. Two of the Knitting Circle pulled the hooded Shadowrunner to her feet, and the Windfinders hurriedly formed a line behind Renaile din Calon. The servants began bringing horses out of the stables. Lan, Birgitte, and one of Careane's Warders, a lanky man called Cieryl Arjuna, immediately darted through the gateway, one behind the other. Like *Far Dareis Mai*, Warders always claimed the right to scout ahead. Aviendha's feet itched to run after them, but there was no point. Unlike Elayne, she could not move more than five or six steps without this weave beginning to weaken, and the same if she tried to tie it off. It was very frustrating.

This time there was no real expectation of danger, so the Aes Sedai followed immediately, Elayne and Nynaeve as well. Farms dotted that treed area thickly, and a wandering shepherd or a young couple seeking privacy might need guidance away from seeing too much, but no Shadowsouled or Shadowrunner could know that clearing; only she, Elayne, and Nynaeve did, and they had not spoken in the choosing, for fear of eavesdroppers. Standing in the opening, Elayne gave Aviendha a questioning look, but Aviendha motioned her to go on. Plans were meant to be followed unless there was reason to change them.

The Windfinders began filing slowly through to the clearing, each suddenly irresolute as she approached this thing she had never dreamed of, taking a breath before she entered. And abruptly, the prickling returned.

Aviendha's eyes rose to the windows overlooking the stableyard. Anyone might be hidden behind the white screens of intricate wrought iron and piercework carving. Tylin had ordered the servants to stay away from those windows, but who would stop Teslyn, or Joline, or. . . . Something made her look higher, to the domes and towers. Narrow walks ringed some of those slim spires, and on one, very high, was a black shape haloed by a sharp nimbus from the sun behind. A man.

Her breath caught. Nothing in his stance, hands on the stone railing, spoke of danger, yet she knew he was the one who put that crawling between her shoulder blades. One of the Shadowsouled would not stand there simply watching, but that creature, that *gholam*. . . . Ice formed in her belly. He could be just a palace servant. He could be, but she did not believe it. No shame in knowing fear.

Anxiously she glanced at the women still edging through the gateway with agonizing slowness. Half the Sea Folk were gone, and the Knitting Circle waited behind the rest with the Shadowrunner firmly in hand, their own unease at the passage warring with resentment that the Sea Folk women were allowed to go first. If she voiced her suspicions, the Kinswomen surely would run—mere mention of the Shadowsouled dried their mouths and turned their bowels to water—while the Windfinders might well try to claim the Bowl straightaway. With them, the Bowl stood above anything else. But only a blind fool stood scratching herself while a lion crept up on the herd she had been set to guard. She caught one of the Atha'an Miere by a red silk sleeve.

"Tell Elayne—" A face like smooth black stone turned to her; the woman somehow made full lips seem thin; her eyes were black pebbles, flat and hard. What message could she send that would not bring down all the troubles she feared from them? "Tell Elayne and Nynaeve to be wary. Tell them enemies always come when you least want them. You must say this to her, without fail." The Windfinder nodded with barely concealed impatience, but surprisingly, she waited for Aviendha to release her before making her hesitant way through the gateway.

The walk up on the tower stood empty. Aviendha felt no relief. He could be anywhere. Making his way down to the stableyard. Whoever he was, whatever he was, he *was* dangerous; this was *not* a dust-funnel dancing in her imagination.

The last four Warders had formed a square around the gate-way, a guard who would be last to leave, and much as she despised their swords, she was grateful that someone there besides herself knew the use of sharp metal. Not that they would have any more chance against a *gholam*, or worse, one of the Shadowsouled, than the servants waiting with the horses. Or than she herself.

Grimly she drew the Power, until the sweetness of *saidar* grew near to pain. A hair beyond, and pain would almost become blinding agony for the moments needed to die or lose the ability completely. Would those shuffling women quicken their feet! No shame in feeling fear, but she was very much afraid that hers was painted on her face.

CHAPTER

2

Unweaving

Elayne stepped to one side as soon as she was through the gateway, but Nynaeve trampled across the clearing, kicking up brown grasshoppers from the dead grass and peering this way and that for evidence of the Warders. Of one Warder, anyway. A bright red bird flashed across the clearing and was gone. Nothing else moved except the sisters; a squirrel barked somewhere in the mostly leafless trees, and then there was silence. To Elayne it seemed impossible those three could have passed this way without leaving paths as wide as that behind Nynaeve, yet she could not make out any sign that they had been there at all.

She sensed Birgitte somewhere off to her left, roughly southwest she thought, and feeling quite content, clearly in no immediate danger. Careane, part of a protective circle gathered around Sareitha and the Bowl, cocked her head almost as if listening. Apparently her Cieryl was to the southeast. Which meant Lan was north. Oddly enough, north was the direction Nynaeve had settled down to watch, all the while muttering under her breath. Perhaps being married had created some sense of him in her. More likely, she had noticed a track that escaped Elayne. Nynaeve was as skilled at woodscraft as she was with herbs.

From where Elayne stood at first, Aviendha was clearly visible through the gateway, studying the palace rooftops as if she expected an ambush. By her stance, she could have been carrying spears, ready to leap into battle in her riding dress. She made Elayne smile, hiding how distressed she was about her problems with the gateway, so much braver

than she herself. But at the same time she could not help
worrying. Aviendha *was* brave, and no one Elayne knew
was better able to keep her head. She also might decide that
ji'e'toh required her to fight when there was no chance except in running. The light around her shone so brightly it
was obvious she could not draw much more of *saidar*. If
one of the Forsaken did appear. . . .

I should have stayed with her. Elayne rejected the
thought immediately. Whatever excuse she gave, Aviendha
would know the truth, and she was touchy as a man, sometimes. Most of the time. Especially when it bore upon her
honor. With a sigh, Elayne let the Atha'an Miere crowd her
farther from the gateway as they filed through. She stayed
close enough to hear any shout on the other side, though.
Close enough to leap to Aviendha's aid in a heartbeat. And
for another reason.

The Windfinders came through in order of rank, striving
to keep their faces smooth, but even Renaile relaxed tight
shoulders once her bare feet were beating down the tall
brown grass. Some gave a little shiver, quickly suppressed,
or glanced back with round eyes at the opening hanging in
midair. One and all, they stared at Elayne suspiciously as
they stepped by her, and two or three opened their mouths,
perhaps to ask what she was doing, perhaps to ask—or
tell—her to move. She was just as glad that they hurried
on in obedience to Renaile's curt urgings. They would have
their chance to tell Aes Sedai what to do soon enough; it did
not have to start with her.

That thought made her stomach sink, and the number
of them made her shake her head. They had the knowledge of weather to use the Bowl properly, yet even Renaile agreed—if reluctantly—that the more Power directed
through the Bowl, the better the chances of being able to
heal the weather. It must be directed with a precision impossible except for one woman alone or a circle, though. A
full circle of thirteen it had to be. That thirteen certainly
would include Nynaeve and Aviendha and Elayne herself,
and probably a few of the Kin, but Renaile plainly intended
to jump on the part of the bargain that said they would be
allowed to learn any abilities the Aes Sedai could teach.
The gateway had been the first, and forming a circle would
be the second. A wonder she had not brought every Wind-

finder in the harbor. Imagine trying to deal with three or
four hundred of these women! Elayne offered a small prayer
of thanks that there were only twenty.

She was not standing there to count them, though. As
each Windfinder passed, barely more than a pace away, she
let herself feel the woman's strength in the Power. Earlier
there had been time to get close enough to only a handful,
what with all the trouble of convincing Renaile to come at
all. Apparently achieving rank among the Windfinders had
nothing to do with either age or strength; Renaile was far
from the strongest even in the first three or four, while one
woman toward the rear, Senine, had weathered cheeks and
thickly grayed hair. Strangely, by the marks in her ears it
seemed that Senine might once have worn more than six
earrings, and thicker ones than she did now.

Elayne sorted and stored away faces and the names she
knew with a growing sense of complacency. The Windfinders might have secured an upper hand of sorts, and she and
Nynaeve might be in deep trouble, very deep, with both
Egwene and the Hall of the Tower once the terms of their
bargain became known, but none of these women would
stand particularly high among Aes Sedai. Certainly not low,
but not high. She told herself not to feel smug—it changed
nothing in what they had agreed—yet it was very hard not
to. These were the best the Atha'an could produce, after all.
Here in Ebou Dar, anyway. And if they had been Aes Sedai,
every one of them, from Kurin, with her stony black stare,
to Renaile herself, would have listened when she spoke and
stood when she entered a room. If they were Aes Sedai and
behaving as they should.

And then the end of the line appeared, and she gave a
start as a young Windfinder off one of the smaller ships
passed her, a round-cheeked woman called Rainyn, in plain
blue silks, with barely a half-dozen ornaments hanging
from her nose chain. The two apprentices, boyishly slim
Talaan and big-eyed Metarra, scurried at the very tail with
harried expressions. They had not earned the nose ring yet,
much less the chain, and only a single thin gold earring in
the left ear balanced the three in the right. Her eyes followed the three of them just short of staring. Perhaps not
short of it, at that.

The Atha'an Miere clustered with Renaile again, most,

like her, glaring hungrily at the Aes Sedai and the Bowl. The last three women stood at the rear, the apprentices with the air of those uncertain whether they had a right to be there at all, Rainyn folding her arms in imitation of Renaile, yet doing little better than the other two. The Windfinder on a darter, the least of the Sea Folk vessels, likely seldom found herself in company with the Windfinder to her clan Wavemistress, not to mention the Windfinder to the Mistress of the Ships. Rainyn was easily as strong as Lelaine or Romanda, and Metarra on a level with Elayne herself, while Talaan. . . . Talaan, so meek in her red linen blouse, with eyes that seemed permanently downcast, came very close to Nynaeve. Very close. More, Elayne knew she herself had not yet reached her full potential, and neither had Nynaeve. How close were Metarra and Talaan? She had grown accustomed to knowing that only Nynaeve and the Forsaken were stronger than she. Well, Egwene, but she had been forced, and her own potential, and Aviendha's, matched Egwene's. *So much for complacency,* she told herself ruefully. Lini would have said it was what she deserved for taking things for granted.

Laughing softly at herself, Elayne turned back to check on Aviendha, but the Knitting Circle stood rooted to one spot in front of the gateway, twitching at cold stares from Careane and Sareitha. All but Sumeko, and she did not move away either for all that she had met the sisters' gazes. Kirstian appeared ready to burst into tears.

Suppressing a sigh, Elayne herded the Kinswomen out of the way of the stable folk waiting to bring the horses through. The Knitting Circle went along like sheep—she was the shepherd, Merilille and the rest the wolves—and they would have moved faster if not for Ispan.

Famelle, one of only four among the Knitting Circle without a touch of gray or white in her hair, and Eldase, a fierce-eyed woman when she was not looking at an Aes Sedai, held Ispan by the arms. They could not seem to decide between holding her firmly enough to keep her upright and not clutching her too tightly, with the result that the Black sister moved in a bobbing fashion, sagging halfway to her knees when they loosened their grips, then pulled back up just before she fell completely.

"Forgive me, Aes Sedai," Famelle kept murmuring to Is-

pan with a faint Taraboner accent. "Oh, I am sorry, Aes
Sedai." Eldase winced and gave a little moan every time
Ispan stumbled. Just as if Ispan had not helped murder two
of their number and the Light alone knew how many others.
They were fussing over a woman who was going to die.
The killings in the White Tower that Ispan had conspired at
were enough to condemn her by themselves.

"Take her over there somewhere," Elayne told them, waving away from the gateway into the clearing. They obeyed,
bobbing curtsies and nearly dropping Ispan, murmuring
apologies to Elayne and to the hooded prisoner. Reanne and
the rest scurried along, anxiously eyeing the sisters around
Merilille.

Almost immediately the war of glares started up again,
the Aes Sedai at the Kinswomen, the Knitting Circle at the
Windfinders, and the Atha'an Miere at anybody their eyes
fell on. Elayne clamped her teeth shut. She was *not* going to
shout at them. Nynaeve always got better results with yells,
anyway. But she did want to shake some sense into every
one of them, shake them until their teeth rattled. Including
Nynaeve, who was supposed to be getting everyone organized instead of staring into the trees. But what if it had
been Rand who was going to die unless she could find a
way to save him?

Suddenly tears trembled on the edge of falling, stinging
her eyes. Rand *was* going to die, and there was nothing she
could do to stop it. *Peel the apple in your hand, girl, not the
one on the tree,* Lini's thin voice seemed to whisper in her
ear. *Tears are for after; they just waste time before.*

"Thank you, Lini," Elayne murmured. Her old nurse was
an irritating woman sometimes, never admitting that any of
her charges had really grown up, but her advice was always
good. Just because Nynaeve was slacking her duties was no
reason for Elayne to slack hers.

Servants had started trotting horses through right on the
heels of the Knitting Circle, beginning with the packhorses.
None of those first animals carried anything so frivolous as
clothes. They could walk if the riding horses needed to be
abandoned on the other side of the gateway, and wear what
they stood up in if the rest of the pack animals had to be
left behind, but what was on those first horses could not be
left for the Forsaken. Elayne motioned the leather-cheeked

woman leading the very first to follow her aside, out of the way of the others.

Untying and tossing back the stiff canvas cover on one of the wide wicker panniers revealed a great heap of what appeared to be rubbish stuffed in every which way, right up to the top, some of it wrapped in cloth that was falling to pieces. The greater part of it probably was rubbish. Embracing *saidar*, Elayne began sorting. A rusted breastplate quickly went onto the ground, along with a broken table leg, a cracked platter, a badly dented pewter pitcher, and a bolt of rotted, unidentifiable cloth that almost broke apart in her hands.

The storeroom where they found the Bowl of the Winds had been stuffed full, things that should have been on a refuse heap jumbled in with more objects of the Power than just the Bowl, some in beetle-riddled casks or chests, some carelessly stacked. For hundreds and hundreds of years the Kin had hidden away all things they found that were connected to the Power, fearful of using them and fearful of delivering them to Aes Sedai. Until that very morning. This was the first chance Elayne had had to see what was worth keeping. The Light send that the Darkfriends had not gotten away with anything important; they had taken some, but certainly less than a quarter of what the room had held, rubbish included. The Light send she found something they could use. People had died to bring these things out of the Rahad.

She did not channel, just held the Power as she lifted each item. A chipped clay cup, three broken plates, a child's moth-eaten dress, and an old boot with a hole worn through the side all fell to the ground. A stone carving a little larger than her hand—it *felt* like stone; it *might* have been a carving, though it did not exactly look carved, for some reason—all deep blue curves vaguely like roots. It seemed to warm faintly at her touch; it held a . . . resonance . . . to *saidar*. That was the closest word she could think of. What it was meant to do, she had no idea, but it was a *ter'angreal* without any doubt. It went on the other side of her, away from the pile of rubbish.

The heap of refuse continued to grow, but so did the other, if more slowly, things that had nothing in common except the faint warmth and the sense of echoing the Power.

A small box that felt like ivory, covered in wavering red and green stripes; she set it down carefully without opening the hinged lid. You could never tell what might trigger a *ter'angreal*. A black rod no thicker than her little finger, a pace in length, stiff yet so flexible she thought she could have doubled it into a circle. A tiny stoppered vial that might have been crystal, with a dark red liquid inside. The figure of a stout, bearded man with a jolly smile, holding a book; two feet tall, it appeared to be age-darkened bronze and took both of her hands to move. Other things. Most was trash, though. And none was what she truly wanted. Not yet.

"Is this the time to be doing that?" Nynaeve asked. She straightened hastily from the small cluster of *ter'angreal*, grimacing and rubbing her hand on her skirt. "That rod feels like . . . pain," she muttered. The hard-faced woman holding the packhorse's head blinked at the rod and edged away.

Elayne eyed the rod—Nynaeve's occasional impressions about objects she touched could be useful—but she did not stop sorting. There had been too much pain lately to need any more, surely. Not that what Nynaeve sensed was always that straightforward. The rod might have been present when a great deal of pain was caused without being the cause in itself. The pannier was almost empty; some of what was on the other side of the horse would have to be shifted to balance the weight. "If there's an *angreal* in this somewhere, Nynaeve, I would like to find it before Moghedien taps one of us on the shoulder."

Nynaeve grunted sourly, but she peered into the wicker basket.

Dropping another table leg—that made *three*, none of which matched—Elayne spared a glance for the clearing. All of the packhorses were out, and the mounts were coming through the gateway, now, filling the open space between the trees with bustle and confusion. Merilille and the other Aes Sedai already sat their saddles, barely concealing their impatience to be off, while Pol fussed hurriedly with her mistress's saddlebags, but the Windfinders. . . .

Graceful afoot, graceful on their ships, they were unused to horses. Renaile was trying to mount from the wrong side, and the gentle bay mare chosen for her danced slow circles around the liveried man who was gripping the bridle with one hand while tugging his hair in frustration with the other and vainly trying to correct the Windfinder. Two of the stablewomen were attempting to hoist Dorile, who served the Wavemistress of Clan Somarin, into her saddle, while a third, holding the gray's head, wore the tight face of someone trying not to laugh. Rainyn was on the back of a leggy brown gelding, but somehow without either foot in the stirrups or the reins in her hands and having considerable trouble finding any of them. And those three seemed to be having the easiest time of it. Horses whinnied and danced and rolled their eyes, and Windfinders shouted curses in voices that could have been heard over a gale. One of them knocked a serving man flat with her fist, and three more stable folk were trying to catch mounts that had gotten free.

There was also what she had expected to see, if Nynaeve was no longer keeping her private watch. Lan stood by his black warhorse, Mandarb, dividing his gaze between the treeline, the gateway, and Nynaeve. Birgitte came striding out of the woods shaking her head, and a moment later, Cieryl, trotted from the trees, but with no sense of urgency. There was nothing out there to threaten or inconvenience them.

Nynaeve was watching her, eyebrows raised high.

"I didn't say anything," Elayne said. Her hand closed on something small, wrapped in rotting cloth that might have been white once. Or brown. She knew immediately what was inside.

"A good thing for you," Nynaeve grumbled, not quite far enough under her breath. "I can't abide women who poke their noses into other people's business." Elayne let it pass without so much as a start; she was proud that she did not have to bite her tongue.

Stripping away the decayed cloth revealed a small amber brooch in the shape of a turtle. It looked like amber, anyway, and it might have been amber once, but when she opened herself to the Source through it, *saidar* rushed into her, a torrent compared to what she could draw safely on her own. Not a strong *angreal*, but far better than nothing. With it, she could handle twice as much of the Power as Nynaeve, and Nynaeve herself would do better still. Releasing the extra flow of *saidar*, she slipped the brooch

into her belt pouch with a smile of delight and went back to
searching. Where there was one, there might be more. And
now that she had one to study, she might be able to reason
out how to *make* an *angreal*. That was something she had
wished for. It was all she could do not to take the brooch out
again and begin probing it right there.

Vandene had been eyeing Nynaeve and her for some
time, and now she heeled her slab-sided gelding over to
them and dismounted. The groom at the packhorse's head
managed a decent if awkward curtsy, more than she had for
Elayne or Nynaeve. "You're being careful," Vandene said
to Elayne, "and that's very good. But it might be better to
leave these things alone until they're in the Tower."

Elayne's mouth tightened. In the Tower? Until they could
be examined by someone else, was what she meant. Someone older and supposedly more experienced. "I *do* know
what I'm doing, Vandene. I have *made ter'angreal*, after all.
Nobody else living has done *that*." She had taught the basics
to some sisters, but no one had managed the trick of it by
the time she left for Ebou Dar.

The older Green nodded, flipping her reins idly against
the palm of her riding glove. "Martine Janata also knew
what she was doing, so I understand," she said casually.
"She was the last sister to really make a business of studying *ter'angreal*. She did it for over forty years, almost from
the time she reached the shawl. She was careful, too, so I
was told. Then one day, Martine's maid found her uncon-
scious on the floor of her sitting room. Burned out." Even
in a conversational tone, those words were a sharp slap.
Vandene's voice did not alter a hair, though. "Her Warder
was dead from the shock. Not unusual in cases like that.
When Martine came to, three days later, she couldn't recall
what she had been working with. She couldn't remember
the preceding week at all. That was more than twenty-five
years ago, and no one since has had the nerve to touch any
of the *ter'angreal* that were in her rooms. Her notes mentioned every last one, and everything she had discovered
was innocuous, innocent, even frivolous, but. . . ." Vandene
shrugged. "She found something she wasn't expecting."

Elayne peeked at Birgitte, and found Birgitte looking
back at her. She did not need to see the worried frown on
the other woman's face; it was mirrored in her mind, in the

small patch of her mind that *was* Birgitte and in the rest. Birgitte felt her worry, and she felt Birgitte's, until sometimes it was hard to say which was which. She risked more than herself. But she *did* know what she was doing. More than anyone else there, at least. And even if none of the Forsaken appeared, they *needed* all the *angreal* she could find.

"What happened to Martine?" Nynaeve asked quietly. "Afterward, I mean." She could seldom hear of anyone being hurt without wanting to Heal them; she wanted to Heal everything.

Vandene grimaced. She might have been the one to bring up Martine, but Aes Sedai did not like talking about women who had been burned out or stilled. They did not like remembering them. "She vanished once she was well enough to slip out of the Tower," she said hurriedly. "The important thing to remember is that she was cautious. I never met her, but I've been told she treated every *ter'angreal* as if she had no idea what it might do next, even the one that makes the cloth for Warders' cloaks, and nobody has ever been able to make that do anything else. She was careful, and it did her no good."

Nynaeve laid an arm across the nearly empty pannier. "Maybe you really should," she began.

"*No-o-o-o!*" Merilille shrieked.

Elayne spun, instinctively opening herself through the *angreal* again, only half conscious of *saidar* flooding into Nynaeve and Vandene. The glow of the Power sprang up around every woman in the clearing who could embrace the Source. Merilille was straining forward in her saddle, eyes bulging, one hand reaching toward the gateway. Elayne frowned. There was nothing there except Aviendha, and the last four Warders, startled in the middle of walking away, searching for the threat with swords half-drawn. Then she realized what Aviendha was doing and nearly lost *saidar* in her shock.

The gateway trembled as Aviendha carefully picked apart the weave that had made it. It shivered and flexed, the edges wavering. The last flows came loose, and instead of winking out, the opening shimmered, the view through it of the courtyard fading away until it evaporated like mist in the sun.

"That is impossible!" Renaile said incredulously. An

astonished murmur of agreement broke out among the Windfinders. The Kinswomen gaped at Aviendha, mouths working soundlessly.

Elayne nodded slowly in spite of herself. Clearly it *was* possible, but one of the first things she had been told as a novice was that never, ever, under any circumstances was she to try what Aviendha had just done. Picking apart a weave, any weave, rather than simply letting it dissipate, could not be done, she had been told, not without inevitable disaster. Inevitable.

"You fool girl!" Vandene snapped, her face a thunderhead. She strode toward Aviendha dragging her gelding behind. "Do you realize what you almost did? One slip—one!—and there's no saying what the weave will snap into, or what it will do! You could have completely destroyed everything for a hundred paces! Five hundred! Everything! You could have burned yourself out and—"

"It was necessary," Aviendha cut in. A babble erupted from the mounted Aes Sedai crowding around her and Vandene, but she glared at them and raised her voice over theirs. "I know the dangers, Vandene Namelle, but it was necessary. Is this another thing you Aes Sedai cannot do? The Wise Ones say any woman can learn, if she is taught, some women more and some less, but any woman, if she can pick out embroidery." She did not quite sneer. Not quite.

"This is *not* embroidery, girl!" Merilille's voice was deep winter ice. "Whatever so-called training you received among your people, you cannot possibly know what you are *playing* with! You will promise me—swear to me!—that you will never do this again!"

"Her name should be in the novice book," Sareitha said firmly, glaring across the Bowl still held firmly to her bosom. "I've always said it. She should be entered in the book." Careane nodded, her stern gaze measuring Aviendha for a novice dress.

"That might not be necessary for the moment," Adeleas told Aviendha, leaning forward in her saddle, "but you must let yourself be guided by us." The Brown sister's tone was much milder than the others', yet she was not making a suggestion.

A month or so earlier, Aviendha might have begun to wilt under all that Aes Sedai disapproval, but not now. Elayne hurriedly pushed in among the horses before her friend decided to draw the knife she was fondling. Or to do something worse. "Maybe somebody should ask *why* she thought it was necessary," she said, slipping an arm around Aviendha's shoulders as much to keep her arms at her sides as for comfort.

Aviendha did not quite include her in the exasperated look she gave the other sisters. "This leaves no residue," she said patiently. Too patiently. "The residues of a weave this large might be read two days from now."

Merilille snorted, a very strong sound to come from that slight body. "That is a rare Talent, girl. Neither Teslyn nor Joline has it. Or do you Aiel wilders all learn that as well?"

"Few can do it," Aviendha admitted calmly. "But I can." That produced a different sort of stare, from Elayne as well; it was a *very* rare Talent. She did not seem to notice. "Do *you* claim that none of the Shadowsouled can?" she went on. The tightness of her shoulder under Elayne's hand said she was not so cool as she pretended. "Are you such fools that you leave tracks for your enemies to follow? Any who could read the residues could make a gateway to this spot."

That would have taken great dexterity, very great dexterity, but the suggestion was enough to leave Merilille blinking. Adeleas opened her mouth, then closed it without speaking, and Vandene frowned thoughtfully. Sareitha simply looked worried. Who could say what Talents the Forsaken had, what skill?

Strangely, all the fierceness drained out of Aviendha. Her eyes fell, her shoulders loosened. "Perhaps I should not have taken the risk," she muttered. "With that man watching me, I could not think clearly, and when he disappeared. . . ." A little of her spirit returned, but not a great deal. "I do not think a man could read my weaves," she said to Elayne, "but if he was one of the Shadowsouled, or even the *gholam*. . . . The Shadowsouled know more than any of us. If I was wrong, I have great *toh*. But I do not think I was. I do not think it."

"What man?" Nynaeve demanded. Her hat had been knocked askew in pushing among the horses, and that, with the tight frown she directed at everyone impartially, made her look ready for a fight. Perhaps she was. Careane's geld-

ing accidentally nudged her with a shoulder, and she swatted the blue dun's nose.

"A servant," Merilille said dismissively. "Whatever orders Tylin gave, Altaran servants are an independent lot. Or
perhaps her son; that boy is too curious by half."

The sisters around her nodded, and Careane said, "One
of the Forsaken would hardly have stood and watched. You
said so yourself." She was patting her gelding's neck and
frowning accusingly at Nynaeve—Careane was one of
those who gave her horse the sort of affection most people
reserved for infants—she was frowning at Nynaeve, and
Nynaeve took the words for her, too.

"Maybe it was a servant, and maybe it was Beslan.
Maybe." Nynaeve's sniff said she did not believe it. Or that
she wanted them to believe she did not; she could tell you
to your face that you were a blind idiot, yet let anyone else
say it, and she would defend you until she went hoarse. Of
course, she did not seem ready to decide whether she liked
Aviendha, but she definitely did not like the older Aes Sedai. She tugged her hat almost straight, and her frown swept
across them, then started over. "Whether it was Beslan or
the Dark One, there's no call to stand here all day. We need
to get ready and move on to the farm. Well? Move!" She
clapped her hands sharply, and even Vandene gave a little
start.

There was little preparation left to do when the sisters
moved their horses away. Lan and the other Warders had
not sat on their heels once they realized there was no
danger. Some of the servants had gone back through the
gateway before Aviendha disposed of it, but the rest stood
with the three dozen or so packhorses, occasionally glancing at the Aes Sedai, clearly wondering what marvel they
might produce next. The Windfinders were all mounted,
if awkwardly, and holding their reins as though expecting
their horses to bolt any moment, or perhaps sprout wings
and take flight. So were the Knitting Circle, with a good
deal more grace, unconcerned that their skirts and petticoats were pushed up past their knees, and with Ispan still
hooded and tied across a saddle like a sack. She could not
possibly have sat upright on a horse, yet even Sumeko's eyes
popped whenever they touched her.

Glaring about her, Nynaeve looked ready to tongue-lash everybody into doing what they had already done, but only until Lan handed her the reins of her plump brown mare. She had adamantly refused the gift of a better horse from Tylin. Her hand trembled a little when it touched Lan's, and her face changed color as she swallowed the anger she had been about to unleash. When he offered a hand for her foot, she stared at him for a moment as if wondering what he was about, then colored again when he boosted her to her saddle. Elayne could only shake her head. She hoped she did not turn into an idiot when she married. If she married.

Birgitte brought her silvery-gray mare and the yellow dun Aviendha rode, but she seemed to understand that Elayne wanted a private word with Aviendha. She nodded almost as if Elayne had spoken, swung up onto her mouse-colored gelding, and rode to where the other Warders were waiting. They greeted her with nods and began discussing something in low voices. By the glances directed at the sisters, the "something" had to do with taking care of Aes Sedai whether Aes Sedai wanted care taken or not. Including herself, Elayne noted grimly. There was no time now for that, though. Aviendha stood fiddling with her horse's reins, staring at the animal like a novice staring at a kitchen full of greasy pots. Very likely, Aviendha saw small difference between having to scrub pots and having to ride.

Snugging her green riding gloves, Elayne casually shifted Lioness to block them from the others' view, then touched Aviendha's arm. "Talking to Adeleas or Vandene might help," she said gently. She had to be very careful here, as careful as with any *ter'angreal.* "They're old enough to know more than you might suspect. There has to be a reason you've been . . . having trouble . . . with Traveling." That was a mild way of putting it. Aviendha almost had failed to make the weave work at all, in the beginning. Careful. Aviendha was far more important than any *ter'angreal* ever could be. "They might be able to help."

"How can they?" Aviendha stared stiffly at the saddle on her gelding. "They cannot Travel. How could any of them know how to help?" Abruptly her shoulders slumped, and she turned her head to Elayne. Shockingly, unshed tears glistened in her green eyes. "That isn't the truth, Elayne. Not the whole truth. They cannot help, but. . . . You are my near-sister; you have the right to know. They think I panicked at a servant. If I ask for help, it must all come out. That I Traveled once to run from a man, a man I hoped in my soul would catch me. To run like a rabbit. To run, wanting to be caught. How could I let them know such shame? Even if they really could help, how could I?"

Elayne wished she did not know. About the catching part, at least. About the fact that Rand *had* caught her. Snatching the flecks of jealousy that suddenly were floating through her, she pushed them into a sack and stuffed it into the back of her head. Then she jumped up and down on it for good measure. *When a woman plays the fool, look for the man.* That was one of Lini's favorites. Another was, *Kittens tangle your yarn, men tangle your wits, and it's simple as breathing for both.* She drew a deep breath. "No one will know from me, Aviendha. I'll help you as much as I can. If I can figure out how." Not that there was much she could think to do. Aviendha was remarkably quick at seeing how weaves were formed, much quicker than she herself.

Aviendha merely nodded and scrambled clumsily into her saddle, showing a bit more grace than the Sea Folk. "There was a man watching, Elayne, and he was no servant." Looking Elayne right in the eye, she added, "He frightened me." An admission she likely would have made to no one else in the world.

"We're safe from him now, whoever he was," Elayne said, turning Lioness to follow Nynaeve and Lan from the clearing. In truth, it very likely had been a servant, but she would never tell that to anyone, Aviendha least of all. "We're safe, and in a few more hours, we will reach the Kin's farm, we'll use the Bowl, and the world will be right again." Well, somewhat. The sun seemed lower than it had in the stableyard, but she knew that was only imagination. For once, they had gained a clear jump on the Shadow.

From behind a screen of white wrought iron, Moridin watched the last of the horses vanish through the gateway, and then the tall young woman and the four Warders. It was possible they were carrying away some item he could use—an *angreal* attuned to men, perhaps—but the chances were small. For the rest, the *ter'angreal*, the greatest likelihood was that they would kill themselves trying to puzzle out how to use them. Sammael was a fool to have risked so much to seize a collection of no one knew what. But then, Sammael had never been half as clever as he thought. He himself would not disrupt his own plans merely on the off chance, to see what scraps of civilization he could find. Only idle curiosity had brought him here. He liked to know what others thought important. But it was dross.

He was about to turn away when the outlines of the gateway suddenly began to flex and tremble. Transfixed, he watched until the opening simply—melted. He had never been a man to give way to obscenities, but several rose in his mind. What had the woman done? These barbarous rustics offered too many surprises. A way to Heal being severed, however imperfectly. That was impossible! Except that they had done it. Involuntary rings. Those Warders and the bond they shared with their Aes Sedai. He had known of that for a long, long time, but whenever he thought he had the measure of them, these *primitives* revealed some new skill, did something that no one in his own Age had dreamed of. Something the pinnacle of civilization had not known! What had the girl done?

"Great Master?"

Moridin barely turned his head from the window. "Yes, Madic?" Her soul be damned, what had the girl done?

The balding man in green-and-white who had slipped into the small room bowed deeply before falling to his knees. One of the upper servants in the palace, Madic, with his long face, possessed a pompous dignity that he tried to maintain even now. Moridin had seen men who stood far higher do far worse. "Great Master, I have learned what the Aes Sedai brought to the palace this morning. It is said they found a great treasure hidden in ancient days, gold and jewels and heartstone, artifacts from Shiota and Eharon and even the Age of Legends. There are said to be things among them that use the One Power. It is said that one can control the weather. No one knows where they are going, Great Master. The palace is aquiver with talk, but ten tongues name ten different destinations."

Moridin went back to studying the stableyard below as soon as Madic spoke. Ridiculous tales of gold and *cuendillar* held no interest. Nothing would make a gateway behave that way. Unless. . . . Could she actually have *unraveled* the web? Death held no fear for him. Coldly he considered the possibility that he had been within sight of an unraveling web. One that had been unmade successfully. Another impossibility casually offered up by these . . .

Something Madic had said caught his ear. "The weather, Madic?" The shadows of the palace spires had barely lengthened from their bases, but there was not a cloud to shield the baking city.

"Yes, Great Master. It is called the Bowl of the Winds."

The name meant nothing to him. But . . . a *ter'angreal* to control the weather. . . . In his own Age, weather had been carefully regulated with the use of *ter'angreal*. One of the surprises of this Age—one of the smaller, it had seemed— was that there were those who could manipulate weather to a degree that should have required one of those *ter'angreal*. One such device should not be enough to affect even a large part of a single continent. But what could these women do with it? What? If they used a ring?

He seized the True. Power without thought, the *saa* billowing black across his sight. His fingers tightened in the wrought-iron grille across the window; the metal groaned, twisting, not from his grip but from the tendrils of the True Power, drawn from the Great Lord himself, that wreathed around the grillework, flexing as he flexed his hand in anger. The Great Lord would not be pleased. He had strained from his prison to touch the world enough to fix the seasons in place. He was impatient to touch the world more, to shatter the void that contained him, and he would not be pleased. Rage enveloped Moridin, blood pounding in his ears. A moment past, he had not cared where those women went, but now. . . . Somewhere far from here. People fleeing ran as far and as fast as they could. Somewhere they felt safe. No use sending Madic to ask questions, no use squeezing anyone here; they would not have been fool enough to leave anyone behind alive who knew their destination. Not to Tar Valon. To al'Thor? To that band of rebel Aes Sedai? In all three places he had eyes, some that did not know they served him. All would serve him, before the end. He would not allow chance slips to spoil his plans now.

Abruptly he heard something other than the thundering drumbeat of his own fury. A bubbling sound. He looked at

Madic curiously, and stepped back from the spreading puddle on the floor. It seemed that in his anger he had seized at more than the wrought-iron screen with the True Power. Remarkable how much blood could be squeezed from a human body.

He let what remained of the man fall without regret; indeed, thinking only that when Madic was found, the Aes Sedai would surely be blamed. A small addition to the chaos growing in the world. Ripping a hole in the fabric of the Pattern, he Traveled with the True Power. He had to find those women before they used this Bowl of the Winds. And failing that. . . . He disliked people meddling with his carefully laid plans. Those who did so and lived, lived to pay.

The *gholam* stepped into the room cautiously, nostrils already twitching with the scent of still hot blood. The livid burn on its cheek seemed like a live coal. The *gholam* appeared to be merely a slender man, a little taller than average in this time, yet it had never encountered anything that could harm it. Until that man with the medallion. What might have been smile or snarl bared its teeth. Curious, it peered around the room, but there was nothing beyond the crushed corpse on the floor tiles. And a . . . feel . . . of something. Not the One Power, but something that made it . . . itch, if not quite in the same way. Curiosity had brought it here. Parts of the grille over the window were crushed, pulling the whole thing loose at the sides. The *gholam* seemed to remember something that made it itch in that manner, yet so much of what it recalled was fogged and dim. The world had changed, as it seemed, in the blink of an eye. There had been a world of war and killing on a huge scale, with weapons that reached across miles, across thousands of miles, and then there was . . . this. But the *gholam* had not changed. It was still the most dangerous weapon of all.

Its nostrils flared again, though it was not by scent that it tracked those who could channel. The One Power had been used below, and miles to the north. To follow, or not? The man who had wounded it was not with them; it had made sure of that before leaving the high vantage place. The one who commanded it wanted the man who had wounded it dead perhaps as much as he did the women, but the women were an easier target. The women had been named, too, and for the time being, it was constrained. For its entire existence it had been compelled to obey one or another human, but its mind held the concept of not being constrained. It must follow the women. It wanted to follow. The moment of death, when it felt the ability to channel vanish along with life, produced ecstasy. Rapture. But it was hungry, too, and there was time. Where they could run, it could follow. Settling fluidly beside the mangled body, it began to feed. Fresh blood, hot blood, was a necessity, but human blood always held the sweetest savor.

CHAPTER

3

A Pleasant Ride

Farms and pastures and olive groves covered most of the land around Ebou Dar, but many small forests stretched a few miles across as well, and while the ground was much flatter than the Rhannon Hills to the south, it rolled and sometimes rose in a prominence of a hundred feet or higher, sufficient to cast deep shadows in the afternoon sun. All in all, the country provided more than enough cover to keep unwanted eyes from what might have passed as some odd merchant's pack train, nearly fifty people mounted and almost as many afoot, especially when it had Warders to find unfrequented paths through the undergrowth. Elayne did not sight a mark of human habitation beyond a few goats cropping on some of the hills.

Even plants and trees used to heat were beginning to wither and die, yet at any other time she might have enjoyed merely seeing the countryside. It could have been a thousand leagues from the land she had seen riding down the other bank of the Eldar. The hills were strange, knobby shapes, as though squeezed together by huge, careless hands. Flocks of brilliantly hued birds soared up at their passing, and a dozen sorts of hummingbirds flitted away from the horses, hovering jewels on blurred wings. Thick vines hung like ropes in some places, and there were trees with bundles of narrow fronds at the top for foliage, and things that looked like green feather dusters as tall as a man. A handful of plants, fooled by the heat, struggled to put out blossoms, bright reds and vivid yellows, some twice as wide as her two hands. Their perfume was lush and—"sultry" came to mind. She saw some boulders she would have wagered had once been toes on a statue, though why anyone would make a statue that large with bare feet she could not imagine, and another time the way led through a forest of thick fluted stones among the trees, the weathered stumps of columns, many toppled and all long since mined almost to the ground for their stone by local farmers. A pleasant ride despite the dust the horses' hooves raised from parched soil. The heat did not touch her, of course, and there were not very many flies. All the dangers lay behind them; they had outrun the Forsaken, and no chance any of them or their servants could catch up now. It *could* have been a pleasant ride, except. . . .

For one thing, Aviendha learned that the message she had sent about enemies coming when least expected had not been delivered. At first Elayne felt relief at anything to change the topic from Rand. It was not the jealousy come back; rather, more and more she found herself wanting what Aviendha had shared with him. Not jealousy. Envy. She would almost have preferred the other. Then she began really hearing what her friend was saying in a low monotone, and the hair on the back of her neck tried to stand.

"You can't do that," she protested, reining her horse closer to Aviendha's. Actually, she supposed Aviendha would not have much trouble drubbing Kurin, or tying her up, or any of the rest. If the other Sea Folk women stood still for it, anyway. "We can't start a war with them, certainly not before we use the Bowl. And not over this," she added hastily. "Not at all." They certainly were not going to start a war before or after the Bowl was used. Not just because the Windfinders were behaving more high-handedly by the hour. Not just because. . . . Drawing breath, she hurried on. "If she *had* told me, I would not have known what you meant. I understand why you couldn't speak more clearly, but you do see, don't you?"

Aviendha glared ahead at nothing, absently brushing flies away from her face. "Without fail, I told her," she grumbled. "Without fail! What if he had been one of the Shadowsouled? What if he had managed to get by me through the gateway, and you with no warning? What if . . . ?" She turned a suddenly forlorn gaze on Elayne. "I will bite my knife," she said sadly, "but my liver may burst for it."

Elayne was about to say that swallowing her anger was

the right thing to do and she could pitch as large a fit as she
wanted so long as she did not hurl it at the Atha'an Miere—
that was what all that about knives and livers meant—but
before she could open her mouth, Adeleas brought her
rangy gray up on her other side. The white-haired sister had
acquired a new saddle in Ebou Dar, a gaudy thing worked
with silver on pommel and cantle. The flies seemed to avoid
her, for some reason, though she wore a scent as strong as
any of the flowers.

"Pardon me. I could not help overhearing that last." Adeleas did not sound at all apologetic, and Elayne wondered
just how much she had overheard. She felt her cheeks coloring. Some of what Aviendha had said about Rand had been
remarkably frank and straightforward. Some of what she
had said had been, too. It was one thing to talk that way
with your nearest friend, quite another to suspect someone
else had been listening. Aviendha seemed to feel the same
way; she did not blush, but the sour look she shot at the
Brown would have done Nynaeve proud.

Adeleas merely smiled, a vague smile as bland as water
soup. "It might be best if you gave your friend there free
rein with the Atha'an Miere." She peered past Elayne at
Aviendha, blinking. "Well, a loose rein. Putting the fear of
the Light into them ought to be sufficient. They're almost
there already, in case you haven't noticed. They're much
more wary of the 'savage' Aiel—forgive me, Aviendha—
than they are of Aes Sedai. Merilille would have suggested
it, but her ears are still burning."

Aviendha's face rarely gave much away, but right then
she looked as puzzled as Elayne felt. Elayne twisted in her
saddle to frown behind her. Merilille rode abreast with
Vandene, Careane, and Sareitha not far back, all very studi-
ously looking at anything except Elayne. Beyond the sisters
were the Sea Folk, still in single file, and then would come
the Knitting Circle, keeping themselves out of sight for the
moment just ahead of the packhorses. They were threading
their way through the glades of truncated columns. Fifty
or a hundred long-tailed red-and-green birds winged over
their heads, filling the air with chattering cries.

"Why?" Elayne asked curtly. It seemed foolish to add to
the turmoil already bubbling just below the surface—and
sometimes on the surface—but she had seen no hint of the

fool in Adeleas. The Brown sister's eyebrows rose in apparent surprise. Maybe she was surprised; Adeleas usually thought anyone should see what she saw. Maybe.

"Why? To restore a little balance, that is why. If the Atha'an Miere feel they need us to protect them from an Aiel, it might be a useful balance against. . . ." Adeleas paused slightly, suddenly absorbed in adjusting her pale gray skirts. ". . . other things."

Elayne's face tightened. Other things. The bargain with the Sea Folk was what Adeleas meant. "You may ride with the others," she said coolly.

Adeleas made no protest, no attempts to press her argument. She just inclined her head and let her horse fall back. Her small smile never altered a whit. The older Aes Sedai accepted that Nynaeve and Elayne stood above them and spoke with Egwene's authority at their backs, but the truth was, that changed little beyond the surface. Perhaps nothing. They were outwardly respectful, they obeyed, and yet. . . .

After all was said and done, Elayne, at least, was Aes Sedai at an age when most initiates of the Tower still wore novice white and very few had reached the Accepted. And she and Nynaeve had agreed to that bargain, hardly a display of wisdom and acumen. Not just the Sea Folk getting the Bowl, but twenty sisters going to the Atha'an Miere, subject to their laws, required to teach anything the Windfinders wanted to learn and unable to leave until others came to replace them. Windfinders allowed to enter the Tower as guests, allowed to learn whatever they wished, leave whenever they wished. Those alone would make the Hall scream, and probably Egwene as well, yet the rest. . . . Every last one of the older sisters thought she would have found a way around making that bargain. Perhaps they really could have. Elayne did not believe it, but she was not sure.

She did not say anything to Aviendha, but after a few moments, the other woman spoke. "If I can serve honor and help you at the same time, I do not care whether it serves some Aes Sedai end." She never seemed to take it in that Elayne was also Aes Sedai, not completely.

Elayne hesitated, then nodded. Something had to be done to temper the Sea Folk. Merilille and the others had displayed a remarkable forbearance so far, but how long would that last? Nynaeve might explode, once she actually turned her attentions to the Windfinders. Matters had to be kept as smooth as possible for as long as possible, but if the Atha'an Miere went on believing they could stare down any Aes Sedai, there would be trouble. Life was more complex than she had imagined back in Caemlyn, no matter how many lessons she had received as Daughter-Heir. So much more complicated since she entered the Tower.

"Just don't be too . . . emphatic," she said softly. "And please have a care. There are twenty of them, after all, and only one of you. I wouldn't want anything to happen before I could help you." Aviendha gave her a grin with a good bit of wolf in it and drew her dun mare off at the edge of the stones to wait for the Atha'an Miere.

From time to time Elayne glanced back, but all she saw through the trees was Aviendha riding next to Kurin, speaking quite calmly and not even looking at the Sea Folk woman. Certainly not glaring, though Kurin seemed to stare at her with considerable astonishment. When Aviendha thumped her horse back up to join Elayne, flapping her reins—she would never be a horsewoman—Kurin rode forward to speak with Renaile, and a short time later Renaile angrily sent Rainyn to the head of the column.

The most junior of the Windfinders sat her horse even more awkwardly than Aviendha, whom she pretended to ignore on Elayne's other side just as she ignored the small green flies buzzing around her dark face. "Renaile din Calon Blue Star," she said stiffly, "demands that you snub the Aiel woman, Elayne Aes Sedai." Aviendha grinned toothily at her, and Rainyn must have been watching at least a little, because her cheeks reddened beneath the sheen of sweat.

"Tell Renaile that Aviendha is not Aes Sedai," Elayne replied. "I will ask her to be careful," no lie there; she had, and would again, "but I can't *make* her do anything." On impulse, she added, "You know how Aiel are." The Sea Folk had some very odd ideas of how the Aiel were. Rainyn stared wide-eyed at a still-grinning Aviendha, her face going gray, then jerked her horse around and galloped back to Renaile, bouncing in her saddle.

Aviendha gave a pleased chuckle, but Elayne wondered whether the whole notion had been a mistake. Even with a good thirty paces between them, she could see Renaile's face swell up at Rainyn's report, and the others began to buzz like bees. They did not look frightened, they looked angry, and the glares they directed at the Aes Sedai ahead of them grew baleful. Not at Aviendha, at the sisters. Adeleas nodded thoughtfully when she saw that, and Merilille just barely failed to hide a smile. At least they were pleased.

If that had been the only incident during the ride it would have taken the edge off any enjoyment of flowers and birds, but it was not even the first. Beginning shortly after leaving the clearing, the Knitting Circle had made their way forward to Elayne one by one, all but Kirstian, and no doubt she would have come too had she not been ordered to keep Ispan shielded. One by one they came, each hesitant, smiling timorously until Elayne wanted to tell them to act their ages. They certainly made no demands, and they were too smart to ask straight out for what already had been denied, but they found other paths.

"It occurred to me," Reanne said brightly, "that you must want to question Ispan Sedai quite urgently. Who can say what else she was up to in the city besides trying to find the storeroom?" She pretended to just be making conversation, but from time to time she darted quick looks at Elayne to see how she was taking it. "I'm sure we'll take over an hour to reach the farm, the way we're going, perhaps two, and you certainly don't want to waste two hours. The herbs Nynaeve Sedai gave her make her quite talkative, and I'm sure she would sit up for sisters."

The bright smile faded when Elayne said that questioning Ispan could wait and would. Light, did they really expect anyone to ask questions riding through forests on paths that barely deserved the name? Reanne rode back to the other Kinswomen muttering to herself.

"Forgiveness, Elayne Sedai," Chilares murmured a short time later, the traces of Murandy clinging to her accent. Her green straw hat matched some of her layered petticoats exactly. "Your forgiveness, if I intrude." She did not wear the red belt of a Wise Woman; most of the Knitting Circle did not. Ivara was a goldsmith, and Eldase supplied lacquerware to the merchants for export; Chilares was a rug seller, while Reanne herself arranged shipping for small traders. Some worked at simple tasks—Kirstian ran a tiny weaver's shop, and Dimana was a seamstress, though a prosperous one—but then, in the course of their lives, they had all followed many crafts. And used many names. "Ispan Sedai appears to be unwell," Chilares said, shifting uneasily in her saddle. "Perhaps the herbs are affecting her more than Nynaeve Sedai thought. It would be terrible if anything happened to her. Before she can be questioned, I mean. Perhaps the sisters would look at her? Healing, you know. . . ." She trailed off, blinking those big brown eyes nervously. As well she might, with Sumeko among her companions.

A glance back showed the stout woman standing in her stirrups to peer past the Windfinders, until she saw Elayne looking and sat back down hurriedly. Sumeko, who knew more of Healing than any sister except Nynaeve. Perhaps *more* than Nynaeve. Elayne simply pointed to the rear until Chilares colored and reined her mount around.

Merilille joined Elayne only moments after Reanne left, and the Gray sister made a much better pretense at simple chat than the Kinswoman had. In her manner of speaking, at least, she was poise itself. What she had to say was another matter. "I wonder how trustworthy those women are, Elayne." Her lips pursed in distaste as she brushed dust from her divided blue skirts with a gloved hand. "They say they do not take in wilders, but Reanne herself may well be a wilder, whatever she claims about failing her test for Accepted. Sumeko, as well, and certainly Kirstian." A slight frown for Kirstian, a dismissive shake of her head. "You must have noticed how she leaps at any mention of the Tower. She knows no more than she might have picked up in conversation with someone who really was put out." Merilille sighed, regretting what she had to say; she really was very good. "Have you considered that they may be lying about other things? They could be Darkfriends, for all we know, or dupes of Darkfriends. Perhaps not, but they are hardly to be trusted very far. I believe there is a farm, whether they really use it for a retreat or not, or I would not have agreed to this, but I will not be surprised to find a few ramshackle buildings and a dozen or so wilders. Well, not ramshackle—they do seem to have coin—but the principle is the same. No, they are simply not trustworthy."

Elayne began a slow burn as soon as she realized the direction Merilille was taking, and it grew hotter. As this slipping around, all this "may" and "could" so the woman could insinuate things she herself did not believe. Darkfriends? The Knitting Circle had *fought* Darkfriends. Two had died. And without Sumeko and Ieine, Nynaeve might be dead instead of Ispan a prisoner. No, the reason they were not to be trusted was not because Merilille feared they were sworn to the Shadow, or she would have said so. They were not to be trusted because if they were not trusted, then they could not be allowed to hold Ispan.

She swatted a big green fly that had settled on Lioness's neck, punctuating Merilille's last word with a loud crack, and the Gray sister jerked in surprise. "How dare you?" Elayne breathed. "They faced Ispan and Falion in the Rahad, and the *gholam,* not to mention two dozen or more toughs with swords. *You* weren't there." That was hardly fair. Merilille and the rest had been left behind because Aes Sedai in the Rahad, obvious Aes Sedai, might as well be trumpets and drums for the attention they attracted. She did not care. Her anger grew by the moment, and her voice rose by the word. "You will *never* suggest such a thing to me again. *Never*! Not without hard evidence! Not without *proof*! If you do, I'll set you a penance that will make your eyes pop!" No matter how high she stood above the other woman, she had no authority to set her any penance at all, but she did not care about that, either. "I'll make you *walk* the rest of the way to Tar Valon! Eating nothing but bread and water the entire way! I'll put *you* in their charge, and tell them to slap you down if you say boo to a *goose*!"

It dawned on her that she was shouting. Some sort of gray-and-white birds went flittering past overhead in a broad band, and she was drowning out their cries. Drawing a deep breath, she tried to calm herself. She did not have a voice for shouting; it always came out as a shriek. Everyone was looking at her, most in astonishment. Aviendha nodded approvingly. Of course, she would have done the same had Elayne plunged a knife into Merilille's heart. Aviendha stood beside her friends no matter what. Merilille's Cairhienin paleness had become dead white.

"I mean what I say," Elayne told her, in a much cooler tone. It seemed to make even more blood leave Merilille's face. She did mean every word; they could not afford that sort of rumor floating among them. One way or another she would see it done, though the Knitting Circle very likely would faint.

She hoped that was the end of it. It should have been. But when Chilares left, Sareitha replaced her, and she too had a reason the Kinswomen were not to be trusted. Their ages. Even Kirstian claimed to be older than any living Aes Sedai, while Reanne was over a hundred years more than that and not even the oldest of the Kin. Her title of Eldest went to the oldest of them in Ebou Dar, and the rigid schedule they followed to avoid notice had a number of still older women off in other places. It was obviously impossible, Sareitha maintained.

Elayne did not shout; she very carefully did not shout. "We will learn the truth eventually," she told Sareitha. She did not doubt the Kinswomen's word, but there had to be a reason why the Kinswomen looked neither ageless nor anything near the ages they claimed. If she could only puzzle it out. Something told her it was obvious, but nothing leaped up that said what. "Eventually," she added firmly when the Brown opened her mouth again. "That will be enough, Sareitha." Sareitha nodded uncertainly and fell back. Not ten minutes later, Sibella replaced her.

Every time one of the Kinswomen came to make her roundabout plea to be relieved of Ispan, one of the sisters came soon after to offer the same plea. All save Merilille, who still blinked whenever Elayne looked at her. Perhaps shouting did have its uses. Certainly no one else tried to be so straightforward in attacking the Kin.

For instance, Vandene began with discussing the Sea Folk and how to counter the effects of the bargain made with them, why it was necessary to counter them as much as possible. She was quite matter-of-fact, with never a word or gesture to lay any blame. Not that she needed any; the subject did that, however delicately handled. The White Tower, she said, maintained its influence in the world not by force of arms, or persuasion, or even by plotting or manipulation, though those two she brushed past lightly. Rather the White Tower controlled or influenced events to whatever extent they did because everyone saw the Tower as standing apart and above, more even than kings or queens. That in turn depended on every Aes Sedai being seen that way, as mysterious and apart, different from everyone else. A different flesh. Historically, Aes Sedai who could not manage that—and there were a few—were kept out of public view as much as possible.

It took Elayne a little while to realize that the thrust of the conversation had shifted away from the Sea Folk, and to see where it was headed. A different flesh, mysterious and apart, could not have a sack thrust over its head and be tied across a saddle. Not where anyone who was not Aes Sedai could see, anyway. In truth, the sisters would be rougher on Ispan than the Knitting Circle could possibly make themselves be, just not in public. The argument might have borne more weight had it come first, but as it was, Elayne sent Vandene packing as quickly as she did anyone else. And saw her replaced by Adeleas, right after Sibella was told that if none of the Knitting Circle could understand what Ispan was mumbling, then none of the sisters was likely to either. Mumbling! Light! The Aes Sedai took their repeated turns, and even knowing what they were up to, sometimes it was hard to see the connection at first. By the time Careane began by telling her that those boulders really had been toes once, supposedly on a statue of some warrior queen nearly two hundred feet high. . . .

"Ispan stays where she is," she told Careane coolly without waiting for more. "Now, unless you really want to tell me why the Shiotans thought of putting up a statue like that. . . ." The Green said ancient records claimed it had worn little more than armor, and not a great deal of that! A queen! "No? Then, if you don't mind, I'd like to talk with Aviendha alone. Thank you so much." Even being curt did not stop them, of course. She was surprised they did not send Merilille's *maid* to take a turn.

None of this would have happened had Nynaeve been where she was meant to be. At least, Elayne was sure that Nynaeve could have quelled the Knitting Circle and the sisters both, in short order. She was a great one for quelling. The problem was that Nynaeve had glued herself tight to Lan's side before they left the first clearing. The Warders scouted ahead and to both sides of their path, and sometimes to the rear, only riding back to the column long enough to report what they had seen or give directions on how to avoid a farm or a shepherd. Birgitte ranged far, never spending more than moments with Elayne. Lan ranged farther. And where Lan went, Nynaeve went.

"No one's making any trouble, are they?" she demanded with a dark stare for the Sea Folk, the first time she followed Lan back. "Well, that's all right, then," she said before Elayne had a chance to open her mouth. Spinning her round-bellied mare like a racer, she flicked the reins and galloped after Lan holding her hat on with one hand, catching up to him just as he vanished around the flank of the hill ahead. Of course, then there really was nothing to complain about. Reanne had made her visit, and Merilille hers, and everything seemed settled.

By the next time Nynaeve appeared, Elayne had suffered through a number of disguised attempts to have Ispan turned over to the sisters, Aviendha had spoken to Kurin, and the Windfinders were on a slow boil, but when Elayne explained, Nynaeve simply looked around, frowning. Of course, right at that moment everyone had to be where they belonged. The Atha'an Miere wore glares, true, but the Knitting Circle were all behind them, and as for the other sisters, no group of novices could have appeared more well-behaved and innocent. Elayne wanted to shriek!

"I'm sure you can handle everything, Elayne," Nynaeve said. "You *have* had all that training to be a queen. This can't be anywhere near so—Drat the man! He's going again! You can handle it." And off she went, galloping that poor mare as though it were a warhorse.

That was when Aviendha chose to discuss how Rand seemed to like kissing the sides of her neck. And incidentally how much she had liked it. Elayne had liked that when he did it to her, too, but however used to discussing this sort of thing she had become—uncomfortably used to it—she did not want to talk about it right then. She was angry with Rand. It was unfair, but if not for him, she could have told Nynaeve to stop treating Lan like a child who might trip over his own feet and attend to her own duties. She almost wanted to blame him for the way the Knitting Circle was behaving, too, and the other sisters, and the Windfinders. *It's one of the things men are for, taking the blame*, she remembered Lini saying once, and laughing while she did. *They usually deserve it, even if you don't know exactly how.*

Not fair, yet she wished he were there long enough for her to box his ears, just once. Long enough to kiss him, to have him kiss the sides of her neck softly. Long enough to. . . .

"He will listen to advice, even when he doesn't like hearing it," she said abruptly, her face reddening. Light, for all her talk about shame, in some areas Aviendha had none. And it seemed that she herself no longer had any, either! "But if I tried to push him, he dug in his heels even when it was plain that I was right. Was he that way with you?"

Aviendha glanced at her and appeared to understand. Elayne was not sure whether she liked that or not. At least there was no more talk of Rand and kissing. For a while, anyway. Aviendha had some knowledge of men—she had traveled with them as a Maiden of the Spear, fought beside them—but she had never wanted to be anything but *Far Dareis Mai,* and there were . . . gaps. Even with her dolls as a child she had always played at the spears and raiding. She had never flirted, did not understand it, and she did not understand why she felt the way she did when Rand's eyes fell on her, or a hundred other things Elayne had begun learning the first time she noticed a boy looking at her differently than he did at the other boys. She expected Elayne to teach her all of it, and Elayne tried. She really could talk to Aviendha about anything. If only Rand had not been the example used quite so often. If he had been there, she *would* have boxed his ears. And kissed him. Then boxed his ears again.

Not a pleasant ride at all. A miserable ride.

Nynaeve made several more brief visits, before finally coming to announce that the Kin's farm lay just ahead, out of sight around a low rounded hill that appeared ready to fall on its side. Reanne had been pessimistic in her estimate; the sun had not fallen nearly two hours' worth.

"We'll be there very quickly, now," Nynaeve told Elayne, not seeming to notice the sullen stare Elayne gave in return. "Lan, fetch Reanne up here, please. Best if they see a familiar face right off." He whirled his horse away, and Nynaeve turned in her saddle briefly to fix the sisters with a firm eye. "I don't want you frightening them, now. You hold your tongues until we have a chance to explain what's what. And hide your faces. Pull up the hoods of your cloaks." Straightening without waiting for any reply, she gave a satisfied nod. "There. All settled, and all right. I vow, Elayne, I don't know what you were moaning so about. Everyone's doing exactly as they should, so far as I can see."

Elayne ground her teeth. She wished they were in Caemlyn already. That was where they were heading once this was done. She had duties long overdue in Caemlyn. All she had to deal with there was convincing the stronger Houses that the Lion Throne was hers despite her long absence, that and handling a rival claimant or two. There might not have been any had she been there when her mother vanished, when she died, but the history of Andor said there would be by now. Somehow, it seemed ever so much easier than this.

CHAPTER

4

A Quiet Place

The Kin's farm lay in a broad hollow surrounded by three low hills, a sprawling affair of more than a dozen large, white-plastered buildings with flat roofs, gleaming in the sun. Four great barns were built right into the slope of the highest hill, a flat-topped thing with one side that fell away in steep cliffs beyond the barns. A few tall trees that had not lost all of their leaves provided a modicum of shade in the farmyard. To the north and east, olive groves marched away and even up the sides of the hills. A sort of slow bustle enveloped the farm, with easily over a hundred people in evidence despite the afternoon heat, carrying on all the everyday tasks but none quickly.

It might almost have passed for a small village instead of a farm, except that there was not a man or a child to be seen. Elayne did not expect any. This was a waypoint for Kinswomen passing through Ebou Dar to elsewhere, so there would not be too many in the city itself at one time, but that was a secret matter, as secret as the Kin themselves. Publicly this farm was known for two hundred miles or more as a retreat for women, a place for contemplation and escape from the cares of the world for a time, a few days, a week, sometimes longer. Elayne could almost feel serenity in the air. She might have regretted bringing the world into this quiet place, except that she also brought new hope.

The first appearance of the horses coming around the leaning hill produced far less stir than she expected. A number of the women stopped to watch, but no more than that. Their clothing varied widely—Elayne even saw a sheen of silk here and there—but some carried baskets and others buckets, or great white bundles of what had to be wash. One held a pair of bound ducks by the feet in either hand. Noblewoman and craftswoman, farmer and beggar, all were equally welcome here, but everyone did a share of the work during her stay. Aviendha touched Elayne's arm, then pointed to the top of one of the hills, a thing like an inverted funnel skewed to one side. Elayne added a hand to the shade of her hat and after a moment saw movement. Small wonder no one was surprised. Lookouts up there could see anyone coming from a long way.

A middling woman walked out to meet them short of the farm buildings. Her dress was in the Ebou Dari style, with a deep narrow neckline, but her dark skirts and brightly colored petticoats were short enough that she did not need to hold them up out of the dust. She did not wear a marriage knife; the Kin's rules prohibited marriage. The Kin had too many secrets to keep.

"That's Alise," Reanne murmured, reining in between Nynaeve and Elayne. "She runs the farm this turn. She's very intelligent." Almost like an afterthought, she added, even more quietly, "Alise does not suffer fools gladly." As Alise approached, Reanne drew herself up in her saddle, squaring her shoulders as though for an ordeal.

Middling was exactly how Elayne thought of Alise, not someone to give Reanne pause, certainly, even had she not been the Eldest of the Knitting Circle. Straight-backed, Alise appeared to be somewhere in her middle years, neither slender nor stout, tall nor short, a little gray flecking dark brown hair that was tied back with a piece of ribbon, but in a very practical manner. Her face was unremarkable, though pleasant enough, a mild face, perhaps a little long in the jaw. When she saw Reanne, she gave a fleeting look of surprise, then smiled. That smile transformed everything. It did not make her beautiful or even pretty, but Elayne felt warmed by it, comforted.

"I hardly expected to see you . . . Reanne," Alise said, barely hesitating over the name. Obviously she was unsure whether to use Reanne's rightful title in front of Nynaeve and Elayne and Aviendha. She studied them with quick glances as she spoke. There seemed to be a bit of Tarabon in her voice. "Berowin brought word of trouble in the city, of course, but I didn't think it was so bad you would have to leave. Who are all these. . . ." Her words trailed off, and her eyes widened, staring beyond them.

Elayne glanced back, nearly loosing a few of the choice phrases she had picked up in various places, most recently from Mat Cauthon. She did not understand all of them, not most of them really—nobody ever wanted to explain what they meant exactly—but they did have a way of relieving emotion. The Warders had doffed their color-shifting cloaks, and the sisters had drawn up the hoods of their dustcloaks as instructed, even Sareitha, who had no need to hide her youthful face, but Careane had not pulled hers forward far enough. It simply framed her ageless features. Not everyone would know what they were seeing, yet anyone who had been in the Tower surely would. Careane jerked the hood forward at Elayne's glare, but the damage was done.

Others at the farm beside Alise possessed sharp eyes. "Aes Sedai!" a woman howled in tones suitable for announcing the end of the world. Perhaps she was, for her world. Shrieks spread like dust blown on the wind, and that quickly, the farm became a kicked anthill. Here and there a woman simply fainted dead away, but most ran wildly, screaming, dropping what they carried, bumping into one another, falling down and scrambling up to run on. Flapping ducks and chickens and short-horned black goats darted wildly to avoid being trampled. In the midst of it all, some women stood gaping, plainly those who had come to the retreat with no knowledge of the Kin, though a few of them began to move hurriedly, too, caught up in the frenzy.

"Light!" Nynaeve barked, yanking her braid. "Some of them are running into the olive groves! Stop them! The last thing we want is a panic! Send the Warders! Quick, quick!" Lan raised a questioning eyebrow, but she waved a peremptory hand at him. "Quick! Before they *all* run away!" With a nod that seemed to begin as a shake of his head, he sent Mandarb galloping after the other men, curving to avoid the spreading pandemonium among the buildings.

Elayne shrugged at Birgitte, then motioned her to follow. She agreed with Lan. It seemed a bit late to try stopping a panic, and Warders on horseback attempting to herd frightened women probably was not the best way. But she could not see how to change matters now, and there was no point letting them run off into the countryside. They would all want to hear the news she and Nynaeve brought.

Alise gave no sign of running, or even fidgeting. Her face paled slightly, but she stared up at Reanne with a steady gaze. A firm gaze. "Why?" she breathed. "Why, Reanne? I could not have imagined you doing this! Did they give you bribes? Offer immunity? Will they let you walk free while we pay the price? They probably won't allow it, but I vow I'll ask them to let me call you down. Yes, you! The rules apply even to you, *Eldest*! If I can find a way to manage it, I vow you won't walk away from this smiling!" A very firm gaze. Steely, in fact.

"It isn't what you think," Reanne said hurriedly, dismounting and dropping her reins. She caught both of Alise's hands in hers despite the other woman's efforts to free them. "Oh, I did not want it to be like this. They know, Alise. About the Kin. The Tower has *always* known. Everything. Almost everything. But that isn't what is important." Alise's eyebrows tried to climb onto her scalp at that, but Reanne rushed on, beaming eagerly from under her large straw hat. "We can go back, Alise. We can try again. They *said* we can." The farm buildings seemed to be emptying as well, women rushing out to learn what the commotion was, then joining the flight without a pause for more than hiking skirts. Shouts from the olive groves said the Warders were at work, but not how much they were achieving. Perhaps not a great deal. Elayne sensed growing frustration from Birgitte, and irritation. Reanne eyed the turmoil and sighed. "We must gather them in, Alise. We can go back."

"That's all very well for you and some of the others," Alise said doubtfully. "If it's true. What about the rest of us? The Tower would not have let me stay as long as I did had I been quicker to learn." She darted a frown at the now well-hooded sisters, and the stare she returned to Reanne held no little anger. "What would we go back *for*? To be told again we aren't strong enough and be sent on our way? Or will they just keep us as novices the rest of our lives? Some might accept that, but I won't. What for, Reanne? What for?"

Nynaeve climbed down, tugging her mare forward at the end of her reins, and Elayne imitated her, though leading

Lioness more easily. "To be part of the Tower, if that's what you wish," Nynaeve said impatiently before even reaching the two Kinswomen. "Maybe to be Aes Sedai. Myself, I don't know why you have to be a certain strength, if you can pass the fool tests. Or don't go back; run away, for all I care. Once I'm done here, anyway." Planting her feet, she pulled off her hat and planted her fists on her hips. "This is wasting time, Reanne, and we have work to do. Are you sure there's anybody here we can use? Speak up. If you're not sure, then we might as well get on with it. The hurry might be out of the way, but now we have the thing, I'd as soon it was over and done with."

When she and Elayne were introduced as Aes Sedai, the Aes Sedai who had given the promises, Alise made a choked sound and began smoothing her woolen skirts as though her hands wanted to latch on to Reanne's throat. Her mouth opened angrily—then snapped shut without a sound when Merilille joined them. That stern gaze did not fade completely, but it became mixed with a touch of wonder. And more than a touch of wariness.

"Nynaeve Sedai," Merilille said calmly, "the Atha'an Miere are . . . impatient . . . to be off their horses. I think some may ask for Healing." A brief smile flickered across her lips.

That settled that question, though Nynaeve grumbled extravagantly about what she was going to do to the next person who doubted her. Elayne might have said a few choice words herself, but the truth was, Nynaeve looked more than a little silly carrying on that way with Merilille and Reanne both waiting attentively for her to finish and Alise staring at all three. That settled it, or perhaps it was the Windfinders, afoot and pulling their horses behind them. Every shred of grace had vanished during the ride, worn away by hard saddles—their legs seemed as stiff as their faces—yet no one could mistake them for anything but who they were.

"If there are twenty Sea Folk this far from the sea," Alise muttered, "I'll believe anything." Nynaeve snorted but said nothing, for which Elayne was grateful. The woman seemed to be having a hard enough time accepting even with Merilille naming them Aes Sedai. Neither tirade nor tantrum would help.

"Then Heal them," Nynaeve told Merilille. Their eyes

went to the hobbling women together, and Nynaeve added, "If they ask. Politely." Merilille smiled again, but Nynaeve had already abandoned the Sea Folk and gone back to frowning at the now all but empty farm. A few goats still trotted around a farmyard littered with dropped wash and rakes and brooms, spilled buckets and baskets, not to mention the crumpled forms of Kinswomen who had fainted, and a handful of chickens had gone back to scratching and pecking, but the only conscious women still in sight among the farm buildings were plainly not of the Kin. Some wore embroidered linen or silk and some rough country woolens, yet the fact that they had not run spoke that much of them. Reanne said that at any given time as many as half those at the farm might fall into that group. Most appeared stunned.

Despite her grumbling, Nynaeve wasted no time taking charge of Alise. Or perhaps Alise took charge of Nynaeve. It was difficult to tell, since the Kinswoman showed little of the deference toward Aes Sedai that the Knitting Circle did. Perhaps she was still just too numbed by the sudden turn of events. In any case, they moved off together, Nynaeve leading her mare and gesturing with the hat in her other hand, instructing Alise on how to bring in the scattered women and what to do with them once they were collected. Reanne had been sure that at least one woman strong enough to join the circle was there, Garenia Rosoinde, and possibly two more. In truth, Elayne was hoping they had all gone. Alise alternated between nodding and giving Nynaeve very level looks that Nynaeve seemed not to notice.

Now, in the wait while the gathering was done, seemed a good time to do a bit more searching through the panniers, but when Elayne turned toward the packhorses, which were just beginning to be led toward the farm buildings, she noticed the Knitting Circle, Reanne and the whole lot of them, making their own way into the farm on foot, some hurrying toward women lying on the ground, others toward those standing about gaping. The whole lot of them, and no sign of Ispan. It took only a glance to find her, though. Between Adeleas and Vandene, each holding an arm as they half-dragged her along, their dust-cloaks streaming behind.

The white-haired sisters were linked, the glow of *saidar* somehow encompassing them both without including Ispan. There was no way to tell which led the small circle and held

the shield on the Darkfriend, but not even one of the Forsaken could have broken it. They stopped to speak to a stout
woman in plain brown wool, who gaped at the leather sack
covering Ispan's head but still curtsied and pointed toward
one of the white-plastered buildings.

Elayne exchanged angry glances with Aviendha. Well,
hers was angry, anyway. Sometimes Aviendha gave away
no more than a stone. Handing their horses over to two of
the palace stablemen, they hurried after the three. Some of
the women who were not of the Kin tried to question them
about what was happening, a few in rather overbearing
fashion, but Elayne gave them short shrift, leaving behind a
wake of indignant sniffs and snorts. Oh, what she would not
give to have the ageless face already! That tweaked a thread
in the back of her thoughts, but it vanished as soon as she
tried to examine it.

When she pushed open the plain wooden door where the
trio had vanished, Adeleas and Vandene had Ispan seated
in a ladder-back chair with her head bare, the sack lying
atop a narrow trestle table with their linen cloaks. The room
possessed only one window, set in the ceiling, but with the
sun still high it let in a good light. Shelves lined the walls,
stacked with large copper pots and big white bowls. By
the smell of bread baking, the only other door led into a
kitchen.

Vandene looked around sharply at the sound of the door,
but seeing them, she smoothed her face to a total lack of
expression. "Sumeko said the herbs Nynaeve gave her were
wearing off," she said, "and it seemed best to question her
a little before fuzzing her brain again. We do seem to have
time, now. It would be good to know what the . . . the Black
Ajah," her mouth twisted in distaste, "was up to in Ebou
Dar. And what they know."

"I doubt they are aware of this farm, since we were not,"
Adeleas said, tapping a finger thoughtfully on her lips as
she studied the woman in the chair, "but it is better to be
sure than to weep later, as our father used to say." She might
have been examining an animal she had never seen before,
a creature she could not fathom existing.

Ispan's lip curled. Sweat rolled down her bruised face,
and her dark, beaded braids were disheveled and her clothing all disarrayed, but despite bleary eyes, she was not

nearly so woozy as she had been. "The Black Ajah, it is a fable, and a filthy one," she sneered, a trifle hoarsely. It must have been very hot inside that leather sack, and she had had no water since leaving the Tarasin Palace. "Me, I am surprised that you will give it voice. And to cast the charge on me! What I have done, I have done on the orders of the Amyrlin Seat."

"Elaida?" Elayne spat incredulously. "You have the nerve to claim that *Elaida* ordered you to murder sisters and steal from the Tower? *Elaida* ordered what you did in Tear and Tanchico? Or do you mean Siuan? Your lies are pathetic! You've forsaken the Three Oaths, somehow, and that names you Black Ajah."

"I do not have to answer the questions from you," Ispan said sullenly, hunching her shoulders. "You are rebels against the lawful Amyrlin Seat. You will be punished, perhaps stilled. Especially if you harm me. I serve the true Amyrlin Seat, and you will be punished severely if you harm me."

"You will answer any questions my near-sister asks." Aviendha tested her belt knife on a thumbnail, but her eyes were on Ispan's. "Wetlanders fear pain. They do not know how to embrace it, accept it. You will answer as you are asked." She did not glare or snarl, she just spoke, but Ispan shrank back in the chair.

"I fear that is proscribed, even were she not an initiate of the Tower," Adeleas said. "We are forbidden to shed blood in questioning, or to allow others to do so in our name." She sounded reluctant, though whether over the prohibition or over admitting that Ispan was an initiate, Elayne could not say. She herself had not really considered that Ispan might still be considered one. There was a saying that no woman was finished with the Tower until it was finished with her, but truthfully, once the White Tower touched you, it never was finished.

Her brow furrowed as she studied the Black sister, so bedraggled, and still so sure of herself. Ispan sat up a little straighter, and darted glances full of amused contempt at Aviendha—and Elayne. She had not been so poised earlier, when she thought it was Nynaeve and Elayne alone who had her; regained composure had come with remembering that there were older sisters present. Sisters who would hold

White Tower law as part of themselves. That law forbade
not only shedding blood, but breaking bones and a number
of other things that any Whitecloak Questioner would be
more than ready to do. Before any session began, Healing
had to be given, and if the questioning started after sunrise,
it had to end before sundown; if after sunset, then before
sunrise. The law was even more restrictive when it came
to initiates of the Tower, the sisters and Accepted and novices, banning the use of *saidar* in questioning, punishment,
or penance. Oh, a sister might flick a novice's ear with the
Power if she was exasperated, or even give her a swat on
the bottom, but not very much more. Ispan smiled at her.
Smiled! Elayne took a deep breath.

"Adeleas, Vandene, I want you to leave Aviendha and
me alone with Ispan." Her stomach tried to tie itself into a
knot. There had to be a way to press the woman sufficiently
to learn what was needed without breaking Tower law.
But how? People who were to be questioned by the Tower
usually began talking before a finger was laid on them—
everyone *knew* that no one held out against the Tower; *no
one!*—but they were very seldom initiates. She could hear
another voice, not Lini's this time, but her mother's. *What
you order done, you must be willing to do with your own
hand. As a queen, what you order done, you* have *done.* If
she did break the law. . . . Her mother's voice again. *Even
a queen cannot be above the law, or there is no law.* And
Lini's. *You can do whatever you wish, child. So long as
you're willing to pay the price.* She dragged her hat off
without untying the ribbons. Keeping her voice steady took
an effort. "When we are—when we are done talking with
her, you can take her back to the Knitting Circle." Afterward, she would submit herself to Merilille. Any five sisters
could sit in judgment to set a penance, if they were asked.

Ispan's head swung, swollen eyes going from Elayne
to Aviendha and back, slowly widening until the whites
showed all the way around. She was not so sure of herself
now.

Silent glances passed between Vandene and Adeleas,
in the manner of people who had spent so much time together they hardly needed to speak aloud any longer; then
Vandene took Elayne and Aviendha each by an arm. "If I
may speak with you outside a moment," she murmured. It

sounded a suggestion, but she was already urging them to the door.

Outside in the farmyard, perhaps two dozen or so Kins-women were huddled together like sheep. Not all wore Ebou Dari clothes, but two had the red belts of Wise Women, and Elayne recognized Berowin, a stout little woman who normally showed a pride far greater than her strength in the Power. Not now. Like the rest, her face was frightened, her eyes darting, despite the entire Knitting Circle surrounding them and talking urgently. Down the way, Nynaeve and Alise were trying to herd perhaps twice as many women inside one of the larger buildings. "Trying" did seem to be the word.

". . . don't care *what* estates you hold," Nynaeve was shouting at a proud-necked woman in pale green silk. "You get in there and stay in there, out of the way, or I'll *kick* you inside!"

Alise simply seized the green-clad woman by the scruff of the neck and ran her through the doorway despite voluble and heated protests. There was a loud squawk like a huge goose being stepped on, then Alise reappeared, dusting her hands. The others seemed to give no trouble after that.

Vandene released them, studying their eyes. The glow still enveloped her, yet Adeleas must have been focusing their combined flows. Vandene could have maintained the shield, once woven, without being able to see it, but had she been the one, it was much likelier that Adeleas would have brought them out. Vandene could have gone several hundred paces before the link began to attenuate—it would not break if she and Adeleas went to opposite corners of the earth, though it would have been useless long before that—but she remained close to the door. She seemed to sort words in her head.

"I've always thought it best if women with experience handle this sort of thing," she said finally. "The young can easily be caught up in hot blood. Then they do too much. Or sometimes, they realize they can't bring themselves to do enough. Because they haven't really seen enough, yet. Or worst of all, they find a . . . taste for it. Not that I believe either of you has that flaw." She gave Aviendha a weighing glance without pausing; Aviendha hastily sheathed her belt knife. "Adeleas and I have seen enough to know why we must do what must be done, and we left hot blood behind long ago. Perhaps you will leave this to us. Much better that way, all around." Vandene seemed to take the recommendation as accepted. She nodded and turned back toward the door.

No sooner had she disappeared behind it, than Elayne felt the use of the Power within, a weave that must have blanketed the room inside. A ward against eavesdropping, certainly. They would not want stray ears to catch whatever Ispan said. Then another use hit her, and suddenly the silence from within was more ominous than any shrieks that ward would contain.

She crushed her hat back onto her head. The heat she could not feel, but the sun's glare suddenly made her queasy. "Maybe you'll help me look over what the packhorses are carrying," she said breathily. She had not ordered it done— whatever *it* was—but that did not seem to change anything. Aviendha nodded with surprising quickness; she seemed to want to be away from that silence, too.

The Windfinders were waiting not far from where the servants had the pack animals, waiting impatiently and staring about imperiously, arms folded beneath their breasts, copying Renaile. Alise marched up to them, marking Renaile out as the leader after one sweeping glance. Elayne and Aviendha she ignored.

"Come with me," she said in brisk tones that brooked no argument. "The Aes Sedai say you will want to be out of the sun until matters are more settled." The words "Aes Sedai" held as much bitterness as they did the awe Elayne was used to from Kinswomen. Maybe more. Renaile stiffened, her dark face growing darker, but Alise plowed on. "You wilders can sit out here and sweat if that's what you want, for all of me. If you *can* sit." It was obvious none of the Atha'an Miere had received Healing for their saddle soreness; they stood like women who wanted to forget they existed below the waist. "What you will not do is keep me waiting."

"Do you know who I am?" Renaile demanded in a tight fury, but Alise was already walking away and not looking back. Struggling with herself visibly, Renaile dashed sweat from her forehead with the back of her hand, then angrily ordered the other Windfinders to leave the "shore-cursed" horses and follow her. They made a spraddle-legged line wobbling along after Alise, everyone but the two apprentices muttering to herself—Alise included.

Instinctively, Elayne began to plan how to smooth matters over, how to get the Atha'an Miere's pains Healed without them having to ask. Or a sister having to offer too strenuously; Nynaeve had to be appeased, too, and the other sisters. To her surprise, she suddenly realized that for once in her life she had no real desire to smooth anything. Watching the Windfinders limp toward one of the farm buildings, she decided that matters were fine just as they were. Aviendha wore a large, open grin as she watched the Atha'an Miere. Elayne snatched the much smaller smile from her own face and turned to the packhorses. They did deserve it, though. Not grinning was very hard.

With Aviendha's help, the searching went more quickly than before, though Aviendha did not recognize what they were after as quickly as she did. Not a great surprise. A few of the sisters Elayne had trained showed a greater skill in this than she did herself, but most came nowhere near. Still, two sets of hands found more than one, and there was a great deal to be found. Liveried stablemen and women carried away the rubbish, while a collection of *ter'angreal* grew on the broad stone lid of a square cistern.

Four more horses were unloaded quickly, and they accumulated a selection that would have caused a celebration, brought into the Tower. Even with no one studying *ter'angreal*. They took every form imaginable. Cups and bowls and vases, no two the same size or design or in the same material. A flat, worm-eaten box, half-falling apart and whatever had lined it long since gone to dust, held pieces of jewelry—a necklace and bracelets set with colored stones, a slim gem-studded belt, several finger rings— and there were spaces for more. Every single one was a *ter'angreal*, and they all matched, meant to be worn together, though Elayne could not imagine why any woman would want to carry so many about her at one time. Aviendha found a dagger with gold wire wrapped around a hilt of rough deerhorn; the blade was dull, and by all evidence, always had been. She kept turning that over and over in her fingers—her hands actually began to tremble—until Elayne took it away from her and put it with the others on the cistern's lid. Even then Aviendha stood for a time, looking at it and licking her lips as though they had gone dry. There were finger rings, earrings, necklaces, bracelets and buckles, many of very peculiar pattern indeed. There were statuettes and figures of birds and animals and people, several knives that did have edges, half a dozen large medallions in bronze or steel, most worked with strange patterns and not one carrying an image Elayne could really understand, a pair of peculiar hats seemingly made of metal, too ornate and too thin to be helmets, and any number of items she could not think what to call. A rod, as thick as her wrist, bright red and smooth and rounded, firm rather than hard for all that it seemed to be stone; it did not warm slightly in her hand, it almost felt hot! Not real heat any more than the warmth was real, but still! What about a set of metal basketwork balls, one inside the other? Any movement produced a faint musical chime, a different tone every time, and she had the feeling that no matter how hard she looked into it, there would always be a still smaller ball waiting to be discovered. A thing that looked like a blacksmith's puzzle made of glass? It was heavy enough that she dropped it, and it broke a chip off the edge of the cistern cover. A collection to stir amazement in any Aes Sedai. More important, they found two more *angreal*. Those Elayne set very carefully aside, within arm's reach.

One was an odd piece of jewelry, a golden bracelet attached by four flat chains to finger rings, every bit of it engraved in an intricate mazelike pattern. That was the stronger of the two, stronger than the turtle still in her pouch. It was made for a smaller hand than hers or Aviendha's. Strangely, the bracelet had a tiny lock, complete with a minuscule, tubular key dangling from a fine chain that was obviously made to be removed. Along with the key! The other was a seated woman in age-darkened ivory, her legs folded in front of her, her exposed knees bare, but with hair so long and luxuriant she could not have been more muffled in the heaviest cloak. It was not even as strong as the turtle, but she found it very appealing. One hand rested on a knee, palm up and fingers arranged so the thumb touched the tips of the middle two fingers, while the other hand was lifted, the first two fingers raised and the others folded. The whole figure carried an air of supreme dignity, yet the delicately worked face showed amusement and delight. Maybe it had been made for a particular woman? It seemed personal, somehow. Perhaps they had done that, in the Age of Legends. Some *ter'angreal* were immense, needing men and horses, or even the Power, to move, but most *angreal* were small enough to carry about your person; not all, but most.

They were tossing back the canvas covers on another set of wicker panniers when Nynaeve came striding up. The Atha'an Miere began filing out of one of the farm buildings, no longer limping. Merilille was talking with Renaile, or rather, the Windfinder was talking and Merilille listening. Elayne wondered what had happened in there. The slim Gray did not look so satisfied anymore. The huddle of Kinswomen had grown larger, but even as Elayne looked up, three more came hesitantly into the farmyard, and another two stood at the edge of the olive trees, peering about indecisively. She could sense Birgitte, somewhere out among the groves and only a little less irritated than earlier.

Nynaeve glanced at the display of *ter'angreal* and gave her braid a tug. Her hat had gone missing somewhere. "That can wait," she said, sounding disgusted. "It's time."

CHAPTER

5

The Breaking Storm

The sun stood little more than halfway down toward the horizon by the time they clambered up the well-worn, snaking path to the top of the steep-sided hill above the barns. That was the spot Renaile had chosen. It did make sense from what Elayne knew of working weather, all learned from a Sea Folk Windfinder, to be sure. Changing anything beyond your immediate vicinity required working over long distances, which meant being able to *see* a long distance, much easier on the ocean than on land. Except from a mountain or hilltop. It also needed a deft hand to avoid causing torrential rains or whirlwinds or the Light alone knew what elsewhere. Whatever you did, the effects spread like ripples from a stone tossed into a pond. She had no desire whatsoever to lead the circle that would use the Bowl.

The top of the hill was clear of brush and flat, if far from level, a rough stone table, fifty paces long and broad, with plenty of room for everybody who needed to be there, and some who did not, strictly speaking. From at least fifty paces above the farm, the spectacular view stretched for miles over a patchwork quilt of farms and pastures, forests and olive groves. Far too many browns and sere yellows were mixed in with a hundred shades of green, crying the need for what they were to do, yet even so, the beauty of it struck Elayne. Despite dust in the air like a faint mist, she could see so *far*! The land really was quite flat here except for those few hills. Ebou Dar lay just out of sight to the south even if she embraced the Power, yet it seemed she should be able to see it, by straining just a little. Surely with a little effort she could see the River Eldar. A marvelous view. Not everyone was interested.

"An hour wasted," Nynaeve grumbled, glaring sideways at Reanne. And at just about everyone else. With Lan not there, it seemed she might take the opportunity to unleash her temper. "Almost an hour. Maybe more. Completely wasted. Alise is capable enough, I suppose, but you'd think Reanne would *know* who was there! Light! If that fool woman faints on me again . . . !" Elayne hoped she held on a little longer. It looked to be quite a storm once she let it break.

Reanne tried to keep a cheerful, eager face, yet her hands were never still on her skirts, constantly plucking and smoothing. Kirstian simply clutched hers and sweated, appearing ready to empty her stomach any minute; when anyone looked at her, anyone at all, she shivered. The third Kinswoman, Garenia, was a Saldaean merchant with a strong nose and a wide mouth, a short slim-hipped woman, stronger than the other two, who looked not that much older than Nynaeve. A greasy dampness glistened on her pale face, and her dark eyes grew wider whenever they fell on an Aes Sedai. Elayne thought she might soon discover whether someone's eyes actually *could* pop out of her head. At least Garenia had stopped moaning, which she had done all the way up the hill.

There really had been another pair who might have been strong enough—possibly; the Kin did not pay much attention to that—but the last had gone on her way three days past. No one else at the farm even came close. Which was why Nynaeve was still disgusted. One reason. The other was that Garenia had been one of the very first found, passed out in the farmyard. For that matter, she fainted again the first two times she was roused, as soon as her eyes fell on one of the sisters. Of course, Nynaeve being Nynaeve, she was not about to admit that she should have done anything so simple as ask Alise who was still at the farm. Or even tell Alise what she was looking for before the woman inquired. Nynaeve never expected anyone to have sense to know up from down. Except herself.

"We could be done by now!" Nynaeve growled. "We could be shut of—!" She almost quivered with the effort of not scowling at the Sea Folk as they gathered near the east end of the stone table. Renaile, gesturing emphatically, appeared to be giving instructions. Elayne would have given a pretty to hear those.

Nynaeve's glares certainly took in Merilille and Careane and Sareitha, who still clutched the silk-wrapped Bowl tightly. Adeleas and Vandene had remained below, sequestered with Ispan. The three sisters stood chatting together, not paying any mind to Nynaeve unless she spoke to them directly, but Merilille's gaze sometimes slipped to the Windfinders, then jerked away; her mask of serenity faltered slightly, and she licked her lips with the tip of her tongue.

Had she made some mistake down below while Healing them? Merilille had negotiated treaties and mediated disputes between nations; few in the White Tower were better than she. But Elayne remembered hearing a story once, a joke of sorts, about a Domani merchant, a Sea Folk Cargomaster and an Aes Sedai. Not many people told jokes involving Aes Sedai; telling one might not be entirely safe. The merchant and the Cargomaster found an ordinary rock on the shore and proceeded to sell it back and forth between them, somehow making a profit each time. Then an Aes Sedai came along. The Domani convinced the Aes Sedai to buy the simple stone for twice what she herself had last paid. After which the Atha'an Miere convinced the Aes Sedai to buy the *same* rock from him for twice that again. Only a joke, but it showed what people believed. Maybe the older sisters would *not* have done any better bargaining with the Sea Folk.

Aviendha strode straight to the edge of the cliffs as soon as she reached the hilltop, and stood staring north, motionless as a statue. After a moment, Elayne realized that she was not admiring the view; Aviendha was simply staring. Gathering her skirts a bit awkwardly with the three *angreal* in hand, she joined her friend.

The cliff fell in fifty-foot steps to olive groves, steep swathes of ridged gray stone, bare except for a few small, dying bushes. The drop was not really bothersome, but it was hardly the same as looking at the ground from the top of a tree, either. Strangely, looking down made Elayne feel a trifle dizzy. Aviendha did not seem to notice that the edge was right at her toes.

"Is something troubling you?" Elayne asked quietly.

Aviendha kept her gaze on the distance. "I have failed you," she said finally. Her voice was flat, empty. "I cannot form the gateway properly, and all saw me shame you. I thought a servant was one of the Shadowwrought, and behaved worse than foolishly. The Atha'an Miere ignore me and glare at the Aes Sedai, as if I am an Aes Sedai dog yapping at their command. I pretended I could make the Shadowrunner talk for you, but no *Far Dareis Mai* is allowed to question prisoners until she has been wed to the spear for twenty years, or even to watch until she has carried it ten. I am weak and soft, Elayne. I cannot bear to shame you further. If I fail you again, I will die."

Elayne's mouth went dry. That sounded too close to a promise. Gripping Aviendha's arm firmly, she drew her back from the edge. Aiel could be almost as peculiar as the Sea Folk thought they were. She did not really think Aviendha would jump off—not really—but she was not about to take any chances. At least the other woman did not try to resist.

Everyone else seemed to be engrossed in themselves, or in each other. Nynaeve had begun speaking to the Atha'an Miere, both hands tight on her braid and her face almost as dark as theirs from the strain of not shouting, while they listened with contemptuous arrogance. Merilille and Sareitha still guarded the Bowl, but Careane was attempting to talk with the Kinswomen, without much success. Reanne answered, if blinking uneasily and licking her lips, but Kirstian stood trembling and silent, while Garenia's eyes were squeezed shut. Elayne kept her voice low anyway; this was none of their business.

"You haven't failed anyone, least of all me, Aviendha. Nothing you've done has *ever* shamed me, and nothing you do ever could." Aviendha blinked at her doubtfully. "And you're about as weak and soft as a stone." That had to be the oddest compliment she had ever paid anyone, yet Aviendha actually looked gratified. "I'll bet the Sea Folk are scared silly of you, too." Another strange one; it made Aviendha smile, if only faintly. Elayne drew a breath. "As for Ispan. . . ." She did not like even thinking about this. "I thought I could do what was necessary, too, but just letting my mind dwell on it makes my hands sweat and my stomach roil. I'd throw up if I even tried. So we share that."

Aviendha made the Maiden handtalk sign for "You startle me"; she had started teaching some of them to Elayne, though she said it was forbidden. Apparently, being near-sisters who were learning to be more changed that. Except that it did not, really. Aviendha seemed to think her explanation had been perfectly clear. "I did not mean I could not," she said aloud, "only that I do not know how. Likely I would have killed her, trying." Suddenly she smiled, much wider and warmer than before, and lightly touched Elayne's cheek. "We both have weakness in us," she whispered, "but it brings no shame so long as only we two know."

"Yes," Elayne said weakly. She just did not know *how*! "Of course it doesn't." This woman contained more surprises than any gleeman. "Here," she said, pressing the woman-wrapped-in-her-hair into Aviendha's hand. "Use this in the circle." Letting the *angreal* go was not easy. She had intended to use it herself, but smiles or no smiles, her friend's spirits—her near-sister's spirits—needed raising. Aviendha turned the small ivory figure over in her hands; Elayne could almost see her trying to decide how to give it back. "Aviendha, you know how it feels when you hold as much of *saidar* as you can? Think of holding almost twice as much. *Really* think of it. I want you to use it. Please?"

Perhaps Aiel did not show a great deal on their faces, but Aviendha's green eyes widened. They had discussed *angreal*, considering their search, but she probably never had thought what it would be like to use one before this. "Twice as much," she murmured. "To hold all that. I can barely make myself imagine. This is a very great gift, Elayne." She touched Elayne's cheek again, pressing her fingertips; that was the Aiel equivalent of a kiss and a hug.

Whatever Nynaeve had to say to the Sea Folk, it did not take long. She stalked away from them twitching at her skirts furiously. Approaching Elayne, she frowned equally at Aviendha and at the edge of the cliff. Usually she denied her poor head for heights, but she kept them between herself and the drop. "I have to talk to you," she muttered, guiding Elayne a little distance along the hilltop. And farther from the edge. A little way, but far enough from anyone to avoid being overheard. She drew several deep breaths before beginning, in a low voice, and she did not look at Elayne.

"I. . . . I've been behaving like a fool. It's that bloody

man's fault! When he's not right in front of me, I can hardly think of anything else, and when he is, I can hardly think at all! You . . . you have to tell me when I . . . when I'm acting the fool. I depend on you, Elayne." Her voice stayed low, but her tone became almost a wail. "I can't afford to lose my wits in a man, not now."

Elayne was so shocked, she could not speak for a moment. Nynaeve, admitting she had been a fool? She almost looked to see whether the sun had turned green! "It isn't Lan's fault, and you know it, Nynaeve," she said at last. She pushed away memories of her own recent thoughts about Rand. This was not the same. And the opportunity was a gift of the Light. Tomorrow, Nynaeve would likely try to box her ears if she said Nynaeve was being foolish. "Take hold of yourself, Nynaeve. Stop behaving like a giddy girl." Definitely not thoughts of Rand! *She* had not been mooning over him *that* badly! "You're an Aes Sedai, and you are supposed to be leading us. Lead! And think!"

Folding her hands at her waist, Nynaeve actually hung her head. "I'll try," she mumbled. "I will, truly. You don't know what it's like, though. I. . . . I'm sorry."

Elayne nearly swallowed her tongue. Nynaeve, *apologizing* on top of the other? Nynaeve, *abashed*? Maybe she was ill.

It did not last, of course. Abruptly frowning at the *angreal*, Nynaeve cleared her throat. "You gave one to Aviendha, did you?" she said briskly. "Well, I suppose she's all right. A pity we have to let the Sea Folk use one. I'll wager they try to hang on to it! Well, just let them try! Which one is mine?"

With a sigh, Elayne handed her the bracelet-and-rings, and she stalked away, fumbling the piece of jewelry onto her left hand and calling loudly for everyone to take their places. Sometimes, it was difficult to tell Nynaeve leading from Nynaeve bullying. As long as she *did* lead, though.

The Bowl of the Winds sat atop its unfolded white wrappings in the center of the hilltop, a shallow, heavy disc of clear crystal two feet across, worked inside with thick swirling clouds. An ornate piece, yet simple when you thought of what it could do. What they hoped it could do. Nynaeve took up her place nearby, the *angreal* finally clicking shut on her wrist. She worked her hand, looking surprised that the chains did not seem to inconvenience her; it fit as if made for her hand. The three Kinswomen were already there, Kirstian and Garenia huddling at Reanne's back and appearing more frightened than ever, if that was possible. The Windfinders still stood arrayed behind Renaile, almost twenty paces away.

Lifting her divided skirts, Elayne met Aviendha at the Bowl and eyed the Sea Folk suspiciously. Did they intend to create a fuss? She had been afraid of exactly that from the first mention of women at the farm who might be strong enough to join the link. The Atha'an Miere were sticklers for rank enough to shame the White Tower, and Garenia's presence meant that Renaile din Calon Blue Star, Windfinder to the Mistress of the Ships to the Atha'an Miere, would not be part of the circle. Should not be.

Renaile frowned searchingly at the women around the Bowl. She seemed to be weighing them, judging their capabilities. "Talaan din Gelyn," she barked suddenly, "take your station!" It was like a whip-crack! Even Nynaeve jumped.

Talaan bowed low, touching her heart, then ran to the Bowl. As soon as she moved, Renaile barked again. "Metarra din Junalle, take your station!" Metarra, plump yet solid, sped on Talaan's heels. Neither apprentice was old enough to have earned what the Sea Folk called a "salt name."

Once begun, Renaile rattled off names quickly, sending Rainyn and two other Windfinders, all of whom moved quickly, yet not so fast as the apprentices. By the number of their medallions, Naime and Rysael were higher in rank than Rainyn, dignified women with a quiet air of command, but markedly weaker. Then Renaile paused, only for a heartbeat, yet in that rapid listing it stood out. "Tebreille din Gelyn South Wind, take your station! Caire din Gelyn Running Wave, assume the command!"

Elayne felt a moment of relief that Renaile had not named herself, but it lasted about as long as Renaile's pause had. Tebreille and Caire exchanged one look, Tebreille grim and Caire smug, before moving to the Bowl. Eight earrings and a multitude of overlapping medallions marked each Windfinder to a Clan Wavemistress. Only Renaile stood above them; only Dorile among the Sea Folk on the hilltop was their equal. In brocaded yellow silks, Caire was slightly the taller, Tebreille in brocaded green somewhat sterner of face, both more than handsome women, and it did not take their names to know them blood sisters. They had the same big, almost black eyes, the same straight nose, the same strong chin. Caire silently pointed to a spot at her right side; Tebreille did not speak either, nor did she hesitate in standing where her sister pointed, but her face was stone. With her, a circle of thirteen women surrounded the Bowl nearly shoulder-to-shoulder. Caire's eyes almost sparkled. Tebreille's were leaden. Elayne was reminded of another of Lini's sayings. *No knife is sharper than a sister's hate.*

Caire glared around the circle of women surrounding the Bowl, not yet truly a circle, as though trying to fix each face in her mind. Or maybe to fix her scowl in theirs. Remembering herself, Elayne hurriedly passed the last *angreal*, the small amber turtle, to Talaan and started to explain how it was used. The explanation was simple, yet anyone who tried without knowing how could fumble for hours. She was not given the chance for five words.

"Silence!" Caire roared. Tattooed fists on her hips and bare feet apart, she belonged on the deck of a ship going into battle. "There will be no talking on station without my permission. Talaan, report yourself immediately on returning to your ship." Nothing in Caire's tone suggested that she was speaking to her own daughter. Talaan bowed deeply, touching her heart, and murmured something inaudible. Caire snorted contemptuously—and gave Elayne a glare that suggested a wish that she could order her to report herself to someone as well—before going on in a voice that might have been heard at the base of the hill. "Today, we shall do what has not been done since the Breaking of the World, when our ancestors fought wind and wave gone mad. By the Bowl of the Winds and the mercy of the Light, they survived. Today, we will use the Bowl of the Winds, lost to us for more than two thousand years, and now returned. I have studied the ancient lore, studied the records of the days when our foremothers first learned the sea and the Weaving of the Winds, and the salt entered our blood. What is known of the Bowl of the Winds, I know, more than anyone else." Her eyes cut toward her sister, a satisfied glance that Tebreille did not acknowledge. Which seemed to satisfy Caire even more. "What the Aes Sedai cannot do,

I will do today, if it pleases the Light. I expect every woman to stand her station to the last. I will not accept failure."

The rest of the Atha'an Miere seemed to accept that speech as expected and proper, but the Kinswomen gaped at Caire in astonishment. In Elayne's opinion, grandiose did not begin to describe it; plainly Caire fully expected that the Light *would* be pleased, and *she* would be most displeased if it was not! Nynaeve rolled her eyes to the heavens and opened her mouth. Caire forestalled her.

"Nynaeve," the Windfinder announced loudly, "you will now demonstrate your skill at linking. Be about it, woman, and quickly!"

In response, Nynaeve shut her eyes tight. Her lips . . . writhed. She looked about to burst a blood vessel. "I assume that means I have *permission* to speak!" she murmured. Fortunately too low to be heard by Caire, on the far side of the circle. Opening her eyes, she put on a smile that was quite horrible when added to the rest of her expression. She was a sour stomach and several other complaints rolled into one.

"The first thing is to embrace the True Source, Caire." The light of *saidar* suddenly shone bright around Nynaeve; she was using the *angreal* on her hand already, by what Elayne could feel. "I assume you know how to do that, of course." Ignoring the abrupt tightening of Caire's mouth, Nynaeve went on. "Elayne will now assist me in the *demonstration*. If we have your *permission*?"

"I prepare myself to embrace the Source," Elayne put in quickly, before Caire could erupt, "but I don't actually embrace it." She opened herself, and the Windfinders leaned forward, peering at her, though there really was nothing to see yet. Even Kirstian and Garenia forgot their fear enough to show interest. "While I'm at this point, the rest is up to Nynaeve."

"Now I will reach out to her. . . ." Nynaeve paused, looking at Talaan. Elayne had not had a chance to tell her anything, really. "It's much the same as with an *angreal*," Nynaeve said, addressing the slender apprentice. Caire growled, and Talaan tried to watch Nynaeve with her head down. "You open yourself to the Source *through* an *angreal*, just as I will through Elayne. As though you mean to embrace the *angreal* and the Source at the same time. It isn't very difficult, really. Watch, and you'll see. When it's time to bring you into the circle, just put yourself on the brink. That way, when I embrace through you, I'll embrace through the *angreal* as well."

Concentration or no concentration, sweat began to bead on Elayne's forehead. But then, the heat had nothing to do with it. The True Source beckoned; it throbbed, and she throbbed with it. It demanded. The longer she hung just a hairsbreadth from touching the Power, the worse the desire, the need, would grow. Hanging, she began to tremble slightly. Vandene had told her that the longer you channeled, the worse that anticipation grew.

"Watch with Aviendha," Nynaeve told Talaan. "She knows how to—" She caught sight of Elayne's face and finished hurriedly. "Watch!"

It was not exactly the same as using an *angreal*, though very close. It was not meant to be done hurriedly, either; Nynaeve did not have a soft touch, at best. Elayne felt as though she were being shaken; nothing happened physically, but inside her head she seemed to be bouncing around, tumbling wildly downhill. Worse, she was jostled toward embracing *saidar* with excruciating slowness. It took less than a heartbeat, and seemed to take hours, days. She wanted to howl, but she could not breathe. Abruptly, like a dam bursting, the One Power flowed through her, a rush of life and joy, of bliss, and breath left her in a long gasp of pleasure and relief so overwhelming that her legs wobbled. It was all she could do to keep from panting. Tottering, pulling herself up, she gave Nynaeve a stern look, and Nynaeve shrugged apologetically. Twice in one day! The sun *had* to be turning green.

"I now control the flow of *saidar* from her as well as my own," Nynaeve went on, not quite meeting Elayne's eyes, "and will until I let her go. Now, don't fear that whoever leads the circle," she shot a frown at Caire and sniffed, "can make you draw too much. This really is a great deal like an *angreal*. The *angreal* buffers you against the extra Power, and in somewhat the same way, in a circle you can't be made to draw too much. In fact, in a circle you can't draw quite as much as you can otherwi—"

"This is dangerous!" Renaile broke in, shouldering roughly

between Caire and Tebreille. Her scowl took in Nynaeve, Elayne, and the sisters standing off from the circle as well. "You say that one woman can simply seize another, hold her captive, use her? How long have you Aes Sedai known this? I warn you, if you try to use it on one of us—" It was her turn to be cut off.

"It doesn't work that way, Renaile." Sareitha touched Garenia, and she and Kirstian leaped apart to make room. The young Brown eyed Nynaeve uncertainly, then folded her hands and took on a lecturing tone, as if addressing a class. With it came composure; perhaps she did see Renaile as a pupil right then. "The Tower studied this for many years, long before the Trolloc Wars. I have read every page that survives in the Tower Library of those studies. It was proven conclusively that one woman cannot form a link with another against her will. It simply cannot be done; nothing happens. A willing surrender is necessary, just as in embracing *saidar* itself." She sounded absolutely definite, but Renaile still frowned; too many people knew how Aes Sedai could sidestep the Oath against lying.

"And why did they study it?" Renaile demanded. "Why was the White Tower so interested in such a thing? Perhaps you Aes Sedai still study?"

"That is ridiculous." Exasperation dripped from Sareitha's voice. "If you must know, it was the problem of men who can channel that drew them to it. The Breaking of the World was a living memory to some, then. I don't suppose even very many sisters remember—it hasn't been part of the required instruction since before the Trolloc Wars— but men can be brought into a circle, too, and as the circle doesn't break even if you go to sleep. . . . Well, you can see the advantages. That was an utter failure, unfortunately. More to the point here, I say again that it is impossible to force a woman into a circle. If you doubt, try it yourself. You will see."

Renaile nodded, accepting at last; there was very little else to do when an Aes Sedai made a simple statement of fact. Yet Elayne wondered. What was in the pages that had *not* survived? She had noticed a slight change in Sareitha's inflection at one point. She had questions. For later, when there were fewer ears around.

When Renaile and Sareitha withdrew, Nynaeve twitched her divided skirts straight, plainly irritated at the interruption, and opened her mouth again.

"Continue your demonstration, Nynaeve," Caire commanded harshly. Her dark face might have been smooth as a frozen pond, but she was not very pleased, either.

Nynaeve's mouth worked before she could make any sound come out, and when it did, she went on in a rush, as though afraid someone else might break in.

The next part of the lesson was passing control of the circle. That had to be done voluntarily, too, and even as she reached out toward Nynaeve, Elayne held her breath until she felt the subtle shift that meant she now controlled the Power flowing into her. And that flowing through Nynaeve, of course. She had not been sure it would work. Nynaeve could form a circle easily, if not with any finesse, but passing guidance also involved a form of surrender; Nynaeve had *considerable* difficulties relinquishing control or being brought into a circle, just as she had once had difficulty surrendering to *saidar*. Which was why Elayne kept the guidance for now. It would have to be passed to Caire, and Nynaeve might not be able to manage letting go twice. Those apologies must have been much easier for her.

Elayne linked next with Aviendha, so Talaan could actually see how it was done with an *angreal*, as much as there was to see, and it went perfectly; Aviendha was a very quick study, blending in easily. Talaan was quick as well, it turned out, adding her still greater *angreal* aided flow without a hitch. One by one, Elayne brought them in, and she herself almost shivered at the river of the Power that streamed into her. No one yet was drawing nearly as much as she could, but it added up, especially with *angreal* involved. Elayne's awareness climbed higher with each addition of *saidar*. She could smell the heavy scents in the lacework gold boxes that the Windfinders wore around their necks, and separate one from another. She could make out each fold and crease in everyone's clothes as sharply as if she had her nose pressed to the cloth, more sharply. She was aware of the faintest movement of the air against her hair and skin, caresses she never would have noticed without the Power.

That was not the whole of her awareness, of course. The link had a certain kinship to the Warder bond, just as intense and somehow even more intimate. She knew that a tiny blister from climbing the hill made a spot of pain on Nynaeve's right heel; Nynaeve always talked about good stout shoes, but she had a weakness for slippers with a great deal of embroidery. Nynaeve wore a fixed frown, directed at Caire, her arms were crossed, her fingers wearing the *angreal* played on the braid pulled over her right shoulder, every line of her of a piece, yet inside she was a maelstrom of emotions. Fear, worry, anticipation, irritation, wariness and impatience bounced over each other, and washing through it all, sometimes submerging the rest, ripples of warmth and waves of heat that threatened to burst into flame. Those last Nynaeve suppressed quickly, especially the heat, but they always returned. Elayne almost thought she could recognize them, but it was like something glimpsed from the corner of your eye that was gone when you turned your head.

Surprisingly, Aviendha felt fear, too, but small and tightly contained, and all but swallowed by determination. Garenia and Kirstian, shaking visibly, were nearly pure terror, so strong it was amazing that they could even have begun to embrace the Source. What filled Reanne to overflowing was eagerness, and no matter her skirt smoothing. As for the Atha'an Miere. . . . Even Tebreille exuded a wary alertness, and it did not take the quick darting of Metarra's eyes, and Rainyn's, to know the focus was Caire, watching them all, impatient and commanding.

Her, Elayne left to last, and it was no real surprise that she had to make four tries—four!—to bring the woman into the circle. Caire was no better at yielding than Nynaeve. Elayne desperately hoped the woman had been chosen for ability, not rank.

"I will now pass the circle to you," she told the Windfinder when it finally was done. "If you recall what I did with Ny—" Words froze momentarily in her throat as guidance of the circle was torn from her surrender, a sensation like having a sudden burst of wind rip all of her clothes off or yank the bones out of her. She exhaled fiercely, and if it sounded close to spitting, well, so be it.

"Good," Caire said, rubbing her hands together. "Good." Her attention focused on the Bowl, her head twisting this way and that as she studied it. Well, perhaps not all her attention. Reanne started to sit down, and without looking up,

Caire snapped, "Hold your station, woman! This isn't a fish lolly! Stand till you're told to move!"

Startled, Reanne jerked back to her feet, muttering under her breath, but she might as well have ceased to exist as far as Caire was concerned. The Windfinder's eyes remained on the flattened crystal shape. Elayne felt resolve in her great enough to move a mountain. And something else, tiny and quickly stamped out. Uncertainty. Uncertainty? If after all of this, the woman really did not know what to do—

At that moment, Caire drew deeply. *Saidar* flooded through Elayne, almost as much as she could hold; an unbroken ring of light blazed into being, joining the women in the circle, brighter wherever one used an *angreal*, but nowhere faint. She watched closely as Caire channeled, forming a complex weave of all Five Powers, a four-pointed star that she laid atop the Bowl with what Elayne somehow was sure was exquisite precision. The star touched, and Elayne gasped. Once, she had channeled a trickle into the Bowl—in *Tel'aran'rhiod*, to be sure, and only a reflection of the Bowl, though still a dangerous thing to do—and that clear crystal had turned a pale blue, and the carved clouds moved. Now, the Bowl of the Winds *was* blue, the bright blue of a summer sky, and fleecy white clouds billowed across it.

The four-point star became five-pointed, the composition of the weave altered slightly, and the Bowl was a green sea with great heaving waves. Five points became six, and it was another sky, a different blue, darker, winter perhaps, with purple clouds heavy with rain or snow. Seven points, and a gray-green sea raged in storm. Eight points and sky. Nine and sea, and suddenly, Elayne felt the Bowl itself drawing *saidar*, a wild torrent far greater than all the circle together could manage.

The changes continued unabated inside the Bowl, sea to sky, waves to clouds, but a writhing, braided column of *saidar* shot up from that flattish crystal disc, Fire and Air, Water and Earth and Spirit, a column of intricate lace as wide as the Bowl, climbing up and up into the sky, until its top rose out of sight. Caire continued her weaving, sweat streaming down her face; she paused seemingly only to blink salty drops away from her eyes as she examined the images in the Bowl, then laid a new weave. The pattern of

pped her arms around herself and drew
. Queen Tylin she left to the mercies of the
ould survive if it was possible. But Mat Cau-
y strange, very instructive subject; her most
ner. He had come for her, too, and offered
om Merrilin; dear Thom, who she sometimes
vould turn out to be her real father, and the
hat that would make of her mother. And the
d Chel Vanin, and. . . . She had to think like
Rose Crown is heavier than a mountain, her
ld her, *and duty will make you weep, but you
l do what must be done.*

said, then more firmly, "No. Look at you,
can hardly stand. Even if we all went, what
How many of the Forsaken are there? We'd
for no gain. The Forsaken have no reason to
or the others. It's us they will be after."

ped at her, stubborn Nynaeve with sweat run-
er face and her legs unsteady. Wonderful, gal-
Nynaeve. "You're saying leave him, Elayne?
k to her. Tell her about that honor you're al-
n about!"

esitated, then shook her head. She was almost
Nynaeve, and from the way she moved, just as
are times to fight without hope, Nynaeve, but
nt. The Shadowsouled will not be looking for
; they will be after us, and the Bowl. He may
city already. If we go, we risk giving them
lo what we have done. Wherever we send the
ill be able to make us tell them who we sent it
re."

face crumpled in pain. Elayne reached to put
und her.

awn!" someone screamed, and suddenly
embracing *saidar* all over the hilltop. Balls
p from Merilille's hands, from Careane's and
fast as they could throw. A huge winged shape
flame tumbled out of the sky trailing oily
falling just beyond the cliff.

nother one!" Kirstian shouted, pointing. A
ed creature dove away from the hill, body as
, ribbed wings spanning thirty paces or more,

the braiding in the thick column altered with every weave,
subtly echoing what Caire wove.

It was a very good thing she had not wanted to focus the
flows for this circle, Elayne realized; what the woman was
doing required *years* more study than she had. Many years
more. Suddenly, she realized something else. That ever-
changing lacework of *saidar* bent itself around something
else, something unseen that made the column solid. She
swallowed, hard. The Bowl was drawing *saidin* as well as
saidar.

Her hope that no one else had puzzled that out vanished with one glance at the other women. Half stared at
the twisting column with a revulsion that should have been
reserved for the Dark One. Fear grew stronger among the
emotions shared in her head. Some were approaching the
level of Garenia and Kirstian, and it was a wonder those
two had not fainted. Nynaeve was a hair from sicking up,
for all her suddenly too smooth face. Aviendha appeared
just as calm outwardly, but inside, that tiny fear quivered
and pulsed, trying to grow.

From Caire came only determination, as steely hard as
her expression. Nothing was going to stand in Caire's way,
certainly not the mere presence of Shadow-tainted *saidin*
mixed into her weaving. Nothing was going to stop her.
She worked the flows, and abruptly spiderwebs of *saidar*
blossomed from the unseen top of the column, like uneven
spokes of a wheel, almost a solid fan to the south, sparser
fans reaching north and northwest, single lacy spokes
stretching in other directions. They changed as they grew,
never the same from one moment to the next, spreading
across the sky, farther and farther, until the ends of the
pattern also passed out of sight. Not just *saidar* there either, Elayne was certain; in places that spiderweb caught
and curved around something she could not see. Still Caire
wove, and the column danced to her bidding, *saidar* and
saidin together, and the spiderweb altered and flowed like a
lopsided kaleidoscope spinning across the heavens, vanishing into the distance, on and on and on.

Without warning, Caire straightened, knuckling her
back, and released the Source completely. Column and spiderweb evaporated, and she collapsed as much as sat down,
breathing hard. The Bowl turned clear again, but small

patches of *saidar* flashed and crackled around its edges. "It is done, the Light willing," she said tiredly.

Elayne hardly heard. That was *not* the way to end a circle. When Caire let go in that way, the Power disappeared from every woman simultaneously. Elayne's eyes popped. For one instant, it was as though she stood atop the highest tower in the world, and suddenly the tower was not there anymore! Just an instant, yet hardly pleasant. She felt tired, if not anywhere near what she would have had she actually done anything beyond serve as a conduit, but what she felt most was loss. Letting go of *saidar* was bad enough; having it simply vanish out of you went beyond thinking about.

Others had suffered far worse than she. As the glow joining the circle winked out, Nynaeve sat down right where she stood as though her legs had melted, sat stroking the bracelet-and-rings, staring at it and panting. Sweat rolled down her face. "I feel like a kitchen sieve that just had the whole mill poured through it," she murmured. Carrying that much of the Power had its cost even if you did nothing, even with an *angreal*.

Talaan wavered, a reed in the wind, casting surreptitious glances at her mother, plainly afraid to sit. Aviendha stood straight, her fixed expression saying that willpower had as much to do with that as anything else. She gave a slight smile, though, and made a gesture in Maiden handtalk— worth the price—and then another—more—right behind. More than worth the price. Everyone looked weary, if not so much as those who had used *angreal*. The Bowl of the Winds went quiet at last, just a wide bowl of clear crystal, but decorated now with towering waves. *Saidar* still seemed to be there, though, not being wielded by anyone, not visible, but in dimly felt flashes like those that had played around the Bowl at the end.

Nynaeve raised her head to glower at the cloudless sky, then lowered her gaze to Caire. "All that, for what? Did we do anything, or not?" A breath of air stirred across the hilltop, warm as the air in a kitchen.

The Windfinder struggled to her feet. "Do you think Weaving the Winds is like throwing the helm over on a darter?" she demanded contemptuously. "I just moved the rudder on a skimmer with a beam as broad as the world! He will take time to turn, time to know he is *supposed* to

turn. That he *must* turn. Bu Storms himself will be able it, Aes Sedai, and the Bowl

Renaile moved into the Carefully she began folding take this to the Mistress of "We have fulfilled our par Sedai must fulfill the rest of in her throat, but when Elay peared a study in composur

"Maybe you've done you steadily. "Maybe. We'll see yours turns. If it turns!" R the Bowl, but Nynaeve ign tered, rubbing her temple. T her hair, and she grimaced *saidar*. It must be this thing

"No," Elayne said slowly. dimly perceived crackling i actly. More the shadow of a she were feeling someone u On the horizon to the south bolts vivid silver-blue again to Ebou Dar.

"A rainstorm?" Sareitha s be righting itself already." E sky even where the lightning not strong enough to sense s tance.

Elayne shivered. *She* wa someone was using as muc Fifty or even a hundred Aes Or. . . . "Not one of the Fors one behind her moaned.

"One couldn't do that," Ny they didn't feel us the way w have seen, unless they're a luck!" Quiet or not, she w Elayne down for using langu who will go to Andor with you there. Mat's in the city. I the boy; he came for me, and

Elayne w a deep breat Light; Tylin thon, her ve unlikely rese more. And T still wished Light burn v boy, Olver, a a queen. *The* mother had *must bear a*

"No," she Nynaeve; yc could we do die, or wors look for Mat

Nynaeve ning down h lant, foolish Aviendha, t ways going

Aviendha as sweaty as tired. "Ther Elayne is ri Mat Cautho have left th what can u Bowl, they with and wh

Nynaeve' her arms ar

"Shadows women wer of fire shot Sareitha's, a enveloped black smok

"There's second win big as a hor

long neck stretched out before and longer tail streaming behind. Two figures crouched low on its back. A storm of fire rained after it, quickest of all from Aviendha and the Sea Folk, who made no throwing gesture as part of their weaving. A hail of fire so thick it seemed that Fire must be forming itself out of the air, and the thing dodged behind the hill on the other side of the farm and appeared to vanish.

"Did we kill it?" Sareitha asked. Her eyes shone bright, and she breathed hard in agitation.

"Did we even hit it?" one of the Atha'an Miere growled disgustedly.

"Shadowspawn," Merilille murmured in amazement. "Here! At least that proves it's the Forsaken in Ebou Dar."

"Not Shadowspawn," Elayne said hollowly. Nynaeve's face was a picture of anguish; she knew, too. "They call it a *raken*. It's the Seanchan. We must go, Nynaeve, and take every woman at the farm with us. Whether we killed that thing or not, more will come. Anyone we leave behind will be wearing a *damane* leash by tomorrow morning." Nynaeve nodded, slowly, painfully; Elayne thought she murmured, "Oh, Mat."

Renaile strode up with the Bowl in her arms, once more swathed in its white covering. "Some of our ships have encountered these Seanchan. If they are in Ebou Dar, then the ships beat to sea. My ship fights for his life, and I am not on his deck! We go now!" And she formed the weave for a gateway, right there.

It tangled uselessly, of course, flared bright for an instant then collapsed into nothing, but Elayne squeaked in spite of herself. Right there in the middle of them! "You aren't going anywhere from here unless you mean to stay long enough to learn this hilltop!" she snapped. She hoped none of the women who had been in the circle tried the weave; holding *saidar* was the fastest way to learn a place. She could have made it work here, and very likely so could they. "You aren't going to a moving ship from *anywhere*; I don't think it's even *possible!*" Merilille nodded, though that meant little; Aes Sedai believed a great many things to be true, and some of them actually were. As well if the Sea Folk believed it proven, in any case. Nynaeve, haggard and staring, was in no condition to do any leading at the moment, so Elayne went on. She hoped she managed to do her mother's memory proud. "But most of all, you aren't going anywhere except with us, because our bargain isn't complete; the Bowl of the Winds is not yours until the weather is right." Not precisely true unless you twisted the words of the bargain a little, and Renaile opened her mouth, but Elayne plowed on. "*And* because you made a bargain with Matrim Cauthon, my subject. You go voluntarily where I want you to, or you go tied to a packsaddle. Those were the choices you accepted. So, get down this hill now, Renaile din Calon Blue Star, before the Seanchan sweep down on us with an army and a few hundred women who can channel and would like nothing better than to see us collared alongside them. Now! Run!"

To her astonishment, they ran.

CHAPTER
6

Threads

Elayne ran, too, of course, holding her skirts up, and
quickly took the lead on the well-worn dirt path.
Only Aviendha stayed close, though she seemed to
have no idea how to run in a dress, divided or not; tired as
she was, she certainly would have passed Elayne otherwise.
Everyone else strung out behind them along the narrow,
winding track. None of the Atha'an Miere would push by
Renaile, and despite her silk trousers she could not move
very fast carrying the Bowl hugged to her chest. Nynaeve
had no such compunctions, elbowing past and running
hard, shouting for people to get out of her way when she
stumbled into them whether they were Windfinders, Kinswomen, or Aes Sedai.

Bounding down the hillside, tripping and catching herself, Elayne wanted to laugh despite the urgency. Despite
the danger. Lini and her mother had been death on running
and climbing trees from the time she was twelve, but it was
not just the sheer pleasure of running again that made delight bubble up in her middle. She had behaved as a queen
was supposed to behave, and it had worked *exactly* as it was
supposed to! She had taken charge, to lead people out of
danger, and they *followed*! Her whole life had been training
for this. It was satisfaction that made her laugh, and the hot
glow of pride seemed about to burst through her skin like
the radiance of *saidar*.

Rounding the last curve, she pounded down the final
straight beside one of the tall white-plastered barns. And
her toe caught an almost buried stone. She pitched forward
heavily, windmilling her arms, and suddenly she was

somersaulting head-over-heels through the air. No time even to yell. With a thump that jarred her teeth and took all the wind out of her, she landed hard at the foot of the path, sitting right in front of Birgitte. For an instant she could not even think, and when she could, little satisfaction remained. So much for queenly dignity. Brushing her hair out of her face, she tried to catch her breath as she waited for Birgitte's cutting comment. This was a chance for the other woman to play the older and wiser sister with a vengeance, and she seldom let an opportunity pass.

To Elayne's surprise, Birgitte heaved her to her feet even before Aviendha could reach her, and without so much as the faint grin on Aviendha's face. All Elayne could feel from her Warder was a sense of . . . focus; she thought an arrow nocked on a drawn bowstring might feel that way. "Do we run or fight?" Birgitte asked. "I recognized those Seanchan fliers from Falme, and truth for true, I suggest running. My bow is the ordinary sort, today." Aviendha gave her a slight frown, and Elayne sighed; Birgitte *had* to learn to guard her tongue if she really intended to hide who she was.

"Of course we run," Nynaeve panted, laboring down the final stretch of path. "Fight or run! Fool question! Do you think we're utter—? Light! What are they doing?" Her voice started climbing and kept right on. "Alise! Alise, where are you? Alise! Alise!"

With a start, Elayne realized the farm was boiling as badly as it had when Careane's face was recognized. Maybe worse. A hundred and forty-seven Kinswomen inhabited the place at present, Alise had reported, including fifty-four red-belted Wise Women sent out days ago and a number of others who had been passing through the city; now it looked as though every last one was running somewhere, and a good many of the other women, too. Most of the Tarasin Palace servants in their green-and-white livery dashed this way and that carrying burdens. Ducks and chickens darted through the tumult, flapping and squawking, adding to the apparent confusion. Elayne even saw a *Warder*, Vandene's grizzled Jaem, trot by with his wiry arms wrapped around a big jute sack!

Alise appeared as though from the air, poised and collected despite the perspiration on her face. Every strand of her hair was in place, and her dress looked as if she were merely out for a stroll. "There's no need to screech," she said calmly, planting hands on hips. "Birgitte told me what those big birds are, and I thought we might be leaving sooner rather than later, especially with all of you galloping down the hill like the Dark One himself was after you. I told everybody to collect one clean dress apiece, three changes of shift and stockings, soap, mending baskets, and all the coin they have. That, and no more. The last ten to finish will do the washing-up till we get where we're going; that will speed their feet. I told those servants to gather all the food they could, too, just in case. And your Warders. Sensible fellows, most of them. Surprisingly sensible, for men. Does being a Warder do something to them?"

Nynaeve stood there with her jaw hanging, ready to issue orders and none left to give. Emotions played across her face too fast to catch. "Very good," she mumbled finally. And sourly. Suddenly she brightened. "The women who aren't Kin. Yes! They have to be—"

"Calm yourself," Alise broke in, making a soothing gesture. "They are already gone, for the most part. Mainly those with husbands or families they're worried about. I couldn't have held those back had I wanted. But a good thirty think those birds really are Shadowspawn, and want to stay as close to Aes Sedai as they can get." A sharp sniff said what she thought of that. "Now, you just gather yourself. Drink some cool water; not too fast. Put a little on your face. I have to keep an eye on things." Casting her eye over the bustle, everybody running in bounds, Alise shook her head. "Some would slack off if Trollocs were coming over the hill, and most of the noblewomen never really do get used to our rules. For sure, I'll need to remind two or three before we go." With that, she waded serenely back into the turmoil of the farmyard and left Nynaeve gaping.

"Well," Elayne said, brushing her skirt, "you did say she was a very capable woman."

"I never said that," Nynaeve snapped. "I never said 'very.' Hmmph! Where did my hat get to? Thinks she knows everything. I'll wager she doesn't know *that*!" She flounced off in a different direction than Alise.

Elayne stared after her. Her *hat*? She would have liked to know where her own hat had gone to—it was a beautiful thing—but really! Maybe being in a circle working that much of the Power, using an *angreal* doing it, had unsettled Nynaeve's wits temporarily. She still felt a trifle odd, herself, as though she could pluck little bits of *saidar* out of the air around her. In any case, she had other matters to worry about right then. Like being ready to get away before the Seanchan descended. From what she had seen in Falme, they really might bring a hundred *damane*, or more, and based on the little Egwene would let herself say of her captivity, most of those women really would be eager to help collar others. She said that what had turned her stomach most had been the sight of *damane* from Seanchan laughing with their *sul'dam*, fawning and playing with them, well-trained hounds with their affectionate handlers. Egwene said some of the women collared in Falme had been that way, too. It made Elayne's blood run cold. She would die before letting them put that leash on her! And she would as soon let the Forsaken have what she had found as the Seanchan. She went running to the cistern, Aviendha at her side breathing almost as hard as she was herself.

It seemed Alise really had thought of everything, though. The *ter'angreal* were already stowed away on the packhorses. The unsearched panniers remained full of jumbled odds and ends and the Light knew what, but those she and Aviendha had emptied now bulged with coarse sacks of flour and salt, beans and lentils. A handful of stablefolk minded the pack animals instead of running about with their arms full. Doing Alise's bidding, no doubt. Even Birgitte went trotting off at the woman's call with no more than a rueful grin!

Elayne lifted canvas covers to examine the *ter'angreal* as well as she could without unloading them again. Everything appeared to be there, a bit tumbled together in two panniers, not enough to fill them, but nothing broken. Not that anything short of the One Power itself *could* break most *ter'angreal*, yet even so. . . .

Aviendha took a seat cross-legged on the ground, blotting sweat from her face with a large, plain linen handkerchief that seemed very much at odds with her pretty silk riding dress. Even she was beginning to show weariness. "What are you muttering about, Elayne? You sound like Nynaeve. This Alise has only saved us the trouble of packing those things ourselves."

Elayne colored faintly. She had not meant to speak aloud. "I just don't want anyone handling them who doesn't know what they are doing, Aviendha." Some *ter'angreal* could trigger even for people unable to channel, if they did the wrong thing, but the truth was, she did not want *anyone* handling them. They were hers! The Hall was *not* going to hand these over to some other sister just because she was older and more *experienced*, or hide them away because studying *ter'angreal* was too dangerous. With this many examples to study, maybe she could finally figure out how to make *ter'angreal* that worked every time; there had been far too many failures and half-successes. "They need someone who knows what she's doing," she said, lashing the stiff canvas back in place.

Order began to appear out of pandemonium more rapidly than Elayne expected, though not as fast as she could have wished. Of course, she admitted reluctantly, nothing slower than instantaneous could have matched her wishes. Unable to keep her eyes off the sky, she sent Careane running back to the top of the hill to watch toward Ebou Dar. The stocky Green grumbled a bit under her breath before curtsying, and even frowned at the Kinswomen dashing about as if on the point of suggesting one of them instead, but Elayne wanted someone who would not faint at the sight of "Shadowspawn" approaching, and Careane stood lowest among the sisters. Adeleas and Vandene brought out Ispan between them, firmly shielded and the leather sack back over her head. She walked quite easily, and nothing visible said that anything at all had been done to her, except. . . . Ispan kept her hands folded at her waist, never so much as trying to raise the sack for a peek, and when she was boosted into a saddle, she held out her wrists to be corded to the pommel without being told. If she was that amenable, perhaps they had learned something from her. Elayne just did not want to contemplate how the learning might have been achieved.

There were . . . bumps, of course, of sorts, even with what might be rushing toward them. What surely was rushing toward them. Nynaeve getting her blue-plumed hat back was not really a bump, though it almost turned into one; Alise *had* found it, and handed it back telling Nynaeve she needed to shield her face from the sun if she wanted to keep that smooth pretty skin. An openmouthed Nynaeve watched the graying woman hurry off to deal with one of the numerous small problems, then ostentatiously shoved the hat under a strap of her saddlebags.

From the beginning Nynaeve set about flattening the real bumps, but Alise was nearly always there first, and where Alise met a bump, the bump flattened itself. Several noble-women demanded help packing their belongings, only to be informed in no uncertain terms that she had meant what she said and if they did not hop to it, they could live in what they stood in. They hopped. Some, and not only nobles, changed their minds about going when they learned the destination was Andor, and were literally chased away. Afoot, and told to keep running as long as they could. Every horse was needed, but they had to be well away before the Seanchan appeared; at the very least they could be expected to put anyone near the farm to the question. As should have been expected, Nynaeve got into a shouting match with Renaile over the Bowl, and the turtle Talaan had used, which Renaile apparently had tucked behind her sash. Hardly had they reached the stage of waving arms, however, than Alise was right there, and in short order the Bowl was back in Sareitha's care and the turtle in Merilille's. Following which, Elayne was treated to the sight of Alise shaking her finger under the astonished nose of the Windfinder to the Mistress of the Ships to the Atha'an Miere, delivering a tongue-lashing on the subject of theft that left Renaile spluttering indignantly. Nynaeve did a little spluttering, too, stalking away empty-handed, yet Elayne thought she had never seen anyone look so forlorn.

All in all, it did not take very long, though. The remaining women who had been at the farm gathered under the watchful eyes of the Knitting Circle—and of Alise, who carefully noted the last ten to arrive, all but two in fine embroidered silks, not much different from Elayne's. Definitely not Kinswomen. Elayne felt sure they really would do the washing-up anyway; Alise would not let a little thing like noble birth stand in her way. The Windfinders lined up with their horses, surprisingly silent except for Renaile, who muttered imprecations whenever she saw Alise. Careane was summoned back from the hilltop. The Warders brought the sisters their mounts. Almost everyone kept an eye on the sky, and *saidar* made halos around all of the older Aes Sedai and most of the Windfinders. Around a few of the Kin, as well.

Leading her mare to the head of the line, at the cistern, Nynaeve fingered the *angreal* still on her hand as if she were going to be the one to make the gateway, ridiculous as the very idea might be. For one thing, though she had washed her face—and donned her hat; strangely, all things considered—she still tottered whenever her self-control slipped. Lan stayed practically at her shoulder, stone-faced as always, but if ever there was a man ready to catch a woman when she fell, it was he. Even with the bracelet-and-rings, Nynaeve might not be able to manage enough to weave a gateway. More important, she had been dashing about the farm ever since they first arrived; Elayne had spent a considerable time holding *saidar* right where they now stood. She knew that spot. Nynaeve scowled sulkily when Elayne embraced the Source, but at least she had sense enough to say nothing.

Right from the first Elayne wished that she had asked Aviendha for the woman-cloaked-in-her-own-hair; she was weary, too, and all the *saidar* she could draw was barely enough to form the weave so it would work. The flows wavered in her grasp almost as if trying to twist free, then snapped into place so suddenly that she jumped; channeling when you were tired was not at all like other times, but this was the worst ever. At least the familiar vertical slash of silver appeared as it should, and widened into an opening right alongside the cistern. An opening no bigger than the one Aviendha had made, and at that, Elayne was grateful it was large enough to fit a horse through. At the last, she had not been certain it would be. Gasps rose from the Kinswomen, seeing a view of an upland meadow suddenly standing between them and the familiar gray bulk of the cistern.

"You should have let me try," Nynaeve said softly. Softly, but with a sharp point even so. "You nearly flubbed it altogether."

Aviendha gave Nynaeve a flat look that almost made Elayne grab her arm. The longer they remained near-sisters, the more she seemed to think she had to defend Elayne's honor; if they did become first-sisters, Elayne could see having to keep her away from Nynaeve, and Birgitte, completely!

"It's done, Nynaeve," she said quickly. "That's all that counts." Nynaeve directed a flat look at her and muttered something about the day being prickly, as if *Elayne* were the one showing her snappish side.

Birgitte was the first through, grinning impudently at Lan, leading her horse with her bow already in her other hand. Elayne could sense eagerness in her, a touch of satisfaction, perhaps that this time she had the lead instead of Lan—there was always a bit of rivalry between Warders— and a small measure of wariness. Very small. Elayne knew that meadow well; Gareth Bryne had taught her to ride not far from there. About five miles over those first sparsely treed hills lay the manor house of one of her mother's estates. One of *her* estates; she had to get used to that. The seven families who tended the house and its grounds would be the only people for half a day's journey in any direction.

Elayne had chosen that destination because they could reach Caemlyn in two weeks from there. And because the estate was so isolated, she might be entering Caemlyn before anyone knew she was in Andor. That could be a very necessary precaution; at various times in Andor's history, rivals for the Rose Crown had been kept as "guests" until they relinquished their claims. Her mother had kept two, until she took the throne. With luck, she could have a solid base established by the time Egwene and the others arrived.

Lan took Mandarb right behind Birgitte's brown gelding, and Nynaeve lurched as if to rush after the black warhorse, then pulled herself up short with a level stare that dared Elayne to say a word. Fiddling furiously with her reins, she made a visible effort to look anywhere except through the gateway after Lan. Her lips moved. After a moment, Elayne realized that she was *counting*.

"Nynaeve," she said quietly, "we really don't have time for—"

"Move along," Alise called from the rear, the sound of her hands clapping a sharp punctuating crack. "No pushing or shoving, now, but I'll have no laggards either! Move along."

Nynaeve's head swung wildly, pained indecision painting her face. For some reason she touched her wide hat, a few of its blue plumes broken and drooping, before pulling her hand away. "Oh, that goat-kissing old . . . !" she growled, the rest lost as she dragged her mare through the gateway. Elayne sniffed. And Nynaeve had the *nerve* to speak to anybody about *their* language! She wished she could have heard the rest, though; she already knew the first bit.

Alise continued her urging, but there really did not seem to be much need after the first. Even the Windfinders hurried, glancing worriedly over their shoulders at the sky. Even Renaile, who mumbled something about Alise that Elayne noted in the back of her head. Though calling some- one "a fish-loving scavenger" did seem rather mild. She would have expected the Sea Folk to eat fish all the time.

Alise herself brought up the very rear, except for the re- maining Warders, as if to herd even the packhorses along. She paused long enough to hand Elayne her green-plumed hat. "You'll want to keep the sun off that sweet face of yours," she said with a smile. "Such a pretty girl. No need to turn to leather before your time."

Aviendha, sitting on the ground nearby, fell over back- ward and kicked her heels laughing.

"I think I'll ask her to find *you* a hat. With lots of plumes, and big bows," Elayne said in dulcet tones before quickly following the Kinswoman. That certainly cut off Aviend- ha's laughter.

The gently rolling meadow was broad and nearly a mile long, surrounded by hills taller than those she had left be- hind, and by trees she knew, oak and pine and blackwood, sourgum and leatherleaf and fir, thick forest with good, tall timber to south and west and east, though there might not be any cutting this year. Most of the more scattered trees to the north, toward the manor, were better suited for firewood. Small gray boulders dotted the thick brown grass here and there, and not even a withered stalk marked the death of a wildflower. That was not so different from the south.

For once Nynaeve was not peering at the surrounding countryside trying to find Lan. He and Birgitte would not be gone long anyway, not here. Instead she strode briskly among the horses, ordering people to mount in a loud, com- manding voice, chivvying the servants with the pack ani- mals, curtly telling some of the Kinswomen who had no horses that any child could walk five miles, shouting at a slender Altaran noblewoman with a scar on her cheek and carrying a bundle nearly as big as herself that if she had been fool enough to bring all of her dresses then she could carry them. Alise had gathered the Atha'an Miere around her and was instructing them on how to mount a horse. For a wonder, they actually appeared to be paying attention. Nynaeve glanced her way and seemed pleased to see Alise standing in one spot. Until Alise smiled encouragingly and motioned her to go on with what she was doing.

For an instant Nynaeve stood stock-still, staring at the woman. Then she came striding through the grass to Elayne. Reaching up to her hat with both hands, she hesitated, glowering up at it through her lashes before giving it a twitch straight. "I'll just let her take care of everything this time," she said in a suspiciously reasonable tone. "We'll just see how well she does with those . . . Sea Folk. Yes, we will." Too reasonable a tone by half. Abruptly she frowned at the still-open gateway. "Why are you holding it? Let go." Aviendha was frowning, too.

Elayne drew a deep breath. She had thought about this, and there was no other way, but Nynaeve would try to argue her out of it, and there was no time for arguing. Through the gateway, the farmyard stood empty, even the chickens finally frightened away by the hubbub, yet how long before it filled up again? She studied her weave, melded together so snugly that only a few threads remained distinct. She could see every flow, of course, but except for those few, they appeared inseparably combined. "Take everyone to the manor house, Nynaeve," she said. The sun did not have very much farther to fall; perhaps two hours of light remained. "Master Hornwell will be surprised at so many visitors arriving at dark, but tell him you're guests of the girl who cried over the redbird with the broken wing; he'll remember that. I will be along as soon as I can."

"Elayne," Aviendha began in a surprisingly anxious voice, and at the same time, Nynaeve said sharply, "Just what do you think you're—"

There was only one way to stop it. Elayne plucked one of the discernible threads free of the weave; it wavered and flailed like a living tentacle; it fuzzed and spluttered, tiny fluffs of *saidar* breaking off and fading away. She had not noticed that when Aviendha unmade her weave, but she had only seen the tail of that, really. "Go on," she told Nynaeve. "I'll wait for the rest until you are all out of sight." Nynaeve

stared out, her jaw hanging. "It has to be done," Elayne
sighed. "The Seanchan will be at the farm in hours, for
sure. Even if they wait until tomorrow, what if one of the
damane has the Talent to read residues? Nynaeve, I won't
give Traveling to the Seanchan. I won't!"

Nynaeve growled something under her breath about the
Seanchan that must have been particularly pithy, judging
by her tone. "Well, *I* won't let you burn yourself out!" she
said aloud. "Now, put that back! Before the whole thing ex-
plodes the way Vandene said. You could kill all of us!"

"It cannot be put back," Aviendha said, laying a hand on
Nynaeve's arm. "She has begun, and now she must finish.
You must do as she says, Nynaeve."

Nynaeve's brows drew down. "Must" was a word she did
not like hearing one bit, not applied to her. She was not
a fool, though, so after a bit of glaring—at Elayne, at the
gateway, at Aviendha, at the world in general—she flung
her arms around Elayne in a hug that made her ribs creak.

"You be careful, you hear me," she whispered. "If you
get yourself killed, I swear I'll skin you alive!" In spite of
everything, Elayne burst out laughing. Nynaeve snorted,
pushing her out to arm's length by her shoulders. "You
know what I mean," she grumbled. "And don't think I don't
mean it, because I do! I do," she added in a softer voice.
"You take care."

It took Nynaeve a moment to gather herself, blinking
and pulling her blue riding gloves tight. There seemed to
be a hint of moisture in her eyes, though that could not have
been; Nynaeve made other people cry, she did not cry herself. "Well, then," she said loudly. "Alise, if you don't have
everyone ready yet—" Turning, she cut off with a strangled
croak.

Those who were supposed to be mounted were, even the
Atha'an Miere. The Warders were all gathered around the
other sisters; Lan and Birgitte had returned, and Birgitte
watched Elayne worriedly. The servants had the pack animals in a line, and the Kinswomen were waiting patiently,
most afoot except for the Knitting Circle. A number of
horses that could have been used for riding were loaded
with sacks of food and bundles of belongings. Women who
had brought more than Alise allowed—none of them Kin—
carried their bundles on their own backs. The slender noble

with the scar was bent at an awkward angle beneath hers, and glaring at anyone but Alise. Every woman who could channel was staring at the gateway. And every woman who had been there to hear Vandene tell of the dangers watched that one whipping filament as she would have a red adder.

It was Alise herself who brought Nynaeve her horse. And straightened the blue-plumed hat as Nynaeve put a foot in the stirrup. Nynaeve turned the plump mare north with Lan riding Mandarb at her side and a look of utter mortification on her face. Why she did not just set Alise down, Elayne did not understand. To hear Nynaeve tell it, she had been putting women older than herself in their place since she was little more than a girl. And she was Aes Sedai, now, after all; that should carry mountains of weight with any Kinswoman.

As the column began to wend its way toward the hills, Elayne looked at Aviendha and Birgitte. Aviendha simply stood there with her arms folded beneath her breasts; she had the woman-wrapped-in-her-own-hair *angreal* clutched in one hand. Birgitte took Lioness's reins from Elayne, adding them to those of her own horse and Aviendha's, then walked over to a small boulder twenty paces away and sat down.

"You two must," Elayne began, then coughed when Aviendha's eyebrows shot up in surprise. Sending Aviendha out of danger was impossible without shaming her. Perhaps impossible altogether. "I want you to go with the others," she told Birgitte. "And take Lioness. Aviendha and I can take turns riding her gelding. I'd like a walk before bedtime."

"If you ever treat a man half as well as you do that horse," Birgitte said dryly, "he'll be yours for life. I think I'll just sit awhile; I've ridden long enough today. I'm not at your beck and call all the time. We can play that game in front of the sisters and the other Warders, to spare your blushes, but you and I know better." Despite the mocking words, what Elayne felt from her was affection. No; stronger than affection. Her own eyes stung suddenly. Her death would hurt Birgitte to the bone—the Warder bond made that certain— but it was friendship that made her stay now.

"I am thankful to have two friends such as you," she said simply. Birgitte grinned at her as if she had said something silly.

Aviendha, however, blushed furiously and stared at Birgitte, wide-eyed and flustered, as though the Warder's presence were to blame for her fiery cheeks. Hurriedly she shifted her gaze to the people still short of the first hill, perhaps half a mile distant. "Best to wait until they are out of sight," she said, "but you cannot wait too long. Once you have started the unweaving, the flows begin to grow ... slick ... after a time. Letting one slip free before it is out of the weave is the same as letting go of the weave; it will fall into whatever it wishes, then. But you must not hurry, either. Each thread must be pulled free as far as it will go. The more that come loose, the easier others will be to see, but you must always pick the thread that is easiest to see." Smiling warmly, she pressed her fingers firmly against Elayne's cheek. "You will do well, if you are careful."

It did not sound that difficult. She just had to be careful. It seemed to take a long time for the last woman to vanish over the hill, the slender noble bent under the bulk of her dresses. The sun barely appeared to settle any at all, but it seemed like hours. What did Aviendha mean precisely by "slick"? She could not explain beyond variations on the word; they became difficult to hold, that was all.

Elayne found out as soon as she began again. "Slick" was what you would get if you coated a live eel with grease. She gritted her teeth just holding on to that first thread, and that was on top of trying to pull it free. All that stopped her from gasping in relief when the thread of Air began whipping about, finally loose, was that there were more to go. If they became much more "slick," she was not sure she could manage it. Aviendha watched closely, but did not say another word, though she always had an encouraging smile when Elayne needed one. Elayne could not see Birgitte—she did not dare look away from her work—yet she could feel her, a small knot of rock-solid confidence in her own head, enough confidence to fill her.

Sweat slid down her face, down her back and belly, until she began to feel "slick" herself. A bath tonight would be *most* welcome. No, she could not think of that. All attention on the weaves. They *were* getting harder to handle, quivering in her grip as soon as she touched one, but they still came free, and every time one thread began to lash about, another seemed to leap out of the mass, to suddenly be clearly perceptible where there had only been solid *saidar* before. To her eye the gateway resembled some monstrous, distorted hundred-heads on the bottom of a pond, surrounded by flailing tendrils, every one thickly haired with threads of the Power that grew and writhed and vanished only to be replaced by new. The opening visible to anyone flexed along its edges, changing shape and even size continuously. Her legs began to tremble; strain stung her eyes as much as sweat did. She did not know how much longer she could go on. Gritting her teeth, she fought. One thread at a time. One thread at a time.

A thousand miles away, less than a hundred paces away through the shuddering gateway, dozens of soldiers swept around the white farm buildings, short men carrying crossbows, in brown breastplates and painted helmets that looked like the heads of huge insects. Behind them came a woman with red panels bearing silver lightning on her skirts, a bracelet on her wrist linked by a silvery leash to the collar around the neck of a woman in gray, and then another *sul'dam* and her *damane*, then another pair. One of the *sul'dam* pointed at the gateway, and the glow of *saidar* abruptly enveloped her *damane*.

"Get down!" Elayne screamed, falling backward, out of sight of the farmyard, and silver-blue lightning shot through the gateway with a roar that filled her ears, forking savagely in every direction. Her hair lifted, every strand trying to stand on its own, and thunderous fountains of earth erupted wherever one of the forks struck. Dirt and pebbles rained down on her.

Hearing returned suddenly, and a man's voice from the other side of the opening, a slurred, drawling accent that made her skin crawl as much as the words. ". . . must take them alive, you fools!"

Abruptly one of the soldiers was leaping into the meadow right in front of her. Birgitte's arrow punched through the clenched fist embossed on his leather breastplate. A second Seanchan soldier stumbled over the first as he fell, and Aviendha's belt knife stabbed into his throat before he could recover. Arrows flew from Birgitte's bow like hail; with one boot on the horses' reins, she grinned grimly as she shot. The trembling horses tossed their heads and danced as if they would jerk free and run, but Birgitte simply stood and shot as fast as she could draw. Shouts from beyond the gateway said Birgitte Silverbow still struck home with every shaft she loosed. Answer came, quick as bad thought, black streaks, crossbow bolts. So quick, all happening so fast. Aviendha fell, blood running over the fingers clutching her right arm, but she let go of her wound immediately, crawling clear, scrabbling on the ground for the *angreal*, her face set. Birgitte cried out; dropping her bow, she grabbed her thigh where a quarrel stuck out. Elayne felt the stab of agony as sharply as if it were her own.

Desperately, she seized another thread from where she lay half on her back. And realized to her horror after one tug that it was all she could do to hold on. Had the thread moved? Had it slipped free any at all? If it had, she did not dare let go. The thread trembled greasily in her grasp.

"Alive, I said!" that Seanchan voice roared. "Anyone who kills a woman gets no share of the taking gold!" The flurry of crossbow bolts ceased.

"You wish to take me?" Aviendha shouted. "Then come and dance with me!" *Saidar*'s glow abruptly surrounded her, dim even with the *angreal*, and balls of fire sprang into being in front of the gateway and sprayed through again and again. Not very large balls, but the blasts as they burst back in Altara sounded in a steady stream. Aviendha panted with effort, though; her face glistened with sweat. Birgitte had recovered her bow; she looked every inch the hero of legend, blood streaming down her leg, barely able to stand, but an arrow half drawn, searching for a target.

Elayne tried to control her breathing. She could not embrace one shred more of the Power, nothing to help. "The two of you must get away," she said. She could not believe how she sounded, calm as ice; she knew she should have been wailing. Her heart was trying to pound through her ribs. "I don't know how much longer I can hold this." That held true for the entire weave as much as for that single thread. Was it sliding? Was it? "Go, as fast as you can. The other side of the hills should be safe, but every span you can cover gains something. Go!"

Birgitte growled in the Old Tongue, but nothing that Elayne knew. It sounded like phrases she would like to learn. If there was ever a chance. Birgitte went on in words Elayne could understand. "You let that bloody thing go

before I tell you, and you won't have to worry about waiting for Nynaeve to skin you; I'll do it myself. And then
let her have a turn. Just be quiet and hang on! Aviendha,
get around here—behind that thing!—can you keep that
up from behind it?—get around here and on one of these
bloody horses."

"As long as I can see where to weave," Aviendha replied,
staggering to her feet. She wobbled sideways and barely
caught herself short of falling. Blood flowed down her
sleeve from a wicked gash. "I think I can." She vanished
behind the gateway, and the fireballs continued. You could
see through a gateway from the other side, though it appeared to be a heat haze hanging in the air. You could not
walk through from that side, though—the attempt would
be extremely painful—and when Aviendha reappeared, she
was stumbling well wide. Birgitte helped her mount her
gelding, but *backward*, of all things!

When Birgitte motioned fiercely to her, Elayne did not
bother with shaking her head. For one thing, she feared
what might happen if she did. "I'm not certain I can hold
on if I try to get up." In truth, she was not certain she *could*
get up; tired was no longer in it; her muscles were water.
"Ride as fast as you can. I'll hold on as long as I'm able.
Please, go!"

Muttering curses in the Old Tongue—they had to be;
nothing else ever had the sound!—Birgitte shoved the
horses' reins into Aviendha's hands. Nearly falling twice,
she hobbled to Elayne and bent to take her by the shoulders. "You can hang on," she said, her voice filled with the
same conviction Elayne felt from her. "I never met a Queen
of Andor before you, but I've known queens like you. A
backbone of steel and a lion's heart. You can do it!"

Slowly she pulled Elayne up, not waiting for an answer,
her face tight, every stab in her leg echoing in Elayne's
head. Elayne quivered with the effort of holding the weave,
holding that one thread; she was surprised to find herself
erect. And alive. Birgitte's leg throbbed madly in her head.
She tried not to lean on Birgitte, but her own trembling
limbs would not support her completely. As they lurched
toward the horses, each half leaning on the other, she kept
looking back over her shoulder. She could hold a weave
without looking at it—she could normally—but she needed

to reassure herself that she really did still have a grip on that one thread, that it was not slipping. The gateway now appeared like no weave she had ever seen, twisting wildly, wreathed with fuzzed tentacles.

With a groan, Birgitte heaved her into her saddle more than helped her. Backward, just like Aviendha! "You have to see," she explained, limping to her gelding; holding the reins of all three horses, she pulled herself up painfully. Without a sound, but Elayne felt the agony. "You do what needs doing and leave where we're going to me." The horses leaped away, perhaps as much from eagerness to be gone as from Birgitte's heel in her own mount's flank.

Elayne hung on to the high cantle of her saddle as grimly as she did to the weave, to *saidar* itself. The galloping horse flung her about, and it was all she could do to remain in the saddle. Aviendha used her saddle's cantle as a prop to keep herself upright; her mouth hung open, sucking air, and her eyes seemed fixed. The glow surrounded her, though, and that stream of fireballs continued. Not as fast as before, true, and some shot wide of the gateway, streaking trails of flame through the grass or exploding on the ground beyond, but they still formed and flew. Elayne took strength, made herself take strength; if Aviendha could keep on when she looked ready to fall on her face, she could, too.

At a gallop, the gateway began to dwindle, brown grass stretching out between them and the opening, and then the ground was slanting upward. They were climbing the hill! Birgitte was again the arrow in the bow, all focus, fighting down the agony in her legs, urging her horses for more speed. All they had to do was reach the crest, reach the other side.

With a gasp, Aviendha sagged onto her elbows, bouncing on her saddle like a loose sack; the light of *saidar* flickered around her and was gone. "I cannot," she panted. "I cannot." That was all she could get out. Seanchan soldiers began leaping into the meadow almost as soon as the hail of fire ceased.

"It's all right," Elayne managed. Her throat was sand; all the moisture that had been in her now coated her skin and soaked her clothes. "Using an *angreal* is tiring. You did well, and they can't catch us now."

As if to mock her, a *sul'dam* appeared in the meadow

below; even at half a mile there was no mistaking the two women. The sun, low in the west, still flashed glints off the *a'dam* linking them. Another pair joined them, then a third, and a fourth. A fifth.

"The crest!" Birgitte shouted joyfully. "We made it! It's good wine and a well set-up man tonight!"

In the meadow, a *sul'dam* pointed, and time seemed to slow for Elayne. The glow of the One Power sprang up around the woman's *damane*. Elayne could see the weave forming. She knew what it was. And there was no way to stop it. "Faster!" she shouted. The shield struck her. She should have been too strong for it—she should have been!—but exhausted as she was, barely clinging to *saidar* as she was, it sliced between her and the Source. Down in the meadow, the weave that had been a gateway fell in on itself. Haggard, looking as though she could not possibly move, Aviendha hurled herself from her saddle at Elayne, carrying them both off. Elayne had just time to see the far slope of the hill below her as she fell.

The air turned white, blanking her sight. There was sound—she knew there was sound, a great roar—but it lay beyond hearing. Something struck her, as if she had fallen from a rooftop onto hard pavement, from a tower top.

Her eyes opened, staring at the sky. The sky looked, strange somehow, blurry. For a moment she could not move, and when she did, she gasped. She hurt everywhere. Oh, Light, she hurt! Slowly she raised a hand to her face; her fingers came away red. Blood. The others. She had to help the others. She could feel Birgitte, feel pain as bad as what gripped her, but at least Birgitte was alive. And determined, and angry apparently; she could not be injured too badly. Aviendha.

With a sob, Elayne rolled over, then pushed up to hands and knees, her head spinning, agony stabbing her side. Vaguely she recalled that moving with even one broken rib could be dangerous, but the thought was as hazy as the hillside. Thinking seemed . . . difficult. Blinking appeared to help her sight, though. Some. She was almost to the bottom of the hill! High above, a haze of smoke rose from the meadow beyond. Unimportant, now. Not important at all.

Thirty paces up the slope, Aviendha was on her hands and knees, too, almost falling over when she raised a hand to wipe away blood that poured down her face, but search-ing anxiously. Her gaze fell on Elayne, and she froze, star-ing. Elayne wondered how bad she looked. Surely no worse than Aviendha herself; half of the other woman's skirt was gone, her bodice torn nearly off, and everywhere skin showed, there seemed to be blood.

Elayne crawled to her. With her head, it seemed much easier than trying to stand and walk. As she came close, Aviendha gave a relieved gasp.

"You are all right," she said, touching bloody fingers to Elayne's cheek. "I was so afraid. So afraid."

Elayne blinked in surprise. What she could see of herself appeared in every bit as bad shape as Aviendha. Her own skirts remained intact, but half of her bodice was ripped away entirely, and she seemed to be bleeding from two dozen gashes. Then it struck her. She had not been burned out. She shivered at the thought. "We are both all right," she said softly.

Well off to one side, Birgitte wiped her belt knife on the mane of Aviendha's gelding and straightened from the still horse. Her right arm dangled, her coat was gone, along with one boot, and the rest of her garments torn; as much blood stained her skin and clothes as either of theirs. The crossbow bolt standing out from her thigh seemed to be the worst of her injuries, but the rest certainly added up to as much again. "His back was broken," she said, gesturing to the horse at her feet. "Mine's well, I think, but the last I saw of him, he was running fit to win the Wreath of Megairil. I always thought he had a turn of speed. Lioness." She shrugged, and winced. "Elayne, Lioness was dead when I found her. I'm sorry."

"We are alive," Elayne said firmly, "and that is what counts." She would weep for Lioness later. The smoke above the hilltop was not thick, but it rose over a wide area. "I want to see exactly what it was that I did."

It took clinging to one another for all three of them to stand, and laboring up the hillside was an effort of panting and groans, even from Aviendha. They sounded as though they had been thrashed within an inch of their lives—which Elayne supposed they had been—and looked as though they had wallowed in a butcher's shambles. Aviendha still carried the *angreal* tight in her fist, but even if she or Elayne had possessed more than their small Talent with Healing, neither could have managed to embrace the Source, much less channel. At the top of the hill, they stood leaning on each other and stared at devastation.

Fire ringed the meadow, but the heart of it was blackened, smoldering and swept clear even of boulders. Half the trees on the surrounding slopes were broken or leaning away from the meadow. Hawks began to appear, riding the hot air rising from the fire; hawks often hunted so, looking for small animals chased into the open by the flames. Of the Seanchan there was no sign. Elayne wished there were bodies, so she could be certain they were all dead. Especially all of the *sul'dam*. Gazing down at the burned, smoking ground, though, she was suddenly glad there was no evidence. It had been a terrible way to die. *The Light have mercy on their souls*, she thought. *On all of their souls.*

"Well," she said aloud, "I did not do as well as you, Aviendha, but I suppose it worked out for the best, considering. I will try to do better next time."

Aviendha glanced at her sideways. There was a gash on her cheek, and another across her forehead, as well as a long one laying open her scalp. "You did much better than I, for a first try. I was given a simple knot tied in a flow of Wind the first time. It took me fifty tries to unweave even that without having a clap of thunder in my face, or a blow that made my ears ring."

"I suppose I should have started with something simpler," Elayne said. "I have a habit of leaping in over my head." Over her head? She had leaped before looking to see whether there was *water*! She stifled a chuckle, but not before it sent a stab through her side. So instead of chuckling, she moaned through her teeth. She thought some of them might be loose. "At least we've found a new weapon. Perhaps I should not be happy about that, but with the Seanchan back again, I am."

"You do not understand, Elayne." Aviendha gestured toward the center of the meadow, where the gateway had been. "That could have been no more than a flash of light, or even less. You cannot tell until it happens. Is a flash of light worth the risk of burning out yourself and every woman closer to you than a hundred paces or more?"

Elayne stared at her. She had stayed, knowing that? To

risk your life was one thing, but to risk losing the ability to channel. . . . "I want us to adopt each other as first-sisters, Aviendha. As soon as we can find Wise Ones." What they were to do about Rand, she could not imagine. The very idea that they would *both* marry him—and Min, too!—was worse than ridiculous. But of this, she was sure. "I don't need to know any more about you. I want to be your sister." Gently, she kissed Aviendha's blood-stained cheek.

She had only thought Aviendha blushed fiercely before. Even Aiel lovers did not kiss where anyone could see. Fiery sunsets paled beside Aviendha's face. "I want you for my sister, too," she mumbled. Swallowing hard—and eyeing Birgitte, who was pretending to ignore them—she leaned over and quickly pressed her lips to Elayne's cheek. Elayne loved her as much for that gesture as for the rest.

Birgitte had been gazing behind them, over her shoulder, and perhaps she had not been pretending after all, because she suddenly said, "Someone's coming. Lan and Nynaeve, unless I miss my guess."

Awkwardly, they turned, hobbling and stumbling and groaning. It seemed quite ludicrous; heroes in stories never got hurt so they could barely stand. In the distance to the north, two riders appeared briefly through the trees. Briefly, but long enough to make out a tall man on a tall horse, galloping hard, and a woman on a shorter animal running just as hard at his side. Gingerly, the three of them sat down to wait. That was another thing heroes in stories never did, Elayne thought with a sigh. She hoped she could be a queen to make her mother proud, but it was clear that she would never make a hero.

Chulein moved the reins slightly, and Segani banked smoothly, turning on a ribbed wing. He was a well-trained *raken*, swift and agile, her favorite, though she had to share flying him. There were always more *morat'raken* than *raken*; a fact of life. Down in the farm below, balls of fire were leaping out of the air apparently, scattering in every direction. She tried to pay no attention; her job was to watch for trouble approaching from the area around the farm. At least the smoke had stopped rising from where Tauan and Macu had died in the olive grove.

A thousand paces above the ground, she had a very long view. All the other *raken* were off scouting the countryside; any woman who ran would be marked for checking, to see whether she was one of those who had caused all the excitement, though truth for sure, anyone in these lands who saw a *raken* in the air likely would run. All Chulein had to do was watch for approaching trouble here. She wished she did not feel an itch between her shoulder blades; it always meant trouble *was* on the way. The wind of Segani's flight was not bad at this speed, but she drew the drawstring of her waxed linen hood tighter under her chin, tested the leather safety straps that held her in the saddle, adjusted her crystal goggles, snugged her gauntlets.

Over a hundred Fists of Heaven were on the ground already, and more important, six *sul'dam* with *damane* and another dozen carrying shoulder bags full of spare *a'dam*. The second flight would be lifting from the hills to the south with reinforcements. Better if more had come in the first strike, but there were few enough *to'raken* with the Hailene, and strong rumor had it that many of those had been given the task of ferrying the High Lady Suroth and her entire entourage down from Amadicia. Bad to think ill of the Blood, yet she wished more *to'raken* had been sent to Ebou Dar. No *morat'raken* could think well of the huge, ungainly *to'raken*, fit only to carry burdens, but they could have put more Fists of Heaven on the ground faster, more *sul'dam*.

"Rumor says there are hundreds of *marath'damane* down there," Eliya said loudly against her back. In the sky, you had to speak loudly, over the rush of wind. "Do you know what I'm going to do with my share of the taking gold? Buy an inn. This Ebou Dar looks a likely place, what I saw of it. Maybe I'll even find a husband. Have children. What do you think of that?"

Chulein grinned behind her wind-scarf. Every flier talked of buying an inn—or a tavern, sometimes a farm— yet who could leave the sky? She patted the base of Segani's long, leathery neck. Every woman flier—three in four were women—talked of a husband and children, but children meant an end to flying, too. More women left the Fists of Heaven in a month than left the sky in half a year.

"I think you should keep your eyes open," she said. But there was no harm in a little talk. She could have seen a child move in the olive groves below, much more anything that might threaten Fists of Heaven. The most lightly armored of soldiers, they were about as hard as the Deathwatch Guard; some said harder. "I'll use my share to buy a *damane* and hire a *sul'dam*." If there were half as many *marath'damane* down there as rumor claimed, her share would buy two *damane*. Three! "A *damane* trained to make Sky Lights. When I leave the sky, I'll be as rich as one of the Blood." They had something called "fireworks" here—she had seen some fellows vainly trying to interest the Blood in Tanchico—but who would watch such a pitiful thing compared to the Sky Lights? Those fellows had been bundled out and dumped in the road outside the city.

"The farm!" Eliya shouted, and suddenly something hit Segani hard, harder than the worst storm gust Chulein had ever felt, tumbling him wing over wing.

Down the *raken* plunged, screaming his raucous cry, spinning so fast that Chulein was pulled tight against her safety straps. She left her hands on her thighs, tensed on the reins but still. Segani had to pull out of this himself; any twitch on the reins would only hinder him. Rolling like a gambling wheel, they fell. *Morat'raken* were taught not to watch the ground if a *raken* fell, whatever the reason, but she could not help estimating her height every time a whiplike tumble brought the ground into sight. Eight hundred paces. Six hundred. Four. Two. The Light illumine her soul, and the infinite mercy of the Creator protect her from—

With a snap of his broad wings that jerked her sideways and rattled her teeth, Segani leveled out, the tips of his pinions brushing treetops as they swept down. With a calmness born of hard training, she checked the motion of his wings for strain. Nothing, but she would have a *der'morat'raken* examine him thoroughly anyway. A tiny thing that might slip by her eyes would not escape a master.

"It seems we've escaped the Lady of the Shadows one more time, Eliya." Turning to look over her shoulder, she let her words trail off. A length of broken safety strap trailed back from the empty seat behind her. Every flier knew that the Lady waited at the bottom of the long fall, but knowing never made seeing easier.

Offering a quick prayer for the dead, she firmly pushed herself back to duty and urged Segani to climb. A slow, spiraling climb, in case of some hidden strain, but as quick as she thought safe. Maybe a little quicker than safe. Smoke rising from beyond the knobby hill ahead made her frown, but what she saw as she cleared the crest dried her mouth. Her hands stilled on the reins, and Segani continued to climb on powerful sweeps of his wings.

The farm was . . . gone. Foundations scoured clean of the white buildings that had stood on them, the big structures built into a hillside smashed heaps of rubble. Gone. Everything was blackened and burned. Fire raged through the undergrowth on the slopes and made fans a hundred paces long into the olive groves and the forest, stretching from the spaces between the hills. Beyond lay broken trees for another hundred or more, all leaning away from the farm. She had never seen anything like it. Nothing could be alive down there. Nothing could have lived through that. Whatever it had been.

Quickly she came to herself and turned Segani south. In the distance she could make out *to'raken*, each one crowded with a dozen Fists of Heaven over this short distance, Fists of Heaven and *sul'dam*, coming too late. She began composing her report in her head; there was certainly no one else to make one. Everyone said this was a land full of *marath'damane* waiting to be collared, but with this new weapon, these women who called themselves Aes Sedai were a true danger. Something had to be done about them, something decisive. Perhaps, if the High Lady Suroth was on her way to Ebou Dar, she would see the need, too.

CHAPTER
7

A Goatpen

The Ghealdanin sky was cloudless, the forested hills hammered by a fierce morning sun. Even short of midday, the land sweltered. Pines and leatherleaf were yellowing in the drought, and others Perrin suspected also were evergreens. Not a whisper of air stirred. Sweat dripped down his face, ran into his short beard. His curly hair was matting on his head. He thought he heard thunder somewhere to the west, but he had almost stopped believing it would ever rain again. You hammered the iron that lay on your anvil instead of daydreaming about working silver.

From the vantage of his sparsely treed ridge, he studied the walled town of Bethal through a brass-bound looking glass. Even his eyes could use help over this distance. It was a good-sized town of slate-roofed buildings, with half a dozen tall stone structures that might have been minor nobles' palaces or the homes of well-to-do merchants. He could not make out the scarlet banner hanging limply atop the tallest tower of the largest palace, the only flag in sight, but he knew who it belonged to. Alliandre Maritha Kigarin, Queen of Ghealdan, far from her capital in Jehannah.

The town gates stood open, with a good twenty guards at each, yet no one came out, and the roads he could see were empty except for a lone rider galloping hard toward Bethal from the north. The soldiers were on edge, some shifting pikes or bows at sight of the horseman as though he waved a blood-dripping sword. More soldiers on watch crowded the wall towers or marched the walls between. Plenty of nocked arrows up there, too, and raised crossbows. Plenty of fear.

A storm had swept over this part of Ghealdan. It still did. The Prophet's bands created chaos, bandits took advantage, and Whitecloaks raiding across the border from Amadicia might easily strike this far. A few scattered columns of smoke farther south probably marked burning farms, Whitecloak work or the Prophet's. Bandits seldom bothered with burning, and the other two left little for them in any case. Adding to the jumble, rumor in every village he had passed the last few days said that Amador had fallen, to the Prophet or Taraboners or Aes Sedai, depending on who told the tale. Some claimed Pedron Niall himself was dead in the fighting to defend the city. All in all, reason enough for a queen to be concerned for her own safety. Or the soldiers could be down there because of him. Despite his best efforts, his passage south had hardly gone unnoticed.

He scratched his beard, considering. A pity the wolves in the surrounding hills could not tell him anything, but they seldom paid heed to men's doings except to stay clear of them. And since Dumai's Wells he had not felt right in asking any more of them than he absolutely had to. It might be best after all if he rode in alone, with just a few of the Two Rivers men.

He often thought Faile could read his mind, usually when he least wanted her to, and she proved it now, heeling her night-black mare Swallow close to his dun. Her narrow-skirted riding dress was nearly as dark as the mare, yet she seemed to be taking the heat better than he. She smelled faintly of herbal soap and clean perspiration, of herself. Of determination. Her tilted eyes were very determined, and with her bold nose, she was very much her namesake falcon.

"I would not like to see holes in that fine blue coat, husband," she said softly, for his ears alone, "and those fellows look as if they might just shoot at a group of strange men before asking who they are. Besides, how will you reach Alliandre without announcing your name to the world? This must be done quietly, remember." She did not say that she should be the one to go, that the gate guards would take a woman alone for a refugee from the troubles, that she could reach the Queen using her mother's name without exciting too much comment, but she did not need to. He had had all that and more from her every night since entering Ghealdan. He was here in part because of Alliandre's cautious letter to Rand, offering. . . . Support? Allegiance? Her desire for secrecy had been paramount, in any case.

Perrin doubted that even Aram, sitting his leggy gray a few paces behind them, could have heard a word Faile said, yet before she finished speaking, Berelain brought her white mare up on his other side, sweat glistening on her cheeks. She also smelled determined, through a cloud of rose perfume. To him, it seemed a cloud. For a wonder, her green riding dress showed no more flesh than it had to.

Berelain's two companions stayed back, though Annoura, her Aes Sedai advisor, studied him with an unreadable expression from beneath her cap of thin shoulder-long beaded braids. Not him and the two women at his sides; him in particular. No sweat there. He wished he were close enough to smell the beak-nosed Gray sister; unlike the other Aes Sedai, she had made no promises to anyone. For whatever those promises were worth. Lord Gallenne, commander of Berelain's Winged Guards, was seemingly busy examining Bethal through a looking glass raised to his one eye, and fiddling with his reins in a way Perrin had come to know meant that he was deep in calculations. Probably how to take Bethal by force; Gallenne always saw the worst possibility first.

"I still think I should be the one to approach Alliandre," Berelain said. This, too, Perrin had heard every day. "It is why I came, after all." That was one of the reasons. "Annoura will be granted an audience at once, and take me in with none the wiser save Alliandre." A second wonder. There had not been a hint of flirtation in her voice. She seemed to be paying as much attention to smoothing her red leather gloves as to him.

Which one? The trouble was, he did not want to choose either.

Seonid, the second Aes Sedai who had come to the ridgeline, stood beside her bay gelding a little way off, near a tall drought-withered blackwood, looking not at Bethal but the sky. The two pale-eyed Wise Ones with her made a sharp contrast, faces sun-dark to her pale complexion, fair-haired to her dark, tall to her short, not to mention their dark skirts and white blouses contrasting to her fine blue wool. Necklaces and bracelets of gold and silver and ivory draped Edarra and Nevarin, while Seonid wore only her Great

Serpent ring. They were young to her ageless. The Wise Ones matched the Green sister for self-possession, though, and they were studying the sky, too.

"Do you see something?" Perrin asked, putting off the decision.

"We see the sky, Perrin Aybara," Edarra said calmly, her jewelry making a soft clatter as she adjusted the dark shawl looped over her elbows. The heat seemed to touch the Aiel as little as it did the Aes Sedai. "If we saw more, we would tell you." He hoped they would. He thought they would. At least, if it was something they believed Grady and Neald might see, too. The two Asha'man would not keep it secret. He wished they were there instead of back in the camp.

More than half a week ago, now, a lace of the One Power streaking high across the sky had created quite a stir among the Aes Sedai and Wise Ones. And with Grady and Neald. Which fact had made a bigger stir still, as close to panic as any Aes Sedai was likely to come. Asha'man, Aes Sedai and Wise Ones *all* claimed they could still feel the Power faintly in the air long after that bar of lace vanished, but nobody knew what it meant. Neald said it made him think of wind, though he could not tell why. No one would voice more of an opinion than that, yet if both the male and female halves of the Power were visible, it had to be the Forsaken at work, and on a huge scale. Wondering what they were up to had kept Perrin awake late most nights since.

In spite of himself, he glanced to the sky. And saw nothing, of course, except a pair of pigeons. Abruptly a hawk plummeted into his sight, and one of the pigeons was gone in a spray of feathers. The other winged on frantically toward Bethal.

"Have you reached a decision, Perrin Aybara?" Nevarin asked, a touch sharply. The green-eyed Wise One appeared even younger than Edarra, perhaps no older than he was, and she did not quite have the blue-eyed woman's serenity. Her shawl slid down her arms as she planted hands on hips, and he half expected her to shake a finger at him. Or a fist. She reminded him of Nynaeve, though they surely looked nothing alike. Nevarin would have made Nynaeve look plump. "What use our advice if you will not listen?" she demanded. "What use?"

Faile and Berelain sat straight in their saddles, both as

proud as they could be, both smelling expectant and uncertain at the same time. And irritated at being uncertain;
neither liked that one speck. Seonid was too far to send
her scent, but compressed lips gave her mood well enough.
Edarra's command not to speak unless spoken to infuriated
her. Still, she certainly wanted him to take the Wise Ones'
counsel; she stared at him intently, as though the pressure
of her eyes could push him the way they wanted him to go.
In truth, he wanted to choose her, yet he hesitated. How
far did her oath of fealty to Rand truly hold? Further than
he would have believed, by the evidence seen so far, but
still, how far could he trust an Aes Sedai? The arrival of
Seonid's two Warders spared him for another few minutes.

They rode up together, though they had gone out sepa-
rately, keeping their horses well back into the trees along
the ridgeline so they would not be seen from the town.
Furen was a Tairen, nearly as dark as good soil, with gray
streaking his curly black hair, while Teryl, a Murandian,
was twenty years younger, with dark reddish hair, curled
mustaches, and eyes bluer than Edarra's, yet they were
stamped from the same mold, tall and lean and hard. They
dismounted smoothly, cloaks shifting colors and vanishing
in a queasy-making way, and made their reports to Seonid,
deliberately ignoring the Wise Ones. And Perrin.

"It's worse than back north," Furen said disgustedly. A
few drops of sweat beaded on his forehead, but neither man
appeared much affected by the heat. "The local nobles are
shut up in their manors or the town, and the Queen's soldiers keep inside the town walls. They've abandoned the
countryside to the Prophet's men. And the bandits, though
those seem scarce around here. The Prophet's people are all
over. I think Alliandre will be happy to see you."

"Rabble," Teryl snorted, slapping his reins on his palm.
"I never saw more than fifteen or twenty in one place,
armed with pitchforks and boar spears mainly. Ragged as
beggars, they were. Fit for scaring farmers, to be sure, but
you'd think the lords would be rooting them out and hanging them in bunches. The Queen will kiss your hand to see
a sister."

Seonid opened her mouth, then glanced up at Edarra,
who nodded. If anything, gaining permission to speak
tightened the Green's mouth more. Her tone was mild as

butter, though. "There is no more reason to put off your decision, Lord Aybara." She emphasized that title a bit, knowing exactly how much right he had to it. "Your wife can claim a great House, and Berelain is a ruler, yet Saldaean Houses count little here, and Mayene is the smallest of nations. An Aes Sedai for an emissary will put the weight of the White Tower behind you in Alliandre's eyes." Perhaps recalling that Annoura would do for that as well as she, she hurried on. "Besides, I have been in Ghealdan before, and my name is well known. Alliandre will not only receive me immediately, she will listen to what I say."

"Nevarin and I will go with her," Edarra said, and Nevarin added, "We will make sure she says nothing she should not." Seonid ground her teeth audibly, to Perrin's ears, and busied herself smoothing her divided skirts, eyes carefully down. Annoura made a sound, very nearly a grunt, and turned her head from the sight; she herself stayed away from the Wise Ones, and did not like seeing the other sisters with them.

Perrin wanted to groan. Sending the Green would lift him off a spike, yet the Wise Ones trusted Aes Sedai less than he did and kept Seonid and Masuri on short leashes. There had been tales about Aiel in the villages recently, too. None of those folk had ever seen an Aiel, but rumors about the Aiel following the Dragon Reborn drifted in the air, half of Ghealdan was sure there were Aiel just a day or two away, and each story was stranger and more horrible than the last. Alliandre might be too frightened to let him near her once she saw a pair of Aiel women telling an Aes Sedai when to hop. And Seonid was hopping, however much she ground her teeth! Well, he was not about to risk Faile without more assurance of her greeting than a vaguely worded letter received months ago. That spike dug deeper, right between his shoulder blades, yet he had no choice at all.

"A small party will get through those gates easier than a large," he said finally, stuffing the looking glass into his saddlebags. It would set fewer tongues wagging, as well. "That means just you and Annoura, Berelain. And maybe Lord Gallenne. Likely they'll take him for Annoura's Warder."

Berelain chortled in delight, leaning to clasp his arm with both hands. She did not leave it at that, of course.

Her fingers squeezed caressingly, and she flashed a heated smile of promise, then straightened before he could move, her face suddenly innocent as a babe's. Expressionless, Faile focused on pulling her gray riding gloves snug. By her scent, she had not noticed Berelain's smile. She hid her disappointment well.

"I'm sorry, Faile," he said, "but—"

Outrage flared in the smell of her like thorns. "I am certain you have matters to discuss with the First before she goes, husband," she said calmly. Her tilted eyes were pure serenity, her scent sand burrs. "Best you see to her now." Pulling Swallow around, Faile walked the mare over to a plainly fuming Seonid and the tight-faced Wise Ones, but she did not dismount or speak to them. Instead she frowned down at Bethal, a falcon staring from her eyrie.

Perrin realized he was feeling at his nose and pulled his hand down. There was no blood, of course; his nose only felt as if there should be.

Berelain needed no last-minute instructions—the First of Mayene and her Gray advisor were all impatience to be off, all certainty they knew what to say and do—yet Perrin stressed caution anyway, and emphasized that Berelain and only Berelain was to speak with Alliandre. Annoura gave him one of those cool Aes Sedai looks and nodded. Which might have been agreement or might not; he doubted he could get more out of her with a prybar. Berelain's lips curled in amusement, though she agreed with everything he said. Or said she did. He suspected she would say anything to get what she wanted, and those smiles in all the wrong places bothered him. Gallenne had put his looking glass away, but he was still playing with his reins, no doubt calculating how to carve a way out of Bethal for the two women. Perrin wanted to growl.

He watched them ride down to the road with worry. The message Berelain carried was simple. Rand understood Alliandre's caution, but if she wanted his protection she must be willing to announce support for him openly. That protection would come, soldiers and Asha'man to make it plain to everyone, and even Rand himself if need be, once she agreed to make the announcement. Berelain had no reason to change the message a hair, despite her smiles—he thought they might be another way of flirting—but Annoura. . . .

Aes Sedai did what they did, and the Light alone knew why half the time. He wished he knew some way to reach Alliandre without using a sister or rousing talk. Or risking Faile.

The three riders reached the gates with Annoura in the lead, and guards quickly raised pikes, lowered bows and crossbows, no doubt as soon as she named herself Aes Sedai. Not many people had the nerve to challenge that particular claim. There was barely a pause before she was leading the way into the town. In fact, the soldiers seemed eager to hurry them through, out of sight of anyone watching from the hills. Some peered at the distant heights, and Perrin did not need to smell them to sense their unease over who might be hidden up there, who might, improbably, have recognized a sister.

Turning north, toward their camp, Perrin led the way along the ridge until they were out of sight from Bethal's towers, then slanted down to the hard-packed road. Scattered farms lined the road, thatch-roofed houses and long narrow barns, withered pastures and stubbled fields and high-walled stone goatpens, but there was little livestock to be seen and fewer people. Those few watched the riders warily, geese watching foxes, stopping chores where they stood until the horses passed on. Aram kept as close an eye on them in return, sometimes fingering the sword hilt rising above his shoulder, perhaps wishing to find more than farmfolk. Despite his green-striped coat, little Tinker remained in him.

Edarra and Nevarin walked beside Stepper, seemingly out for a stroll yet keeping pace easily despite their bulky skirts. Seonid heeled them on her gelding, Furen and Teryl at her own back. The pale-cheeked Green pretended that she simply wanted to ride a careful two paces behind the Wise Ones, but the men scowled openly. Warders often had a greater care for their Aes Sedai's dignity than the sister did herself, and Aes Sedai had enough for queens.

Faile kept Swallow on the far side of the Aiel women, riding in silence, apparently studying the drought-scarred landscape. Slim and graceful, she made Perrin feel a little clumsy at the best of times. She was quicksilver, and he loved it in her, usually, but. . . . A slight breath of air had begun to stir, enough to keep her scent mingled with the rest. He knew he should be thinking about Alliandre and what her answer would be, or better still, the Prophet and how to find him once Alliandre replied, however she did, but he could not find room in his head.

He had expected Faile to be angry when he chose Berelain, for all that Rand supposedly had sent her for the purpose. Faile knew he did not want to send her into danger, into any risk of danger, a fact she disliked more than she did Berelain. Yet her scent had been soft as a summer morning—until he tried to apologize! Well, apologies usually stoked her anger if she already was angry—except when they melted her temper, anyway—but she had not *been* angry! Without Berelain, everything ran smooth as silk satin between them. Most of the time. But explanations that he did nothing to encourage the woman—far from it!—earned only a curt "Of course you don't!" in tones that called him a fool for bringing it up. But she still grew angry—with him!—every time Berelain smiled at him or found an excuse to touch him, no matter how brusquely he put her off, and the Light knew he did that. Short of tying her up, he did not know what more he could do to discourage her. Ginger attempts to find out from Faile what he was doing wrong received a light "Why do you think you've done anything?" or a not-so-light "What do *you* think you've done?" or a flat "I do not want to talk about it." He *was* doing something wrong, but he could not puzzle out what! He had to, though. Nothing was more important than Faile. Nothing!

"Lord Perrin?"

Aram's excited voice cut into his brown study. "Don't call me that," he muttered, following the direction of the man's pointing finger, to yet another abandoned farm some distance ahead, where fire had taken the roof from house and barn. Only rough stone walls stood. An abandoned farm, but not deserted. Angry shouts rose up there.

A dozen or more rough-clad fellows carrying spears and pitchforks were trying to force their way over the chest-high stone wall of a goatpen, while a handful of men within tried to keep them out. Several horses ran loose inside, frightened at the noise and dodging about, and there were three women mounted. They were not simply waiting to see how it would all turn out, though; one of the women appeared to be hurling rocks, and even as he looked, another dashed close to the wall to lash out with a long cudgel while the third reared her horse, and a tall fellow toppled back off the wall to get clear of flashing hooves. But there were too many attackers, too much wall to defend.

"I advise you to ride wide," Seonid said. Edarra and Nevarin turned grim stares on her, but she plowed on, hurry overwhelming her matter-of-fact tone. "Those are surely the Prophet's men, and killing his people is a bad way to begin. Tens of thousands, hundreds of thousands, may die if you fail with him. Is it worth risking that to save a handful?"

Perrin did not intend to kill anyone if he could help it, but he did not intend to look the other way either. He wasted no time in explanations, though. "Can you frighten them?" he asked Edarra. "Just frighten?" He remembered all too well what the Wise Ones had done at Dumai's Wells. And the Asha'man. Maybe as well Grady and Neald were not there.

"Perhaps," Edarra replied, studying the crowd around the pen. She half-shook her head, shrugged a fraction. "Perhaps." That would have to be good enough.

"Aram, Furen, Teryl," he snapped, "with me!" He dug in his heels, and as Stepper leaped forward, he was relieved to see the Warders following closely. Four men charging made a better show than two. He kept his hands on the reins, away from his axe.

He was not so pleased when Faile galloped Swallow up alongside him. He opened his mouth, and she arched an eyebrow at him. Her black hair was beautiful, streaming in the wind of their rush. She was beautiful. An arched eyebrow; no more. He changed what he had been about to say. "Guard my back," he told her. Smiling, she produced a dagger from somewhere. With all the blades she carried hidden away, sometimes he wondered how he missed being stabbed just trying to hug her.

As soon as she looked ahead again, he gestured frantically to Aram, trying to keep the motion where she could not see. Aram nodded, but he was leaning forward, sword bared, ready to skewer the first of the Prophet's folk he reached. Perrin hoped the man understood he was to guard Faile's back, and the rest of her, if they actually came to grips with those fellows.

None of the ruffians had noticed them yet. Perrin shouted,

but they seemed not to hear over their own yelling. A man in a coat too big for him managed to scramble atop the wall, and two others appeared about to get over. If the Wise Ones were going to do anything, it was past—

A thunderclap nearly over their heads almost deafened Perrin, a mountainous crack that made Stepper stumble before regaining his pace. The attackers certainly noticed that, staggering and looking around wildly, some clapping hands over their ears. The man on the wall overbalanced and fell off outside. He leaped up immediately, though, angrily gesturing to the enclosure, and some of his companions leaped back at it. Others saw Perrin then and pointed, their mouths working, but still no one ran. A few hefted weapons.

Suddenly a horizontal wheel of fire appeared above the goatpen, as wide as a man was tall, flinging off sputtering tufts of flame as it spun with a moan that rose and fell, mournful groan to keening wail and back.

The rough-clad men broke in every direction like scattering quail. For a moment longer the man in a too-big coat waved his arms and shouted at them, then with one last glance at the fiery wheel, he too darted away.

Perrin almost laughed. He would not have to kill anyone. And he would not have to worry about Faile getting a pitchfork through her ribs.

Apparently the people in the pen were as frightened as those outside, one of them at least. The woman who had reared her horse at the attackers slipped open the gate and kicked her mount to an awkward gallop. Up the road, away from Perrin and the others.

"Wait!" Perrin shouted. "We won't harm you!" Whether she heard or not, she kept whipping her reins. A bundle tied behind her saddle bounced wildly. Those men might be running as hard as they could now, but if she went off by herself, even two or three could do her injury. Lying flat on Stepper's neck, Perrin dug in his heels, and the dun shot forward like an arrow.

He was a big man, yet Stepper had earned his name for more than prancing feet. Besides, by its lumbering run, the woman's mount was hardly fit for a saddle. With every stride Stepper closed the gap, nearer, nearer, until Perrin was able to reach out and seize the other horse's bridle. Up close, her hammer-nosed bay was little better than crow-bait, lathered and worn out more than the short run could account for. Slowly he drew both horses to a halt.

"Forgive me if I frightened you, Mistress," he said. "Truly, I mean you no harm."

For the second time that day an apology did not get the response he expected. Angry blue eyes glared at him from a face surrounded by long red-gold curls, a face as regal as any queen's for all that it was plastered with sweat and dust. Her dress was plain wool, travel-stained and as dusty as her cheeks, but her face was furious as well as queenly. "I do not need," she began in chill tones, trying to jerk her horse free, then cut off as another of the women, white-haired and bony, galloped up on a slab-sided brown mare in worse condition than the bay. They had been riding hard for some time, these folk. The older woman was just as worn and dust-covered as the younger.

She alternated between beaming at Perrin and scowling at the woman whose bridle he still held. "Thank you, my Lord." Her voice, thin but strong, gave a hitch as she noticed his eyes, but golden-yellow eyes on a man slowed her only an instant. Not a woman fazed by much. She still carried the stout stick she had been using for a weapon. "A most timely rescue. Maighdin, whatever were you thinking? You could have gotten yourself killed! And the rest of us, too! She's a headstrong girl, my Lord, always leaping before she looks. Remember, child, a fool abandons friends, and gives up silver for shiny brass. We do thank you, my Lord, and Maighdin will, too, when she comes to her senses."

Maighdin, a good ten years older than Perrin, could only be called a girl in comparison to the older woman, but despite weary grimaces that matched her scent, frustration tinged with anger, she accepted the tirade, only pulling once more in a halfhearted attempt to free her horse, then giving up. Letting her hands rest on her cantle, she frowned at Perrin accusingly, then blinked. The yellow eyes again. Yet despite that strangeness, she still did not smell afraid. The old woman did, but Perrin did not think it was of him.

Another of Maighdin's companions, an unshaven man mounted on yet another bedraggled horse, this a knob-kneed gray, approached while the old woman was talking, but kept back. He was tall, as tall as Perrin if not nearly so wide, in a travel-worn dark coat with a sword belted over. Like the women, he had a bundle tied on behind his saddle. That tiny breeze swirled to bring Perrin his scent. He was not afraid; he was wary. And if the way he looked at Maighdin was any guide, it was she he was wary of. Maybe this was not so simple as rescuing travelers from a gang of ruffians after all.

"Perhaps you should all come to my camp," Perrin said, finally releasing the bridle. "You'll be safe from . . . brigands . . . there." He half expected Maighdin to make a break for the nearest tree line, but she turned her horse with his, back toward the goatpen. She smelled . . . resigned.

Even so, she said, "I thank you for the offer, but I . . . we . . . must continue our journey. We will go on, Lini," she added firmly, and the older woman frowned at her so sternly that he wondered whether they were mother and daughter despite her use of the woman's name. They certainly looked nothing alike. Lini was narrow-faced and parchment-skinned, all sinew, while Maighdin might be beautiful under that dust. If a man liked fair hair.

Perrin glanced over his shoulder at the man trailing after. A hard-looking fellow, in need of a razor. Perhaps he liked fair hair. Perhaps he liked it too much. Men had made trouble for themselves as well as others for that reason before this.

Ahead, Faile was sitting Swallow and peering over the wall of the pen at the people inside. Perhaps one of them had been hurt. Seonid and the Wise Ones were nowhere in sight. Aram had understood, apparently; he was close to Faile, though looking impatiently toward Perrin. The danger was clearly past, though.

Before Perrin was halfway to the goatpen, Teryl appeared with a narrow-eyed, stubble-cheeked man stumbling along beside his roan, the collar of his coat gripped in the Warder's fist. "I thought we should catch one of them," Teryl said with a hard grin. "Always best to hear both sides, whatever you thought you saw, my old da always said." Perrin was surprised; he had thought Teryl could not think beyond the end of his sword.

Even hiked up as it was, the stubble-cheeked fellow's

frayed coat was plainly too big for him. Perrin doubted anyone else had been able to see well enough at the distance,
but he recognized that thrusting nose, too. This man had
been the last to run, and he was not cowed now, either. His
sneer took them all in. "You're all in deep muck, for this,"
he rasped. "We was doing the Prophet's bidding, we was.
The Prophet says if a man bothers a woman as doesn't want
him, he dies. This lot was chasing after her"—he jerked
his chin at Maighdin—"and she was running hard. The
Prophet'll have your ears for this!" He spat for emphasis.

"That is ridiculous," Maighdin announced in a clear
voice. "These people are my friends. This man completely
misunderstood what he saw."

Perrin nodded, and if she thought he was agreeing with
her, all well and good. But putting what this fellow said
alongside what Lini had. . . . Not simple at all.

Faile and the others joined them, followed by the rest of
Maighdin's traveling companions, three more men and another woman, all leading worn-down horses with few miles
left in them. Not that they had been prime horseflesh in
some years, if ever. A finer collection of buck knees, bow
hocks, spavins, and swaybacks, Perrin could not recall. As
always, his gaze went first to Faile—his nostrils strained
for her scent—but Seonid snagged his eyes. Slumped in
her saddle, flushing scarlet, she wore a sullen glower, and
her face looked odd, her cheeks puffed out and her mouth
not quite closed. There was something, a bit of red-and-
blue. . . . Perrin blinked. Unless he was seeing things, she
had a wadded-up *scarf* stuffed into her mouth! Apparently
when Wise Ones told an apprentice to be quiet, even an Aes
Sedai apprentice, they meant it.

He was not the only one with sharp eyes; Maighdin's
mouth fell open when she saw Seonid, and she gave him
a long, considering look as if he were responsible for the
scarf. So she knew an Aes Sedai on sight, did she? Uncommon, for the country woman she appeared. She did not
sound like one, though.

Furen, riding behind Seonid, wore a thunderhead for a
face, but it was Teryl who made everything even less simple
by tossing something to the ground. "I found this behind
him," he said, "where he might have dropped it, running."

At first, Perrin did not know what he was looking at, a

long loop of rawhide thickly strung with what appeared to be tags of shriveled leather. Then he did know, and his teeth bared in a snarl. "The Prophet would have our ears, you said."

The stubble-cheeked man stopped gaping at Seonid and licked his lips. "That . . . that's Hari's work!" he protested. "Hari's a mean one. He likes to keep count, take trophies, and he . . . uh. . . ." Shrugging in his captive coat, he sank in on himself like a cornered dog. "You can't tie that to me! The Prophet'll hang you if you touch me! He's hanged nobles before, fine lords and ladies. I walk in the Light of the blessed Lord Dragon!"

Perrin walked Stepper to the man, careful to keep the dun's hooves clear of the . . . thing . . . on the ground. He wanted nothing less than to have the fellow's scent in his nose, but he bent down, putting his face closer. Sour sweat warred with fear, panic, a tinge of anger. A pity he could not sniff out guilt. "Might have dropped" was not "had dropped." Close-set eyes widened, and the man pressed back against Teryl's gelding. Yellow eyes had their uses.

"If I *could* tie that to you, you'd hang from the nearest tree," he growled. The fellow blinked, began to brighten as he understood what that meant, but Perrin gave him no time to regain his bluster. "I'm Perrin Aybara, and your precious Lord Dragon *sent* me here. You spread the word. He sent me here, and if I find a man with . . . *trophies* . . . he hangs! If I find a man burning a farm, he hangs! If one of you looks at me cross-eyed, he hangs! And you can tell Masema I said so, too!" Disgusted, Perrin straightened. "Let him go, Teryl. If he isn't out of my sight in two shakes . . . !"

Teryl's hand opened, and the fellow dashed off at a dead run for the nearest trees, never so much as glancing back. Part of Perrin's disgust was for himself. Threatening! If one of them looked at him cross-eyed? But if the nameless man had not cut off ears himself, he watched it and done nothing.

Faile was smiling, pride shining through the sweat on her face. Her look washed away some of Perrin's revulsion. He would walk barefoot through fire for that look.

Not everyone approved, of course. Seonid's eyes were squeezed shut, and her gloved fists quivered on her reins as though she desperately wanted to yank that scarf from her mouth and tell him what she thought. He could guess anyway. Edarra and Nevarin had gathered their shawls around them and were eyeing him darkly. Oh, yes; he could guess.

"I thought it was to be all secrecy," Teryl said casually, watching the stubble-cheeked man run. "I thought Masema wasn't to know you were here till you spoke in his pink ear."

That had been the plan. Rand had suggested it as a precaution, Seonid and Masuri had insisted on it every chance they got. After all, Prophet of the Lord Dragon or no, Masema might not *want* to come face-to-face with someone Rand sent, considering the things he was said to have allowed. Those ears were not the worst, if the tenth part of rumor was to be believed. Edarra and the other Wise Ones saw Masema as a possible enemy, to be ambushed before he could set his own trap.

"I'm supposed to stop . . . that," Perrin said, gesturing angrily to the rawhide string on the ground. He had heard the rumors, and done nothing. Now he had seen. "I might as well start now." And if Masema decided *he* was an enemy? How many thousands followed the Prophet, out of belief or fear? It did not matter. "It stops, Teryl. It stops!"

The Murandian nodded slowly, eyeing Perrin as though seeing him for the first time.

"My Lord Perrin?" Maighdin said. He had forgotten all about her and her friends. The others had gathered with her a little way off, most still afoot. There were three men aside from the fellow who had followed Maighdin, and two of those were hiding behind their horses. Lini appeared the wariest of all, eyes focused on him worriedly; she had her horse close to Maighdin's and seemed ready to seize the bridle herself. Not to stop the younger woman bolting, but to bolt herself and take Maighdin with her. Maighdin herself appeared completely at ease, but she also studied Perrin. Little wonder, after all that talk of the Prophet and the Dragon Reborn, on top of his eyes. Not to mention an Aes Sedai gagged. He expected her to say that they wanted to go now, immediately, but what she said instead was "We will accept your kind offer. A day or two resting in your camp might be just the thing."

"As you say, Mistress Maighdin," he said slowly. Masking his surprise was difficult. Especially since he had just recognized the two men trying to keep their horses between them and him. *Ta'veren* work, to bring them here? A strange twist in any case. "It might be just the thing at that."

CHAPTER
8

A Simple Country Woman

The camp lay about a league farther on, well back from the road among low, wooded hills, just beyond a stream that was ten paces' width of stones and only five of water never deeper than a man's knees. Tiny green and silver fish darted away from the horses' hooves. Casual passersby were unlikely to come on them here. The nearest inhabited farm was over a mile away, and Perrin had checked personally to make sure those folk took their animals to water elsewhere.

He truly had been trying to avoid notice as much as possible, traveling by back roads and the smallest country paths when they could not keep to the forests. A futile effort, really. The horses could be pastured wherever there was grass, but they required at least some grain, and even a small army had to buy food, and a lot of it. Every man needed four pounds a day, in flour and beans and meat. Rumors must have been floating all over Ghealdan, though with luck, no one suspected who they were. Perrin grimaced. Perhaps they had not, until he went and opened his mouth. Still, he would have done nothing differently.

It was three camps really, close to one another and none far from the stream. They traveled together, all following him, obeying him supposedly, but there were too many personalities involved, and no one was entirely sure the others aimed at the same goal. Some nine hundred or so Winged Guards had their cook fires crowded between rows of picketed horses in a broad meadow of trampled brown grass. He tried to close his nose to the mingled smells of horses, sweat, dung and boiling goat meat, an unpleasant combination on a hot day. A dozen mounted sentries rode a slow circuit in pairs, their long, red-streamered lances all at precisely the same angle, but the rest of the Mayeners had shed breastplates and helmets. Coatless and often shirtless in the sun, they lay sprawled on their blankets or diced as they waited on the food. Some looked up as Perrin passed, a number straightened from what they were doing to study the additions to his party, but none came running, so the patrols were still out. Small patrols, without lances, who could see without being seen. Well, that was the hope. It had been.

A handful of *gai'shain* moved at various chores among the Wise Ones' low gray-brown tents on the sparsely wooded crest of the hill above the Mayeners. At this distance, the white-robed figures appeared harmless, eyes downcast and meek. Up close, they would look the same, but most were Shaido. The Wise Ones claimed *gai'shain* were *gai'shain*; Perrin did not trust any Shaido out of his sight. Off to one side on the slope, beneath a bedraggled sourgum, perhaps a dozen Maidens in *cadin'sor* knelt in a circle around Sulin, the toughest of them despite her white hair. She had sent out scouts, too, women who could move as fast afoot as the Mayeners on their horses and were much more likely to escape unwanted attention. None of the Wise Ones up there were in the open, but a slender woman stirring a large stew kettle straightened, knuckling her back as she watched Perrin and the others pass. A woman in a green silk riding dress.

He could see the glare on Masuri's face. Aes Sedai did not stir kettles, nor perform twenty other tasks the Wise Ones had her and Seonid doing. Masuri laid it at Rand's feet, but he was not here, and Perrin was. Given half a chance, she would peel his hide for him.

Edarra and Nevarin turned up that way, even in those bulky skirts barely disturbing the layers of dead leaves that carpeted the ground. Seonid followed, her cheeks still bulging around that scarf. She twisted in her saddle, peering back at Perrin. If he could have believed an Aes Sedai looking anxious, that was what he would have called her. Riding behind her, Furen and Teryl wore scowls.

Masuri saw them coming and hastily bent back to the black kettle, stirring with renewed vigor, trying to make out that she had never stopped. So long as Masuri stayed in the Wise Ones' charge, Perrin thought he did not have to worry about his hide. The Wise Ones seemed to keep a very short leash.

Nevarin looked back over her shoulder at him, another of those dark stares he had been getting from her and Edarra since sending his warning, his threat, by the stubble-cheeked fellow. Perrin exhaled in exasperation. He did not have to worry about his pelt unless the Wise Ones decided *they* wanted it. Too many personalities. Too many goals.

Maighdin rode at Faile's side, seemingly paying no attention to what they passed, but he would not have wagered a split copper on it. Her eyes had widened a hair at sight of the Mayener sentries. She knew what red breastplates and helmets like rimmed pots meant, as surely as she had recognized an Aes Sedai face. Most people would not have known either, especially not folk dressed as she was. She was a mystery, this Maighdin. For some reason, she seemed vaguely familiar.

Lini and Tallanvor—that was what he had heard Maighdin call the fellow who had ridden after her; "young" Tallanvor, though there could not have been more than four or five years between them if that—stayed as close behind Maighdin as possible, with Aram in the way trying to heel Perrin. So did a little stick of a fellow with a pursed mouth, called Balwer, who seemed to pay less heed to their surroundings than Maighdin pretended. Even so, Perrin thought Balwer saw more than she did. He could not say why, precisely, but the few times he had caught the bony little man's scent, he had been minded of a wolf testing the air. Strangely, there was no fear in Balwer, only quickly suppressed ridges of irritation shot through with the quivery smell of impatience. The remainder of Maighdin's companions trailed along well back. The third woman, Breane, was whispering fiercely to a hulking fellow who kept his eyes down and sometimes nodded silently, sometimes shook his head. A shoulderstriker and street tough if ever there was one, but the short woman had an edge of toughness about her, too. The last man sheltered behind those two, a stout man with a battered straw hat pulled low to hide his face. On him, the sword the men all wore looked as strange as it did on Balwer.

The third part of the camp, spread out among the trees just around the curve of the hill from the Mayeners, covered as much ground as the Winged Guards' though it held far fewer people. Here, the horses were picketed well away from the cook fires, so the unblemished smell of dinner filled the air. Roasting goat, this time, and hard turnips the farmers probably had intended to feed to their pigs even with times as hard as they were. Close on to three hundred Two Rivers men who had followed Perrin away from home were tending meat on spits, mending clothes, checking over arrows and bows, all scattered in haphazard clumps of five or six friends around a fire. Nearly every one of them waved and shouted greetings, though there was too much of "Lord Perrin" and "Perrin Goldeneyes" to suit him. Faile had a right to the titles they gave her.

Grady and Neald, unsweating in their night-black coats, did not cheer; standing beside the cook fire they had built a little away from everyone else, they merely looked at him. Expectant looks, he thought. Expecting what? That was the question he always asked himself about them. The Asha'man made him uneasy, more than Aes Sedai or Wise Ones. Women channeling the Power was natural, if not exactly anything a man could be comfortable around. Plainfaced Grady appeared a farmer despite his coat and sword, and Neald a popinjay with his curled mustaches, yet Perrin could not forget what they were, what they had done at Dumai's Wells. But then, he had been there, too. The Light help him, he had. Pulling his hand from the axe at his belt, he dismounted.

Servants, men and women from Lord Dobraine's estates in Cairhien, came running from the lines where the horses were picketed, to take their mounts. None stood taller than Perrin's shoulder, country-clad folk, forever bowing and curtsying obsequiously. Faile said he just upset them when he tried to make them stop, or at least not to bob around him so often; in truth, that was how they smelled when he did, and they always went back to bobbing in an hour or two. Others, nearly as many as the Two Rivers men, were working with the horses or around the long rows of high-wheeled carts that hauled all their supplies. A few were darting in and out of a large red-and-white tent.

As usual, that tent made Perrin grunt gloomily. Berelain

had a larger one back in the Mayener part of the camp, plus
one for her two maids and another for the pair of thief-
catchers she had insisted on bringing. Annoura had a tent
of her own, and Gallenne as well, but only he and Faile possessed one here. For himself, he would have slept under the
sky like the other men from home. They had nothing over
them at night but a blanket. There was certainly no fear
of rain. The Cairhienin servants bedded down beneath the
carts. He could not ask Faile to do that, though, not when
Berelain had a tent. If only he could have left Berelain in
Cairhien. But then he would have had to send Faile into
Bethal.

A pair of banners on tall, fresh-cut poles in the middle
of a clear space near the tent soured his mood further. The
breeze had picked up a trifle, though it was still too warm;
he thought he heard that thunder again, faint in the west.
The flags unfolded in slow waves, collapsed of their own
weight, rippled open again. His crimson-bordered Red
Wolfhead and the Red Eagle of long-dead Manetheren, out
in the open again despite his orders. Perhaps he had stopped
trying to hide, after a fashion, but what was now Ghealdan had been part of Manetheren; Alliandre would not be
soothed by hearing of *that* banner! He managed a pleasant
face and a smile for the stocky little woman who curtsied
deeply and took Stepper away, but it was a near thing. Lords
were supposed to be obeyed, and if he was supposed to be a
lord, well, he seemed to be making a poor job of it.

Fists on her hips, Maighdin stood studying those rippling
flags as her horse was taken off with the rest. Surprisingly,
Breane had both their bundles, held awkwardly; she wore a
petulant scowl, directed at the other woman. "I have heard
about banners like those," Maighdin said suddenly. And
angrily; there was no anger in her voice, and her face was
smooth as ice, but her fury filled Perrin's nose. "They were
raised by men in Andor, in the Two Rivers, who rebelled
against their lawful ruler. Aybara is a Two Rivers name, I
think."

"We don't know much about lawful rulers in the Two
Rivers, Mistress Maighdin," he growled. He was going to
skin whoever had put them up this time. If stories about
rebellion had spread this far. . . . He faced too many complications already without adding more. "I suppose Mor-

gase was a good queen, but we had to fend for ourselves, and we did." Abruptly he knew who she reminded him of. Elayne. Not that it meant anything; he had seen men a thousand miles from the Two Rivers who could have belonged to families he knew back home. Still, she had to have some reason for anger. Her accent could be Andoran. "Things aren't as bad in Andor as you might have heard," he told her. "Caemlyn was quiet, last I was there, and Rand—the Dragon Reborn—means to put Morgase's daughter Elayne on the Lion Throne."

Far from being mollified, Maighdin rounded on him, blue eyes blazing. "He intends to *put* her on the throne? *No* man *puts* a queen on the Lion Throne! Elayne will claim the throne of Andor by her *right*!"

Scratching his head, Perrin wished Faile would stop watching the woman so calmly and say something. But all she did was tuck her riding gloves behind her belt. Before he could think of what to say, Lini darted in, seizing Maighdin's arm and giving her a shake fit to rattle her teeth.

"You apologize!" the old woman barked. "This man saved your life, Maighdin, and you forget yourself, a simple country woman speaking so to a lord! Remember who you are, and don't let your tongue land you in hotter water! If this young lord was at odds with Morgase, well, everyone knows she's dead, and it's none of your affair in any event! Now apologize before he grows angry!"

Maighdin stared at Lini, her mouth working, even more startled than Perrin. Again she surprised him, though. Instead of erupting at the white-haired woman, she slowly drew herself up, shoulders squared, and looked him in the eye. "Lini is entirely right. I have no right to speak to you so, Lord Aybara. I apologize. Humbly. And I ask your pardon." Humble? Her jaw was stubborn, her tone proud enough for an Aes Sedai, and her scent said she was ready to chew a hole in something.

"You have it," Perrin said hastily. Which did not seem to placate her one bit. She smiled, and maybe she intended gratitude, but he could hear her teeth grinding. Were women *all* crazy?

"They are hot and dirty, husband," Faile said, putting a hand in at last, "and the last few hours have been trying for them, I know. Aram can show the men where to clean themselves. I will take the women with me. I'll have damp cloths brought to wash your hands and faces," she told Maighdin and Lini. Gathering up Breane with a gesture, she began herding them toward the tent. At a nod from Perrin, Aram motioned the men to follow him.

"As soon as you finish your wash, Master Gill, I'd like to talk with you," Perrin said.

He might as well have made that spinning wheel of fire. Maighdin whipped around to gape at him, and the other two women froze in their tracks. Tallanvor was suddenly gripping his sword hilt again, and Balwer rose on his toes, peering over his bundle, head tilting this way then that. Not a wolf, perhaps; some sort of bird, watching for cats. The stout man, Basel Gill, dropped his belongings and leaped a foot in the air.

"Why, Perrin," he stammered, snatching off the straw hat. Sweat made tracks in the dust on his cheeks. He bent to pick up his bundle, changed his mind and straightened again hastily. "I mean, Lord Perrin. I . . . ah . . . I thought it was you, but . . . but with them calling you lord, I wasn't sure you'd want to know an old innkeeper." Scrubbing a handkerchief across his nearly bald head, he laughed nervously. "Of course, I'll talk to you. Washing can wait a little longer."

"Hello, Perrin," the hulking man said. With his heavy-lidded eyes, Lamgwin Dorn appeared lazy despite his muscles and the scars on his face and hands. "We heard about young Rand being the Dragon Reborn, Master Gill and me. Should have figured you'd have come up in the world, too. Perrin Aybara's a good man, Mistress Maighdin. I think you could trust him with anything you've a mind to." He was not lazy, and he was not stupid, either.

Aram jerked his head impatiently, and Lamgwin and the other two followed, but Tallanvor and Balwer dragged their feet, casting wondering glances back at Perrin and Master Gill. Concerned glances. And at the women. Faile had them moving again, as well, though with plenty of darted looks at Perrin and Master Gill, at the men trailing Aram. Suddenly they were not so pleased at being separated.

Master Gill mopped his forehead and smiled uneasily. Light, why did he smell afraid? Perrin wondered. Of him? Of a man tied to the Dragon Reborn, calling himself lord and leading an army, however small, threatening the Prophet. Might as well throw gagging Aes Sedai into it, too; he would take the blame for that, one way or another. *No*, Perrin thought wryly; *nothing in that to frighten anybody.* The whole lot of them were probably afraid he might murder them all.

Trying to put Master Gill at ease, he led the man to a large oak a hundred paces from the red-and-white tent. Most of the great tree's leaves were gone and half those left were brown, but massive limbs spreading low provided a little shade, and some of the gnarled roots stood high enough to serve as benches. Perrin had used one for just that, twiddling his thumbs while camp was being set. Whenever he tried to do anything useful, there were always ten hands snatching it away from him.

Basel Gill was not eased, however much Perrin asked after the Queen's Blessing, his inn in Caemlyn, or recalled his own visit there. But then, perhaps Gill was remembering that that visit was not the thing to calm a man, with Aes Sedai and talk of the Dark One and a flight in the night. He paced anxiously and hugged his bundle to his chest, shifted it from one arm to the other and answered in a bare handful of words, licking his lips between.

"Master Gill," Perrin told him finally, "stop calling me Lord Perrin. I'm not. It's complicated, but I'm not a lord. You know that."

"Of course," the round man replied, at last seating himself on one of the oak roots. He appeared reluctant to set his bundled things down, drawing his hands from them slowly. "As you say, Lord Perrin. Ah, Rand . . . the Lord Dragon . . . he really means the Lady Elayne to have the throne? Not that I doubt your word, of course," he added hurriedly. Pulling off his hat, he began mopping his forehead again. Even for such a round man, he seemed to be sweating twice as much as the heat called for. "I'm sure the Lord Dragon will do just as you say." His laugh was shaky. "You wanted to talk to me. And not about my old inn, I'm sure."

Perrin exhaled wearily. He had thought nothing could be worse than old friends and neighbors bowing and scraping, but at least they forgot sometimes and spoke their minds. And none of them was afraid of him. "You're a long way from home," he said in a gentle voice. No need to go too fast, not with a man ready to jump out of his skin. "I wondered what brought you here. Not troubles of any kind, I hope."

"You tell him right, Basel Gill," Lini said sharply, marching up to the oak. "No embroidery, mind." She had not been gone very long, yet somehow she had found time to wash her face and hands and work her hair into a neat white bun on the back of her head. And to beat most of the dust from her plain woolen dress. Bobbing a perfunctory curtsy in Perrin's direction, she turned to shake a gnarled finger at Gill. "'Three things annoy to distraction: a tooth that aches, a shoe that pinches, and a man that chatters.' So you hold to the point and don't go telling the young lord more than he wants to hear." For a moment she held the gaping innkeeper with an admonitory stare, then abruptly gave Perrin another quick curtsy. "He does love the sound of his own voice—most men do—but he'll tell it to you properly, now, my Lord."

Master Gill glowered at her, and muttered under his breath when she waved sharply for him to speak. "Bony old . . ." was what Perrin heard. "What happened—the *simple* and *straight* of it—" The round man glared at Lini again, but she did not appear to notice, "was that I had some business down to Lugard. A chance to import wine. But you're not interested in that. I took Lamgwin along, of course, and Breane, because she won't let him out of her sight an hour she doesn't have to. Along the way, we met Mistress Dorlain, Mistress Maighdin as we call her, and Lini, and Tallanvor. And Balwer, of course. On the road. Near to Lugard."

"Maighdin and I were in service in Murandy," Lini put in impatiently. "Until the troubles. Tallanvor was an armsman to the House, and Balwer the secretary. Bandits burned the manor, and our lady couldn't afford to keep us, so we decided to travel together for protection."

"I was telling it, Lini," Master Gill grumbled, scratching behind his ear. "The wine merchant had left Lugard for the country, for some reason, and . . ." He shook his head. "It's all too much to go into, Perrin. Lord Perrin, I mean. Forgive me. You know there's trouble everywhere nowadays, one kind or another. Seems like every time we ran from one kind, we found another, and always getting farther from Caemlyn. Till here we are, tired and grateful for a rest. And that's the short of it."

Perrin nodded slowly. That could be simple truth, though he had learned that people had a hundred reasons for lying, or just shading the truth. Grimacing, he raked fingers through his hair. Light! He was becoming suspicious as a Cairhienin, and the deeper Rand tangled him, the worse it got. Why on earth would Basel Gill, of all people, lie to him? A lady's maid, accustomed to privilege and fallen on hard times; that explained Maighdin. Some things were simple.

Lini's hands were folded at her waist, but she watched with a keen eye, no little like a falcon herself, and Master Gill began fidgeting as soon as he stopped talking. He seemed to take Perrin's grimace as a demand for more. He laughed, more on edge than amused. "I haven't seen so much of the world since the Aiel War, and I was considerably skinnier, then. Why, we've been as far as Amador. Of course, we left after those Seanchan took the city, but truth, they aren't any worse than the Whitecloaks, that I could—" He cut off as Perrin leaned forward abruptly and seized his lapel.

"Seanchan, Master Gill? Are you sure of that? Or is it one of those rumors, like the Aiel, or Aes Sedai?"

"I saw them," Gill replied, exchanging uncertain looks with Lini. "And that's what they call themselves. I'm surprised you don't know. Word's been running ahead of us all the way from Amador. These Seanchan want people to know what they're about. Strange people, with strange creatures." His voice picked up intensity. "Like Shadowspawn. Big leathery things that fly, and carry men, and these things like lizards, only they're big as horses, and they have three eyes. I saw them! I did!"

"I believe you," Perrin said, releasing the man's coat. "I've seen them, too." At Falme, where a thousand Whitecloaks died in minutes and it had taken dead heroes of legend, called by the Horn of Valere, to throw the Seanchan back. Rand had said they would return, but how could they have so soon? Light! If they held Amador, they had to have Tarabon as well, or most of it. Only a fool killed a deer when he knew there was a wounded bear behind his back.

How much had they taken? "I can't send you to Caemlyn right away, Master Gill, but if you stay with me a while longer, I'll see you there safely." If staying with him any length of time was safe. The Prophet, Whitecloaks, and now maybe Seanchan added in.

"I think you're a good man," Lini said suddenly. "I'm afraid we didn't tell you the whole truth, and maybe we should."

"Lini, what are you saying?" Master Gill exclaimed, bounding to his feet. "I think the heat's getting to her," he told Perrin. "And all the travel. She has strange fancies, sometimes. You know how old folks can get. Hush, now, Lini!"

Lini slapped away the hand he was trying to put over her mouth. "You mind yourself, Basel Gill! I'll 'old' you! Maighdin *was* running from Tallanvor, in a manner of speaking, and he *was* chasing her. We all were, four days now, and near killing us and the horses both. Well, it's no wonder she doesn't know her own mind half the time; you men snarl up a woman's wits so she can hardly think, then you pretend you've done nothing at all. The lot of you ought to have your ears boxed on general principle. The girl's afraid of her own heart! Those two should be married, and the quicker the better."

Master Gill gaped at her, and Perrin was not sure his own mouth might not be hanging open. "I'm not certain I understand what it is you want of me," he said slowly, and the white-haired woman leaped in before he was well finished.

"Don't pretend to be dense. I won't believe it in you for a moment. I can see you have more wits than most men. That's the worst habit you men have, making believe you don't see what's plain under your noses." What had happened to all those curtsies? Folding thin arms across her chest, she eyed him sternly. "Well, if you must pretend, I'll set it out for you. This Lord Dragon of yours does whatever he wants, the way I hear. Your Prophet picks out people and marries them on the spot. Very well; you snatch up Maighdin and Tallanvor and marry them. He'll thank you, and so will she. When her mind settles."

Stunned, Perrin glanced at Master Gill, who shrugged and made a sickly grin. "If you will forgive me," Perrin told the frowning woman, "I have some matters I must see to." He hurried away, only looking back once. Lini was shaking a finger at Master Gill, berating him despite his protests. The breeze was wrong for Perrin to hear what they were saying. In truth, he did not want to. They *were* all crazy!

Berelain might have her two maids and her thief-catchers, but Faile had her own attendants, of a sort. Close on twenty young Tairens and Cairhienin were sitting cross-legged near the tent, the women in coats and breeches with swords belted on just like the men. None wore their hair longer than the shoulder, and men and women both had it tied back with a ribbon, imitating the Aiel tail. Perrin wondered where the rest were; they seldom strayed far from the sound of Faile's voice. Not causing trouble, he hoped. She had taken them under her wing to keep them *out* of trouble, she said, and the Light knew they would have gotten into it, left back in Cairhien with a great lot of young fools just like them. In Perrin's opinion, the whole lashing of them needed a swift kick in the bottom to knock some sense into them. Dueling, playing at *ji'e'toh*, pretending to be some sort of Aiel. Idiocy!

Lacile rose to her feet as Perrin came closer, a pale little woman with red ribbons pinned to her lapels, small gold hoops in her ears, and a challenging stare that sometimes made the Two Rivers men think she might like a kiss despite her sword. Right then, the challenge was stony hard. A moment behind her, Arrela stood too, tall and dark, with her hair cut short as a Maiden's and her clothes plainer than most of the men's. Unlike Lacile, Arrela made it clear she would as soon kiss a dog as any man. The pair made as if to move in front of the tent, to block Perrin's way, but a square-chinned fellow in a puffy-sleeved coat barked an order and they sat again. Reluctantly. For that matter, Parelean thumbed that block of a chin as though he might be reconsidering. He had worn a beard the first time Perrin saw him—several of the Tairen men had had them—but Aiel did not wear beards.

Perrin muttered about foolishness under his breath. They were Faile's to the bone, and the fact that he was her husband meant little. Aram might be jealous of his attentions, yet Aram at least shared his affections with Faile. He could feel the young idiots' eyes on him as he strode inside. Faile would skin him if she ever learned that he hoped they would keep *her* from trouble.

The tent was tall and spacious, with a flowered carpet for a floor and sparse furnishings that folded for storage on a cart, most of them. The heavy stand-mirror certainly could not. Except for brass-bound chests draped with embroidered cloths and doubling as extra tables, straight lines of bright gilt decorated everything down to the washstand and its mirror. A dozen mirrored lamps made the interior nearly as bright as outside, if considerably cooler, and there were even a pair of silk hangings dangling from the roof poles, too ornate for Perrin's taste. Too rigid, with the birds and flowers marching in lines and angles. Dobraine had set them up to travel like Cairhienin nobles, though Perrin had managed to "lose" the worst of it. The huge bed, for one, a ridiculous thing to travel with. It had taken up almost a whole cart to itself.

Faile and Maighdin were sitting alone together, worked silver cups in hand. They had the air of women feeling one another out, all smiles on the outside yet with a hint of sharpness to the eyes, a hint of listening for something behind the words, and not a clue as to whether they would hug in the next instant or draw knives. Well, he thought most women would not actually go as far as knives, but Faile could. Maighdin appeared much less travel-worn than she had, washed and combed, the dust brushed from her dress. A small mosaic-topped table between them held more cups and a tall sweating silver pitcher that gave off the minty scent of herb tea. Both women looked around at his entrance, and for an instant, they had almost exactly the same expression, coolly wondering who was barging in and not at all pleased with the interruption. At least Faile softened hers immediately with a smile.

"Master Gill told me your story, Mistress Dorlain," he said. "You've faced hard days, but you can be sure you're safe here till you decide to leave." The woman murmured thanks over the rim of her cup, but she smelled wary, and her eyes tried to read him like a book.

"Maighdin also told me their story, Perrin," Faile said, "and I have an offer to make her. Maighdin, you and your friends have had trying months behind, and you tell me of no prospects ahead. Enter my service, all of you. You will still have to journey, but the circumstances will be much better. I pay well, and I am not a harsh mistress." Perrin voiced his approval immediately. If Faile wanted to indulge her fancy for taking in strays, at least he wanted to help this lot, too. Maybe they would be safer with him than wandering around alone at that.

Choking on her tea, Maighdin nearly dropped her cup. She blinked at Faile, dabbing at the damp on her chin with a lace-edged linen handkerchief, and her chair creaked faintly as she turned, strangely, to study Perrin. "I . . . thank you," she said at last, slowly. "I think. . . ." Another moment's perusal of Perrin, and her voice picked up. "Yes, I thank you, and I accept your kind offer gratefully. I must tell my companions." Rising, she hesitated in setting her cup on the tray, then straightened only to spread her skirts in a curtsy suitable for any palace. "I will try to give good service, my Lady," she said levelly. "May I withdraw?" At Faile's assent, she curtsied again and backed away two steps before turning to go! Perrin scratched his beard. Somebody else who would be bobbing at him every time she turned around.

No sooner had the tentflap dropped behind Maighdin than Faile put her cup down and laughed, drumming her heels on the carpet. "Oh, I like her, Perrin. She has spirit! I'll wager she would have singed your beard over those banners if I hadn't saved you. Oh, yes. Spirit!"

Perrin grunted. Just what he needed; another woman to singe his beard. "I promised Master Gill to look after them, Faile, but. . . . Can you guess what that Lini asked? She wanted me to marry Maighdin to that fellow Tallanvor. Just stand them up and marry them whatever they said! She claimed they want it." He filled a silver cup with tea and dropped into the chair Maighdin had vacated, ignoring its alarming groans under his sudden weight. "In any case, that nonsense is the least of my worries. Master Gill says it was the Seanchan took Amador, and I believe him. Light! The Seanchan!"

Faile tapped her fingertips together, staring across them at nothing. "That might be just the thing," she mused. "Most servants do better married than not. Perhaps I should arrange it. And for Breane, too. The way she went running out of here to check on that big fellow as soon as her face was clean, I suspect they should be already. There was a gleam in her eye. I won't have that kind of behavior in my servants, Perrin. It just leads to tears and recriminations and sulking. And Breane will be worse than he is."

Perrin stared at her. "Did you hear me?" he said slowly. "The Seanchan have captured Amador! The Seanchan, Faile!"

She gave a start—she really had been thinking about marrying off those women!—then smiled at him, amused. "Amador is a long way, yet, and if we do meet with these Seanchan, I'm sure you will deal with them. After all, you taught me to perch on your wrist, didn't you?" That was what she claimed, though he had never seen any sign of it.

"They might be a touch more difficult than you were," he said dryly, and she smiled again. She smelled extremely pleased, for some reason. "I'm thinking about sending Grady or Neald to warn Rand, no matter what he said." She shook her head fiercely, smiles evaporating, but he pushed on. "If I knew how to find him, I would. There has to be some way to get word to him without anyone learning of it." Rand had insisted on that more than he had on secrecy about Masema. Perrin had been exiled from Rand's presence, and no one was to know anything remained between them except enmity.

"He knows, Perrin. I'm sure of it. Maighdin saw pigeon-cotes everywhere in Amador, and apparently the Seanchan didn't look at them twice. By this time, any merchant who has business with Amador has heard, and so has the White Tower. Believe me, Rand must have, too. You have to trust that he knows best. In this, he does." She was not always so certain of that.

"Maybe," Perrin muttered irritably. He tried not to worry about Rand's sanity, but Rand made Perrin at his most suspicious look like a child skipping in a meadow. How much did Rand trust even him? Rand kept things back, had plans he never let on.

Exhaling, Perrin settled back in the chair, gulped a swallow of tea. The truth of it was, mad or sane, Rand *was* right. If the Forsaken caught a suspicion of what he was up to, or the White Tower did, they would find some way to overturn the anvil on his feet. "At least I can give the Tower's eyes-and-ears less to talk about. This time, I'm *burning* that bloody banner." And the Wolfhead, too. He might have to play at being a lord, but he could do it without a bloody flag!

Faile's full lips pursed judiciously, and she shook her head slightly. Slipping from her chair, she knelt beside him, took his wrist in her hands. Perrin met her level gaze warily. When she looked at him so intently, so seriously, she was about to tell him something important. That, or pull the wool over his eyes and spin him around till he did not know front from back. Her scent told him nothing. He tried to stop smelling her; it was all too easy to lose himself in that, and then she *would* pull the wool over his eyes. One thing he had learned since marrying: a man needed all of his wits dealing with a woman. Too often even that was not enough; women did what they wanted as surely as Aes Sedai.

"You might want to reconsider, husband," she murmured. A tiny smile quirked her mouth as if she once again knew what he was thinking. "I doubt anyone who's seen us since we entered Ghealdan knew what the Red Eagle is. Around a town the size of Bethal, some will, though. And the longer we have to hunt for Masema, the greater the chance."

He did not bother with saying that was all the more reason to get rid of the banner. Faile was no fool, and she thought much faster than he. "Then why keep it," he asked slowly, "when all it'll do is draw eyes to the idiot everybody will think is trying to pull Manetheren out of the grave?" Men had tried that in the past, and women, too; the name of Manetheren carried powerful memories, and it was convenient for anyone who wanted to start a rebellion.

"Because it *will* draw eyes." She leaned toward him intently. "To a man trying to raise up Manetheren again. Lesser folk will smile to your face, hope you ride on soon, and try to forget you as soon as you do. As for the greater, they've too much in front of their faces right now to look twice unless you pinch their noses. Compared to the Seanchan, or the Prophet, or the Whitecloaks, a man trying to raise Manetheren is small turnips. And I think it's safe to say the Tower won't look twice either, not now." Her smile widened, and the light in her eyes said she was about to make her most telling point. "But most important, no one will think that man is doing anything else." Abruptly her smile vanished; she stuck a finger against his nose, hard.

"And don't call yourself an idiot, Perrin t'Bashere Aybara. Not even sideways, like that. You aren't, and I do not like it." Her scent was tiny spikes, not true anger but definitely displeased.

Quicksilver. A kingfisher flashing by faster than thought. Certainly faster than his thoughts. It would never have occurred to him to hide so . . . flagrantly. But he could see the sense. It was like concealing the fact that you were a murderer by claiming to be a thief. Yet it might work.

Chuckling, he kissed her fingertip. "The banner stays," he said. He supposed that meant the Wolfhead did, too. Blood and bloody ashes! "Alliandre has to know the truth, though. If she thinks Rand means to set me up as King of Manetheren and take her lands. . . ."

Faile rose so suddenly, turning away, that he was afraid he had made a mistake bringing up the Queen. Alliandre could lead to Berelain all too easily, and Faile smelled . . . prickly. Wary. But what she said, over her shoulder, was "Alliandre won't be a bit of trouble for Perrin Goldeneyes. That bird's as good as netted, husband, so it's time to put our minds on how to find Masema." Kneeling gracefully beside a small chest against the tent wall, the only chest without draperies, she lifted the lid and began removing rolled maps.

Perrin hoped she was right about Alliandre, because he did not know what to do if she was wrong. If only he were half what she thought him. Alliandre was a netted bird, the Seanchan would fall over like dolls for Perrin Goldeneyes, and he would snatch up the Prophet and take him to Rand if Masema had ten thousand men around him. Not for the first time he realized that however much her anger hurt and confused him, it was her disappointment he feared. If he ever saw that in her eyes, it would rip the heart out of his chest.

He knelt beside her and helped her spread out the largest map, covering the south of Ghealdan and the north of Amadicia, and studied it as though Masema's name would leap off the parchment at him. He had more reason than Rand to want to succeed. Whatever else, he could not fail Faile.

Faile lay in the darkness, listening until she was sure that Perrin's breath had the deep rhythm of sleep, then slipped

ut Berelain. It was not Perrin's fault. She repeated that
erself twenty times a day, like a prayer. But why was
man so blind? "What kind of bother?" She drew a cha-
ed breath. Troubles with your husband should never af-
t your tone with your vassals.

'Nothing of note, my Lady." Selande buckled her sword
t and settled it on her hips. "They let some fellows ahead
us drive their wagons through without a second look,
t they were worried about letting women go out into the
ght." Some of the other women laughed. The five men
ho had gone into Bethal stirred irritably, no doubt because
ey had not been thought enough protection. The rest of
ha Faile made a thick semicircle behind those ten, watch-
g Faile closely, listening closely. Moonlight shadowed
eir faces.

"Tell me what you saw," Faile commanded in a calmer
one. Much better.

Selande made her report concisely, and for all Faile's
wishes that she had gone herself, she had to admit they had
seen almost as much as she could have wished. The streets
of Bethal were nearly empty even at the busiest hours of the
day. People stayed to their own homes as much as possible.
A little commerce trickled in and out, but few merchants
ventured into this part of Ghealdan, and barely enough
food came in from the countryside to keep everyone fed.
Most of the townspeople seemed stunned, afraid of what
lay outside the walls, sinking deeper and deeper into apathy
and despair. Everyone kept their mouths closed for fear of
the Prophet's spies, and their eyes as well, for fear of being
taken for spies. The Prophet had a deep effect. For instance,
however many bandits roamed the hills, cutpurses and footpads had vanished from Bethal. It was said the Prophet's
penalty for a thief was to cut off the man's hands. Though
hat did not seem to apply to his own people.

"The Queen tours the city every day, showing herself to
ep spirits up," Selande said, "but I do not think it helps
uch. She is making a progress here in the south to re-
nd people they have a Queen; maybe she has had more
ccess elsewhere. The Watch has been added to the wall
rds, and all but a handful of her soldiers, too. Perhaps it
es the townsfolk feel safer. Until she moves on. Unlike
yone else, Alliandre herself apparently feels no fear

out from the blankets they shared. Rueful amusement
touched her as she pulled her linen nightdress up over her
head. Did he really think she would not find out that he had
hidden the bed deep in a copse one morning while the carts
were being loaded? Not that she minded; not a great deal,
at least. She was sure she had slept on the ground as often
as he. She had pretended surprise, of course, and made light
of it. Anything else, and he would have apologized, perhaps
even gone back to fetch the bed. Managing a husband was
an art, so her mother said. Had Deira ni Ghaline ever found
it so difficult?

Scuffing her bare feet into slippers, she shrugged into a
silk robe, then hesitated, looking down at Perrin. He would
be able to see her clearly, if he woke, but to her, he was
just a shadowed mound. She wished her mother were there,
now, to advise her. She loved Perrin with every fiber of her
being, and he confused every fiber. Actually understanding
men was impossible, of course, but he was so unlike anyone
she had grown up with. He never swaggered, and instead
of laughing at himself, he was . . . modest. She had not believed a man *could* be modest! He insisted that only chance
had made him a leader, claimed he did not know how to
lead, when men who met him were ready to follow after an
hour. He dismissed his own thinking as slow, when those
slow, considering thoughts saw so deeply that she had to
dance a merry jig to keep any secrets at all. He was a wonderful man, her curly-haired wolf. So strong. And so gentle.
Sighing, she tiptoed from the tent. His ears had caused her
difficulties before.

The camp lay quiet beneath a gibbous moon that gave
as much light in a cloudless sky as it normally would have
full, a brightness that washed out the stars. Some sort of
night-bird cried shrilly, then fell silent at an owl's deep
hoot. There was a small breeze, and for a wonder, it actually seemed a little cool. Probably her imagination. The
nights were cool only in comparison to the days.

Most of the men were asleep, dark humps among the
shadows beneath the trees. A few remained awake, talking
around the handful of fires still burning. She made no effort
to hide, but none noticed her. Some appeared half asleep
where they sat, heads nodding. If she had not known how
well the men on sentry duty would be keeping watch, she

might have thought the camp could be surprised by a herd of wild cattle. Of course, the Maidens would be on guard in the night, too. But it did not matter if they saw her, either.

The high-wheeled carts made long, shadowed rows, the servants already snug and snoring beneath. Most of the servants. One fire still crackled there. Maighdin and her friends sat around it. Tallanvor was talking, gesturing fiercely, but only the other men seemed to be paying him any mind, though he appeared to be addressing himself to Maighdin. That they had had better garb in their bundles than those near rags was not surprising, but their former mistress must have had a very free hand to give out silk to her people, and Maighdin wore finely cut silk indeed, in a muted blue. None of the others was dressed so well, so perhaps Maighdin had been their lady's favorite.

A twig snapped under Faile's foot, and heads whipped around, Tallanvor starting to his feet, half drawing his sword before he saw her gathering her robe in the moonlight. They were more alert than the Two Rivers men behind her. For an instant the lot of them just stared at her; then Maighdin rose gracefully and made a deep curtsy, and the others hastily followed her example with varying degrees of skill. Only Maighdin and Balwer appeared at all at ease. A nervous smile split Gill's round face.

"Go on with what you were doing," Faile told them kindly. "But don't stay up too late; tomorrow will be full." She walked on, but when she glanced back, they were still standing, still peering after her. Their travels must have made them wary as rabbits, always watching for a fox. She wondered how well they would fit in. Over the next few weeks, she would be busy training them to her ways, learning theirs. One was as important as the other for a well-run household. The time would have to be found.

They did not stay long in her thoughts tonight. Soon she was beyond the carts, not quite out to where Two Rivers men would be keeping sharp watch from up in the trees. Nothing larger than a mouse would get by them unseen—even some of the Maidens had been spotted upon occasion—but they were watching for anyone attempting to sneak in. Not for those who had a right to be there. In a small moonlit clearing, her people were waiting.

Some of the men bowed, and Parelean nearly went to one

knee before stopping himself. Several women made curtsies that looked quite peculiar in me dropped their eyes or shifted in embarrassmen what they had done. The manners of the cou bred into them, though they tried very hard to customs. What they believed were Aiel custom Sometimes they horrified the Maidens with wh lieved. Perrin called them fools, and they wer ways, but they had sworn fealty to her, these Cair Tairens—water oath, they named it, copying the ing to—and that made them hers. Among themse had taken to calling their "society" *Cha Faile,* the Talon, though they had seen the necessity of keep quiet. They were not fools in all ways. In fact, are edges anyway, they were not too unlike the young women she had grown up with.

Those she had sent off early that morning had turned, for the women among them were still chang of the dresses they had worn of necessity. Even one v dressed as a man would have roused notice in Bethal, mention five. The clearing was a great flurry of skirts shifts, coats and shirts and breeches. The women made lieve they did not mind being unclothed in front of other including men, since the Aiel apparently did not, but haste and labored breathing gave them the lie. The men were all shifting feet and turning heads, torn between looking away decently and watching, as they thought the Aiel did, while pretending they were not looking at half-dressed women Faile held her robe close over her nightdress; she could have dressed further without waking Perrin for sure, she made no pretense at comfort. She was no Doman receive her retainers in her bath.

"Forgive us for being late, my Lady Faile," S panted, tugging her coat on. The accents of Cairhie sharp in the short woman's voice. Even for a Cai she was not tall. She managed a credible swagger a suitable boldness in the tilt of her head and the shoulders. "We would have returned sooner, b guards made a bother letting us out."

"A bother?" Faile said sharply. If only she seen with her own eyes, on top of theirs; if on let her go instead of that trollop. No, she w the Prophet will come storming over the walls. She walks alone in the gardens of Lord Telabin's palace, morning and evening, and keeps only a few soldiers, who spend most of their time in the kitchens. Everybody in the city seems as concerned with food, with how long there will be enough, as they are with the Prophet. In truth, my Lady, for all the guards on the walls, I think if Masema appeared at the gates alone, they might give him the town."

"They would," Meralda put in contemptuously, buckling her own sword round her waist, "and beg for mercy." Dark and stocky, Meralda was as tall as Faile, but the Tairen woman ducked her head at a frown from Selande and murmured an apology. There were no doubts who led *Cha Faile*, after Faile herself.

She had been pleased there was no need to change the precedence they had established. Selande was the brightest of them except perhaps for Parelean, and only Arrela and Camaille were quicker. And Selande had something extra, a steadiness, as if she had already faced the worst fear in her life and nothing could ever be that bad again. Of course, she wanted a scar like those some of the Maidens had. Faile possessed several small scars, badges of honor most of them, but actually seeking one was idiocy. At least the woman was not too very eager in the matter.

"We made a map, as you required, my Lady," the diminutive woman finished with a last, warning glance at Meralda. "We marked out Lord Telabin's palace on the back as much as we could, but I fear that is not much more than the gardens and stables."

Faile did not try to make out the lines on the paper she unfolded in the moonlight. A pity she had not been able to go herself; she could have mapped the interior, too. No. Done was done, as Perrin liked to say. And it was enough. "You are certain no one searches wagons leaving the city?" Even in the pale light, she could see confusion on many of the faces in front of her. None knew why she had sent some of them into Bethal.

Selande did not look confused. "Yes, my Lady," she said calmly. Quite bright, and more than quick enough.

The wind gusted for a moment, rustling leaves on the trees, rustling dead leaves on the ground, and Faile wished she had Perrin's ears. His nose and eyes, too. It did not matter if anyone saw her here with her retainers, but eavesdroppers would be something else. "You've done very well, Selande. All of you have." Perrin knew the dangers here, as real as any farther south; he knew, but like most men, he thought with his heart as often as his head. A wife had to be practical, to keep her husband out of trouble. That had been her mother's very first piece of advice on married life. "At first light, you will return to Bethal, and if you receive word from me, this is what you will do. . . ."

Even Selande's eyes widened in shock as she went on, but no one murmured the slightest protest. Faile would have been surprised if anyone had. Her instructions were to the point. There would be some danger, but under the circumstances, not nearly what might have been.

"Are there any questions?" she said finally. "Does everyone understand?"

With one voice, *Cha Faile* answered. "We live to serve our Lady Faile." And that meant they would serve her beloved wolf, whether he wanted them to or not.

Maighdin shifted in her blankets on the hard ground, sleep eluding her. That was her name, now; a new name for a new life. Maighdin, for her mother, and Dorlain, for a family on an estate that had been hers. A new life for an old life gone, but ties of the heart could not be cut. And now. . . . Now. . . .

A faint crackle of dead leaves brought her head up, and she watched a dim shape pass through the trees. The Lady Faile, returning to her tent from wherever she had gone. A pleasant young woman, kindhearted and well spoken. Whatever her husband's stock, she almost certainly was nobly born. But young. Inexperienced. That might be a help.

Maighdin let her head fall back on the cloak she had wadded up for a pillow. Light, what was she doing here? Taking service as a lady's maid! No. She would hold on to her confidence in herself, at least. She could still find that. She could. If she dug deeply. Her breath caught at the sound of footsteps close by.

Tallanvor knelt gracefully at her side. He was shirtless, moonlight gleaming on the smooth muscles of his chest and shoulders, his face in shadows. A slight breeze ruffled his hair. "What madness is this?" he asked softly. "Entering *service*? What are you up to? And don't tell me that nonsense about making a new life; I don't believe it. No one does."

She tried to turn away, but he laid a hand on her shoulder. He exerted no pressure, yet it stopped her as surely as a halter. Light, please let her not tremble. The Light did not listen, but at least she managed to keep her voice steady. "If you haven't noticed, I must make my way in the world, now. Better as a lady's maid than a tavern maid. You may feel free to go on alone if service here doesn't suit."

"You didn't abdicate your wits or your pride when you gave up the throne," he muttered. Burn Lini for revealing that! "If you mean to pretend that you did, I suggest you avoid letting Lini get you alone." The man chuckled at her! He chuckled, oh, so richly! "She wants a word with Maighdin, and I suspect she won't be as gentle with Maighdin as she was with Morgase."

Angrily she sat up, brushing his hand away. "Are you blind, and deaf as well? The Dragon Reborn has *plans* for Elayne! Light, I wouldn't like it if he simply knew her name! It must be more than chance that brought me to one of his henchmen, Tallanvor. It has to be!"

"Burn me, I knew it must be that. I hoped I was wrong, but. . . ." He sounded as angry as she. He had no right to be angry! "Elayne is safe in the White Tower, the Amyrlin Seat won't let her anywhere near a man who can channel, even if he is the Dragon Reborn—especially if he is!—and Maighdin Dorlain can do nothing about the Amyrlin Seat, the Dragon Reborn, *or* the Lion Throne. All she can do is get her neck snapped, or her throat cut, or—!"

"Maighdin Dorlain can watch!" she broke in, at least partly to stop that awful litany. "She can listen! She can . . . !" Irritably, she trailed off. What *could* she do? Suddenly she realized she was sitting there in a thin shift and hurriedly folded her blankets around her. The night actually seemed a little cool. Or maybe the goose bumps on her skin were from Tallanvor's unseen eyes on her. The thought roused a flush in her cheeks she hoped he could not see. Luckily, it put a heat in her voice, too. She was not a girl, to go blushing because a man looked at her! "I will do what I

can, whatever that is. The chance will come to learn something or do something that will help Elayne, and I will
take it!"

"A dangerous decision," he told her calmly. She wished
she could make out his face in the darkness. Only to read
his expression, of course. "You heard him threaten to hang
anyone who looked at him the wrong way. I can believe it,
in a man with those eyes. Like a beast. I was surprised he
let that fellow go; I thought he'd rip his throat out! If he dis-
covers who you are, who you used to be. . . . Balwer might
betray you. He never really explained why he helped us
escape Amador. Maybe he thought Queen Morgase would
give him a new position. Now he knows there's no chance
of that, and he might want to curry favor with his new master and mistress."

"Are you afraid of *Lord* Perrin Goldeneyes?" she demanded contemptuously. Light, the man frightened her!
Those eyes belonged on a wolf. "Balwer knows enough to
hold his tongue. Anything he says will reflect on him; he
came with me, after all. If you're afraid, then ride on!"

"You always fling that in my face," he sighed, settling
back on his heels. She could not see his eyes, but she could
feel them. "Ride on if you wish, you say. Once, there was
a soldier loved a queen from afar, knowing it was hopeless,
knowing he could never dare speak. Now the queen is gone,
and only a woman remains, and I hope. I burn with hope!
If you want me to leave, Maighdin, say it. One word. 'Go!'
A simple word."

She opened her mouth. *A simple word,* she thought.
Light, it's only one word! Why can't I say it! Light, please!
For the second time that night, the Light failed to hear. She
sat there huddled in her blankets like a fool, her mouth
open, her face growing hotter and hotter.

If he had chuckled again, she would have put her belt
knife in him. If he had laughed, or given any sign of triumph. . . . Instead, he leaned forward and gently kissed
her eyes. She made a sound deep in her throat; she could
not seem to move. Wide-eyed, she watched him stand. He
loomed in the moonlight. She was a queen—she had been
a queen—used to command, used to hard decisions in hard
times, but right then the pounding of her heart drummed
thought from her head.

"Had you said 'go,'" he told her, "I'd have buried hope, but I could never leave you."

Not until he was back in his own blankets could she make herself lie down and draw hers around her. She breathed as if she had been running. The night *was* cool; she was shivering, not trembling. Tallanvor was too young. Too young! Worse, he was right. Burn him for that! A lady's maid could do nothing to affect events, and if the Dragon Reborn's wolf-eyed killer learned that he had Morgase of Andor in his hands, she could be used against Elayne instead of helping her. He had no right to be right when she wanted him to be wrong! The illogic of that thought infuriated her. There *was* a chance she might do some good! There had to be!

In the back of her head, a small voice laughed. *You can't forget that you're Morgase Trakand, it told her scornfully, and even after she's abdicated her throne, Queen Morgase can't stop trying her hand in the affairs of the mighty, no matter how much ruin she's made of it so far. And she can't tell a man to go away, either, because she can't stop thinking how strong his hands are, and how his lips curve when he smiles, and—*

Furious, she pulled the blanket over her head, trying to shut out the voice. She was *not* staying because she could not walk away from power. As for Tallanvor. . . . She would set him firmly in his place. This time she would! But. . . . What was his place, with a woman who was no longer a queen? She tried to put him out of her mind and tried to ignore that mocking voice that would not be quiet, yet when sleep finally came, she could still feel the pressure of his lips on her eyelids.

CHAPTER
9

Tangles

P errin woke before first light as usual, and as usual, Faile was already up and about. She could make a mouse seem noisy when she wanted to, and he suspected that if he woke an hour after lying down, she would still manage to be up first. The door-flaps were tied back, the side panels raised a little at the bottom, and a stir of air rose through the venthole in the peak, enough to create an illusion of coolness. Perrin actually shivered while searching for his shirt and breeches. Well, it was supposed to be winter, even if the weather did not know it.

He dressed in the dark and scrubbed his teeth with salt, needing no lamps, and when he left the tent, stamping his feet into his boots, Faile had her new servants gathered around her in the deep grayness of early morning, some holding lighted lanterns. A lord's daughter needed servants; he should have arranged for it before this. There were Two Rivers folk in Caemlyn that Faile had trained herself, but with the need for secrecy there had been no way to fetch them along. Master Gill would want to go home as soon as possible, and Lamgwin and Breane with him, but maybe Maighdin and Lini would stay.

Aram straightened from where he had been sitting cross-legged beside the tent, and waited silently on Perrin. If Perrin had not stopped him, Aram would have slept across the entrance. This morning his coat was striped red-and-white, though the white was a trifle dingy, and even here that wolfhead-pommeled sword hilt rose over his shoulder. Perrin had left his axe in the tent, and grateful to be rid of it.

Tallanvor still wore his sword belted over his coat, but not
Master Gill or the other two.

Faile must have been watching, because no sooner did
Perrin come out than she gestured toward the tent, clearly
issuing orders. Maighdin and Breane came bustling past
him and Aram with lanterns, their jaws set, smelling of
determination for some reason. Neither curtsied, a pleasant surprise. Lini did, a quick bend of the knee before she
darted after the other two muttering about "knowing their
place." Perrin suspected Lini was one of those women who
saw her "place" as being in charge. Come to think of it,
most women did. That was the way of the world, it seemed,
not just the Two Rivers.

Tallanvor and Lamgwin followed close behind the
women, and Lamgwin was as serious about bowing as Tallanvor, who was almost grim. Perrin sighed and bowed
back, and they both gave a start, gaping at him. A curt shout
from Lini jerked them into the tent.

With only a quickly flashed smile for him, Faile strode
off toward the carts, talking alternately to Basel Gill on
one side of her and Sebban Balwer on the other. The men
each held a lantern out to light her way. Of course, a double
handful of those idiots kept pace where they could hear if
she raised her voice, strutting and stroking sword hilts and
staring about in the dimness as though they expected an attack or hoped for one. Perrin tugged at his short beard. She
always found plenty of work to fill her hours, and nobody
took it out of her hands. Nobody would dare.

Not so much as the first fingers of dawn showed on
the horizon yet, but the Cairhienin were beginning to stir
around the carts, and moving more quickly the closer Faile
came. By the time she reached them, they appeared to be
trotting, their lanterns bobbing and swinging in the dimness. The Two Rivers men, used to farmers' days, were already making breakfast, some laughing and roughhousing
around their cook fires, some grumping, but most getting
the work done. A few tried to stay in their blankets and
were unceremoniously tumbled out. Grady and Neald were
up, too, as always off by themselves, shadows in black coats
among the trees. Perrin could not recall seeing them without those coats, always buttoned to the neck, always clean and

unwrinkled come sunrise, whatever they had looked like the
night before. Stepping through the forms in unison, the pair
were practicing the sword as they did every morning. That
was better than their evening practice, when they would sit
cross-legged, hands on knees, staring at some distant nothing. They never did anything then that anyone could see,
yet not a man in the camp but knew what they were about
and kept as far off as possible. Not even the Maidens would
step into their line of sight then.

Something was missing, Perrin realized with a start.
Faile always had one of the men meet him first thing with
a bowl of the thick porridge they breakfasted on, but it
seemed she had been too busy this morning. Brightening,
he hurried toward the cook fires, hoping at least to be able
to dip up his own porridge for once. A small hope.

Flann Barstere, a lanky fellow with a dent in his chin,
met him halfway and shoved a carved bowl into his hands.
Flann was from up toward Watch Hill, and Perrin did not
know him well, but they had been hunting together a time
or two, and once Perrin had helped him dig one of his father's
cows out of a boghole in the Waterwood. "The Lady Faile
told me to bring this to you, Perrin," Flann said anxiously.
"You won't tell her I forgot, will you? You won't tell? I
found some honey, and I put in a good dollop." Perrin tried
not to sigh. At least Flann had remembered his name.

Well, maybe he could not get away with doing the sim-
plest chores for himself, but he was still responsible for the
men eating beneath the trees. Without him, they would
be with their families, getting ready for the day's chores
around the farm, milking cows and cutting firewood instead of wondering whether they might have to kill or be
killed before sunset. Gulping down the honeyed porridge
quickly, he told Aram to take his ease over breakfast, but
the man looked so miserable that he relented, so Aram followed as he made his way around the camp. The journey
was not one Perrin enjoyed.

Men put down their bowls when he approached, or even
stood until he passed. He gritted his teeth whenever somebody he had grown up with, or worse, a man who had sent
him on errands as a boy, called him Lord Perrin. Not everyone did, but too many. Far too many. After a time, he gave
up telling them to stop out of sheer weariness; all too often

the reply was "Oh! Whatever you say, Lord Perrin." It was
enough to make a man howl!

Despite that, he made himself pause to speak a word or
two to every man. Mainly, though, he kept his eyes open.
And his nose. They all knew enough to keep their bows
in good repair and tend the fletching and points on their
arrows, but some would wear the soles out of their boots
or the bottom out of their breeches without noticing, or let
blisters fester because they could not be bothered to do anything about them just yet. Several had the habit of picking
up brandy when they could, and two or three of those had
no head for it at all. There had been a small village the day
before reaching Bethal that held no fewer than three inns.

It was very strange. Having Mistress Luhhan or his
mother tell him he needed new boots or his breeches
mended had always been embarrassing, and he was sure he
would have been irritated at the same from anybody else,
but from grizzled old Jondyn Barran on down, the Two
Rivers men just said "Why, right you are, Lord Perrin; I'll
see to it straightaway" or some such. He caught a number of
them grinning at one another when he moved on. And they
smelled pleased! When he rooted a clay jar of pear brandy
out of Jori Congar's saddlebags—a skinny fellow who ate
twice as much as anyone else and always looked as if he
had not had a bite in a week, Jori was a good shot with a
bow, but given a chance he would drink until he could not
stand, and he had light fingers besides—Jori gave him a
wide-eyed look and spread his hands as if he did not know
where the jar had come from. But as Perrin walked on,
emptying the brandy onto the ground, Jori laughed, "You
can't put anything over on Lord Perrin!" He sounded proud!
Sometimes, Perrin thought he was the only sane person left.

Another thing, he noticed. One and all, they were very
interested in what he did not say. Man after man cast an eye
toward the two banners that occasionally flapped atop their
poles in a brief gust, Red Wolfhead and Red Eagle. They
eyed the banners and watched him, waiting for the order he
had given every time the things had come out since reaching Ghealdan. And often enough before that. Except that
he had said nothing yesterday, and he said nothing today,
and he saw speculation blooming on men's faces. He left
behind clusters of men peering at the banners and at him,

murmuring excitedly among themselves. He did not try to listen. What would they say if he was wrong, if the Whitecloaks or King Ailron decided they could look away from the Prophet and the Seanchan long enough to snuff out a supposed rebellion? They were his responsibility, and he had already gotten too many of them killed.

The sun was more than peeking above the horizon, spreading a sharp morning light, by the time he finished, and over at the tent, Tallanvor and Lamgwin were lugging out chests under Lini's direction, while Maighdin and Breane appeared to be sorting the contents out on a broad patch of dead grass, blankets and linens mainly, and long bright swaths of silk satin that had been intended to drape the bed he had misplaced. Faile must have been inside, because that gaggle of idiots were cooling their heels not far off. No carrying and hauling for them. Useful as rats in the barn.

Perrin thought about taking a look at Stayer and Stepper, but when he glanced through the trees at the horselines, he was seen. No fewer than three of the farriers stepped out anxiously, watching him. They were blocky men in leather aprons, alike as eggs in a basket, though Falton had only a fringe of white around his head, Aemin was graying, and Jerasid had not yet come into his middle years. Perrin growled at the sight of them. They would hover if he laid a hand on either horse, and goggle if he lifted a hoof. The one time he had tried to change a worn shoe, on Stayer, all *six* farriers had darted about grabbing up tools before he could touch them, nearly knocking the bay over in their rush to do the work themselves.

"They're afraid you don't trust them," Aram said suddenly. Perrin looked at him in surprise, and Aram shifted his shoulders in his coat. "I've talked to them, some. They think if a lord tends his own horses, it must be because he doesn't trust them. You might send them off, with no way to get home." His tone said they were fools to think that, but he gave Perrin a sideways glance and shrugged again, uncomfortably. "I think they're embarrassed, too. If you don't behave the way they think a lord should, it reflects on them, as they see it."

"Light!" Perrin muttered. Faile had said the same—about them being embarrassed, anyway—but he had believed it just a lord's daughter talking. Faile had grown up surrounded by servants, yet how could a lady know the thoughts of a man who had to work for his bread? He frowned toward the horselines. Five of the farriers stood together watching him, now. Embarrassed that he wanted to look after his own horses, and upset that he did not want them pulling wool and scratching gravel all over the place. "Do *you* think I ought to act like a fool in silk small-clothes?" he asked. Aram blinked, and began studying his boots. "Light!" Perrin growled.

Spotting Basel Gill hurrying from the direction of the carts, Perrin moved to meet him. He did not think he had done very well at making Gill feel at ease yesterday. The stout man was talking to himself and once more mopping his head with a kerchief, sweating away in a rumpled dark gray coat. The day's heat was beginning to take hold already. He did not see Perrin until Perrin was nearly on him, and then he gave a jump, stuffing the kerchief into a coat pocket and making a bow. He looked curried and brushed fit for a feastday.

"Ah. My Lord Perrin. Your Lady told me to take a cart into Bethal. She says I'm to find you some Two Rivers tabac, if I can, but I don't know that's possible. Two Rivers leaf has always been dear, and trade isn't what it was."

"She's sending you for tabac?" Perrin said, frowning. He supposed secrecy had gone down the well, but still. "I bought three casks, two villages back. Enough for everybody."

Gill shook his head firmly. "Not Two Rivers leaf, and your Lady says you like that above any other. The Gheal-danin leaf will do for your men. I'm to be your *shambayan*, she called it, and keep you and her supplied with what you need. Not much different from what I did running the Blessing, really." The similarity seemed to amuse him; his belly shook with quiet chuckles. "I have quite a list, though I can't say how much of it I'll find. Good wine, herbs, fruit, candles and lamp oil, oilcloth and wax, paper and ink, needles, pins, oh, all sorts of things. Tallanvor and Lamgwin and I are going, with some of your Lady's other retainers."

His Lady's other retainers. Tallanvor and Lamgwin were bringing out yet another chest for the women to sort

through. They had to pass by the squatting clump of young
fools, who never offered to lend a hand. In fact, the lay-
abouts ignored them completely.

"You keep an eye on that lot," Perrin cautioned. "If one
of them starts any trouble—if he even looks as if he will—
you have Lamgwin crack his head." And if it was one of
the women? They were just as likely, maybe more so. Perrin grunted. Faile's "retainers" were going to tie his belly
into permanent knots yet. Too bad she could not be satisfied
with the likes of Master Gill and Maighdin. "You didn't
mention Balwer. Has he decided to go on alone?" Just then,
a shift in the breeze brought him Balwer's scent, an alert
smell very much at odds with the fellow's almost desiccated
exterior.

Even for so reedy a man, Balwer made surprisingly little
noise on the dried leaves underfoot. In a sparrow-brown
coat, he offered a quick bow, and his tilted head added to
the image of a bird. "I am staying, my Lord," he said cautiously. Or maybe that was just his manner. "As your gracious Lady's secretary. And yours, if it pleases you." He
stepped closer, very nearly a hop. "I am well versed, my
Lord. I possess a good memory and write a good hand, and
my Lord can be assured that whatever he confides in me
will never pass my lips to another. The ability to keep secrets is a primary skill of a secretary. Don't you have pressing duties for our new mistress, Master Gill?"

Gill frowned at Balwer, opened his mouth, then closed it
with a snap. Spinning on his heel, he trotted away toward
the tent.

For a moment Balwer watched him go, head to one side,
lips pursed thoughtfully. "I can offer other services, as well,
my Lord," he said finally. "Knowledge. I overheard some
of my Lord's men speaking, and I understand that my Lord
may have had some . . . difficulties . . . with the Children of
the Light. A secretary learns many things. I know a surprising amount about the Children."

"With any luck I can avoid Whitecloaks," Perrin told
him. "Better if you knew where the Prophet is. Or the Seanchan." He did not expect any of that, of course, but Balwer
surprised him.

"I cannot be certain, of course, but I think the Seanchan
have not spread far beyond Amador as yet. Fact is difficult

to sift from rumor, my Lord, but I keep my ears open. Of course, they do seem to move with unexpected suddenness. A dangerous people, with large numbers of Taraboner soldiers. I believe from Master Gill that my Lord knows of them, but I observed them closely in Amador, and what I saw is at my Lord's disposal. As to the Prophet, there are as many rumors concerning him as the Seanchan, but I believe I can say reliably that he was recently at Abila, a largish town some forty leagues south of here." Balwer smiled thinly, a brief self-satisfied smile.

"How can you be so sure?" Perrin said slowly.

"As I said, my Lord, I keep my ears open. The Prophet reportedly closed a number of inns and taverns, and tore down those he considered too disreputable. Several were mentioned, and by chance, I happen to know there are inns of those names in Abila. I think there is little chance another town would have inns with the same names." He flashed another narrow smile. He certainly smelled pleased with himself.

Perrin scratched his beard thoughtfully. The man just happened to remember where some inns that Masema supposedly had torn down were located. And if Masema turned out not to be there after all, well, these days rumors sprouted like mushrooms after rain. Balwer sounded a man trying to build up his own importance. "Thank you, Master Balwer. I'll keep that to mind. If you hear any more, be sure to tell me." As he turned to go, the man caught his sleeve.

Balwer's skinny fingers leaped away immediately, as though burned, and he made one of those birdlike bows, dry-washing his hands. "Forgive me, my Lord. I hesitate to press, but do not take the Whitecloaks too lightly. Avoiding them is wise, but it may not be possible. They are much closer than the Seanchan. Eamon Valda, the new Lord Captain Commander, led most of their numbers toward northern Amadicia before Amador fell. He was hunting the Prophet, also, my Lord. Valda is a dangerous man, and Rhadam Asunawa, the Grand Inquisitor, makes Valda seem pleasant. And I fear neither has any love for your own Lord. Forgive me." He bowed again, hesitated, then went on smoothly. "If I may say so, my Lord's display of Manetheren's banner is inspired. My Lord will be more than a match for Valda and Asunawa, if he takes care."

Watching him bow himself away, Perrin thought he knew part of Balwer's story now. Clearly, he also had run afoul of the Whitecloaks. That could take no more than being on the same street with them, a frown at the wrong time, but it seemed Balwer had a grudge. A sharp mind, too, seeing right away about the Red Eagle. And a sharp tongue with Master Gill.

Gill was on his knees beside Maighdin, talking rapidly despite Lini's effort to hush him. Maighdin had turned to stare after Balwer as the fellow hurried through the trees toward the carts, but now and then her gaze swung to Perrin. The rest of them clustered close to her, peering now at Balwer, now at Perrin. If he had ever seen a group of people worried about what somebody else had said, it was they. But what were they worried he might have heard? Backbiting, probably. Tales of resentments and misdeeds, real or imagined. People cooped up together tended to start pecking at one another. If that was it, maybe he could put a stop to it before somebody drew blood. Tallanvor was fondling his sword hilt again! What did Faile intend to do with the fellow?

"Aram, I want you to go talk to Tallanvor and that lot. Tell them what Balwer said to me. Just slide it into the talk, but tell everything." That should soothe fears of talebearing. Faile said servants needed to be made to feel at home. "Make friends with them if you can, Aram. But if you decide to moon over one of the women, be sure it's Lini. The other two are taken."

The man had a smooth tongue for any pretty woman, but he managed to look surprised and offended, both. "As you wish, Lord Perrin," he muttered sulkily. "I'll catch you up quickly."

"I will be over with the Aiel."

Aram blinked. "Ah. Yes. Well, it might take a while, at that, if I'm to make friends with them. They don't look like they much want friends, to me." This from a fellow who stared suspiciously at anyone except Faile who came near Perrin and never smiled for anyone not wearing a skirt.

Nevertheless, he went over and squatted on his heels where he could speak to Gill and the others. Even from a distance their standoffishness was plain. They continued with their work, only now and then saying a word to Aram, and they looked at each other as often as at him. Skittish as green quail in summer, when the foxes were teaching the cubs to hunt. But at least they were talking.

Perrin wondered what mischief Aram had gotten up to with the Aiel—there did not seem to have been any time for it!—but he did not wonder long. Any serious trouble with Aiel usually meant someone dead, and not the Aiel. In truth, he was not so eager to meet the Wise Ones himself. He walked around the curve of the hill, but instead of climbing the slope, his feet carried him all the way to the Mayeners. He had stayed away from their camp as much as possible, too, and not simply because of Berelain. There were disadvantages to having too keen a nose.

Fortunately, a freshening breeze was carrying most of the stink away, though it did little for the heat. Sweat rolled down the faces of the mounted sentries in their red armor. At the sight of him, they sat up even more rigidly in their saddles, which was saying something. Where the Two Rivers men rode like fellows heading out to the fields, the Mayeners usually were statues on horseback. They could fight, though. The Light send there was no need.

Havien Nurelle came running, buttoning up his coat, before Perrin was well past the sentries. The dozen or so other officers followed at Nurelle's heels, all coated and some fastening the straps of their red breastplates. Two or three carried helmets with thin red plumes tucked under their arms. Most were years older than Nurelle, some twice his age, graying men with hard, scarred faces, but Nurelle's reward for helping to rescue Rand had been to be named Gallenne's second, his First Lieutenant, they called it.

"The First hasn't returned, yet, Lord Perrin," Nurelle said, making a bow mirrored by the others. A tall slender man, he did not look as young as he had before Dumai's Wells. There was an edge to his eyes, which had seen more blood than most veterans of twenty battles. But if his face was harder, there was still an eagerness to please in his scent. To Havien Nurelle, Perrin Aybara was a man who could fly or walk on water as he chose. "The morning patrols saw nothing, those that are back. I would have reported, otherwise."

"Of course," Perrin told him. "I . . . just wanted to look about a bit."

He simply meant to walk around until he could work up his

nerve to face the Wise Ones, but the young Mayener followed him with the rest of the officers, anxiously watching
for Lord Perrin to find some flaw in the Winged Guards,
wincing whenever they came on bare-chested men tossing dice on a blanket or some fellow snoring away with
the sun on the climb. He need not have bothered; to Perrin,
the camp looked laid out with a plumb line and level. Each
man had his blankets, and his saddle for a pillow, not more
than two paces from where his horse was tied to one of the
long ropes drooping between chest-high poles set upright
in the ground. A cook fire stood every twenty paces, with
lances stacked in steel-tipped cones between. The whole
made a sort of box around five peaked tents, one striped
gold-and-blue and larger than the other four combined. All
very different from the Two Rivers men's every-which-way
arrangement.

Perrin walked along briskly, trying not to look too much
a fool. He was not sure how much success he was having. He itched to stop and look over a horse or two—just
to be able to pick up a hoof without somebody practically
fainting—but mindful of what Aram had said, he kept his
hands to himself. Everyone seemed as startled as Nurelle at
his pace. Tough-eyed bannermen chivvied men to their feet
only to have Perrin stride by with a nod before they were all
upright. A puzzled murmur trailed in the air behind him,
and his ears caught a few comments about officers, lords in
particular, that he was just as glad Nurelle and the others
missed. Finally, he found himself on the verge of the camp,
staring up the brushy slope toward the Wise Ones' tents.
Only a few of the Maidens were visible among the scattered
trees up there, and some of the *gai'shain.*

"Lord Perrin," Nurelle said hesitantly. "The Aes Sedai. . . ." He stepped closer and lowered his voice to a hoarse
whisper. "I know they swore to the Lord Dragon, and. . . .
I've seen things, Lord Perrin. They do *camp chores*! Aes
Sedai! This morning, Masuri and Seonid came down to
fetch water! And yesterday, after you returned. . . . Yesterday, I thought I heard someone up there . . . crying out. It
couldn't have been one of the sisters, of course," he added
hurriedly, and laughed to show how ridiculous the idea was,
a very shaky laugh. "You. . . . You will see that everything
is . . . all right . . . with them?" He had ridden into forty

thousand Shaido leading two hundred lancers, but talking about this had him hunching his shoulders and shifting his feet. Of course, he had ridden into forty thousand Shaido because an Aes Sedai wanted him to.

"I'll do what I can," Perrin muttered. Maybe matters were worse than he had thought. Now he had to stop them getting worse still. If he could. He would rather have faced the Shaido again.

Nurelle nodded as though Perrin had promised all he asked and more. "That is well, then," he said, sounding relieved. Casting sideways glances at Perrin, he worked himself up to say something else, but apparently this was not so touchy as the Aes Sedai. "I heard that you let the Red Eagle stay."

Perrin very nearly jumped. Even for just around the hill, news had traveled fast. "It seemed the thing to do," he said slowly. Berelain would have to know the truth, yet if too many knew, that truth would spread from the next village they passed, the next farm. "This used to be part of Manetheren," he added, as if Nurelle did not know that perfectly well. Truth! He had gotten so he could bend truth like an Aes Sedai, and to men on his side. "Not the first time that flag's been raised around here, I'll warrant, but none of those fellows had the Dragon Reborn behind him." And if that did not set the necessary seeds, he did not know how to plow a furrow.

Abruptly he realized that what seemed every last one of the Winged Guards was watching him with their officers. No doubt wondering what he was saying, after all but running through that way. Even the lean balding old soldier Gallenne called his dogrobber had come out to stare, and Berelain's maids, a pair of plump plain-faced women garbed to match their mistress's tent. Perrin had hardly seen a thing, but he knew he had to give some sort of praise.

Raising his voice enough to carry, he said, "The Winged Guards will do Mayene proud if we ever face another Dumai's Wells." Those were the first words that came to mind, but he winced at saying them.

To his shock, shouting rose straightaway among the soldiers, cheering, "Perrin Goldeneyes!" and "Mayene for Goldeneyes!" and "Goldeneyes and Manetheren!" Men danced and capered, and some snatched lances from the

stacks to shake them so the red streamers waved in the
breeze. Grizzled bannermen watched them with arms
folded, nodding approval. Nurelle beamed, and not only
him. Officers with gray in their hair and scars on their faces
grinned like boys praised at their lessons. Light, he *was* the
only sane man left! He *prayed* never to see another battle!

Wondering whether this was going to cause trouble with
Berelain, he made his goodbyes with Nurelle and the others
and tramped up the slope through dead or dying brush,
none of it waist-high. Brown weeds crackled beneath his
boots. Shouting still filled the Mayener camp. Even after
she learned the truth, the First might not be pleased to have
her soldiers cheering him this way. Of course, that could
have good points. Maybe she would be angry enough to
stop pestering him.

Short of the crest, he paused, listening to the cheers finally fade away. No one was going to cheer him here. All of
the side flaps were down on the Wise Ones' low gray-brown
tents, closing them in. Only a few of the Maidens were in
sight, now. Squatting easily on their heels beneath a leatherleaf that still showed some green, they eyed him curiously.
Their hands moved quickly in that way they had of talking
among themselves with signs. After a moment Sulin rose,
shifting her heavy belt knife, and strode in his direction,
a tall, wiry woman with a pink scar across her sun-dark
cheek. She glanced back down the way he had come and
seemed relieved that he was alone, though it was often hard
to tell with Aiel.

"This is good, Perrin Aybara," she said quietly. "The
Wise Ones have not been pleased that you make them come
to you. Only a fool displeases Wise Ones, and I have not
taken you for a fool."

Perrin scrubbed at his beard. He had been keeping clear
of the Wise Ones—and the Aes Sedai—as much as possible, but he had had no intention of forcing them to come
to him. He just found their company uncomfortable. To
put it mildly. "Well, I need to see Edarra now," he told her.
"About the Aes Sedai."

"Perhaps I was mistaken after all," Sulin said dryly.
"But I will tell her." Turning, she paused. "Tell me some-
thing. Teryl Wynter and Furen Alharra are close to Seonid
Traighan—like first-brothers with a first-sister; she does

not like men as men—yet they offered to take her punishment for her. How could they shame her so?"

He opened his mouth, but nothing came out. A pair of *gai'shain* appeared from the reverse slope, each leading two of the Aiel's pack mules; the white-robed men passed within a few paces, heading down toward the stream. He could not be sure, but he thought both were Shaido. The pair kept their eyes meekly down, barely looking up enough to see where they were going. They had had every opportunity to run away, doing chores like that without anyone to watch. A peculiar people.

"I see you are shocked, too," Sulin said. "I had hoped you could explain. I will tell Edarra." As she started for the tents, she added over her shoulder, "You wetlanders are very strange, Perrin Aybara."

Perrin frowned after her, and when she vanished into one of the tents, he turned to frown at the two *gai'shain* leading the horses to water. *Wetlanders* were strange? Light! So Nurelle had been right in what he heard. It was beyond time to stick his nose into what was going on between the Wise Ones and the Aes Sedai. He should have before this. He wished he did not think it would be the same as sticking his nose into a hornet's nest.

It seemed to take a long time for Sulin to reappear, and she did little to help his mood when she did. Holding the tentflap for him, she flicked his belt knife contemptuously with a finger as he ducked through. "You should be better armed for this dance, Perrin Aybara," she said.

Inside, he was surprised to find all six Wise Ones sitting cross-legged on colorful tasseled cushions, their shawls tied around their waists and their skirts making carefully arranged fans across the layered rugs. He had hoped for just Edarra. None looked to be more than four or five years older than he, some no older at all, yet somehow they always made him feel as if he were facing the oldest members of the Women's Circle, the ones who had spent years learning to sniff out whatever you wanted to hide. Separating one woman's scent from another's was all but impossible, but he hardly needed to. Six sets of eyes latched on to him, from Janina's pale sky blue to Marline's purple twilight, not to mention Nevarin's sharp green. Every eye could have been a skewer.

Edarra brusquely motioned him to take a cushion himself, which he did with gratitude, though it put him facing
them all in a semicircle. Maybe Wise Ones had designed
these tents, to make men bend their necks if they wanted
to stand upright. Strangely, it was cooler in the dim interior, but he still felt like sweating. Maybe he could not pick
one from another, yet these women smelled like wolves
studying a tethered goat. A square-faced *gai'shain* who
was half again as big as he was knelt to offer a golden cup
of dark wine-punch on an elaborate silver tray. The Wise
Ones already held mismatched silver cups and goblets. Unsure what it meant that he was being offered gold—maybe
nothing, yet who could say, with Aiel?—Perrin took it cautiously. It gave off the scent of plums. The fellow bowed
meekly enough when Edarra clapped her hands, and bent
himself out of the tent backward, but the half-healed slash
down his hard face had to date from Dumai's Wells.

"Now that you are here," Edarra said as soon as the tentflap dropped behind the *gai'shain,* "we will explain again
why you must kill the man called Masema Dagar."

"We should not have to explain again," Delora put in. Her
hair and eyes were nearly the same shade as Maighdin's,
but no one would call her pinched face pretty. Her manner was pure ice. "This Masema Dagar is a danger to the
Car'a'carn. He must die."

"The dreamwalkers have told us, Perrin Aybara." Carelle
certainly was pretty, and though her fiery hair and piercing
eyes made her look as though she had a temper, she was
always mild. For a Wise One. And certainly not soft. "They
have read the dream. The man must die."

Perrin took a swallow of plum punch to gain a moment.
Somehow, the punch was cool. It was always the same
with them. Rand had not mentioned any warning from the
dreamwalkers. The first time, Perrin had mentioned that.
Only the once; they had thought he was casting doubt on
their word, and even Carelle had gone hot-eyed. Not that
Perrin thought they would lie. Not exactly. He had not
caught them in one, anyway. But what they wanted for the
future and what Rand wanted—what he himself wanted,
for that matter—might be very different things. Maybe it
was Rand who was keeping secrets. "If you could just give
me some idea what this danger is," he said, finally. "The

Light knows, Masema's a madman, but he *supports* Rand.
A fine thing, if I go around killing people on our side. That
will certainly convince people to join Rand."

Sarcasm was lost on them. They looked at him, unblinking. "The man must die," Edarra said at last. "It is enough
that three dreamwalkers have said so, and six Wise Ones
tell you." The same as always. Maybe they did not know
any more than that. And maybe he should get on with why
he had come.

"I want to talk about Seonid and Masuri," he said, and
six faces turned to frost. Light, these women could stare
down a stone! Setting the winecup beside him, he leaned
toward them stubbornly. "I'm supposed to show people Aes
Sedai sworn to Rand." He was supposed to show Masema,
actually, but this did not seem a good time to mention that.
"They aren't going to be very cooperative if you lot beat
them! Light! They're Aes Sedai! Instead of making them
haul water, why don't you learn from them? They must
know all sorts of things you don't." Too late, he bit his
tongue. The Aiel women did not take offense, though; not
that it showed, anyway.

"They know some things we do not," Delora told him
firmly, "and we know some they do not." As firmly as a
spearpoint in the ribs.

"We learn what there is to learn, Perrin Aybara," Marline
said calmly, combing nearly black hair with her fingers. She
was one of the few Aiel he had seen with such dark hair,
and she often toyed with it. "And we teach what there is to
teach."

"In any event," Janina said, "it is none of your affair.
Men do not interfere between Wise Ones and apprentices."
She shook her head over his foolishness.

"You may stop listening outside and come in, Seonid
Traighan," Edarra said suddenly. Perrin blinked in surprise,
but none of the women batted an eye.

There was a moment of silence, then the tentflap twitched
aside, and Seonid ducked inside, kneeling quickly on the
rugs. That vaunted Aes Sedai serenity was shattered in her.
Her mouth was a thin line, her eyes tight, her face red. She
smelled of anger, frustration, and a dozen more emotions all
whirling about so quickly that Perrin could barely separate
any out. "May I speak to him?" she asked in a stiff voice.

"If you take care what you say," Edarra told her. Sipping her wine, the Wise One watched over the rim of her cup. A teacher watching a pupil? A hawk watching a mouse? Perrin could not be sure. Except that Edarra was very sure of *her* place, whatever the pairing. So was Seonid. But that did not carry over to him.

She twisted around to face him on her knees, back going straight, eyes heated. Anger raged in the smell of her. "Whatever you know," she said angrily, "whatever you *think* you know, you will forget!" No, there was not a shred of serenity left in her. "Whatever is between the Wise Ones and us is for us alone! You will stand aside, avert your eyes, and keep your mouth closed!"

Amazed, Perrin raked his fingers through his hair. "Light, you're upset because I know you got a switching?" he said incredulously. Well, he would have been, too, but not alongside the rest. "Don't you know these women would as soon cut your throat as look at you? Slit your throat and leave you by the side of the road! Well, I promised myself I wouldn't let that happen! I don't like you, but I promised to protect you from the Wise Ones, or the Asha'man, or Rand himself, so come down off that high horse!" Realizing that he was shouting, he drew a deep, embarrassed breath and settled back on his cushion, snatched up his winecup and took a long drink.

Seonid went stiffer by the word with indignation, and her lip curled well before he finished. "You promised?" she sneered. "You think Aes Sedai need *your* protection? You—?"

"Enough," Edarra said quietly, and Seonid's jaw snapped shut, though her hands made white-knuckled fists clutching her skirts.

"What makes you think we would kill her, Perrin Aybara?" Janina asked curiously. Aiel seldom showed much on their faces, but the others frowned at him or looked with open incredulity.

"I know how you feel," he replied slowly. "I've known since I saw you with the sisters after Dumai's Wells." He was not about to explain that he had smelled their hatred, their contempt, every time a Wise One looked at an Aes Sedai back then. He did not smell it now, but no one could maintain that level of fury for long without bursting. That did not mean it was gone, only that it had sunk deep, maybe into the bone.

Delora snorted, a sound like linen ripping. "First you say they must be coddled because you need them, and now because they are Aes Sedai and you have promised to protect them. Which is truth, Perrin Aybara?"

"Both." Perrin met Delora's hard gaze for a long moment, then eyed each of the others in turn. "Both are true, and I mean both."

The Wise Ones exchanged glances, the sort where every flicker of an eyelid held a hundred words and no man could make out a one. Finally, in a shifting of necklaces and readjusting of tied shawls, they appeared to reach agreement.

"We do not kill apprentices, Perrin Aybara," Nevarin said. She sounded shocked at the idea. "When Rand al'Thor asked us to apprentice them, perhaps he thought it was just to make them obey us, but we do not speak empty words. They *are* apprentices, now."

"They will remain so until five Wise Ones agree they are ready to be more," Marline added, sweeping her long hair over her shoulder. "And they are treated no differently than any others."

Edarra nodded over her winecup. "Tell him the advice you would give him concerning Masema Dagar, Seonid Traighan," she said.

The kneeling woman had practically writhed during Nevarin and Marline's short speeches, gripping her skirt until Perrin thought the silk might rip, but she wasted no time complying with Edarra's instructions. "The Wise Ones are right, whatever their reasons. I do not say this because they wish it." She drew herself up again, smoothing her features with a visible effort. A touch of heat still flared in her voice, though. "I saw the work of so-called Dragonsworn before I ever met Rand al'Thor. Death and destruction, to no purpose. Even a faithful dog must be put down if it begins to foam at the mouth."

"Blood and ashes!" Perrin grumbled. "How can I even let you in sight of the man after that? You swore fealty to Rand; you know that isn't what he wants! What about that 'thousands will die if you fail'?" Light, if Masuri felt the same, then he had to put up with Aes Sedai and Wise Ones for nothing! No, worse. He would have to guard Masema from them!

"Masuri knows Masema for rabid as well as I," Seonid replied when he put the question to her. All of her serenity had returned. She regarded him with a cool, unreadable face. Her scent was sharply alert. Intent. As if he needed his nose, with her eyes fixed on his, big and dark and bottomless. "I swore to serve the Dragon Reborn, and the best service I can give him now is to keep this animal from him. Bad enough that rulers know Masema supports him; worse if they see him embrace the man. And thousands *will* die if you fail—to get close enough to Masema to kill him."

Perrin thought his head would spin. Again an Aes Sedai whirled words about like a top, made it seem she had said black when she meant white. Then the Wise Ones added their bit.

"Masuri Sokawa," Nevarin said calmly, "believes the rabid dog can be leashed and bound so he may be used safely." For an instant, Seonid looked as surprised as Perrin felt, but she recovered quickly. Outside, she did; her scent was suddenly wary, as if she sensed a trap where she had not expected one.

"She also wishes to fit you for a halter, Perrin Aybara," Carelle added, even more casually. "She thinks you must be bound also, to make you safe." Nothing on her freckled face told whether she agreed.

Edarra raised a hand toward Seonid. "You may go, now. You will not listen further, but you may ask Gharadin again to let you Heal the wound on his face. Remember, if he still refuses, you must accept it. He is *gai'shain*, not one of your wetlander servants." She invested that last word with depths of scorn.

Seonid stared icy augers at Perrin. She looked at the Wise Ones, her lips trembling on the brink of speech. In the end, though, all she could do was go with as good a grace as she could muster. Outwardly, that was considerable, an Aes Sedai being Aes Sedai fit to shame a queen. But the scent she trailed behind her was frustration sharp enough to cut.

As soon as she was gone, the six Wise Ones focused on Perrin again.

"Now," Edarra said, "you can explain to us why you would put a rabid animal next to the *Car'a'carn*."

"Only a fool obeys another's command to push him over a cliff," Nevarin said.

"You will not listen to us," Janina said, "so we will listen to you. Speak, Perrin Aybara."

Perrin considered making a break for the doorflaps. But if he did, he would leave behind one Aes Sedai who might possibly be of some doubtful help, and another, along with six Wise Ones, who were all set to ruin everything he had come to do. He put his winecup down again, and settled his hands on his knees. He needed a clear head if he was to show these women he was no tethered goat.

CHAPTER

10

Changes

When Perrin left the Wise Ones' tent, he considered removing his coat to see whether his hide was still attached and whole. Not a tethered goat, maybe, but a stag with six she-wolves on his heels, and he was unsure what fast feet had gained him. For certain, none of the Wise Ones had changed her mind, and their promises not to take any action on their own had been vague at best. About the Aes Sedai, there had been no promises, even foggy ones.

He looked for either of the sisters, and found Masuri. A narrow rope had been tied between two trees and a fringed red-and-green rug draped over it. The slender Brown was flailing away with a bent-wood beater, raising thin clouds of dust motes that floated glittering in the midmorning sun. Her Warder, a compact man with dark receding hair, sat on a fallen tree trunk nearby, watching her glumly. Rovair Kirklin normally had a ready grin, but it was buried deep today. Masuri caught sight of Perrin, and with barely a pause in her rug-beating shot him a look of such frozen malevolence that he sighed. And she was the one who thought as he did. As close to it as he was likely to find, anyway. A red-tailed hawk passed overhead, riding rising currents of hot air from hill to hill without flapping its outstretched wings. It would be very nice to soar away from all this. The iron in front of him, not dreams of silver.

Nodding to Sulin and the Maidens, who might have taken root under that leatherleaf, Perrin turned to go, and stopped. Two men were climbing the hill, one an Aiel in the grays and browns and greens of the *cadin'sor*, his cased bow on his back, a bristling quiver at his belt, and his spears and round hide buckler in hand. Gaul was a friend, and the only man among the Aiel who did not wear white. His companion, a head shorter in a broad-brimmed hat and coat and breeches of a plain dull green, was no Aiel. He had a full quiver at his belt, too, and a knife even longer and heavier than the Aielman's, but he carried his bow, much shorter than a Two Rivers longbow though longer than the horn bows of the Aiel. Despite his clothes, he did not have the look of a farmer, or a city man either. Perhaps it was the graying hair tied at the nape of his neck and hanging to his waist, the beard fanning across his chest, or perhaps just the way he moved, much like the man at his side, slipping around the brush on the hill so that you were sure no twig snapped in his passing, no weeds broke under his foot. Perrin had not seen him in what seemed a very long time.

Reaching the hilltop, Elyas Machera regarded Perrin, golden eyes shining faintly in the shadow of his hat brim. His eyes had been that way years before Perrin's; Elyas had introduced Perrin to the wolves. He had been dressed in hides, then. "Good to see you again, boy," he said quietly. Sweat glistened on his face, but little more than on Gaul's. "You give away that axe, finally? I didn't think you'd ever stop hating it."

"I still do," Perrin said just as quietly. A long time ago the onetime Warder had told him to keep the axe until he stopped hating to use it. Light, but he still hated it! And he had added new reasons, now. "What are you doing in this part of the world, Elyas? Where did Gaul find you?"

"He found me," Gaul said. "I did not know he was behind me until he coughed." He spoke loudly enough to be heard by the Maidens, and the sudden stillness among them was solid as a touch.

Perrin expected at least a few cutting comments—Aiel humor could near draw blood, and the Maidens seized any chance to dig at the green-eyed man—but instead, some of the women took up spears and bucklers to rattle them together in approbation. Gaul nodded approval.

Elyas grunted ambiguously and tugged his hat down, yet he smelled pleased. The Aiel did not approve of much this side of the Dragonwall. "I like to keep moving," he told Perrin, "and I just happened to be in Ghealdan when some mutual friends told me you were traveling with this parade." He did not name the mutual friends; it was unwise to speak openly about talking to wolves. "Told me a lot of things. Told me they smell a change coming. They don't know what. Maybe you do. I hear you've been running with the Dragon Reborn."

"I don't know," Perrin said slowly. A change? He had not thought to ask the wolves anything more than where large groups of men were, so he could go around them. Even here in Ghealdan, sometimes he felt blame among them for the wolves dead at Dumai's Wells. What kind of change? "Rand is surely changing things, but I couldn't say what they mean. Light, the whole world is turning somersaults, and never mind him."

"All things change," Gaul said dismissively. "Until we wake, the dream drifts on the wind." For a moment he studied Perrin and Elyas, comparing their eyes, Perrin was sure. He said nothing about them, though; the Aiel seemed to take golden eyes as just one more peculiarity among wetlanders. "I will leave you two to talk alone. Friends long separated need to talk by themselves. Sulin, are Chiad and Bain about? I saw them hunting yesterday, and thought I might show them how to draw a bow before one of them shoots herself."

"I was surprised to see you come back today," the white-haired woman replied. "They went out to set snares for rabbits." Laughter rippled through the Maidens, and fingers flickered rapidly in handtalk.

Sighing, Gaul rolled his eyes ostentatiously. "In that case, I think I must go cut them loose." Almost as many Maidens laughed at that, including Sulin. "May you find shade this day," he told Perrin, a casual farewell between friends, but he clasped forearms formally with Elyas and said, "My honor is yours, Elyas Machera."

"Odd fellow," Elyas murmured, watching Gaul lope back down the hill. "When I coughed, he turned around ready to kill me, I think, then he just started laughing instead. You have any objections to going somewhere else? I don't know the sister who's trying to murder that rug, but I don't like taking chances with Aes Sedai." His eyes narrowed. "Gaul says there are three with you. You don't expect to be meeting up with any more, do you?"

"I hope not," Perrin replied. Masuri was glancing their way between slashes with the beater; she would learn about Elyas' eyes soon enough and start trying to ferret out what else linked him to Perrin. "Come on; it's time I was back in my own camp anyway. Are you worried about meeting an Aes Sedai who knows you?" Elyas' days as a Warder had ended when it was learned he could talk to wolves. Some sisters thought it a mark of the Dark One, and he had had to kill other Warders to get away.

The older man waited until they were a dozen paces from the tents before he replied, and even then, he spoke quietly, as though he suspected someone behind them might have ears as good as theirs. "One who knows my name will be bad enough. Warders don't run off often, boy. Most Aes Sedai will free a man who really wants to go—most will—and anyway, she can track you down however far you run if she decides to hunt. But any sister who finds a renegade will spend her idle moments making him wish he'd never been born." He shivered slightly. His smell was not fear, but anticipation of pain. "Then she'll turn him over to his own Aes Sedai to drive the lesson home. A man's never quite the same after that." At the edge of the slope, he looked back. Masuri did seem to be trying to kill the carpet, focusing all her rage on attempting to beat a hole through it. Elyas shivered again, though. "Worse thing would be to run into Rina. I'd rather be caught in a forest fire with both legs broken."

"Rina's your Aes Sedai? But how could you run into her? The bond lets you know where she is." That nudged something in Perrin's memory, but whatever it was melted away at Elyas' reply.

"A fair number can fuzz the bond, in a manner of speaking. Maybe they all can. You don't know much more than she's still alive, and I know that anyway, because I haven't gone crazy." Elyas saw the question on his face and barked a laugh. "Light, man, a sister's flesh-and-blood, too. Most are. Think about it. Would you want somebody inside your head while you cuddled up with a likely wench? Sorry; I forgot you were married, now. No offense meant. I was surprised to hear you'd married a Saldaean, though."

"Surprised?" Perrin had never considered *that* about the Warder bond. Light! For that matter, he had never really thought about Aes Sedai that way. It seemed about as possible as . . . as a man talking to wolves. "Why surprised?" They started down through the trees on this side of the hill, not hurrying and making little noise. Perrin had always been a good hunter, accustomed to the forests, and Elyas hardly disturbed the leaves underfoot, gliding smoothly through the undergrowth without shifting a branch. He might have slung his bow on his back now, but he still carried it ready. Elyas was a wary man, especially around people.

"Why, because you're a quiet sort, and I thought you'd marry somebody quiet, too. Well, you know by now Saldaeans aren't quiet. Except with strangers and outsiders. Set the sun on fire one minute, and the next, it's all blown away and forgotten. Make Arafellin look stolid and Domani downright dull." Elyas grinned suddenly. "I lived a year with a Saldaean, once, and Merya shouted my ears off five days in the week, and maybe heaved the dishes at my head, too. Every time I thought about leaving, though, she'd want to make up, and I never seemed to get to the door. In the end, she left me. Said I was too restrained for her taste." His rasping laugh was reminiscent, but he rubbed at a faint, age-faded scar along his jaw reminiscently, too. It looked to have been made by a knife.

"Faile's not like that." It sounded like being married to Nynaeve! Nynaeve with sore teeth! "I don't mean she doesn't get angry now and then," he admitted reluctantly, "but she doesn't shout and throw things." Well, she did not shout very often, and instead of flaring hot and vanishing, her anger started hot and dragged on till it turned cold.

Elyas glanced at him sideways. "If I ever smelled a man trying to dodge hail. . . . You've been giving her soft words all the time, haven't you? Mild as milk-water and never lay your ears back? Never raise your voice to her?"

"Of course not!" Perrin protested. "I love her! Why would I shout at her?"

Elyas began muttering under his breath, though Perrin could hear every word, of course. "Burn me, a man wants to sit on a red adder, it's his affair. Not my business if a man wants to warm his hands when the roof's on fire. It's his life. Will he thank me? No, he bloody well won't!"

"What are you going on about?" Perrin demanded. Catching Elyas' arm, he pulled him to a stop beneath a winterberry tree, its prickly leaves still mostly green. Little else nearby was, except for some struggling creepers. They had come less than halfway down the hill. "Faile isn't a red adder *or* a roof on fire! Wait until you meet her before you start talking like you know her."

Irritably, Elyas raked fingers through his long beard. "I know Saldaeans, boy. That year wasn't the only time I've been there. I've only ever met about five Saldaean women I'd call meek, or even mild-mannered. No, she isn't an adder; what she is is a leopard, I'll wager. Don't growl, burn you! I'll bet my boots she'd smile to hear me say it!"

Perrin opened his mouth angrily, then closed it again. He had not realized he was growling deep in his throat. Faile *would* smile at being called a leopard. "You can't be saying she wants me to shout at her, Elyas."

"Yes, I am. Most likely, anyway. Maybe she's the sixth. Maybe. Just hear me out. Most women, you raise your voice, and they go bulge-eyed or ice, and next thing you know, you're arguing about you being angry, never mind what put the ember down your back in the first place. Swallow your tongue with a Saldaean, though, and to her, you're saying she isn't strong enough to stand up to you. Insult her like that, and you're lucky she doesn't feed you your own gizzard for breakfast. She's no Far Madding wench, to expect a man to sit where she points and jump when she snaps her fingers. She's a leopard, and she expects her husband to be a leopard, too. Light! I don't know what I'm doing. Giving a man advice about his wife is a good way to get your innards spilled."

It was Elyas' turn to growl. He jerked his hat straight unnecessarily and looked around the slope frowning, as though considering whether to vanish back into the forests, then poked a finger at Perrin. "Look here. I always knew you were more than a stray, and putting what the wolves told me together with you just happening to be heading toward this Prophet fellow, I thought maybe you could use a friend to watch your back. Of course, the wolves didn't mention you were *leading* those pretty Mayener lancers. Neither did Gaul, till we saw them. If you'd like me to stay, I will. If not, there's plenty of the world I haven't seen yet."

"I can always use another friend, Elyas." *Could* Faile really *want* him to shout? He had always known he might hurt somebody if he was not careful, and he always tried to keep a tight rein on his temper. Words could hurt as hard as fists, the wrong words, words you never meant, let loose in a temper. It had to be impossible. It just stood to reason. No woman would stand for that, from her husband or any man.

A bluefinch's call brought Perrin's head up, ears pricking. It was just at the edge of hearing even for him, but a moment later the trill was repeated closer, then again, nearer still. Elyas cocked an eyebrow at him; he would know the call of a Borderland bird. Perrin had learned it from some Shienarans, Masema among them, and taught the Two Rivers men.

"We have visitors coming," he told Elyas.

They came quickly, four riders at a fast canter, arriving before he and Elyas reached the bottom of the hill. Berelain led the way, splashing across the stream with Annoura and Gallenne close behind and a woman in a pale, hooded dust-cloak at her side. They swept right by the Mayener camp without a glance, not drawing rein until they were in front of the red-and-white striped tent. Some of the Cairhienin servants rushed to take bridles and hold stirrups, and Berelain and her companions were inside before the dust of their arrival settled.

All in all, the arrival created quite a stir. A buzz rose among the Two Rivers men that Perrin could only call anticipatory. The inevitable gathering of Faile's young fools scratched their heads and stared at the tent, chattering excitedly among themselves. Grady and Neald watched the tent through the trees, too, now and then leaning together to talk though nobody was close enough to hear anything they said.

"Looks like your visitors are more than casual," Elyas said quietly. "Watch Gallenne; he could be trouble."

"You know him, Elyas? I'd like you to stay, but if you think he might tell one of the sisters who you are. . . ." Perrin shrugged in resignation. "I might be able to stop Seonid and Masuri"—he thought he could—"but I think Annoura will do whatever she wants." And what did *she* really think about Masema?

"Oh, Bertain Gallenne doesn't know the likes of Elyas Machera," Elyas replied with a wry grin. "'More fools know Jak Fool than Jak Fool knows.' I know him, though.

He won't go against you or behind your back, but Berelain
has the brains between them. She's kept Tear out of Mayene by playing the Tairens against the Illianers since she
was sixteen. Berelain knows how to maneuver; all Gallenne
knows is attack. He's good at it, but he never sees anything
else, and sometimes he doesn't stop to think."

"I'd figured that out about both of them," Perrin muttered. At least Berelain had brought a messenger from Alliandre. She would not have come rushing in that way with
a new maid. The only question was why Alliandre's reply
needed a messenger. "I had best find out whether the news
is good, Elyas. Later, we'll talk about what lies south. And
you can meet Faile," he added before turning away.

"The Pit of Doom lies south," the other man called after him, "or as close to it as I expected to see below the
Blight." Perrin imagined he heard that faint thunder in the
west again. Now, that would be a pleasant change.

In the tent, Breane was carrying a silver tray about with
a bowl of rose-scented water and cloths for washing faces
and hands, curtsying stiffly as she presented it. With even
stiffer curtsies, Maighdin was offering a tray holding cups
of wine-punch—made with the last of the dried blueber-
ries, by the smell—while Lini folded the newcomer's dust-
cloak. There seemed something odd in the way Faile and
Berelain stood to either side of the new woman, and Annoura hovered behind them, all focused on her. Somewhere
in her middle years, with a cap of green net gathering dark
hair that fell almost to her waist, she might have been pretty
if her nose had not been so long. And if she had not carried
it so high. Shorter than Faile or Berelain either one, she still
managed to look down that nose at Perrin, coolly examining him from hair to boots. She did not blink at sight of his
eyes, although nearly everyone did.

"Majesty," Berelain pronounced in a formal voice as
soon as Perrin entered, "may I present Lord Perrin Aybara
of the Two Rivers, in Andor, the personal friend and emissary of the Dragon Reborn." The long-nosed woman nodded carefully, coolly, and Berelain went on with scarcely a
pause. "Lord Aybara, give greetings and welcome to Alliandre Maritha Kigarin, Queen of Ghealdan, Blessed of the
Light, Defender of Garen's Wall, who is pleased to receive you
in person." Gallenne, standing near the tent wall, adjusted

his eyepatch and raised his winecup to Perrin with a smile of triumph.

For some reason Faile shot Berelain a hard look. Perrin's mouth nearly dropped open. Alliandre herself? He wondered whether he should kneel, then settled for a bow after too long a pause. Light! He had no notion how to deal with a queen. Especially one who turned up out of the blue with no escort, without a jewel in sight. Her dark green riding dress was plain wool, lacking a single stitch of embroidery.

"After the recent news," Alliandre said, "I thought I should come to you, Lord Aybara." Her voice was calm, her face smooth, her eyes aloof. And observant, or he was a Taren Ferry man. Best to step warily till he knew how the path lay. "You may not have heard," she continued, "but four days ago Illian fell to the Dragon Reborn, blessed be his name in the Light. He has taken the Laurel Crown, though I understand it is now called the Crown of Swords."

Faile, taking a cup from Maighdin's tray, whispered under her breath, "And seven days gone, the Seanchan took Ebou Dar." Even Maighdin did not notice.

If Perrin had not already taken hold of himself, he truly would have gaped. Why did Faile tell him this way instead of waiting for it to come from the woman who must have told her? In a voice that everyone could hear, he repeated her words. A hard voice, but that was the only way to keep it from shaking. Ebou Dar, too? Light! And seven days ago? The day Grady and the others had seen the One Power in the sky. Coincidence, maybe. But would he *rather* it had been the Forsaken?

Annoura frowned over her cup, pursing her lips, before he finished speaking, and Berelain gave him a startled look that vanished quickly. They knew he had not known about Ebou Dar when they rode into Bethal.

Alliandre merely nodded, every bit as self-possessed as the Gray. "You seem remarkably well informed," she said, coming closer to him. "I doubt the first rumors are reaching Jehannah with the river trade, yet. I myself learned of it only a few days ago. Several of the merchants keep me abreast of events. I believe," she added dryly, "that they hope I can intercede for them with the Prophet of the Lord Dragon, if such becomes necessary."

At last he could pick out her scent, and his opinion of her

changed, though not for the worse. Outwardly, the Queen was all cool reserve, but uncertainty shot through with fear filled the smell of her. He did not believe he could have held his face so calm had he felt that.

"Always best to know as much as you can," he told her, half distracted. *Burn me*, he thought, *I have to let Rand know about* this*!*

"In Saldaea we find merchants useful for information, too," Faile said. Implying that was how Perrin knew about Ebou Dar. "They seem to learn what happened a thousand miles off weeks before the rumors begin."

She did not look at Perrin, but he knew she spoke to him as much as Alliandre. Rand knew, she was saying. And anyway, there *was* no way to get word to him in secret. *Could* Faile really want him to . . . ? No, it was unthinkable. Blinking, he realized he had missed something Alliandre had said. "Your pardon, Alliandre," he said politely. "I was thinking about Rand—the Dragon Reborn." Of course it was unthinkable!

Everyone stared at him, even Lini and Maighdin and Breane. Annoura's eyes had gone wide, and Gallenne's mouth hung open. Then it hit him. He had just called the Queen by name. He took a cup from Maighdin's tray, and she rose from her curtsy so quickly that she nearly knocked it from his hand. Waving her away absently, he wiped his damp hand on his coat. He had to concentrate here, not let his mind wander in nine directions. No matter what Elyas thought he knew, Faile would never. . . . No! Concentrate!

Alliandre recovered her equilibrium quickly. In truth, she had appeared the least surprised of anyone, and her scent never wavered. "I was saying that coming to you in secret seemed the wisest course, Lord Aybara," she said in that cool voice. "Lord Telabin believes I am keeping private in his gardens, which I left by a seldom-used gate. Passing out of the city, I was Annoura Sedai's maid." Brushing fingertips across one skirt of her riding dress, she gave a small laugh. Even that about her was cool, so at odds with what his nose told him. "A number of my own soldiers saw me, but with the hood of my cloak pulled up, none knew me."

"Times being what they are, that probably was wisest," Perrin said carefully. "But you will have to come into the open sooner or later. One way or another." Polite and to the point, that was the thing. A queen would not want to waste time with a man who blathered. And he did not want to disappoint Faile by acting the hayfoot again. "Why come at all? All you had to do was send a letter, or just tell Berelain your answer. Will you declare for Rand or not? Either way, have no fear about getting back to Bethal safely." A good point, that. Whatever else frightened her, being here alone must.

Faile was watching him, pretending not to, sipping her punch and directing her smiles at Alliandre, but he caught the quick flickers of her eyes in his direction. Berelain made no pretense, watching quite openly, eyes slightly narrowed and never leaving his face. Annoura was just as intent, just as thoughtful. Did they *all* believe he was going to trip over his own tongue again?

Instead of answering the important question, Alliandre said, "The First told me a great deal about you, Lord Aybara, and about the Lord Dragon Reborn, blessed be his name in the Light." That last sounded by rote, an addition she no longer had to think about. "I cannot see him before I make my decision, so I wished to see you, to take a measure of you. It's possible to tell much about a man by those he chooses to speak for him." Tilting her face down toward the cup in her hands, she peered at him through her lashes. From Berelain, that would have been flirtatious, but Alliandre was cautiously watching a wolf sure as he was standing in front of her. "I also saw your banners," she said quietly. "The First did not mention them."

Perrin scowled before he could stop himself. Berelain had told her a great deal about him? What had she said? "The banners are meant to be seen." Anger put a roughness in his voice that required some effort to force down. Now, Berelain was a woman who *needed* shouting at. "Believe me, there are no plans to set up Manetheren again." There; his tone was as cool as Alliandre's. "What is your decision? Rand can have ten thousand soldiers, a hundred thousand, here in the blink of an eye, or near enough." And he might have to. The Seanchan in Amador *and* Ebou Dar? Light, how many were they?

Alliandre sipped delicately at her wine-punch before speaking, and again she dodged the question. "There are a thousand rumors, as you must know, and even the wildest is believable when the Dragon is Reborn, strangers appear claiming to be Artur Hawkwing's armies returned, and the Tower itself is broken by rebellion."

"A matter for Aes Sedai," Annoùra said sharply. "It concerns no one else." Berelain flashed an exasperated look at her, which she affected not to notice.

Alliandre flinched and turned her shoulder to the sister. Queen or not, no one wanted to hear that tone from an Aes Sedai. "The world is turned upside down, Lord Aybara. Why, I've even had reports of Aiel sacking a village right here in Ghealdan." Abruptly Perrin realized there was more here than anxiety over offending Aes Sedai. Alliandre watched him, waiting. But for what? Reassurance?

"The only Aiel in Ghealdan are with me," he told her. "The Seanchan may be descendants of Artur Hawkwing's army, but Hawkwing is a thousand years dead. Rand dealt with them once already, and he will again." He remembered Falme as clearly as Dumai's Wells, though he had tried forgetting. Surely there had not been enough of them there to take Amador *and* Ebou Dar, even with their *damane*. Balwer claimed they had Taraboner soldiers, too. "And it might cheer you to hear that those rebel Aes Sedai support Rand. They will, soon, at least." That was what Rand said, a handful of Aes Sedai with nowhere to go except to him. Perrin was not so sure. Rumor in Ghealdan put an army with those sisters. Of course, the same rumors counted more Aes Sedai in that handful than there were in the world, but still. . . . Light, he wished someone would reassure him! "Why don't we sit," he said. "I'll answer any questions you have, to help you make your decision, but we might as well be comfortable." Drawing one of the folding chairs to him, he remembered at the last instant not to just drop into it, but it creaked under him just the same.

Lini and the other two servants rushed about, pulling chairs into a circle with his, but none of the other women moved toward them. Alliandre stood looking at him, and the rest looked at her. Except for Gallenne, who merely poured himself another cup of punch from the silver pitcher.

It came to Perrin that Faile had not opened her mouth since speaking of the merchants. He was as grateful for Berelain's silence as he was that she had not decided to flutter her lashes at him in front of the Queen, but he could have used some help from Faile right then. A little advice. Light, she knew ten times what he did about what he should say and do here.

Wondering whether he should stand with the others, he set his wine-punch on one of the small tables and asked her to speak to Alliandre. "If anyone can make her see the right way to go, you can," he said. Faile gave him a pleased smile, but held her tongue.

Abruptly Alliandre put out her cup to one side without looking, as if expecting a tray to be there. One was, barely in time to catch the cup, and Maighdin, who held it, muttered something Perrin hoped Faile had not heard. Faile was death on servants using that sort of language. He started to rise as Alliandre approached him, but to his shock, she knelt gracefully in front of him, catching his hands with hers. Before he knew what she was doing, she twisted so her hands were back-to-back between his palms. She clung so hard her hands must have hurt; for sure, he was not certain he could loose himself without hurting her.

"Under the Light," she said firmly, looking up at him, "I, Alliandre Maritha Kigarin, pledge my fealty and service to Lord Perrin Aybara of the Two Rivers, now and for all time, save that he chooses to release me of his own will. My lands and throne are his, and I yield them to his hand. So I do swear."

For an instant there was a silence broken only by Gallenne's gasp and the muted thud of his winecup hitting the rug.

Then Perrin heard Faile, once more whispering so softly no one next to her could have made out her words. "Under the Light, I do accept your pledge and will defend and protect you and yours through battle's wrack and winter's blast and all that time may bring. The lands and throne of Ghealdan, I give to you as my faithful vassal. Under the Light, I do accept. . . ." That must have been the Saldaean manner of accepting. Thank the Light she was too busy concentrating on him to see Berelain nodding at him furiously, urging the same. The pair of them looked almost as if they had expected this! Annoura, though, with her mouth hanging open, appeared as stunned as he, like a fish who had just seen the water vanish.

"Why?" he asked gently, ignoring Faile's frustrated

hiss and Berelain's exasperated grunt alike. *Burn me,* he thought, *I'm a bloody blacksmith!* Nobody swore fealty to blacksmiths. Queens did not swear fealty to anyone! "I've been told I'm *ta'veren*; you might want to reconsider this in an hour."

"I hope you are *ta'veren*, my Lord." Alliandre laughed, but not in amusement, and gripped his hands even more tightly, as though fearful he might pull away. "With all my heart, I hope it. I fear nothing less will save Ghealdan. I all but reached this decision as soon as the First told me why you are here, and meeting you only confirmed me in it. Ghealdan needs protection I cannot give, so duty demands I find it. You can give it, my Lord, you and the Lord Dragon Reborn, blessed be his name in the Light. In truth, I would swear directly to him if he were here, but you are his man. Swearing to you, I also swear to him." Drawing a deep breath, she forced out another word. "Please." She smelled desperate, now, and her eyes shone with fear.

Still, he hesitated. This was everything Rand could want and more, but Perrin Aybara was just a blacksmith. He was! Could he still tell himself that if he did this thing? Alliandre stared up at him pleadingly. Did *ta'veren* work on themselves, he wondered. "Under the Light, I, Perrin Aybara, accept your pledge. . . ." His throat was dry by the time he finished the words Faile had whispered. Too late to stop and think now.

With a gasp of relief, Alliandre kissed his hands. Perrin did not think he had ever been so embarrassed in his life. Standing hurriedly, he drew her to her feet. And realized he did not know what to do next. A proudly beaming Faile whispered no further hints. Berelain smiled, too, relief so strong on her face she might have just been pulled from a fire.

He was sure Annoura would speak—Aes Sedai always had plenty to say, especially when it gave an opportunity to take charge—but the Gray sister was holding out a winecup for Maighdin to refill. Annoura watched him with an unreadable expression, and for that matter, so did Maighdin, so much so that she continued tilting her pitcher until punch slopped over onto the Aes Sedai's wrist. At which Annoura gave a start, staring at the cup in her hand as though she had forgotten it was there. Faile frowned, and Lini frowned even harder, and Maighdin scurried for a cloth to dry the sister's hand, all the while muttering under her breath again. Faile was going to have fits if she ever heard those mutters.

Perrin knew he was taking too long. Alliandre licked her lips anxiously; she expected more, but what? "Now that we're done here, I have to find the Prophet next," he said, and winced. Too abrupt. He had no feel for dealing with nobles, much less queens. "I suppose you'll want to get back to Bethal before anyone learns you're gone."

"The last I heard," Alliandre told him, "the Prophet of the Lord Dragon was in Abila. That's a largish town in Amadicia, perhaps forty leagues south of here."

In spite of himself, Perrin frowned, though he smoothed his brow quickly. So Balwer had been right. Right in one thing did not mean right in all, but it might be worthwhile hearing what the man had to say about the Whitecloaks. And the Seanchan. How many Taraboners?

Faile glided to his side, laying a hand on his arm and directing a warm smile at Alliandre. "You cannot mean to send her away now, my heart. Not when she has just arrived. Leave us to talk here out of the sun before she must face the ride back. I know you have important matters to see to."

He managed not to stare, with a little effort. What could be more important than the Queen of Ghealdan? Certain sure, nothing anyone would let him lay hand to. Clearly she wanted to talk with Alliandre without him. With luck, she would tell him why later. With luck, she would tell him all of it. Elyas might think he knew Saldaeans, but Perrin had learned on his own that only a fool tried to root out all of his wife's secrets. Or let her know about those he had unearthed already.

Leaving Alliandre should no doubt involve as much ceremony as meeting her, but he managed a credible leg and made his bow, asking her pardon for going off, and she curtsied deeply, murmuring that he honored her too much, and that was that. Except for jerking his head at Gallenne to follow him. He doubted that Faile would send him off and want that one to stay. What *did* she want to talk about alone?

Outside, the one-eyed man gave Perrin a clap on the shoulder that would have staggered a smaller man. "Burn me, I've never heard of the like! Now I can say I've seen a *ta'veren* at work for true. What did you want with me?" And what was he to say to that?

Just then, he heard shouting from the Mayener camp, the sound of arguing, loud enough that Two Rivers men stood to peer through the trees, though the side of the hill hid everything.

"First let's see what all that is about," Perrin replied. That would give him time to think. About what to say to Gallenne, and other things.

Faile waited a few moments after Perrin left before telling the servants that she and the others would see to themselves. Maighdin was so busy staring at Alliandre that Lini had to pluck at her sleeve before she moved. That would have to be handled later. Setting her cup down, Faile followed the three women to the door of the tent as if hurrying them, but she paused there.

Perrin and Gallenne were striding off through the trees toward the Mayener camp. Good. Most of *Cha Faile* was squatting not far off. Catching Parelean's eye, she gestured low in front of her waist, where no one behind her could see. A quick circular motion followed by a clenched fist. Immediately the Tairens and Cairhien broke apart in groups of two or three and spread out. Far less elaborate than Maiden handtalk, *Cha Faile*'s signals sufficed. In moments a scattered ring of her people had surrounded the tent, apparently at random, talking idly or playing at cat's cradle. But no one would come nearer than twenty paces without her receiving warning before they reached the threshold.

It was Perrin who worried her most. She had expected something momentous as soon as Alliandre appeared in the flesh, if not what came, but he had been stunned by her vow. If he took it into his head to return, to take another stab at making Alliandre feel comfortable in her decision. . . . Oh, he did think with his heart when he should use his head. And with his head when he should use his heart! Guilt pricked her at the thought.

"Peculiar servants you found by the side of the road," Berelain said in tones of mock sympathy at her side, and Faile gave a start. She had not heard the woman come up

behind her. Lini and the others were walking toward the
carts, Lini shaking a finger at Maighdin, and Berelain
shifted her gaze from Faile to them. She kept her voice
low, but the mocking tone remained. "The oldest at least
seems to know her duties instead of simply having heard
about them, but Annoura tells me the youngest is a wilder.
Very weak, Annoura says, negligible, but wilders always
cause problems. The others will carry tales about her, if
they know, and sooner or later, she will run away. Wilders
always do, I hear. That's what comes of picking up your
maids like stray dogs."

"They suit me well enough," Faile replied coolly. Still,
a long conversation with Lini was definitely needed. A
wilder? Even if weak, that might prove useful. "I always
thought you were fit for hiring servants." Berelain blinked,
uncertain what that meant, and Faile carefully did not let
her satisfaction show. Turning away, she said, "Annoura,
will you make us private with a ward against listeners?"

There seemed little chance that Seonid or Masuri would
find any opportunity to eavesdrop using the Power—she
was waiting for the explosion when Perrin found out just
how tightly the Wise Ones had that pair haltered—yet the
Wise Ones themselves might have learned. Faile was sure
Edarra and the others were wringing Seonid and Masuri
dry.

The Gray sister's beaded braids clicked softly as she nodded. "It is done, Lady Faile," she said, and Berelain's lips
compressed briefly. Quite satisfying. The temerity of making the presentations here in Faile's own tent! She deserved
more than having someone step between her and her advisor, but it was satisfying.

Childishly satisfying, Faile admitted, when she should
be focused on the matter at hand. She almost bit her lip
in aggravation. She did not doubt her husband's love, but
she could not treat Berelain as the woman deserved, and
that forced her, against her will, to play a game with Perrin
too often as the gaming board. And the prize, so Berelain
believed. If only Perrin did not sometimes behave as if he
might be. Firmly she put all that out of her head. There was
a wife's work to be done here. The practical side.

Alliandre glanced thoughtfully at Annoura when a ward
was mentioned—she had to realize it meant serious talk—

but what she said was "Your husband is a formidable man, Lady Faile. I mean no offense when I say his bluff exterior belies a shrewd mind. With Amadicia on our doorstep, we in Ghealdan play *Daes Dae'mar* of necessity, but I do not think I have ever been danced so swiftly or so deftly to a decision as your Lord did. The hint of a threat here, a frown there. A very formidable man."

This time hiding her smile took some effort on Faile's part. These southlanders set a great store by the Game of Houses, and she did not think Alliandre would appreciate learning that Perrin simply said what he believed—too freely by half, at times—and people with devious minds saw calculation in his honesty. "He spent some time in Cairhien," she said. Let Alliandre make of that what she would. "We can speak freely here, safe behind Annoura Sedai's warding. It is plain you do not want to return to Bethal yet. Is your oath to Perrin, and his to you, not enough to tie him to you?" Some here in the south had peculiar ideas of what fealty entailed.

Berelain silently took a position to Faile's right, and a moment later Annoura did the same on her left, so that Alliandre found herself confronted by all three. It surprised Faile that the Aes Sedai fell in with her plan without knowing what it was—without doubt Annoura had her own reasons, and Faile would have given a pretty to know what they were—but she felt no surprise that Berelain did so. One casual mocking sentence could spoil everything, especially about Perrin's skill in the Great Game, yet she was sure it would not come. In a way, that irritated her. Once she had despised Berelain; she still hated her, deep and hot, but grudging respect had replaced contempt. The woman knew when their "game" had to be put aside. If not for Perrin, Faile thought she might actually have *liked* her! Briefly, to extinguish that hateful thought, she pictured herself shaving Berelain bald. She was a jade and a trull! And not something Faile could allow to divert her now.

Alliandre studied each of the women in front of her in turn, but she gave no evidence of nervousness. Taking up her winecup again, she sipped casually and spoke with sighs and rueful smiles as if her words were not really as important as they sounded. "I mean to keep my oath, of course, but you must understand that I hoped for more. Once your husband goes, I am left as I was. Worse, perhaps, until some tangible aid comes from the Lord Dragon, blessed be his name in the Light. The Prophet could ruin Bethal or even Jehannah itself as he did Samara, and I cannot stop him. And if he somehow learns of my oath. . . . He says he has come to show us how to serve the Lord Dragon in the Light, but *he* is the one who shows that way, and I cannot think he will be pleased with anyone who finds another."

"It is good that you will keep your oath," Faile told her dryly. "If you want more of my husband, perhaps you should do more. Perhaps you should accompany him when he goes south to meet the Prophet. Of course, you will want your own soldiers with you, but I suggest no more than the First has with her. Shall we sit?" Taking the chair Perrin had vacated, she motioned Berelain and Annoura to those on either side, and only then gestured toward another for Alliandre.

The Queen sat slowly, staring wide-eyed at Faile, not nervous but astounded. "Why in the Light would I do that?" she exclaimed. "Lady Faile, the Children of the Light will take any excuse to increase their depredations in Ghealdan, and King Ailron might decide to send an army north as well. It's impossible!"

"The wife of your liege lord asks it of you, Alliandre," Faile said firmly.

It didn't seem possible that Alliandre's eyes could widen farther, yet they did. She looked to Annoura and found only imperturbable Aes Sedai calm looking back. "Of course," she said after a moment. Her voice was hollow. Swallowing, she added, "Of course, I will do as you . . . ask . . . my Lady."

Faile hid her relief behind a gracious nod of acceptance. She had expected Alliandre to balk. That Alliandre could swear fealty without realizing what that meant—that she felt it necessary to say that she intended to keep her oath!—had only confirmed Faile's belief that the woman could not be left behind. By all accounts, Alliandre had dealt with Masema by yielding to him. Slowly, to be sure, with little other choice and only when she had to, yet submission could become a habit. Back in Bethal, with nothing visible changed, how soon before she would decide to hedge with a warning to Masema? She had felt the weight of her oath; now Faile could lighten her burden.

"I am happy that you will be accompanying us," she said warmly. And truly, she was. "My husband does not forget those who render him service. One such service would be to write to your nobles, telling them that a man in the south has raised the banner of Manetheren." Berelain's head half jerked around in surprise, and Annoura went so far as to blink.

"My Lady," Alliandre said urgently, "half of them will send word to the Prophet as soon as they receive my letter. They are terrified of him, and the Light alone knows what he might do." Just the response Faile had hoped for.

"Which is why you will write him also, saying that you have gathered a few soldiers to deal with this man personally. After all, the Prophet of the Lord Dragon is too important to have to turn his attention to such a minor matter."

"Very good," Annoura murmured. "No one will know who is who."

Berelain laughed in delighted approval, burn her!

"My Lady," Alliandre breathed, "I said that my Lord Perrin is formidable. May I add that his wife is every bit as formidable?"

Faile tried not to bask too visibly. Now she had to send word to her people in Bethal. In a way, she regretted that. Explaining to Perrin would have been more than difficult, but even he could not have kept his temper if she had kidnapped the Queen of Ghealdan.

Most of the Winged Guards appeared to be gathered on the edge of their camp, surrounding ten of their number on horseback. The absence of lances said the riders were scouts. The men afoot milled and pushed, trying to get closer. Perrin thought he heard thunder again, not so distant, but it only touched the edge of awareness.

As he prepared to push his way through, Gallenne roared, "Make way, you mangy hounds!" Heads whipped around, and men wriggled sideways in the mass, opening a narrow path. Perrin wondered what would happen if he called the Two Rivers men mangy hounds. Probably earn him a punch in the nose. It might be worth a try.

Nurelle and the other officers were with the scouts. So were seven men afoot with their hands tied behind them

and lead ropes around their necks, all shuffling their feet
and hunching their shoulders and scowling defiance or
fear or both. Their clothes were stiff with old filth, though
some had been fine once. Strangely, they smelled heavily
of woodsmoke. For that matter, some of the mounted soldiers had soot on their faces, and one or two seemed to be
nursing burns. Aram stood studying the prisoners, frowning slightly.

Gallenne took a stance with his feet apart and fists on
his hips, his one eye doing as good a job of glaring as most
men's two. "What happened?" he demanded. "My scouts
are supposed to bring back information, not ragpickers!"

"I will let Ortis report, my Lord," Nurelle said. "He was
there. Squadman Ortis!"

A soldier in his middle years scrambled down from his
saddle to bow, gauntleted hand pressed to heart. His helmet was plain, without the thin plumes and wings that were
worked in the sides of officers' helmets. Beneath the rim,
a livid burn stood out plainly on his face. The other cheek
had a scar that pulled up the corner of his mouth. "My Lord
Gallenne, my Lord Aybara," he said in a gravelly voice.
"We came on these turnip-eaters about two leagues to the
west, my Lords. Burning a farm, with the farm folk inside.
A woman tried to get out a window, and one of these scum
bashed her head in. Knowing how Lord Aybara feels, we
put a stop to it. We were too late to save anybody, but we
caught these seven. The rest got away."

"People are often tempted to slide back into the Shadow,"
one of the prisoners said suddenly. "They must be reminded
of the cost." A tall, lean man with a stately air, his voice
was smooth and educated, but his coat was as dirty as any
of the others, and he had not shaved in two or three days.
The Prophet did not seem to approve of wasting time on
things like razors. Or washing. With his hands bound and
a rope around his neck, he glared at his captors without the
least bit of fear. He was all supercilious defiance. "Your soldiers do not impress me," he said. "The Prophet of the Lord
Dragon, blessed be his name in the Light, has destroyed
greater armies by far than your tag end. You may kill us,
but we will be avenged when the Prophet spills your blood
on the ground. None of you will survive us long. He will

triumph in fire and in blood." He finished on a ringing tone, his back straight as an iron rod. Murmurs ran through the listening soldiers. They knew very well that Masema had destroyed larger armies than theirs.

"Hang them," Perrin said. Again, he heard that thunder.

Having given the order, he made himself watch. Despite the murmurs, there was no lack of ready hands. Some of the prisoners began to weep as their lead ropes were thrown over tree limbs. A once-fat man whose wattles hung in folds shouted that he repented, that he would serve any master they named. A bald-headed fellow who looked as tough as Lamgwin thrashed and screamed until the rope cut off his howls. Only the smooth-voiced man did not kick or fight, even when the noose drew tight on his neck. To the end he glared defiance.

"At least one of them knew how to die," Gallenne growled as the last body went limp. He frowned at the men decorating the trees as if regretting they had not put up more fight.

"If those people were serving the Shadow," Aram began, then hesitated. "Forgive me, Lord Perrin, but will the Lord Dragon approve of this?"

Perrin gave a start and stared at him, aghast. "Light, Aram, you heard what they did! Rand would've put the ropes on their necks himself!" He thought Rand would have, hoped he would have. Rand was fixed on welding the nations together before the Last Battle, and he had done little counting of cost to do so.

Men's heads jerked up as thunder pealed loud enough for all to hear, then closer, and again closer still. A wind gusted, fell, rose again, tugging Perrin's coat as it slashed this way and that. Lightning forked in a cloudless sky. In the Mayener camp, horses whinnied and reared at their ties. Thunder tolled repeatedly, and lightning writhed in silver-blue snakes, and beneath a burning sun, rain fell, fat scattered drops that splashed fountains of dust where they hit bare ground. Perrin wiped one from his cheek and peered at damp fingers in amazement.

In moments the storm was gone, thunder and lightning rolling on eastward. Thirsty ground absorbed the raindrops that had fallen, the sun baked as fiercely as ever, and only flickering lights in the sky and fading booms said that anything had happened. Soldiers stared at each other uncertainly. Gallenne pried his fingers from the hilt of his sword with an obvious effort.

"This . . . this can't be the Dark One's work," Aram said, and flinched. No one had ever seen a natural storm like that. "It means the weather is changing, doesn't it, Lord Perrin? The weather is going to be right again?"

Perrin opened his mouth to tell the man not to call him that, but he closed it again with a sigh. "I don't know," he said. What was it Gaul had said? "Everything changes, Aram." He had just never thought that he would have to change, too.

CHAPTER

II

Questions and an Oath

The air in the huge stable smelled of old hay and horse dung. And blood, and burned flesh. With all the doors closed, the air felt thick. Two lanterns gave little light, and shadows filled most of the interior. In the long rows of stalls, horses whickered nervously. The man hanging by his wrists from a roof beam gave a low moan, then a ragged cough. His head fell down on his chest. He was a tall man, well-muscled, if rather the worse for wear.

Abruptly Sevanna realized that his chest no longer moved. The gem-studded rings on her fingers glittered red and green as she gestured curtly to Rhiale.

The flame-haired woman pushed the man's head up and thumbed back one eyelid, then pressed an ear to his chest, careless of the still-smoldering splinters that peppered him. With a sound of disgust, she straightened. "He is dead. We should have left this to the Maidens, Sevanna, or the Black Eyes. I do not doubt we killed him by ignorance."

Sevanna's mouth tightened, and she shifted her shawl in a clatter of bracelets. They ran nearly to her elbows, a no-ticeable weight in gold and ivory and gems, yet she would have worn every one she owned if she could. None of the other women said anything. Putting prisoners to the question was *not* the work of Wise Ones, but Rhiale knew why they had to do this themselves. The lone survivor of ten mounted men who thought they could defeat twenty Maidens because they rode horses, the man had also been the first Seanchan captured in the ten days since their arrival in this land.

"He would have lived if he had not fought the pain so hard, Rhiale," Someryn said finally, shaking her head. "A strong man for a wetlander, but he could not accept pain. Still, he told us much."

Sevanna eyed her sideways, trying to see whether she hid sarcasm. As tall as most men, Someryn wore more bracelets and necklaces than any woman there except Sevanna herself, layers of firedrops and emeralds, rubies and sapphires, almost concealing a too-full bosom that otherwise would have been half bared with her blouse undone almost to her skirt. Her shawl, tied around her waist, hid nothing. At times it was difficult for Sevanna to tell whether Someryn was copying her or competing with her.

"Much!" Meira exclaimed. In the light of the lantern she held, her long face was grimmer than usual, though that hardly seemed possible. Meira could find the dark side of the noonday sun. "That his people lie two days west in the city called Amador? We knew that. All he has told us are wild tales. Artur Hawkwing! Bah! The Maidens should have kept him and done what was needed."

"Would you . . . risk letting everyone learn too much too soon?" Sevanna bit her lip in vexation. She had almost called them "you fools." Too many already knew too much, in her opinion, Wise Ones among them, but she could not risk offending these women. That knowledge grated on her! "The people are frightened." There was no need to hide her contempt for that, at least. What shocked her, outraged her, was not that they were afraid, but how few made any effort to hide the fact. "Black Eyes, or Stone Dogs, or even Maidens, would have talked of what he said. You know they would! His lies would only have spread more fear." They had to be lies. In Sevanna's mind a sea was like the lakes she had seen in the wetlands, but with its far side beyond sight. If hundreds of thousands more of his people were coming, even from the other side of so large a body of water, the other prisoners she had questioned would have known of them. And no prisoner was questioned without her present.

Tion raised the second lantern and regarded her with unblinking gray eyes. Nearly a head shorter than Someryn, Tion was still taller than Sevanna. And twice as wide. Her round face often appeared placid, but thinking her so was a mistake. "They are right to fear," she said in a stony voice. "*I* am afraid, and take no shame in it. The Seanchan are many if they are no more than took Amador, and we are few. You have your sept around you, Sevanna, but where is *my* sept? Your wetlander friend Caddar and his tame Aes Sedai sent us through his holes in the air to die. Where are the rest of the Shaido?"

Rhiale moved to stand defiantly beside Tion, and they were quickly joined by Alarys, even now toying with her black hair to draw attention to it. Or perhaps it was to avoid meeting Sevanna's eyes. After a moment, a scowling Meira added herself to the cluster, and then Modarra. Modarra might have been called slim if she were not even taller than Someryn; as it was, lean was the best that could be said of her. Sevanna had thought Modarra as firmly in her grasp as any of the rings on her fingers. As firmly in her grasp as. . . . Someryn looked at her and sighed, looked at the others. Slowly she walked over to stand beside them.

Sevanna was left standing on the very edge of the lantern's light. Of all the women tied to her by the killing of Desaine, she trusted these most. Not that she trusted anyone very far, of course. But Someryn and Modarra she had been sure were hers as tightly as if they had sworn water oath to follow where she led. And now they dared face her with accusing eyes. Even Alarys looked up from playing with her hair.

Sevanna met their stares with a cool smile just short of a sneer. Now, she decided, was not the time to remind them of the crime that bound their fates together. Not the bludgeon, this time. "I suspected Caddar might try to betray us," she said instead. Rhiale's blue eyes widened at the admission, and Tion opened her mouth. Sevanna went on, not leaving them room to speak. "Would you rather have remained in Kinslayer's Dagger to be destroyed? To be hunted like animals by four clans whose Wise Ones know how to make those holes without the traveling boxes? Instead, we are in the heart of a rich, soft land. Richer even than the lands of the tree-killers. Look at what we have taken in only ten days. How much more will we take in a wetlander city? You fear the Seanchan because they have numbers? Remember that I brought every Shaido Wise One who can channel with me." That she could not channel herself seldom occurred to her, now. Soon that lack would be remedied. "We are as strong as any force these wetlanders can send against us. Even if they do have flying lizards." She sniffed forcefully to show what she thought of those! None of them had seen one, nor any of the scouts, but nearly every prisoner had been full of the ridiculous tales. "After we find the other septs, we will take this land for our own. *All* of it! We will extract a tenfold repayment from the Aes Sedai. And we will find Caddar and make him die screaming for mercy."

That should have rallied them, restored their hearts as she had had to do before. Not one woman's face changed. Not one.

"And there is the *Car'a'carn*," Tion said calmly. "Unless you have given up your plan to marry him."

"I have given up nothing," Sevanna replied irritably. The man—and more important, the power that came with him—would be hers someday. Somehow. Whatever it took. Smoothing her voice, she went on. "Rand al'Thor is hardly of consequence now." At least to these blind simpletons. With him in her hands, anything would be possible for her. "I do not intend to stand here all day discussing my bridal wreath. I have matters to see to that *are* important."

As she stalked away from them through the gloom, toward the doors of the stable, an unpleasant thought suddenly occurred to her. She was alone with these women. How far *could* she trust them, now? Desaine's death remained all too vivid in her mind; the Wise One had been . . . butchered . . . using the One Power. By the women behind her, among others. The thought twisted her belly tight. She listened for the faint rustle of straw that would announce feet following her and heard nothing. Were they just standing there watching? She refused to look over her shoulder. Keeping the same slow pace required only a little effort—*she* would not display fear and shame herself!—yet when she pushed one of the tall doors open on its well-oiled hinges and stepped into bright midday light, she could not stop from drawing a relieved breath.

Efalin was pacing outside, *shoufa* draped around her neck, bow cased on her back, spears and buckler in hand. The gray-haired woman turned abruptly, the worry on her face fading only a little at sight of Sevanna. The leader of all the Shaido Maidens, and she let her distress show! She was not Jumai, but she had come with Sevanna using the excuse that Sevanna spoke as the chief until a new chief of the Shaido could be chosen. Sevanna was sure that Efalin suspected that would never happen. Efalin knew where the power lay. And when to keep her mouth closed.

"Bury him deeply and hide the grave," Sevanna told her.

Efalin nodded, signaling the Maidens ringing the stable to their feet, and they vanished inside behind her. Sevanna studied the building, with its sharp-peaked red roof and blue walls, then turned to the field in front of it. A low stone fence with a single opening, right before the stable, enclosed a circle of hard-packed dirt perhaps a hundred paces across. The wetlanders had used it for training horses. Why it had been placed so far from everything else, surrounded by trees so tall that Sevanna still sometimes stared at them, she had not thought to ask the former owners, but the isolation served her purposes. The Maidens with Efalin were those who had captured the Seanchan. No one not here knew he existed. Or would know. Were the other Wise Ones talking in there? About her? In front of the Maidens? What were they saying? She would not wait on them or anyone!

They came out of the stable just as she started off toward the forest, Someryn and the others, and followed her into the trees arguing among themselves about the Seanchan, and Caddar, and where the rest of the Shaido had been sent. Not about her, but then, they would not where she could listen. What she did hear made her grimace. There were over three hundred Wise Ones with the Jumai, and it was the same whenever three or four started talking. Where were the rest of the septs, and had Caddar been a spear hurled by Rand al'Thor, and how many Seanchan were there, and even did they really ride lizards? Lizards! These women had been with her from the first. She had guided their feet step by step, but they believed they had helped plan every move, believed they knew the destination. If she was losing them now. . . .

The forest gave way to a huge clearing that could have swallowed the circle back at the stable fifty times over, and Sevanna felt ill temper slipping away as she stopped to look. Low hills rose to the north, and mountains a few leagues beyond them were capped with clouds, great masses of white streaked with dark gray. She had never seen so many clouds in her life. Closer at hand, thousands of Jumai went about the day's work. The ring of hammer on anvil rose from blacksmiths, and sheep and goats were being slaughtered for the evening meal, their bleating mixed with the laughter of the children as they ran at play. Given more time to prepare for their flight from Kinslayer's Dagger than the other septs, the Jumai had brought the flocks gathered in Cairhien, and added to them here.

Many people had set up their tents, but there was no need. Colorful structures nearly filled the clearing like a large wetlander village, tall barns and stables, a large forge and the squat roofs that had sheltered servants, all painted red and blue, surrounding the great roof itself. The manor house that was called, three floors high beneath a dark green tile roof, all of it a paler green trimmed with yellow, atop a broad man-made stone hill ten paces tall. Jumai and *gai'shain* climbed the long ramp that led to the great building's door and walked the ornately carved balconies that ringed it.

The stone walls and palaces she had seen in Cairhien had not impressed her half so much. This one was painted like a wagon of the Lost Ones, but even so, marvelous. She should have realized that with so many trees, these people could afford to build *anything* of wood. Could no one but she see how fat this land was? More white-clad *gai'shain* scurried about their tasks than any twenty septs had ever had before, nearly half as many as there were Jumai! No one complained about making wetlanders *gai'shain* anymore. They were so docile! A wide-eyed young man in rough-sewn white hurried past clutching a basket, gaping at the people around him and stumbling over the hem of his robe. Sevanna smiled. That one's father had called himself the lord of this place and blustered that she and her people would be hunted down—by children, of all things!—for this outrage, yet now he wore white and worked as hard as his son, as did his wife and his daughters and his other sons. The women had possessed many fine gems and beautiful silks, and Sevanna had only taken the first pick for herself. A fat land, so soft it oozed rich oils.

The women behind her had stopped short to talk among themselves at the edge of the trees. She caught what they were saying, and it turned her mood again.

". . . how many Aes Sedai fight for these Seanchan," Tion was saying. "We must learn that." Someryn and Modarra murmured agreement.

"I do not think it matters," Rhiale put in. At least her contrariness extended to the others, too. "I do not think they will fight unless we attack them. Remember, they did nothing until we moved against them, not even to defend themselves."

"And when they did," Meira said sourly, "twenty-three of us died. And more than ten thousand *al-gai'd'siswai* did not return either. Here, we have little more than a third of that number even counting the Brotherless." She soaked the last word in scorn.

"That was Rand al'Thor's work!" Sevanna told them sharply. "Instead of thinking what he did against us, think what we can do when he is ours!" *When he is mine*, she thought. The Aes Sedai had been able to take and hold him as long as they had, and she had something the Aes Sedai had not, else they would have used it. "Remember instead that we had the Aes Sedai beaten until he took their side. Aes Sedai are nothing!"

Once again her effort to strengthen their hearts produced no visible effect. All they could remember was that the spears had been broken trying to capture Rand al'Thor, and they with them. Modarra might have been staring into the grave of all her sept, and even Tion frowned uneasily, doubtless recalling that she, too, had run like a frightened goat.

"Wise Ones," a man's voice said behind Sevanna, "I have been sent to ask for your judgment."

Instantly every woman's face regained its equanimity. What she could not do, he had done with his very presence. No Wise One would allow any but another Wise One to see her out of countenance. Alarys stopped stroking her hair, which she had pulled over her shoulder. Plainly none of them recognized him. Sevanna thought she did.

He regarded them gravely, with green eyes much older than his smooth face. He had full lips, but there was a set to his mouth, as if he had forgotten how to smile. "I am Kinhuin, of the *Mera'din*, Wise Ones. The Jumai say we may not take our full share from this place because we are not Jumai, but it is because they will have less since we are two for every Jumai *al-gai'd'siswai*. The Brotherless ask your judgment, Wise Ones."

Now that they knew who he was, some could not hide their dislike of the men who had abandoned clan and sept to come to the Shaido rather than follow Rand al'Thor, a wetlander and no true *Car'a'carn*, as they thought. Tion's face merely went flat, but Rhiale's eyes flashed, and Meira teetered on the edge of a scowl. Only Modarra showed concern, but then, she would have tried to settle a dispute between treekillers.

"These six Wise Ones will give judgment after hearing both sides," Sevanna told Kinhuin with a graveness to match his.

The other women looked at her, barely concealing their surprise that she intended to stand aside. It had been she who arranged for ten times the number of *Mera'din* to accompany the Jumai as went with any other sept. She really had suspected Caddar, if not of what he had done, and she had wanted as many spears around her as possible. Besides, they could always die in place of Jumai.

She affected surprise at the others' surprise. "It would not be fair for me to take part since my own sept is involved," she told them before turning back to the green-eyed man. "They will give fair judgment, Kinhuin. And I am certain they will speak in favor of the *Mera'din*."

The other women gave her hard looks before Tion motioned abruptly for Kinhuin to lead the way. He had to tear his eyes away from Sevanna to comply. Wearing a faint smile—he had been staring at her, not Someryn—she watched them vanish into the mass of people moving about the manor grounds. For all their misliking the Brotherless—and her making predictions to the man about their decision—the chances were they *would* decide that way. Either Way, Kinhuin would remember and tell the others of his so-called society. The Jumai were already in her belt pouch, but anything that tied the *Mera'din* to her was welcome.

Turning, Sevanna strode back into the trees, though not toward the stable. Now that she was alone, she could see to something much more important than the Brotherless. She checked what she had tucked into her skirt at the small of her back, where her shawl hid it. She would have felt if it slipped a hair, but she wanted to touch its smooth length with her fingers. No Wise One would dare think her less than they, once she used that, perhaps today. And one day, it would give her Rand al'Thor. After all, if Caddar had lied in one thing, maybe he had lied in others.

Through a blur of tears Galina Casban glared at the Wise One shielding her. As if there were any need for the slender woman's shield. Right then she could not have so much as embraced the Source. Sitting cross-legged on the ground between two squatting Maidens, Belinde adjusted her shawl and gave a thin smile, as if she knew Galina's thoughts. Her face was narrow and foxlike, and her hair and eyebrows had been bleached nearly white by the sun. Galina wished she had crushed her skull instead of merely slapping her.

It had not been an attempt at escape, merely more frustration than she could bear. Her days began and ended with exhaustion, every day more than the last. She could not remember how long since they had stuffed her into that coarse black robe; the days ran together like an everlasting stream. A week? A month? Maybe not that long. Surely not more. She wished she had never touched Belinde. If the woman had not stuffed rags into her mouth to silence her sobbing, she would have begged to be allowed to carry rocks again, or move a pile of pebbles stone by stone, or any of the tortures they filled her hours with. Anything rather than this.

Only Galina's head stuck out of the leather sack that hung suspended from the stout limb of an oak. Directly beneath the sack, coals glowed in a bronze brazier, a slow burn, heating the air inside the sack. She huddled in that sweltering heat with her thumbs tied to her toes, sweat slicking her nakedness. Her hair clung damply to her face, and she panted, nostrils flaring for air, when she was not sobbing. Even so, this would have been better than the endless, senseless, backbreaking labor they subjected her to except for one thing. Before snugging the neck of the sack beneath her chin, Belinde had emptied a pouch of some fine powder over her, and as she had begun to sweat, it had begun to burn like pepper flung in the eyes. It seemed to coat her from the shoulders down, and, oh, Light, it burned!

That she called on the Light measured her desperation,

but they had not broken her for all their trying. She *would* get free—she would!—and once she did, she would make these savages pay in blood! Rivers of blood! Oceans! She would have them all skinned alive! She would . . . ! Flinging back her head, she howled; the wadded rags in her mouth muffled the sound, but she howled, and she did not know whether it was a shriek of rage or a scream for mercy.

When her howls died and her head fell forward, Belinde and the Maidens were on their feet, and Sevanna was with them. Galina attempted to stifle her sobbing in front of the golden-haired woman, but she could as soon have plucked the sun from the sky with her fingers.

"Listen to her whine and snivel," Sevanna sneered, coming to look up at her. Galina tried to put an equal contempt in her own stare. Sevanna decked herself with enough jewelry for ten women! She wore her blouse unlaced to nearly bare her bosom, except for all those mismatched necklaces, and breathed deep when men looked at her! Galina tried, but contempt was hard to manage with tears rolling down her cheeks along with her sweat. She shook with weeping, making the sack sway.

"This *da'tsang* is tough as an old ewe," Belinde cackled, "but I always found even the toughest old ewe was made tender if cooked slowly, with the right herbs. When I was a Maiden, I softened Stone Dogs with enough cooking." Galina closed her eyes. *Oceans* of blood, to pay for . . . !

The sack lurched, and Galina's eyes popped open as it began to settle. The Maidens had undone the rope running over the limb, and the pair of them were lowering her slowly. Frantically she thrashed about, trying to look down, and almost began sobbing anew, with relief, when she saw that the brazier had been moved aside. With Belinde's talk of cooking. . . . That would be Belinde's fate, Galina decided. Tied to a spit and turned over a fire until her juices dripped! That to begin!

With a thud that made Galina grunt, the leather bag hit the ground and toppled over. As unconcerned as if they were handling a sack of potatoes, the Maidens tumbled her out onto the brown weeds, sliced the cords that held her thumbs and toes, plucked the gag from between her teeth. Dirt and dead leaves stuck to the sweat coating her.

She very much wanted to stand, to meet them all eye-to-eye and glare-for-glare. Instead, she rose only as far as hands and knees, then dug her fingers into the mulch of the forest floor, dug her toes in. Any farther, and she would not be able to stop her hands from flying to soothe her red, flaming skin. Her sweat felt like the juice of ice peppers. All she could do was crouch there and quiver, try to work some moisture back into her mouth and daydream of what she would do to these savages.

"I believed you were stronger than this," Sevanna said above her in thoughtful tones, "but perhaps Belinde is right. Perhaps you are soft enough, now. If you swear to obey me, you can stop being *da'tsang*. Perhaps you will not even have to be *gai'shain*. Will you swear to obey me in all things?"

"Yes!" The hoarse word flew from Galina's tongue without hesitation, though she had to swallow before speaking more. "I will obey you! I swear it!" And so she would obey. Until they gave the opening she needed. Was this all that had been necessary? An oath she would have made the first day? Sevanna would learn what it was like to hang over hot coals. Oh, yes, she. . . .

"Then you will not object to swearing your oath on this," Sevanna said, tossing something down in front of her.

Galina's scalp crawled as she stared at it. A white rod like polished ivory, a foot long and no thicker than her wrist. Then she saw the flowing marks carved into the end toward her, numerals used in the Age of Legends. One hundred eleven. She had thought it was the Oath Rod, somehow stolen from the White Tower. That also was marked, but with the numeral three, which some thought stood for the Three Oaths. Maybe this was not what it seemed. Maybe. Yet no hooded viper from the Drowned Lands coiled there could have frozen her so still.

"A fine oath, Sevanna. When did you intend to tell the rest of us?"

That voice jerked Galina's head up. It could have pulled her eyes away from a hooded viper, too.

Therava appeared among the trees leading a dozen cold-faced Wise Ones. When they stopped behind her, confronting Sevanna, every woman present except for the Maidens had been there when Galina was sentenced to wear the black robe. A word from Therava, a short nod from Sevanna, and the Maidens departed swiftly. Sweat still oozed from Galina, but suddenly the air seemed cold.

Sevanna glanced at Belinde, who avoided her eye. Sevanna's lip curled, half sneer, half snarl, and she planted fists on hips. Galina did not understand where she found the nerve, a woman who could not channel at all. Some of these women possessed not inconsiderable strength. No, she could not afford to think of them only as wilders if she was to escape and have her revenge. Therava and Someryn were stronger than any woman in the Tower, and any of them could have been Aes Sedai easily.

But Sevanna faced them defiantly. "It seems you rendered justice quickly," she said in a voice dry as dust.

"The matter was simple," Tion replied calmly. "The *Mera'din* received the justice they deserved."

"And they were told they received it in *spite* of your attempt to sway us," Rhiale added with some heat. Sevanna nearly *did* snarl at that.

Therava would not be diverted from her purpose, though. In one swift step she reached Galina, gripped a handful of her hair and jerked her up to her knees, bent her head back. Therava was not the tallest of these women by at least a head, yet she loomed taller than most men, staring down with a hawk's eyes, driving away every thought of revenge or defiance. The white streaks touching her dark red hair only made her face more commanding. Galina's hands clenched into fists on her thighs, nails digging into her palms. Even the burning of her skin paled under that stare. She had daydreamed about breaking every one of these women, making them plead for death, laughing as she denied their begging. About every one except Therava. At night, Therava filled her dreams and all Galina could do was try to flee; the only escape was to wake screaming. Galina had broken strong men and strong women, but she stared up at Therava wide-eyed and whined.

"This one has no honor to shame." Therava almost spat the words. "If you want her broken, Sevanna, let me have her. When I am done, she will obey without the need for your friend Caddar's toy."

Sevanna spoke up heatedly, denying friendship with this Caddar, whoever he was, and Rhiale barked that Sevanna had brought him to the others, and others began arguing about whether the "binder" would work any better than the "traveling box."

A small part of Galina's mind seized on mention of the traveling box. She had heard it spoken of before, longed to lay hands on it if only for a moment. With a *ter'angreal* that enabled her to Travel, however imperfectly it seemed to work, she would be able to. . . . Even hope of escape could not stand against thoughts of what Therava would do to her if the others decided to give in to the woman's request. When the hawk-eyed Wise One loosed her hair to join the argument, Galina hurled herself at the rod, landing flat on her belly. Anything, even having to obey Sevanna, was better than being handed over to Therava. If she had not been shielded, she would have channeled to operate the rod herself.

No sooner did her fingers close on the smooth rod than Therava's foot came down on it hard, trapping her hands painfully against the ground. None of the Wise Ones so much as glanced at her where she lay writhing, trying futilely to pull free. She could not make herself pull too hard; dimly she could recall making rulers pale with fear, but she did not dare disturb this woman's foot.

"If she is to swear," Therava said, staring hard at Sevanna, "it should be to obey all of us here." The others nodded, some voicing agreement, all but Belinde, and she pursed her lips thoughtfully.

Sevanna stared back just as hard. "Very well," she acceded finally. "But me first among us. I am not only a Wise One; I speak as the clan chief."

Therava smiled thinly. "So you do. Two among us first, Sevanna. You and I." Not a whisper of defiance faded from Sevanna's face, but she nodded. Grudgingly. Only then did Therava move her foot. The light of *saidar* surrounded her, and a flow of Spirit touched the numerals at the end of the rod in Galina's hands. Just as was done with the Oath Rod.

For an instant, Galina hesitated, flexing mashed fingers. It felt the same as the Oath Rod, too; not quite like ivory, not quite like glass, distinctly cool on her palms. If it was a second Oath Rod, it could be used to remove any oath she swore now. If she were given the opportunity. She did not want to take the chance, did not want to swear to Therava in any case. Always before this in her life, *she* had commanded; life since her capture had been misery, but Therava would make her a lapdog! Yet if she did not, would they let Therava break her? She could not find the smallest particle of doubt that the woman would do just that. Utterly.

"Under the Light and by my hope of salvation and rebirth"—she no longer believed in the Light or a hope of salvation, and there was no need to speak more than a simple promise, but they expected a strong oath—"I swear to obey every Wise One present here in all things, and first among them, Therava and Sevanna." The last hope that this "binder" was something else vanished as Galina felt the oath settle on her, as if she suddenly wore a garment that covered her far too tightly from her scalp to the soles of her feet. Throwing back her head, she screamed. In part that was because it suddenly seemed as if the burning of her skin was being pressed deep into her flesh, but mainly, it was pure despair.

"Be quiet!" Therava said sharply. "I do not want to listen to you wailing!" Galina's teeth clicked shut, nearly biting her tongue, and she struggled to swallow her sobs. Nothing but obedience was possible, now. Therava frowned at her. "Let us see if this truly works," she muttered, bending closer. "Have you planned violence against any Wise One here? Answer truthfully, and ask to be punished if you have. The penalty for violence against a Wise One," she added like an afterthought, "can be to be killed like an animal." She drew a finger expressively across her throat then gripped her belt knife with the same hand.

Gulping air in horrified panic, Galina shied back from the woman. She could not take her eyes away from Therava's, though, and she could not stop the words that chattered through her teeth. "I d-did, ag-g-gainst all of you! P-please p-punish me f-for it!" Would they kill her, now? After all of this, was she to die here?

"It seems this binder does as your friend claimed after all, Sevanna." Plucking the rod from Galina's limp hands, Therava tucked it behind her belt as she straightened. "It also seems that you will wear white after all, Galina Casban." For some reason, she gave a pleased smile at that. But she issued other commands, too. "You will behave meekly, as a *gai'shain* should. If a *child* tells you to jump, you will jump unless one of us has said otherwise. And you will not touch *saidar* or channel unless one of us tells you. Release the shield on her, Belinde."

The shield vanished, and Galina knelt there, staring hollowly. The Source shone just out of sight, tantalizing. And she could have sprouted wings as easily as she could stretch out for it.

Bracelets clattered as Sevanna shifted her shawl in anger. "You take too much on yourself, Therava. That is mine; give it to me!" She held out her hand, but Therava merely folded her arms beneath her breasts.

"There have been meetings among the Wise Ones," the stern-eyed woman told Sevanna. "We have reached certain decisions." The women who had come with her gathered behind her, all of them facing Sevanna, and Belinde hurried to join them.

"Without me?" Sevanna snapped. "Do any of you dare reach a decision without me?" Her tone remained as strong as ever, but her eyes flickered to the rod in Therava's belt, and Galina thought there was a touch of uneasiness there. Another time, she would have been delighted to see it.

"One decision had to be reached without you," Tion said in a flat voice.

"As you so often point out, you speak as the clan chief," Emerys added, a mocking light in her big gray eyes. "Sometimes, Wise Ones must talk without a clan chief listening. Or someone who speaks as a chief."

"We decided," Therava said, "that just as a clan chief must have a Wise One to advise him, so must you have a Wise One's advice. *I* will advise you."

Gathering her shawl around her, Sevanna studied the women confronting her. Her expression was unreadable. How did she do it? They could crush her like an egg beneath a hammer. "And what *advice* do you offer me, Therava?" she said at last in an icy voice.

"My strong advice is that we move without delay," Therava replied, as cool as Sevanna. "These Seanchan are too close and too many. We should move north into these Mountains of Mist and establish a hold. From there, we can send parties to find the other septs. It may take long to

reunite the Shaido, Sevanna. Your wetlander friend may
have scattered us to the nine corners of the world. Until we
do that, we are vulnerable."

"We will move tomorrow." If Galina had not been sure
she knew Sevanna inside and out, she would have thought
the woman sounded petulant as well as angry. Those green
eyes flashed. "But east. That also is away from the Seanchan, and the lands to the east are in turmoil, ripe for plucking."

There was a long silence, then Therava nodded. "East."
She said the word softly, the softness of silk laid over steel.
"But remember that clan chiefs have lived to regret reject-
ing a Wise One's advice too often. You may, as well." The
threat on her face was plain as that in her voice, yet Sevanna
laughed!

"*You* remember, Therava! All of you remember! If I am
left for the vultures, so will you be! I have made assurance
of that."

The other women exchanged worried glances, all but
Therava, and Modarra and Norlea frowned.

Slumped on her knees, whimpering and trying in vain to
soothe her skin with her hands, Galina found herself wondering what these threats meant. It was a small thought,
worming its way through bitterness and self-pity. Anything
she could use against these women would be welcome. If
she dared use it. A bitter thought.

Abruptly she realized that the sky was turning dark. Billowing clouds were rolling down from the north, streaked
gray and black, obscuring the sun. And beneath the clouds
fell flurries of snow, swirling in the air. None reached the
ground—few fell as far as the treetops—but Galina gaped.
Snow! Had the Great Lord loosened his grip on the world
for some reason?

The Wise Ones stared at the sky, too, mouths hanging
open as if they had never seen clouds, much less snow.

"What is this, Galina Casban?" Therava demanded.
"Speak if you know!" She did not look away from the sky
until Galina told her it was snow, and when she did it was
to laugh. "I always thought the men who ran down La-
man Treekiller lied about snow. This could not hamper a
mouse!"

Galina clamped her jaws shut on explaining about snowfalls, aghast that her instinct had been to curry favor. Aghast as well at the small pang of pleasure that keeping the information back gave. *I am the Highest of the Red Ajah!* she reminded herself. *I sit on the Supreme Council of the Black Ajah!* They sounded like lies. This was not fair!

"If we are done here," Sevanna said, "I will take the *gai'shain* back to the great roof and see her put in white. You can remain and stare at the snow if you wish." Her tone was so smooth, like butter in the tub, that no one would have thought her at daggers' points only moments earlier. She looped her shawl over her elbows and adjusted some of her necklaces; nothing in the world concerned her more.

"We will take care of the *gai'shain*," Therava told her just as smoothly. "Since you speak as the chief, you have a long day and most of the night ahead of you if we are to move tomorrow." For an instant, Sevanna's eyes flashed again, but Therava merely snapped her fingers and gestured sharply at Galina before turning to go. "Come with me," she said. "And stop pouting."

Head down, Galina scrambled to her feet and scurried after Therava and the other women who could channel. Pouting? She might have been scowling, but never pouting! Her thoughts scrabbled like rats in a cage, finding no hope of escape. There had to be one! There had to be! One thought that surfaced in the middle of that turmoil almost made her begin weeping again. Were *gai'shain* robes softer than the scratchy black wool she had been forced to wear so far? There had to be a way out! A hasty glance back through the trees showed Sevanna still standing there, glaring after them. Overhead, the clouds swirled, and the falling snow melted like Galina's hopes.

CHAPTER
12

New Alliances

Graendal wished there had been even a simple transcriber among the things she had removed from Illian after Sammael's death. This Age was frightful usually, primitive and uncomfortable. Still, some of it suited her. In a large bamboo cage at the far end of the room a hundred brightly plumaged birds sang melodiously, almost as beautiful in their multicolored flitting as her two pets in transparent robes who waited on either side of the door, their gazes locked on her, eager to serve her pleasure. If oil lamps did not give the same light as glowbulbs, aided by large mirrors on the walls they produced a certain barbaric splendor with the gilded fish-scale ceiling. It would have been nice to need only speak the words, but actually putting them on paper with her own hand produced a pleasure akin to that she felt in sketching. The script of this Age was quite simple, and learning to duplicate another's style had been no more difficult.

Signing with a flourish—not her own name, of course—she sanded the thick page, then folded it and sealed it with one of the signet rings of various sizes that made a decorative line across the writing table. The Hand and Sword of Arad Doman impressed on an irregular circle of blue-and-green wax.

"Take this to Lord Ituralde with all speed," she said, "and say only what I told you."

"As fast as horses can carry me, my Lady." Nazran bowed as he took the letter, one finger stroking thin black mustaches above a winning smile. Square and deeply brown in a well-fitting blue coat, he was handsome; just not sufficiently handsome. "I received this from the Lady Tuva, who died of her wounds after telling me that she was a courier from Alsalam and had been attacked by a Gray Man."

"Make sure there is human blood on it," she admonished. She doubted anyone in this time could tell human blood from any other, but she had found too many surprises to take an unnecessary chance. "Enough for realism; not enough to spoil what I wrote."

His black eyes lingered warmly on her as he bowed again, but as soon as he straightened he hurried to the door, boots thudding on the pale yellow marble floor. He did not notice the servants with their eyes fixed ardently on her, or affected not to notice, though he had once been a friend of the young man. Only a touch of Compulsion had been needed to make Nazran nearly as avid to obey as they, not to mention certain that he might yet taste her charms again. She laughed softly. Well, he believed he had tasted them; just a little prettier, and he might have. Of course, he would have been useless for anything else then. He would ride horses to death reaching Ituralde, and if that message, delivered by Alsalam's close cousin, supposedly coming from the King himself and with Gray Men trying to stop it, did not satisfy the Great Lord's command to increase chaos, nothing would, short of balefire. And it would serve her own ends very nicely as well. Her own ends.

Graendal's hand went to the only ring on the table that was not a signet, a plain golden band too small for any but her little finger. It had been a pleasant surprise to find an *angreal* attuned to women among Sammael's possessions. A pleasant surprise to have time to find much of anything useful with al'Thor and those puppies who called themselves Asha'man constantly in and out of Sammael's chambers in the Great Hall of the Council. They had stripped it bare of what she had not taken. Dangerous puppies, all of them, especially al'Thor. And she had not wanted to risk *anyone* being able to draw a line from Sammael to her. Yes, she must increase the pace of her own plans, and distance herself from Sammael's disaster.

Abruptly a vertical slash of silver appeared at the far end of the room, bright against the tapestries hanging between the heavy gilded mirrors, and a crystalline chime rang loud. Her eyebrows rose in surprise. Someone remembered the courtesies of a more civilized Age, it seemed. Standing, she forced the plain band of gold down against the ruby ring on her smallest finger and embraced *saidar* through it before channeling the web that would sound an answering chime for whoever wanted to open a gateway. The *angreal* did not offer much, yet anyone who thought they knew her strength would find a shock.

The gateway opened, and two women in nearly identical red-and-black silk dresses stepped through warily. At least, Moghedien moved cautiously, dark eyes flickering in search of traps, hands smoothing her wide skirts; the gateway winked out after a moment, but she held on to *saidar*. A sensible precaution, though Moghedien had always been a great one for precautions. Graendal did not let go of the Source, either. Moghedien's companion, a short young woman with long silver hair and vivid blue eyes, stared about her coldly, hardly more than glancing in Graendal's direction. By her demeanor, she might have been a Prime Counselor forced to endure the company of common laborers and intent on ignoring their existence. A foolish girl, to imitate the Spider. Red and black did not suit her coloring, and she should have made better use of such an impressive bosom.

"This is Cyndane, Graendal," Moghedien said. "We are . . . working together." She did not smile when she named the haughty young woman, but Graendal did. A pretty name for a more than pretty girl, but what twist of fate had led some mother of this time to give her daughter a name that meant "Last Chance"? Cyndane's face remained cold and smooth, but her eyes flared. A beautiful doll carved from ice, with hidden fires. It seemed she knew the meaning and did not like it.

"What brings you and your friend, Moghedien?" Graendal asked. The Spider was the very last she had expected to come out from the shadows. "Have no fear of speaking in front of my servants." She gestured, and the pair by the door sank to their knees, pressed their faces to the floor. They would not quite fall dead by her simple command, but close.

"What interest can you find in them when you destroy anything that might make them interesting?" Cyndane demanded, striding arrogantly across the floor. She held herself very straight, striving for every hair of height. "Do you know that Sammael is dead?"

Graendal kept her own face smooth, with a little effort. She had supposed this girl some Friend of the Dark whom Moghedien had picked up to run errands, perhaps a noble who thought her title counted, but now that she was close. . . . The girl was stronger in the One Power than she herself! Even in her own Age, that had been uncommon among men, and very rare indeed among women. On the instant, on instinct, she changed her intention to deny any contact with Sammael.

"I suspected," she replied, directing a false smile over the young woman's head at Moghedien. How much did she know? Where had the Spider found a girl so much stronger than she, and why was she traveling with her? Moghedien had always been jealous of anyone with more strength. Or more of anything. "He used to visit me, importuning my help in one mad plan or another. I never rejected him outright; you know Sammael is—was a dangerous man to reject. He appeared every few days without fail, and when he stopped, I assumed something dire had happened to him. Who is this girl, Moghedien? A remarkable find."

The young woman stepped closer, staring up at her with eyes like blue fire. "She told you my name. That is all you need know." The girl knew she spoke to one of the Chosen, and yet her tone remained frost. Even given her strength, this was no simple Friend of the Dark. Unless she was insane. "Have you paid attention to the weather, Graendal?"

Abruptly, Graendal realized that Moghedien was letting the girl do all the talking. Hanging back until a weakness became apparent. And Graendal had been letting her! "I do not suppose you came to tell me of Sammael's death, Moghedien," she said sharply. "Or to talk about weather. You know I seldom go outside." Nature was unruly, lacking order. There were not even windows in this room, nor in most that she used. "What do you want?" The dark-haired woman was edging sideways along the wall; the glow of the One Power still surrounded her. Graendal stepped casually so that both remained in her sight.

"You make a mistake, Graendal." A chilly smile barely curved Cyndane's full lips; she was enjoying this. "I lead between us. Moghedien is in a bad odor with Moridin for *her* recent mistakes."

Wrapping her arms around herself, Moghedien shot the silver-haired little woman a scowl as good as any spoken confirmation. Suddenly Cyndane's big eyes opened even wider, and she gasped, shuddering.

Moghedien's glare turned malicious. "You lead for the moment," she sneered. "Your place in his eyes is not far better than mine." And then *she* gave a start and shivered, biting her lip.

Was she being toyed with, Graendal wondered. The pure hatred for each other on the two women's faces seemed unfeigned. Either way, she would see how they enjoyed being played. Unconsciously rubbing her hands together, rubbing the *angreal* on her finger, she moved to a chair without taking her eyes from the pair. The sweetness of *saidar* flowing into her was a comfort. Not that she needed comfort, but there was something odd here. The high straight back, thickly carved and gilded, made the chair seem a throne, though it was no different from any other in the room. Such things affected even the most sophisticated on levels they never knew consciously.

She sat leaning back with her legs crossed, one foot kicking idly, the picture of a woman at her ease, and made her voice bored. "Since you lead, child, tell me, when this man who calls himself Death is in his skin, who is he? What is he?"

"Moridin is Nae'blis." The girl's voice was calm and cold and arrogant. "The Great Lord has decided it is time for you to serve the Nae'blis, too."

Graendal jerked upright. "This is preposterous." She could not keep the anger from her voice. "A man I've never *heard* of has been named the Great Lord's Regent on Earth?" She did not mind when others tried to manipulate her—she always found a way to turn their schemes against them—but Moghedien must take her for a half-wit! She had no doubt that Moghedien was directing this obnoxious girl, whatever they claimed, whatever looks they stabbed at each other. "I serve the Great Lord and myself, no other! I think the two of you should go, now, and play your little game elsewhere. Demandred might be diverted by it. Or Semirhage? Be careful how you channel in leaving; I have set a few inverted webs, and you would not want to trigger one."

That was a lie, but a very believable one, so it came as a shock when Moghedien suddenly channeled and every lamp in the room went out, plunging them into darkness. Instantly Graendal flung herself from the chair so as not to be where they had last seen her, and she also channeled even as she moved, weaving a web of light that hung to one side, a sphere of pure white that cast lurid shadows about the room. And revealed the pair clearly. Without hesitation, she channeled again, drawing the full strength of the little ring. She did not need it all, or even most, but she wanted every advantage she could find. Attack her, would they! A net of Compulsion tightened on each of them before they could twitch.

She had spun the nets strong, for anger's sake, nearly strong enough to do harm, and the women stood staring at her adoringly, eyes wide and mouths hanging open in adulation, intoxicated with worship. They were hers to command, now. If she told them to cut their own throats, they would. Suddenly Graendal realized that Moghedien was no longer embracing the Source. This much Compulsion might have shocked her into letting go. The servants by the door had not moved, of course.

"Now," she said a touch breathlessly, "you will answer my questions." She had a number, including who was this Moridin fellow, if there was such a man, and where had Cyndane come from, but one piqued her more than the rest. "What did you hope to gain by this, Moghedien? I may decide to knot those webs on you. You can pay for your game by serving *me*."

"No, please," Moghedien groaned, wringing her hands. She actually began to weep! "You will kill us all! Please, you must serve the Nae'blis! That is what we came for. To bring you to Moridin's service!" The silver-haired little woman's face was a shadowed mask of terror in the pale light, her bosom heaving as she gulped breath.

Suddenly uneasy, Graendal opened her mouth. This made less and less sense by the moment. She opened her mouth, and the True Source vanished. The One Power vanished from her, and blackness swallowed the room again. Abruptly the caged birds broke into a frenzy of chirruping; their wings fluttered frantically against the bamboo bars.

Behind her, a voice rasped like rock being ground to dust.

"The Great Lord thought you might not take their word, Graendal. The time when you could go your own way has passed." A ball of . . . something . . . appeared in the air, a dead black globe, but a silver light filled the room. The mirrors did not shine; they seemed to dull in that light. The birds went still, silent; somehow, Graendal knew they had frozen in terror.

She gaped at the Myrddraal standing there, pale and eyeless and clothed in black deeper than the ball, but larger than any she had ever seen. It had to be the reason she could not sense the Source, but that was impossible! Except. . . . Where had that strange sphere of black light come from if not from it? She had never felt the same fear others did at a Myrddraal's gaze, not to the same degree, yet her hands rose on their own, and she had to snatch them down to keep from covering her face. Glancing toward Moghedien and Cyndane, she flinched. They had adopted the same pose as her servants, crouching on their knees, heads to the floor toward the Myrddraal.

She had to work moisture into her mouth. "You are a messenger from the Great Lord?" Her voice was steady, but weak. She had never heard of such a thing, the Great Lord sending a message by Myrddraal, and yet. . . . Moghedien was a physical coward, but still one of the Chosen, and she groveled as assiduously as the girl. And there was the light. Graendal found herself wishing her dress were not cut so low. Ridiculous, of course; Myrddraal's appetites for women were well known, but she was one of the. . . . Her eyes drifted to Moghedien once more.

The Myrddraal strode by her sinuously, seeming not to pay her any heed. Its long black cloak hung undisturbed by its movements. Aginor had thought the creatures were not quite in the world in the same way everything else was; "slightly out of phase with time and reality," he had called it, whatever that meant.

"I am Shaidar Haran." Stopping by her servants, the Myrddraal bent to grip them by the backs of their necks, one hand to each. "When I speak, you may consider that you hear the voice of the Great Lord of the Dark." Those hands tightened to the surprisingly loud sound of cracking bone. The young man spasmed as he died, kicking out; the young woman merely went limp. They had been two of her prettiest. The Myrddraal straightened from the corpses. "I am his hand in this world, Graendal. When you stand before me, you stand before him."

Graendal considered carefully, if quickly. She was afraid, an emotion she was far more used to inspiring in others, but she knew how to control her fear. While she had never commanded armies as some of the others had, she was neither a stranger to hazard nor a coward, yet this was more than a mere threat. Moghedien and Cyndane still knelt with their heads to the marble floor, Moghedien actually trembling visibly. Graendal believed this Myrddraal. Or whatever it truly was. The Great Lord *was* taking a more direct hand in events, as she had feared. And if he learned of her scheming with Sammael. . . . If he chose to take action, that was; betting that he did not know was a foolish wager at this point.

She knelt smoothly before the Myrddraal. "What would you have me do?" Her voice had regained its strength. A necessary flexibility was not cowardice; those who did not bend for the Great Lord were bent. Or snapped in two. "Should I call you Great Master, or would you prefer another title? I would not feel comfortable addressing even the Great Lord's hand as I would him."

Shockingly, the Myrddraal laughed. It sounded like ice crumbling. Myrddraal never laughed. "You are braver than most. And wiser. Shaidar Haran will do for you. So long as you remember who I am. So long as you do not let bravery overcome your fear too far."

As it issued its commands—a visit to this Moridin was first, it seemed; she would need to be on her guard against Moghedien, and perhaps Cyndane also, taking revenge for her brief use of Compulsion; she doubted the girl was any more forgiving than the Spider—she decided to keep to herself the letter she had sent to Rodel Ituralde. Nothing she was told indicated that her actions would be displeasing to the Great Lord, and she still had to consider her own position. Moridin, whoever he was, might be Nae'blis today, but there was always tomorrow.

Bracing herself against the rocking of Arilyn's coach, Cadsuane moved one of the leather window curtains far enough

to see out. A light rain fell on Cairhien from a gray sky full
of blustering clouds and rough, swirling winds. Not only
the sky was full of wind. Howling gusts rocked the coach
more than did its forward motion. Tiny droplets stung her
hand, cold as ice. If the air cooled a little more, there would
be snow. She drew her woolen cloak closer; she had been
pleased to find it, shoved to the bottom of her saddlebags.
The air would cool.

The city's steep slate roofs and stone-paved streets glistened wetly, and though the rain was not hard, few were
willing to brave the strong winds. A woman guiding an ox-
cart with taps of a long goad moved as patiently as her ox,
but most people afoot clutched cloaks tightly, hoods pulled
down, and stepped quickly as the bearers of a sedan chair
rushed by, its stiff *con* fluttering. Others beside the woman
and her ox saw no reason for haste, though. In the middle
of the street a towering Aielman stood gaping at the sky
in disbelief while the drizzle soaked him, so absorbed that
a daring cutpurse sliced away his belt pouch and darted
off unnoticed by his victim. A woman whose elaborately
curled, high-piled hair marked her as noble walked along
slowly, her cloak flapping wildly, and its long hood as well.
This might have been the first time ever that she had actually walked in the streets, but she was laughing as the rain
slicked her cheeks. From the doorway of a perfumer's shop,
the shopkeeper stared out disconsolately; she would do little business today. Most of the hawkers had vanished for
the same reason, but a handful still hopefully cried hot tea
and meat pies from barrows beneath makeshift awnings.
Though anyone who bought a meat pie in the street these
days deserved the bellyache she would get.

A pair of starving dogs ran out from an alley, stiff-legged
and hackles up, barking and snarling at the coach. Cadsuane
let the curtain fall. Dogs seemed to know women who could
channel as easily as cats did, but dogs appeared to think
the women *were* cats, if unnaturally large ones. The pair of
women seated across from her were still in conversation.

"Forgive me," Daigian was saying, "but the logic is ines-
capable." She ducked her head apologetically, making the
moonstone dangling on a fine silver chain from her long
black hair sway across her forehead. Her fingers plucked
the white slashes in her dark skirts, and she spoke rapidly,

as though afraid of being interrupted. "If you accept that the lingering heat was the Dark One's work, the change must be by some other agency. He would not have relented. You might say that he has decided to freeze or drown the world instead of baking it, but why? Had the heat continued through spring, the dead might well have outnumbered the living, no different than if snow falls into the summer. Therefore, logically, some other hand is at work." The plump woman's diffidence was trying at times, but as always, Cadsuane found her logic impeccable. She just wished she knew whose hand and to what end.

"Peace!" Kumira muttered. "I would rather an ounce of hard proof than a hundredweight of your White Ajah logic." She was Brown, herself, though little given to their usual failings. A handsome woman with short-cut hair, she was hardheaded and practical, a keen observer, and never lost herself so deeply in thought that she lost sight of the world around her as well. No sooner had Kumira spoken than she patted Daigian's knee with a graceful hand, and gave a smile that changed her blue eyes from sharp to warm. Shienarans were a polite people, by and large, and Kumira took care not to offend. By accident, at least. "Put your mind to what we can do about the sisters held by the Aiel. I know you'll reason out something if anyone can."

Cadsuane snorted. "They deserve whatever happens to them." She had not been allowed near the Aiel tents herself, nor had any of her companions, but some of the fools who had sworn fealty to the al'Thor boy had ventured out to the sprawling encampment and come back white-faced and torn between outrage and sicking up. Normally, she also would have been furious over the affront to Aes Sedai dignity, whatever the circumstances; not now. To achieve her goal, she would have run the entire White Tower through the streets naked. How could she concern herself with the discomfort of women who might have ruined everything?

Kumira opened her mouth to protest despite knowing her feelings, but Cadsuane went on, calm yet relentless. "Perhaps they'll weep enough to atone for the dog's dinner they made of matters, but I doubt it. They are out of our hands, and if they were in mine, I might just *give* them to the Aiel. Forget them, Daigian, and put that fine mind of yours on the track I set you."

The Cairhienin woman's pale cheeks flushed red at the compliment. Thank the Light she was not this way except with other sisters. Kumira sat silently, very smooth-faced, her hands in her lap. She might be subdued now, but little could subdue Kumira for long. They were exactly the pair Cadsuane wanted with her today.

The coach tilted as the team started up the long ramp leading to the Sun Palace. "Remember what I told you," she told the other two firmly. "And have a care!"

They murmured that they would, as well they might, and she nodded. If need demanded, she would use them both for mulch, and others too, but she did not intend to lose either because they grew careless.

There was no bother or delay in letting the coach through the Palace gates. The guards recognized Arilyn's sigil on the doors, and they knew who would be riding inside. That coach had been to the Palace often enough in the past week. The moment the horses halted, an anxious-eyed footman in unadorned black opened the coach door, holding out a broad flat parasol of dark oiled cloth. Rain dripped from the edge onto his bare head, but then, it was not intended for his shelter.

Quickly touching the ornaments dangling from the bun atop her head to be sure they were all there—she had never lost one, but that was because she was careful of them—Cadsuane gathered the handles of her square wicker sewing basket from beneath her seat and stepped down. Half a dozen footmen stood waiting behind the first, parasols at the ready. So many passengers would have crowded the coach beyond comfort, but the footmen were not about to be caught short, and the extra did not hurry away until it was plain there were only the three of them.

Obviously the coach had been seen coming. Dark-garbed serving men and women made a neat array on the deep blue and gold tiles of the great entry hall with its square-vaulted ceiling five spans high. They leaped forward, taking cloaks, offering small, warm linen towels in case anyone needed to dry face or hands, proffering Sea Folk porcelain goblets of mulled wine that gave off a heady scent of spices. A winter drink, yet the sudden drop in temperature made it suitable. And after all, it *was* winter. Finally.

Three Aes Sedai stood waiting to one side among the

massive square columns of dark marble, in front of tall, pale friezes depicting battles no doubt important to Cairhien, but Cadsuane ignored the women for the time being. One of the young serving men had a small red-and-gold figure embroidered on the left breast of his coat, what people were calling a Dragon. Corgaide, the grave-faced, gray-haired woman who ordered the servants in the Sun Palace, wore no ornament save for the large ring of heavy keys at her waist. Nor did anyone else have any decoration on their clothes, and despite the young man's apparent enthusiasm, it was Corgaide, the Holder of the Keys, who would set the mood among the servants. Still, she had allowed the young fellow his embroidery; a point to remember. Cadsuane spoke to her quietly, asking after a room where she might work her embroidery hoop undisturbed, and the woman did not blink at the request. But then, doubtless she had heard stranger, serving in this place.

As the servants with the cloaks and trays bowed and curtsied themselves off, Cadsuane finally turned to the three sisters among the columns. They were all looking at her, ignoring Kumira and Daigian. Corgaide remained, but she stayed well back, giving the Aes Sedai privacy. "I hardly expected to find you strolling about at your ease," Cadsuane said. "I thought the Aiel worked their apprentices hard."

Faeldrin barely reacted, merely a slight jerk of her head that softly rattled the colored beads in her thin braids, but Merana colored with embarrassment, and her hands clenched in her skirts. Events had shaken Merana so deeply that Cadsuane was unsure she would ever recover. Bera, of course, was very nearly unflappable.

"Most of us were given a freeday because of the rain," Bera replied calmly. A sturdy woman in plain wool—fine and well-cut, but decidedly plain—you might have thought her more at home on a farm than in a palace. You might if you were a fool; Bera had a keen mind, a strong will, and Cadsuane did not believe she ever made the same mistake twice. Like most sisters, she had not entirely gotten over meeting Cadsuane Melaidhrin, alive and in the flesh, yet she did not let awe rule her. After only the slightest of deep breaths, she went on. "I cannot understand why you keep coming back, Cadsuane. Clearly, you want something from us, but unless you tell us what it is, we cannot help you. We know what you did for the Lord Dragon"—she stumbled a little over the title; they still were not quite sure what to call the boy—"but it's obvious you came to Cairhien because of him, and until you tell us why and what you intend, you must understand that you'll find no aid from us." Faeldrin, another Green, gave a start at Bera's bold tone, but she was nodding agreement before Bera finished.

"You must understand this, too," Merana added, her serenity regained. "If we decide we must oppose you, we will." Bera's face did not change, but Faeldrin's mouth tightened briefly. Perhaps she disagreed, and perhaps she did not want to reveal too much.

Cadsuane favored them with a thin smile. Tell them why and what? If *they* decided? So far they had managed to stuff themselves into young al'Thor's saddlebags tied hand and foot, even Bera. Small recommendation for letting them decide so much as what to wear in the morning! "I did not come to see you," she said. "Though I suppose Kumira and Daigian would enjoy a visit, since you have a freeday. You will excuse me."

Motioning Corgaide to lead on, she followed the woman across the entry hall. She only glanced back once. Bera and the others had already gathered up Kumira and Daigian and were hustling them away, but hardly like welcome guests. More like herded geese. Cadsuane smiled. Most sisters considered Daigian little better than a wilder and treated her little better than a servant. In that company, Kumira hardly stood much higher. The most suspicious could not think they were there to try to convince anyone of anything. So Daigian would pour the tea and sit quietly except when addressed—and apply her excellent mind to everything she heard. Kumira would let everyone except Daigian speak before her—and sort and file away every word, every gesture and grimace. Bera and the rest would keep their oaths to the boy, of course—that went without saying—but how assiduously was another question. Even Merana might be unwilling to go too far beyond bare obedience. That was bad enough, yet it left considerable room for them to maneuver. Or be maneuvered.

Dark-liveried servants hurrying at their tasks along the broad, tapestry-hung hallways darted aside for Cadsuane and Corgaide, and the two of them progressed to a flurry of deep bows and curtsies made over baskets and trays and armloads of towels. From the way eyes watched Corgaide, Cadsuane suspected the deference was as much for the Holder of the Keys as for an Aes Sedai. There were a few Aiel about, too, huge men like cold-eyed lions and women like colder-eyed leopards. Some of those gazes followed her icily enough to bring on the snow threatened by the rain outside, but other Aiel nodded to her gravely, and here and there one of the fierce-eyed women went so far as to smile. She had never claimed to be responsible for saving their *Car'a'carn*, but tales became twisted in retelling, and the belief granted her more respect than any other sister, and certainly more freedom of movement around the Palace. She wondered how they would feel if they knew that had she had the boy in front of her right then, she would have been hard-pressed to stop herself from blistering his hide for him! Barely more than a week since he nearly got himself killed, and not only had he managed to elude her completely, he had made her task even more difficult, if half what she heard was true. A pity he had not been raised in Far Madding. But then, that might have led to its own catastrophe.

The room Corgaide took her to was comfortably warm, with fires blazing in marble fireplaces at either end of the chamber and lamps lit, mirrored flames in glass towers that chased away the day's gloom. Plainly Corgaide had sent orders ahead to prepare while she was waiting in the entry hall. A serving woman appeared almost as soon as they, with both hot tea and spiced wine on a tray, and small cakes glazed with honey.

"Will there be anything else, Aes Sedai?" Corgaide asked as Cadsuane set her sewing basket beside the tray on a table with edge and legs thickly gilded. Rigidly carved, too, as was the wide cornice, also covered with gilt. Cadsuane always felt she was in a golden fish weir when she visited Cairhien. Despite the light and warmth inside, rain dripping outside the tall narrow windows and the gray sky outside heightened the sensation.

"The tea will do nicely," she said. "If you will, tell Alanna Mosvani that I want to see her. Tell her, without delay."

Corgaide's keys jingled as she curtsied, murmuring respectfully that she would find "Alanna Aes Sedai" herself.

Her grave expression never altered as she left. Very likely she was examining the request for subtleties. Cadsuane preferred to be direct, when possible. She had tripped up any number of clever people who had not believed she meant exactly what she said.

Opening the lid of her sewing basket, she took out her embroidery hoop with a less than half-done piece of work wrapped around it. The basket had pockets woven inside to hold items that had nothing to do with sewing. Her ivory hand mirror and hairbrush and comb, a pen case and tightly stoppered ink bottle, a number of things that she had found useful to have at hand over the years, including some that would have surprised anyone with nerve enough to search the basket. Not that she often left it out of her sight. Setting the polished silver thread box carefully on the table, she selected the skeins she needed and sat with her back to the door. The major image on her piece of embroidery was finished, a man's hand clutching the ancient symbol of the Aes Sedai. Cracks ran across the black-and-white disc, and there was no telling whether the hand was trying to hold it together or crush it. She knew what she intended, but time would tell what was truth.

Threading a needle, she set to work on one of the surrounding images, a bright red rose. Roses and star-blaze and sunburst alternated with daisies and hearts-blush and snowcap, all separated by bands of stark nettles and long-thorned briars. It would be a disturbing piece, when completed.

Before she had finished half a petal on the rose, a flash of motion reflected on the flat lid of the thread box caught her eye. It had been carefully placed to reflect the doorway. She did not raise her head from the hoop. Alanna stood there glaring at her back. Cadsuane continued the slow work of her needle, but she watched that reflection from the corner of her eye. Twice Alanna half turned as if to go, then finally drew herself up, visibly steeling herself.

"Come in, Alanna." Still not raising her head, Cadsuane pointed to a spot in front of her. "Stand there." She smiled wryly as Alanna jumped. There were advantages to being a legend; people seldom noticed the obvious when dealing with a legend.

Alanna stalked into the room in a swish of silk skirts

and took the place Cadsuane had indicated, but there was a sulky twist to her mouth. "Why do you persist in badgering me?" she demanded. "I cannot tell you any more than I have. And if I could, I don't know that I would! He belongs to—!" She cut off abruptly, biting her lower lip, but she might as well have finished. The al'Thor boy belonged to her; her Warder. She had the gall to think that!

"I have kept your crime to myself," Cadsuane said quietly, "but only because I saw no reason to complicate matters." Lifting her eyes to the other woman, she kept her voice soft. "If you think that means I won't core you like a cabbage, think again."

Alanna stiffened. The light of *saidar* suddenly shone around her.

"If you wish to be truly foolish." Cadsuane smiled, a cold smile. She made no move to embrace the Source herself. One of her dangling hair ornaments, intertwined golden crescents, was cool on her temple. "You keep a whole hide at present, but my sufferance is not infinite. In fact, it dangles by a thread."

Alanna struggled with herself, unconsciously smoothing blue silk. Abruptly the glow of the Power winked out, and she turned her head away from Cadsuane so swiftly that her long black hair swung. "I don't know any more to tell." The sullen words rushed out of her breathily. "He was injured, and then not, but I don't think a sister Healed him. The wounds no one could Heal are still there. He leaps about, Traveling, but he's still in the south. Somewhere in Illian, I think, but at this distance, he could be in Tear for all I know. He's full of rage, and pain, and suspicion. There isn't any more, Cadsuane. There isn't!"

Careful of the silver pitcher's heat, Cadsuane poured a cup of tea, testing the thin green porcelain cup for warmth. As might have been expected in silver, the tea had cooled quickly. Channeling briefly, she heated it again. The dark tea tasted too much of mint; Cairhienin used mint entirely too freely in her opinion. She did not offer a cup to Alanna. Traveling. How *could* the boy have rediscovered what had been lost to the White Tower since the Breaking? "You will keep me fully informed, however, won't you, Alanna." That was not a question. "Look at me, woman! If you *dream* of him, I want every detail!"

Unshed tears glistened in Alanna's eyes. "In my place, you would have done the same!"

Cadsuane scowled over the cup at her. She might have. There was no difference between what Alanna had done and a man forcing himself on a woman, but, the Light help her, she might have, had she believed it would help her reach her goal. Now, she no longer considered even making Alanna pass the bond to her. Alanna had proved how useless that was in controlling him.

"Do not keep me waiting, Alanna," she said in an icy tone. She had no sympathy for the other woman. Alanna was another in a line of sisters, from Moiraine to Elaida, who had bungled and worsened what they should have been mending. While she herself had been off chasing first Logain Ablar and then Mazrim Taim. Which did not soothe her mood.

"I will keep you fully informed," Alanna sighed, pouting like a girl. Cadsuane itched to slap her. Alanna had worn the shawl over twenty years; she should have grown up more than this. Of course, she was Arafellin. In Far Madding, few girls of twenty sulked and pouted as much as an Arafellin could on her aged deathbed.

Abruptly, Alanna's eyes widened in alarm, and Cadsuane saw another face reflected in the lid of her thread box. Setting the cup back on the tray and her embroidery hoop on the table, Cadsuane stood and turned to the door. She did not hurry, but she did not dally or play games as she had with Alanna, either.

"Are you done with her, Aes Sedai?" Sorilea asked, stepping into the room. The leathery, white-haired Wise One spoke to Cadsuane, but her eyes remained on Alanna. Ivory and gold clicked softly at her wrists as she planted hands on her hips, and her dark shawl slid to her elbows.

When Cadsuane said that she was indeed done, Sorilea gestured curtly to Alanna, who stalked from the room. Flounced might have been a better word, with sullen irritation on her face. Sorilea frowned after her. Cadsuane had encountered the woman before, and interesting encounters they had been, if brief. She had not met many people she considered formidable, but Sorilea was one. Perhaps even a match for herself, in some ways. She also suspected the woman was as old as she was, maybe older, and that, she had never expected to find.

No sooner had Alanna vanished than Kiruna appeared in the doorway, kicking gray silk skirts in her hurry and peering down the hall in the direction Alanna had gone. And carrying an intricately worked golden tray that held an even more elaborate golden pitcher with a high neck, and, incongruously, two small, white-glazed pottery cups. "Why is Alanna running?" she said. "I would have been faster, Sorilea, but—" She saw Cadsuane then, and her cheeks went the deepest possible crimson. Embarrassment looked quite odd on the statuesque woman.

"Put the tray on the table, girl," Sorilea said, "and go to Chaelin. She will be waiting to give you your lessons."

Stiffly, Kiruna set her burden down, avoiding Cadsuane's eyes. As she turned to go, Sorilea caught her chin in sinewy fingers. "You have begun to make a true effort, girl," the Wise One told her firmly. "If you continue, you will do very well. Very well. Now, go. Chaelin is not as patient as I."

Sorilea waved toward the corridor, but Kiruna stood staring at her for a long moment, a strange expression on her face. If Cadsuane had had to make a wager, she would have called Kiruna pleased at the praise and surprised at being pleased. The white-haired woman opened her mouth, and Kiruna gave herself a shake and hurried from the room. A remarkable show.

"Do you really think she will learn your ways of weaving *saidar*?" Cadsuane asked, hiding her incredulity. Kiruna and the others had told her of these lessons, but many of the Wise Ones' weaves were very different from those taught in the White Tower. The first way you learned the weave for a particular thing imprinted itself on you; learning a second was all but impossible, and even when you could learn, the second-learned weave almost never worked nearly as well. That was one reason some sisters did not welcome wilders to the Tower at any age; too much might have been learned already, and could not be unlearned.

Sorilea shrugged. "Perhaps. Learning a second way is hard enough without all the hand-waving you Aes Sedai do. The main thing Kiruna Nachiman must learn is that she owns her pride; it does not own her. She will be a very strong woman once she learns that." Pulling a chair around to face the one Cadsuane had been sitting in, she eyed it doubtfully, then sat down. She appeared almost as stiff and uncomfortable as Kiruna had, but she motioned authoritatively for Cadsuane to sit, a strong-willed woman used to command.

Cadsuane swallowed a rueful chuckle as she took her chair. It was well to be reminded that, wilders or not, the Wise Ones were far from ignorant savages. Of course they would know the difficulties. As for hand-waving. . . . Few had channeled where she could see, but she had noticed that they created some weaves without the gestures that sisters used. The hand movements were not truly part of the weave, but in a way they were, because they had been part of learning the weave. Perhaps, once, there had been Aes Sedai who could, say, hurl a ball of fire without some sort of throwing motion, but if so, they were long dead, and their teachings with them. Today, some things just could not be done without the appropriate gestures. There were sisters who claimed they could tell who had taught another sister by which motions she used for which weaves.

"Teaching any of our new apprentices anything has been difficult at best," Sorilea went on. "I do not speak to offend, but you Aes Sedai give oath, it seems, and immediately try to find a way around it. Alanna Mosvani is particularly difficult." Suddenly her clear green eyes were very sharp on Cadsuane's face. "How can we punish her willful failings if it means harming the *Car'a'carn*?"

Cadsuane folded her hands in her lap. Masking surprise was not easy. So much for the secret of Alanna's crime. But why had the woman let her know that she knew? Perhaps one revelation called for another. "The bond does not work in that fashion," she said. "If you kill her, he will die, then or soon after. Short of that, he will be aware of what happens to her, but he will not really feel it. As far away as he is now, he will only be vaguely aware, at that."

Sorilea nodded slowly. Her fingers touched the golden tray on the table, then came away. Her expression was as hard to read as the face of a statue, but Cadsuane suspected that Alanna would find an unpleasant surprise the next time she let her temper flare, or threw one of her Arafellin sulks. That was unimportant, though. Only the boy was important.

"Most men will take what is offered, if it seems attractive and pleasant," Sorilea said. "Once, we thought of Rand al'Thor so. Unfortunately, it is too late to change the path we walk. Now, he suspects whatever is offered freely. Now, if I wanted him to accept something, I would pretend I did not want him to have it. If I wanted to stay close to him, I would pretend indifference to whether I ever saw him again." Once more, those eyes focused on Cadsuane, green augers. Not trying to see what lay inside her head. The woman knew. Some, at least. Enough, or too much.

Still, Cadsuane felt a rising thrill of possibility. If she had had any doubts that Sorilea wanted to feel her out, they were gone. And you did not feel out someone in this manner unless you hoped for some agreement. "Do you believe a man must be hard?" she asked. She was taking a chance. "Or strong?" By her tone, she left no doubt she saw a difference.

Again Sorilea touched the tray; the smallest of smiles might have quirked her lips for an instant. Or not. "Most men see the two as one and the same, Cadsuane Melaidhrin. Strong endures; hard shatters."

Cadsuane drew breath. A chance she would have scoured anyone else for taking. But she was not anyone else, and sometimes chances had to be taken. "The boy confuses them," she said. "He needs to be strong, and makes himself harder. Too hard, already, and he will not stop until he is stopped. He has forgotten how to laugh except in bitterness; there are no tears left in him. Unless he finds laughter and tears again, the world faces disaster. He must learn that even the Dragon Reborn is flesh. If he goes to Tarmon Gai'don as he is, even his victory may be as dark as his defeat."

Sorilea listened intently, and kept silent even after Cadsuane finished. Those green eyes studied her. "Your Dragon Reborn and your Last Battle are not in our prophecies," Sorilea said at last. "We have tried to make Rand al'Thor know his blood, but I fear he sees us as only another spear. If one spear breaks in your hand, you do not pause to mourn before taking up another. Perhaps you and I aim at targets not too far apart."

"Perhaps we do," Cadsuane said cautiously. Targets even a hand apart might be not at all alike.

Abruptly, the glow of *saidar* surrounded the leather-faced woman. She was weak enough to make Daigian look at least moderately strong. But then, Sorilea's strength did not lie in the Power. "There is a thing you may find useful," she said. "I cannot make it work, but I can weave the flows to show you." She did just that, laying feeble skeins that fell into place and melted, too poor to do what they were intended for. "It is called Traveling," Sorilea said.

This time, Cadsuane's jaw dropped. Alanna and Kiruna and the rest denied teaching the Wise Ones how to link, or a number of other skills they suddenly seemed to have, and Cadsuane had assumed the Aiel had managed to wring them out of the sisters held in the tents. But this was. . . .

Impossible, she would have said, yet she did not believe Sorilea was lying. She could hardly wait to try the weave herself. Not that it was of much use immediately. Even if she knew exactly where the wretched boy was, she had to make him come to her. Sorilea was right about that. "A very great gift," she said slowly. "I have nothing I can give you to compare."

This time, there was no doubt of the brief smile that flashed across Sorilea's lips. She knew very well that Cadsuane was in her debt. Taking up the heavy golden pitcher with both hands, she carefully filled the small white cups. With plain water. She did not spill a drop.

"I offer you water oath," she said solemnly, picking up one of the cups. "By this, we are bound as one, to teach Rand al'Thor laughter and tears." She sipped, and Cadsuane imitated her.

"We are bound as one." And if their targets turned out not to be the same at all? She did not underestimate Sorilea as ally or opponent, but Cadsuane knew which target had to be struck, at any cost.

CHAPTER

13

Floating Like Snow

The northern horizon was purple with the fierce rain that had hammered the east of Illian through the night. Overhead, a morning sky of dark boiling clouds threatened, and strong winds flung cloaks about, made banners snap and crack like whips on the crest of the ridge, the white Dragon Banner and the crimson Banner of Light, and the bright standards of nobility from Illian and Cairhien and Tear. The nobles kept to their own kind, three widely spaced knots awash in gilt and silver-plated steel, silks and velvets and laces, but in common they looked around uneasily. Even the best-trained of their horses tossed heads and stamped hooves on the muddy ground. The wind was cold, and colder seeming for the heat it had replaced so abruptly, just as the rain had been a shock after so long without. From whatever nation, they had prayed for the baking drought to break, but none knew what to make of unrelenting storms in answer to their prayers. Some glanced at Rand when they thought he would not notice. Perhaps wondering if *he* had answered them so. The thought made him laugh softly, bitterly.

He patted his black gelding's neck with a leather-gauntleted hand, glad that Tai'daishar did not show nerves. The massive animal might have been a statue, awaiting the pressure of reins or knees to move. It was good that the Dragon Reborn's horse seemed as cold as he did, as though they floated in the Void together. Even with the One Power raging through him, fire and ice and death, he was barely aware of the wind, though it flailed his gold-embroidered cloak about and cut through his coat, green silk thickly worked with gold and not intended for wear in such weather. The wounds in his side ached and throbbed, the old and the new cutting across it, the wounds that would never heal, but that was distant, too, another man's flesh. The Crown of Swords might have been pricking someone else's temples with the sharp points of the tiny blades among its golden laurel leaves. Even the filth woven through *saidin* seemed less obtrusive than it once had; still vile, still loathsome, but no longer worth notice. The nobles' eyes on his back were palpable, though.

Shifting his sword hilt, he leaned forward. He could see the tight cluster of low, wooded hills half a mile to the east as clearly as if he were using a looking glass. The land was flat, here, the only prominences those forested hills and this long ridge, thrusting up from the heath. The next thicket dense enough to truly deserve the name lay close to ten miles off. Only storm-battered half-leafless trees and tangles of undergrowth were visible on the hills, but he knew what they hid. Two, perhaps three thousand of the men Sammael had gathered to try to stop him from taking Illian.

That army had disintegrated once they learned that the man who had summoned them was dead, that Mattin Stepaneos had vanished, perhaps into the grave as well, and that there was a new king in Illian. Many had scattered back to their homes, yet just as many clung together. Usually no more than twenty here, thirty there, but a great army if they came together again, and countless armed bands otherwise. Either way, they could not be allowed to roam the countryside. Time weighed down on his shoulders like lead. There was never enough time, but maybe this once. . . . Fire and ice and death.

What would you do? he thought. *Are you there?* And then, doubtfully, hating the doubt, *Were you ever there?* Silence answered, deep and dead in the emptiness that surrounded him. Or was there mad laughter somewhere in the recesses of his mind? Did he imagine it, like the feel of someone looking over his shoulder, someone just on the brink of touching his back? Or the colors that swirled just out of sight, more than colors, and were gone? A thing of madmen. His gloved thumb slid along the carvings that serpentined the Dragon Scepter. The long green-and-white

tassels below the polished spear-point fluttered in the wind.
Fire and ice, and death would come.

"I will go talk to them myself," he announced. Which
produced a furor.

Lord Gregorin, the green sash of the Council of Nine
slanted across his ornately gilded breastplate, hurried his
fine-ankled white gelding forward from the Illianers, followed closely by Demetre Marcolin, First Captain of the
Companions, on a solid bay. Marcolin was the only man
among them without silk or a speck of lace, the only man
in plain if brightly burnished armor, though the conical helmet resting on his saddle's high pommel did bear three thin
golden plumes. Lord Marac lifted his reins, then let them
fall uncertainly when he saw no others of the Nine move.
A wide man with a stolid manner, and new to the Council,
he often seemed more craftsman than lord despite the rich
silks beneath his lavish armor and the falls of lace spilling
over. High Lords Weiramon and Tolmeran spurred together
from the Tairens, as crusted with gold and silver as any
of the Nine, and Rosana, newly raised to High Lady and
wearing a breastplate worked with the Hawk-and-Stars of
her House. There, too, others half made as if to follow then
hung back, looking worried. Blade-slender Aracome and
blue-eyed Maraconn and bald-headed Gueyam were dead
men; they did not know that, but however much they wanted
to be at the center of power, they feared Rand would kill
them. Only Lord Semaradrid came from the Cairhienin, on
a gray that had seen better days, his armor battered, its gild-
ing chipped. His face was gaunt and hard, the front of his
head shaved and powdered like a common soldier, and his
dark eyes shone with contempt for the taller Tairens.

There was plenty of contempt to go around. Tairens and
Cairhienin hated one another. Illianers and Tairens despised each other. Only Cairhienin and Illianers got along
to any degree, and there was a certain amount of prickle
even there. Their two nations might not have near the
long history of bad blood shared by Tear and Illian, yet
the Cairhienin still were foreigners, armed and armored
on Illian's soil, welcomed halfheartedly at best and only
that much because they followed Rand. But despite all the
frowning and bristling and trying to talk at once as they

milled about Rand in a flurry of windblown cloaks, they had a common goal now. After a fashion.

"Majesty," Gregorin said hastily, bowing in his gold-tooled saddle, "I do beg you let me go in your stead, or First Captain Marcolin." The square-cut beard that left his upper lip bare framed a round face creased with worry. "These men must know you are King—the proclamations do be read in every village, at every crossroads, as we do speak—yet they may no show proper respect for your crown." Lantern-jawed Marcolin, clean-shaven, studied Rand with dark, deep-set eyes, giving no hint what lay behind his impassive face. The Companions' loyalty was to the crown of Illian, and Marcolin was old enough to remember when Tarn al'Thor had been Second Captain over him, but only he knew what he thought of Rand al'Thor as King.

"My Lord Dragon," Weiramon intoned as he made his bow, not waiting for Gregorin to finish. The man always intoned, and even on horseback he seemed to strut. His worked velvets and striped silks and falls of lace almost overwhelmed his armor, and his pointed gray beard gave off a flowery scent of perfumed oils. "This rabble is too petty to concern the Lord Dragon personally. Set dogs to catch dogs, I say. Let the Illianers root them out. Burn my soul, they've done nothing so far to serve you but talk." Trust him to turn agreement with Gregorin into an insult. Tolmeran was lean enough to make Weiramon appear bulky and somber enough to dim the luster of his garb; he was no fool, and rival to Weiramon besides, yet he nodded slowly in agreement. No love lost there for Illianers, at all.

Semaradrid curled a lip at the Tairens but addressed himself to Rand, cutting in hard on Weiramon's heels. "This gathering is ten times as large as any other we have found so far, my Lord Dragon." He cared nothing for the King of Illian, and little enough for the Dragon Reborn, except that the throne of Cairhien was Rand's to give, and Semaradrid hoped it would be given to one he could follow instead of fight. "Their loyalties must be to Brend, or so many would not have held together. I fear talking to them is a waste of time, but if you must talk, let me ring their position openly with steel so they know the price of putting a foot out of line."

Rosana glared right back at Semaradrid, a lean woman,

not tall yet nearly as tall as he, with eyes like blue ice. She
did not wait for him to finish, either, and she, too, spoke to
Rand. "I've come too far and invested too much in you to
see you die now, for nothing," she said bluntly. No more
a fool than Tolmeran, Rosana had claimed a place in the
councils of the High Lords, though Tairen High Ladies seldom did, and blunt was the word for her. Despite the armor most of the noblewomen wore, none actually led their
armsmen into battle, yet Rosana carried a flanged mace on
her saddle, and sometimes Rand thought she would like a
chance to use it. "I doubt those Illianers lack for bows," she
said, "and it takes only one arrow to kill even the Dragon
Reborn." Pursing his lips thoughtfully, Marcolin nodded
before catching himself, then exchanged startled looks with
Rosana, each more surprised than the other to find themselves of like mind with an ancient enemy.

"These peasants could never have found the mettle to
stay under arms without encouragement," Weiramon continued smoothly, ignoring Rosana. He was skilled at ignoring who, and what, he did not want to see or hear. He *was*
a fool. "May I suggest my Lord Dragon look to these so-
called Nine for the source?"

"I do protest this Tairen pig's insults, Majesty!" Gregorin
growled right atop him, one hand darting to his sword. "I
do protest most heartily!"

"There are too many this time," Semaradrid said at the
same instant. "Most will turn against you as soon as your
back is to them in any case." By his pointed frown, he might
have been speaking of the Tairens as well as the men on the
wooded hills. Perhaps he was. "Better to kill them and be
done!"

"Did I ask for opinions?" Rand snapped harshly. Babble
became silence, except for the crack of cloaks and banners
flapping in the wind. Suddenly expressionless faces regarded him, more than one going gray. They did not know
he held the Power, but they knew him. Not all of what they
knew was truth, but it was just as well they believed. "You
will come with me, Gregorin," he said in a more normal
voice. Still hard, though. Steel was all they understood; go
soft, and they *would* turn on him. "And you, Marcolin. The
rest stay here. Dashiva! Hopwil!"

Everyone not named reined their horses back hurriedly

as the two Asha'man rode to join Rand, and the Illianers eyed the black-coated men as though they would have liked to remain behind, too. Aside from anything else, Corlan Dashiva was glowering and muttering under his breath as he so often did. Everyone was aware that *saidin* drove men mad sooner or later, and plain-faced Dashiva certainly looked the part, lank untrimmed hair flying in the wind, licking his lips and shaking his head. For that matter, Eben Hopwil, just sixteen and still with a few scattered blotches on his cheeks, wore a staring frown that gazed beyond anything in sight. At least Rand knew the why of that.

As the Asha'man drew near, Rand could not help cocking his head to listen, though what he listened for was inside his head. Alanna was there, of course; neither the Void nor the Power altered that a whisker. Distance wore that awareness down to just that—awareness that she existed, somewhere far to the north—yet there was something more today, something he had felt several times recently, dim and barely on the edge of notice. A whisper of shock, perhaps, or outrage, a breath of something sharp he could not quite grasp. She must feel whatever it was very strongly for him to be even that conscious of it at this distance. Maybe she was missing him. A wry thought. He did not miss her. Ignoring Alanna was easier than it had been once. She was there, but not the voice that used to shout of death and killing whenever an Asha'man came into sight. Lews Therin was gone. Unless that feel of someone staring at the back of his head, brushing his shoulder blades with a finger, was him. *Was* there a madman's hoarse laughter deep in his thoughts? Or was it his own? The man *had* been there! He had!

He became aware of Marcolin staring at him, and Gregorin trying very hard not to. "Not yet," he told them wryly, and almost laughed when they clearly understood right away. Relief was too plain on their faces for anything else. He was not insane. Yet. "Come," he told them, and started Tai'daishar down the slope at a trot. Despite the men following, he felt alone. Despite the Power, he felt empty.

Between the ridge and the hills lay patches of thick scrub and long stretches of dead grass, a glistening mat of brown and yellow beaten flat by the rain. Only a few days ago the ground had been so parched that he had thought it could drink a river without changing. Then the torrents came, sent by the Creator finding mercy at last, or maybe by the Dark One in a fit of black humor; he did not know which. Now the horses' hooves splashed mud at every second step. He hoped this did not take long. He had some time, by what Hopwil had reported, but not forever. Perhaps weeks, if he was lucky. He needed months. Light, he needed years he would never have!

His hearing heightened by the Power, he could make out some of what the men behind him were saying. Gregorin and Marcolin rode knee-to-knee, trying to hold their cloaks against the wind and speaking in low tones about the men ahead, about their fears the men might fight. Neither doubted they would be crushed if they resisted, but they feared the effect on Rand, and his on Illian, if Illianers fought him now that Brend was dead. They still could not bring themselves to give Brend his true name, Sammael. The very notion that one of the Forsaken had ruled in Illian frightened them even more than the fact that the Dragon Reborn ruled there now.

Dashiva, slumped in his gray's saddle like a man who had never seen a horse before, muttered angrily under his breath. In the Old Tongue, which he spoke and read as fluently as a scholar. Rand knew a little, though not enough to understand what the fellow was mumbling. Probably complaints about the weather; despite being a farmer, Dashiva disliked being out-of-doors unless the skies were clear.

Only Hopwil rode in silence, frowning at something beyond the horizon, his hair and cloak whipping about as wildly as Dashiva's. Now and then he clutched the hilt of his sword unconsciously. Rand had to speak three times, the last sharply, before Hopwil gave a surprised jerk and booted his lanky dun up beside Tai'daishar.

Rand studied him. The young man—not a boy any longer, no matter his age—had filled out since Rand first saw him, though his nose and ears still seemed made for a bigger man. A Dragon, red-enameled gold, now balanced the silver Sword on his high collar, just like Dashiva's. Once, he had said he would laugh a year for joy when the Dragon was his, but he stared unblinking at Rand as though looking through him.

"What you learned was good news," Rand told him. Only an effort kept him from trying to crush the Dragon Scepter in his fist. "You did well." He had expected the Seanchan to return, but not so soon. He had hoped not so soon. And not leaping out of nowhere, swallowing cities at a gulp. When he found out that merchants in Illian had known for days before any of them thought to inform the Nine—the Light forbid they should lose a chance at profit because too many knew too much!—he had been within a hair of scouring the city to its foundations. But the news was good, or as good as it could be in the circumstances. Hopwil had Traveled to Amador, to the countryside nearby, and the Seanchan appeared to be waiting. Perhaps digesting what they had consumed. The Light send they choked on it! He forced his grip to loosen on the length of Dragon-carved spearhead. "If Morr brings half as good, I have time to settle Illian before dealing with them." Ebou Dar, as well! The Light burn the Seanchan! They were a distraction, one he did not need and could not afford to ignore.

Hopwil said nothing, only looked.

"Are you upset because you had to kill women?" *Desora, of the Musara Reyn, and Lamelle, of the Smoke Water Miagoma, and. . . .* Rand forced down the instinctive litany even as it began floating across the Void. New names had appeared on that list, names he did not remember adding. Laigin Arnault, a Red sister who had died trying to take him a prisoner to Tar Valon. Surely she had no right to a place, but she had claimed one. Colavaere Saighan, who had hanged herself rather than accept justice. Others. Men had died in thousands, by his order or by his hand, but it was the faces of the women that haunted his dreams. Each night, he made himself confront their silently accusing eyes. Maybe it was their eyes he had felt of late.

"I told you about *damane* and *sul'dam*," he said calmly, but inside of him, rage flared, fire spiderwebbing around the emptiness of the Void. *The Light burn me, I've killed more women than all your nightmares could hold! My hands are* black *with the blood of women!* "If you hadn't wiped out that Seanchan patrol, they'd have killed you for sure." He did not say that Hopwil should have avoided them, avoided the need to kill them. Too late for that. "I doubt that *damane* even knew how to shield a man. You had no choice." And better they were all dead than some escaping with word of a man who could channel, scouting them.

Absently, Hopwil touched his left sleeve, where the black color disguised fire-scarred wool. The Seanchan had not died easily or fast. "I piled the bodies in a hollow," he said in a flat voice. "The horses, everything. I burned it all to ash. White ash that floated in the wind like snow. It didn't bother me at all."

Rand heard the lie on the man's tongue, but Hopwil had to learn. After all, he had. They were what they were, and that was all there was to it. All there was. Liah, of the Cosaida Chareen, a name written in fire. Moiraine Damodred, another name that seared to the soul rather than merely burning. A nameless Darkfriend, represented only by a face, who had died by his sword near. . . .

"Majesty," Gregorin said loudly, pointing ahead. A lone man came out of the trees at the foot of the nearest hill to stand waiting in an attitude of defiance. He carried a bow, and wore a pointed steel cap and a belted mail shirt that hung nearly to his knees.

Rand spurred Tai'daishar to meet him seething with the Power. *Saidin* could protect him from men.

Up close, the bowman did not make so brave a sight. Rust streaked his helmet and mail, and he looked sodden, mud to his thighs, damp hair trailing down a narrow face. Coughing hollowly, he scrubbed at a long nose with the back of his hand. His bowstring appeared taut, though; that, he had protected from the rain. And the fletchings on the arrows in his quiver looked dry, too.

"Are you the leader here?" Rand demanded.

"You might say I do speak for him," the narrow-faced man replied warily. "Why?" As the others galloped up behind Rand, he shifted his feet, dark eyes like a cornered badger's. Badgers were dangerous, cornered.

"Watch your tongue, man!" Gregorin snapped. "You do speak to Rand al'Thor, the Dragon Reborn, Lord of the Morning and King of Illian! Kneel to your King! What do your name be?"

"He do be the Dragon Reborn?" the fellow said doubtfully. Eyeing Rand from the crown on his head to his boots, lingering a moment on the gilded Dragon buckling his sword belt, the man shook his head as if he had expected someone older, or grander. "And Lord of the Morning, you do say? Our King did never style himself so." He made no move toward kneeling, or giving his name. Gregorin's face darkened at the man's tone, and maybe at the man's oblique denial of Rand as King. Marcolin gave a slight nod, as though he had expected no more.

Damp rustlings stirred in the undergrowth among the trees. Rand heard easily, and abruptly he felt *saidin* fill Hopwil. No longer staring at nothing, Hopwil studied the woodline intently, a wild light in his eyes. Dashiva, silent, raking dark hair out of his face, looked bored. Leaning forward in his saddle, Gregorin opened his mouth angrily. Fire and ice, but not yet death.

"Peace, Gregorin." Rand did not raise his voice, but he wove flows to carry his words, Air and Fire, so they boomed against the wall of trees. "My offer is generous." The long-nosed man staggered at the sound, and Gregorin's horse shied. Those hidden men would hear clearly. "Lay down your arms, and those who want to return home, can. Those who want to follow me instead, can do that. But no man leaves here under arms unless he *does* follow me. I know most of you are good men, who answered the call of your King and the Council of Nine to defend Illian, but *I* am your King, now, and I'll not have anyone tempted to turn bandit." Marcolin nodded grimly.

"What about your Dragonsworn burning farms?" a man's frightened voice shouted from the trees. "They do be flaming bandits!"

"What about your Aiel?" another called. "I do hear they carry off whole villages!" More voices from unseen men joined in, all shouting the same things, Dragon-sworn and Aiel, murderous brigands and savages. Rand ground his teeth.

When the shouting faded, narrow-face said, "You do see?" He paused to cough, then hawked and spat, maybe for his chest and maybe for emphasis. A pitiful sight, all wet and rust, but his backbone was as tight as his bowstring. He ignored Rand's glare as easily as he did Gregorin's. "You do ask us to go home unarmed, unable to defend ourselves or our families, while your people do burn and steal and kill. They do say the storm be coming," he added, and looked surprised that he had, surprised and confused for a moment.

"The Aiel you've heard about are my enemies!" Not spiderwebs of flame this time, but solid sheets of fury that wrapped tight around the Void. Rand's voice was ice, though; it roared like the crack of winter. The storm was coming? Light, he *was* the storm! "*My* Aiel are hunting them down. My Aiel hunt the Shaido, and they and Davram Bashere and most of the Companions hunt bandits, whatever they call themselves! I am the King of Illian, and I will allow no one to disrupt the peace of Illian!"

"Even if what you say do be true," narrow-face began.

"It is!" Rand snapped. "You have until midday to decide." The man frowned uncertainly; unless the roiling clouds cleared, he might have a difficult time knowing midday. Rand gave him no relief. "Decide wisely!" he said. Whirling Tai'daishar about, he spurred the gelding to a gallop back toward the ridge without waiting for the others.

Reluctantly he let go of the Power, forced himself not to hang on like a man clutching salvation with his fingernails as life and filth drained from him together. For an instant, he saw double; the world seemed to tilt dizzily. That was a recent problem, and he worried it might be part of the sickness that killed men who channeled, but the dizziness never lasted more than moments. It was the rest of letting go that he regretted. The world seemed to dull. No, it did dull, and became somehow less. Colors were washed-out, the sky smaller, compared to what they had been before. He wanted desperately to seize the Source again and wring the One Power out of it. Always it was so when the Power left him.

No sooner had *saidin* gone, though, than rage bubbled in its place, white-hot and searing, nearly as hot as the Power had been. The Seanchan were not enough, and brigands hiding behind his name? Deadly distractions he could not afford. Was Sammael reaching out from the grave? Had he sown the Shaido to sprout like thorns wherever Rand laid a hand? Why? The man could not have *believed* he would die. And if half the tales Rand heard were true, there were more in Murandy and Altara and the Light alone knew where! Many among the Shaido already taken prisoner had spoken of an Aes Sedai. Could the *White Tower* be involved somehow? Would the White Tower never give him peace? Never? Never.

Battling fury, he was blind to Gregorin and the rest catching up. When they topped the ridge among the waiting nobles, he drew rein so abruptly that Tai'daishar reared, pawing the air and flinging mud from his hooves. The nobles edged their mounts back, from his gelding, from him.

"I gave them to midday," he announced. "Watch them. I don't want this lot breaking into fifty smaller bands and slipping away. I'll be in my tent." Except for wind-tossed cloaks they might have been stone, rooted to one spot as if he meant the command to watch for them personally. At that moment, he did not care if they stayed there till they froze or melted.

Without another word he trotted down the back slope of the ridge, followed by the two black-coated Asha'man and his Illianer banner-bearers. Fire and ice, and death was coming. But he was steel. He was steel.

CHAPTER
14

Message from the M'Hael

A mile west of the ridge, the camps began, men and horses and cook fires, wind-flailed banners and a few scattered tents clumped by nationality, by House, each camp a lake of churned mud separated from the others by stretches of brushy heath. Men mounted and afoot watched Rand's streaming banners pass, and peered toward other camps to gauge reactions. When the Aiel had been present, these men had made a single huge camp, driven together by one of the few things they truly shared in common. They were not Aiel, and feared them however much they denied it. The world would die unless he succeeded, but he had no illusions that they shared any loyalty to him, or even believed that the fate of the world could not be made to accommodate their own concerns, their own desires for gold or glory or power. A handful did, perhaps, a bare handful, but for the most part, they followed because they feared him far more than they did the Aiel. Maybe more than they did the Dark One, in whom some did not really believe, not in the depths of their hearts, not that he could and would touch the world harder than he had already. Rand stood before their faces, and they believed in that. He accepted it, now. He had too many battles ahead of him to waste effort on one he could not win. So long as they followed and obeyed, it had to be enough.

The largest of the camps was his own, and here Illianer Companions in green coats with yellow cuffs rubbed shoulders with Tairen Defenders of the Stone in fat-sleeved coats striped black-and-gold and an equal number of Cairhienin drawn from forty-odd Houses, in dark colors, some with *con* stiff above their heads. They cooked at different fires, slept apart, picketed their horses apart, and eyed one another warily, but they mingled. The safety of the Dragon Reborn was their responsibility, and they took the job seriously. Any of them might betray him, but not while the others were there to watch. Old hatreds and new dislikes would bring betrayal of any plot before the betrayer stopped to think.

A ring of steel stood guard around Rand's tent, a huge peaked thing of green silk embroidered all over with bees in thread-of-gold. It had belonged to his predecessor, Mattin Stepaneos, and had come with the crown, in a manner of speaking. Companions in burnished conical helmets stood side by side with Defenders in helmets ridged and rimmed, and Cairhienin in bell-shaped helms, ignoring the wind, barred faceguards hiding their features, halberds slanted precisely. Not one moved a hair when Rand drew rein, but a bevy of servants came running to attend to him and the Asha'man. A bony woman in the green-and-yellow vest of a groom from the Royal Palace in Illian took his bridle, while his stirrup was held by a bulbous-nosed fellow in the black-and-gold livery of the Stone of Tear. They tugged forelocks to him, and cast only one sharp look at one another. Boreane Carivin, a stout pale little woman in a dark dress, self-importantly offered him a silver tray of damp cloths from which steam rose. Cairhienin, she watched the other two, though more as if making sure they did their tasks properly than with the animosity for each other they barely hid. But with care, still. What worked with the soldiers worked with the servants as well.

Drawing off his gauntlets, Rand waved away Boreane's tray. Damer Flinn had risen from an ornately carved bench in front of the tent as Rand dismounted. Bald except for a ragged white fringe, Flinn looked more a grandfather than an Asha'man. A leather-tough grandfather with a stiff leg, who had seen more of the world than a farm. The sword at his hip looked as if it belonged, as well it should on a former soldier of the Queen's Guard. Rand trusted him more than most. Flinn had saved his life, after all.

Flinn saluted, fist to chest, and when Rand acknowledged him with a nod, limped closer and waited until the grooms left with the horses before speaking in a low voice. "Torval's here. Sent by the M'Hael, he says. He wanted to wait in the council tent. I told Narishma to watch him." That had been Rand's command, though he was not sure why he had given it; no one who came from the Black Tower was to be left alone. Hesitating, Flinn fingered the Dragon on his black collar. "He wasn't happy to hear you'd raised all of us."

"Wasn't he, now," Rand said softly, tucking his gloves behind his sword belt. And because Flinn still looked uncertain, he added, "You all earned it." He had been about to send one of the Asha'man to Taim—the Leader, the M'Hael, as the Asha'man all called him—but now Torval could carry the message. In the council tent? "Have refreshments sent," he told Flinn, then motioned Hopwil and Dashiva to follow.

Flinn saluted again, but Rand was already striding away, black mud squelching around his boots. No cheers rose for him in the blustering wind. He could recall when there had been. If that was not one of Lews Therin's memories. If Lews Therin had ever been real. A flash of color just beyond the edge of sight, the feel of someone about to touch him from behind. With an effort, he focused himself.

The council tent was a large red-striped pavilion that had once sat on the Plains of Maredo, now pitched in the middle of Rand's encampment, surrounded by thirty paces of bare ground. There were never guards here, not unless Rand was meeting with the nobles. Anyone trying to slip in would have been seen instantly by a thousand prying eyes. Three banners on tall poles formed a triangle around the tent, the Rising Sun of Cairhien, the Three Crescents of Tear, and the Golden Bees of Illian, and above the crimson roof, higher than the rest, stood the Dragon Banner, and the Banner of Light. The wind made them all stand out, rippling and snapping, and the tent walls shivered in the gusts. Inside, colorful, fringed carpets made a floor, and the only furniture was a huge table, thickly carved and gilded, inlaid with ivory and turquoise. A jumble of maps almost hid the tabletop.

Torval lifted his head from the maps, plainly ready to give the rough side of his tongue to whoever had barged in on him. Close to his middle years and tall beside anyone save Rand or an Aiel, he stared coldly down a sharp nose

that practically quivered with indignation. The Dragon and
the Sword glistened on his coat collar in the light of the
stand-lamps. A silk coat, shining black, cut fine enough for
a lord. His sword had silver mountings washed with gold,
and a glittering red gem capped the hilt. Another gleamed
darkly on a finger ring. You could not train men to be weapons without expecting a certain amount of arrogance, yet
Rand did not like Torval. But then, he had no need of Lews
Therin's voice to be suspicious of any man in a black coat.
How far did he truly trust even Flinn? Yet he had to lead
them. The Asha'man were his making, his responsibility.

When Torval saw Rand, he straightened casually and
saluted, but his expression barely changed. He had had a
sneering mouth the first time Rand ever saw him. "My Lord
Dragon," he said in the accents of Tarabon, and he might
have been greeting an equal. Or being gracious to an in-
ferior. His swaggering bow took in Hopwil and Dashiva
as well. "I give congratulations on the conquest of Illian.
A great victory, yes? There would have been wine to greet
you, but this young . . . Dedicated . . . does not seem to understand orders."

In the corner, silver bells on the ends of Narishma's two
long dark braids made a faint sound as he shifted. He had
tanned darkly in the southern sun, but some things about
him had not changed. Older than Rand, his face made him
seem younger than Hopwil, but the red that rose in his
cheeks was anger, not embarrassment. His pride in the new-
won Sword on his collar was quiet, yet deep. Torval smiled
at him, a slow smile both amused and dangerous. Dashiva
laughed, a short bark, and was still.

"What are you doing here, Torval?" Rand asked roughly.
He tossed the Dragon Scepter and his gauntlets down atop
the maps and followed them with his sword belt and scabbarded sword. The maps that Torval had no reason to be
studying. No need of Lews Therin's voice.

With a shrug, Torval produced a letter from his coat
pocket and handed it to Rand. "The M'Hael, he sent this."
The paper was snowy white and thick, the seal a dragon
impressed in a large oval of blue wax that glittered with
golden flecks. It might almost have been thought to come
from the Dragon Reborn. Taim did think well of himself.
"The M'Hael said to tell you the tales of Aes Sedai in Mu-

randy with an army, they are true. Rumor says they are rebels against Tar Valon"—Torval's sneer thickened with disbelief—"but they are marching toward the Black Tower. Soon, they may become a danger, yes?"

Rand cracked the magnificent seal to bits between his fingers. "They're going to Caemlyn, not the Black Tower, and they're no threat. My orders were clear. Leave Aes Sedai alone unless they come after you."

"But how can you be sure they are not a threat?" Torval persisted. "Perhaps they are going to Caemlyn, as you say, but if you are wrong, we'll not know before they attack us."

"Torval might be right," Dashiva put in thoughtfully. "I can't say I'd trust women who put me in a box, and these haven't sworn any oaths. Or have they?"

"I said leave them alone!" Rand slapped the tabletop, hard, and Hopwil jumped in surprise. Dashiva frowned with irritation before hurriedly smoothing it over, but Rand was not interested in Dashiva's moods. By chance—he was sure it was chance—his hand had come down on the Dragon Scepter. His arm trembled with the desire to take it up and stab Torval through the heart. No need for Lews Therin at all. "The Asha'man are a weapon to be aimed where I say, not to flutter around like hens every time Taim gets frightened over a handful of Aes Sedai having dinner at the same inn. If I must, I can come back to make myself clearer."

"I am sure there is no need of that," Torval said quickly. At last something had wiped the wry twist from his mouth. Eyes tight, he spread his hands, close to diffident, very nearly apologetic. And plainly frightened. "The M'Hael, he merely wanted you informed. Your orders are read aloud every day at Morning Directives, after the Creed."

"That's good, then." Rand kept his voice cool, kept a scowl from his face by main effort. It was his precious M'Hael the man feared, not the Dragon Reborn. Afraid Taim would take it amiss if something he had said brought Rand's anger on Taim's head. "Because I'll kill any one of you who goes near those women in Murandy. You cut where *I* direct."

Torval bowed rigidly, murmuring, "As you say, my Lord Dragon." His teeth were bared in an attempted smile, but his nose was pinched, and he struggled to avoid meeting anyone's eyes while seeming to avoid nothing. Dashiva yelped another laugh, and Hopwil wore a small grin.

Narishma was not enjoying Torval's discomfort, though, or paying it attention. He looked at Rand without blinking, as though he sensed deep currents that the rest missed. Most women and no few men thought him just a pretty boy, but those too-big eyes sometimes seemed more knowing than any others.

Rand pulled his hand from the Dragon Scepter and smoothed open the letter. His hands did not quite shake. Torval smiled weakly, sourly, noticing nothing. Against the tent wall, Narishma shifted, relaxing.

The refreshments arrived, then, borne by a stately procession following Boreane, a line of Illianers and Cairhienin and Tairens in their various liveries. There was a servant bearing a silver tray and pitcher for each kind of wine, and two more with trays of silver mugs for hot punch and spiced wines and fine blown goblets for the others. A pink-faced fellow in green-and-yellow carried a tray on which to do the pouring, and a dark woman in black-and-gold was there to actually handle the pitchers. There were nuts and candied fruits, cheeses and olives, each sort requiring a serving man or woman. Under Boreane's direction, they flowed in a formal dance, bowing, curtsying, one giving way to another as they made their offerings.

Accepting spiced wine, Rand hoisted himself onto the edge of the table and sat the steaming mug beside him untouched as he busied himself with the letter. There was no address, no preamble of any kind. Taim hated giving Rand any sort of title, though he tried to hide the fact.

I have the honor to report that twenty-nine Asha'man, ninety-seven Dedicated and three hundred twenty-two Soldiers are now enrolled at the Black Tower. There have been a handful of deserters, unfortunately, whose names have been stricken, but losses in training remain acceptable.

I now have as many as fifty recruiting parties in the field at any given time, with the result that three or four men are added to the rolls almost every day. In a few months, the Black Tower will equal the White, as

I said it would. In a year, Tar Valon will tremble at our numbers.

I harvested that blackberry bush myself. A small bush, and thorny, but a surprising number of berries for the size.

Mazrim Taim
M'Hael

Rand grimaced, putting the . . . the blackberry bush . . . out of his mind. What had to be done, had to be done. The whole world paid a price for his existence. He would die for it, but the whole world paid.

There were other things to grimace over, anyway. Three or four new men a day? Taim was optimistic. In a few months, at that rate, there would be more men who could channel than Aes Sedai, true, but the newest sister had years of training behind her. And part of that specifically taught how to deal with a man who could channel. He did not want to contemplate any encounter between Asha'man and Aes Sedai who knew what they were facing; blood and regret could be the only outcome, whatever happened. The Asha'man were not aimed at the White Tower, though, no matter what Taim thought. It was a convenient belief, however, if it made Tar Valon step warily. An Asha'man only needed to know how to kill. If there were enough to do that at the right place and time, if they lived long enough to, that was all they had been created for.

"How many deserters, Torval?" he said quietly. He picked up the wine mug and took a swallow, as if the answer were unimportant. The wine should have been warming, but the ginger and sweet sorrel and mace tasted bitter on his tongue. "How many losses in training?"

Torval was recovering himself over the refreshments, rubbing his hands and arching an eyebrow at the choice of wines, making a great show of knowing the best, making a show of lording it. Dashiva had accepted the first offered, and stood glowering into his twist-stemmed goblet as though it held swill. Pointing to one of the trays, Torval cocked his head thoughtfully, but he had the words ready on his tongue. "Nineteen deserters, so far. The M'Hael, he has ordered them killed whenever they are found, and their heads brought back for examples." Plucking a bit of glazed pear from the proffered tray, he popped it into his mouth and smiled brightly. "Three heads hang like fruit on the Traitor's Tree at this moment."

"Good," Rand said levelly. Men who ran now could not be trusted not to run later, when lives depended on them standing. And these men could not be allowed to go their own way; those fellows back on the hills, if they escaped in a body, were less dangerous than one man trained in the Black Tower. The Traitor's Tree? Taim was a great one for naming things. But men needed the trappings, the symbols and the names, the black coats and the pins, to help hold them together. Until it was time to die. "The next time I visit the Black Tower, I want to see every deserter's head."

A second piece of candied pear, halfway to Torval's mouth, dropped from his fingers and streaked the front of his fine coat. "It might interfere with recruiting, making that sort of effort," he said slowly. "The deserters, they do not announce themselves."

Rand held the other man's gaze until it fell. "How many losses in training?" he demanded. The sharp-nosed Asha'man hesitated. "How many?"

Narishma leaned forward, staring intently at Torval. So did Hopwil. The servants continued their smooth, silent dance, offering their trays to men who no longer saw them. Boreane took advantage of Narishma's preoccupation to make sure his silver mug held more hot water than spiced wine.

Torval shrugged, too casually. "Fifty-one, all told. Thirteen burned out, and twenty-eight dead where they stood. The rest. . . . The M'Hael, he adds something to their wine, and they do not wake." Abruptly his tone turned malicious. "It can come suddenly, at any time. One man began screaming that spiders were crawling beneath his skin on his second day." He smiled viciously at Narishma and Hopwil, and nearly so at Rand, but it was to the other two he addressed himself, swinging his head between them. "You see? Not to worry if you slide into madness. You'll not hurt yourselves or a soul. You go to sleep . . . forever. Kinder than gentling, even if we knew how. Kinder than leaving you insane *and* cut off, yes?" Narishma stared back, taut as a harpstring, his mug forgotten in his hand. Hopwil was once more frowning at something only he could see.

"Kinder," Rand said in a flat voice, setting the mug back beside him on the table. Something in the wine. *My soul is black with blood, and damned.* It was not a hard thought, not biting or edged; a simple statement of fact. "A mercy any man might wish for, Torval."

Torval's cruel smile faded, and he stood breathing hard. The sums were easy; one man in ten destroyed, one man in fifty mad, and more surely to come. Early days yet, and no way till the day you died to know you had beaten the odds. Except that the odds would beat you, one way or another, in the end. Whatever else, Torval stood under that threat, too.

Abruptly Rand became aware of Boreane. It took a moment before he recognized the expression on her face, and when he did, he bit back cold words. How dare she feel pity! Did she think Tarmon Gai'don could be won without blood? The Prophecies of the Dragon demanded blood like rain!

"Leave us," he told her, and she quietly gathered the servants. But she still carried compassion in her eyes as she herded them out.

Casting around for a way to change the mood, Rand found nothing. Pity weakened as surely as fear, and they had to be strong. To face what they had to face, they *all* must be steel. His making, his responsibility.

Lost in his own thoughts, Narishma peered into the steam rising from his wine, and Hopwil still tried to stare through the side of the tent. Torval cast sideways glances at Rand and struggled to put the scornful twist back on his mouth. Dashiva alone appeared unaffected, with his arms folded, studying Torval as a man might study a horse offered for sale.

Into the painfully stretching silence burst a husky, windblown young man in black, with the Sword and Dragon on his collar. Of an age with Hopwil, still not old enough to marry most places, Fedwin Morr wore intensity more closely than his shirt; he moved on his toes, and his eyes had the look of a hunting cat that knew itself hunted in turn. He had been different, once, and not so long ago. "The Seanchan will move from Ebou Dar soon," he said as he saluted. "They mean to come against Illian next." Hopwil gave a start and a gasp, jolted out of his dark study. Once again, Dashiva's response was to laugh, mirthlessly this time.

Nodding, Rand took up the Dragon Scepter. After all, he carried it for remembrance. The Seanchan danced to their own tune, not the song he wished for.

If Rand received the announcement in silence, Torval did not. Finding his sneer, he raised a contemptuous eyebrow. "Did they tell you all that, now?" he said mockingly. "Or have you learned to read minds? Let me tell you something, boy. I have fought, against Amadicians and Domani both, and no army takes a city then packs itself up to march a thousand miles! More than a thousand miles! Or do you think they can Travel?"

Morr met Torval's derision calmly. Or if it unsettled him at all, the only sign he gave was running a thumb down his long sword hilt. "I did talk to some of them. Most were Taraboners, and more landing by ship every day, or near enough." Shouldering past Torval to the table, he favored the Taraboner with a level look. "All stepping right quick whenever anybody with a slurring way of speech opened a mouth." The older man opened his, angrily, but the younger pressed on hurriedly, to Rand. "They're putting soldiers all along the Venir Mountains. Five hundred, sometimes a thousand together. All the way to Arran Head already. And they're buying or taking every wagon and cart within twenty leagues of Ebou Dar, and the animals to draw them."

"Carts!" Torval exclaimed. "Wagons! Is it that they mean to hold a market fair, do you think? And what fool would march an army through mountains when there are perfectly good roads?" He noticed Rand watching him, and cut off with a small frown, suddenly uncertain.

"I told you to stay low, Morr." Rand let anger touch his voice. The young Asha'man had to step back as he jumped down from the table. "Not to go asking the Seanchan their plans. To look and stay low."

"I was careful; I didn't wear my pins." Morr's eyes did not change for Rand, still hunter and hunted in one. He seemed to be boiling inside. Had Rand not known better, he would have thought Morr held the Power, struggling to survive *saidin* even as it gave him life ten times over. His face seemed to want to sweat. "If any of the men I talked to knew where they're going next, they didn't say, and I didn't ask, but they were willing to complain over a mug of ale about marching all the time and never standing still. In Ebou Dar, they were soaking up all the ale in the city as fast as they could, because they say they have to march again. And they're gathering wagons, just like I said." That all came out in a rush, and he clamped his teeth at the end as though to trap more words that wanted to fly from his tongue.

Smiling suddenly, Rand clapped him on the shoulder. "You did well. The wagons would have been enough, but you did well. Wagons are important," he added, turning to Torval. "If an army feeds off the country, it eats what it finds. Or not, if it doesn't." Torval had not flickered an eyelid at hearing of Seanchan in Ebou Dar. If that tale had reached the Black Tower, why had Taim not mentioned it? Rand hoped his smile did not look a snarl. "It's harder to arrange supply trains, but when you have one you know there's fodder for the animals and beans for the men. The Seanchan organize everything."

Sorting through the maps, he found the one he wanted and spread it out, weighted at one side with his sword and at the other with the Dragon Scepter. The coast between Illian and Ebou Dar stared up at him, rimmed for most of its length by hills and mountains, dotted with fishing villages and small towns. The Seanchan did organize. Ebou Dar had been theirs barely more than a week, but the merchants' eyes-and-ears wrote of repairs well under way on the damage done to the city in its taking, of clean sickhouses set up for the ill, of food and work arranged for the poor and those driven from their homes by troubles inland. The streets and the surrounding countryside were patrolled so that no one need fear footpads or bandits, day or night, and while merchants were welcome, smuggling had been cut to a trickle if not less. Those honest Illianer merchants had been surprisingly glum about the smuggling. What were the Seanchan organizing now?

The others gathered around the table as Rand perused the map. There were roads hard along the coast, but poor straggling things, marked as little more than cart paths. The broad trade roads lay inland, avoiding the worst of the terrain and the worst of what the Sea of Storms had to offer. "Men raiding out of those mountains could make passage difficult for anyone trying to use the inland roads," he said finally. "By controlling the mountains, they make the roads safe as a city street. You're right, Morr. They are coming to Illian."

Leaning on his fists, Torval glared at Morr, who had been right when he was wrong. A grievous sin, perhaps, in Torval's book. "Even so, it will be months before they can trouble you here," he said sullenly. "A hundred Asha'man, fifty, placed in Illian, could destroy any army in the world before one man crosses the causeways."

"I doubt an army with *damane* is destroyed as easily as one kills Aiel committed to an attack and caught by surprise," Rand said quietly, and Torval stiffened. "Besides, I have to defend all of Illian, not just the city."

Ignoring the man, Rand traced lines across the map with a finger. Between Arran Head and the city of Illian lay a hundred leagues of open water, across the mouth of Kabal Deep, where, ship captains in Illian said, their longest sounding lines could find no bottom just a mile or so from the shore. The waves there could overturn ships as they surged north to pound the coast with breakers fifteen paces high. In this weather, it would be worse. Marching around the Deep was a route of two hundred leagues to reach the city, even keeping to the shortest ways, but if the Seanchan pressed on from Arran Head, they could reach the border in two weeks despite the rainstorms. Maybe less. Better to fight where he chose, not where they did. His finger slid along the south coast of Altara, along the Venir range, until the mountains dwindled to hills short of Ebou Dar. Five hundred here, a thousand there. A tantalizing string of beads dropped along the mountains. A sharp rap might roll them back to Ebou Dar, might even pen them there while they tried to figure out what he was up to. Or. . . .

"There was something else," Morr said abruptly, rushing again. "There was talk about some sort of Aes Sedai weapon. I found where it was used, a few miles from the city. The ground was all burned over, seared clean in the middle, a good three hundred paces wide or more, and ruined orchards further. The sand was melted to sheets of glass. *Saidin* was worst, there."

Torval waved a hand at him dismissively. "There could have been Aes Sedai near when the city fell, yes? Or maybe the Seanchan themselves did it. One sister with an *angreal* could—"

Rand cut in. "What do you mean, *saidin* was worst there?" Dashiva moved, eyeing Morr oddly, reaching as though to seize the young man. Rand fended him off roughly. "What do you mean, Morr?"

Morr stared, mouth shut tight, running his thumb up and down the length of his sword hilt. The heat inside of him seemed ready to burst out. There really was sweat beading on his face now. "*Saidin* was . . . strange," he said hoarsely. His words came in rapid bursts. "Worst there—I could . . . feel it . . . in the air all around me—but strange everywhere around Ebou Dar. And even a hundred miles away. I had to fight it; not like always; different. Like it was alive. Sometimes. . . . Sometimes, it didn't do what I wanted. Sometimes, it . . . did something else. It did. I'm not mad! It did!" The wind gusted, howling for a moment, shivering and snapping the tent walls, and Morr fell silent. Narishma's bells chimed at a jerk of his head, then were still.

"That isn't possible," Dashiva muttered into the silence, but nearly under his breath. "It is not possible."

"Who knows what's possible?" Rand said. "I don't! Do you?" Dashiva's head came up in surprise, but Rand turned to Morr, moderating his tone. "Don't worry, man." Not a mild tone—he could not manage that—yet heartening, he hoped. His making, his responsibility. "You'll be with me to the Last Battle. I promise it."

The young man nodded, and scrubbed at his face with his hand as though surprised to find it damp, but he glanced at Torval, who had gone as still as stone. Did Morr know about the wine? It *was* a mercy, given the alternatives. A small and bitter mercy.

Rand picked up Taim's missive, folded the page, and thrust it into his coat pocket. One in fifty mad already, and more to come. Was Morr next? Dashiva was surely close. Hopwil's stares took on a new meaning, and even Narishma's habitual quiet. Madness did not always mean screaming about spiders. He had asked once, warily, where he knew the answers would be true, how to cleanse the taint from *saidin*. And got a riddle for answer. Herid Fel had claimed the riddle stated "sound principles, in both high philosophy and natural philosophy," but he had not seen any way to apply it to the problem at hand. Had Fel been killed because he might have puzzled out the riddle? Rand had a hint at the answer, or thought he might, a guess that could be disastrously wrong. Hints and riddles were not answers, yet he had to do something. If the taint was not cleansed somehow, Tarmon Gai'don might find a world already ruined by madmen. What had to be done, had to be done.

"That would be wondrous," Torval said in a near whisper, "but how could anyone short of the Creator or . . . ?" He trailed off uneasily.

Rand had not realized he had spoken any of his thoughts aloud. Narishma's eyes, and Morr's, and Hopwil's, belonged in one face, shining with sudden hope. Dashiva looked poleaxed. Rand hoped he had not said too much. Some secrets had to be kept. Including what he would do next.

In short order, Hopwil was running for his horse to ride to the ridge with orders for the nobles, Morr and Dashiva to find Flinn and the other Asha'man, and Torval was striding off to Travel back to the Black Tower with commands for Taim. Narishma was last, and thinking of Aes Sedai and Seanchan and weapons, Rand sent him away as well, with careful instructions that made the young man's mouth tighten.

"Speak to no one," Rand finished softly, gripping Narishma's arm hard. "And don't fail me. Not by a hair."

"I won't fail," Narishma said, unblinking. With a quick salute, he was gone, too.

Dangerous, a voice whispered in Rand's head. *Oh, yes, very dangerous, maybe too dangerous. But it might work; it might. In any event, you must kill Torval now. You must.*

Weiramon entered the council tent, shouldering aside Gregorin and Tolmeran, trying to shoulder aside Rosana and Semaradrid, the lot of them eager to tell Rand that the men in the trees had decided wisely after all. They found him laughing till tears rolled down his face. Lews Therin had come back. Or else he really was mad already. Either way, it was reason to laugh.

CHAPTER
15

Stronger Than Written Law

In the dim, cold dark of deep night, Egwene woke groggily from restless sleep and troubling dreams, the more troubling because she could not remember them. Her dreams were always open to her, as clear as printed words on a page, yet these had been murky and fearful. She had had too many of those, lately. They left her wanting to run, to escape, never able to recall what from, but always queasy and uncertain, even trembling. At least her head was not hurting. At least she could recall the dreams she knew must be significant, though not how to interpret them. Rand, wearing different masks, until suddenly one of those false faces was no longer a mask, but him. Perrin and a Tinker, frenziedly hacking their way through brambles with axe and sword, unaware of the cliff that lay just ahead. And the brambles screamed with human voices they did not hear. Mat, weighing two Aes Sedai on a huge set of balance scales, and on his decision depended. . . . She could not say what; something vast; the world, perhaps. There had been other dreams, most tinged with suffering. Recently, all of her dreams about Mat were pale and full of pain, like shadows cast by nightmares, almost as though Mat himself were not quite real. That made her afraid for him, left behind in Ebou Dar, and gave her agonies of grief for sending him there, not to mention poor old Thom Merrilin. But the unremembered dreams were worse, she was sure.

The sound of low voices arguing had wakened her, and the full moon was still up outside, casting enough light for her to make out two women confronting one another at the tent's entrance.

"The poor woman's head pains her all day, and she gets little rest at night," Halima whispered fiercely, fists on her hips. "Let this wait till morning."

"I don't propose to argue with you." Siuan's voice was winter itself, and she tossed back her cloak with a mittened hand as though preparing to fight. She was dressed for the weather, in stout wool no doubt worn over as many shifts as she could fit underneath. "You stand aside, and right quick, or I'll have your guts for bait! And put on some decent clothes!"

With a soft laugh, Halima drew up and if anything planted herself more squarely in Siuan's way. Her white nightgown clung, but was decent enough for its purpose. Though it did seem a wonder she evaded freezing in that thin silk. The coals in the tripod braziers had died down long since, and neither much-mended tent canvas nor lay-ered carpets on the ground held in warmth any longer. Both women's breath was pale mist.

Throwing off the blankets, Egwene sat up wearily on her narrow cot. Halima was a country woman with a skim of sophistication, and often she did not seem to realize the def-erence due to Aes Sedai, or indeed seem to think she need defer to anyone. She spoke to Sitters as she might to the goodwives in her own village, with a laugh and a level eye and a straightforward earthiness that sometimes shocked. Siuan spent her days giving way to women who had jumped at her word a year earlier, smiling and curtsying for nearly every sister in the camp. Many still laid much of the Tower's troubles at her feet and thought she had hardly suffered enough to atone. Sufficient to keep anyone's pride at a stiff prickle. Together, the pair were a lantern tossed into the back of an Illuminator's wagon, but Egwene hoped to avoid an explosion. Besides, Siuan would not have come in the middle of the night unless it was necessary.

"Go back to bed, Halima." Smothering a yawn, Egwene bent to fumble her shoes and stockings from beneath the cot. She did not channel a lamp alight. Better if no one no-ticed that the Amyrlin was awake. "Go on; you need your rest."

Halima protested, perhaps more strongly than she should have to the Amyrlin Seat, but soon enough she was back on the tiny cot that had been squeezed into the tent for her.

Very little room remained to move in, with a washstand, a stand-mirror and a real armchair, plus four large chests stacked atop one another. Those held the constant flow of clothes from Sitters who had not yet realized that however young Egwene might be, she was not young enough to be dazzled or diverted by silks and laces. Halima lay curled up, watching in the darkness, while Egwene hastily dragged an ivory comb through her hair, donned stout mittens, and pulled a fox-lined cloak over her nightgown. A thick woolen nightgown, and she would not have minded thicker in this weather. Halima's eyes seemed to pick up the faint moonlight and shine darkly, unblinking.

Egwene did not think the woman jealous of her place near the Amyrlin Seat, casual as it was, and the Light knew she did not carry gossip, but Halima had an innocent curiosity about everything, whether or not it was any of her business. Reason enough to hear Siuan out elsewhere. Everyone knew now that Siuan had thrown in her lot with Egwene, after a fashion, as they thought, sullenly and grudgingly. A figure of some amusement and occasional pity, Siuan Sanche, reduced to attaching herself to the woman who held the title once hers, and that woman no more than a puppet once the Hall finished fighting over who would pull her cords. Siuan was human enough to harbor sparks of resentment, but so far they had managed to keep secret that her advice was far from grudging. So she endured pity and snickers as best she could, and everyone believed her as changed by her experiences as her face. That belief had to be maintained, or Romanda and Lelaine and very likely the rest of the Hall, too, would find ways to separate her—and her advice—from Egwene.

The cold outside slapped Egwene in the face and flooded under her cloak; her nightgown might as well have been Halima's for all the protection it offered. Despite stout leather and good wool, her feet felt as if they were bare. Tendrils of frosty air curled around her ears, mocking the thick fur lining her hood. Yearning for her bed as she was, ignoring the iciness took all the concentration she could muster. Clouds scudded across the sky, and moonshadows floated over the gleaming white that covered the ground, a smooth sheet broken by the dark mounds of tents and the taller shapes of canvas-topped wagons that now had long wooden runners in place of wheels. Many of the wagons were no longer parked apart from the tents, but left where they had been unloaded; no one had the heart to make the wagon drivers put out even that much extra effort at the end of the day. Nothing moved except those pale sliding shadows. The wide runnels that had been trampled through the camp for paths lay empty. The silence was crisp and so deep that she almost regretted breaking it.

"What is it?" she asked softly, casting a wary glance at the small tent nearby shared by her maids, Chesa, Meri, and Selame. That was as still and dark as the others. Exhaustion made as thick a blanket over the camp as the snow. "Not another revelation like the Kin, I hope." She clicked her tongue in vexation. She was spent, too, by long freezing days in the saddle and not enough real sleep, or she would not have said that. "I'm sorry, Siuan."

"No need to apologize, Mother." Siuan kept her voice down as well, and glanced about to see whether anyone might be watching from the shadows besides. Neither wanted to find herself discussing the Kin with the Hall. "I know I should have told you beforehand, but it seemed a small thing. I never expected those girls to even speak to one of them. There's so much to tell you. I have to try to pick and choose what's important."

With an effort, Egwene managed not to sigh. That was almost word for word the apology Siuan had offered before. Several times. What she meant was that she was trying to force-feed Egwene over twenty years of experience as Aes Sedai, more than ten of that as Amyrlin, and do it in months. At times Egwene felt like a goose being fattened for market. "Well, what's important tonight?"

"Gareth Bryne's waiting in your study." Siuan did not raise her voice, but it took on an edge, as always when she spoke of Lord Bryne. She tossed her head angrily inside the deep hood of her cloak, and made a sound like a cat spitting. "The man came in dripping snow, scooped me out of my bedding, and barely gave me time to dress before hauling me up behind his saddle. He told me nothing; just tossed me down at the edge of camp and sent me to fetch you like I was a serving girl!"

Firmly, Egwene stifled a rising hope. There had been too many disappointments, and whatever had brought Bryne in the middle of the night was much more likely to be a potential disaster than what she wished for. How far yet to the border with Andor? "Let's see what he wants."

Starting off toward the tent everyone named the Amyrlin's Study, she held her cloak close. She did not shiver, but refusing to let heat or cold touch you did not make them go away. You could ignore them right up to the moment sunstroke cooked your brain or frostbite rotted your hands and feet. She considered what Siuan had said.

"You weren't sleeping in your own tent here?" she said carefully. The other woman's relation to Lord Bryne *was* that of a servant, in a very peculiar way, but Egwene hoped Siuan was not letting her stubborn pride lead her into letting him take advantage. She could not imagine it, of him or her, yet not so long ago she could not have imagined Siuan accepting any part of the situation. She still could not understand why.

Snorting loudly, Siuan kicked her skirts, and nearly fell as her shoes skidded. Snow beaten down by countless feet had quickly become a rough sheet of ice. Egwene was picking her own way cautiously. Every day brought broken bones that travel-weary sisters had to Heal. Half abandoning her cloak, she offered an arm as much for the support she might receive as give. Siuan took it, muttering.

"By the time I finished cleaning the man's spare boots and second saddle, it was too late to tramp back through this. Not that he offered more than blankets in a corner; not Gareth Bryne! Made me dig them out of the chest myself, while *he* went off the Light knows where! Men are a trial, and that one the worst!" Without a pause for breath, she changed the subject. "You shouldn't let that Halima sleep in your tent. She's another pair of ears you have to be careful of, and snoopy with it. Besides, you're lucky you don't walk in to find her *entertaining* some soldier."

"I am very glad that Delana can spare Halima nights," Egwene said firmly. "I need her. Unless you think Nisao's Healing might do better with my headaches a second time around." Halima's fingers seemed to draw the pain out through her scalp; without that, she would not be able to sleep at all. Nisao's effort had had no effect whatsoever, and she was the only Yellow Egwene dared approach with the problem. As for the rest. . . . She made her voice sterner still. "I am surprised you're still listening to that gossip, daughter. The fact that men like looking at a woman doesn't mean she invites it, as you should know well. I've seen more than a few looking at you and grinning." Taking that tone came easier than it once had.

Siuan gave her a startled sidelong glance and, after a moment, grumbled an apology. It might have been sincere. Egwene accepted it, either way. Lord Bryne was very bad for Siuan's temper, and tossing Halima into the bargain, Egwene thought it a good job she was not pushed into taking a stricter stance. Siuan herself had said that she should not put up with nonsense, and she surely could not afford to put up with it from Siuan, of all people.

Trudging arm-in-arm, they went on in silence, the cold fogging their breath and seeping through their flesh. The snow was a curse and a lesson. She could still hear Siuan going on about what she called the Law of Unintended Consequences, stronger than any written law. *Whether or not what you do has the effect you want, it will have three at least you never expected, and one of those usually unpleasant.*

The first, feeble rains had brought astonishment, for all Egwene had already informed the Hall that the Bowl of the Winds had been found and used. That was almost as much as she could risk letting them know of what Elayne had told her in *Tel'aran' rhiod*; too much of what had happened in Ebou Dar was just the thing to cut her feet out from under her here, and her position was precarious enough as it was. An explosion of joy erupted at those first sprinkles. They had halted the march at midday, and there had been bonfires and feasting in the drizzle, prayers of thanksgiving among the sisters and dancing among the servants and the soldiers. For that matter, some of the Aes Sedai had danced, too.

A few days later, the soft rains became downpours, and then howling tempests. The temperature slid downward, plummeted, and tempests became blizzards. Now, the distance once covered in a day, with Egwene gritting her teeth over how slowly they moved, took five when the sky held only clouds, and when the snows fell, they did not move at all. Easy enough to think of three unintended consequences, or more, and the snow might well be the least unpleasant.

As they approached the small, patched tent called the

Amyrlin's Study, a shadow moved beside one of the tall
wagons, and Egwene's breath caught. The shadow became a
figure who slipped back her hood enough to reveal Leane's
face, then pulled back into darkness.

"She'll keep a watch and let us know if anybody comes,"
Siuan said softly.

"That's good," Egwene muttered. The woman *could* have
told her in advance. She had half been afraid it was Romanda or Lelaine!

The Amyrlin's Study was dark, but Lord Bryne stood
waiting patiently inside, wrapped in his cloak, a shadow
among shadows. Embracing the Source, Egwene channeled, not to light the lantern hanging from the center-pole
or one of the candles, but to make a small sphere of pale
light that she suspended in the air over the folding table she
used as a writing desk. Very small, and very pale; unlikely
to be noticed from outside, and quick as thought to extinguish. She could not afford discovery.

There had been Amyrlins who reigned in strength,
Amyrlins who managed an even balance with the Hall, and
Amyrlins who had had as little power as she, or less upon
rare occasions, well-hidden in the secret histories of the
White Tower. Several had frittered away power and influence, falling from strength to weakness, but in over three
thousand years, precious few had managed to move in the
other direction. Egwene very much wished she knew how
Myriam Copan and the rest of that bare handful had managed. If anyone had ever thought to write that down, the
pages were long lost.

Bowing respectfully, Bryne showed no surprise at her
caution. He knew what she put at hazard, meeting him secretly. To a very large degree, she trusted this sturdy, heavily graying man with the bluff, weathered face, and not only
because she had to. His cloak was thick red wool, lined
with marten and bordered with the Flame of Tar Valon, a
gift from the Hall, yet he had made plain a dozen times
in the past weeks that whatever the Hall thought—and he
was not blind enough to have missed that!—she was the
Amyrlin, and he followed the Amyrlin. Oh, he had never
said so right out, but with carefully worded hints that left
no doubts. Expecting more would have been expecting
too much. There were nearly as many undercurrents in the

camp as there were Aes Sedai, some strong enough to pull him down. Several strong enough to mire her deeper than she was, if the Hall learned of this meeting. She trusted him further than anyone except Siuan and Leane, or Elayne and Nynaeve, maybe further than any of the sisters who had sworn fealty to her in secret, and she wished she had the courage to trust him more. The ball of white light cast weak, fitful shadows.

"You have news, Lord Bryne?" she asked, stifling hope. She could think of a dozen possible messages that might bring him in the night, each with its own set of pitfalls and snares. Had Rand decided to add more crowns to that of Illian, or the Seanchan somehow captured still another city, or the Band of the Red Hand suddenly moved on its own instead of shadowing the Aes Sedai, or. . . .

"An army lies north of us, Mother," he replied calmly. His leather-gauntleted hands rested lightly atop his long sword hilt. An army to the north, a little more snow, all the same. "Andorans, mainly, but with a goodly number of Murandians. My deep scouts brought the news less than an hour ago. Pelivar leads, and Arathelle is with him, the High Seats of two of the strongest Houses in Andor, and they've brought twenty more at least. They're pushing south hard, it seems. If you keep on as you are, which I advise against, we should meet head-on in two days, three at the outside."

Egwene kept her face smooth, suppressing her relief. What she had been hoping for, waiting for; what she had begun to fear might never come. Surprisingly, it was Siuan who gasped, and clapped a mittened hand over her mouth too late. Bryne cocked an eyebrow at her, but she recovered quickly, putting on Aes Sedai serenity so thick you almost forgot her youthful face.

"Do you have qualms at fighting your fellow Andorans?" she demanded. "Speak up, man. I'm not your washwoman here." Well, there was a small crack in that serenity.

"As you command, Siuan Sedai." Bryne's tone held no scrap of mockery, yet Siuan's mouth began to tighten, her outward coolness evaporating fast. He made her a small bow, workmanlike but acceptable. "I will fight whoever the Mother wishes me to fight, of course." Even here, he would not be more forthcoming. Men learned caution around Aes

Sedai. So did women. Egwene thought caution had become a second skin for her.

"And if we don't keep on?" she said. So much planning, just her and Siuan and sometimes Leane, and now she still had to feel out each step as carefully as on those icy paths outside. "If we stop here?"

He did not hesitate. "If you have a way to bring them around without fighting, all well and good, but some time tomorrow they'll reach an excellent position to defend, one flank held by the River Armahn, the other by a large peat bog, and small streams in front to break up attacks. Pelivar will settle in there to wait; he knows the work. Arathelle will have her part if there's talking, but she'll leave the pikes and swords to him. We can't reach it ahead of him, and anyway, the terrain is no use to us there, with him to the north. If you mean to fight, I advise making for that ridge we crossed two days back. We can reach it in good order ahead of them if we start at dawn, and Pelivar would think twice about coming at us there if he had three times the numbers he does."

Wriggling near-frozen toes inside her stockings, Egwene let out an annoyed sigh. There was a difference between not letting cold touch you and not feeling it. Picking her way carefully, not letting herself be distracted by the chill, she asked, "*Will* they talk, offered the chance?"

"Probably, Mother. The Murandians hardly count; they're just there for whatever advantage they can wring out of the situation, same as their countrymen under me. It's Pelivar and Arathelle who matter. If I had to wager, I'd say they only mean to keep you out of Andor." He shook his head grimly. "But they'll fight if they have to, if they must, maybe even if it means facing Aes Sedai instead of just soldiers. I expect they've heard the same tales we have about that battle out east somewhere."

"Fish guts!" Siuan growled. So much for calm. "Half-baked rumors and raw gossip are no proof there *was* any battle, you lummox, and if there was, sisters wouldn't have gotten themselves mixed up in it!" The man truly was an occasion of sin for her.

Strangely, Bryne smiled. He often did when Siuan showed her temper. Anywhere else, on anyone else, Egwene would have called the smile fond. "Better for us if they believe," he told Siuan mildly. Her face darkened so, you might have thought he had sneered at her.

Why did a normally sensible woman let Bryne get under her skin? Whatever the reason, Egwene had no time for it tonight. "Siuan, I see someone forgot to take away the mulled wine. It can't have soured in this weather. Warm it for us, please." She did not like setting the other woman down in front of Bryne, but she had to be reined in, and this seemed the gentlest way to do it. Really, they should not have left the silver pitcher on her table.

Siuan did not quite flinch, but from her stricken expression, quickly smoothed over, you would never have believed she washed the man's smallclothes. Without comment she channeled slightly to reheat the wine in the silver pitcher, quickly filled two clean worked-silver cups, and handed the first to Egwene. She kept the second, staring at Lord Bryne as she sipped and leaving him to pour for himself.

Warming her mittened fingers on her own cup, Egwene felt a flash of irritation. Maybe it was part of Siuan's long-delayed reaction to the death of her Warder. She still became weepy for no visible reason now and then, though she tried to hide it. Egwene put the matter out of her head. Tonight, that was an anthill beside mountains.

"I want to avoid a battle if I can, Lord Bryne. The army is for Tar Valon, not fighting a war here. Send to arrange a meeting as soon as possible for the Amyrlin Seat with Lord Pelivar and Lady Arathelle and anyone else you think should be present. Not here. Our ragged camp won't impress them very much. As soon as possible, mind. I wouldn't object to tomorrow, if it could be set."

"That's sooner than I can manage, Mother," he said mildly. "If I send riders out as soon as I return to camp, I doubt they can be back with an answer much before tomorrow night."

"Then I suggest you return quickly." Light, but her hands and feet felt cold. And the pit of her stomach, too. But her voice kept its calm. "And I want you to keep that meeting, and the existence of their army, from the Hall as long as possible."

This time, she was asking him to take as great a risk as she did. Gareth Bryne was one of the best generals living, but the Hall chafed that he did not run the army to suit them. They had been grateful for his name in the beginning, for it helped draw soldiers to their cause. Now the army had more than thirty thousand armed men, with more coming even since the snows had started, and they thought that maybe they did not need Lord Gareth Bryne any longer. And of course, there were those who believed they never had needed him. They would not simply send him away for this. If the Hall chose to act, he might well go to the headsman for treason.

He did not blink, and he did not ask questions. Perhaps he knew she would not give answers. Or maybe he thought he knew them. "There isn't much traffic between my camp and yours, but too many men know already to keep a secret long. I will do what I can, though."

As simple as that. The first step down a road that would see her on the Amyrlin Seat in Tar Valon, or else deliver her firmly into the grasp of the Hall, with nothing left to decide except whether it was Romanda or Lelaine who told her what to do. Somehow, such a pivotal moment should have been accompanied by fanfares of trumpets, or at the least, thunder in the sky. It was always that way in stories.

Egwene let the ball of light vanish, but as Bryne turned to leave, she caught his arm. It was like catching a thick tree branch through his coat. "A thing I have been meaning to ask you, Lord Bryne. You can't want to take men worn down by marching right into a siege of Tar Valon. How long would you want to rest them before you began?"

For the first time, he paused, and she wished she still had the light to see his face. She thought he frowned. "Even leaving people in the pay of the Tower out of it," he said at last, slowly, "news of an army flies as fast as a falcon. Elaida will know to the day when we'll arrive, and she won't give us an hour. You know she's increasing the Tower Guard? To fifty thousand men, apparently. But a month, if I could, to rest and recover. Ten days would do, but a month would be better."

She nodded, releasing him. That casual question about the Tower Guard hurt. He was aware that the Hall and the Ajahs told her what they wanted her to know and no more. "I suppose you're right," she said evenly. "There'll be no time for rest once we reach Tar Valon. Send your fastest

riders. There won't be any difficulty, will there? Pelivar and
Arathelle will hear them out?" She did not feign the touch
of anxiety. More than her plans might be ruined if they had
to fight now.

Bryne's tone did not alter a whit that she could tell, but
somehow, he sounded soothing. "So long as there is light
enough for them to see the white feathers, they'll recognize
a truce and listen. I'd better go, Mother. It's a long way and
hard riding, even for men with extra horses."

As soon as the tentflap fell behind him, Egwene let out
a long breath. Her shoulders were tight, and she expected
her head to start aching any moment. Bryne usually made
her feel relaxed, absorbing his sureness. Tonight, she had
had to manipulate him, and she thought he knew it. He was
very observant for a man. But too much was at stake to trust
him more, until he made an open declaration. Maybe an
oath like the one Myrelle and the others had given. Bryne
followed the Amyrlin, and the army followed Bryne. If he
thought she was going to throw men away uselessly, a few
words from him could hand her to the Hall trussed like a
pig on a platter. She drank deeply, feeling the warmth of the
spiced wine spread through her.

"Better for us if they believed," she muttered. "I wish
there was something *for* them to believe. If I do nothing
else, Siuan, I hope at least I can free us from the Three
Oaths."

"No!" Siuan barked. She sounded scandalized. "Even
trying could be disastrous, and if you succeeded. . . . The
Light help us, if you succeeded, you would destroy the
White Tower."

"What are you talking about? I try to follow the Oaths,
Siuan, since we're stuck with them—for now—but the
Oaths won't help us against the Seanchan. If sisters have
to be in danger of their lives before they can fight back, it's
only a matter of time before we are all dead or collared."
For a moment she could feel the *a'dam* around her throat
again, turning her into a dog on a leash. A well-trained and
obedient dog. She was glad of the darkness, now, hiding her
trembles. Shadows obscured Siuan's face, save for a soundlessly working jaw.

"Don't you look at me like that, Siuan." It was easier to
be angry than afraid, easy to mask fear in anger. She would

never be collared like that again! "You've taken every advantage since you were freed from the Oaths. If you hadn't lied in your teeth, we'd all be in Salidar, without an army, sitting on our hands and waiting for a miracle. Well, you would be. They'd never have summoned me to be Amyrlin without your lie about Logain and the Reds. Elaida would reign supreme, and in a year, nobody would remember how she usurped the Amyrlin Seat. *She'd* destroy the Tower, for sure. You know she'd mishandle everything about Rand. I would not be surprised if she had tried to kidnap him by now, except that she's concerned with us. Well, maybe not kidnap, but she'd have done something. Likely, Aes Sedai would be fighting Asha'man today, and never mind Tarmon Gai'don waiting over the horizon."

"I have lied when it seemed necessary," Siuan breathed. "When it seemed expedient." Her shoulders hunched, and she sounded as though she were confessing crimes she did not want to admit to herself. "Sometimes I think it's become too easy for me to decide that it's necessary and expedient. I've lied to almost everyone. Except you. But don't think it hasn't occurred to me. To nudge you toward a decision, or away from one. It wasn't wanting to keep your trust that stopped me." Siuan's hand stretched out in the dark, pleading. "The Light knows what your trust and friendship mean to me, but it wasn't that. It wasn't knowing that you'd have the hide off me in strips, or send me away, if you found out. I realized that I had to hold on to the Oaths with somebody, or I'd lose myself completely. So I don't lie to you, or to Gareth Bryne, whatever it costs. And as soon I can, Mother, I will swear the Three Oaths on the Oath Rod again."

"Why?" Egwene asked quietly. Siuan had considered lying to her? She *would* have had her hide for that. But her anger was gone. "I don't condone lying, Siuan. Not normally. It's just that sometimes, it really is necessary." Her time with the Aiel flashed through her mind. "So long as you're willing to pay for it, anyway. I've seen sisters take on penance for smaller things. You are one of the first of a new sort of Aes Sedai, Siuan, free and unbound. I believe you when you say you won't lie to me." Or to Lord Bryne? Odd, that. "Why give up your freedom?"

"Give up?" Siuan laughed. "I'll be giving up nothing." Her back straightened, and her voice began to gain strength, and then passion. "The Oaths are what make us more than simply a group of women meddling in the affairs of the world. Or seven groups. Or fifty. The Oaths hold us together, a stated set of beliefs that bind us all, a single thread running through every sister, living or dead, back to the first to lay her hands on the Oath Rod. *They* are what make us Aes Sedai, not *saidar*. Any wilder can channel. Men may look at what we say from six sides, but when a sister says, 'This is so,' they *know* it's true, and they trust. Because of the Oaths. Because of the Oaths, no queen fears that sisters will lay waste to her cities. The worst villain knows he's safe in his life with a sister unless he tries to harm her. Oh, the Whitecloaks call them lies, and some people have strange ideas about what the Oaths entail, but there are very few places an Aes Sedai cannot go, and be listened to, because of the Oaths. The Three Oaths are what it is to *be* Aes Sedai, the *heart* of being Aes Sedai. Throw that on the rubbish heap, and we'll be sand washing away in the tide. Give up? I will be gaining."

Egwene frowned. "And the Seanchan?" What it was to be Aes Sedai. Almost from the day she first arrived in Tar Valon, she had worked to be Aes Sedai, but she had never really thought about what it was that *made* a woman Aes Sedai.

Once more Siuan laughed, though this time it was a touch wry, and weary. She shook her head, and darkness or no, looked tired. "I don't know, Mother. The Light help me, I don't. But we survived the Trolloc Wars, and Whitecloaks, and Artur Hawkwing, and everything in between. We can find a way to deal with these Seanchan. Without destroying ourselves."

Egwene was not so sure. Many of the sisters in camp thought the Seanchan were such a danger that besieging Elaida should wait. As if waiting would not cement Elaida on the Amyrlin Seat. Many others seemed to think that simply uniting the White Tower again, at whatever price, would make the Seanchan vanish. Survival lost some of its attraction if it was survival on a leash, and Elaida's would not be much less confining than the Seanchan's. What it was to *be* Aes Sedai.

"There's no need to keep Gareth Bryne at arm's length," Siuan said suddenly. "The man's a walking tribulation, it's true. If he doesn't count as penance for my lies, being flayed alive wouldn't do. One of these days, I'll box his ears every morning and twice at evenings, on general principle, but you can tell him everything. It would help, if he understood. He's taking *you* on trust, and it ties his stomach in knots, wondering whether you know what you're doing. He doesn't let on, but I see."

Suddenly, pieces clicked in Egwene's mind like a blacksmith's puzzle coming undone. Shocking pieces. Siuan was in *love* with the man! Nothing else made sense. Everything she knew between them altered. Not necessarily for the better. A woman in love often put her brains on the shelf when she was around the man in question. As she herself was all too well aware. Where *was* Gawyn? Was he well? Was he warm? Enough of that. Too much, in light of what she had to say. She put on her best Amyrlin's voice, sure and in command. "You can box Lord Bryne's ears or bed him, Siuan, but you *will* watch yourself with him. You will *not* let slip things he mustn't know yet. Do you understand me?"

Siuan jerked stiffly erect. "I'm not in the habit of letting my tongue flap like a torn sail, Mother," she said heatedly.

"I'm very glad to hear it, Siuan." Despite their looking only a few years apart, Siuan was old enough to be her mother yet at that moment Egwene felt as though their ages had been reversed. This might be the first time that Siuan had ever had to manage with a man not as Aes Sedai, but as a woman. *A few years of thinking I loved Rand*, Egwene thought wryly, *a few months of dangling by my toes for Gawyn, and I know all there is to know.*

"I think we're done here," she went on, slipping an arm through Siuan's. "Almost. Come."

The walls of the tent had seemed little protection, yet stepping outside brought a renewed assault by winter's teeth. The moonlight was almost bright enough to read by, reflected off the snow, but that glow seemed cold. Bryne had vanished as if he had never been. Leane appeared long enough to say she had seen no one, her slimness swallowed in layers of wool, then hurried off into the night looking about her. No one knew of any connection between Leane and Egwene, and everyone thought Leane and Siuan were practically at daggers' points.

Gathering her cloak as best she could one-handed, Egwene

focused on ignoring the icy chill as she and Siuan walked in the opposite direction from Leane. Ignoring the chill, and keeping an eye out for anyone who happened to be out. Not that anyone who was outside now was likely to be there by happenstance.

"Lord Bryne was right," she told Siuan, "about it being better if Pelivar and Arathelle believed those stories. Or at least if they were uncertain. Too uncertain to fight, or do anything except talk. Do you think they would welcome a visit from Aes Sedai? Siuan, are you listening to me?"

Siuan gave a start, and stopped staring into the distance ahead of them. She had been walking ahead without missing a step, but now she slipped and nearly sat down in the frozen path, barely regaining her balance in time to keep from pulling Egwene down. "Yes, Mother. Of course I'm listening. They might not be exactly welcoming, but I doubt they'll turn sisters away."

"Then I want you to wake Beonin, Anaiya, and Myrelle. They are to ride north inside the hour. If Lord Bryne expects a reply as soon as tomorrow evening, time is short." A pity she had not found out exactly where this other army was located, but asking Bryne might have roused suspicion. Finding it should not be too hard for Warders, and those three sisters had five between them.

Siuan listened in silence to her instructions. Not only those three were to be rooted out of their sleep. Come dawn, Sheriam and Carlinya, Morvrin and Nisao would all know what to say over breakfast. Seeds had to be planted, seeds that could not have been placed earlier for fear of them sprouting too soon, but now they had all too little time to grow.

"It will be a pleasure to haul them out of their blankets," Siuan said when she was done. "If I have to tramp around in this. . . ." Releasing Egwene's arm, she started to turn away, then stopped, her face serious, even grim. "I know you want to be a second Gerra Kishar—or maybe Sereille Bagand. You have it in you to match either. But be careful you don't turn out to be another Shein Chunla. Good night, Mother. Sleep well."

Egwene stood watching her go, a cloak-shrouded figure sometimes skidding on the path and muttering angrily almost loud enough to make out. Gerra and Sereille were remembered as among the greatest Amyrlins. Both had raised the influence and prestige of the White Tower to levels seldom equaled since before Artur Hawkwing. Both controlled the Tower itself, too, Gerra by skillfully playing one faction in the Hall against another, Sereille by the sheer force of her will. Shein Chunla was another matter, one who had squandered the power of the Amyrlin Seat, alienating most of the sisters in the Tower. The world believed that Shein had died in office, close on four hundred years ago, but the deeply hidden truth was that she had been deposed and sent into exile for life. Even the secret histories treaded lightly in certain areas, yet it was fairly obvious that, after the fourth plot to restore her to the Amyrlin Seat was uncovered, the sisters guarding Shein had smothered her in her sleep with a pillow. Egwene shivered, and told herself it was the cold.

Turning, she began making her slow way back to her tent alone. Sleep well? The fat moon hung low in the sky, and there were hours yet till sunrise, but she was not sure she was going to be able to sleep at all.

CHAPTER
16

Unexpected Absences

Before the sun made a rim on the horizon the next morning, Egwene convened the Hall of the Tower. In Tar Valon, that would have been accompanied by considerable ceremony, and even since leaving Salidar they had held to some despite the difficulties of travel. Now, Sheriam simply went from Sitter's tent to Sitter's tent while it was still dark to announce that the Amyrlin Seat had called the Hall to Sit. In fact, they did not sit at all. In the grayness just before true sunrise, eighteen women stood in a semicircle on the snow to hear Egwene, all bundled against the cold that misted their breath.

Other sisters began appearing behind them to listen, only a few at the start, but when no one told them to leave, the group thickened and spread out to a soft buzz of talk. A very muted buzz. Few sisters would risk bothering a lone Sitter, much less the entire Hall. The Accepted in banded dresses and cloaks who had appeared behind the Aes Sedai were quieter, of course, and even quieter the gathering novices who had no chores, though there were a good many more of them. The camp now held half again as many novices as sisters, so many that few possessed a proper white cloak and most made do with a simple white skirt instead of a novice dress. Some sisters still believed they should go back to the old ways and let girls seek them out, but most regretted the lost years, when Aes Sedai numbers dwindled. Egwene herself almost shivered whenever she thought of what the Tower could have been. This was one change not even Siuan could object to.

In the midst of all the gathering, Carlinya came around

the corner of a tent and stopped short at the sight of Egwene and the Sitters. Normally composure to her toenails, the White sister gaped, and her pale face reddened before she hurried away, looking back over her shoulder. Egwene stifled a grimace. Everyone was too concerned with what she herself was about this morning to have noticed, but sooner or later, someone was going to, and wonder.

Flinging back her delicately embroidered cloak to reveal the narrow blue stole of the Keeper, Sheriam made Egwene as much of a formal curtsy as her bulky garments allowed before taking a place at her side. Wrapped in layers of fine wool and silk, the flame-haired woman was the very picture of equanimity. At Egwene's nod, she took one step forward to intone the ancient formula in a clear, high voice.

"She comes; she comes! The Watcher of the Seals, the Flame of Tar Valon, the Amyrlin Seat. Attend you all, for she comes!" It seemed a little out of place here, and besides, she was already there, not coming. The Sitters stood in silence, waiting. A few frowned impatiently, or fiddled restlessly with cloaks or skirts.

Egwene pushed back her own cloak, uncovering the seven-striped stole draped around her neck. These women needed any reminder she could give that she was indeed the Amyrlin Seat. "Everyone is weary from travel in this weather," she announced, not quite so loudly as Sheriam, but loud enough that everyone could hear. She felt a tingle of anticipation, an almost light-headed thrill. It was not much different from being queasy. "I have decided to stop here for two days, perhaps three." That brought heads up and sparked interest. She hoped Siuan was in the listening crowd. She did try to hold to the Oaths. "The horses need rest, too, and many of the wagons badly need repairs. The Keeper will see to the necessary arrangements." It truly was begun, now.

She expected neither argument nor discussion, and there was none. What she had told Siuan was no exaggeration. Too many sisters hoped for a miracle, so they would not have to march on Tar Valon with the world watching. Even among those convinced in their souls that Elaida must be ousted for the good of the Tower, despite everything they had done, too many would grasp any chance of delay, any chance for that miracle to appear.

One of those last, Romanda, did not wait for Sheriam to speak the closing lines. As soon as Egwene finished speaking, Romanda, looking quite youthful with her tight gray bun hidden by her hood, simply strode away. Cloaks flapping, Magla, Saroiya, and Varilin scurried after her. As well as anyone could scurry, when every other step sank ankle-deep. They did a good job of it anyway; Sitters or no, they hardly seemed to breathe without Romanda's permission. When Lelaine saw Romanda leaving, she gathered up Faiselle, Takima, and Lyrelle from the semicircle with a gesture and went without a backward glance, like a swan with three anxious goslings. If they were not so firmly in Lelaine's grasp as the other three were in Romanda's, they did not fall far short. For that matter, the rest of the Sitters barely waited on the final "Depart now in the Light" to leave Sheriam's lips. Egwene turned to go with her Hall of the Tower already scattering in every direction. That tingle was stronger. And *very* like being queasy.

"Three days," Sheriam murmured, offering Egwene a hand to help her down into one of the rutted paths. The corners of her tilted green eyes crinkled quizzically. "I'm surprised, Mother. Forgive me, but you dug in your heels nearly every time I wanted to stop for more than one."

"Speak to me again after you've talked to the wheelwrights and farriers," Egwene told her. "We'll not go far with horses dropping dead and wagons falling apart."

"As you say, Mother," the other woman replied, not precisely meekly, but in perfect acceptance.

The footing was no better now than it had been the night before, and their steps sometimes slid. Linking arms, they walked on slowly. Sheriam offered more support than Egwene required, but she did so almost surreptitiously. The Amyrlin Seat should not fall on her bottom in the full view of fifty sisters and a hundred servants, but neither should she seem propped up like an invalid.

Most of the Sitters who had sworn to Egwene, Sheriam included, had done so out of simple fear, really, and self-preservation. If the Hall learned they had sent sisters to sway the Aes Sedai in Tar Valon, and worse, kept the fact from the Hall for fear of Darkfriends among the Sitters, they surely and certainly would spend the rest of their lives in penance and exile. So the women who had believed they could somehow twitch Egwene about like a puppet, after the greater part of their influence with the Hall melted, instead found themselves sworn to obey her. That was rare even in the secret histories; sisters were expected to obey the Amyrlin, but swearing fealty was something else again. Most still seemed unsettled by it, though they did obey. Few were as bad as Carlinya, but Egwene had actually heard Beonin's teeth chatter the first time she saw Egwene with Sitters after swearing. Morvrin looked astonished anew whenever her eyes fell on Egwene, as if she still did not quite believe, and Nisao hardly seemed to stop frowning. Anaiya clicked her tongue over the secrecy, and Myrelle often flinched, though for more reason than taking an oath. But Sheriam simply had settled into the role of Egwene's Keeper of the Chronicles in truth, not just name.

"May I suggest using this opportunity to see what the surrounding country offers in way of food and fodder, Mother? Our stocks are low." Sheriam frowned anxiously. "Especially tea and salt, though I doubt we'll find those."

"Do what you can," Egwene said in a soothing tone. Odd now, to think that once she had gone in awe of Sheriam, and in no little fear of her displeasure. Strange as it seemed, now that she was no longer Mistress of Novices, no longer trying to tug and push Egwene to do as she wished, Sheriam actually seemed happier. "I have every confidence in you, Sheriam." The woman positively beamed at the compliment.

The sun still did not show above the tents and wagons to the east, but the camp was already bustling. In a manner of speaking. Breakfast done, the cooks were cleaning up, helped by a horde of novices. From the vigor they put into it, the young women seemed to find some warmth in scrubbing kettles with snow, but the cooks moved laboriously, knuckling their backs, stopping to sigh and sometimes to pull their cloaks close and stare bleakly at the snow. Shivering serving men, wearing most of the clothes they owned, had begun striking tents and loading wagons automatically as soon as they finished their hasty meal, and were now stumbling about to raise the tents and haul chests out of the wagons. Animals that had been being harnessed were now being led away by weary horsehandlers who walked with heads down. Egwene heard a few grumbles from men who failed to notice there were sisters nearby, but the greater number seemed too tired to voice a complaint.

Most of the Aes Sedai whose tents were up had vanished inside, but a good many still directed workers, and others hurried along the sunken paths on errands of their own. Unlike everyone else, they showed as little outward weariness as the Warders, who somehow managed to appear as if they had had all the sleep they needed for this fine spring day. Egwene suspected that was a real part of how a sister drew strength from her Warder, quite aside from what she could do with the bond. When your Warder would not admit to himself that he was cold or tired or hungry, you just had to bear up as well.

On one of the crossing paths, Morvrin appeared, clutching Takima's arm. Perhaps it was for support, though Morvrin was wide enough to make the shorter woman seem more diminutive than she actually was. Perhaps it was to keep Takima from escaping; Morvrin was dogged once she set a goal. Egwene frowned. Morvrin might well be expected to seek out a Sitter for her Ajah, the Brown, yet Egwene would have thought Janya or Escaralde more likely. The two passed out of sight behind a canvas-topped wagon on runners, Morvrin bending to talk in her companion's ear. There was no way to tell whether Takima was paying any mind.

"Is something the matter, Mother?"

Egwene put on a smile that felt tight. "No more than usual, Sheriam. No more than usual."

At the Amyrlin's Study, Sheriam departed to see to the tasks Egwene had given her, and Egwene went in to find everything in readiness. She would have been surprised at anything else. Selame was just setting a tea tray on the writing table. Brightly colored beadwork ran across the rail-thin woman's bodice and down her sleeves, and with her long nose carried high, she hardly seemed a servant at first glance, but she had seen to what needed doing. Two braziers full of glowing coals had taken some of the chill off the air, though most of the heat rushed out through the smoke hole. Dried herbs sprinkled on the coals gave a pleasant scent to the smoke that did not escape, the tray from the night before was gone, and the lantern and tallow candles had been trimmed and lit. No one was about to leave a tent open enough to let in light from outside.

Siuan was already there, too, with a stack of papers in her hands, a harried expression on her face, and a smudge of ink on her nose. The post of secretary provided the two of them another reason to be seen talking, and Sheriam had not minded at all giving up the work. Siuan herself grumbled frequently, however. For a woman who had seldom left the Tower since entering as a novice, she had a remarkable dislike for staying inside. At the moment she was the picture of a woman being patient and wanting everyone to know it.

For all her high nose, Selame simpered and bobbed so many curtsies that taking Egwene's cloak and mittens turned into an elaborate little ceremony. The woman nattered on about the Mother putting her feet up, and perhaps she should fetch the Mother a lap robe, and maybe she should stay in case the Mother wanted anything else, until Egwene practically chased her out. The tea tasted of mint. In this weather! Selame was a trial, and she could hardly be called loyal, but she did try.

There was no time for lounging and sipping tea, though. Egwene straightened her stole and took her place behind the writing desk, absentmindedly giving a yank to the leg of her chair so it would not fold beneath her as it often did, Siuan perched atop a rickety stool on the other side of the table, and the tea cooled. They did not speak of plans, or Gareth Bryne, or hopes; what could be done there for now, had been. Reports and problems piled up when they were on the move and weariness overcame attempts to deal with them, and now that they were stopped, all had to be gone through. An army ahead did not change that.

At times, Egwene wondered how so much paper could be found when everything else seemed so difficult. The reports Siuan handed her detailed shortages and little else. Not simply those Sheriam had mentioned, but coal and nails and iron for the farriers and wheelwrights, leather and oiled thread for the harnessmakers, lamp oil and candles and a hundred other things, even soap. And whatever was not running out was wearing out, from shoes to tents, all listed in Siuan's bold hand, which grew more aggressive the more glaring the need she wrote about. Her account of the coin remaining looked to have been slashed onto the paper in a positive fury. And not a thing to be done about it.

Among Siuan's papers were several addresses from Sitters suggesting ways to solve the problem of money. Or rather, informing Egwene what they intended to lay before the Hall. There were few advantages to any of the schemes, however, and many pitfalls. Moria Karentanis proposed stopping the soldiers' pay, a notion Egwene thought the Hall had already realized would cause the army to melt away like dew under a midsummer sun. Malind Nachenin presented an appeal to nearby nobles that sounded more a demand and might well turn the whole countryside against them, as would Salita Toranes' intention to levy a tax on the towns and villages they passed.

Crumpling the three addresses together in her fist, Egwene shook them at Siuan. She wished it were three Sitters' throats she was gripping. "Do they *all* think everything has to go the way they wish, and never mind realities? Light, *they're* the ones behaving like children!"

"The Tower has managed to make its wishes become realities often enough," Siuan said complacently. "Remember, some would say you're ignoring reality, too."

Egwene sniffed. Luckily, whatever the Hall voted, none of the proposals could be carried forward without a decree from her. Even in her straitened circumstances, she had a little power. Very little, but that was more than none. "Is the Hall always this bad, Siuan?"

Siuan nodded, shifting slightly to try to find a better balance. No two of her stool's legs were the same length. "But it could be worse. Remind me to tell you about the Year of the Four Amyrlins; that was about a hundred and fifty years after the founding of Tar Valon. In those days, the normal workings of the Tower nearly rivaled what's happening today. Every hand tried to snatch the tiller, if they could. There were actually two rival Halls of the Tower in Tar Valon for part of that year. Almost like now. Just about everyone came to grief in the end, including a few who thought they were going to save the Tower. Some of them might have, if they hadn't stepped in quicksand. The Tower survived anyway, of course. It always does."

A great deal of history grew up in over three thousand

years, much suppressed, hidden from all but a few eyes, yet Siuan seemed to have every detail at her fingertips. She must have spent a good part of her years in the Tower *burying* herself in those secret histories. Of one thing, Egwene was certain. She would avoid Shein's fate if she could, but she would not remain as she was, little better off than Cemaile Sorenthaine. Long before the end of her reign, the most important decision left to Cemaile's discretion was what dress to wear. She *was* going to have to ask Siuan to tell her about the Year of the Four Amyrlins, and she did not look forward to it.

The shifting beam of light from the smoke hole in the roof showed morning toward midday, but Siuan's stack of papers seemed hardly diminished. Any interruption at all would have been welcome, even premature discovery. Well, maybe not that.

"What's next, Siuan?" she growled.

A flicker of movement caught Aran'gar's eye, and she peered through the trees toward the army's camp, an obscuring ring around the tents of the Aes Sedai. A line of wagon-sledges was moving slowly east, escorted by men on horseback. The pale sun glinted from armor and the points of lances. She could not help sneering. Spears and horses! A primitive rabble that could move no faster than a man could walk, led by a man who did not know what was happening a hundred miles away. Aes Sedai? She could destroy the lot of them, and even dying they would never suspect who was killing them. Of course, she would not survive them long. That thought made her shiver. The Great Lord gave very few a second chance at life, and she was not about to throw away hers.

Waiting until the riders moved out of sight into the forest, she started back toward the camp, thinking idly of tonight's dreams. Behind her, smooth snow would hide what she had buried until the spring thaw, more than long enough. Ahead, some of the men in the camp finally noticed her and straightened from their tasks to watch. In spite of herself, she smiled and smoothed her skirt over her hips. It was difficult now to really remember what life had been like as a man; had she been such an easily manipulated fool, then?

Getting through that swarm with a corpse unseen had been
difficult, even for her, but she enjoyed the walk back.

The morning went on in a seemingly endless wading
through paper, until what Egwene had known would happen, did. Certain daily events were sure. There would be
bitter cold, there would be snow, there would be clouds, and
gray skies, and wind. And there would be visits from Lelaine and Romanda.

Weary of sitting, Egwene was stretching her legs when
Lelaine swept into the tent with Faolain at her heels. Frigid
air rolled in with them before the tentflap fell shut. Looking around with a faintly disapproving air, Lelaine plucked
off blue leather gloves, while allowing Faolain to remove
the lynx-lined cloak from her shoulders. Slender and dignified in deep blue silk, with penetrating eyes, she might have
been in her own tent. At a casual gesture, Faolain retreated
deferentially to a corner with the garment, merely shrugging her own cloak back. Plainly, she was ready to go on
the instant at another wave of the Sitter's hand. Her dark
features wore a cast of resigned meekness, not very much
like her.

Lelaine's reserve cracked for a moment, in a surprisingly
warm smile for Siuan. They had been friends, once, years
ago, and she had even offered something like the patronage
that Faolain had accepted, a Sitter's protection and shelter-
ing arm against the sneers and accusations of other sisters.
Touching Siuan's cheek, Lelaine softly murmured something that sounded sympathetic. Siuan blushed, a startling
uncertainty flashing across her face. It was not pretense,
Egwene was sure. Siuan found it difficult to deal with what
really had changed in her, and more, with how easily she
was adapting.

Lelaine eyed the stool in front of the writing table and, as
usual, visibly rejected such an unsteady seat. Only then did
she acknowledge Egwene's presence, with the barest dip of
her head. "We need to speak of the Sea Folk, Mother," she
said in a tone a bit firm to be directed at the Amyrlin Seat.

Not until Egwene's heart sank down from her throat did
she realize she had been afraid that Lelaine already knew
what Lord Bryne had told her. Or even the meeting he was

arranging. The next instant, her heart leaped back again. The Sea Folk? Surely the Hall could not have learned of the insane bargain Nynaeve and Elayne had made. She could not imagine what had led them into such a disaster, or how she was to deal with it.

Her stomach roiling, she took her place behind the table without revealing anything of what she felt. And that fool chair leg folded, nearly dropping her onto the carpets before she could jerk it straight again. She hoped her cheeks were not coloring. "The Sea Folk in Caemlyn, or in Cairhien?" Yes; that sounded suitably calm and collected.

"Cairhien." Romanda's high voice rang like sudden chimes. "Definitely Cairhien." Her entry made Lelaine's seem almost diffident, the force of her personality abruptly filling the tent. There were no warm smiles in Romanda; handsome as her face was, it did not seem made for them.

Theodrin followed her in, and Romanda swung her cloak off with a flourish and tossed it to the slim, apple-cheeked sister with a peremptory gesture that sent Theodrin hurrying to a corner opposite Faolain. Faolain was distinctly subdued, but Theodrin's tilted eyes were very wide, as though she was permanently startled, and her lips seemed ready to gasp. Like Faolain, her proper place in the hierarchy of Aes Sedai demanded better employment, but neither was likely to receive it soon.

Romanda's compelling gaze rested a moment on Siuan, as if considering whether to send her to a corner as well, then brushed past Lelaine almost dismissively before settling on Egwene. "It seems that young man has been talking with the Sea Folk, Mother. The Yellow eyes-and-ears in Cairhien are most excited about it. Do you have any idea what might interest him in the Atha'an Miere?"

Despite the title, Romanda hardly sounded as if she were addressing the Amyrlin Seat, but then, she never did. There was no doubt who "that young man" was. Every sister in the camp accepted that Rand was the Dragon Reborn, but anyone who heard them talk would have believed they were speaking of an unruly young lout who might come to dinner drunk and throw up on the table.

"She can hardly know what's in the boy's head," Lelaine said before Egwene could open her mouth. Her smile was not at all warm this time. "If an answer is to be found,

Romanda, it will be in Caemlyn. The Atha'an Miere there are not sequestered on a ship, and I seriously doubt that high ranking Sea Folk came so far from the sea on different errands. I've never heard of them doing so for any reason. It may be they have an interest in him. They must know who he is by now."

Romanda smiled back, and frost should have appeared on the tent walls. "There's hardly need to state the obvious, Lelaine. The first question is how to find out."

"I was about to resolve that when you barged in, Romanda. The next time the Mother encounters Elayne or Nynaeve in *Tel'aran'rhiod*, she can pass on instructions. Merilille can discover what the Atha'an Miere want, or maybe what the boy does, when she reaches Caemlyn. A pity the girls didn't think to set a regular schedule, but we must work around that. Merilille can meet with a Sitter in *Tel'aran'rhiod* when she knows." Lelaine made a small gesture; plainly, she herself was the intended Sitter. "I thought Salidar might be a suitable place."

Romanda snorted with amusement. Even in that, there was no warmth. "Easier to instruct Merilille than to see she obeys, Lelaine. I expect she knows she faces sharp questions. This Bowl of the Winds should have been brought to us for study first. None of the sisters in Ebou Dar had much ability in Cloud Dancing, I believe, and you can see the result, all this hurly-burly and suddenness. I have a thought to call a question before the Hall concerning everyone involved." Abruptly the gray-haired woman's voice became smooth as butter. "As I recall, you supported the choice of Merilille."

With a jerk, Lelaine drew herself up. Her eyes flashed. "I supported who the Gray put forward, Romanda, and no more," she said indignantly. "How could I have imagined she would decide to use the Bowl there? And to include Sea Folk wilders in the circle! How could she believe they know as much of working weather as Aes Sedai?" Abruptly her ire slipped. She was defending herself to her fiercest adversary in the Hall, her only real adversary. And, no doubt worse in her view, she was agreeing with her about the Sea Folk. There was no question that she did agree, but giving the fact voice was another matter.

Romanda let her cold smile deepen as Lelaine's face

paled with fury. She straightened her bronze-colored skirts with meticulous care as Lelaine searched for a way to turn matters about. "We will see how the Hall stands, Lelaine," she said finally. "Until the question is called, I think it best if Merilille does *not* meet with any of the Sitters involved in her selection. Even a suggestion of collusion would be looked at askance. I'm sure you will agree I should be the one to speak with her."

Lelaine's face paled differently. She was not afraid, not visibly, yet Egwene could almost see her counting who might stand for her, or against. Collusion was almost as serious as a charge of treason, and required only the lesser consensus. Likely, she could avoid that, but the arguments would be deep and acrimonious. Romanda's faction might even increase. That would cause untold problems whether or not Egwene's own plans bore fruit. And there was nothing she could do to stop it, short of revealing what really had happened in Ebou Dar. As well ask them to let her accept the same offer Faolain and Theodrin had.

Egwene drew breath. At least she might be able to prevent the use of Salidar as a meeting place in *Tel'aran'rhiod*. That was where she met Elayne and Nynaeve, now. When she did, anyway; she had not in days. With Sitters popping in and out of the World of Dreams, finding anywhere you could be sure they would not appear was difficult. "The next time I encounter Elayne or Nynaeve, I will pass on your instructions regarding Merilille. I can let you know when she's ready to meet you." Which would be never, once she was done with those instructions.

The Sitters' heads whipped around, and two sets of eyes stared at her. They had forgotten she was there! Struggling to keep her face smooth, she realized her foot was tapping irritably, and stopped it. She had to go along with what they thought of her a while longer, yet. A little while longer. At least she no longer felt nauseated. Just angry.

Into that moment of silence, Chesa came bustling with Egwene's midday meal on a cloth-covered tray. Dark-haired, plump and pretty in her middle years, Chesa managed to convey a proper respect without cringing. Her curtsy was as simple as her dark gray dress, with just a touch of plain lace at the throat. "Forgive me for intruding, Mother, Aes Sedai. I *am* sorry this is late, Mother, but Meri seems to have wandered off." She clicked her tongue in exasperation as she set the tray in front of Egwene. Wandering seemed very unlike the misnamed Meri. That dour woman was as disapproving of faults in herself as she was of those in others.

Romanda frowned, but she said nothing. After all, she could hardly show too much interest in one of Egwene's maids. Especially when the woman was her spy. Just as Selame was Lelaine's. Egwene avoided looking at Theodrin or Faolain, both still standing dutifully in their corners like Accepted, rather than Aes Sedai themselves.

Chesa half-opened her mouth, but closed it again, perhaps intimidated by the Sitters. Egwene was relieved when she dipped another curtsy and left with a murmured "By your leave, Mother." Chesa's advice was always indirect enough for any sister when anyone else was present, but right then, the last thing Egwene wanted was even a circumspect reminder to eat while her food was hot.

Lelaine took up as if there had been no interruption. "The important thing," she said firmly, "is to learn what the Atha'an Miere want. Or what the boy does. Maybe he wants to be their king, too." Holding out her arms, she allowed Faolain to restore her cloak, which the dark young woman did with care. "You will remember to let me know if you have any thoughts on it, Mother?" That was just barely a request.

"I will think hard," Egwene told her. Which was not to say she would share her thoughts. She wished she had a glimmer of the answer. That the Atha'an Miere believed Rand was their prophesied Coramoor, she knew, though the Hall did not, but what he wanted from them, or them from him, she could not begin to imagine. According to Elayne, the Sea Folk with them had no clue. Or said not. Egwene almost wished one of the handful of sisters who had come from the Atha'an Miere was in the camp. Almost. One way or another, those Windfinders *were* going to cause trouble.

At a wave of Romanda's hand, Theodrin leaped forward with the Sitter's cloak as though goosed. By Romanda's expression, Lelaine's recovery did not best please her. "You will remember to tell Merilille I wish to speak with her, Mother," she said, and that was not a request at all.

For a brief moment the two Sitters stood staring at each other, Egwene forgotten again in their mutual animosity.

They departed without a word to her, very nearly jostling for precedence before Romanda slipped out first, drawing Theodrin in her wake. Baring her teeth, Lelaine practically pushed Faolain from the tent ahead of her.

Siuan heaved a hearty sigh, and made no attempt to hide her relief.

"By your leave, Mother," Egwene muttered mockingly. "If you please, Mother. You may go, daughters." Letting out a long breath, she settled back in her chair. Which promptly pitched her onto the carpets in a heap. She picked herself up slowly and jerked her skirts straight, put her stole to rights. At least it had not happened in front of those two. "Go get something to eat, Siuan. And bring it back. We've a long day, yet."

"Some falls hurt less than others," Siuan said as if to herself before ducking outside. It was a good thing she went so quickly, or Egwene might have given her an earful.

She returned soon, though, and they ate hard rolls and lentil stew laced with tough carrot and scraps of meat Egwene did not look at closely. There were only a few interruptions, intrusions where they fell silent and pretended to study reports. Chesa came to take away the tray, and later to replace the candles, a task she grumbled over, which was not like her.

"Who'd expect Selame to go missing, too?" she muttered, half to herself. "Off canoodling with the soldiers, I expect. That Halima's a bad influence."

A skinny young fellow with a dripping nose renewed the already dead coals in the braziers—the Amyrlin got more warmth than most, but that was not a great deal—and he stumbled over his own boots and gaped at Egwene in a manner quite gratifying after the two Sitters. Sheriam appeared to ask whether Egwene had any further instructions, of all things, and then seemed to want to stay. Perhaps the few secrets she knew made her nervous; her eyes certainly darted uneasily.

That was the lot, and Egwene was not sure whether it was because no one bothered the Amyrlin without cause, or because everyone knew the real decisions were made in the Hall.

"I don't know about this report of soldiers moving south out of Kandor," Siuan said as soon as the tentflap fell behind

Sheriam. "There's just the one, and Borderlanders seldom go far from the Blight, but every fool knows that, so it's hardly the kind of tale anyone would make up." She was not reading from a page, now.

Siuan had managed to keep very tenuous control of the Amyrlin's network of eyes-and-ears so far, and reports, rumors, and gossip flowed to her in steady streams, to be studied before she and Egwene decided what to pass on to the Hall. Leane had her own network, to add to the flow. Most of it was passed on—some things the Hall had to know, and there was no guarantee that the Ajahs would pass on what their own agents learned—but it all had to be sieved for what might be dangerous, or serve to divert attention from the real goal.

Few of those streams carried anything good, of late. Cairhien had produced any number of rumors of Aes Sedai allied with Rand, or, worse, serving him, yet at least those could be dismissed out of hand. The Wise Ones would not say much at all about Rand or anyone connected to him, but according to them, Merana was awaiting his return, and certainly sisters in the Sun Palace, where the Dragon Reborn kept his first throne, were more than seed enough to grow those tales. Others were not easily ignored, even when it was hard to know what to make of them. A printer in Illian asserted that he had proof Rand had killed Mattin Stepaneos with his own hands and destroyed the body with the One Power, while a laborer on the docks there claimed she had seen the former King carried, bound and gagged and rolled in a rug, aboard a ship that had sailed in the night with the blessings of the captain of the Port Watch. The first was far more likely, but Egwene hoped none of the Ajahs' agents had picked up the same tale. There were already too many black marks against Rand's name in the sisters' books.

It went on like that. The Seanchan seemed to be taking a firm hold in Ebou Dar, against very little resistance. That might have been expected in a land where the Queen's true rule ended a few days' ride from her capital, yet it was hardly heartening. The Shaido seemed to be everywhere, though word of them always came from someone who had heard from someone who had heard. Most sisters seemed to believe the scattered Shaido were Rand's work despite the

Wise Ones' denials, carried by Sheriam. No one wanted to probe the Wise Ones' supposed lies too closely, of course. There were a hundred excuses, but no one was willing to meet them in *Tel'aran'rhiod* except the sisters sworn to Egwene, and they had to be ordered. Anaiya dryly called the encounters "quite compact lessons in humility," and she did not seem at all amused.

"There can't *be* that many Shaido," Egwene muttered. No herbs had been added to the second batch of charcoal, which was dying down in faint embers, and her eyes ached from the smoke that hung thin in the air. Channeling to get rid of it would disperse the last warmth, too. "Some of this must be bandits' work." After all, who could tell a village emptied by people fleeing brigands from one emptied by Shaido? Especially at third hand, or fifth. "There are certainly enough bandits around to account for some of it." Most calling themselves Dragonsworn, which was no help at all. She worked her shoulders to loosen a few of the knots in her muscles.

Abruptly she realized that Siuan was staring at nothing so intently that she appeared ready to slip off of her stool. "Siuan, are you falling asleep? We may have worked most of the day, but it's still light out." There was light at the smoke hole, though it did appear to be fading.

Siuan blinked. "I'm sorry. I've been thinking about something lately, and trying to decide whether to share it with you. About the Hall."

"The Hall! Siuan, if you know something about the Hall—!"

"I don't *know* anything," Siuan cut in. "It's what I suspect." She clicked her tongue in annoyance. "Not even suspect, really. At least, I don't know what to suspect. But I see a pattern."

"Then you had best tell me about it," Egwene said. Siuan had shown herself very skilled at detecting patterns where others saw only a jumble.

Shifting on her stool, Siuan leaned forward intently. "It's this. Aside from Romanda and Moria, the Sitters chosen in Salidar are . . . they're too young." Much had changed in Siuan, but speaking of other sisters' ages clearly made her uncomfortable. "Escaralde is the oldest, and I'm sure she isn't much past seventy. I can't be certain without going into the novice book in Tar Valon, or her telling us, but I'm as sure as I can be. It isn't often the Hall has held more than one Sitter under a hundred, and here we have eight!"

"But Romanda and Moria *are* new," Egwene said gently, resting her elbows on the table. It had been a long day. "And neither is young. Maybe we should be grateful the others are, or they might not have been willing to raise me." She could have pointed out that Siuan herself had been chosen Amyrlin at less than half Escaralde's age, but the reminder would have been cruel.

"Maybe," Siuan said stubbornly. "Romanda was certain for the Hall as soon as she showed up. I doubt there's a Yellow who would dare speak against her for a chair. And Moria. . . . She doesn't cling to Lelaine, but Lelaine and Lyrelle probably thought she would. I don't know. Mark me, though. When a woman is raised too young, there's a reason." She took a deep breath. "Including when I was." The pain of loss flashed across her face, the loss of the Amyrlin Seat certainly, maybe of all the losses she had suffered. It was gone almost as soon as it came. Egwene did not think she had ever known a woman as strong as Siuan Sanche. "This time, there were more than enough sisters of proper age to choose from, and I can't see five Ajahs deadlocking on all of them. There is a pattern, and I mean to pick it out."

Egwene did not agree. Change hung in the air whether Siuan wanted to see it or not. Elaida had broken custom, come very close to breaking law, in usurping Siuan's place. Sisters had fled the Tower and let the world know of it, and that last certainly had never happened before. Change. Older sisters were more likely to be tied to the old ways, but even some of them had to see that everything was shifting. Surely that was why younger women, more open to the new, had been chosen. Should she order Siuan to stop wasting her time with this? Siuan had enough else to do. Or would it be a kindness to let her continue? She wanted so deeply to prove that the change she saw was not really occurring at all.

Before Egwene could make a decision, Romanda ducked into the tent and stood holding the tentflap open. Long shadows stretched across the snow outside. Evening was coming fast. Romanda's face was as dark as those shadows.

She fixed Siuan with a stern gaze and snapped one word. "Out!"

Egwene gave an infinitesimal nod, but Siuan was already on her feet. She missed a step, then all but ran from the tent. A sister who stood where Siuan did was expected to obey any sister of Romanda's strength in the Power, not just a Sitter.

Throwing down the tentflap, Romanda embraced the Source. The glow of *saidar* surrounded her, and she wove a ward against eavesdropping around the inside of the tent without so much as a pretense of asking Egwene's permission. "You are a fool!" she grated. "How long did you think you could keep this a secret? Soldiers talk, child. Men always talk! Bryne will be lucky if the Hall doesn't put his head on a pike."

Egwene stood slowly, smoothing her skirt. She had been waiting for this, but she still needed to be careful. The game was far from played out, and everything could still turn against her in a flash. She had to pretend innocence, until she could afford to stop pretending. "Must I remind you that rudeness to the Amyrlin Seat is a crime, daughter," she said instead. She had been pretending so long, and she was so close.

"The Amyrlin Seat." Romanda strode across the carpets to within arm's reach of Egwene, and by her glare, the thought of reaching more crossed her mind. "You're an infant! Your bottom still remembers the last switching it had as a novice! After this, you'll be lucky if the Hall doesn't put you in a corner with a few play pretties. If you want to avoid that, you will listen to me, and do as I tell you. Now, sit down!"

Egwene seethed inside, but she sat. It was too soon.

With a sharp, satisfied nod, Romanda planted her fists on her hips. She stared down at Egwene like a stern aunt lecturing a misbehaving niece. A very stern aunt. Or a headsman with a toothache. "This meeting with Pelivar and Arathelle has to go forward, now it's been arranged. They expect the Amyrlin Seat, and they will see her. You will attend with all the pomp and dignity your title deserves. And you will tell them I am to speak for you, after which, you will hold your tongue! Getting them out of our way will require a firm hand, and someone who knows what she's about. No doubt Lelaine will be here any minute, trying to put herself forward, but you just remember the trouble she's in. I've spent the day speaking with other Sitters, and it appears very likely that Merilille and Merana's failures will be quite firmly attached to Lelaine when the Hall sits next. So, if you have any hope of gaining the experience you'll need to grow into that stole, it lies with me! Do you understand me?"

"I understand perfectly," Egwene said, in what she hoped was a meek voice. If she let Romanda speak in her place, there would no longer be any doubts. The Hall and the whole world would know who held Egwene al'Vere by the scruff of her neck.

Romanda's eyes seemed to bore into her head before the woman gave a curt nod. "I hope that you do. I intend to remove Elaida from the Amyrlin Seat, and I won't see that ruined because a child thinks she knows enough to find her way across the street without her hand held." With a snort, she flung her cloak around her and flung herself out of the tent. The ward vanished as she did.

Egwene sat and frowned at the tent's entrance. A child? Burn the woman, she was the Amyrlin Seat! Whether they liked it or not, they had raised her, and they were going to have to live with it! Eventually. Snatching up the stone ink-well, she hurled it at the tentflap.

Lelaine dodged back, barely avoiding the splash. "Temper, temper," she chided, coming on in.

No more asking permission than Romanda had, she embraced the Source and wove a ward to stop anyone over-hearing what she had to say. Where Romanda had been in a fury, Lelaine appeared pleased with herself, rubbing her gloved hands and smiling.

"I don't suppose I need tell you your little secret is out. Very bad of Lord Bryne, but I think he's too valuable to kill. A good thing for him I do. Let me see. I suppose Romanda told you that there will be a meeting with Pelivar and Arathelle, but you are to let her do all the talking. Am I right?" Egwene stirred, but Lelaine waved a hand at her. "No need to answer. I know Romanda. Unfortunately for her, I learned about this before she did, and instead of running to you straightaway, I've been polling the other Sitters. Do you want to know what they think?"

Egwene balled her fists in her lap, where she hoped they would not be noticed. "I expect you're going to tell me."

"You are in no position to take that tone with me," Lelaine said sharply, but the next instant, her smile returned. "The Hall is displeased with you. Very displeased. Whatever Romanda has threatened you with—and it's easy enough to imagine—I can deliver. Romanda, on the other hand, has upset a number of Sitters with her bullying. So, unless you want to find yourself with less authority than the little you have now, Romanda is going to be surprised tomorrow when you name me to speak for you. It's hard to believe Arathelle and Pelivar were foolish enough to put a thing like this in motion, but they'll slink away with their tails between their legs once I'm done with them."

"How do I know you won't carry out those threats anyway?" Egwene hoped her angry mutter sounded like sullenness. Light, but she was tired of this!

"Because I say I won't," Lelaine snapped. "Don't you know by now that you aren't really in charge of anything? The Hall is, and that is between Romanda and me. In another hundred years, you may grow into the stole, but for now, sit quietly, fold your hands, and let someone who knows what she is about see to pulling Elaida down."

After Lelaine left, Egwene once more sat staring. This time, she was not letting anger boil. *You may grow into the stole.* Almost the same thing Romanda had said. *Someone who knows what she is about. Was* she deceiving herself? A child, ruining what a woman with experience could handle easily?

Siuan slipped into the tent and stood looking worried. "Gareth Bryne just came to tell me the Hall knows," she said dryly. "Under cover of asking about his shirts. Him and his bloody shirts! The meeting is set for tomorrow, at a lake about five hours to the north. Pelivar and Arathelle are already on the way. Aemlyn, too. That's a third strong House."

"That's more than Lelaine or Romanda saw fit to tell me," Egwene said, just as dryly. No. A hundred years of being led by the hand, pushed by the scruff of her neck, or fifty years, or five, and she would be fit for nothing more. If she had to grow, she had to grow *now*.

"Oh, blood and bloody ashes," Siuan groaned. "I can't stand it! What did they say? How did it go?"

"About as we expected." Egwene smiled with a wonder that touched her voice, too. "Siuan, they couldn't have handed me the Hall better if I had told them what to do."

The last light was failing as Sheriam approached her tiny tent, smaller even than Egwene's. If she had not been Keeper, she would have had to share. Ducking inside, she had only time to realize she was not alone when she was shielded and flung facedown on her cot. Stunned, she tried to cry out, but a corner of one of her blankets wadded itself into her mouth. Dress and shift burst away from her body like a pricked bubble.

A hand stroked her head. "You were supposed to keep me informed, Sheriam. That girl is up to something, and I want to know what."

It took a long time to convince her questioner that she had already told all she knew, that she would never hold back a word, not a whisper. When she was left alone at last, it was to lie curled up and whimpering from her welts, bitterly wishing that she had never in her life spoken to a single sister in the Hall.

CHAPTER

17

Out on the Ice

The next morning, a column rode north from the Aes Sedai camp well before dawn, near silent except for the creak of saddles and the crunch of hooves breaking through the snow's crisp crust. Occasionally a horse snorted, or metal jingled and was quickly muffled. The moon was already down, the sky glistening with stars, but the pale blanket lying over everything below lightened the darkness. When the first glimmers of day appeared in the east, they had been riding a good hour or more. Which was not to say they had traveled far. Over some open stretches, Egwene could let Daishar go at a slow canter that sprayed white like splashing water, but for the most part, the horses walked, and not quickly, through sparse forest where the snow made deep drifts below and clung to branches overhead. Oak and pine, sourgum and leatherleaf and trees she did not recognize all looked even more bedraggled than they had in the heat and drought. Today was the Feast of Abram, but there would be no prizes baked in honeycakes. The Light send some people found surprises in the day, though.

The sun rose and climbed, a pale golden ball that gave no warmth. Every breath still bit the throat and produced a puff of mist. A sharp wind blew, not hard, but cutting, and to the west dark clouds rolled north on their way to Andor. She felt a touch of pity for whoever would know the burden of those clouds. And relief that they were heading away. Waiting another day would have been maddening. She had been unable to sleep at all, for fidgety restlessness, not headaches. Restlessness, and tendrils of fear that had crept in like cold air under the edges of the tent. She was not tired, though. She felt like a compressed spring, a tight-wound clock, full of energy that wanted desperately to find release. Light, everything could still go horribly wrong.

It was an impressive column, behind the standard of the White Tower, the white Flame of Tar Valon centered on a spiral of seven colors, one for each Ajah. Sewn secretly in Salidar, it had lain in the bottom of a chest ever since, with the keys in the keeping of the Hall. She did not think they would have produced it except for this morning's need for pomp. A thousand heavy cavalry in plate-and-mail pro-vided a close escort, a panoply of lances, swords, maces and axes seldom seen south of the Borderlands. Their com-mander was a one-eyed Shienaran with a vividly painted eyepatch, a man she had met once, what seemed an Age ago. Uno Nomesta glared at the trees through the steel bars of his helmet's faceguard as if he expected every last one to hide an ambush, and his men seemed nearly as watchful, erect in their saddles.

Almost out of sight ahead through the trees rode a knot of men who wore helmets, breast- and backplates, but no other armor. Their cloaks whipped about freely; a gaunt-leted hand for the reins and a hand for the short bow they each carried left nothing to grasp at warmth. There were more farther on, and beyond sight to left and right and be-hind, another thousand altogether, to scout and screen. Ga-reth Bryne did not expect trickery from the Andorans, but he had been wrong before, so he said, and the Murandians were another matter. And then there was the possibility of assassins in Elaida's pay, or even Darkfriends. The Light alone knew when a Darkfriend might decide to kill, or why. For that matter, though the Shaido were supposedly far away, no one ever seemed to know they were there until the killing began. Even bandits might have tried their hand with too small a party. Lord Bryne was not a man to take chances unnecessarily, and Egwene was very glad. Today, she wanted as many witnesses as possible.

She herself rode ahead of the banner, with Sheriam and Siuan and Bryne. The others appeared caught in their own thoughts. Lord Bryne sat his saddle easily, the mist of his even breath forming a light frost on his faceguard, yet Egwene could see him calmly marking terrain in his mind.

In case he had to fight over it. Siuan rode so stiffly that she would be sore long before reaching their destination, but she stared north as though she could already see the lake, and sometimes she nodded to herself, or shook her head. She would not have done that unless she was uneasy. Sheriam knew no more of what was to come than the Sitters did, yet she appeared even more nervous than Siuan, shifting constantly in her saddle and grimacing. Anger shone in her green eyes, too, for some reason.

Close behind the banner came the entire Hall of the Tower in double column, wearing embroidered silks and rich velvets and furs and cloaks with the Flame large on the back. Women who seldom wore more ornaments than the Great Serpent ring were decked today in the finest gems the camp's jewelry caskets could supply. Their Warders made a more splendid display simply by wearing their color-shifting cloaks; parts of the men seemed to vanish as the disquieting cloaks swirled in the stiff breeze. Servants followed, two or three for every sister, on the best horses that could be found for them. They might have passed for lesser nobility themselves if a number had not been leading pack animals; every chest in the camp had been ransacked to outfit them in bright colors.

Perhaps because she was one of the Sitters without a Warder, Delana had brought Halima along, on a spirited white mare. The two rode almost knee-to-knee. Sometimes Delana would lean toward Halima to speak privately, though Halima appeared too excited to listen. Supposedly, Halima was Delana's secretary, but everyone believed it a case of charity, or possibly friendship, however unlikely, between the dignified, pale-haired sister and the hot-natured, raven-haired country woman. Egwene had seen Halima's hand, and it had the unformed look of a child's just learning her letters. Today, she was in garments as fine as any sister's, with gems that easily equaled Delana's, who must have been their source. Whenever a gust opened her velvet cloak, she displayed a shocking amount of bosom, and she always laughed and took her time about gathering it around her again, refusing to admit that she felt the cold any more than the sisters did.

For once, Egwene was glad of all the gifts of clothing she had been given, allowing her to surpass the Sitters. Her green-and-blue silk was slashed with white and worked with seed pearls. Pearls even decorated the backs of her gloves. At the last minute a cloak lined with ermine had been provided by Romanda, and a necklace and earrings of emeralds and white opals by Lelaine. The moonstones in her hair came from Janya. The Amyrlin had to be resplendent today. Even Siuan appeared ready for a ball, in blue velvets and cream lace, with a wide band of pearls at her throat and more laced through her hair.

Romanda and Lelaine led the Sitters, riding so closely behind the soldier bearing the banner that he glanced over his shoulder nervously and sometimes edged his horse nearer the riders ahead of him. Egwene managed not to look back more than once or twice, yet she could feel their eyes pressing between her shoulder blades. Each thought her tied in a neat bundle, but each had to be wondering whose cords had done the binding. Oh, Light, this could not go wrong. Not now.

Other than the column, little moved in all that snow-covered landscape. A broad-winged hawk wheeled overhead against the cold blue sky for a time before winging eastward. Twice Egwene saw black-tailed foxes trotting in the distance, still in their summer fur, and once, a large deer with tall forked antlers ghosted away and vanished amid the trees. A hare, starting up right under Bela's hooves and bounding off, made the shaggy mare toss her head, and Siuan yelped and grabbed at the reins as if she expected Bela to bolt. Of course, Bela only gave a reproachful snort and plodded onward. Egwene's tall roan gelding shied more, and the hare had not gone near him.

Siuan began grumbling under her breath after the hare scampered away, and it took quite some time before she eased Bela's reins. Being on a horse always made her grumpy—she traveled in one of the wagons whenever possible—but she was seldom this bad. There was no need to look further than Lord Bryne, or her fierce glances at him, to know why.

If he noticed Siuan's looks, he gave no sign. The only one not in fine array, he looked as he always did, plain and slightly battered. A rock that had weathered storms and would outlast more to come. For some reason, Egwene was glad he had resisted their efforts to dress him in finer garb.

They truly did need to make an impression, yet she thought he made an excellent one as he was.

"It's a fine morning to be in the saddle," Sheriam said after a time. "Nothing like a good ride in the snow to clear the head." Her voice was not low, and she cut her eyes at the still-muttering Siuan with a tiny smile.

Siuan did not say anything—she hardly could do that in front of so many eyes—but she did give Sheriam a hard look that promised sharp words for later. The fire-haired woman twisted away abruptly with very close to a wince. Wing, her dappled gray mare, pranced a few steps, and Sheriam settled her down with almost too firm a hand. She had shown little gratitude to the woman who had named her Mistress of Novices, and like most in that position, she found reasons to blame Siuan. It was the only flaw Egwene had found in her since the swearing. Well, she had protested that, as Keeper, she should not have to take orders from Siuan the way the others who had sworn did, but Egwene had seen right away where that would lead. This was not the first time Sheriam had tried to plant a barb. Siuan insisted on handling Sheriam herself, and her pride was too fragile for Egwene to deny the request unless matters got out of hand.

Egwene wished there were some way to make more speed. Siuan went back to her grumbling, and Sheriam was obviously thinking of something else to say that would not quite bring a rebuke. All that muttering and cutting of eyes began to find their way under Egwene's skin. After a while, even Bryne's levelheaded poise began to wear. She found herself thinking of things she might say that would shake his aplomb. Unfortunately—or perhaps fortunately—she did not believe anything could. But if she had to wait much longer, she thought she might burst from sheer impatience.

The sun climbed toward midday, the painfully slow miles passed behind, and at last one of the riders ahead turned and raised his hand. With a hasty apology to Egwene, Bryne galloped forward. It was really more of a lumber through the snow for his sturdy bay gelding, Traveler, but he caught up to the outriders, exchanged a few words, then sent them on through the trees and waited for Egwene and the others to reach him.

As he fell in beside her once more, Romanda and Lelaine joined them. The two Sitters barely acknowledged

Egwene's presence, fixing Bryne with the cool serenity that had shaken so many men facing Aes Sedai. Except that now and then, each glanced sideways at the other in a considering way. They hardly seemed to realize what they were doing. Egwene hoped they were half as nervous as she; she would be satisfied with that.

Coolly serene stares washed over Bryne like rain over that rock. He made slight bows to the Sitters, but he spoke to Egwene. "They've already arrived, Mother." That had been expected. "They brought almost as many men as we did, but they're all on the north side of the lake. I've put scouts out to make sure nobody tries circling around, but in truth, I don't expect it."

"Let us hope you're right," Romanda told him sharply, and Lelaine added in a much colder tone, "Your judgment has not been all it should be, of late, Lord Bryne." A frigid, cutting tone.

"As you say, Aes Sedai." He made another slight bow without really turning from Egwene. Like Siuan, he was tied to her openly now, at least so far as the Hall was concerned. If only they did not know how tightly. If only she could be sure how tightly. "One thing more, Mother," he went on. "Talmanes is there at the lake, too. There are about a hundred of the Band on the east side. Not enough to cause trouble even if he wanted to, and small chance he would, I think."

Egwene merely nodded. Not enough to cause trouble? Talmanes alone might be enough! She tasted bile. It—could—not—go—wrong—now!

"Talmanes!" Lelaine exclaimed, serenity shattering. She *must* have been as much on edge as Egwene. "How did he find out? If you've included Dragonsworn in your scheming, Lord Bryne, you truly will learn what going too far means!"

Right on top of her, Romanda growled, "This is disgraceful! You say you've only learned of his presence now? If that's so, your reputation is puffed up like a boil!" Aes Sedai calm was a thin layer for some today, it seemed.

They continued in that vein, but Bryne rode on, only murmuring the occasional "As you say, Aes Sedai," when he had to say something. He had received worse in Egwene's hearing this morning, and reacted no more. It was Siuan who finally snorted, and then blushed crimson when the Sitters looked at her in surprise. Egwene almost shook her head. Siuan was very definitely in love. And she *very* definitely needed talking to! For some reason, Bryne smiled, but that might just have been because he was no longer the object of the Sitters' attention.

Trees gave way to another open space, larger than most, and there was no more time for frivolous thoughts.

Aside from a wide rim of tall brown reeds and cattails poking through the snow, nothing named this a lake. It could have been a big meadow, flat and very roughly oval in shape. Some distance from the treeline, on the frozen lake, stood a large blue canopy on tall poles, with a small crowd of people milling about it and dozens of horses held by servants behind. The breeze ruffled a bright thicket of pennants and banners, and carried muffled shouts that could only have been orders. More servants darted about hastily. Apparently, they had not been there long enough to finish their preparations.

Perhaps a mile away the trees began again, and the feeble sunlight glinted off metal there. Quite a lot of metal, stretching the length of the far shore. To the east, almost as close as the pavilion, the hundred men of the Band made no effort at concealment, standing beside their mounts just short of where the cattails began. A few of them pointed when the flag of Tar Valon appeared. The people at the pavilion stopped to look.

Egwene did not pause before riding out onto the snow-covered ice. She did imagine herself a rosebud opening to the sun, though, that old novice exercise. She did not actually embrace *saidar*, but the calm that came was very welcome.

Siuan and Sheriam followed, and the Sitters with their Warders, and the servants. Lord Bryne and the banner-man were the only two soldiers who went. Shouts rising behind her told of Uno putting his armored horsemen into position along the shoreline. The more lightly armored men were arrayed to either side, those not off guarding against treachery. One reason the lake had been chosen was that the ice was thick enough to hold a fair number of horses, but not hundreds, much less thousands. That cut down on the chance of chicanery. Of course, a pavilion beyond bowshot was not beyond the range of the One Power, not if it could be seen. Except that the worst man in the world knew himself safe from that unless he threatened a sister. Egwene exhaled sharply, and began acquiring calm all over again.

A proper greeting for the Amyrlin Seat should have had servants rushing forward with warm drinks and cloths wrapped around hot bricks, and the lords and ladies themselves to take reins and offer a kiss in token of Abram. Any visitor of rank at all would have had the servants, but no one stirred from the pavilion. Bryne himself dismounted and came to hold Daishar's bridle, and the same lanky young man who had come with fresh charcoal the day before ran to hold Egwene's stirrup. His nose still dripped, but in a red velvet coat only a little too large for him and a bright blue cloak, he outshone any of the nobles who stood staring from under the canopy. They appeared to be in stout woolens for the most part, with not much embroidery and very little silk or lace. Likely they had had to scramble to find suitable clothes once the snows began, and them already on the march. Though the simple truth was that the young man might have outshone a Tinker.

Carpets had been laid to floor the pavilion, and braziers lit, though the breeze carried away heat and smoke alike. Chairs stood in two facing lines for the delegations, eight in each. They had not expected so many sisters. Some of the waiting nobles exchanged looks of consternation, and a number of their servants actually wrung their hands, wondering what to do. They need not have.

The chairs were a mismatched miscellany, but they were all alike in size, and none was noticeably more worn or battered than another. None had noticeably more or less gilded carving. The lanky young man and a number of others trotted in and under the frowns of the nobles, without so much as a by-your-leave, carried those meant for Aes Sedai out into the snow, then rushed to help with unloading the packhorses. Still, no one spoke a word.

Quickly, seats were set up sufficient for the entire Hall, and Egwene. Only simple benches, though polished till they gleamed, but each stood on a wide box covered with cloth in the color of the Sitter's Ajah, in a long row as wide as the canopy. The box placed in front, for Egwene's bench, was striped like her stole. There had been a great flurry of activity in the night, beginning with finding beeswax for polish and good cloth of the right colors.

When Egwene and the Sitters took their places, they sat a foot higher than anyone else. She had had her doubts about that, but the lack of any word of welcome had settled those. The meanest farmer would have offered a cup and a kiss to a vagabond on the Feast of Abram. They were not supplicants, and they were not equals. They were Aes Sedai.

Warders stood behind their Aes Sedai, and Siuan and Sheriam flanked Egwene. The sisters ostentatiously flung back cloaks and tucked gloves away to emphasize that the cold did not touch them, a sharp contrast to the nobles clutching their own cloaks close. Outside, the Flame of Tar Valon lifted in the stiffening breeze. Only Halima, lounging beside Delana's chair on the edge of the gray-covered box, at all spoiled the grand image, and her big green eyes stared at the Andorans and Murandians so challengingly that she did not spoil it much.

There were a few stares when Egwene took the seat in front, but only a few. No one really looked surprised. *I suppose they've heard all about the* girl *Amyrlin*, she thought dryly. Well, there had been queens younger, including queens of Andor and Murandy. Calmly, she nodded, and Sheriam gestured to the line of chairs. No matter who had arrived first or provided the pavilion, there was no doubt who had called this meeting. Who was in charge.

Her action was not well received, of course. There was a moment of silent hesitation while the nobles cast their minds about for some way to regain an equal footing, and no few grimaces as they realized it could not be done. Grim-faced, eight of them sat down, four men and four women, with much angry gathering of cloaks and adjusting of skirts. Those of lesser rank stood behind the chairs, and clearly there was little love lost between Andoran and Murandian. For that matter, the Murandians, men and women alike, muttered and jostled one another for precedence as fiercely as they did their "allies" from the north. The Aes Sedai received a good many dark looks as well, and a few folk spared scowls for Bryne, who stood off to one side with his helmet under his arm. He was well known on both sides of the border, and respected even by most of those who would have liked to see him dead. At least, that had been the case before he turned up leading the Aes Sedai's army. He ignored their acid glares as he had the Sitters' acid tongues.

Another man did not join with either party. A pale man, less than a hand taller than Egwene, in a dark coat and breastplate, he wore the front of his head shaved, and there was a long red scarf tied around his left arm. His deep gray cloak had a large red hand worked on the breast. Talmanes stood opposite Bryne, leaning against one of the pavilion's poles with an arrogant casualness, and watched without revealing a hint of his thoughts. Egwene wished she knew what he was doing there. She wished she knew what he had said before she arrived. In any case, she had to speak with him. If it could be managed without a hundred ears listening.

A lean, weathered man in a red cloak, sitting in the middle of the row of chairs, leaned forward and opened his mouth, but Sheriam forestalled him in a clear, carrying voice.

"Mother, may I present to you, of Andor, Arathelle Renshar, High Seat of House Renshar. Pelivar Coelan, High Seat of House Coelan. Aemlyn Carand, High Seat of House Carand, and her husband, Culhan Carand." They acknowledged their names sourly, with bare nods and no more. Pelivar was the lean man; he was losing his dark hair from the front. Sheriam went on without pause; it was a good thing Bryne had been able to supply the names of those who had been chosen to speak. "May I present, of Murandy, Donel do Morny a'Lordeine. Cian do Mehon a'Macansa. Paitr do Fearna a'Conn. Segan do Avharin a'Roos." The Murandians seemed to feel the lack of titles even more than the Andorans. Donel, wearing more lace than most of the women, twisted his curled mustaches fiercely, and Paitr appeared to be trying to yank his loose. Segan pursed full lips and her dark eyes caught fire, while Cian, a stocky, graying woman, snorted quite loudly. Sheriam took no notice. "You are beneath the eyes of the Watcher of the Seals. You are before the Flame of Tar Valon. You may present your supplications to the Amyrlin Seat."

Well. They did not like that, not in the least. Egwene had thought them sour before, but now they looked stuffed full of green persimmons. Perhaps they had believed they could

pretend she was not the Amyrlin at all. They would learn.
Of course, first she had to teach the Hall.

"There are ancient ties between Andor and the White
Tower," she said, loudly and firmly. "Sisters have always
expected welcome in Andor or Murandy. Why then do
you bring an army against Aes Sedai? You meddle where
thrones and nations fear to step. Thrones have fallen, meddling in the affairs of Aes Sedai."

That sounded suitably threatening, whether or not
Myrelle and the others had managed to prepare her way.
With luck, they were well on their way back to the camp,
with no one the wiser. Unless one of these nobles spoke the
wrong name. That would lose her an advantage against the
Hall, but alongside everything else, it was a straw beside a
hayloft.

Pelivar exchanged looks with the woman seated beside
him, and she stood. Creases in her face could not disguise
the fact that Arathelle had been a beautiful, fine-boned
woman when young; now, gray threaded thickly through
her hair, and her gaze struck as hard as any Warder's. Her
red-gloved hands gripped the edges of her cloak at her
sides, but plainly not in worry. Mouth compressed to a thin
line, she scanned the line of Sitters, and only then spoke.
Past Egwene, to the sisters behind her. Gritting her teeth,
Egwene put on an attentive expression.

"We are here precisely because we do not want to become entangled in the White Tower's affairs." Arathelle's
voice held tones of authority, unsurprising in the High Seat
of a powerful House. There was no hint of the diffidence
that might have been expected, even from a powerful High
Seat, facing so many sisters, not to mention the Amyrlin
Seat. "If all we've heard is true, then at best, allowing you
to pass through Andor unhindered may seem like giving
aid, or even alliance, in the eyes of the White Tower. Failure
to oppose you might mean learning what the grape learns
in the winepress." Several of the Murandians turned their
scowls on her. No one in Murandy had tried to hinder the
sisters' passage. Very likely, no one had considered the possibilities beyond the day they passed onto another's lands.

Arathelle continued as if she had not noticed, but Egwene
doubted that. "At worst. . . . We have heard . . . reports . . .

of Aes Sedai making their way into Andor in secret, and
Tower Guards. Rumors might be a better word, but they
come from many places. None of us would like to see a
battle between Aes Sedai in Andor."

"The Light preserve and protect us!" Donel burst out,
red-faced. Paitr nodded encouragement, sliding to the edge
of his seat, and Cian looked ready to jump in herself. "No
one wants to see it here, either!" Donel spat. "Not between
Aes Sedai! For sure, we've heard what happened out east!
And those sisters—!"

Egwene breathed a little more easily when Arathelle
stepped on him firmly. "If you please, Lord Donel. You will
have your turn to speak." She turned back to Egwene—to
the Sitters once more, really—without waiting on his reply, leaving him spluttering and the other three Murandians
glowering. She herself looked quite undisturbed, simply a
woman laying out the facts. Laying them out, and meaning
that they should be seen as she saw them.

"As I was saying. That is the worst we fear, if the tales
are true. And also if they are not. Aes Sedai may be gathering secretly in Andor, with Tower Guards. Aes Sedai with
an army are ready to enter Andor. Often enough the White
Tower has seemed to aim at one target, only for the rest of
us to learn later it was aiming at another all along. I can
hardly imagine even the White Tower going this far, but
if ever there was a target you might twist yourselves into a
knot for, it's the Black Tower." Arathelle shivered slightly,
and Egwene did not think it was the cold. "A battle between
Aes Sedai might ruin the land for miles around. *That* battle
might ruin half of Andor."

Pelivar sprang to his feet. "The plain of it is, you must
go another way." His voice was surprisingly high, but no
less firm than Arathelle's. "If I must die to defend my lands
and my people, then better here than where my lands and
people die, too."

He subsided at Arathelle's soothing gesture, sinking back
into his chair. Hard-eyed, he did not look mollified. Aemlyn, a plump woman wrapped in dark wool, nodded agreement with him, as did her square-faced husband.

Donel stared at Pelivar as though he had never had this
thought either, and he was not the only one. Some of the
standing Murandians began to argue out loud until others

quieted them. Sometimes with a shaken fist. Whatever had possessed these people to join forces with the Andorans?

Egwene drew breath. A rosebud, opening to the sun. They had not acknowledged her as the Amyrlin Seat—Arathelle had come as close to ignoring her as was possible without pushing her aside!—yet they had given her everything else she could have wished for. Calm. Now was when Lelaine and Romanda would be expecting her to name one of them to handle the negotiations. She hoped their stomachs were tied in knots with wondering which of them it would be. There would be no negotiations. There could be none.

"Elaida," she said levelly, eyeing Arathelle and the seated nobles in turn, "is a usurper who has violated what lies at the very heart of the White Tower. I am the Amyrlin Seat." She was surprised at how stately she managed to sound, how cool. But not as surprised as she once would have been. The Light help her, she *was* the Amyrlin Seat. "We go to Tar Valon to remove Elaida and try her, but that is the White Tower's business, and none of yours except to know the truth. This so-called Black Tower also is our business; men who can channel have always been the White Tower's affair. We will deal with them as we choose, when the time is ripe, but I assure you, that time is not now. More important matters must take precedence."

She heard movement among the Sitters behind her. An actual shifting on benches and the crisp swishing of divided skirts being adjusted. At least some must be severely agitated. Well, several had suggested that the Black Tower might be dealt with in passing. Not one believed there could be more than a dozen or so men there at most, no matter what they heard; after all, it simply was not possible that *hundreds* of men would *want* to channel. Then again, it might have been the realization that Egwene was not going to name either Romanda or Lelaine.

Arathelle frowned, perhaps catching a hint of something in the air. Pelivar moved, on the point of rising again, and Donel drew himself up querulously. There was nothing for it but to press on. There never had been.

"I understand your concerns," she continued in the same formal tone, "and I will address them." What was that strange call to arms the Band used? Yes. It was time to toss the dice. "I give you this assurance as the Amyrlin Seat.

For one month we will stay here, resting, and then we will leave Murandy, but we will not cross the border into Andor. Murandy will be troubled by us no more after that, and Andor will not be troubled at all. I'm certain," she added, "the Murandian lords and ladies here will be happy to supply our wants in exchange for good silver. We will pay fair prices." There was no point mollifying the Andorans if it meant Murandians raiding the horses and supply trains.

The Murandians, looking around uneasily, appeared decidedly torn in any case. There was coin to be made, and a great deal of it supplying an army so large, but on the other hand, who could haggle successfully with whatever an army so large offered? Donel actually seemed ready to sick up, while Cian seemed to be doing sums in her head. Mutters rose among the onlookers. More than mutters; nearly loud enough for Egwene.

She wanted to look over her shoulder. The silence from the Sitters was deafening. Siuan was staring straight ahead and gripping her skirts as if to keep herself looking forward by main force. At least she had known what was coming. Sheriam, who had not, eyed the Andorans and Murandians regally, calmly, as though she had expected every word.

Egwene needed to make them forget the girl they saw before them, and hear a woman with the reins of power firmly in hand. If they were not in her hands now, they would be! She firmed her voice. "Mark me well. I have made my decision; it is for you to accept it. Or face what surely will come from your failure." As she fell silent, the wind gusted to a brief howl, rattling the canopy, tugging at garments. Egwene straightened her hair calmly. Some of the watching nobles shivered and twitched their cloaks around them, and she hoped their shivers came from more than the weather.

Arathelle exchanged looks with Pelivar and Aemlyn, and all three studied the Sitters before slowly nodding. They believed she was merely mouthing words the Sitters had put on her tongue! Even so, Egwene very nearly sighed with relief.

"It will be as you say," the hard-eyed noblewoman said. Again, to the Sitters. "We do not doubt the word of Aes Sedai, of course, but you will understand if we also remain. Sometimes, what you hear isn't what you think you heard. Not that that's the case here, I'm sure. But we will stay while you do." Donel truly looked ready to empty himself. Very likely his lands lay nearby. Andoran armies in Murandy had seldom been known to pay for anything.

Egwene stood, and she could hear the rustle of the Sitters rising behind her. "It is agreed, then. We must all depart soon, if we are to return to our own beds before dark, but we should spare a few moments. Getting to know one another a little better now might avoid misunderstandings later." And talk might give her a chance to reach Talmanes. "Oh. One other thing you should all be aware of. The novice book is now open to any woman, whatever her age, if she tests true." Arathelle blinked. Siuan did not, yet Egwene thought she heard a faint grunt. This was not part of what they had discussed, but there would never be a better time. "Come. I'm sure you would all like to speak with the Sitters. Let formality go."

Without waiting for Sheriam to offer a hand, she stepped down. She almost felt like laughing. Last night she had been afraid she might never reach her goal, but she was halfway there, almost halfway, and it had not been nearly as difficult as she had feared. Of course, the other half remained.

CHAPTER
18

A Peculiar Calling

For a moment after Egwene descended, no one else moved. And then the Andorans and Murandians headed for the Sitters, almost as one. Apparently, a girl Amyrlin—a girl puppet and figurehead!—held no interest, not with ageless faces in front of them that at least said they actually were speaking to Aes Sedai. Two or three lords and ladies clustered around each Sitter, some thrusting their chins demandingly, others diffidently bending their necks, yet every one insistent on being heard. The sharp breeze whisked away the mist of their breath and fluttered cloaks forgotten in the importance of asking their questions. Sheriam was buttonholed too, by red-faced Lord Donel, who blustered and jerked bows by turns.

Egwene pulled Sheriam away from the narrow-eyed man. "Find out discreetly all you can about these sisters and Tower Guards in Andor," she whispered hastily. As soon as she released the woman, Donel reclaimed her. Sheriam actually looked put-upon, but her frown disappeared quickly. Donel blinked uneasily as she began questioning *him*.

Romanda and Lelaine gazed at Egwene through the crowd with faces carved from ice, but each had acquired a pair of nobles who wanted. . . . Something. Reassurance that there was no hidden trick in Egwene's words, perhaps. How they would hate doing that, but dodge and duck as they would—and they would!—there was no way to really avoid that reassurance without repudiating her on the spot. Even those two would not go that far. Not here, not publicly.

Siuan slipped close to Egwene, features set in meekness. Except that her eyes darted, maybe looking for Romanda or Lelaine coming to seize them where they stood, and forget law, custom, propriety *and* who was watching. "Shein Chunla," she all but hissed in a whisper.

Egwene nodded, but *her* eyes searched for Talmanes. Most of the men and some of the women were tall enough to hide him. With everyone shifting about. . . . She went up on her toes. Where had he gone to?

Segan planted herself in front of her, fists on her hips, eyeing Siuan doubtfully. Egwene let her heels down hurriedly. The Amyrlin could not bob about like a girl at a dance looking for a boy. A rosebud unfolding. Calm. Serenity. Drat all men!

A slender woman with long dark hair, Segan seemed to have been born petulant, her full mouth fixed in a pout. Her dress was good blue wool and made for warmth, but it had far too much vivid green embroidery across her bosom, and her gloves were bright enough for a Tinker. She looked Egwene up and down, pursing her lips, with as much incredulity on her face as she had given Siuan. "What you said about the novice book," she said abruptly. "Were you meaning any woman of any age at all? Any can become Aes Sedai, then?"

A question close to Egwene's heart, and an answer she dearly wanted to give—along with a box on the ear for the doubt—but just then a small gap in the flow of people showed her Talmanes near the back of the pavilion. Talking with Pelivar! They stood stiffly, mastiffs not quite ready to show teeth, yet they were keeping a watch to make sure no one came close enough to overhear what they had to say. "Any woman of any age at all, daughter," she agreed absently. Pelivar?

"Thank you," Segan said, and haltingly added, "Mother." She sketched a curtsy, the barest hint of one, before hurrying off. Egwene stared after her. Well, it was a beginning.

Siuan snorted. "I don't mind sailing the Fingers of the Dragon in the dark if I must," she muttered half under her breath. "We discussed that; we weighed the dangers, and anyway, there doesn't seem to be a gull's last dinner for choice. But you have to set a fire on deck just to make things interesting. Netting lionfish isn't enough for you. You have to stuff a prickleback down your dress, too. You aren't content trying to wade a school of silverpike—"

Egwene broke in. "Siuan, I think I should tell Lord Bryne you're head over heels in love with him. It's only fair that he know, don't you agree?" Siuan's blue eyes bulged, and her mouth worked, but all that came out was a sort of gobbling. Egwene patted her shoulder. "You're Aes Sedai, Siuan. Try to maintain at least a little dignity. And try to find out about those sisters in Andor." The crowd parted again. She saw Talmanes in a different place, but still on the edge of the pavilion. And alone, now.

Trying not to hurry, she walked in his direction, leaving Siuan still gobbling. A pretty, black-haired serving man, whose bulky woolen breeches could not quite hide neatly turned calves, offered Siuan a steaming silver cup from a tray. Other servants were moving about with other silver trays. Refreshment was being offered, if a bit late. It was much too late for the kiss of peace. She did not hear what Siuan said as she snatched a cup, but from the way the fellow jerked and started bobbing bows, he had received sharp shards of her temper at the least. Egwene sighed.

Talmanes stood with arms folded, observing the goings-on with an amused smile that did not reach his eyes. He seemed poised to explode into motion, but his eyes were tired. At her approach, he made a respectful leg, but there was a wry touch to his voice when he said, "You changed a border today." He gathered his cloak against the icy breeze. "It has always been . . . fluid . . . between Andor and Murandy, no matter what maps say, but Andor has never come south in such numbers before. Except for the Aiel War, and the Whitecloak War, anyway, but they were only passing through, then. Once they have been here a month, new maps will show a new line. Look at the Murandians scramble, fawning over Pelivar and his companions as much as they do the sisters. They are hoping to make new friends for the new day."

To Egwene, trying to conceal her careful watch on those who might be watching her, it seemed that all of the nobles, Murandian and Andoran, were intent on the Sitters, crowding around them. In any case, she had slightly more important matters in mind than borders. To her, if not to the nobles. Except for brief moments, none of the Sitters were visible beyond the tops of their heads. Only Halima and Siuan seemed to notice her, and a babble like that of a flock of excited geese filled the air. She lowered her voice, and chose her words carefully.

"Friends are always important, Talmanes. You've been a good friend to Mat, and I think to me. I hope that hasn't changed. I hope you've not told anyone what you shouldn't." Light, she *was* anxious, or she would not have been so direct. Next, she would come right out and ask what he and Pelivar had been talking about!

Luckily, he did not laugh at her for a blunt-tongued village woman. Though he might have been thinking it. He studied her seriously before speaking. In a soft voice. He also knew caution. "Not all men gossip. Tell me, when you sent Mat south, did you know what you would do here today?"

"How could I know that two months ago? No, Aes Sedai aren't omniscient, Talmanes." She had hoped for something that would put her in the place she was, had planned for it, but she had not known, not back then. She also hoped he did not gossip. Some men did not.

Romanda started toward her with a firm stride and a frozen face, but Arathelle intercepted her, catching the Yellow Sitter's arm and refusing to be put off despite Romanda's astonishment.

"Will you at least tell me where Mat is?" Talmanes asked. "On his way to Caemlyn with the Daughter-Heir? Why are you surprised? A serving woman will speak to a soldier when fetching water from the same stream. Even when he is a horrible Dragonsworn," he added dryly.

Light! Men really were . . . inconvenient . . . at times. The best of them found ways to say exactly the wrong thing at the wrong moment, to ask the wrong question. Not to mention inveigling serving women into prattle. So much easier if she could just lie, but he had given her plenty of room within the Oaths. Half the truth would suffice, and keep him from haring off to Ebou Dar. Maybe less than half.

Over in the far corner of the pavilion, Siuan stood conversing with a tall young redhead with curled mustaches who was eyeing her as dubiously as Segan had. Nobles usually knew the look of Aes Sedai. But he held only a part of Siuan's attention. Her gaze constantly flickered toward Egwene. It seemed to shout, loud as conscience. Easier.

Expedient. What it was to be Aes Sedai. She had *not* known about today, only hoped! Egwene expelled an irritated breath. Burn the woman!

"He was in Ebou Dar, the last I heard," she muttered. "But he must be hurrying north as fast as he can by now. He still thinks he has to save me, Talmanes, and Matrim Cauthon wouldn't miss the chance to be on the spot so he can say I told you so."

Talmanes did not look at all surprised. "I thought it might be so," he sighed. "I have . . . felt . . . something, for weeks now. Others in the Band have, too. Not urgent, but always there. As if he needed me. As if I should look south, anyway. It can be peculiar, following a *ta'veren*."

"I suppose it can," she agreed, hoping none of her incredulity showed. It was strange enough to think of Mat the wastrel as leader of the Band of the Red Hand, much less as *ta'veren*, but surely a *ta'veren* had to be present, nearby at least, to have any effect.

"Mat was wrong about you needing rescue. You never had any intention of coming to me for help, did you?"

He still spoke softly, but she looked around hurriedly anyway. Siuan was still watching them. And so was Halima. Paitr stood much too close to her, puffing and preening and stroking his mustaches—from the way he stared down her dress, he had not mistaken her for a sister, that was certain!—but she was giving him only half her mind, darting sidelong glances in Egwene's direction while she smiled up at him warmly. Everyone else appeared occupied, and no one stood close enough to hear.

"The Amyrlin Seat could hardly go running for sanctuary, now could she? But there have been times it's been a comfort knowing you were there," she admitted. Reluctantly. The Amyrlin Seat was hardly supposed to need a bolt-hole, but it could do no harm so long as none of the Sitters knew. "You *have* been a friend, Talmanes. I hope that continues. I truly do."

"You have been more . . . open . . . with me than I expected," he said slowly, "so I will tell you something." His face did not change—to any watcher, he must have seemed as casual as before—but his voice dropped to a whisper. "I have had approaches from King Roedran about the Band. It seems he has hopes of being Murandy's first real king. He wants to hire us. I would not have considered it, normally, but there is never enough coin, and with this . . . this *feel* of Mat needing us. . . . It might be better if we remain in Murandy. Clear as good glass, you are where you want to be and have everything in hand."

He fell silent as a young serving woman curtsied to offer mulled wine. She wore finely embroidered green wool and a cloak plush with spotted rabbit. Other servants from the camp were helping out now, as well, no doubt for something to do besides stand and shiver. The young woman's round face was decidedly pinched from the cold.

Talmanes waved her off and pulled his cloak back around him, but Egwene took a silver cup to gain a moment for thought. Truly there was little need for the Band any longer. Despite all the muttering, the sisters took their presence as a matter of course now, Dragon-sworn or not; they no longer feared an attack, and there had been no real need to use the Band's presence to prod them into moving since leaving Salidar. The only true purpose *Shen an Calhar* served now was to draw recruits into Bryne's army, men who thought two armies meant a battle and wanted to be on the side with the greatest numbers. She had no need of them, but Talmanes had acted as a friend. And she was Amyrlin. Sometimes friendship and responsibility pushed in the same direction.

As the serving woman moved off, Egwene laid a hand on Talmanes' arm. "You must not do that. Even the Band can't conquer all of Murandy by itself, and every hand will be against you. You know very well the one thing that makes Murandians stand together is foreigners on their soil. Follow us to Tar Valon, Talmanes. Mat will come there; I have no doubt of that." Mat would not really believe she was the Amyrlin until he saw her wearing the stole in the White Tower.

"Roedran is no fool," he said placidly. "All he wants us to do is sit and wait, a foreign army—without Aes Sedai—and nobody knowing what it is up to. He should not have much trouble uniting the nobles against us. Then, so he says, we quietly slip across the border. He thinks he can hold on to them afterward."

She could not stop a touch of heat entering her voice. "And what is to stop him betraying you? If the threat goes away without a fight, his dream of a united Murandy might, too." The fool man seemed *amused*!

"I am not a fool either. Roedran cannot be ready before spring. This lot would never have stirred from their manors if the Andorans had not come south, and they were on the march before the snows began. Before then, Mat will find us. If he is coming north, he must hear of us. Roedran will have to be satisfied with whatever he has managed by then. So if Mat does intend to go to Tar Valon, I may see you there yet."

Egwene made a vexed sound. It was a remarkable plan, the sort of thing Siuan might devise, and hardly a scheme she thought Roedran Almaric do Arreloa a'Naloy could carry off. The fellow was said to be so dissolute he made Mat look wholesome. But then, it was hardly a scheme she would have believed Roedran could think up. The only certainty was that Talmanes had made up his mind.

"I want your word, Talmanes, that you won't let Roedran pull you into a war." Responsibility. The narrow stole around her neck seemed to weigh ten times more than her cloak. "If he moves sooner than you think, you will leave whether or not Mat has joined you."

"I wish I could promise, but it is not possible," he protested. "I expect the first raid against my foragers three days at most after I start moving away from Lord Bryne's army. Every lordling and farmer will think he can pick up a few horses in the night, give me a pinprick, and run off to hide."

"I'm not talking about defending yourself, and you know it," she said firmly. "Your word, Talmanes. Or I will not allow your agreement with Roedran." The only way to stop it was to betray it, but she would not leave a war in her wake, a war she had started by bringing Talmanes here.

Staring at her as if for the first time, he finally bent his head. Strangely, that seemed more formal than his bow had. "It will be as you say, Mother. Tell me, are you sure you are not *ta'veren*, too?"

"I am the Amyrlin Seat," she replied. "That is quite enough for anyone." She touched his arm again. "The Light shine on you, Talmanes." His smile nearly touched his eyes this time.

Inevitably, despite their whispers, their talk had been noticed. Maybe because of their whispers. The girl who claimed to be Amyrlin, a rebel against the White Tower, in conversation with the leader of ten thousand Dragonsworn. Had she made Talmanes' scheme with Roedran harder, or easier? Was war in Murandy less likely, or more? Siuan and her bloody Law of Unintended Consequences! Fifty gazes followed her, then darted away, as she moved through the crowd warming her fingers on her cup. Well, most darted away. The Sitters' faces were all ageless Aes Sedai serenity, but Lelaine might have been a brown-eyed crow watching a fish struggle in the shallows, while Romanda's slightly darker eyes could have drilled holes through iron.

Trying to keep a watch on the sun outside, she made a slow circuit through the pavilion. The nobles were still importuning Sitters, but they moved from one to another as if seeking better answers, and she began to notice small things. Donel paused on his way from Janya to Moria, bowing low to Aemlyn, who acknowledged him with a gracious nod. Cian, turning away from Takima, curtsied deeply to Pelivar and received a slight bow in return. There were others, always a Murandian deferring to an Andoran who responded just as formally. The Andorans tried to ignore Bryne except for the odd scowl, but any number of Murandians sought him out, one by one and well away from everyone else, and from the directions their eyes went, it was plain they were discussing Pelivar, or Arathelle, or Aemlyn. Perhaps Talmanes had been right.

She received bows and curtsies, too, though none so deep as those given Arathelle and Pelivar and Aemlyn, much less the Sitters. Half a dozen women told her how thankful they were that matters had been resolved peacefully, though in truth, almost as many made noncommittal noises or shrugged uneasily when she expressed the same sentiment, as though they were uncertain it all *would* end peacefully. Her assurances that it would were met with a fervent "The Light send it so!" or a resigned "If the Light wills." Four called her Mother, one without hesitating first. Three others said that she was quite lovely, that she had beautiful eyes, and that she had a graceful carriage, in that order; suitable compliments perhaps for Egwene's age but not her station.

At least she found one unalloyed pleasure. Segan was not

alone in being intrigued by her announcement concerning
the novice book. Plainly that was why most of the women
spoke to her in the first place. After all, the other sisters
might be in rebellion against the Tower, but she claimed
to be the Amyrlin Seat. Their interest had to be strong
to overcome that, though no one wanted to let it show.
Arathelle made the inquiry with a frown that put more
creases in her cheeks. Aemlyn shook her graying head at
the answer. Blocky Cian asked, followed by a sharp-faced
Andoran lady named Negara, then a pretty, big-eyed Murandian called Jennet, and others. None wanted to know
for herself—several made that clear quickly, especially
the younger women—but before long, every single noblewoman there had asked, and several servants as well, under
cover of offering more spiced wine. One, a wiry woman
named Nildra, had come from the Aes Sedai camp.

Egwene felt quite pleased with the seed she had planted
there. She was not so pleased with the men. A few spoke
to her, but only when they came face-to-face and seemed
to have no other choice. A murmured word about the
weather, either praising the end of the drought or deplor-
ing the sudden snows, a muttered hope that the bandit
problem would end soon, perhaps with a significant look
toward Talmanes, and they slipped away like greased
pigs. A bear of an Andoran by the name of Macharan
tripped over his own boots to avoid her. In a way, it was
hardly surprising. The women had the justification, if only
to themselves, of the novice book, but the men had only
the thought that being seen conversing with her might tar
them with the same brush.

It was really quite discouraging. She did not care what
the men thought about novices, but she very much wanted
to know if they were as fearful as the women that this
would come to blows in the end. Fears like that could fulfill
themselves very easily. At last, she decided there was only
one way to find out.

Pelivar turned from taking a fresh cup of wine from a
tray and started back, with a muffled oath, to keep from
bumping into her; had she stood any closer, she would have
had to stand on his boots. Hot wine splashed over his gloved
hand and ran down under his coatsleeve, producing a curse

not so muted. Tall enough to loom over her, he made a good job of it. His scowl belonged on a man wanting to send an annoying young woman briskly out of his way. Or on a man who had nearly stepped on a red adder. She held herself erect and focused on an image of him as a small boy up to no good; that always helped; most men seemed to feel it. He muttered something—it might have been a polite greeting, or another oath—and dipped his head slightly, then tried to step around her. She side-stepped to stay in front of him. He moved back, and she followed. He began to look hunted. She decided to try putting him at ease before pressing the important question. She wanted answers, not more mumbling.

"You must be pleased to hear that the Daughter-Heir is on her way to Caemlyn, Lord Pelivar." She had heard several of the Sitters mention that.

His face went blank. "Elayne Trakand has a right to put in her claim to the Lion Throne," he replied in a flat voice.

Egwene's eyes widened, and he stepped back again, uncertainly. Perhaps he thought her angry over the absence of her title, but she barely noticed that. Pelivar had supported Elayne's mother in her claim for the throne, and Elayne had been sure he would support her, too. She spoke of Pelivar fondly, like a favorite uncle.

"Mother," Siuan murmured at her elbow, "we must leave if you want to be sure of reaching the camp before sunset." She managed to put considerable urgency into those quiet words. The sun had passed its peak.

"This is no weather to be in the open at nightfall," Pelivar said hurriedly. "If you will excuse me, I must make ready to leave." Shoving his cup onto the tray of a passing servant, he hesitated before halfway making a leg, and stalked off with the air of a man who had wriggled free of a trap.

Egwene wanted to grind her teeth with frustration. What *did* the men think of their agreement? If it could be called that, the way she had forced it on them. Arathelle and Aemlyn had more power and influence than most of the men, yet it was Pelivar and Culhan and the like who rode with the soldiers; they could still make this flare up in her face like a barrel of lamp oil.

"Find Sheriam," she growled, "and tell her to get everyone

mounted *now*, no matter what it takes!" She could not give the Sitters a night to think about what had happened today, to plan and plot. They *had* to be back in camp before the sun went down.

CHAPTER
19

The Law

Getting the Sitters to their mounts proved no bother; they were as eager to be away as Egwene, especially Romanda and Lelaine, both cold as the wind and with eyes like thunderclouds. The rest were the very image of cool-eyed Aes Sedai serenity, giving off composure like a heavy scent, yet they glided to their horses so quickly that the nobles were left gaping and the brightly clad servants scrambled in loading the packhorses to catch up as best they could.

Egwene had Daishar set a hard pace in the snow, and with no more than a look and a nod from her Lord Bryne made sure the armored escorts moved as fast. Siuan on Bela and Sheriam on Wing rushed to join her. For long stretches they churned through fetlock-deep cover, the horses stepping high at near to a trot, the Flame of Tar Valon rippling in the icy breeze, and even when it was necessary to slow, when the horses were sinking knee-deep through the snow crust, they kept to a fast walk.

The Sitters had no choice except to keep up, and their speed cut down their opportunity to talk on the way. At that tiring pace, a lack of attention to your horse could bring a broken leg for the animal and a broken neck for you. Even so, Romanda and Lelaine each managed to gather her coterie around her, and those two knots floundered through the snow surrounded by wards against eavesdropping. The pair seemed to be delivering tirades. Egwene could imagine the topic. For that matter, other Sitters managed to ride together for a time, exchanging a few words quietly and casting cool glances sometimes at her and sometimes at the sisters wrapped around by *saidar*. Only Delana never joined one of those brief conversations. She stayed close beside Halima, who at last admitted that she was cold. Face tight, the country woman held her cloak close around her, but she still tried to comfort Delana, whispering to her almost constantly. Delana seemed to need comforting; her brows were drawn down, putting a crease in her forehead that actually made her seem aged.

She was not the only one worried. The others masked the feeling rigidly, radiating absolute poise, but the Warders rode like men expecting the worst to leap out of the snow at the next step, eyes shifting in an unceasing watch, disquieting cloaks streaming in the wind to leave hands free. When an Aes Sedai worried, her Warder worried, and the Sitters were too absorbed to think of calming the men. Egwene was just as glad to see it. If the Sitters were troubled, they had not yet made up their minds.

When Bryne rode out to confer with Uno, she took the opportunity to ask what the two women had learned about Aes Sedai and Tower Guards in Andor.

"Not much," Siuan replied in a tight voice. Shaggy Bela did not seem to be having any difficulty with the pace, but Siuan did, gripping her reins tightly in one hand and the pommel of her saddle with the other. "As near as I can make out, there are fifty rumors and no facts. It's a likely sort of tale to spring up, but it might still be true." Bela lurched, her front hooves sinking deep, and Siuan gasped. "The Light burn all horses!"

Sheriam had learned no more. She shook her head, and sighed irritably. "It sounds all feathers and nonsense to me, Mother. There are *always* rumors of sisters sneaking about. Didn't you ever learn to ride, Siuan?" she added, her voice suddenly dripping derision. "By tonight, you'll be too sore to walk!" Sheriam's nerves must have been ragged for her to burst out so openly. From the way she kept shifting in her saddle, she had already achieved her prediction for Siuan.

Siuan's eyes hardened, and she opened her mouth already half snarling, never mind who was watching from behind the banner.

"Be still, both of you!" Egwene snapped. She took a deep, calming breath. She was a bit ragged herself. Whatever Arathelle believed, any force Elaida sent to interfere with them would be too large for sneaking. That left the Black Tower, a disaster in the making. You got further plucking the chicken in front of you than trying to start on one up a tree. Especially when the tree was in another country and there might not even be another chicken.

Still, she bit off her words in giving Sheriam instructions for once they reached the camp. She was the Amyrlin Seat, and that meant *all* Aes Sedai were her responsibility, even those following Elaida. Her voice was rock steady, though. It was too late to be frightened once you grabbed the wolf by the ears.

Sheriam's tilted eyes went wide at the orders. "Mother, if I may ask, why . . . ?" She trailed off under Egwene's level gaze, and swallowed. "It will be as you say, Mother," she said slowly. "Strange. I remember the day you and Nynaeve came to the Tower, two girls who couldn't decide whether to be excited or frightened. So much has changed since then. Everything."

"Nothing stays the same forever," Egwene told her. She gave Siuan a significant look, but Siuan refused to see. She appeared to be sulking. Sheriam looked sick.

Lord Bryne returned then, and he must have sensed the mood among them. Aside from saying that they were making good time, he kept his mouth shut. A wise man.

Making good time or not, the sun was sitting almost on the treetops when they finally rode through the army's sprawling camp. Wagons and tents cast long shadows across the snow, and a number of men were hard at work building yet more low shelters out of brush. There were not nearly enough tents, even for all the soldiers, and the camp held almost as many harnessmakers and laundresses and fletchers and the like, all those who inevitably followed any army. The ringing of anvils spoke of farriers and armorers and blacksmiths still at their labors. Cook fires were burning everywhere, and the cavalry peeled away, eager for warmth and hot food as soon as their wearily plodding animals were cared for. Surprisingly, Bryne rode on at Egwene's side after she dismissed him.

"If you will allow, Mother," he said, "I thought I might accompany you a while longer." Sheriam actually twisted in her saddle to stare in astonishment. Siuan stared, too, straight ahead, as if not daring to turn her suddenly wide eyes toward him.

What did he think he could do? Act as her bodyguard? Against *sisters*? That fellow with the drippy nose would do as well. Reveal just how completely he was on her side? Tomorrow was time enough for that, if all went well tonight; that revelation now might easily stampede the Hall in directions she hardly dared contemplate.

"Tonight is for Aes Sedai business," she told him firmly. But, silly as the suggestion was, he had offered to put himself at risk for her. There was no telling his reasons—who knew why a man did *anything*?—yet she owed him for that. Among other things. "Unless I send Siuan to you tonight, Lord Bryne, you should leave before morning. If blame for today attaches itself to me, it might reflect on you, too. Staying could prove dangerous. Even fatal. I don't think they would need much excuse." No need to name who "they" were.

"I gave my word," he replied quietly, patting Traveler's neck. "To Tar Valon." Pausing, he glanced toward Siuan. It was less a hesitation than a consideration. "Whatever tonight's business is," he said finally, "remember that you have thirty thousand men and Gareth Bryne behind you. That should count for something, even among Aes Sedai. Until tomorrow, Mother." Reining his big-nosed bay around, he called over his shoulder, "I expect to see you tomorrow, too, Siuan. *Nothing* changes that." Siuan stared at his back as he rode away. There was anguish in her eyes.

Egwene could not help staring, too. He had never been so open before, not nearly. Why now, of all times?

Crossing the forty or fifty paces that separated the army's camp from the Aes Sedai's, she nodded to Sheriam, who drew rein at the first tents. She and Siuan rode on. Behind them, Sheriam's voice rose, surprisingly clear and steady. "The Amyrlin Seat calls the Hall to sit this day in formal session. Let preparations be made with all speed." Egwene did not look back.

At her tent, a bony groom kicking her layered woolen skirts came running to take Daishar and Bela. Her face was pinched, and she barely ducked her head before hurrying away with the horses as quickly as she had come. The warmth of the glowing braziers inside was like a fist closing down. Egwene had not realized how cold it was outside until then. Or how cold she was.

Chesa took her cloak, and exclaimed when she felt her hands. "Why, you're ice to the bone, Mother." Chattering away, she bustled around folding Egwene's cloak and Siuan's, smoothing the neatly turned-down blankets on Egwene's cot, touching a tray set on one of the chests that had been pulled down from the stack. "I'd jump right into bed, with hot bricks all around, if I was that chilled. As soon as I'd eaten, anyway. Warm outside does only so much good without warm inside. I'll fetch a few extra bricks to tuck under your feet while you sup. And for Siuan Sedai, of course. Oh, if I was as hungry as you must be, I know I'd be tempted to gulp my food, but that always gives me pains in the stomach." Pausing by the tray, she eyed Egwene, and nodded with satisfaction when she said that she would not eat too fast.

Making a sober answer was not easy. Chesa was always refreshing, but after today, Egwene almost laughed with pleasure. There were no complications to Chesa. Two white bowls of lentil stew stood on the tray, along with a tall pitcher of spiced wine, two silver cups, and two large rolls. Somehow, the woman had known Siuan would be eating with her. Steam rose from the bowls and pitcher. How often had Chesa had to change that tray to make sure warm food greeted Egwene straightaway? Simple and uncomplicated. And as caring as a mother. Or a friend.

"I must forgo bed for now, Chesa. I've work yet tonight. Would you leave us?"

Siuan shook her head as the tentflap fell behind the plump woman. "Are you sure she hasn't been in your service since you were a babe?" she muttered.

Taking one of the bowls, a roll, and a spoon, Egwene settled into her chair with a sigh. She also embraced the Source and warded the tent against listeners. Unfortunately, *saidar* made her all that much more aware of half-frozen hands and feet. The bits in between were not much warmer. The bowl seemed almost too warm to handle, and the roll, as well. Oh, how she would have loved to have those hot bricks.

"Is there anything more we can do?" she asked, and

promptly gulped down a spoonful of stew. She was raven-ous, and no wonder, with nothing since breakfast and that early. Lentils and woody carrots tasted like her mother's finest cooking. "I can't think of anything, but can you?"

"What can be done, has been. There isn't anything else, short of the Creator putting a hand in." Siuan took the other bowl and dropped onto the low stool, but then she sat staring into her stew and stirring it with her spoon. "You wouldn't really tell him, would you?" she said finally. "I couldn't bear if he knew."

"Why on earth not?"

"He'd take advantage," Siuan said darkly. "Oh, not *that*. I don't think *that*." She was quite prudish in some areas. "But the man would make my life the Pit of Doom!" And wash-ing his smallclothes and polishing his boots and his saddle every day was not?

Egwene sighed. How *could* such a sensible, intelligent, capable woman turn into a scatterbrain over this one sub-ject? Like a hissing viper, an image rose in her head. Her-self, sitting on Gawyn's knee playing kissing games. In a tavern! She shoved it away, hard. "Siuan, I need your ex-perience. I need your brain. I can't afford to have you half-witted because of Lord Bryne. If you can't pull yourself together, I'll pay him what you owe, and forbid you to see him. I will."

"I said I'd work off the debt," Siuan said stubbornly. "I have as much honor as Lord Gareth bloody Bryne! As much and more! He keeps his word, and I keep mine! Besides, Min told me I have to stay close to him or we'll both die. Or something like that." A pinkness in her cheeks gave her away, though. Her honor and Min's viewing notwithstand-ing, she was simply willing to put up with anything to be near the man!

"Very well. You're besotted, and if I tell you to stay away from him, you'll either disobey or mope and wrap the rest of your brains in a cloud. What are you going to do about him?"

Scowling indignantly, Siuan went on for some little time, growling what she would like to do about Gareth bloody Bryne. He would have enjoyed none of it. Some, he might not have survived.

"Siuan," Egwene said warningly. "You deny one more

time what's plain as your nose, and I'll tell him *and* give him the money."

Siuan pouted sullenly. She pouted! Sullenly! Siuan! "I don't have time to be in love. I barely have time to think, between working for you *and* him. And even if everything goes right tonight, I'll have twice as much to do. Besides. . . ." Her face fell, and she shifted on the stool. "What if he doesn't . . . return my feelings?" she muttered. "He's never even tried to kiss me. All he cares about is whether his shirts are clean."

Egwene scraped her spoon through her bowl, and was surprised when it came up empty. Nothing remained of the roll but a few crumbs on her dress. Light, her middle still felt hollow. She eyed Siuan's bowl hopefully; the woman seemed to have little interest in anything but drawing circles in the lentils.

A sudden thought occurred to her. Why had Lord Bryne insisted that Siuan work off her debt even after learning who she was? Just because she had said she would? It was a preposterous arrangement. Except that it did keep her close to him when nothing else would have. For that matter, she herself had often wondered why Bryne had agreed to build the army. He had to have known there was a very good chance he was laying his head on the chopping block. And why he had offered that army to her, a girl Amyrlin with no real authority and not a friend among the sisters except Siuan, as far as he knew? Could the answer to all of those questions be as simple as . . . he loved Siuan? No; most men were frivolous and flighty, but that was *truly* preposterous! Still, she offered the suggestion, if only to amuse Siuan. It might cheer her a little.

Siuan snorted in disbelief. It sounded odd, coming from that pretty face, but no one could put quite so much expression into a snort as she did. "He's not a total idiot," she said dryly. "In fact, he has a good head on his shoulders. He thinks like a woman, most of the time."

"I still haven't heard you say you'll straighten up, Siuan," Egwene persisted. "You have to, one way or another."

"Well, of course I will. I don't know what's been the matter with me. It isn't as if I never kissed a man before." Her eyes narrowed suddenly, as if she expected Egwene to challenge her on that. "I haven't spent my *whole* life in the

Tower. This is ridiculous! Chattering about *men*, tonight of all nights!" Peering into her bowl, she seemed to realize for the first time that it held food. She filled her spoon, gesturing with it at Egwene. "You have to be careful of your timing, more now than ever. If Romanda or Lelaine grabs the tiller, you'll never get your hands on it."

Ridiculous or not, something certainly had restored Siuan's appetite. She went through her stew faster than Egwene had hers, and not a crumb of the roll escaped her. Egwene found that she had drawn her fingers through her own empty bowl. There was nothing for it then but to lick off the last few lentils, of course.

Discussing what was to happen tonight served no real point. They had honed and refined what Egwene was to say, and when, so many times that she was surprised she had not dreamed of it. She certainly could have done her part in her sleep. Siuan insisted anyway, skirting very near the point where Egwene would have to call her down, going over it again and again, bringing up possibilities they had discussed before a hundred times. Strangely, Siuan had found herself a very good mood. She even essayed a little humor, unusual for her of late, though some was on the gallows side.

"You know Romanda wanted to be Amyrlin herself once," she said at one point. "I've heard it was Tamra getting the stole and staff that made her stalk off into retirement like a gull with her tail feathers clipped. I'll lay a silver mark I don't have to a fish scale that her eyes bulge twice as much as Lelaine's."

And later. "I wish I could be there to hear them howl. Somebody's going to before much longer, and I'd rather it was them than us. I never had the voice for singing." She actually sang a little snatch about staring across the river at a boy and having no boat. She was right; her voice was pleasant in its fashion, but she could not carry a tune in a bucket.

And later still. "A good thing I have such a sweet face now. If this goes badly, they'll dress the pair of us for dolls and sit us on a shelf to admire. Of course, we might have 'accidents' instead. Dolls do get broken. Gareth Bryne will have to find someone else to bully." She *really* laughed at that.

Egwene felt considerable relief when the tentflap bulged

inward briefly, announcing someone who knew enough not to enter where there was a ward. She really did not want to hear where Siuan's humor went from there!

As soon as she released the ward, Sheriam stepped inside, accompanied by a rush of air that seemed ten times as cold as earlier. "It's time, Mother. Everything is ready." Her tilted eyes were wide, and she licked her lips with the tip of her tongue.

Siuan bounded to her feet and seized her cloak from Egwene's cot, but she paused in the act of draping it on her shoulders. "I *have* sailed the Fingers of the Dragon in the dark, you know," she said seriously. "And netted a lionfish once, with my father. It can be done."

Sheriam frowned as Siuan darted out, letting in more cold. "Sometimes, I think," she began, but whatever she sometimes thought, she did not share. "Why are you doing this, Mother?" she asked instead. "All of it, today at the lake, calling the Hall tonight. Why did you have us spend all day yesterday talking about Logain to everybody we met? I'd think you might share it with me. I *am* your Keeper. I *did* swear fealty."

"I tell you what you need to know," Egwene said, swinging her cloak around her shoulders. There was no need to say that she trusted a forced oath only so far, even a sister's. And Sheriam might find a reason to let a word slip into the wrong ear despite that oath. After all, Aes Sedai were noted for finding loopholes in what they had said. She did not really believe that would happen, but just as with Lord Bryne, she could not take even small chances unless she had to.

"I have to tell you," Sheriam said bitterly, "I think tomorrow Romanda or Lelaine will be your Keeper of the Chronicles, and I'll be serving a penance for not warning the Hall. And I think you might envy me."

Egwene nodded. All too possible. "Shall we go?"

The sun made a red dome on the treetops to the west, and a lurid light shone off the snow. Servants marked Egwene's passage along the deep paths with silent bows and curtsies. Their faces were troubled or else blank; servants could pick up the moods of those they served almost as quickly as Warders.

Not a sister was to be seen, at first, and then they all were, in a great gathering three deep around a pavilion set up in the only open space in the camp large enough, the area used by sisters Skimming to the dovecotes in Salidar and Traveling back with reports from the eyes-and-ears. A large much-mended piece of heavy canvas, not a patch on the splendor of the canopy at the lake, it had been a great deal of effort to set up. Most often in the past two months, the Hall had convened much as they had yesterday morning, or perhaps squeezed into one of the larger tents. The pavilion had been erected only twice since leaving Salidar. Both times for a trial.

Noticing Egwene and Sheriam's approach, sisters in the back murmured to those ahead, and a gap opened to let them through. Expressionless eyes watched the pair of them, giving not a clue to whether the watching sisters knew or even suspected what was happening. Not a clue to what they thought. Butterflies stirred in Egwene's stomach. A rosebud. Calm.

She stepped onto the layered carpets, woven in bright flowers and a dozen different patterns, and moved through the ring of braziers set up around the canopy's rim, and Sheriam began. "She comes; she comes. . . ." If she sounded a little less grand than usual, a touch nervous, it was small wonder.

The polished benches and cloth-covered boxes from the lake were in use again. They made a much more formal sight than the mismatched gaggle of chairs that had been used previously, two slanting lines of nine, grouped by threes; Green, Gray and Yellow to one side, White, Brown and Blue to the other. At the wide end, farthest from Egwene, stood the striped box and bench for the Amyrlin Seat. Sitting there, she would be the focus of every eye, very much aware that she was one facing eighteen. As well she had not changed her clothes; every Sitter still wore her finery from the lake, only adding her shawl. A rosebud. Calm.

One of the benches was empty, though only for a moment longer. Delana came running in just as Sheriam finished her litany. Looking breathless and flustered, the Gray Sitter scrambled up to her seat, between Varilin and Kwamesa, with little of her usual grace. She wore a sickly grin, and toyed nervously with the firedrops around her neck. Anyone might have thought she was the one on trial. Calm. No one was on trial. Yet.

Egwene started slowly across the carpets, between the two rows, with Sheriam close behind, and Kwamesa stood. The light of *saidar* suddenly shone around the dark slender woman, youngest of the Sitters. Tonight there would be no skimping of the formalities. "What is brought before the Hall of the Tower is for the Hall alone to consider," Kwamesa announced. "Whosoever intrudes unbidden, woman or man, initiate or outsider, whether they come in peace or in anger, I will bind according to the law, to face the law. Know that what I speak is true; it will and shall be done."

That formula was older than the oath against speaking untruth, from a time when almost as many Amyrlins died by assassination as by all other causes put together. Egwene continued her measured tread. It was an effort not to touch her stole, for a reminder. She tried to concentrate on the bench ahead.

Kwamesa resumed her seat, still shining with the Power, and among the Whites, Aledrin rose, the glow surrounding her as well. With her dark golden hair and big pale brown eyes, she was quite lovely when she smiled, but tonight a stone had more expression than she. "There are those within earshot who are not of the Hall," she said in a cool voice strong with the accents of Tarabon. "What is spoken in the Hall of the Tower is for the Hall alone to hear, until and unless the Hall decides otherwise. I will make us private. I will seal our words to our ears only." Weaving a ward that walled the entire pavilion, she sat. There was a stir among the sisters outside, who now must watch the Hall move in utter silence.

Strange, that so much among Sitters depended on age, when distinction by age was next to anathema among the rest of Aes Sedai. *Could* Siuan have seen a pattern in the Sitters' ages? No. Focus. Calm, and focus.

Gripping the edges of her cloak, Egwene stepped up onto the brightly striped box and turned. Lelaine was already on her feet, blue-fringed shawl looped across her arms, and Romanda was rising, without even waiting for Egwene to sit. She dared not let either seize the tiller. "I call a question before the Hall," she said in a loud, firm voice. "Who will stand to declare war against the usurper Elaida do Avriny a'Roihan?"

And then she sat, throwing off her cloak and letting it fall across the bench. Standing beside her on the carpets, Sheriam appeared quite cool and collected, but she made a small sound, almost a whimper. Egwene did not think anyone else had heard. She hoped not.

There was a brief moment of shock, women frozen on their seats, staring at her in amazement. Perhaps as much because she had asked at all as what she had asked. No one put a question before the Hall before sounding out the Sitters; it just was not done, for practical reasons as much as tradition.

At last Lelaine spoke. "We do not declare war on *individuals*," she said in a dry voice. "Not even on traitors like Elaida. In any case, I call to shelve your question while we deal with more immediate matters." She had had time to gather herself since the ride back; her face was merely hard now, not thunderous. Brushing blue-slashed skirts as if brushing away Elaida—or perhaps Egwene—she turned her attention to the other Sitters. "What brings us to sit tonight is. . . . I was about to say simple, but it isn't. Open the novice book? We would have *grandmothers* clamoring to be tested. Remain here a month? I hardly need list the difficulties, beginning with spending half our gold without coming a foot nearer Tar Valon. And as for not crossing into Andor—"

"My sister Lelaine, in her anxiety, has forgotten who has the right to speak first," Romanda cut in smoothly. Her smile managed to make Lelaine appear merry. Still, she took her time adjusting her shawl just as she wanted, a woman with all the time in the world. "I have two questions to call before the Hall, and in the second I will address Lelaine's concerns. Unfortunately for her, my first question concerns Lelaine's own fitness to continue in the Hall." Her smile widened without growing the slightest bit warmer. Lelaine sat slowly, her scowl quite open.

"A question of war cannot be shelved," Egwene said in a carrying tone. "It must be answered before any question called after it. That is the law."

Quick, questioning glances passed between Sitters.

"Is that so?" Janya said finally. Squinting thoughtfully, she twisted on her bench to address the woman next to her. "Takima, you remember everything you read, and I'm sure

I remember you saying you had read the Law of War. Is that what it says?"

Egwene held her breath. The White Tower had sent soldiers to any number of wars over the last thousand years, but always in response to a plea for help from at least two thrones, and it always had been their war, not the Tower's. The last time the Tower itself actually declared war had been against Artur Hawkwing. Siuan said that now only a few librarians knew much more than that there *was* a Law of War.

Short, with long dark hair to her waist and skin the color of aged ivory, Takima often reminded people of a bird, tilting her head in thought. Now she looked like a bird that wanted to take flight, shifting on her seat, adjusting her shawl, unnecessarily straightening her cap of pearls and sapphires. "It is," she said finally, and clamped her mouth shut.

Egwene quietly started breathing again.

"It seems," Romanda said in a clipped tone, "that Siuan Sanche has been teaching you well. Mother. How speak you in support of declaring war? On a woman." She sounded as if she were trying to push something disagreeable out of her way, and she dropped onto her seat waiting for it to depart.

Egwene nodded graciously anyway, and rose. She met the Sitters' gazes one by one, levelly, firmly. Takima avoided her eyes. Light, the woman knew! But she had not said anything. Would she hold silent long enough? It was too late to change plans.

"Today we find ourselves confronted by an army, led by people who doubt us. That army would not be there otherwise." Egwene wanted to put passion into her voice, to let it burst out, but Siuan had advised utter coolness, and finally she had agreed. They needed to see a woman in control of herself, not a girl being ridden by her heart. The words came from her heart, though. "You heard Arathelle say she did not want to become entangled in Aes Sedai affairs. Yet they were willing to bring an army into Murandy and stand in our way. Because they are not certain who we are, or what we are about. Did any of you feel that they truly believe you are Sitters?" Malind, round-faced and fierce-eyed, shifted on her bench among the Greens, and so did Salita, twitching her yellow-fringed shawl, though her dark face managed to hide any expression. Berana, another Sitter chosen in Salidar, frowned thoughtfully. Egwene did not mention the reaction to her as Amyrlin; if that thought was not already in their heads, she did not want to plant it.

"We've listed Elaida's crimes to countless nobles," she went on. "We've told them we intend to remove her. But they doubt. They think that maybe—maybe—we are what we say. And maybe there's a trick in our words. Perhaps we are only Elaida's hand, weaving some elaborate scheme. Doubt leaves people floundering. Doubt gave Pelivar and Arathelle the nerve to stand before Aes Sedai and say, 'You cannot go further.' Who else will stand in our way, or interfere, because they aren't certain, and uncertainty leads them to act in a cloud of confusion? There's only one way for us to dispel their confusion. We have already done everything else. Once we declare ourselves at war with Elaida, there can be no doubts. I don't say that Arathelle and Pelivar and Aemlyn will march away as soon as we do so, but they and everyone else will know who we are. No one will dare again to show doubt so openly when you say you are the Hall of the Tower. No one will dare stand in our way, meddling in the affairs of the Tower through uncertainty and ignorance. We have walked to the door and put our hands on the latch. If you are afraid to walk through, then you all but ask the world to believe that you are nothing but Elaida's puppets."

She sat, surprised at how calm she felt. Beyond the two rows of Sitters, sisters outside stirred, putting their heads together. She could imagine the excited murmurs that Aledrin's ward blocked off. Now if only Takima kept her mouth shut long enough.

Romanda grunted impatiently, and stood only long enough to say, "Who stands for declaring war against Elaida?" Her gaze returned to Lelaine, and her cold, smug smile returned. It was clear what she considered important, once this nonsense was done with.

Janya rose immediately, the long brown fringe on her shawl swaying. "We might as well," she said. She was not supposed to speak, but her set jaw and sharp gaze dared anyone to call her down. She was not normally so forceful, but as usual, her words nearly tripped over one another. "Mending what the world knows won't be any harder than

it is for this. Well? Well? I don't see the point of waiting."
On the other side of Takima, Escaralde nodded and stood.

Moria all but bounded to her feet, frowning down at
Lyrelle, who gathered her skirts as if to rise, then hesitated
and looked at Lelaine questioningly. Lelaine was too busy
frowning across the carpets at Romanda to notice.

Among the Greens, Samalin and Malind stood together,
and Faiselle looked up with a jerk. A stocky, copper-skinned
Domani, Faiselle was not a woman startled by much, but
she looked startled now, her square face swinging wide-
eyed from Samalin to Malind and back.

Salita rose, carefully adjusting the yellow fringe of her
shawl and just as carefully avoiding Romanda's sudden
frown. Kwamesa stood, and then Aledrin, drawing Berana up by her sleeve. Delana twisted completely around
on her bench, peering at the sisters outside. Even in silence
the spectators' excitement communicated itself in constant
shifting, heads going together, eyes darting toward the Sitters. Delana rose slowly, both hands pressed to her middle,
looking ready to sick up on the spot. Takima grimaced and
stared at her hands on her knees. Saroiya studied the other
two White Sitters, tugging at her ear the way she did when
deep in thought. But no one else moved to stand.

Egwene felt bile rising in her own throat. Ten. Just ten.
She had been so sure. Siuan had been so sure. Logain alone
should have been enough, given their ignorance of the law
involved. Pelivar's army and Arathelle refusing to admit
that they *were* Sitters should have primed them like a pump.

"For the love of the Light!" Moria burst out. Rounding
on Lyrelle and Lelaine, she planted her fists on her hips. If
Janya's speaking had gone against custom, this tied it in a
knot. Displays of anger were strictly forbidden in the Hall,
but Moria's eyes blazed, and her Illianer accent was thick
with it. "Why do you wait? Elaida did steal the stole and
the staff! Elaida's Ajah did make Logain a false Dragon,
and only the Light knows how many other men! No woman
in the history of the Tower did ever deserve this declaration
more! Stand, or hold silent from now about your *resolve* to
remove her!"

Lelaine did not quite stare, but by her expression you
might have thought she had found herself attacked by a

sparrow. "This is hardly worth a vote, Moria," she said in a tight voice. "We will speak later about decorum, you and I. Still, if you need a demonstration of resolve. . . ." With a sharp sniff, she rose, and gave a jerk of her head that pulled Lyrelle to her feet like strings. Lelaine seemed surprised that it did not pull up Faiselle and Takima, too.

Far from standing, Takima grunted as if struck. Disbelief bright on her face, she ran her eyes along the women on their feet, obviously counting. And then did it again. Takima, who remembered *everything* the first time.

Egwene breathed deep in relief. It was done. She could hardly believe. After a moment, she cleared her throat, and Sheriam actually jumped.

Green eyes as big as teacups, the Keeper cleared her throat, too. "The lesser consensus standing, war is declared against Elaida do Avriny a'Roihan." Her voice was none too steady, but it sufficed. "In the interest of unity, I ask for the greater consensus to stand."

Faiselle half-moved, then clenched her hands in her lap. Saroiya opened her mouth, then closed it without speaking, her face troubled. No one else stirred.

"You won't get it," Romanda said flatly. The sneer she directed across the pavilion at Lelaine was as good as a statement of why she, at least, would not stand. "Now that little business is finished, we can go on with—"

"I don't think we can," Egwene cut in. "Takima, what does the Law of War say about the Amyrlin Seat?" Romanda was left with her mouth hanging open.

Takima's lips writhed. The diminutive Brown looked more than ever a bird wishing to take flight. "The Law . . ." she began, then took a deep breath and sat up straight. "The Law of War states, 'As one set of hands must guide a sword, so the Amyrlin Seat shall direct and prosecute the war by decree. She shall seek the advice of the Hall of the Tower, but the Hall shall carry out her decrees with all possible speed, and for the sake of unity, they shall. . . .'" She faltered, and had to visibly force herself to go on. ". . . they shall and must approve any decree of the Amyrlin Seat regarding prosecution of the war with the greater consensus."

A long silence stretched. Every eye seemed to be goggling. Turning abruptly, Delana vomited onto the carpets behind her bench. Kwamesa and Salita both climbed down and started toward her, but she waved them off, plucking a scarf from her sleeve to wipe her mouth. Magla and Saroiya and several others still seated looked as though they might follow her example. No others who had been chosen in Salidar, though. Romanda appeared ready to bite through a nail.

"Very clever," Lelaine said at last in clipped tones, and after a deliberate pause, added, "Mother. Will you tell us what the great wisdom of your vast experience tells you to do? About the war, I mean. I want to make myself clear."

"Let me make myself clear, too," Egwene said coldly. Leaning forward, she fixed the Blue Sitter sternly. "A certain degree of respect is *required* toward the Amyrlin Seat, and from now on, I *will* have it, daughter. This is no time for me to have to unchair you and name a penance." Lelaine's eyes crept wider and wider with shock. Had the woman really believed everything would continue as before? Or after so long not daring to show more than the tiniest backbone, had Lelaine simply believed she had none? Egwene really did not want to unchair her; the Blues would almost certainly return the woman, and she still had to deal with the Hall on matters that could not be convincingly disguised as part of the war against Elaida.

From the corner of her eye, she saw a smile pass across Romanda's lips at seeing Lelaine set down. Small profit if all she did was raise Romanda's stock with the others. "That holds for everyone, Romanda," she said. "If need be, Tiana can find two birches as easily as one." Romanda's smile vanished abruptly.

"If I may speak, Mother," Takima said, rising slowly. She attempted a smile, but she still looked decidedly ill. "I myself think you have begun well. There may be benefits to stopping here a month. Or longer." Romanda's head jerked around to stare at her, but for once, Takima did not appear to notice. "Wintering here, we can avoid worse weather farther north, and also plan carefully—"

"There's an end to delays, daughter," Egwene cut in. "No more dragging our feet." Would she be another Gerra, or another Shein? Either was still possible. "In one month, we will Travel from here." No; she was Egwene al'Vere, and whatever the secret histories would say of her faults and virtues, the Light only knew, but they would be hers, not copies of some other woman's. "In one month, we will begin the siege of Tar Valon."

This time, the silence was broken only by the sound of Takima weeping.

CHAPTER
20

Into Andor

Elayne hoped that the journey to Caemlyn would go smoothly, and in the beginning, it seemed to do so. She thought that even as she and Aviendha and Birgitte sat bone-weary and huddled in the rags that remained of their clothing, filthy with dirt and dust and the blood of the injuries they had received when the gateway exploded. In two weeks at most, she would be ready to present her claims to the Lion Throne. There on the hilltop, Nynaeve Healed their numerous hurts and spoke barely a word, certainly not berating them. Surely that was a pleasant sign, if unusual. Relief at finding them alive battled worry on her face.

Lan's strength was necessary to remove the Seanchan crossbow bolt from Birgitte's thigh before she could be Healed of that wound, but although her face drained of blood and Elayne felt a stab of agony through the bond, agony that made her want to cry out, her Warder barely groaned through her gritted teeth.

"*Tai'shar* Kandor," Lan murmured, tossing the pile-head quarrel, made to punch through armor, aside on the ground. True blood of Kandor. Birgitte blinked, and he paused. "Forgive me, if I erred. I assumed from your clothes you were Kandori."

"Oh, yes," Birgitte breathed. "Kandori." Her sickly grin might have been from her injuries; Nynaeve was impatiently shooing Lan out of the way so she could lay hands on her. Elayne hoped the woman knew more of Kandor than the name; when Birgitte had last been born, there had been no Kandor. She should have taken it as an omen.

For the five miles to the small slate-roofed manor house, Birgitte rode behind Nynaeve on the latter's stout brown mare—named Loversknot, of all things—and Elayne and Aviendha rode Lan's tall black stallion. At least, Elayne sat Mandarb's saddle with Aviendha's arms around her waist while Lan led the fiery-eyed animal. Trained warhorses were as much weapons as a sword, and dangerous mounts for strange riders. *Be sure of yourself, girl*, Lini had always told her, *but not too sure*, and she did try. She should have realized events were no more in her control than Mandarb's reins.

At the three-story stone house, Master Hornwell, stout and gray-haired, and Mistress Hornwell, slightly less round and slightly less gray but otherwise resembling her husband remarkably, had every last person who worked the estates, and Merilille's maid, Pol, and the green-and-white liveried servants who had come from the Tarasin Palace as well, all bustling to find sleeping accommodations for over two hundred people, most women, who had appeared out of no-where with dark near to falling. The work went with surprising swiftness, in spite of the estates' people stopping to gawk at an Aes Sedai's ageless face, or a Warder's shifting cloak making parts of him vanish, or one of the Sea Folk with all of her bright silks, her earrings and nosering and medallioned chain. Kinswomen were deciding that now it was safe to be frightened and cry no matter what Reanne and the Knitting Circle said to them; Windfinders were snarling over how far from the salt they had come, against their will as Renaile din Calon loudly claimed; and nobles and craftswomen who had been all too willing to flee whatever lay back in Ebou Dar, willing to carry their bundled possessions on their backs, were now balking at being shown a hayloft for a bed.

All that was going on when Elayne and the others arrived with the sun red on the western horizon, a great upheaval and milling all about the house and thatch-roofed outbuildings, but Alise Tenjile, smiling pleasantly and implacable as an avalanche, seemed to have everything more in hand than even the capable Hornwells. Kinswomen who wept harder for all of Reanne's attempts at comfort dried their tears at a murmur from Alise and began moving with the purposeful air of women who had been caring for themselves in a hostile world for many years. Haughty nobles with marriage knives dangling into the oval cutouts in their lace-trimmed bodices and craftswomen who displayed almost as much arrogance and nearly as much bosom, if not in silk, flinched at the sight of Alise approaching, and went scurrying for the tall barns hugging their bundles and announcing loudly that they had always thought it might be amusing to sleep on straw. Even the Windfinders, many of them important and powerful women among the Atha'an Miere, muffled their complaints when Alise came near. For that matter, Sareitha, still lacking the Aes Sedai agelessness, eyed Alise askance and touched her brown-fringed shawl as if to remind herself it was there. Merilille—unflappable Merilille—watched the woman go about her work with a blend of approval and open amazement.

Clambering down from her saddle at the front door of the house, Nynaeve glared toward Alise, gave her dark braid one deliberate, measured tug that the other woman was far too busy to notice, and stalked inside, stripping off her blue riding gloves and muttering to herself. Watching her go, Lan chuckled softly, then stifled his laughter immediately when Elayne dismounted. Light, but his eyes were cold! For Nynaeve's sake, she hoped the man could be saved from his fate, yet looking into those eyes, she did not believe it.

"Where is Ispan?" she murmured, helping Aviendha scramble down. So many of the women knew an Aes Sedai—a Black sister—was being held prisoner that the news was bound to spread through the estates like fire in dry grass, but better if the manor's folk had a little preparation.

"Adeleas and Vandene took her to a small woodcutter's hut about half a mile away," he replied just as quietly. "In all this, I don't think anyone noticed a woman with a sack over her head. The sisters said they would stay there with her tonight."

Elayne shivered. The Darkfriend was to be questioned again once the sun went down, it seemed. They were in Andor, now, and that made her feel more deeply as if she had given the order for it.

Soon she was in a copper bathtub, luxuriating in perfumed soap and clean skin again, laughing and splashing water at Birgitte, who lolled in another tub except when she was splashing back, both of them giggling over the wincing horror Aviendha could not quite conceal at sitting up to her breasts in water. She thought it was a very good joke on herself, though, and told a most improper story about a man getting *segade* spines in his bottom. Birgitte told one still more improper, about a woman getting her head caught between the slats of a fence, that made even Aviendha blush. They *were* funny, though. Elayne wished she knew one to tell.

She and Aviendha combed and brushed each other's hair—a nightly ritual for near-sisters—and then they snuggled tiredly into the canopied bed in a small room. She and Aviendha, Birgitte and Nynaeve, and lucky there were no more. Larger rooms had cots and pallets covering the floors, including the sitting rooms, the kitchens, and most of the halls. Nynaeve muttered half the night about the indecency of making a woman sleep apart from her husband, and for the other half, her elbows seemed to wake Elayne every time she dropped off. Birgitte flatly refused to change places, and she could not ask Aviendha to endure the woman's sharp prodding, so she did not get a great deal of sleep.

Elayne was still groggy when they prepared to depart the next morning, with the rising sun a molten ball of gold. The manor had few animals to spare unless she stripped the estates bare, so while she rode a black gelding named Fireheart, and Aviendha and Birgitte had new mounts, those who had been afoot when they fled the Kin's farm remained afoot. That included most of the Kinswomen themselves, the servants leading the pack animals, and the twenty-odd women who plainly were beyond regretting their visit to the Kin's farm in hopes of peace and contemplation. The Warders rode ahead to scout the way across rolling hills covered in drought-starved forest, and the rest of them stretched out in a most peculiar snake, with Nynaeve and herself and the other sisters at the head. And Aviendha, of course.

It was hardly a group that could escape notice, so many women traveling with so few men for guards, not to mention twenty dark Windfinders, awkward on their horses and as bright as exotically plumaged birds, and eight Aes Sedai, five of them recognizably so to anyone who knew what to look for. Though one did ride with a leather sack over her head, of course. As if that would not attract eyes by itself. Elayne had hoped to reach Caemlyn unnoticed, but that no longer seemed possible. Still, there was no reason that anyone would suspect that the Daughter-Heir, Elayne Trakand herself, was one of this group. In the beginning, she thought that the greatest difficulty they might face would be someone who opposed her claims learning of her presence, sending armed men to try taking her into custody until the succession was settled.

In truth, she expected the first trouble to come from the footsore craftswomen and nobles, proud women all, and none used to tramping dusty hills. Especially since Merilille's maid had her own plump mare to ride. The few farmwives among them did not seem to mind too much, but nearly half their number were women who possessed lands and manors and palaces, and most of the rest could have afforded to buy an estate if not two or three. They included two goldsmiths, three weavers who owned over four hundred looms between them, a woman whose manufactories produced a tenth of all the lacquerware Ebou Dar produced, and a banker. They walked, their possessions strapped to their backs, while their horses bore packsaddles laden with food. There was real need. Every last coin in everyone's purse had been pooled together and given into Nynaeve's tightfisted keeping, but all might not be sufficient to buy food, fodder and lodgings for so large a party all the way to Caemlyn. They did not seem to understand. They complained loudly and incessantly through the first day's march. Loudest of all was a slim lady with a thin scar on one cheek, a stern-faced woman named Malien, who was nearly bent double under the weight of a huge bundle containing a dozen or more dresses and all the changes that went with them.

When they made camp that first night, with their cook fires glowing in the twilight and everyone full of beans and bread if not entirely satisfied with them, Malien gathered the noblewomen around her, their silks more than travel-stained. The craftswomen joined in, too, and the banker, and the farmers stood close. Before Malien could say a word, Reanne strode into the group. Her face full of smile lines, in plain brown woolens with her skirts sewn up on the left to expose bright layered petticoats, she might have been one of the farm women.

"If you wish to go home," she announced in that surprisingly high voice, "you may do so at any time. I regret that we must keep your horses, though. You will be paid for them as soon as can be arranged. If you choose to remain, please remember that the rules of the farm still apply." A number of the women around her gaped. Malien was not alone in opening her mouth angrily.

Alise just seemed to appear at Reanne's side, fists planted on her hips. She was not smiling now. "I said the last ten to be ready would do the washing up," she told them firmly. And she named them off; Jillien, a plump goldsmith; Naiselle, the cool-eyed banker; and all eight of the nobles. They stood staring at her until she clapped her hands and said, "Don't make me invoke the rule on failure to do your share of the chores."

Malien, wide-eyed and muttering in disbelief, was the last to dart off and begin gathering dirty bowls, but the next morning she pared her bundle down, leaving lace-trimmed silk dresses and shifts to be trampled on the hillside as they departed. Elayne continued to expect an explosion, but Reanne kept a firm hand on them, Alise kept a firmer, and if Malien and the others glared and muttered over the grease stains that grew on their clothes day by day, Reanne had only to speak a few words to send them to their work. Alise only had to clap her hands.

If the rest of the journey could have gone as smoothly, Elayne would have been willing to join those women in their greasy labors. Long before reaching Caemlyn, she knew that for a fact.

Once they reached the first narrow dusty road, little more than cart track, farms began to appear, thatched stone houses and barns clinging to the hillsides or nestled in hollows. From then on, whether the land was hilly or flat, forested or cleared, they rarely spent many hours beyond sight of a farm or a village. At each of those, while the local folk goggled at the very strange strangers, Elayne tried to learn how much support House Trakand had, and what concerned the people most. Addressing those concerns would be important in making her claim to the throne strong enough to stand, as important as the backing of other Houses. She heard a great deal, if not always what she wished to hear. Andorans claimed the right to speak their minds to the Queen herself; they were hardly shy with a young noblewoman, no matter how peculiar her traveling companions.

In a village called Damelien, where three mills sat beside a small river shrunken to leave their tall water-wheels dry, the square-jawed innkeeper at The Golden Sheaves allowed as how he thought Morgase had been a good queen, the best that could be, the best that ever was. "Her daughter might've been a good ruler, too, I suppose," he muttered, thumbing his chin. "Pity the Dragon Reborn killed them. I suppose he had to—the Prophecies or some such—but he had no call to dry up the rivers, now did he? How much grain did you say your horses need, my lady? It's dreadful dear, mind."

A hard-faced woman, in a worn brown dress that hung on her as if she had lost weight, surveyed a field surrounded by a low stone wall, where the hot wind sent sheets of dust marching into the woods. The other farms around Buryhill looked as bad or worse. "That Dragon Reborn's got no right to do this to us, now has he? I ask you!" She spat and frowned up at Elayne in her saddle. "The throne? Oh, Dyelin's as good as any, now Morgase and her girl are dead. Some around here still speak up for Naean or Elenia, but I'm for Dyelin. Any lookout, Caemlyn's a long way off. I've got crops to worry about. If I ever make another crop."

"Oh, it's true, my lady, so it is; Elayne's alive," a gnarled old carpenter told her in Forel Market. He was bald as a leather egg, his fingers twisted with age, but the work standing among the shavings and sawdust that littered his shop looked as fine as any Elayne had seen. She was the only person in the shop besides him. From the look of the village, half the residents had left. "The Dragon Reborn is having her brought to Caemlyn so he can put the Rose Crown on her head himself," he allowed. "The news is all over. 'Tisn't right, if you ask me. He's one of them black-eyed Aielmen, I hear. We ought to march on Caemlyn and drive him and all them Aiel back where they come from. Then Elayne can claim the throne her own self. If Dyelin lets her keep it, anyway."

Elayne heard a great deal about Rand, rumors ranging from him swearing fealty to Elaida to him being the King of Illian, of all things. In Andor, he was blamed for everything bad that happened for the last two or three years, including stillbirths and broken legs, infestations of grasshoppers, two-headed calves, and three-legged chickens. And even people who thought her mother had ruined the country and an end to the reign of House Trakand was good riddance still believed Rand al'Thor an invader. The Dragon Reborn was supposed to fight the Dark One at Shayol Ghul, and he should be driven out of Andor. Not what she had hoped to hear, not a bit of it. But she heard it all again and again. It was not a pleasant journey at all. It was one long lesson in one of Lini's favorite sayings. *It isn't the stone you see that trips you on your nose.*

She thought a number of things beside the nobles might cause trouble, some sure to be explosions as great as the gateway. The Windfinders, smug in the bargain made with Nynaeve and herself, behaved in an irritatingly superior manner toward the Aes Sedai, especially after it came out that Merilille had let herself agree to be one of the first sisters to go on the ships. Yet if the sizzling there continued like the burning of an Illuminator's fuse-cord, the explosion never quite came. The Windfinders and the Kinswomen, in particular the Knitting Circle, seemed as certain to blow up. They cut one another dead when not sneering openly, the Kin at "Sea Folk wilders getting above themselves," the Windfinders at "cringing sandlappers kissing Aes Sedai feet." But it never went beyond lips curled or daggers caressed.

Ispan certainly presented problems that Elayne was sure would grow, yet after a few days, Vandene and Adeleas let her ride unhooded if not unshielded, a silent figure with colored beads in her thin braids, ageless face turned down and hands still on her reins. Renaile told everyone who would listen that among the Atha'an Miere, a Darkfriend was stripped of his or her names as soon as proven guilty, then thrown over the side tied to ballast stones. Among the Kinswomen, even Reanne and Alise paled every time they saw the Taraboner woman. But Ispan grew meeker and meeker, eager to please and full of ingratiating smiles for the two white-haired sisters no matter what it was they did to her when they carried her away from the others at night. On the other hand, Adeleas and Vandene grew more and more frustrated. Adeleas told Nynaeve in Elayne's hearing that the woman spilled out volumes about old plots of the Black Ajah, those she had not been involved in much more enthusiastically than those she was, yet even when they pressed her hard—Elayne could not quite make herself ask how they pressed—and she let slip the names of Darkfriends, most were certainly dead and none was a sister. Vandene said they were beginning to fear she had taken an Oath—the capital was audible—against betraying her cohorts. They continued to isolate Ispan as much as possible and continued with their questions, but it was plain they were feeling their way blindly, now, and carefully.

And there was Nynaeve, and Lan. Most definitely Nynaeve and Lan, with her near to bursting at the effort of holding her temper around him, mooning over him when they had to sleep apart—which was nearly always, the way accommodations divided up—and torn between eager and afraid when she could sneak him off to a hayloft. It was her own fault for choosing a Sea Folk wedding, in Elayne's estimation. The Sea Folk believed in hierarchy as they did in the sea, and they knew a woman and her husband might be promoted one past the other many times in their lives. Their marriage rites took that into account. Whoever had the right to command in public, must obey in private. Lan never took advantage, so Nynaeve said—"not really," whatever that was supposed to mean! She always blushed when she said it—but she kept waiting for him to do so, and he just seemed to grow more and more amused. This amusement, of course, screwed Nynaeve's temper to a fever pitch. Nynaeve did erupt, out of all the explosions Elayne had expected. She snapped at anyone and everyone who got in her way. Except at Lan; with him, she was all honey and cream. And not at Alise. She came close once or twice, but even Nynaeve could not seem to make herself snap at Alise.

Elayne had hopes, not worries, about the things brought out of the Rahad along with the Bowl of the Winds. Aviendha helped her search, and so did Nynaeve once or twice, but she was entirely too slow and ginger about it and showed little skill at finding what they were searching for. They found no more *angreal*, yet the collection of *ter'angreal* grew; once all the rubbish had been thrown away, objects that used the One Power filled five entire panniers on the packhorses.

Careful as Elayne was, though, her attempts to study them did not go so well. Spirit was the safest of the Five Powers to use in this—unless, of course, Spirit happened to be what triggered the thing!—yet at times she had to use other flows, as fine as she could weave. Sometimes her delicate probing did nothing, but her first touch at the thing that looked like a blacksmith's puzzle made of glass left her dizzy and unable to sleep for half the night, and a thread of Fire touching what looked like a helmet made of fluffy metal feathers gave everyone within twenty paces a blinding headache. Except for herself. And then there was the crimson rod that felt hot; hot, in a way.

Sitting on the edge of her bed at an inn called The Wild Boar, she examined the smooth rod by the light of two polished brass lamps. Wrist-thick and a foot long, it looked like stone, but felt firm rather than hard. She was alone; since the helmet, she had tried to do her studying away from the others. The heat of the rod made her think of Fire. . . .

Blinking, she opened her eyes and sat up in the bed. Sunlight streamed in at the window. She was in her shift, and Nynaeve, fully dressed, stood frowning down at her. Aviendha and Birgitte were watching from beside the door.

"What happened?" Elayne demanded, and Nynaeve shook her head grimly.

"You don't want to know." Her lips twitched.

Aviendha's face gave away nothing. Birgitte's mouth might have been a little tight, but the strongest emotion Elayne felt from her was a combination of relief and—hilarity! The woman was doing her utmost not to roll on the floor laughing!

The worst of it was, *no* one would tell what had happened. What she had said, or done; she was sure it was that, by the quickly hidden grins she saw, from Kinswomen and Windfinders as well as sisters. But no one would tell her! After that, she decided to leave studying the *ter'angreal* to somewhere more comfortable than a inn. Somewhere definitely more private!

Nine days after their flight from Ebou Dar, scattered clouds appeared in the sky and a sprinkling of fat raindrops splashed dust in the road. An intermittent drizzle fell the next day, and the day after, a deluge kept them huddled in the houses and stables of Forel Market. That night, the rain turned to sleet, and by morning, thick flurries of snow drifted from a cloud-dark sky. More than halfway to Caemlyn, Elayne began to wonder whether they could make it in two weeks from where they stood.

With the snow, clothes became a worry. Elayne blamed herself for not thinking of the fact that everyone might need warm clothes before they reached their destination. Nynaeve blamed herself for not thinking of it. Merilille thought she was at fault, and Reanne thought she was. They actually stood in the main street of Forel Market that morning with snowflakes drifting down on their heads, arguing over who could claim the blame. Elayne was not sure which of them saw the absurdity first, who was the first to laugh, but all were laughing as they settled around a table in The White Swan to decide what to do. A solution turned out to be no laughing matter. Providing one warm coat or cloak for everyone would take a large bite out of their coin, if so many could be found. Jewelry could be sold or traded, of course, but no one in Forel Market seemed to be interested in necklaces or bracelets, however fine.

Aviendha solved that difficulty by producing a small sack that bulged with clear, perfect gemstones, some quite large. Strangely, the same folk who had said with bare politeness that they had no use for be-gemmed necklaces went round-eyed at the unset stones rolling about in Aviendha's palm. Reanne said they saw one as frippery, the other as wealth, but whatever their reasons, in return for two rubies of moderate size, one large moonstone, and a small firedrop, the people of Forel Market were more than willing to provide as many thick woolens as their visitors desired, some of them hardly worn.

"Very generous of them," Nynaeve muttered sourly as people began rooting clothes out of their chests and attics. A steady stream marched into the inn with their arms full. "Those stones could buy the whole village!" Aviendha shrugged slightly; she would have surrendered a handful of the gems if Reanne had not intervened.

Merilille shook her head. "We have what they want, but they have what we need. I'm afraid that means they set the price." Which was entirely too much like the situation with the Sea Folk. Nynaeve looked positively ill.

When they were alone, in a hallway of the inn, Elayne asked Aviendha where she had gotten such a fortune in jewels, and one she seemed eager to be rid of. She expected her near-sister to say they were her takings from the Stone of Tear, or perhaps Cairhien.

"Rand al'Thor tricked me," Aviendha muttered sullenly. "I tried to buy my *toh* from him. I know that is the least honorable way," she protested, "but I could see no other. And he stood me on my head! Why is it, when you reason things out logically, a man always does something completely illogical and gains the upper hand?"

"Their pretty heads are so fuzzy, a woman can't expect to follow how they skitter," Elayne told her. She did not inquire what *toh* Aviendha had tried to buy, or how the attempt had ended with her near-sister possessing a sack full of rich gems. Talking about Rand was hard enough without where *that* might lead.

Snow brought more than a need for warm clothing. At midday, with the snow flurries falling thicker by the minute, Renaile strode down the stairs into the common room, proclaimed that her part of the bargain had been met, and demanded not only the Bowl of the Winds, but Merilille. The Gray sister stared in consternation, and so did a great many others. The benches were filled with Kinswomen taking their turn at the midday meal, and serving men and women ran to serve this third lot of meals. Renaile did not keep her voice down, and every head in the common room swiveled toward her.

"You can begin your teaching, now," Renaile told the wide-eyed Aes Sedai. "Up the ladder with you to my quarters." Merilille started to protest, but face suddenly cold, the Windfinder to the Mistress of the Ships planted fists on her hips. "When I give a command, Merilille Ceandevin," she said icily, "I expect every hand on deck to jump. Now jump!"

Merilille did not precisely jump, but she did gather herself and go, with Renaile practically chivvying her up the stairs from behind. Given her promise, she had no other choice. Reanne's face was aghast. Alise and stout Sumeko, still wearing her red belt, watched thoughtfully.

In the days that followed, whether laboring along a snow-covered road on their horses, walking the streets of a village, or trying to find room for everyone at a farm, Renaile kept Merilille at her heels except when she told her off to follow another Windfinder. The glow of *saidar* surrounded the Gray sister and her escort almost constantly, and Merilille demonstrated weaves unceasingly. The pale Cairhienin was markedly shorter than any of the dark Sea Folk women, but at first Merilille managed to stand taller by the sheer force of Aes Sedai dignity. Soon, though, she began to wear a permanently startled expression. Elayne learned that when they all had beds to sleep in, which they did not always, Merilille was sharing with Pol, her maid, and the two apprentice Windfinders, Talaan and Metarra. What that said of Merilille's status, Elayne was not sure. Clearly, the Windfinders did not put her on a level with the apprentices. They just expected her to do as she was told, when she was told, with no delays or equivocations.

Reanne remained appalled at the turn of events, but Alise and Sumeko were not the only ones among the Kin to watch closely, not the only ones to nod thoughtfully. And suddenly, another problem came to Elayne's notice. The Kinswomen saw Ispan made more and more malleable in her captivity, but she was the prisoner of other Aes Sedai. The Sea Folk were not Aes Sedai, and Merilille not a prisoner, yet she was starting to jump when Renaile issued a command, or, for that matter, when Dorile, or Caire, or Caire's blood-sister Tebreille did. Each of those was Windfinder to a clan Wavemistress, and none of the others made her hop with such alacrity, but that was enough. More and more of the Kin slid from horrified gaping to thoughtful observation. Perhaps Aes Sedai were not a different flesh after all. If Aes Sedai were just women like themselves, why should they subject themselves once more to the rigors of the Tower, to Aes Sedai authority and Aes Sedai discipline? Had they not survived very well on their own, some for more years than any of the older sisters were quite ready to believe? Elayne could practically see the idea forming in their heads.

When she mentioned it to Nynaeve, though, Nynaeve just muttered, "About time some of the sisters learned what it's like trying to teach a woman who thinks she knows more than her teacher. Those who have a chance at a shawl will still want it, and for the rest, I don't see why they shouldn't

grow some backbone." Elayne refrained from mention-
ing Nynaeve's complaints about Sumeko, who had certainly grown backbone; Sumeko had criticized several of
Nynaeve's Healing weaves as "clumsy," and Elayne had
thought Nynaeve was going to have apoplexy on the spot.
"In any case, there's no need to tell Egwene about this. If
she's there. Any of it. She has enough on her plate." Without
doubt, "any of it" referred to Merilille and the Windfinders.

They were in their shifts, seated on their bed on the second floor of The New Plow, with the twisted-ring dream
ter'angreal hanging about their necks, Elayne's on a simple
leather cord, Nynaeve's alongside Lan's heavy signet ring
on a narrow golden chain. Aviendha and Birgitte, still fully
dressed, sat on two of their clothing chests. Standing guard,
they called it, until she and Nynaeve returned from the
World of Dreams. Both wore their cloaks until they could
climb under the blankets. The New Plow was definitely not
new; cracks spidered across the plastered walls, and unfortunate drafts crept in everywhere.

The room itself was small, and the chests and stacked
bundles left room for little beyond the bed and washstand.
Elayne knew she had to present herself properly in Caemlyn,
but sometimes she felt guilty, with her belongings on pack
animals when most others had to make do with what they
could carry on their backs. Nynaeve certainly never showed
any regrets over *her* chests. They had been sixteen days on
the road, the full moon outside the narrow window shone on
a white blanket of snow that would make traveling tomorrow
slow even if the sky remained clear, and Elayne thought another week to Caemlyn was an optimistic estimate.

"I have enough sense not to remind her," she told
Nynaeve. "I don't want my nose snapped off again."

That was a mild way of putting it. They had not been
in *Tel'aran'rhiod* since informing Egwene, the night after
leaving the estate, that the Bowl had been used. Reluctantly, they also had told her of the bargain they had been
forced into with the Sea Folk, and found themselves facing
the Amyrlin Seat with the striped stole on her shoulders.
Elayne knew it was necessary and right—a Queen's closest friend among her subjects knew she was the Queen as
well as a friend, *had* to know—but she had not enjoyed her
friend telling them in a heated voice that they had behaved

like witless loobies who might have brought ruin down on all their heads. Especially when she herself agreed. She had not liked hearing that the only reason Egwene did not set them both a penance that would curl their hair was that she could not afford to have them waste the time. Necessary and right, though; when she sat on the Lion Throne, she would still be Aes Sedai, and subject to the laws and rules and customs of Aes Sedai. Not for Andor—she would not give her land to the White Tower—but for herself. So, unpleasant as it had been, she accepted her castigation calmly. Nynaeve had writhed and stammered with embarrassment, protested and all but pouted, then apologized so profusely that Elayne hardly believed it was the same woman she knew. Quite rightly, Egwene had remained the Amyrlin, cool in her displeasure even while giving pardon for their mistakes. At best, tonight could not be pleasant or comfortable if she was there.

But when they dreamed themselves into the Salidar of *Tel'aran'rhiod*, into the room in the Little Tower that had been called the Amyrlin's Study, she was not there, and the only sign she had visited since their meeting was some barely visible words roughly scratched on a beetle-riddled wall panel, as if by an idle hand that did not want to spend the effort to carve deeply.

STAY IN CAEMLYN

And a few feet away:

KEEP SILENT AND BE CAREFUL

Those had been Egwene's final instructions to them. Go to Caemlyn, and stay there until she could puzzle out how to keep the Hall from salting all of them down and nailing them into a barrel. A reminder they had no way to erase.

Embracing *saidar,* Elayne channeled to leave her own message, the number fifteen seemingly scratched on the heavy table that had been Egwene's writing desk. Inverting the weave and tying it off meant that only someone who ran her fingers across the numerals would realize they were not really there. Perhaps it would not take fifteen days to reach Caemlyn, but more than a week, she was certain.

Nynaeve strode to the window and peered out both ways, careful not to put her head out through the open casement. It was night out there as in the waking world, a full moon gleaming on bright snow, though the air did not feel cold. No one else should be there except them, and if anyone was, it was someone to avoid. "I hope she isn't having trouble with her plans," she muttered.

"She told us not to mention those even to each other, Nynaeve. 'A secret spoken finds wings.'" That had been another of Lini's many favorites.

Nynaeve grimaced over her shoulder, then returned to peering down the narrow alley. "It's different for you. I tended her as a child, changed her swaddling, smacked her bottom a time or two. And now I have to leap when she snaps her fingers. It's hard."

Elayne could not help herself. She snapped her fingers.

Nynaeve spun so fast that she blurred, her face popeyed with horror. Her dress blurred, too, from blue riding silks to an Accepted's banded white to what she referred to as good, stout Two Rivers wool, dark and thick. When she realized Egwene was not there, had not been listening, she almost fainted with relief.

When they stepped back to their bodies and woke long enough to tell the others they could come to bed, Aviendha certainly thought it a good joke, and Birgitte laughed as well. Nynaeve had her revenge, though. The next morning, she woke Elayne with an icicle. Elayne's shrieks woke everybody else in the whole village.

Three days later, the first explosion came.

CHAPTER
21

Answering the Summons

The great winter tempests called the cemaros continued to roll up out of the Sea of Storms, harsher than any in memory. Some said this year the cemaros was trying to make up for the months of delay. Lightning crackled across the skies, enough to make the darkness patchy at night. Wind lashed the land and rain flailed it, turning all but the hardest roads to rivers of mud. Sometimes the mud froze after nightfall, but sunrise always brought a thaw, even under a gray sky, and the ground became bogs once more. Rand was surprised at how much all that hampered his plans.

The Asha'man he had sent for came quickly, at midmorning the next day, riding out of a gateway into a driving downpour that obscured the sun so, it might as well have been twilight. Through the hole in the air, snow fell back in Andor, fat white flakes swirling about thickly and hiding what lay behind them. Most of the men in the short column were bundled in heavy black cloaks, but the rain seemed to slip around them and their horses. It was not obvious, yet anyone who noticed would look twice, if not three times. Keeping dry required only a simple weave, so long as you did not mind flaunting what you were. But then, the black-and-white disc worked on a crimson circle on the breast of their cloaks did that. Even half-hidden by the rain, there was a pride about them, an arrogance in the way they sat their saddles. A defiance. They gloried in what they were.

Their commander, Charl Gedwyn, was a few years older than Rand, of middling height and wearing the Sword and Dragon, like Torval, on a very well cut, high-collared coat of the best black silk. His sword was mounted lushly with silver, his silver-worked sword belt fastened with a silver buckle shaped in a clenched fist. Gedwyn termed himself Tsorovan'm'hael; in the Old Tongue, Storm Leader, whatever that was supposed to mean. It seemed appropriate to the weather, at least.

Even so, he stood just inside the entrance to Rand's ornate green tent and scowled out at the cascading rain. A guard of mounted Companions encircled the tent, no more than thirty paces away, yet they were barely visible. They might have been statues, ignoring the torrent.

"How do you expect me to find anyone in this?" Gedwyn muttered, glancing back over his shoulder at Rand. A tick late, he added, "My Lord Dragon." His eyes were hard and challenging, but they always were, whether looking at a man or a fencepost. "Rochaid and I brought eight Dedicated and forty Soldiers, enough to destroy an army or cow ten kings. We might even make an Aes Sedai blink," he said wryly. "Burn me, the pair of us could do a fair job alone. Or you could. Why do you need anyone else?"

"I expect you to obey, Gedwyn," Rand said coldly. Storm Leader? And Manel Rochaid, Gedwyn's second, called himself Baijan'm'hael, Attack Leader. What was Taim up to, creating new ranks? The important thing was that the man made weapons. The important thing was that the weapons stayed sane long enough to be used. "And I don't expect you to waste time questioning my orders."

"As you command, my Lord Dragon," Gedwyn muttered. "I'll send men out immediately." With a curt salute, fist to chest, he strode out into the storm. The deluge bent away from him, sheeting down the small shield he wove around himself. Rand wondered whether the man suspected how close he had come to dying when he seized *saidin* without warning.

You must kill him before he kills you, Lews Therin giggled. *They will, you know. Dead men can't betray anyone.* The voice in Rand's head turned wondering. *But sometimes they don't die. Am I dead? Are you?*

Rand pushed the words down to a fly's buzzing, just on the edge of notice. Since his reappearance inside Rand's head, Lews Therin seldom went silent unless forced. The man seemed madder than ever most of the time, and usu-

ally angrier as well. Stronger sometimes, too. That voice
invaded Rand's dreams, and when he saw himself in a
dream, it was not always himself at all that he saw. It was
not always Lews Therin, either, the face he had come to
recognize as Lews Therin's. Sometimes it was blurred, yet
vaguely familiar, and Lews Therin seemed startled by it,
too. That was an indication how far the man's madness
went. Or maybe his own.

Not yet, Rand thought. *I can't afford to go mad yet.*

When, then? Lews Therin whispered before Rand could
mute him again.

With the arrival of Gedwyn and the Asha'man, his plan
to sweep the Seanchan westward got under way. Got under
way, and crept forward as slowly as a man laboring along
one of those mired roads. He shifted his own camp at once,
making no effort to hide his movements. There was little
point to straining for secrecy. Word traveled slowly by pi-
geon, and far slower by courier, once the cemaros came, yet
he had no doubts he was watched, by the White Tower, by
the Forsaken, by anyone who saw gain or loss in where the
Dragon Reborn went and could afford to slip coin to a soldier. Maybe even by the Seanchan. If he could scout them,
why not they him? But not even the Asha'man knew why he
was moving.

While Rand was idly watching men fold his tent onto a
high-wheeled cart, Weiramon appeared on one of his many
horses, a prancing white gelding of the finest Tairen blood-
stock. The rain had cleared, though gray clouds still veiled
the noonday sun and the air felt as if you could squeeze
water out of it with your hands. The Dragon Banner and the
Banner of Light hung limp and sodden on their tall staffs.

Tairen Defenders had replaced the Companions, and as
Weiramon rode through their mounted ring, he frowned
at Rodrivar Tihera, a lean fellow, dark even for a Tairen,
with a short beard trimmed to a very sharp point. A very
minor noble who had had to rise through his abilities, Tihera was punctilious in the extreme. The fat white plumes
bobbing on his rimmed helmet added embellishment to the
elaborate bow he gave Weiramon. The High Lord's frown
deepened.

There was no need for the Captain of the Stone to be personally in charge of Rand's bodyguard, but he frequently

was, just as Marcolin often commanded the Companions himself. An often bitter rivalry had grown up between Defenders and Companions, centering on who should guard Rand. The Tairens claimed the right because he had ruled longer in Tear, the Illianers because he was, after all, King of Illian. Perhaps Weiramon had heard some of the mutters among the Defenders that it was time Tear had a king of its own, and who better than the man who had taken the Stone? Weiramon more than agreed with the need, but not with the choice of who should wear the crown. He was not the only one.

The man smoothed his features as soon as he saw Rand looking, and swung down from his gold-tooled saddle to offer a bow that made Tihera's seem simple. Iron-spined as he was, he could puff up and strut in his sleep. Though he did grimace slightly at putting his polished boot into the mud. He wore a rain cape, to keep the mist off his fine clothes, but even that was encrusted with gold embroidery and had a collar of sapphires. For all of Rand's coat of deep green silk, with golden bees climbing the sleeves and lapels, anyone might have been forgiven for thinking the Crown of Swords belonged on the other's head, not his.

"My Lord Dragon," Weiramon intoned. "I cannot express how happy I am to see you guarded by Tairens, my Lord Dragon. Surely the world would weep if anything untoward happened." He was too intelligent to come out and call the Companions untrustworthy. By a hair, he was.

"Sooner or later it would," Rand said dryly. After a good part of it finished celebrating. "I know how hard you'd cry, Weiramon."

The fellow actually preened, stroking the point of his gray-streaked beard. He heard what he wanted to hear. "Yes, my Lord Dragon, you can be assured of my constancy. Which is why I'm concerned by the orders your man brought me this morning." That was Adley; many of the nobles thought pretending the Asha'man were merely Rand's servants would somehow make them less dangerous. "Wise of you to send away most of the Cairhienin. And the Illianers, of course; that goes without saying. I can even understand why you limit Gueyam and the others." Weiramon's boots squelched in the mud as he stepped nearer, and his voice took on a confiding tone. "I do believe some of them—I wouldn't say *plotted* against you, but I think perhaps their loyalty has not always been without question. As mine is. Without question." His voice shifted again, to strong and confident, a man concerned only with the needs of the one he served. The one who surely would make *him* the first King of Tear. "Allow me to bring all of my armsmen, my Lord Dragon. With them, and the Defenders, I can assure the honor of the Lord of the Morning, and his safety."

In all of the individual camps across the heath, wagons and carts were being loaded, horses saddled. Most tents were already down. The High Lady Rosana was riding north, her banner heading a column large enough to raise havoc among the bandits and at least give the Shaido pause. But not enough to plant notions in her head, especially not when half were Gueyam's and Maraconn's retainers mixed with Defenders of the Stone. Much the same applied to Spiron Narettin, riding eastward over the tall ridge with as many Companions and men sworn to others of the Council of Nine as his own liegemen, not to mention a hundred more tailing behind on foot, some of the fellows who had surrendered in the woods beyond that ridge the day before. A surprising number had chosen to follow the Dragon Reborn, but Rand did not trust them enough to leave them together. Tolmeran was just starting south with the same kind of blend, and others would be marching off as soon as they had their carts and wagons loaded. Each in a different direction, and none able to trust the men at their backs far enough for them to do more than follow the orders Rand had given. Bringing peace to Illian was an important task, yet every last lord and lady regretted being sent away from the Dragon Reborn, plainly wondering whether it meant they had slipped in his trust. Though a few might have considered why he chose to keep those he did under his eye. Rosana had certainly looked thoughtful.

"Your concern touches me," Rand told Weiramon, "but how many bodyguards does one man need? I'm not off to start a war." A fine point, perhaps, yet this war was well under way. It had begun at Falme, if not before. "Get your people ready."

How many have died for my pride? Lews Therin moaned. *How many have died for my mistakes?*

"May I at least ask *where* we are going?" Weiramon's question, not quite exasperated, came right atop the voice in Rand's head.

"The City," Rand snapped. He did not know how many had died for his mistakes, but none for his pride. He was sure of that.

Weiramon opened his mouth, plainly confused as to whether he meant Tear or Illian, or maybe even Cairhien, but Rand gestured him away with the Dragon Scepter, a sharp stabbing motion that made the green-and-white tassel swing. He half wished he could stab Lews Therin with it. "I don't intend to sit here all day, Weiramon! Go to your men!"

Less than an hour later he took hold of the True Source and prepared to make a gateway for Traveling. He had to fight the dizziness that gripped him lately whenever he seized or loosed the Power; he did not quite sway in Tai'daishar's saddle. What with the molten filth floating on *saidin*, the frozen slime, touching the Source came close to emptying his stomach. Seeing double, even for only a few moments, made weaving flows difficult if not impossible, and he could have told Dashiva or Flinn or one of the others to do it, but Gedwyn and Rochaid were holding their horses' reins in front of a dozen or so black-coated Soldiers, all who had not been out to search. Just standing there patiently. And watching Rand. Rochaid, no more than a hand shorter than Rand and maybe two years younger, was also full Asha'man, and his coat, too, was silk. A small smile played on his face, as if he knew things others did not and was amused. What did he know? About the Seanchan, surely, if not Rand's plans for them. What else? Maybe nothing, but Rand was not about to show any weakness in front of that pair. The dizziness faded quickly, the twinned sight a little more slowly, as it always did, these last few weeks, and he completed the weave, then, without waiting, dug in his heels and rode through the opening that unfolded before him.

The City he had meant was Illian, though the gateway opened to the north of that city. Despite Weiramon's supposed concerns, he hardly went unprotected and alone. Nearly three thousand men rode through that tall square hole in the air, into rolling meadowland not far from the broad muddy road that led down to the Causeway of the

Northern Star. Even when every lord had only been allowed a handful of armsmen—to men accustomed to leading a thousand if not thousands, a hundred or so were a
handful—they added up. Tairens and Cairhienin and Illianers, Defenders of the Stone under Tihera and Companions under Marcolin, Asha'man heeling Gedwyn. The
Asha'man who had come with him, anyway. Dashiva and
Flinn and the rest kept their horses close behind Rand. All
but Narishma. Narishma had not come back yet. The man
knew where to find him, but Rand did not like it.

Each kind kept to themselves as much as possible.
Gueyam and Maraconn and Aracome rode with Weiramon, all eyeing Rand more than where they were going,
and Gregorin Panar with three others of the Council of
Nine, leaning in their saddles to speak softly and uneasily among themselves. Semaradrid, with a knot of tight-
faced Cairhienin lords behind him, watched Rand almost
as closely as the Tairens did. Rand had chosen those who
came with him as carefully as those he sent away, not always for the reasons others might have used.

Had there been any onlookers, it would have been a
brave display, with all their bright banners and pennants,
and small *con* rising from some of the Cairhienin's backs.
Bright and brave and very dangerous. Some *had* plotted
against him, and he had learned that Semaradrid's House
Maravin had old alliances with House Riatin, which stood
in open rebellion against him in Cairhien. Semaradrid did
not deny the connection, but he had not mentioned it before
Rand heard, either. The Council of Nine were just too new
to him to risk leaving them all behind. And Weiramon was
a fool. Left to his own devices, he might well try to gain the
Lord Dragon's favor by marching an army against the Seanchan, or Murandy, or the Light alone knew who or where.
Too stupid to leave behind, too powerful to shove aside, so
he rode with Rand and thought himself honored. It was almost a pity he was not stupid enough to do something that
would get him executed.

Behind came the servants and carts—no one understood
why Rand had sent all of the wagons with the others, and
he was not about to explain; who owned the next pair of
ears that would hear?—and then the long strings of spare
mounts led by horse handlers, and straggling files of men in

battered breastplates that did not quite fit or leather jerkins sewn with rusty steel discs, carrying bows or crossbows or spears, and even a few pikes; more of the fellows who had obeyed "Lord Brend's" summons and decided against going home unarmed. Their leader was the runny-nosed man Rand had spoken to on the edge of the woods, Eagan Padros by name and much brighter than he looked. It was difficult for a commoner to rise very far, most places, but Rand had marked Padros out. The fellow gathered his men off to one side, but the whole lot of them milled about, elbowing one another aside for a better view southward.

The Causeway of the Northern Star stretched arrow-straight through the miles of brown marsh that surrounded Illian, a wide road of hard-packed dirt broken by flat stone bridges. A wind from the south carried sea salt and a hint of tanneries. Illian was a sprawling city, easily as large as Caemlyn or Cairhien. Brightly colored roof tiles and hundreds of thrusting towers, gleaming in the sun, were just visible across that sea of grass where long-legged cranes waded and flocks of white birds flew low uttering shrill cries. Illian had never needed walls. Not that walls would have done the City any good against him.

There was considerable disappointment that he did not mean to enter Illian, though no one spoke a complaint, at least not where he could hear. Still, there were plenty of glum faces and sour mutters as hasty camps began going up. Like most of the great cities, Illian had a name for exotic mystery, free-handed tapsters, and willing women. At least among men who had never been there, even when it was their own capital. Ignorance always inflated a city's reputation for such things. As it was, only Morr galloped off across the causeway. Men straightened from hammering tent pegs or setting picket lines for the horses, and followed him with jealous eyes. Nobles watched curiously, while trying to pretend they were not.

The Asha'man with Gedwyn paid Morr no mind as they made their own camp, which consisted of a pitch-black tent for Gedwyn and Rochaid and a space where damp brown grass and mud were squeezed flat and dry, for the rest to sleep wrapped in their cloaks. That was done with the Power, of course; they did everything with the Power, not even bothering to build cook fires. A few in the other camps stared at them, wide-eyed, as the tent seemed to spring up of its own accord and hampers floated away from packsaddles, but most looked anywhere else at all once they realized what was going on. Two or three of the black-coated Soldiers appeared to be talking to themselves.

Flinn and the others did not join Gedwyn's lot—they had a pair of tents that went up not far from Rand's—but Dashiva wandered over to where the "Storm Leader" and the "Attack Leader" were standing at their ease, and occasionally issuing a sharp order. A few words, and he wandered back shaking his head and muttering angrily under his breath. Gedwyn and Rochaid were not a friendly pair. As well they were not.

Rand took to his tent as soon as it was pitched, and sprawled fully clothed on his cot, staring at the sloped ceiling. There were bees embroidered on the inside as well, on a false roof made of silk. Hopwil brought a steaming pewter mug of mulled wine—Rand had left his servants behind—but the wine grew cold on his writing table. His mind worked feverishly. Two or three more days, and the Seanchan would have been dealt a blow that knocked them on their heels. Then it was back to Cairhien to see how negotiations with the Sea Folk had gone, to learn what Cadsuane was after—he owed her a debt, but she was after something!—maybe to put a final end to what remained of the rebellion there. Had Caraline Damodred and Darlin Sisnera slipped away in the confusion? The High Lord Darlin in his hands might finish the rebellion in Tear, as well. Andor. If Mat and Elayne were in Murandy, the way it appeared, it would be weeks more at best before Elayne could claim the Lion Throne. Once that happened, he would have to stay clear of Caemlyn. But he had to talk to Nynaeve. *Could* he cleanse *saidin*? It might work. It might destroy the world, too. Lews Therin gibbered at him in stark terror. Light, where *was* Narishma?

A cemaros storm swept in, all the fiercer this near the sea. Rain beat his tent like a drum. Lightning flashes filled the entrance with blue-white light, and thunder rumbled, the sound like mountains tumbling across the land.

Out of that, Narishma stepped into the tent, dripping wet, dark hair plastered to his head. His orders had been to avoid notice at all cost. No flaunting for him. His sodden coat was plain brown, and his dark hair was tied back, not braided. Even without bells, near waist-length hair on a man attracted eyes. He wore a scowl, too, and under his arm he carried a cylindrical bundle tied with cord, fatter than a man's leg, like a small carpet.

Springing from the cot, Rand snatched the bundle before Narishma could proffer it. "Did anyone see you?" he demanded. "What took you so long? I expected you last night!"

"It took a while to figure out what I had to do," Narishma replied in a flat voice. "You didn't tell me everything. You nearly killed me."

That was ridiculous. Rand *had* told him everything he needed to know. He was sure of it. There was no point to trusting the man as far as he had, only to have him die and ruin everything. Carefully he tucked the bundle beneath his cot. His hands trembled with the urge to strip the wrappings away, to make sure they held what Narishma had been sent for. The man would not have dared return if they did not. "Get yourself into a proper coat before you join the others," he said. "And Narishma. . . ." Rand straightened, fixing the other man with a steady gaze. "You tell anyone about this, and I *will* kill you."

Kill the whole world, Lews Therin laughed, a moan of derision. Of despair. *I killed the world, and you can, too, if you try hard.*

Narishma struck himself hard on the chest with his fist. "As you command, my Lord Dragon," he said sourly.

Bright and early the next morning, a thousand men of the Legion of the Dragon marched out of Illian, across the Causeway of the Northern Star, stepping to the steady beat of drums. Well, it was early, anyway. Thick gray clouds roiled across the sky, and a stiff sea breeze sharp with salt whipped cloaks and banners, muttering of another storm on the way. The Legion attracted a good bit of attention from the armsmen already in the camp, with their blue-painted Andoran helmets and their long blue coats worked on the chest with a red-and-gold Dragon. A blue pennant bearing the Dragon and a number marked each of the five companies. The Legionmen were different in many ways. For instance, they wore breastplates, but beneath their coats, so as not to hide the Dragons—the same reason the coats buttoned up one side—and every man carried a short-sword at his hip and a steel-armed crossbow, every one shouldered exactly the same as every other. The officers walked, each with a tall red plume on his helmet, just ahead of drum and pennant. The only horses were Morr's mouse-colored gelding, at their head, and pack animals at the rear.

"Foot," Weiramon muttered, slapping his reins on a gauntleted hand. "Burn my soul, they're no good, foot. They'll scatter at the first charge. Before." The first of the column strode off the causeway. They had helped take Illian, and they had not scattered.

Semaradrid shook his head. "No pikes," he muttered. "I have seen well-led foot hold, with pikes, but without. . . ." He made a sound of disgust in his throat.

Gregorin Panar, the third man sitting his saddle near Rand to watch the new arrivals, said nothing. Perhaps he had no prejudice against infantry—though if he did not, he would be one of only a handful of noblemen Rand had met without it—but he tried hard not to frown and almost succeeded. Everyone knew by now that the men with the Dragon on their chests bore arms because they had chosen to follow Rand, chosen to follow the Dragon Reborn, for no other reason than that they wanted to. The Illianer had to be wondering where they were going that Rand wanted the Legion and the Council of Nine was not trusted to know. For that matter, Semaradrid eyed Rand sideways. Only Weiramon was too stupid to think.

Rand turned Tai'daishar away. Narishma's package had been rewrapped, into a thinner bundle, and tied beneath his left stirrup leather. "Strike the camp; we're moving," he told the three nobles.

This time, he let Dashiva weave the gateway to take them all away. The plain-faced fellow frowned at him and mumbled to himself—Dashiva actually seemed affronted, for some reason!—and Gedwyn and Rochaid, their horses shoulder-by-shoulder, watched with sardonic smiles as the silvery slash of light rotated into a hole in nothing. Watched Rand more than Dashiva. Well, let them watch. How often could he seize *saidin* and risk falling dizzily on his face before he really did fall? It could not be where they could see.

This time, the gateway took them to a wide road carved through the low, brushy foothills of mountains to the west.

The Nemarellin Mountains. Not the equals of the Mountain of Mist, and not a patch on the Spine of the World, but they rose dark and severe against the sky, sharp peaks that walled the west coast of Illian. Beyond them lay Kabal Deep, and beyond that. . . .

Men began to recognize the peaks soon enough. Gregorin Panar took one look around and nodded in sudden satisfaction. The other three Councilors and Marcolin reined close to him to talk while horsemen were still pouring through the gateway. Semaradrid required only a bit longer to puzzle it out, and Tihera, and they also looked as if they understood now.

The Silver Road ran from the City to Lugard, and carried all of the inland trade for the west. There was a Gold Road, too, that led to Far Madding. Roads and names alike dated from before there had been an Illian. Centuries of wagon wheels, hooves and boots had beaten them hard, and the cemaros could only skim them with mud. They were among the few reliable highways in Illian for moving large groups of men in winter. Everyone knew about the Seanchan in Ebou Dar by this time, though a good many of the tales Rand had heard among the armsmen made the invaders seem Trollocs' meaner cousins. If the Seanchan intended to strike into Illian, the Silver Road was a good place to gather for defense.

Semaradrid and the others thought they knew what he planned: he must have learned that the Seanchan were coming, and the Asha'man were there to destroy them when they did. Given the stories about the Seanchan, no one seemed too upset that that left little for them to do. Of course, Weiramon had to have it explained to him finally, by Tihera, and he *was* upset, though he tried to mask it behind a grand speech about the wisdom of the Lord Dragon and the military genius of the Lord of the Morning, along with how he, personally, would lead the first charge against these Seanchan. A pure bull-goose fool. With luck, anyone else who learned of a gathering on the Silver Road would at least not be too much brighter than Semaradrid or Gregorin. With luck, no one who mattered would learn before it was too late.

Settling in to wait, Rand thought it would only be another

day or so, but as the days stretched out, he began to wonder whether he might be nearly as big a fool as Weiramon.

Most of the Asha'man were out searching across Illian and Tear and the Plains of Maredo for the rest of those Rand wanted. Searching through the cemaros. Gateways and Traveling were all very well, but even Asha'man took time to find who they sought when downpours hid anything fifty paces away and quagmires dragged rumor to a near halt. Searching Asha'man passed within a mile of their quarry in ignorance, and turned only to learn the men had moved on again. Some had farther to go, seeking people not necessarily eager to be found. Days passed before the first brought news.

The High Lord Sunamon joined Weiramon, a fat man with an unctuous manner—toward Rand, at least. Smooth in his fine silk coat, always smiling, he was voluble in his declarations of loyalty, but he had plotted against Rand so long that he probably did so in his sleep. The High Lord Torean came, with his lumpy farmer's face and his vast wealth, stammering about the honor of riding once more at the Lord Dragon's side. Gold concerned Torean more than anything else, except possibly the privileges Rand had taken away from the nobles in Tear. He seemed particularly dismayed to learn there were no serving girls in the camp, and not so much as a village nearby where compliant farmgirls might be found. Torean had schemed against Rand every bit as often as Sunamon. Maybe even more than Gueyam, or Maraconn, or Aracome.

There were others. There was Bertome Saighan, a short, ruggedly handsome man with the front of his head shaved. He supposedly did not mourn the death of his cousin Colavaere too greatly, both because that made him the new High Seat of House Saighan and because rumor said Rand had executed her. Or murdered her. Bertome bowed and smiled, and his smile never reached his dark eyes. Some said he had been very fond of his cousin. Ailil Riatin came, a slim dignified woman with big dark eyes, not young but quite pretty, protesting that she had a Lance-captain to lead her armsmen and no desire to take the field in person. Protesting her loyalty for the Lord Dragon, too. But her brother Toram claimed the throne Rand meant for Elayne, and it was whispered that she would do anything for Toram, anything at all. Even join with his enemies; to hamper or to spy or both, of course. Dalthanes Annallin came, and Amondrid Osiellin, and Doressin Chuliandred, lords who had supported Colavaere's seizure of the Sun Throne when they thought Rand would never return to Cairhien.

Cairhienin and Tairen, they were brought in one by one, with fifty retainers, or at most a hundred. Men and women he trusted even less than he did Gregorin or Semaradrid. Most were men, not because he thought the women any less dangerous—he was not *that* big a fool; a woman would kill you twice as fast as a man, and usually for half the reason!—but because he could not bring himself to take any woman except the most dangerous, where he was going. Ailil could smile warmly while she calculated where to plant the knife in your ribs. Anaiyella, a willowy simpering High Lady who gave a fair imitation of a beautiful goosebrain, had returned to Tear from Cairhien and openly begun talking of herself for the as-yet-nonexistent throne of Tear. Perhaps she *was* a fool, but she had managed to gain a great deal of support, both among nobles and in the streets.

So he gathered them in, all the folk who had been too long out from under his eye. He could not watch all of them all the time, but he could not afford to let them forget that he *did* watch sometimes. He gathered them, and he waited. For two days. Gnashing his teeth, he waited. Five days. Eight.

Rain was beating a diminishing drum on his tent when the last man he was waiting for finally arrived.

Shaking a small torrent from his oiled-cloth cape, Davram Bashere blew out his thick, gray-streaked mustaches in disgust and tossed the cape over a barrel chair. A short man with a great hooked beak of a nose, he seemed larger than he was. Not because he strutted, but because he assumed that he was as tall as any man present, and other men took him so. Wise men did. The wolf-headed ivory baton of the Marshal-General of Saldaea, tucked carelessly behind his sword belt, had been earned on scores of battlefields and at as many council tables. He was one of the very few men Rand would trust with his life.

"I know you don't like explaining," Bashere muttered, "but I could use a little illumination." Adjusting his serpentine sword, he sprawled in another chair and flung a leg over the arm of it. He always seemed at his ease, but he could uncoil faster than a whip. "That Asha'man fellow wouldn't say more than you needed me yesterday, yet he said not to bring more than a thousand men. I only had half that with me, but I brought them. It can't be a battle. Half the sigils I saw out there belong to men who'd bite their tongues if they saw a fellow behind you with a knife, and most of the rest to men who'd try to hold your attention. If they hadn't paid the knife man in the first place."

Seated behind his writing table in his shirtsleeves, Rand wearily pressed the heels of his palms against his eyes. With Boreane Carivin left behind, the lamp wicks needed proper trimming, and a faint haze of smoke hung in the air. Besides, he had been awake most of the night poring over the maps scattered across the table. Maps of southern Altara. No two agreed on very much.

"If you're going to fight a battle," he told Bashere, "who better to pay the butcher's bill than men who want you dead? Anyway, it isn't soldiers who'll win this battle. All they have to do is keep anybody from sneaking up on the Asha'man. What do you think of that?"

Bashere snorted so hard that his heavy mustaches stirred. "I think it's a deadly stew, is what I think. Somebody's going to choke to death on it. The Light send it isn't us." And then he laughed as if that were a fine joke.

Lews Therin laughed, too.

CHAPTER
22

Gathering Clouds

Under a steady drizzle Rand's small army formed columns across the low folded hills facing the Nemarellin peaks, dark and sharp against the western sky. There was no real need to face the direction you intended to Travel, but it always felt askew to Rand otherwise. Despite the rain, rapidly thinning gray clouds let through startlingly bright sunshine. Or maybe the day only seemed bright, after all the recent gloom.

Four of the columns were headed by Bashere's Saldaeans, bandy-legged unarmored men in short coats standing patiently beside their mounts beneath a small forest of shining lance heads, the other five by blue-coated men with the Dragon on their chests, commanded by a short stocky fellow named Jak Masond. When Masond moved, it was always with surprising quickness, but he was utterly still now, feet planted astride and hands folded behind his back. His men were in place, and so were the Defenders and Companions, grumpy about being behind infantry. It was the nobles and their folk, mainly, who milled about as if unsure where to go. Thick mud sucked at hooves and boots, and mired cart wheels; shouted curses rose. It took time to line up nearly six thousand soaked men, getting wetter by the minute. And that was not counting the supply carts, and the remounts.

Rand had donned his finest, so he would stand out at a glance. A lick with the Power had polished the Dragon Scepter's spearhead to mirror brightness, and another had burnished the Crown of Swords so the gold gleamed. The gilded Dragon buckle of his sword belt caught the light, and so did the thread-of-gold embroidery that covered his blue silk coat. For a moment, he regretted giving away the gems that once had decked his sword's hilt and scabbard. The dark boarhide was serviceable, but any armsman could have worn that. Let men know who he was. Let the Seanchan know who had come to destroy them.

Sitting Tai'daishar on a broad flat, he impatiently watched the nobles roil about on the hills. A little way off on the flat, Gedwyn and Rochaid sat their saddles in front of their men, all formed into a precise box, Dedicated in the front rank, Soldiers lined up behind. They looked ready to parade. As many had gray hair or nearly none as were young—several were as young as Hopwil or Morr—but every one was strong enough to make a gateway. That had been a requirement. Flinn and Dashiva waited behind Rand in a casual cluster with Adley and Morr, Hopwil and Narishma. And a rigid pair of mounted bannermen, one Tairen and one Cairhienin, their breastplates and helmets and even their steel-backed gauntlets buffed and polished till they shone. The crimson Banner of Light and the long white Dragon Banner hung limp and dripping. Rand had assumed the Power in his tent, where his momentary stagger would not be seen, and the sparse rain failed by an inch to touch him or his horse.

The taint on *saidin* felt especially heavy today, a thick foul oil that oozed into his pores and stained his bones deep. Stained his soul. He had thought himself accustomed to the vileness, after a fashion, yet today it was nauseating, stronger than the frozen fire and molten cold of *saidin* itself. He held on to the Source as often as possible now, accepting the vileness to avoid the new sickness of seizing it. It could be deadly, if he let sickness distract him from *that* struggle. Maybe it was connected to the dizzy spells, somehow. Light, he could not go mad yet, and he could not die. Not yet. There was too much still to be done.

He pressed his left leg against Tai'daishar's flank just to feel the long bundle strapped between stirrup leather and scarlet saddle cloth. Every time he did that, something wriggled across the outside of the Void. Anticipation, and maybe a touch of fear. Well trained, the gelding started to turn left, and Rand had to rein him back. When *would* the nobles sort themselves out? He ground his teeth in impatience.

He could remember as a boy hearing men laugh that when rain fell in sunshine the Dark One was beating Semirhage. Some of that laughter had been uneasy, though, and scrawny old Cenn Buie would always snarl that Semirhage would be smarting and angry after that, and come for small boys who did not keep out of their elders' way. That had been enough to send Rand running, when he was little. He wished Semirhage *would* come for him now, right that instant. He would make her weep.

Nothing makes Semirhage weep, Lews Therin muttered. *She gives tears to others, but she has none herself.*

Rand laughed softly. If she came today, he *would* make her weep. Her and the rest of the Forsaken together, if they came today. Most assuredly he would make the Seanchan weep.

Not everyone was pleased with the orders he had given. Sunamon's oily smile vanished when he thought Rand did not see. Torean had a flask in his saddlebags, no doubt brandy, or maybe several flasks, because he drank steadily and never appeared to run dry. Semaradrid and Marcolin and Tihera each appeared in front of Rand to protest the numbers with somber faces. A few years before, close on six thousand men would have been army enough for any war, but they had seen armies in the tens of thousands, now, hundreds of thousands, as in Artur Hawkwing's day, and to go against the Seanchan, they wanted far more. He sent them away disgruntled. They did not understand that fifty-odd Asha'man were as big a hammer as anyone could wish for. Rand wondered what they would have said had he told them *he* was hammer enough by himself. He had considered doing this by himself. It might come to that yet.

Weiramon came; he did not like having to take orders from Bashere, or the fact that they were going into mountains—very hard to mount a decent charge in mountains—or several other things—Rand was certain there were at least several more—that Rand did not let him utter.

"The Saldaean seems to believe I should ride on the right flank," Weiramon muttered disparagingly. He twisted his shoulders as though the right flank were a great insult, for some reason. "And the foot, my Lord Dragon. Really, I think—"

"*I* think you should get your men ready," Rand said coldly. Part of the chill was the effect of floating in emotionless emptiness. "Or you won't be on *any* flank." He meant that he would leave the man behind if he was not ready in time. Surely such a fool could not make much trouble left in this remote spot with only a few armsmen. Rand would be back before he could ride to anything larger than a village.

Blood drained from Weiramon's face, though. "As my Lord Dragon commands," he said, briskly for him, and was whirling his horse away before the words were well out of his mouth. His mount was a tall deep-chested bay, today.

The pale Lady Ailil reined to a stop in front of Rand, accompanied by the High Lady Anaiyella, a strange pair to be in company, and not just because their nations hated one another. Ailil was tall for a Cairhienin woman, if only for a Cairhienin, and everything about her was dignity and precision, from the arch of her eyebrow to the turn of her red-gloved wrist to the way her pearl-collared rain cape lay spread across the rump of her smoke-gray mare. Unlike Semaradrid or Marcolin, Weiramon or Tihera, she did not so much as blink at the sight of raindrops sliding down nothing around him. Anaiyella did blink. And gasp. And titter behind her hand. Anaiyella was willowy and darkly beautiful, her rain cape collared with rubies and embroidered with gold besides, but there any resemblance to Ailil ended. Anaiyella was all mincing elegance and simpers. When she bowed, her white gelding did, too, bending its forelegs. The prancing animal was showy, but Rand suspected it had no bottom. Like its mistress.

"My Lord Dragon," Ailil said, "I must make one more protest against my inclusion in this . . . expedition." Her voice was coolly neutral, if not exactly unfriendly. "I will send my retainers where you command and when, but I have no desire at all to be in the thick of a battle."

"Oh, no," Anaiyella added, with a delicate shudder. Even her tone simpered! "Nasty things, battles. So my Master of the Horse says. Surely you won't really make us go, my Lord Dragon? We've heard you have a particular care for women. Haven't we, Ailil?"

Rand was so astonished that the Void collapsed, and

saidin vanished. Raindrops began to trickle through his hair and seep through his coat, but for a moment, clutching his saddle's high pommel to hold himself upright, seeing four women instead of two, he was too stunned to notice. How much did they know? They had *heard*? How many people knew? How did anyone know? Light, rumor had him killing Morgase, Elayne, Colavaere, a hundred women probably, and each in a worse way than the last! He swallowed against the urge to sick up. That was only partly *saidin*'s fault. *Burn me, how many spies* are *there watching me?* The thought was a growl.

The dead watch, Lews Therin whispered. *The dead never close their eyes.* Rand shivered.

"I do try to be careful of women," he told them when he could speak. "Faster than a man, and for half the reason. That's why I want to keep you close the next few days. But if you really dislike the idea so much, I could tell off one of the Asha'man. You'd be safe at the Black Tower." Anaiyella squeaked prettily, but her face went gray.

"Thank you, no," Ailil said after a moment, absolutely calm. "I suppose I had best confer with my lance-captain about what to expect." But she paused in turning her mare away, and regarded Rand with a sidelong look. "My brother Toram is . . . impetuous, my Lord Dragon. Even rash. I am not."

Anaiyella smiled much too sweetly at Rand, and actually wriggled slightly before following, but once she faced away from him, she dug in her heels and worked her jewel-handled quirt, quickly passing the other woman. That white gelding showed a surprising turn of speed.

At last all was ready, the columns formed, snaking back over the low hills.

"Begin," Rand told Gedwyn, who wheeled his horse and began barking orders to his men. The eight Dedicated rode forward and dismounted on the ground they had memorized, facing the mountains. One of them looked familiar, a grizzled fellow whose pointed Tairen beard appeared odd on his wrinkled countryman's face. Eight vertical lines of sharp blue light turned and became openings that showed slightly different views of a long, sparsely wooded mountain valley rising to a steep pass. In Altara. In the Venir Mountains.

Kill them, Lews Therin wept pleadingly. *They're too dangerous to live!* Without thought, Rand suppressed the voice. Another man channeling often brought that reaction from Lews Therin, or even a man who could. He no longer wondered why.

Rand muttered a command, and Flinn blinked in surprise before hurrying to join the line and weave a ninth gateway. None was as large as Rand could make, but any would pass a cart, if closely. He had intended to do that himself, but he did not want to chance seizing *saidin* again in front of everyone. He noticed Gedwyn and Rochaid watching him, wearing identical knowing smiles. And Dashiva as well, frowning, lips moving as he talked to himself. Was it his imagination, or was Narishma eyeing him askance too? And Adley? Morr?

Rand shivered before he could stop himself. Mistrust of Gedwyn and Rochaid was simple sense, but was he coming down with what Nynaeve had called the dreads? A kind of madness, a crippling dark suspicion of everyone and everything? There had been a Coplin, Benly, who thought everybody was scheming against him. He had starved to death when Rand was a boy, refusing to eat for fear of poison.

Ducking low on Tai'daishar's neck, Rand heeled the gelding through the largest gateway. Flinn's, as it happened, but he would have ridden through one made by Gedwyn right then. He was the first onto Altaran soil.

The others followed quickly, the Asha'man first of all. Dashiva stared in Rand's direction, frowning, and Narishma, too, but Gedwyn immediately began directing his Soldiers. One by one, they rushed forward, opened a gateway and darted through, dragging their mounts behind them. Ahead up the valley, bright flashes of light told of gateways opening and closing. The Asha'man could Travel short distances without first memorizing the ground they left from, and cover ground far faster than riding. In short order, only Gedwyn and Rochaid remained, aside from the Dedicated holding the gateways. The others would be fanning out westward, searching for Seanchan. The Saldaeans were through from Illian, and mounting. Legionmen spread into the trees at a trot, crossbows held ready. In this country, they could move as fast afoot as men on horseback.

As the rest of the army began emerging, Rand rode up

the valley in the direction the Asha'man had gone. Mountains rose high behind him, a wall fronting the Deep, but west the peaks ran almost to Ebou Dar. He quickened the gelding's pace to a canter.

Bashere caught him before he reached the pass. The man's bay was small—most of the Saldaeans rode small horses—but quick. "No Seanchan here, it seems," he said almost idly, stroking his mustaches with a knuckle. "But there could have been. Tenobia's likely to have my head on a pike soon enough for following a live Dragon Reborn, much more a dead one."

Rand scowled. Maybe he could take Flinn, to watch his back, and Narishma, and. . . . Flinn had saved his life; the man had to be true. Men could change, though. And Narishma? Even after . . . ? He felt cold at the risk he had taken. Not the dreads. Narishma *had* proved true, but it still had been a mad risk. As mad as running from stares he was not even sure were real, running to where he had no notion what was waiting. Bashere was right, but Rand did not want to talk about it further.

The slopes leading up into the pass were bare stone and boulders of all sizes, but among the natural stone lay weathered pieces of what must have once been a huge statue. Some were just recognizable as worked stone, others more so. A beringed hand nearly big as his chest, gripping a sword hilt with a broken stub of blade wider than his hand. A great head, a woman with cracks across her face and a crown that seemed to be made of upthrusting daggers, some still whole.

"Who do you think she was?" he asked. A queen, of course. Even if merchants or scholars had worn crowns in some distant time, only rulers and generals earned statues.

Bashere twisted in his saddle to study the head before speaking. "A Queen of Shiota, I'll wager," he said finally. "Not older. I saw a statue made in Eharon once, and it was so worn you couldn't say whether it was man or woman. A conqueror, or they wouldn't have shown her with a sword. And I seem to recall Shiota gave a crown like that to rulers who expanded the borders. Maybe they called it the Crown of Swords, eh? A Brown sister might be able to tell you more."

"It isn't important," Rand told him irritably. They did look like swords.

Bashere went on anyway, graying eyebrows lowered, gravely serious. "I expect thousands cheered her, called her the hope of Shiota, maybe even believed she was. In her time, she might have been as feared and respected as Artur Hawkwing was later, but now even the Brown sisters may not know her name. When you die, people begin to forget, who you were and what you did, or tried to do. Everybody dies eventually, and everybody is forgotten, eventually, but there's no bloody point dying before your time comes."

"I don't intend to," Rand said sharply. He knew where he was meant to die, if not when. He thought he did.

The corner of his eye caught motion, back down where bare stone gave way to brush and a few small trees. Fifty paces away, a man stepped into the open and raised a bow, smoothly drawing fletchings to cheek. Everything seemed to happen at once.

Snarling, Rand hauled Tai'daishar around, watching the archer adjust to follow. He seized *saidin* and sweet life and filth poured into him together. His head spun. There were two archers. Bile rose in his throat as he fought wild, uncontrolled surges of the Power that tried to sear him to the bone and freeze his flesh solid. He *could* not control them; it was all he could do to stay alive. Desperately, he fought to clear his sight, to be able to see well enough to weave the flows he could barely form, with nausea flooding him as strongly as the Power. He thought he heard Bashere shout. Two archers loosed.

Rand should have died. At that range, a boy could have hit his target. Maybe being *ta'veren* saved him. As the archer let fly, a covey of gray-winged quail burst up almost at his feet uttering piercing whistles. Not enough to throw off an experienced man, and indeed, the fellow only flinched a hair. Rand felt the wind of the arrow's passage against his cheek.

Fireballs the size of fists suddenly struck the archer. He screamed as his arm spun away, hand still gripping the bow. Another took his left leg at the knee, and he fell shrieking.

Leaning out of his saddle, Rand vomited onto the ground. His stomach tried to heave up every meal he had ever eaten.

The Void and *saidin* left with a sickening wrench. It was nearly more than he could manage not to fall.

When he could sit upright again, he took the white linen handkerchief Bashere silently offered, and wiped his mouth. The Saldaean frowned with concern, as well he might. Rand's stomach wanted to find more to spew out. He thought his face must be pale. He drew a deep breath. Losing *saidin* that way could kill you. But he could still sense the Source; at least *saidin* had not burned him out. At least he could see properly; there was only one Davram Bashere. But the illness seemed a little worse each time he seized *saidin*.

"Let's see if there's enough left of this fellow to talk," he told Bashere. There was not.

Rochaid was on his knees, calmly searching through the corpse's torn, bloodstained coat. Besides his missing arm and leg, the dead man had a blackened hole as big as his head all the way through his chest. It was Eagan Padros; his sightless eyes stared at the sky in surprise. Gedwyn ignored the body at his feet, studying Rand instead, as cold as Rochaid. Both men held *saidin*. Surprisingly, Lews Therin only moaned.

In a clatter of hooves on stone, Flinn and Narishma came galloping up the rise, followed by nearly a hundred Saldaeans. As they came close, Rand could feel the Power in the grizzled old man and the younger, maybe as much as they could hold. They had both leaped up in strength since Dumai's Wells. That was the way of it with men; women seemed to gain smoothly, but men suddenly jumped. Flinn was stronger than Gedwyn or Rochaid either one, and Narishma not far behind. For the time being; there was no way to know how it would end. None came close to matching Rand, though. Not yet, anyway. There was no way to tell what time would bring. Not the dreads.

"It seems it's well we decided to follow you, my Lord Dragon." Gedwyn's voice assumed concern, just shy of mocking. "Are you suffering from a tender stomach this morning?"

Rand just shook his head. He could not take his eyes from Padros' face. Why? Because he had conquered Illian? Because the man had been loyal to "Lord Brend"?

With a loud exclamation, Rochaid ripped a wash-leather

pouch from Padros' coat pocket and upended it. Bright golden coins spilled onto the stony ground, bouncing and clinking. "Thirty crowns," he growled. "Tar Valon crowns. No doubt who paid him." He snatched a coin and tossed it up for Rand, but Rand made no effort to catch it, and it glanced off his arm.

"There's plenty of Tar Valon coin to be found," Bashere said calmly. "Half the men in this valley have a few in their pockets. I do, myself." Gedwyn and Rochaid swiveled to look at him. Bashere smiled behind his thick mustaches, or at least showed teeth, but some of the Saldaeans shifted uneasily in their saddles and fingered belt pouches.

Up where the pass leveled off for a bit between steep mountain slopes, a slash of light rotated into a gateway, and a top-knotted Shienaran in a plain black coat trotted through, pulling his horse behind him. It appeared the first Seanchan had been found, and not too far away if the man was back so quickly.

"Time to move," Rand told Bashere. The man nodded, but he did not stir. Instead, he studied the two Asha'man standing near Padros. They ignored him.

"What do we do with him?" Gedwyn demanded, gesturing to the corpse. "We ought to send him back to the witches, at least."

"Leave him," Rand replied.

Are you ready to kill now? Lews Therin asked. He did not sound insane at all.

Not yet, Rand thought. *Soon.*

Digging his heels into Tai'daishar's flanks, he galloped back down toward his army. Dashiva and Flinn followed closely, and Bashere and the hundred Saldaeans. They were all looking around as if they expected another attempt on his life. To the east, black clouds were building among the peaks, another cemaros storm. Soon.

The hilltop camp was well laid out, with a meandering stream close by for water and good lines of sight to the likeliest ways into the long mountain meadow. Assid Bakuun did not feel pride in the camp. During thirty years in the Ever Victorious Army, he had made hundreds of camps; he would as soon have felt pride in walking across a

room without falling down. Nor did he feel pride in where
he was. Thirty years serving the Empress, might she live
forever, and while there had been the occasional rebellion
by some mad upstart with eyes on the Crystal Throne, the
bulk of those years had been spent preparing for this. For
two generations, while the great ships were built to carry
the Return, the Ever Victorious Army had trained and prepared. Bakuun certainly had been proud when he learned
he was to be one of the Forerunners. Surely he could be
forgiven dreams of retaking the lands stolen from Artur
Hawkwing's rightful heirs, even wild dreams to completing
this new Consolidation before the Corenne came. Not such
a wild dream after all, as it turned out, but not at all the way
he had imagined.

A returning patrol of fifty Taraboner lancers rode up the
hillside, red and green stripes painted across their solid
breastplates, veils of mail hiding their thick mustaches.
They rode well, and even fought well, when they had decent
leaders. More than ten times as many were already among
the cook fires, or down at the picket lines tending their
mounts, and three patrols were still out. Bakuun had never
expected to find himself with well over half his command
descendants of thieves. And unashamed of it; they would
look you straight in the eyes. The patrol's commander
bowed low to him as their muddy-legged horses passed,
but many of the others went on talking in their peculiar accents, speaking too fast for Bakuun to understand without
listening hard. They had peculiar notions of discipline, too.

Shaking his head, Bakuun strode across to the *sul'dam*'s
large tent. Larger than his, of necessity. Four of them were
sitting on stools outside in their dark blue dresses with the
forked lightning on the skirts, enjoying the sun during this
break in the storms. Those were rare enough, now. The
gray-clad *damane* sat at their feet, with Nerith braiding
her pale hair. Talking to her, as well, all of them joining
in and laughing softly. The bracelet on the end of the silvery
a'dam's leash lay on the ground. Bakuun grunted sourly.
He had a favorite wolfhound, back home, and even talked
to him sometimes, but he never expected Nip to carry on a
conversation!

"Is she well?" he asked Nerith, not for the first time.

Or the tenth. "Is everything well with her?" The *damane* dropped her eyes and went silent.

"She is quite well, Captain Bakuun." A square-faced woman, Nerith put the proper degree of respect into her voice and not a whisker beyond. But she stroked the *damane*'s head soothingly while she talked. "Whatever the indisposition, it is gone, now. A small thing, in any case. Nothing to worry about." The *damane* was trembling.

Bakuun grunted again. Not far from the answer he had received before. Something had been wrong, though, back in Ebou Dar, and not just with this *damane*. The *sul'dam* had all been as tight-lipped as clams—and the Blood would not say anything, of course, not to the likes of him!—but he had heard too many whispers. They said the *damane* were all sick, or insane. Light, he had not seen a single one used around Ebou Dar once the city was secured, not even for a victory display of Sky Lights, and who had ever heard the like of that!

"Well, I hope she . . ." he began, and cut off as a *raken* appeared, sweeping through the eastern pass. Its great leathery wings beat powerfully for height, and right above the hill it suddenly tilted and cut a tight circle, one wingtip pointed almost straight down. A thin red streamer fell away under the weight of a lead ball.

Bakuun swallowed a curse. Fliers were always showing off, but if this pair injured one of his men delivering their scouting report, he would have their hides no matter who he had to face to get them. He would not have wanted to fight without fliers to scout, but they *were* coddled like some Blood's favorite pet.

Arrow-straight the streamer plummeted. The lead weight struck the ground and bounced on the crest, almost beside the tall thin message pole, which was too long to lower unless there was a message to send. Besides, when it was left down somebody was always stepping a horse on the thing and breaking the joins.

Bakuun strode straight to his tent, but his First Lieutenant was already waiting with the mud-stained streamer and the message tube. Tiras was a bony man a head taller than him, with an unfortunate scrap of beard clinging to the point of his chin.

The report rolled up in the thin metal tube, on a slip of paper Bakuun could almost see through, was written simply. He had never been forced to ride on *raken* or *to'raken*—the Light be thanked, and the Empress, might she live forever, be praised!—but he doubted it was easy to handle a pen in a saddle strapped to the back of a flying lizard. What it said made him flip open the lid of his small camp desk and write hurriedly.

"There's a force not ten miles east of here," he told Tiras. "Five or six times our number." Fliers exaggerated sometimes, but not often by much. How had that many penetrated these mountains so far without being spotted before? He had seen the coast to the east, and he wanted his burial prayers paid for before he tried a landing there. Burn his eyes, the fliers boasted they would see a flea move anywhere in the range. "No reason to think they know we're here, but I'd not mind a few reinforcements."

Tiras laughed. "We'll give them a brush of the *damane*, and that will be that if they outnumber us by twenty times." His only real fault was a touch of overconfidence. A good soldier, though.

"And if they have a few . . . Aes Sedai?" Bakuun said quietly, hardly stumbling over the name, as he stuffed the flier's report back into the tube with his own brief message. He had not really believed *anyone* could let those . . . women run free.

Tiras' face showed that he remembered the tales about an Aes Sedai weapon. The red streamer floated behind him as he ran with the message tube.

Soon enough tube and streamer were attached to the tip of the message pole, a tiny breeze stirring the long red strip fifteen paces above the hill crest. The *raken* soared toward it along the valley, outstretched wings still as death. Abruptly one of the fliers swung down from the saddle and hung—upside down!—below the *raken*'s trailing claws. It made Bakuun's stomach hurt to watch. But her hand closed on the streamer, the pole flexed, then vibrated back upright as the message tube pulled free of the clip, and she scrambled back up as the creature climbed in slow circles.

Bakuun thankfully put *raken* and fliers out of his mind as he surveyed the valley. Broad and long, nearly flat except for this hill, and surrounded by steep wooded slopes; only a goat could enter, except by the passes in his sight. With the *damane*, he could cut anybody to pieces before they managed to try attacking across that muddy meadow. He had passed word along, though; if the enemy came straight on, they would arrive before any possible reinforcements by three days at best. How *had* they come this far unseen?

He had missed the last battles of the Consolidation by two hundred years, but some of those rebellions had not been small. Two years fighting on Marendalar, thirty thousand dead, and fifty times that shipped back to the mainland as property. Taking notice of the strange kept a soldier alive. Ordering the camp struck and all signs of it cleared, he began moving his command to the forested slopes. Dark clouds were massing in the east, another of those cursed storms coming.

CHAPTER
23

Fog of War, Storm of Battle

No rain fell, for the moment. Rand guided Tai'daishar around an uprooted tree lying across the slope and frowned down at a dead man sprawled on his back behind the tree trunk. The fellow was short and blocky, his face creased, and his armor all overlapping plates lacquered blue and green, but staring sightlessly at the black clouds overhead, he looked a deal like Eagan Padros, even to the missing leg. An officer, plainly; the sword beside his outflung hand had an ivory hilt carved in the likeness of a woman, and his lacquered helmet, shaped like some huge insect's head, bore two long thin blue plumes.

Uprooted trees and shattered ones, a fair number burning from end to end, littered the slope of the mountain for a good five hundred paces. Bodies, too, men broken or ripped apart when *saidin* harrowed the mountainside. Most wore steel veils across their faces, and breastplates painted in horizontal stripes. No women, thank the Light. The injured horses had been put down, another thing to be thankful for. It was incredible how loudly a horse could scream.

Do you think the dead are silent? Lews Therin's laugh was rasping. *Do you? His voice turned to pained rage. The dead howl at me!*

At me, too, Rand thought sadly. *I can't afford to listen, but how do you shut them up?* Lews Therin began weeping for his lost Ilyena.

"A great victory," Weiramon intoned behind Rand, then muttered, "But small honor in it. The old ways are best." Mud liberally decorated Rand's coat, yet surprisingly, Weiramon appeared as pristine as he had back on the Silver

Road. His helmet and armor shone. How had he managed? The Taraboners charged, at the end, lances and courage against the One Power, and Weiramon had led his own charge to break them. Without orders, and followed by every Tairen save the Defenders, even a half-drunk Torean, surprisingly. By Semaradrid and Gregorin Panar, too, with most of the Cairhienin and Illianers. Standing still had been hard by that time, and every man wanted to come to grips with something he actually could come to grips with. The Asha'man could have done it faster. If somewhat more messily.

Rand had taken no part in the fighting, except to sit his saddle where men could see him. He had been afraid to seize the Power. He did not dare display weakness for them to catch. Not a scrap. Lews Therin gibbered with horror at the very idea.

Equally surprising as Weiramon's unsullied coat, Anaiyella rode with him, and for once not simpering. Her face was pinched and disapproving. Strangely, it did not spoil her looks nearly so much as her unctuous smiles did. She had not joined the charge herself, of course, any more than Ailil, but Anaiyella's Master of the Horse had, and the man was most definitely dead, with a Taraboner lance through his chest. She did not like that one bit. But why did she accompany Weiramon? Just Tairens flocking together? Maybe. She had been with Sunamon, the last Rand had seen.

Bashere walked his bay up the slope, picking his way around the dead while seeming to pay them no more mind than he did a splintered tree trunk or a burning stump. His helmet hung from his saddle, and his gauntlets were stuffed behind his sword belt. He was mud all down his right side, and his horse as well.

"Aracome's gone," he said. "Flinn tried Healing him, but I don't think Aracome wanted to live like that. There's near fifty dead so far, and some of the rest might not survive." Anaiyella paled. Rand had seen her near Aracome, emptying herself. Dead commoners did not affect her so much.

Rand felt a moment of pity. Not for her, and not very much for Aracome. For Min, though she was safely back in Cairhien. Min had foretold Aracome's death from one of her viewings, and Gueyam and Maraconn's, too. Whatever she had seen, Rand hoped it had not been anywhere near the reality.

Most of the Soldiers were off scouting again, but down in the broad meadow, gateways woven by Gedwyn's Dedicated were spilling out the supply carts and the remounts. The men coming with them gaped as soon as they were clear enough to see. The muddy ground was not so well plowed as the mountainside, yet blackened furrows, two paces wide and fifty long, carved through the brown grass, and gaping holes a horse might not be able to leap. They had not found the *damane* so far. Rand thought there had to be only one; more would have done considerably greater damage under the circumstances.

Men moved around a number of small fires where water boiled for tea, among other things. For once, Tairens, Cairhienin and Illianers mingled. Not just the commoners. Semaradrid was sharing his saddle-flask with Gueyam, who wearily rubbed a hand over his bald head. Maraconn and Kiril Drapaneos, a stork of a man whose square-cut beard looked odd on his narrow face, were squatting on their heels near one of the fires. Playing cards, by the look of it! Torean had a whole circle of laughing Cairhienin lordlings around him, though they might have been less amused by his jokes than by the way he swayed and rubbed at his potato nose. The Legionmen kept apart, but they had taken in the "volunteers" who had followed Padros to the Banner of Light. That lot seemed more eager than anyone since learning how Padros died. Blue-coated Legionmen were showing them how to change direction without falling apart like a gaggle of geese.

Flinn was among the wounded with Adley and Morr and Hopwil. Narishma could Heal little more than minor cuts, no better than Rand, and Dashiva not even that. Gedwyn and Rochaid stood talking well apart from anyone else, holding their horses by the reins atop the hill in the middle of the valley. The hill where they had expected to catch the Seanchan by surprise when they rushed out of gateways surrounding it. Near fifty dead, and more to come, but it would have been above two hundred without Flinn and the rest who could manage Healing to one degree or another. Gedwyn and Rochaid had not wanted to dirty their hands and grimaced when Rand drove them to it. One of the dead was a Soldier, and another Soldier, a round-faced Cairhienin, sat slumped beside a fire with a dazed look that Rand hoped came from being tossed through the air by the ground erupting almost under his feet.

Down there on the furrowed flats, Ailil was conferring with her Lance-captain, a pale little man called Denharad. Their horses stood nearly touching, and occasionally they looked up the mountain toward Rand. What were *they* scheming?

"We'll do better next time," Bashere murmured. He ran his gaze around the valley, then shook his head. "The worst mistake is to make the same one twice, and we won't."

Weiramon heard him and repeated the same thing, but using twenty times the words, and flowery enough for a garden in spring. Without admitting that there had been any mistakes, certainly not on his part. He avoided Rand's mistakes with equal adroitness.

Rand nodded, his mouth tight. Next time they would do better. They had to, unless he wanted to leave half his men buried in these mountains. Right then, he was wondering what to do with the prisoners.

Most of those who escaped death on the mountainside had managed to withdraw through the trees that remained standing. With amazingly good order considering, Bashere claimed, yet they were unlikely to be much threat now. Not unless they had the *damane* with them. But a hundred or so men sat huddled on the ground, stripped of weapons and armor, under the watchful eyes of two dozen mounted Companions and Defenders. Taraboners, for the most part, they had not fought like men driven to it by conquerors. A fair number held their heads up, and jeered at their guards. Gedwyn had wanted to kill them, after putting them to the question. Weiramon did not care whether they had their throats slit, but he considered torture a waste of time. None would know anything useful, he maintained; there was not a one nobly born.

Rand glanced at Bashere. Weiramon was *still* going on sonorously. ". . . sweep these mountains clean for you, my Lord Dragon. We'll trample them beneath our hooves, and. . . ." Anaiyella was nodding grim approval.

"Six up, and half a dozen down," Bashere said softly. He scraped mud from one of his thick mustaches with a finger-nail. "Or as some of my tenants say, what you gain on the swings, you lose on the roundabouts." What in the Light was a roundabout? A great help that was!

And then one of Bashere's patrols made matters worse.

The six men came prodding a prisoner along the slope ahead of their horses with the butts of their lances. She was a black-haired woman in a torn and dirty dark blue dress, with red panels on the breast and skirts bearing forked lightning. Her face was dirty, too, and tear-streaked. She stumbled and half-fell, but the prodding was more gesture than actual touching. She glared scornfully at her captors, even spitting once. She sneered at Rand, too.

"Did you hurt her?" he demanded. A strange question, perhaps, about an enemy after what had happened in this valley. About a *sul'dam*. But it popped out.

"Not us, my Lord Dragon," the gruff-faced patrol leader said. "We found her like this." Scratching his chin through a black flowing beard, he eyed Bashere as if for support. "She claims we killed her Gille. A pet dog, or cat, or some such, the way she carries on. Her name's Nerith. We got that much out of her." The woman turned and snarled at him again.

Rand sighed. Not a pet dog. No! That name did not belong on the list! But he could hear the litany of names reciting itself in his head, and "Gille the *damane*" was there. Lews Therin moaned for his Ilyena. Her name also was on the list. Rand thought it had a right.

"This is a Seanchan Aes Sedai?" Anaiyella asked suddenly, leaning over the pommel of her saddle to peer hard at Nerith. Nerith spat at her, as well, eyes widening in out-rage. Rand explained the little he knew of *sul'dam*, that they *controlled* women who could channel with the aid of a leash-and-collar *ter'angreal* but could not themselves chan-nel, and to his surprise, the dainty simpering High Lady said coldly, "If my Lord Dragon feels constrained, I'll hang her for him." Nerith spat at her again! Contemptuously, this time. No shortfall of courage there.

"No!" Rand growled. Light, the things people would do to get on his good side! Or maybe Anaiyella had been closer to her Master of the Horse than was considered proper. The man had been stout and balding—and a commoner; that counted heavily with Tairens—but women did have strange tastes in men. He knew that for a pure fact.

"As soon as we're ready to move again," he told Bashere, "turn the men down there loose." Taking prisoners along when he launched his next attack was out of the question, and leaving a hundred men—a hundred now; more later, for sure—leaving them to follow with the supply carts risked fifty kinds of mischief. They could cause no trouble left behind. Even the fellows who had gotten away on horseback could not carry a warning faster than he could Travel.

Bashere shrugged faintly; he thought it might be so, but then again there was always the odd chance. Strange things happened even without a *ta'veren* around.

Weiramon and Anaiyella opened their mouths almost together, faces set in protest, but Rand pressed on. "I've spoken, and it's done! We'll keep the woman, though. And any more women we capture."

"Burn my soul," Weiramon exclaimed. "Why?" The man appeared dumbfounded, and for that matter, Bashere gave a startled jerk of his head. Anaiyella's mouth twisted in contempt before she managed to turn it to a simpering smile for the Lord Dragon. Plainly, she thought him too soft to send a woman off with the others. They would have hard walking in this terrain, not to mention short rations. And the weather was not weather to turn a woman out in.

"I have enough Aes Sedai against me without sending *sul'dam* back to their trade," he told them. The Light knew that was true! They nodded, if Weiramon was slow about it; Bashere looked relieved, Anaiyella disappointed. But what to do with the woman, and any more he captured? He did not intend to turn the Black Tower into a prison. The Aiel could hold them. Except that the Wise Ones might slit their throats the moment his back was turned. What about the sisters that Mat was taking to Caemlyn with Elayne, though? "When this is done, I'll hand her over to some Aes Sedai I choose." They might see it as a gesture of goodwill, a little honey to sweeten their having to accept his protection.

No sooner were the words out of his mouth than Nerith's face went dead white and she screamed at the top of her lungs. Howling without cease, she flung herself down the slope, scrabbling over downed trees, falling and scrambling back up.

"Bloody—! Catch her!" Rand snapped, and the Saldaean patrol leaped after the woman, jumping their mounts across the tree-littered slope careless of broken legs and necks. Still wailing, she dodged and darted among the horses with even less care.

In the mouth of the easternmost pass, a gateway opened in a flash of silver light. A black-coated Soldier pulled his horse through, jumped to the saddle as the gateway winked out and put his mount to a gallop, toward the hilltop where Gedwyn and Rochaid waited. Rand watched impassively. In his head, Lews Therin snarled of killing, killing all the Asha'man before it was too late.

By the time the three of them started up the slope toward Rand, four of the Saldaeans had Nerith down on the ground, binding her hand and foot. It took four, the way she thrashed and bit at them, and an amused Bashere was offering odds on whether she might not overcome them instead. Anaiyella muttered something about cracking the woman's head. Did she mean cracking it open? Rand frowned at her.

The Soldier between Gedwyn and Rochaid glanced at Nerith uneasily as they rode past. Rand vaguely remembered seeing him at the Black Tower, the day he first handed out the silver Swords, and gave Taim the very first Dragon pin. He was a young man, Varil Nensen by name, still wearing a transparent veil to cover his thick mustaches. He had not hesitated when he found himself facing his countrymen, though. Allegiance was to the Black Tower and the Dragon Reborn, now, so Taim always said. The second part of that always sounded an afterthought.

"You may have the honor of making your report to the Dragon Reborn, Soldier Nensen," Gedwyn said. Wryly.

Nensen sat up straight in his saddle. "My Lord Dragon!" he barked, slapping fist to chest. "There's more of them about thirty miles west, my Lord Dragon." Thirty miles was as far as Rand had told the scouts to go before returning. What good if one Soldier found Seanchan while the rest kept moving ever farther west? "Maybe half what were here," Nensen went on. "And. . . ." His dark eyes flickered toward Nerith again. She was tied, now, the Saldaeans struggling to get her over a horse. "And I saw no sign of women, my Lord Dragon."

Bashere squinted at the sky. Dark clouds lay in a blanket from mountain peak to mountain peak, but the sun should still be high. "Time to feed the men before the rest return," he said, nodding in satisfaction. Nerith had managed to sink her teeth into a Saldaean's wrist and was hanging on like a badger.

"Feed them quick," Rand said irritably. Would every *sul'dam* he captured be as difficult? Very likely. Light, what if they took a *damane*? "I don't want to spend all winter in these mountains." Gille the *damane*. He could not erase a name once it went onto that list.

The dead are never silent, Lews Therin whispered. *The dead never sleep.*

Rand rode down toward the fires. He did not feel like eating.

From the point of a thrusting shoulder of stone, Furyk Karede carefully studied the forested mountains rising all around him, sharp peaks like dark fangs. His horse, a tall dappled gelding, stiffened his ears as though catching a sound he had missed, but otherwise the animal was still. Every so often, Karede had to stop and wipe the lens of his looking glass. A light rain fell from a gray morning sky. His helmet's two black plumes were bent over instead of standing straight, and water ran down his back. A light rain compared to yesterday, anyway, and probably compared to tomorrow. Or this afternoon, perhaps. Thunder rumbled ominously in the south. Karede's concern had nothing to do with weather, though.

Below him, the last of twenty-three hundred men snaked through the winding passes, men gathered from four outposts. Well-mounted, reasonably well-led, yet a bare two hundred were Seanchan, and just two besides himself wore the red-and-green of the Guard. Most of the remainder were Taraboners—he knew their mettle—but a good third were Amadicians and Altarans, too new to their oaths for any to be sure how they would stand up. Some Altarans and Amadicians had switched allegiance two or three times already.

Tried to, anyway. People this side of the Aryth Ocean had no shame. A dozen *sul'dam* rode near the front of the column, and he wished all twelve had leashed *damanes* walking by their horses instead of only two.

Fifty paces farther on, the ten men of the spearhead were watching the slopes above them, though not as carefully as they should have. Too many men who rode spearhead relied on the forward scouts to find any dangers. Karede made a note to speak to them personally. They would do their duties properly after that, or he would send them to the labor levies.

A *raken* appeared in the east ahead, skimming low over the treetops, twisting and turning to follow the curves of the land like a man running his hand down a woman's back. Peculiar. *Morat'raken*, fliers, always liked to soar high unless the sky was actually full of lightning. Karede lowered the looking glass to watch.

"Maybe we'll finally get another scouting report," Jadranka said. To the other officers waiting behind Karede, not to him. Three of the ten matched Karede's rank, yet few except the Blood disturbed a man in the blood-red and nearly black green of the Deathwatch Guard. Not that many among the Blood did.

According to the tales he had heard as a child, one of his ancestors, a noble, had followed Luthair Paendrag to Seanchan at Artur Hawkwing's command, but two hundred years later, with only the north secure, another ancestor tried to carve out a kingdom of his own and ended sold from the block instead. Perhaps it was so; many *da'covale* claimed noble ancestors. Among themselves, at least; few of the Blood found such chatter amusing. In any case, Karede had felt lucky when the Choosers picked him out, a sturdy boy not yet old enough to be assigned duties, and he still felt pride in the ravens tattooed on his shoulders. Many Deathwatch Guards went without coat or shirt whenever possible, to display those. The humans, anyway. Ogier Gardeners were not marked or owned, but that was between them and the Empress.

Karede was *da'covale* and proud of it, like every man of the Guard, the property of the Crystal Throne, body and soul. He fought where the Empress pointed, and would die the day she said die. To the Empress alone did the

Guard answer, and where they appeared, they appeared as her hand, a visible reminder of her. No wonder that some among the Blood could become uneasy watching a detachment of Guardsmen pass. A far better life than mucking out a Lord's stables or serving *kaf* to a Lady. But he cursed the luck that had sent him into these mountains to inspect the outposts.

The *raken* darted on westward, the two fliers crouched low in their saddle. There was no scouting report, no message for him. Furyk knew it was his imagination, but the creature's long, outstretched neck somehow looked . . . anxious. Had he been anyone else, he might have been anxious, too. There had been few messages for him since his orders three days ago to assume command and move east. Each message had thickened the fog more than cleared it.

The locals, these Altarans, had moved into the mountains in force, it seemed, but how? The roads along the northern border of this range were patrolled and watched nearly to the border of Illian, by fliers and *morat'torm* as well as horse-mounted parties. What could have made the Altarans decide to show so many teeth? To stand together? A man might find himself in a duel for a look—though they had begun to learn challenging a Guardsman was just a slower way of cutting your own throat—but he had seen nobles of this so-called nation trying to sell each other *and* their Queen for the mere suggestion that their own lands might be protected and perhaps those of their neighbor added to them.

Nadoc, a big man with a deceptively mild face, twisted in his saddle to watch the *raken*. "I don't like marching blind," he muttered. "Not when the Altarans have managed to put forty thousand men up here. Forty, at least."

Jadranka snorted so hard that his tall white gelding shifted. Jadranka was the senior of the three captains behind Karede, having served as long as Karede himself. A short thin man with a prominent nose and such airs you might have thought him of the Blood. That horse would stand out at a mile. "Forty thousand or a hundred, Nadoc, they're scattered from here to the end of the range, too far apart to support one another. Stab my eyes, likely half are dead already. They must be tangling with outposts everywhere. That's why we aren't getting reports. We're just expected to sweep up the remnants."

Karede swallowed a sigh. He had hoped Jadranka was not a fool atop his airs. Praise of victors spread quickly, whether they were an army or half a Banner. It was the rare defeats that were swallowed in silence and forgotten. So much silence was . . . ominous.

"That last report didn't sound like remnants to me," Nadoc persisted. *He* was no fool. "There are five thousand men not fifty miles ahead of us, and I doubt we'll take them with brooms."

Jadranka snorted again. "We'll crush them, with swords or brooms. The Light burn my eyes, I can hardly wait for a decent engagement. I told the scouts to press on until they found them. I won't have them slipping away from us."

"You did what?" Karede said softly.

Soft or not, his words jerked every eye toward him. Though Nadoc and a few of the others had to struggle to stop gaping at Jadranka. Scouts told to press ahead, scouts told what to look for. What had gone unseen for those orders?

Before anyone could open his mouth shouts rose from the men in the pass, screams and the shrieks of horses.

Karede pressed the leather tube of the looking glass to his eye. Along the pass ahead of him, men and horses were dying under a hail of what he thought must be crossbow bolts, the way they hammered through steel breastplates, exploded through chests protected by mail. Hundreds were down already, hundreds more sagging wounded in their saddles or afoot and running from horses thrashing on the ground. Too many were running. Even as he looked, men still mounted whirled their horses to try fleeing back up the pass. Where in the Light were the *sul'dam*? He could not find them. He had faced rebels who had *sul'dam* and *damane*, and they always had to be killed as fast as possible. Maybe the locals had learned that.

Suddenly, shockingly, the ground began to erupt in roaring fountains all along the writhing snake of his command, fountains that flung men and horses into the air as easily as dirt and stones. Lightning flashed out of the sky, blue-white bolts shattering earth and men alike. Other men simply exploded, ripped to shreds by nothing he could see. Did the locals have *damane* of their own? No, it would be those Aes Sedai.

"What are we going to do?" Nadoc said. He sounded shaken. As well he might.

"Do you think to abandon your men?" Jadranka snarled. "We rally them and attack, you—!" He cut off, gurgling, as Karede's swordpoint went neatly into his throat. There were times fools could be tolerated, and times not. As the man toppled from his saddle, Karede deftly wiped his blade on the gelding's white mane before the animal bolted. There were times for a little show, too.

"We rally what can be rallied, Nadoc," he said as if Jadranka had never spoken. As if he had never been. "We save what can be saved, and fall back."

Turning to ride down into the pass where lightnings flashed and thunders roared, he ordered Anghar, a steady-eyed young man with a fast horse, to ride east and report what had transpired here. Perhaps a flier would see and perhaps not, though Karede suspected he knew why they flew low, now. He suspected the High Lady Suroth and the generals in Ebou Dar already knew what was occurring up here, too. Was today the day he died for the Empress? He dug his heels into his horse's flanks.

From the flat, thinly treed ridge, Rand peered westward over the forest before him. With the Power in him—life, so sweet; vileness, oh, so vile—he could see individual leaves, but it was not enough. Tai'daishar stamped a hoof. The jagged peaks behind, to either side, and all around overtopped the ridge by a mile or more, but the ridge stood well above the treetops below, a rolling wooded valley over a league in length and nearly as wide. All was still down there. As quiet as the Void he floated in. Quiet for the moment, anyway. Here and there plumes of smoke rose from where two or three trees in a clump burned like torches. Only the general wet stopped them turning the valley into a conflagration.

Flinn and Dashiva were the only Asha'man still with him. All the rest were down in the valley. The pair stood a little way from him at the edge of the trees, holding their horses by the reins and staring at the forest below. Well, Flinn stared, as intently as Rand himself. Dashiva glanced occasionally, twisting his mouth, sometimes muttering to himself in a way that made Flinn shift his feet and eye him sideways. The Power filled both men, nearly to overflowing, but for a change, Lews Therin said nothing. The man seemed increasingly to have gone back into hiding over the last few days.

In the sky there was actually sunlight, and the scattered clouds were gray. It was five days since Rand had brought his small army to Altara, five days since he had seen his first Seanchan dead. He had seen quite a few since. Thought slid across the surface of the Void. He could feel the heron branded into his palm pressing against the Dragon Scepter through his glove. Silent. There were none of the flying creatures to be seen. Three of those had died, slashed from the sky by lightning, before their riders learned to stay clear. Bashere was fascinated by the creatures. Quiet.

"Perhaps it is finished, my Lord Dragon." Ailil's voice was calm and cool, but she patted her mare's neck, though the animal did not need soothing. She eyed Flinn and Dashiva sideways and straightened, unwilling to reveal a shred of unease in front of them.

Rand found himself humming and stopped abruptly. That was Lews Therin's habit, looking at a pretty woman, not his. Not his! Light, if he started taking on the fellow's mannerisms, and when he was not there, at that . . . !

Abruptly, hollow thunder boomed up the valley. Fire fountained out of the trees a good two miles away or more, then again, and again, again. Lightning streaked down into the forest not far from where the tall flames had bloomed, single slashes like jagged blue-white lances. A flurry of lightning bolts and fire, and all was still again. No trees had caught fire, this time.

Some of that had been *saidin*. Some of it.

Shouts rose, dim and distant, from another part of the valley, he thought. Too far for even his *saidin*-enhanced ears to hear the crash of steel. Despite everything, not all of the fighting was being done by Asha'man and Dedicated and Soldiers.

Anaiyella let out a long breath she must have been holding since the exchange with the Power began. Men fighting with steel did not disturb her. Then *she* patted her mount's neck. The gelding had only flickered an ear. Rand had noticed that about women. Quite often, when a woman was agitated, she tried to soothe others whether they required soothing or not. A horse would do. Where *was* Lews Therin?

Irritably he leaned forward to study the forest canopy again. A good many of those trees were evergreens—oak and pine and leatherleaf—and despite the late drought, they made an effective screen, even to his intensified vision. As if idly, he touched the narrow bundle under his stirrup leather. He could take a hand. And strike blindly. He could ride down into the woods. And be able to see ten paces at most. Down there, he would be little more effective than one of the Soldiers.

A gateway opened among the trees a little way along the ridge, silvery slash widening into a hole that showed different trees and thick winter brown underbrush. A copper-skinned Soldier with a thin mustache on his upper lip and a small pearl in his ear exited afoot and let the gateway vanish. He was shoving a *sul'dam* ahead of him with her wrists tied behind her, a handsome woman except for the purple knot on the side of her head. That seemed to go along with her scowl, though, as well as it did with her rumpled, leaf-stained dress. She sneered over her shoulder at the Soldier while he pushed her along the ridgetop to Rand, and then she sneered up at Rand.

The Soldier stiffened, saluting smartly. "Soldier Arlen Nalaam, my Lord Dragon," he barked, staring straight at Rand's saddle. "My Lord Dragon's orders were to bring any women captured to him."

Rand nodded. It was only to give him the appearance of doing something, inspecting prisoners to be sure they were what any idiot could see they were. "Take her back to the carts, Soldier Nalaam, then return to the fighting." He almost ground his teeth saying that. Return to the fighting. While Rand al'Thor, Dragon. Reborn and King of Illian, sat his horse and watched treetops!

Nalaam saluted again before pushing away the woman ahead of him, but he was not slow about it. She kept peering over her shoulder again, yet not at the Soldier this time. At Rand. With wide-eyed, openmouthed astonishment. For some reason, Nalaam did not pull her to a halt until he reached the spot where he had come out. All that was necessary was to go far enough to avoid injuring the horses.

"What are you doing?" Rand demanded as *saidin* filled the man.

Nalaam half turned back to him, hesitating briefly. "It seems easier, here, if I use a place I've already made a gateway, my Lord Dragon. *Saidin* . . . *saidin* feels . . . strange . . . to me here." His prisoner turned to frown at him.

After a moment, Rand gestured him to go ahead. Flinn pretended to be interested in his horse's saddle girth, but the balding old man smiled faintly. Smugly. Dashiva . . . giggled. Flinn had been the first to mention an odd feel to *saidin* in this valley. Of course, Narishma and Hopwil had heard him, and Morr added his tales of the "strangeness" around Ebou Dar. Small wonder everyone was claiming to feel something now, though not a one could say what. *Saidin* just felt . . . peculiar. Light, with the taint thick on the male half of the Source, what else would it feel? Rand hoped they were not all coming down with his new sickness.

Nalaam's gateway opened, and vanished behind him and his prisoner. Rand let himself really feel *saidin*. Life and corruption commingled; ice to make winter's heart seem warm, and fire to make a forge's flames cold; death, waiting for him to slip. Wanting him to slip. It did not feel any different. Did it? He scowled at where Nalaam had disappeared. Nalaam and the woman.

She was the fourth *sul'dam* taken this afternoon. That made twenty-three *sul'dam* prisoners with the carts. And two *damane*, each still in her silvery leash and collar, carried on separate carts; in those collars, they could not walk three steps before becoming more violently sick than Rand did seizing the Source. He was not sure the sisters with Mat would be pleased to receive them after all. The first *damane*, three days before, he had not thought of as a prisoner. A slender woman with pale yellow hair and big blue eyes, she was a Seanchan captive to be freed. He thought. But when he forced a *sul'dam* to remove the woman's collar, her *a'dam*, she screamed for the *sul'dam* to help her and immediately began lashing out with the Power. She had even offered her neck for the *sul'dam* to replace the thing! Nine Defenders and a Soldier died before she could be shielded. Gedwyn would have killed her on the spot had Rand not stopped it. The Defenders, nearly as uncomfortable around women who could channel as others were around men who could—the Defenders still wanted her dead. They had taken casualties in the fighting these past days, but having men killed by a prisoner seemed to offend them.

There had been more casualties than Rand had expected. Thirty-one Defenders dead, and forty-six Companions. More than two hundred among the Legionmen and the noble's armsmen. Seven Soldiers and a Dedicated, men Rand had never met before they answered his summons to Illian. Too many, considering that all except the gravest injury could be Healed, if a man could only hang on until there was time. But he was driving the Seanchan west. Driving them hard.

More shouting rose somewhere far off down in the valley. Fire blossomed a good three miles to the west, and lightning struck, toppling trees. Trees and stone erupted from a mountainside farther on, strange fountains marching along the slope. The roaring booms swallowed shouts. The Seanchan were retreating.

"Get down there," Rand told Flinn and Dashiva. "Both of you. Find Gedwyn and tell him I said push! Push!"

Dashiva grimaced at the forest below, then began awkwardly tugging his horse along the ridge. The man was ungainly with horses, riding or leading. He nearly tripped over his sword!

Flinn looked up at Rand worriedly. "You mean to stay here alone, my Lord Dragon?"

"I'm hardly alone," Rand said dryly, glancing at Ailil and Anaiyella. They had ridden back to their armsmen, almost two hundred lancers waiting just short of where the ridge began to slope down to the east. At their head, Denharad frowned through the face-bars of his helmet. He had command of both lots, now, and if his concern was for Ailil and Anaiyella, his fellows still made a show fit to keep away most attackers. Besides, Weiramon had the northern end of this ridge secured so a fly could not pass, he claimed, and Bashere held the south. Without boasting; Bashere just erected a wall of lances without talking about it. And the Seanchan were retreating. "And I'm hardly helpless, anyway, Flinn."

Flinn actually looked doubtful and scratched his fringe

of white hair before saluting and leading his horse toward where Dashiva's gateway was already winking out. Limping along, Flinn shook his head, muttering to himself fit for Dashiva. Rand wanted to snarl. He could not go mad, and neither could they.

Flinn's gateway vanished, and Rand returned to his study of the treetops. It was quiet again. Time stretched in stillness. This notion of taking the outposts in the mountains had been a bad one; he was willing to admit that, now. In this terrain, you could be half a mile from an army without knowing. In those tangled woods down there, you could be ten feet from them without knowing! He needed to face the Seanchan on better ground. He needed. . . .

Abruptly he was fighting *saidin*, fighting wild surges that tried to ream out his skull. The Void was vanishing, melting beneath the onslaught. Frantic, dazed, he released the Source before it could kill him. Nausea twisted his middle. Double vision showed him two Crowns of Swords. Lying on the thick mulch of dead leaves in front of his face! He was on the ground! He could not seem to breathe properly, and struggled to suck in air. There was a chip broken off one of the crown's golden laurel leaves, and blood stained several of the tiny golden swordpoints. A knot of hot pain in his side told him those never-healing wounds had broken open. He tried to push himself up, and cried out. In stunned amazement he stared at the dark fletchings of an arrow stuck through his right arm. With a groan he collapsed. Something ran down his face. Something dripped in front of his eye. Blood.

Vaguely he became aware of ululating cries. Horsemen appeared among the trees to the north, galloping along the ridge, some with lowered lances, some working short bows as fast as they could nock and draw. Horsemen in blue-and-yellow armor of overlapping plates, and helmets like huge insects' heads. Seanchan, several hundred of them it seemed. From the north. So much for Weiramon's fly.

Rand struggled to reach the Source. Too late to worry about sicking up, or falling on his face. Another time, he might have laughed at that. He struggled. . . . It was like fumbling for a pin in the dark with numbed fingers.

Time to die, Lews Therin whispered. Rand had always known Lews Therin would be there at the end.

Not fifty paces from Rand, screaming Tairens and Cairhien plowed into the Seanchan.

"Fight, you dogs!" Anaiyella shrieked, swinging down from her saddle beside him. "Fight!" The willow lady in her silks and laces hurled a string of curses that would have made a wagon driver's tongue go dry.

Anaiyella stood holding her mount's reins, glaring from the mill of men and steel to Rand. It was Ailil who turned him onto his back. Kneeling there, she looked down at him with an unreadable expression in her big dark eyes. He could not seem to move. He felt drained. He was not sure he could blink. Screams and the clash of steel rang in his ears.

"If he dies on our hands, Bashere will hang both of us!" Anaiyella certainly was not simpering now. "If those black-coated monsters get hold of us . . . !" She shuddered, and bent closer to Ailil, gesturing with a belt knife he had not noticed in her hand before. A ruby sparkled blood-red on the hilt. "Your Lance-captain could break off enough men to get us away. We could be miles away before he's found, and back to our estates by the time—"

"I think he can hear us," Ailil broke in calmly. Her red-gloved hands moved at her waist. Sheathing a belt knife? Or drawing one? "If he dies here—" She cut off as sharply as the other woman had, and her head jerked around.

Hooves thundered past Rand on either side in thick streams. Galloping north, toward the Seanchan. Sword in hand, Bashere barely reined in before leaping from his saddle. Gregorin Panar dismounted more slowly, but he waved his sword at the men flooding by. "Strike home for King and Illian!" he shouted. "Strike home! The Lord of the Morning! The Lord of the Morning!" The crash of steel rose higher. And the screaming.

"It would be like this at the last of it," Bashere growled, favoring the two women with suspicious glares. He wasted only an instant, though, before raising his voice above the din of battle. "Morr! Burn your Asha'man hide! Here, now!" He did not shout that the Lord Dragon was down, thank the Light.

With an effort, Rand turned his head perhaps a hand. Enough to see Illianers and Saldaeans driving on north. The Seanchan must have given way.

"Morr!" The name roared through Bashere's mustaches,

and Morr himself dropped from a galloping horse nearly on top of Anaiyella. She looked disgruntled at the lack of an apology as the man knelt beside Rand, scrubbing dark hair out of his face. She moved back quickly enough when she realized he intended to channel, though, practically bounding away. Ailil was much smoother about rising, but not noticeably slower in stepping clear. And she slipped a silver-handled belt knife back into its sheath at her waist.

Healing was a simple matter, if not exactly comfortable. The fletchings were broken off and the arrow drawn the rest of the way through with a sharp jerk that brought a gasp to Rand's lips, but that was just to clear the way. Dirt and lightly embedded fragments would fall away as flesh knit itself up, but only Flinn and a few others could use the Power to remove what was driven deep. Resting two fingers on Rand's chest, Morr caught his tongue between his teeth with a fixed expression and wove Healing. That was how he always did it; it did not work for him, otherwise. It was not the complex weaves that Flinn used. Few could manage that, and none as well as Flinn, so far. This was simpler. Rougher. Waves of heat rushed through Rand, strong enough to make him grunt and send sweat gushing from every pore. He quivered violently from head to foot. A roast in the oven must have felt that way.

The sudden flood of heat ebbed slowly, and Rand lay panting. In his head, Lews Therin panted, too. *Kill him! Kill him!* Over and over.

Muting the voice to a faint buzz, Rand thanked Morr—the young man blinked as if surprised!—then grabbed the Dragon Scepter from the ground and forced himself to his feet. Erect, he swayed slightly. Bashere started to offer an arm, then backed away at a gesture. Rand could stand unaided. Barely. He could as soon have flown by waving his arms as channeled, though. When he touched his side, his shirt slipped on blood, yet the old round scar and the newer slash across it merely felt tender. Half-healed only, but they had never been better than that since he got them.

For a moment, he studied the two women. Anaiyella murmured something vaguely congratulatory and offered him a smile that made him wonder whether she intended to lick his wrist. Ailil stood very straight, very cool, as if nothing had happened. Had they meant to leave him to die?

Or to kill him? But if so, why send their armsmen charging in and rush to check on him? On the other hand, Ailil *had* drawn her knife once the talk of him dying began.

Most of the Saldaeans and Illianers were galloping north or riding down the slope of the ridge, pursuing the last of the Seanchan. And then Weiramon appeared from the north, riding a tall, glossy black at a slow canter that picked up when he saw Rand. His armsmen rode in double file at his back.

"My Lord Dragon," the High Lord intoned as he dismounted. He *still* seemed as clean as he had in Illian. Bashere simply looked rumpled and a bit grimy here and there, but Gregorin's finery was decidedly dirt-stained, and slashed down one sleeve besides. Weiramon flourished a bow to shame a king's court. "Forgive me, my Lord Dragon. I thought I saw Seanchan advancing in front of the ridge and went to meet them. I never suspected this other company. You can't know how it would pain me if you were injured."

"I think I know," Rand said dryly, and Weiramon blinked. Seanchan advancing? Perhaps. Weiramon would always snatch at a chance for glory in the charge. "What did you mean, 'at the last,' Bashere?"

"They're pulling back," Bashere replied. In the valley, fire and lightning erupted for a moment as if to give him the lie, but nearly to the far end.

"Your . . . scouts do say they all do be retreating," Gregorin said, rubbing his beard, and gave Morr a sidelong, uncomfortable glance. Morr grinned at him toothily. Rand had seen the Illianer in the thick of fighting heading his men, shouting encouragement and laying his sword about with wild abandon, but he flinched at Morr's grin.

Gedwyn strode up then, leading his horse carelessly, insolently. He almost sneered at Bashere and Gregorin, frowned at Weiramon as if already knowing the man's blunder, and eyed Ailil and Anaiyella as though he might pinch them. The two women drew back from him hastily, but then, so did the men except for Bashere. Even Morr. Gedwyn's salute to Rand was a casual tap of fist to chest. "I sent scouts out as soon as I saw this lot was done. There are three more columns inside ten miles."

"All headed west," Bashere put in quietly, but he looked

at Gedwyn sharp enough to slice stone. "You've done it," he told Rand. "They're *all* falling back. I doubt they'll stop short of Ebou Dar. Campaigns don't always end with a grand march into the city, and this one is finished."

Surprisingly—or perhaps not—Weiramon began arguing for an advance, to "take Ebou Dar for the glory of the Lord of the Morning," as he put it, but it was certainly a shock to hear Gedwyn say he would not mind taking a few more swipes at these Seanchan and he certainly would not mind seeing Ebou Dar. Even Ailil and Anaiyella added their voices in favor of "putting an end to the Seanchan once and for all," though Ailil did add that she would as soon like to avoid having to return to finish. She was quite sure the Lord Dragon would insist on her company for it. That in a tone as cool and dry as night in the Aiel Waste.

Only Bashere and Gregorin spoke for turning back, and raise their voices they did increasingly as Rand stood silent. Silent and staring west. Toward Ebou Dar.

"We did do what we came for," Gregorin insisted. "Light's mercy, do you think to take Ebou Dar itself?"

Take Ebou Dar, Rand thought. Why not? No one would expect that. A total surprise, for the Seanchan and everybody else.

"Times are, you seize the advantage and ride on," Bashere growled. "Other times, you take your winnings and go home. I say it's time to go home."

I would not mind you in my head, Lews Therin said, sounding almost sane, *if you were not so clearly mad.*

Ebou Dar. Rand tightened his hand on the Dragon Scepter, and Lews Therin cackled.

CHAPTER
24

A Time for Iron

A dozen leagues east of Ebou Dar, *raken* glided in out of the cloud-streaked sunrise to land in a long pasture marked as the fliers' field by colored streamers on tall poles. The brown grasses had been trampled and scored days since. All of the creatures' grace in the air was lost as soon as their claws touched the ground in a lumbering run, leathery pinions thirty paces or more wide held high as if the animal wanted to sweep itself back upward. There was little beauty, either, in the *raken* that ran awkwardly down the field beating ribbed wings, fliers crouching in the saddle as if to pull the beast up by main force, ran on until at last they stumbled into the air, wingtips barely clearing the tops of the olive trees at the end of the field. Only as they gained height and turned toward the sun, soared toward the clouds, did the *raken* regain dignified grandeur. Fliers who landed did not bother to dismount. While a groundling held a basket up for the *raken* to gulp whole shriveled fruits by the double-handful at a time, one of the fliers would hand down their scouting report to a still more senior groundling, and the other bent on the other side to receive new orders from a flier too senior to handle reins personally very often. Almost that quickly after coming to a halt, the creature was reined around to waddle over to where four or five others waited their turn to make that long, ungainly run to the sky.

At a dead run, dodging between moving formations of cavalry and infantry, messengers carried the scouting reports to the huge red-bannered command tent. There were haughty Taraboner lancers and stolid Amadician pikemen in well-ordered squares, breastplates striped horizontally in the colors of the regiments they were attached to. Alta-ran light horse in disordered bunches made their mounts prance, vain of the red slashes crisscrossing their chests, so different from the markings anyone else wore. The Al-tarans did not know those indicated irregulars of doubtful reliability. Among the Seanchan soldiers, named regiments with proud honors were represented, from every corner of the Empire, pale-eyed men from Alqam, honey-brown men from N'Kon, men black as coal from Khoweal and Dalen-shar. There were *morat'torm* on their sinuous bronze-scaled mounts that made horses whicker and dance in fright, and even a few *morat'grolm* with their squat, beak-mouthed charges, but one thing that always accompanied a Seanchan army was conspicuous by it absence. The *sul'dam* and *da-mane* were still in their tents. Captain-General Kennar Miraj thought of *sul'dam* and *damane* a great deal.

From his seat on the dais he could see the map table clearly, where helmetless under-lieutenants checked the re-ports and placed markers to represent the forces in the field. A small paper banner stood above each marker, inked sym-bols giving the size and composition of the force. Finding decent maps in these lands was next to impossible, but the map copied atop the large table was sufficient. And worry-ing, in what it told him. Black discs for outposts overrun or dispersed. Far too many of those, dotting the whole eastern half of the Venir range. Red wedges, for commands on the move, marked the western end as thickly, all pointed back toward Ebou Dar. And scattered among the black discs, seventeen stark white. As he watched, a young officer in the brown-and-black of a *morat'torm* carefully placed an eigh-teenth. Enemy forces. A few might be the same group seen twice, but for the most part they were much too far apart, the timing of the sightings wrong.

Along the walls of the tent, clerks in plain brown coats, marked only with insignia of rank among clerks on the wide collars, waited at their writing tables, pens in hand, for Mi-raj to issue orders that they would copy out for distribution. He had already given what orders he could. There were as many as ninety thousand enemy soldiers in the mountains, nearly twice what he could muster here even with the native levies. Too many for belief, except that scouts did not lie; liars had their throats slit by their fellows. Too many, springing out of the ground like trap-worms in the Sen T'jore. At least they had a hundred miles of mountain yet to cover if they intended to threaten Ebou Dar. Almost two hundred, for the white discs farthest east. And hill country after that for another hundred miles. Surely the enemy general could not mean to let his dispersed forces be confronted one by one. Gathering them together would take more time. Time alone was on his side, right then.

The entry flaps of the tent swept open, and the High Lady Suroth glided in, black hair a proud crest spilling down her back, pleated snow-white gown and richly embroidered over-robe somehow untouched by the mud outside. He had thought her still in Ebou Dar; she must have flown out by *to'raken*. She was accompanied by a small entourage, for her. A pair of Deathwatch Guards with black tassels on their sword hilts held the tentflaps, and more were visible outside, stone-faced men in red-and-green. The embodiment of the Empress, might she live forever. Even the Blood took note of them. Suroth sailed past as if they were as much servants as the lushly bodied *da'covale* in slippers and a nearly transparent white robe, her honey-yellow hair in a multitude of thin braids, who carried the High Lady's gilded writing desk a meek two paces behind. Suroth's Voice of the Blood, Alwhin, a glowering woman in green robes with the left side of her head shaved and the remainder of her pale brown hair in a severe braid, followed close on her mistress's heels. As Miraj stepped down from the dais, he realized with shock that the second *da'covale* behind Suroth, short and dark-haired and slim in her diaphanous robe, was *damane*! A *damane* garbed as property was unheard of, but odder still, it was Alwhin who led her by the *a'dam*!

He let none of his amazement show as he went to one knee, murmuring, "The Light be upon the High Lady Suroth. All honor to the High Lady Suroth." Everyone else prostrated themselves on the canvas groundcloth, eyes down. Miraj was of the Blood, if too low to shave the sides of his scalp like Suroth. Only the nails of his little fingers were lacquered. Much too low to register surprise if a High Lady allowed her Voice to continue acting as *sul'dam* after being raised to the *so'jhin*. Strange times in a strange land, where the Dragon Reborn walked and *marath'damane* ran wild to kill and enslave where they would.

Suroth barely glanced at him before turning to study the map table, and if her black eyes tightened at what she saw, she had cause. Under her, the Hailene had done far more than had been dreamed, reclaiming great stretches of the stolen lands. All they had been sent for was to scout the way, and after Falme, some had thought even that impossible. She drummed fingers on the table irritably, the long blue-lacquered fingernails on the first two clicking. Continued success, and she might be able to shave her head entirely and paint a third nail on each hand. Adoption into the Imperial family was not unheard of for achievements so great. And if she stepped too far, overstepped, she might find her fingernails clipped and herself stuffed into a filmy robe to serve one of the Blood, if not sold to a farmer to help till his fields, or sweat in a warehouse. At worst, Miraj would only have to open his own veins.

He continued to watch Suroth in patient silence, but he had been a scout lieutenant, *morat'raken*, before being raised to the Blood, and he could not help being aware of everything around him. A scout lived or died by what he saw or did not, and so did others. The men lying on their faces around the tent; some hardly seemed to breathe. Suroth should have taken him aside and let them continue with their work. A messenger was being turned back by the soldiers at the entrance. How dire was the message that the woman tried to push past Deathwatch Guards?

The *da'covale* with the writing desk in her arms caught his eye. Scowls flashed across her pretty doll's face, never pushed down for more than moments. Property showing anger? And there was something else. His gaze flickered to the *damane*, who stood with her head down but still looked around with curiosity. Brown-eyed *da'covale* and pale-eyed *damane* looked about as different as two women could, yet there was something about them. Something in their faces. Strange. He could not have said how old either was.

Quick as his glance was, Alwhin noticed. With a twitch of the *a'dam*'s silvery leash she put the *damane* facedown on the groundcloth. Snapping her fingers, she pointed to the canvas with the hand not encumbered by the *a'dam*'s bracelet, then grimaced when the honey-haired *da'covale* did not move. "Down, Liandrin!" she hissed almost under her breath. With a glare for Alwhin—a glare!—the *da'covale* sank to her knees, features painted with sulkiness.

Most strange. But hardly important. Face impassive, and otherwise bursting with impatience, he waited. Impatience and no little discomfort. He had been raised to the Blood after riding fifty miles in a single night with three arrows in him to bring word of a rebel army marching on Seandar itself, and his back still pained him.

Finally, Suroth turned from the map table. She did not give him leave to rise, much less embrace him as one of the Blood. Not that he had expected that. He was far beneath her. "You are ready to march?" she demanded curtly. At least she did not speak to him through her Voice. Before so many of his officers, the shame would have put his eyes on the ground for months if not years.

"I will be, Suroth," he replied calmly, meeting her gaze. He *was* of the Blood, however low. "They cannot combine in fewer than ten days, with at least another ten before they can exit the mountains. Well before then, I—"

"They could be here tomorrow," she snapped. "Today! If they come, Miraj, they will come by the ancient art of Traveling, and it seems very possible that they will come."

He heard men shifting on their bellies before they could restrain themselves. Suroth lost control of her emotions *and* babbled of legends? "Are you certain?" The words popped out of his mouth before he could stop them.

He had only thought she had lost control before. Her eyes blazed. She gripped the edges of her flower-worked robe, white-knuckled, and her hands shook. "Do you question me?" she snarled incredulously. "Suffice it that I have my sources of information." And was furious with them as much as with him, he realized. "If they come, there will be perhaps as many as fifty of these grandly named Asha'man, but no more than five or six thousand soldiers. It seems there have been no more since the beginning, whatever the fliers say."

Miraj nodded slowly. Five thousand men, moved about in some way with the One Power, would explain a great deal. What *were* her sources, that she knew numbers so precisely? He was not fool enough to ask. She certainly had

Listeners and Seekers in her service. Watching her, too. Fifty Asha'man. The very idea of a man channeling made him want to spit in disgust. Rumor claimed they were being gathered from every nation by the Dragon Reborn, this Rand al'Thor, but he had never expected there could be so many. The Dragon Reborn could channel, it was said. That might be true, but he was the Dragon Reborn.

The Prophecies of the Dragon had been known in Seanchan even before Luthair Paendrag began the Consolidation. In corrupted form, it was said, much different from the pure version Luthair Paendrag brought. Miraj had seen several volumes of *The Karaethon Cycle* printed in these lands, and they were corrupted too—not one mentioned him serving the Crystal Throne!—but the Prophecies held men's minds and hearts still. More than a few hoped the Return came soon, that these lands could be reclaimed before Tarmon Gai'don so the Dragon Reborn could win the Last Battle for the glory of the Empress, might she live forever. The Empress surely would want al'Thor sent to her, so she could see what sort of man served her. There would be no difficulty with al'Thor once he had knelt to her. Few easily shook off the awe they felt, kneeling before the Crystal Throne, with the thirst to obey drying their tongues. But it seemed obvious that bundling the fellow onto a ship would be easier if disposing of the Asha'man—they had to be disposed of, certainly—waited until al'Thor was well on his way across the Aryth Ocean to Seandar.

Which brought him back to the problem he had been trying to avoid, he realized with an inward start. He was not a man to shy from difficulties, much less ignore them blindly, but this was different from any he had faced before. He had fought in two dozen battles with *damane* used on both sides; he knew the way of them. It was not only a matter of striking out with the Power. Experienced *sul'dam* could somehow see what *damane* or *marath'damane* did and *damane* would tell the others, so they could defend as well. Could *sul'dam* see what a man did, too? Worse. . . .

"You will release the *sul'dam* and *damane* to me?" he said. Taking a deep breath in spite of himself, he added, "If they're still sick, it will be a short fight and bloody. On our side."

Which produced another stir among the men waiting on

their faces. Every second rumor in the camp was about what illness had confined the *sul'dam* and *damane* to their tents. Alwhin reacted quite openly, most improper in a *so'jhin*, with a furious glare. The *damane* flinched again, and began to shiver where she lay. Oddly, the honey-haired *da'covale* flinched, as well.

Smiling, Suroth glided to where the *da'covale* knelt. Why would she smile at a poorly trained serving girl? She began stroking the kneeling woman's thin braids, and a sullen pout appeared on that rosebud mouth. A former noblewoman of these lands? Suroth's first words supported that, though obviously meant for him. "Small failures bring small costs; great failures bring painfully great costs. You will have the *damane* you require, Miraj. And you will teach these Asha'man they should have remained in the north. You will wipe them from the face of the earth, the Asha'man, the soldiers, all of them. To the man. Miraj. I have spoken."

"It will be as you say, Suroth," he replied. "They will be destroyed. To the man." There was nothing else he could say, now. He wished, though, that she had given him an answer about whether the *sul'dam* and *damane* were still sick.

Rand reined Tai'daishar around near the crest of the bare, stony hill to watch most of his small army spilling out of other holes in the air. He held hard to the True Source, so hard it seemed to tremble in his grasp. With the Power in him, the sharp points of the Crown of Swords pricking his temples felt at once keener than ever and utterly removed, the midmorning chill both colder and beneath notice. The never-healing wounds in his side were a dull and distant ache. Lews Therin seemed to be panting in uncertainty. Or perhaps fear. Maybe after coming so close to death the day before, he did not want so much to die anymore. But then, he did not always want to die. The only constant in the man was the desire to kill. Which just happened to include killing himself, often enough.

There'll be killing enough for anybody, soon, Rand thought. *Light, the last six days were enough to sicken a vulture.* Had it only been six days? The disgust did not touch him, though. He would not let it. Lews Therin did not answer. Yes. It was a time for iron hearts. And iron stomachs, too. He bent a moment to touch the long cloth-wrapped package under his stirrup leather. No. Not time, yet. Maybe not at all. Uncertainty shimmered across the Void, and maybe something else. Not at all, he hoped. Uncertainty, yes, but the other had not been fear. It had not!

Half the surrounding low hills were covered with squat, gnarled olive trees, dappled by the sunlight, where lancers already rode along the rows to make sure they were clear. There was no sign of workers in those orchards, no farmhouse, no structure of any kind in sight. A few miles to the west, the hills were darker, forested. Legionmen, emerging in trotting files below Rand, formed up, trailed by a ragged square of Illianer volunteers, now enlisted into the Legion. As soon as their ranks were aligned, they marched out of the way to make room for Defenders and Companions. The ground seemed mostly clay, and boots and hooves alike skidded in the thin skim of mud. For a wonder, though, only a few clouds hung in the sky, white and clean. The sun was a pale yellow ball. And nothing flew up there larger than a sparrow.

Dashiva and Flinn were among the men holding gateways, as were Adley and Hopwil, Morr and Narishma. Some of the gateways lay out of Rand's sight behind the folded hills. He wanted everyone through as quickly as possible, and except for a few Soldiers scanning the sky, every man in a black coat who was not already out scouting held a weave. Even Gedwyn and Rochaid, though both grimaced over it, at each other and in his direction. Rand thought them no longer used to doing anything so common as holding a gateway for others to use.

Bashere cantered up the slope, very much at ease with himself, and with his short bay. His cloak was flung back despite the morning's coolness, not so cold as the mountains, but still wintery. He nodded casually to Anaiyella and Ailil, who gave bleak stares in return. Bashere smiled through those thick mustaches, like down-curving horns, a not entirely pleasant smile. He had as many doubts of the women as Rand did. The women knew, about Bashere's reservations at least. Turning her head quickly from the Saldaean, Anaiyella returned to stroking her gelding's mane; Ailil held her reins too rigidly.

That pair had not strayed far from Rand since the incident on the ridge, even having their tents pitched in earshot of his the night before. On a brown-grass hillside opposite, Denharad shifted to study the two noblewomen's retainers, arrayed together behind him, then quickly returned to watching Rand. Very likely he watched Ailil, and maybe Anaiyella as well, but he watched Rand without doubt. Rand was unsure whether they still feared to take the blame if he was killed or simply wanted to see it happen. The one thing he was certain of was that if they did want him dead, he would give them no opportunity.

Who knows a woman's heart? Lews Therin chuckled wryly. He sounded in one of his saner moods. *Most women will shrug off what a man would kill you for, and kill you for what a man would shrug off.*

Rand ignored him. The last gateway in Rand's sight winked out. The Asha'man mounting their horses were too far for him to say for sure whether any still held on to *saidin*, but it did not matter so long as he did. Clumsy Dashiva tried to mount quickly and nearly fell off twice before successfully reaching his saddle. Most of the black-coated men in view began riding north or south.

The rest of the nobles gathered quickly with Bashere on the slope just below Rand, the highest ranking and those with the most power in front after a little jostling here and there, where precedence remained uncertain. Tihera and Marcolin kept their horses on the fringes, on opposite sides of the mass of nobles, faces carefully blank; they might be asked for advice, but both knew the final decisions rested with others. Weiramon opened his mouth with a grand gesture, doubtless to begin another splendid peroration on the glories of following the Dragon Reborn. Sunamon and Torean, accustomed to his speeches and powerful enough to take no care around him, reined their horses together and began talking quietly. Sunamon's face wore an unaccustomed hardness, and Torean seemed ready to squabble over a boundary line despite the red satin stripes on his coatsleeves. Square-jawed Bertome and some of the other Cairhienin were not quiet at all, laughing at each other's jokes. Everyone had had a bellyful of Weiramon's grand declamations. Though Semaradrid's scowl deepened every time he looked at Ailil and Anaiyella—he did not like them remaining close to Rand, especially his countrywoman—so perhaps his sourness had more root than Weiramon's windiness.

"About ten miles from us," Rand said loudly, "a good fifty thousand men are preparing to march." They were aware of that, but it pulled every eye to him and silenced every tongue. Weiramon's mouth snapped shut sourly; the fellow did love to hear himself talk. Gueyam and Maraconn, tugging at sharp oiled beards, smiled in anticipation, the fools. Semaradrid looked like a man who had eaten an entire bowl of bad plums; Gregorin and the three lords of the Nine with him merely wore grim determination on their faces. Not fools. "The scouts saw no signs of *sul'dam* or *damane*," Rand went on, "but even without them, even with Asha'man, that's enough to kill a lot of us if anybody forgets the plan. No one *will* forget, though, I'm sure." No charges without orders, this time. He had made that clear as glass, and hard as stone. No haring off because you thought maybe you just might have seen something, either.

Weiramon smiled, managing to put as much oil into it as Sunamon ever could.

It was a simple plan, in its way. They would advance west in five columns, each with Asha'man, and attempt to fall on the Seanchan from every side at once. Or as close to all sides as could be managed. Simple plans were best, Bashere insisted. *If you won't be satisfied with a whole litter of fat piglets,* he had muttered, *if you have to rush into the woods to find the old sow, then don't get too fancy, or she'll gut you.*

No plan of battle survives first contact, Lews Therin said in Rand's head. For a moment, he still seemed lucid. For a moment. *Something is wrong,* he growled suddenly. His voice began to gain intensity, and drift into wild disbelieving laughter. *It can't be wrong, but it is. Something strange, something wrong, skittering, jumping, twitching.* His cackles turned to weeping. *It can't be! I must be mad!* And he vanished before Rand could mute him. Burn him, there was nothing wrong with the plan, or Bashere would have been on it like a duck on a beetle.

Lews Therin *was* mad, no doubt of it. But so long as Rand al'Thor remained sane. . . . A bitter joke on the world, if the Dragon Reborn went mad before the Last Battle even began. "Take your places," he commanded with a wave of the Dragon Scepter. He had to fight down the urge to laugh at that joke.

The large clump of nobles broke apart at his order, milling and muttering as they sorted themselves out. Few liked the way Rand had divided them up. Whatever breaking down of barriers had occurred in the shock of the first fight in the mountains, they had sprung up again almost immediately.

Weiramon frowned over his undelivered speech, but after an elaborate bow that thrust his beard at Rand like a spear he rode north over the hills followed by Kiril Drapaneos, Bertome, Doressin, and several minor Cairhienin lords, every last one of them stony-faced at a Tairen being placed over them. Gedwyn rode by Weiramon's side almost as if he were the one leading, and got dark scowls for it that he affected not to notice. The other groupings were as mixed. Gregorin also headed north, with a sullen Sunamon trying to pretend he was heading in the same direction by happenstance, and Dalthanes leading lesser Cairhienin behind. Jeordwyn Semaris, another of the Nine, followed Bashere south with Amondrid and Gueyam. Those three had accepted the Saldaean almost eagerly for the simple reason that he was not Tairen, or Cairhienin, or Illianer, depending on the man. Rochaid seemed to be trying the same with Bashere that Gedwyn was with Weiramon, but Bashere appeared to ignore it. A little way from Bashere's party, Torean and Maraconn rode with their heads together, likely venting spleen at having Semaradrid placed over them. For that matter, Ershin Netari kept glancing toward Jeordwyn, and standing in his stirrups to look back toward Gregorin and Kiril, though it was improbable he could see them any longer past the hills. Semaradrid, his back iron-rod straight, looked as unflappable as Bashere.

It was the same principle Rand had used all along. He trusted Bashere, and he thought he might be able to trust Gregorin, and none of the others could dare think of turning against him with so many outlanders around him, so many old enemies and so few friends. Rand laughed softly, watching them all ride off from his hillside. They would fight for him, and fight well, because they had no other choice. Any more than he had.

Madness, Lews Therin hissed. Rand shoved the voice away angrily.

He was hardly alone, of course. Tihera and Marcolin had most of the Defenders and Companions mounted in ranks among the olive trees on hills flanking the one where he sat his horse. The rest were out as a screen against surprise. A company of blue-coated Legionmen waited patiently in the hollow below under Masond's eye, and at their rear, as many men in what they had worn surrendering on the heath back in Illian. They were trying to emulate the Legionmen's calm—the other Legionmen, now—trying without a great deal of success.

Rand glanced at Ailil and Anaiyella. The Tairen woman gave him a simpering smile, but it faltered weakly. The Cairhienin woman's face was frost. He could not forget them, or Denharad and their armsmen. His column, in the center, would be the largest, and the strongest by a fair margin. A very fair margin.

Flinn and the men Rand had chosen out after Dumai's Wells rode up the hill toward him. The balding old man always led, though all save Adley and Narishma now wore the Dragon as well as the Sword, and Dashiva had worn it first. In part it was because the younger men deferred to Flinn, with his long experience as a banner-man in the Andoran Queen's Guards. In part it was because Dashiva did not seem to care. He only appeared amused by the others. When he could spare time from talking to himself, that was. Most often, he hardly seemed aware of anything past his own nose.

For that reason, it was something of a shock when Dashiva awkwardly booted his slab-sided mount ahead of the rest. That plain face, so often vague or bemused with the fellow's own thoughts, was fixed in a worried frown. It was *more* than something of a shock when he seized *saidin* as soon as he reached Rand and wove a barrier around them against eavesdropping. Lews Therin did not waste breath—if a disembodied voice *had* breath—on mutters about killing; he lurched for the Source snarling wordlessly, tried to claw the Power away from Rand. And just as abruptly fell silent and vanished.

"There's something askew with *saidin* here, something amiss," Dashiva said, sounding not at all vague. In fact, he sounded . . . precise. And testy. A teacher lecturing a particularly dense pupil. He even stabbed a finger at Rand. "I don't know what it is. Nothing can twist *saidin*, and if it could be twisted, we'd have felt it back in the mountains. Well, there *was* something there, yesterday, but so small. . . . I feel it clearly here, though. *Saidin* is . . . eager. I know; I know. *Saidin* is not alive. But it . . . pulses, here. It is difficult to control."

Rand forced his hand to loosen its grip on the Dragon Scepter. He had always been sure Dashiva was nearly as mad as Lews Therin himself. Usually the man maintained a better hold on himself, though, however precariously. "I've been channeling longer than you, Dashiva. You're just feeling the taint more." He could not soften his tone. Light, he could not go mad yet, and neither could they! "Get to your place. We'll be moving soon." The scouts had to return soon. Even in this flatter country, even limited to no farther than they could see, ten miles would not take long to cover, Traveling.

Dashiva made no move to obey. Instead, he opened his mouth angrily, then snapped it shut. Shaking visibly, he drew a deep breath. "I am well aware how long you have channeled," he said in an icy, almost contemptuous voice, "but surely even you can feel it. Feel, man! I don't like 'strange' applied to *saidin*, and I don't want to die or . . . or be burned out because you're blind! Look at my ward! Look at it!"

Rand stared. Dashiva pushing himself forward was peculiar enough, but Dashiva in a temper? And then he did look at the ward. Really look. The flows should have been as steady as the threads in tight-woven canvas. They vibrated. The ward stood solid as it should be, but the individual threads of the Power shimmered with faint movement. Morr had said *saidin* was strange near Ebou Dar, and for a hundred miles around. They were closer than a hundred miles, now.

Rand made himself feel *saidin*. He was always aware of the Power—anything else meant death or worse—yet he had become used to the struggle. He fought for life, but the fight had become as natural as life. The struggle *was* life. He made himself feel that battle, his life. Cold to make stone shatter into dust. Fire to make stone flash to vapor.

Filth to make a rotten cesspit smell a garden in full flower. And . . . a pulsing, like something quivering in his fist. This was not the sort of throbbing he had felt in Shadar Logoth, when the taint on *saidin* had resonated with the evil of that place, and *saidin* had pulsed with it. The vileness was strong, but steady here. It was *saidin* itself that seemed full of currents and surges. Eager, Dashiva called it, and Rand could see why.

Down the slope, behind Flinn, Morr scrubbed a hand through his hair and looked around uneasily. Flinn alternated shifting on his saddle and easing his sword in its scabbard. Narishma, watching the sky for flying creatures, blinked too often. A muscle twitched in Adley's cheek. Every one of them displayed some sign of nervousness, and little wonder. Relief welled up in Rand. Not madness after all.

Dashiva smiled, a twisted self-satisfied smile. "I cannot believe you didn't notice before." There was very close to a *sneer* in his voice. "You've been holding *saidin* practically day and night since we began this mad expedition. This is a simple ward, but it did not want to form, then it snapped together like pulling out of my hands."

The silver-blue slash of a gateway rotated open atop one of the bare hills, half a mile to the west, and a Soldier pulled his horse through and mounted hurriedly, returning from the scout. Even at a distance, Rand could make out the faint shimmer of the weaves surrounding the gateway before they vanished. The rider had not reached the bottom of the hill before another gateway opened on the crest, and then a third, a fourth, more, one after another, almost as fast as the preceding man could get out of the way.

"But it did form," Rand said. So had the scouts' gateways. "If *saidin* is hard to control, it's always hard, and it still does what you want." But why more difficult here? A question for another time. Light, he wished Herid Fel were still alive; the old philosopher might have had an answer. "Get back with the others, Dashiva," he ordered, but the man stared at him in astonishment, and he had to repeat himself before the fellow let the ward vanish, jerked his horse around without a salute and thumped the animal back down the slope with his heels.

"Some trouble, my Lord Dragon?" Anaiyella simpered. Ailil merely looked at Rand with flat eyes.

Seeing the first scout on the way toward Rand, the others fanned off to north and south, where they would join one of the other columns. Finding them the old-fashioned way would be faster than casting about with gateways. Drawing rein in front of Rand, Nalaam slapped fist to chest—did he look a bit wild-eyed? No matter. *Saidin* still did what the man wielding it made it do. Nalaam saluted and gave his report. The Seanchan were not encamped ten miles away, they were no more than five or six distant, marching east. And they had *sul'dam* and *damane* by the score.

Rand issued his orders as Nalaam galloped away, and his column began moving west. The Defenders and the Companions rode on either flank. The Legionmen marched at the rear, just behind Denharad. A reminder to the noblewomen, and their armsmen, if they needed one. Anaiyella certainly looked over her shoulder often enough, and Ailil's refusal to was pointed. Rand formed the main thrust of the column, Rand and Flinn and the others, just as it would be with the other columns. Asha'man to strike, and men with steel to guard their backs while they killed. The sun still had a long way to climb before midday. Nothing had changed to alter the plan.

Madness waits for some, Lews Therin whispered. *It creeps up on others.*

Miraj rode near the head of his army marching east along a muddy road that wound through hilly olive groves and patchy forest. Not at the head. A full regiment, most Seanchan, rode between him and the forward scouts. He had known generals who wanted to be at the very front. Most were dead. Most had lost the battles they died in. Mud kept down dust, yet word of an army on the move ran like wildfire on the Sa'las Plains, whatever the land. Here and there among the olive trees he spotted an overturned wheelbarrow or an abandoned pruning hook, but the workers had vanished long since. Luckily, they would avoid his opponents as much as they did him. With luck, lacking *raken*, his opponents would not know he was on them until it was too late. Kennar Miraj did not like trusting to luck.

Aside from under-officers ready to produce maps or copy orders and messengers ready to carry them, he rode accompanied only by Abaldar Yulan, small enough to make his quite ordinary brown gelding seem immense, a fiery man with the nails of his little fingers painted green who wore a black wig to conceal his baldness, and Lisaine Jarath, a gray-haired woman from Seandar itself, whose pale plump face and blue eyes were a study in serenity. Yulan was not calm; Miraj's coal-dark Captain of the Air often wore a scowl for the rules that seldom let him touch the reins of a *raken* anymore, but today his frown went bone deep. The sky was clear, perfect weather for *raken*, but by Suroth's command, none of his fliers would be in the saddle today, not here. There were too few *raken* with the Hailene to risk them unnecessarily. Lisaine's calm troubled Miraj more. More than the senior *der'sul'dam* under his command, she was a friend with whom he had shared many a cup of *kaf* and many a game of stones. An animated woman, always bubbling over with enthusiasms and amusement. And she was icy calm, as silent as any *sul'dam* he had tried to question.

Within his sight were twenty *damane* flanking the horsemen, each walking beside her *sul'dam*'s mount. The *sul'dam* bobbed in their saddles, bending to pat a *damane*'s head, straightening only to bend again to stroke her hair. The *damane* looked steady enough to his eye, but plainly the *sul'dam* were on razor's edge. And ebullient Lisaine rode silent as a stone.

A *torm* appeared ahead, racing down the column. Well off to the side, on the edge of the groves, yet horses whickered and shied as the bronze-scaled creature flowed past. A trained *torm* would not attack horses—at least not unless the killing frenzy overtook it, the reason *torm* were no good in battle—but horses trained to be calm around *torm* were in as short supply as *torm* themselves.

Miraj sent a skinny under-lieutenant named Varek to fetch the *morat'torm*'s scouting report. Afoot, and the Light consume whether Varek lost *sei'taer*. He would not waste time on Varek trying to control a mount acquired locally. The man returned faster than he went and made a crisp bow, beginning his report before his back was straight again.

"The enemy is less than five miles due east, my Lord Captain-General, marching in our direction. They are deployed in five columns spaced approximately one mile apart."

So much for luck. But Miraj had considered how he would attack forty thousand with only five himself, and fifty *damane*. Quickly men were galloping with orders to deploy to meet an attempted envelopment, and the regiments behind him began turning into the groves, *sul'dam* riding among them with their *damane*.

Gathering his cloak against a sudden cold wind, Miraj noticed something that made him feel colder still. Lisaine was watching the *sul'dam* vanish into the trees, too. And she had begun to sweat.

Bertome rode easily, letting the wind stream his cloak to one side, but he studied the forested country ahead with a wariness he barely attempted to conceal. Of his four countrymen at his back, only Doressin was truly skilled in the Game of Houses. That fool Tairen dog Weiramon was blind, of course. Bertome glared at the puffed-up buffoon's back. Weiramon rode well ahead of the rest in deep conversation with Gedwyn, and if Bertome needed any further proof that the Tairen would smile at what gagged a goat, it was how he tolerated that hot-eyed young monster. He noticed Kiril glancing sideways at him, and reined his gray farther from the towering man. He had no particular enmity toward the Illianer, but he did hate people looming over him. He could not wait to return to Cairhien, where he did not have to be surrounded by ungainly giants. Kiril Drapaneos was not blind, though, however over-tall. He had sent a dozen scouts forward, too. Weiramon had sent one.

"Doressin," Bertome said softly, then, a little louder, "Doressin, you lump!"

The bony man gave a start in his saddle. Like Bertome, like the other three, he had shaved and powdered the front of his head; the style of marking yourself like a soldier had become quite fashionable. Doressin should have called him a toad in return, the way they had since boyhood, but instead he heeled his gelding up beside Bertome's and leaned close. He was worried, and letting it show, his forehead furrowed deeply. "You realize the Lord Dragon means us to die?" he whispered, glancing at the column trailing behind them. "Blood and fire, I only listened to Colavaere, but I have known I was a dead man since he killed her."

For a moment, Bertome eyed the column of armsmen, snaking back through the rolling hills. The trees were more scattered here than ahead, but still enough to shield an attack until it was right on top of you. The last olive grove lay nearly a mile behind. Weiramon's men rode at the fore, of course, in those ridiculous coats with their fat white-striped sleeves, and then Kiril's Illianers in enough green and red to shame Tinkers. His own people, decently clad in dark blue beneath their breastplates, were still beyond his sight with Doressin's and the others', ahead only of the company of Legionmen. Weiramon had seemed surprised that the foot kept up, though he had hardly set a difficult pace.

It was not really the armsmen Bertome glanced at, though. Seven men rode before even Weiramon's, seven men with hard faces and death-cold eyes, in black coats. One wore a pin in the shape of a silver sword on his tall collar.

"An elaborate way to go about it," he told Doressin dryly. "And I doubt al'Thor would have sent those fellows with us, if we were just being fed into a sausage grinder." Forehead still creased, Doressin opened his mouth again, but Bertome said, "I need to talk to the Tairen." He disliked seeing his childhood friend this way. Al'Thor had unhinged him.

Absorbed in one another, Weiramon and Gedwyn did not hear him riding up on them. Gedwyn was idly playing with his reins, his features cold with contempt. The Tairen was red-faced. "I don't care who you are," he was saying to the black-coated man in a low, hard voice, spittle flying, "I won't take more risk without a command direct from the lips of—"

Abruptly the pair became aware of Bertome, and Weiramon's mouth snapped shut. He glared as if he wanted to kill Bertome. The Asha'man's ever-present smile melted away. The wind gusted, cold and sharp as clouds drifted across the sun, but no colder than Gedwyn's sudden stare. With a small shock Bertome realized the man also wanted to strike him dead on the spot.

Gedwyn's icily murderous gaze did not change, but Weiramon's face underwent a remarkable transformation. The red faded slowly as he produced a smile in an instant, an oily smile with only a trace of mocking condescension. "I've been thinking about you, Bertome," he said heartily. "A pity al'Thor strangled your cousin. With his own hands, I hear. Frankly, I was surprised you came when he called. I've seen him watching you. I fear he plans something more . . . interesting . . . for you than thrashing your heels on the floor while his fingers tighten on your throat."

Bertome suppressed a sigh, and not only at the fool's clumsiness. A good many thought to manipulate him with Colavaere's death. She had been his favorite cousin, but ambitious beyond reason. Saighan had good claims to the Sun Throne, yet she could not have held it against the strength of Riatin or Damodred either one, let alone both together, not without the open blessings of the White Tower or the Dragon Reborn. Still, she *had* been his favorite. What did Weiramon want? Certainly not what it seemed on the surface. Even this Tairen oaf was not *that* simple.

Before he could frame any response, a horseman came galloping toward them through the trees ahead. A Cairhienin, and as he reined to a sudden halt in front of them, that made his horse sit back on its haunches, Bertome recognized one of his own armsmen, a gap-toothed fellow with seamed scars on both cheeks. Doile, he thought. From the Colchaine estates.

"My Lord Bertome," the fellow panted, bowing hastily. "There are two thousand Taraboners hard on my heels. And women with them! With lightning on their dresses!"

"Hard on his heels," Weiramon murmured disparagingly. "We'll see what my man has to say when he gets back. I certainly don't see any—!"

Sudden whoops in the near distance ahead cut him off, and the thunder of hooves, and then quickly galloping lancers appeared, a flowing tide spreading through the trees. Straight toward Bertome and the others.

Weiramon laughed. "Kill whoever you wish, wherever you wish, Gedwyn," he said, drawing sword with a flourish. "I use the methods I use, and that's that!" Racing back toward his armsmen, he waved the blade over his head shouting, "Saniago! Saniago and glory!" It was no surprise he did not add a shout for his country to those for his House and his greatest love.

Spurring in the same direction, Bertome raised his own voice. "Saighan and Cairhien!" No need for sword waving yet. "Saighan and Cairhien!" What *had* the man been after?

Thunder rumbled, and Bertome looked to the sky, perplexed. There were few more clouds than earlier. No; Doile—Dalyn?—had mentioned those women. And then he forgot all about whatever the fool Tairen wanted as steel-veiled Taraboners poured over the wooded hills toward him, the earth blooming fire and the sky raining lightning ahead of them.

"Saighan and Cairhien!" he shouted.

The wind rose.

Horsemen clashed amid thick trees and heavy underbrush, where shadows hung heavily. The light seemed to be failing, the clouds thickening overhead, but it was hard to say with the dense forest canopy for a roof. Booming roars half-drowned the ring of steel on steel, the shouts of men, the screams of horses. Sometimes the ground shook. Sometimes the enemy raised shouts.

"Den Lushenos! Den Lushenos and the Bees!"

"Annallin! Rally to Annallin!"

"Haellin! Haellin! For the High Lord Sunamon!"

The last was the only cry Varek understood in the least, though he suspected any of the locals who named themselves High Lords or Ladies might not be offered the chance to swear the Oath.

He jerked his sword free from where he had jammed it into his opponent's armpit, just above the breastplate, and let the pale little man topple. A dangerous fighter, until he made the mistake of raising his blade too high. The man's bay crashed off through the undergrowth, and Varek spared a moment for regret. The animal looked better than the white-footed dun he was forced to ride. A moment only, and then he was peering through the close-set trees, where it seemed vines dangled from half the branches and bunches of some gray, feathery plant from nearly all.

Sounds of battle rose from every direction, but at first he could see nothing that moved. Then a dozen Altaran lancers appeared at fifty paces, walking their horses and peering about carefully, though the way they talked loudly among themselves more than justified the red slashes crisscrossing their breastplates. Varek gathered his reins, meaning to take them in. An escort, even this undisciplined rabble, might be the difference between the urgent message he carried reaching Banner-General Chianmai and not.

Black streaks flashed from among the trees, emptying Altaran saddles. Their horses dashed in every direction as the riders fell, and then there were only a dozen corpses sprawled on the damp carpet of dead leaves, at least one crossbow bolt jutting from every man. Nothing moved. Varek shivered in spite of himself. Those foot in blue coats had seemed easy at first, with no pikes to stand behind, but they never came into the open, hiding behind trees, in dips in the ground. They were not the worst. He had been sure after the frantic retreat to the ships at Falme that he had seen the worse he ever could see, the Ever Victorious Army in a rout. Not half an hour gone, though, he had seen a hundred Taraboners face one lone man in a black coat. A hundred lancers against one, and the Taraboners had been ripped to shreds. Literally ripped to shreds, men and horses simply exploding as fast he could count; the slaughter had continued after the Taraboners turned to flee, went on so long as one of them remained in sight. Perhaps it was really no worse than having the ground erupt beneath your feet, but at least *damane* usually left enough of you to be buried.

He had been told by the last man he managed to speak to in these woods, a grizzled veteran from home leading a hundred Amadician pikes, that Chianmai was in this direction. Ahead, he spotted riderless horses tied to trees, and men afoot. Maybe they could give him further direction. And he would give them the lash of his tongue for standing about while a battle raged.

When he rode in among them, he forgot tongue-lashings. He had found what he was looking for, but not at all what he wanted to find. A dozen badly burned corpses lay in a row. One, his honey-brown face untouched, was recognizably Chianmai. The men on their feet were all Taraboners, Amadicians, Altarans. Some of them were injured, too. The only Seanchan was a tight-faced *sul'dam* soothing a weeping *damane*.

"What happened here?" Varek demanded. He did not think it was like these Asha'man to leave survivors. Maybe the *sul'dam* had fought him off.

"Madness, my Lord." A hulking Taraboner shrugged away the man who was spreading ointment down his seared left arm. The sleeve appeared to have been burned away clear to the fellow's breastplate, yet despite his burns, he did not grimace. His veil of steel mail hung by a corner from his red-plumed conical helmet, baring a hard face with thick gray mustaches that nearly hid his mouth, and his eyes were insultingly direct. "A group of Illianers, they fell on us without warning. At first, all went well. They had none of the blackcoats with them. Lord Chianmai, he led us bravely, and the . . . the woman . . . channeled lightnings. Then, just as the Illianers broke, the lightnings, they fell among us, too." He cut off with a significant look at the *sul'dam*.

She was on her feet in an instant, shaking her free fist and striding as far toward the Taraboner as the leash attached to her other wrist would allow. Her *damane* lay in a weeping heap. "I will not hear this dog's words against my Zakai! She is a good *damane*! A good *damane*!"

Varek made soothing gestures to the woman. He had seen *sul'dam* make their charges howl for misdeeds, and a few who crippled the recalcitrant, but most would bristle even at one of the Blood who cast aspersions on a favorite. This Taraboner was *not* of the Blood, and by the look of the quivering *sul'dam*, she was ready to do murder. Had the man voiced his ridiculous, unspoken charge, Varek thought she might have killed him on the spot.

"Prayers for the dead must wait," Varek said bluntly. What he was about to do would end with him in the hands of the Seekers, if he failed, but there was not a Seanchan left standing here except the *sul'dam*. "I am assuming command. We will disengage and turn south."

"Disengage!" the heavy-shouldered Taraboner barked. "It will take us *days* to *disengage*! The Illianers, they fight like badgers backed into a corner, the Cairhienin like ferrets in a box. The Tairens, they are not so hard as I have heard, but there are maybe a dozen of these Asha'man, yes? I do not even know where three-quarters of my men are, in this jolly-bag!" Emboldened by his example, the others began giving protest, too.

Varek ignored them. And forbore asking what a "jolly-bag" was; looking at the tangled forest all around, listening

to the clash of battle, the booms of explosions and lightnings, he could imagine. "You will gather your men and
begin pulling back," he said loudly, cutting through their
chatter. "Not too fast; you will act in unison." Miraj's orders
to Chianmai said "with all possible speed"—he had memorized them, in case something happened to the copy in
his saddlebags—"all possible speed," but too much speed
in this, and half the men would be left behind, chopped to
flinders at the enemy's leisure. "Now, move! You fight for
the Empress, may she live forever!"

That last was the sort of thing you told fresh recruits, but
for some reason, the listening men jerked as if he had struck
them all with his quirt. Bowing quickly and deeply, hands
on knees, they all but flew to their horses. Strange. Now
it was up to him to find the Seanchan units. One of those
would be commanded by someone above him, and he could
pass his responsibility.

The *sul'dam* was on her knees, stroking her still weeping *damane*'s hair and crooning softly. "Get her soothed
down," he told her. With all possible speed. And he thought
he had seen a touch of anxiety in Miraj's eyes. What could
make Kennar Miraj anxious? "I think we will be depending
on you *sul'dam* to the south." Now, why would that make
the blood drain from her face?

Bashere stood just inside the edge of the trees, frowning
through his helmet's face-bars at what he saw. His bay nuz-
zled his shoulder. He held his cloak close against the wind.
More to avoid any motion that would draw eyes than for
the cold, though that chilled his flesh. It would have been a
spring breeze back in Saldaea, but months in the southlands
had softened him. Shining bright between gray clouds that
sailed along quickly, the sun still lay a little short of midday. And ahead of him. Just because you began a battle facing west did not mean you ended it that way. Before him
lay a broad pasture where flocks of black-and-white goats
cropped at the brown grass in desultory fashion just as if
there was no battle raging all around them. Not that there
was any sign of it here. For the moment. A man could get
himself cut to doll rags crossing that meadow. And in the
trees, whether forest or olive groves or thickets, you did not

always see the enemy before you were on top of him, scouts or no scouts.

"If we're going to cross," Gueyam muttered, rubbing a wide hand over his bald head, "we should cross. Light's truth, we're wasting time." Amondrid snapped his mouth shut; likely, the moon-faced Cairhienin had been about to say much the same thing. He would agree with a Tairen when horses climbed trees.

Jeordwyn Semaris snorted. The man should have grown a beard to hide that narrow jaw. It made his head look like a forester's splitting wedge. "I do say go around," he muttered. "I've lost enough men to those Light-cursed *damane*, and . . ." He trailed off with an uneasy glance toward Rochaid.

The young Asha'man stood by himself, mouth tight, fingering that Dragon pin on his collar. Maybe wondering whether it was worth it, by the look of him. There was no knowing air about the boy now, only frowning worry.

Leading Quick by the reins, Bashere strode to the Asha'man and drew him farther aside in the trees. Pushed him farther aside. Rochaid scowled, going reluctantly. The man was tall enough to loom over Bashere, but Bashere was having none of it.

"Can I count on your people next time?" Bashere demanded, jerking a mustache in irritation. "No delays?" Rochaid and his fellows seemed to have grown slower and slower in responding when they found themselves opposite *damane*.

"I know what I'm about, Bashere," Rochaid snarled. "Aren't we killing enough of them for you? As far as I can see, we're about done!"

Bashere nodded slowly. Not in agreement with the last. There were plenty of enemy soldiers left, almost anywhere you looked hard enough. But a good many *were* dead. He had patterned his movements on what he had studied of the Trolloc Wars, when the forces of the Light seldom came anywhere near the numbers they had to face. Slash at the flanks, and run. Slash at the rear, and run. Slash, and run, and when the enemy chased after, turn on the ground you had chosen beforehand, where the legionmen lay waiting with their crossbows, turn and cut at him until it was time to run again. Or until he broke. Already today he had broken

Taraboners, Amadicians, Altarans *and* these Seanchan in their strange armor. He had seen more enemy dead than in any fight since the Blood Snow. But if he had Asha'man, the other side had those *damane*. A good third of his Saldaeans lay dead along the miles behind. Nearly half his force was dead, all told, and there were still more Seanchan out there with their cursed women, and Taraboners, and Amadicians and Altarans. They just kept coming, more appearing as soon as he finished the last. And the Asha'man were growing . . . hesitant.

Swinging into Quick's saddle, he rode back to Jeordwyn and the others. "We go around," he ordered, ignoring Jeordwyn's nods as much as he did Gueyam and Amondrid's scowls. "Triple scouts out. I mean to push hard, but I don't want to trip over a *damane*." No one laughed.

Rochaid had gathered the other five Asha'man around him, one with a silver sword pinned to his collar, the others without. There had been two more with bare collars when they started out that morning, but if Asha'man knew how to kill, so did *damane*. Waving his arms angrily, Rochaid appeared to be arguing with them. His face was red, theirs blank and stubborn. Bashere just hoped Rochaid could keep all of them from deserting. Today had been costly enough without adding that sort of man wandering about loose.

A light rain fell. Rand scowled at the thick black clouds gathering in the sky, already beginning to obscure a pale sun halfway down to the far horizon. Light rain now, but it would thicken like those clouds! Irritably he returned to studying the land ahead of him. The Crown of Swords pricked his temples. With the Power in him, the land was clear as a map despite the weather. Clear enough, anyway. Hills sinking away, some covered with thickets or olive trees, others bare grass or just stone and weeds. He thought he saw movement at the edge of a copse, then again among the rows of an olive orchard on another hill a mile from the copse. Thinking was not enough. Dead men lay across the miles behind, dead enemies. Dead women, too, he knew, but he had stayed away from anywhere *sul'dam* and *damane* had died, refused to see their faces. Most thought it was hatred for those who killed so many of his followers.

Tai'daishar frisked a few steps on the hilltop before Rand settled him with a firm hand and the pressure of his knees. A fine thing if a *sul'dam* spotted *his* movement. The few trees around him were not enough to hide much. Vaguely, he realized he did not recognize a one of them. Tai'daishar tossed his head. Rand tucked the Dragon Scepter into his saddlebags, just the carved butt end sticking out, to free both hands in case the gelding was not satisfied. He could have taken weariness from the horse with *saidin*, but he knew no way to make it obey with the Power.

He could not see how the gelding retained enough energy. *Saidin* filled him, bubbled in him, but his distantly felt body wanted to sag with weariness. Part of that was the sheer amount of the Power he had handled today. Part was the strain of fighting *saidin* to make it do what he wanted. Always, *saidin* had to be conquered, forced, but never before like today. The half-healed, never-healing wounds in his left side were agony, the older an auger trying to drill through the Void, the newer a blaze of raw flame.

"It was an accident, my Lord Dragon," Adley said suddenly. "I swear it was!"

"Shut up and watch!" Rand told him harshly. Adley's eyes sank to his hands on his own reins for a moment, then he raked damp hair out of his face and jerked his head up obediently.

Today, here, controlling *saidin* was harder than ever, but letting it slip anytime, anywhere, could kill you. Adley had let it slip, and men had died in uncontrolled bursts of fire, not just the Amadicians he had been aiming at, but near thirty of Ailil's armsmen and almost as many of Anaiyella's.

Except for his slip, Adley would have been with Morr, with the Companions in the woods half a mile to the south. Narishma and Hopwil were with the Defenders, to the north. Rand wanted Adley under his eye. Had any other "accidents" happened, out of his sight? He could not watch everyone, all the time. Flinn's face was grim as day-old death, and Dashiva, far from looking vague, seemed on the point of sweating with concentration. He still muttered to himself under his breath, so low Rand could not hear even with the Power in him, but the man mopped rain from his face continually with a sodden lace-edged linen handkerchief that had grown more than grimy as the day wore on. Rand did not think they had slipped. In any case, neither they nor Adley held the Power now. Nor would until he instructed them to seize it.

"Is it done?" Anaiyella asked behind him.

Heedless of who might be watching out there, Rand wheeled Tai'daishar around to face her. The Tairen woman started back in her saddle, the hood of her richly elaborate rain cape falling to her shoulders. Her cheek gave a twitch. Her eyes might have been full of fear, or hate. At her side, Ailil fingered her reins calmly with red-gloved hands.

"What more can you want?" the smaller woman asked in a cool voice. A lady being polite to a menial. Barely. "If the size of a victory is accounted by dead enemies, I think today alone will put your name in the histories."

"I mean to drive the Seanchan into the sea!" Rand snapped. Light, he *had* to finish them now, when he had the chance! He could not fight the Seanchan and the Forsaken and the Light alone knew who or what else, all at the same time! "I did it before, and I will again!"

Do you have the Horn of Valere hidden in your pocket this time? Lews Therin asked slyly. Rand snarled at him silently.

"There's someone below," Flinn said suddenly. "Riding up this way. From the west."

Rand pulled his mount back around. Legionmen ringed the slopes of the hill, though they hid well enough that he seldom caught sight of a blue coat. None of them had a horse. Who would be riding . . .

Bashere's bay trotted up the slope almost as though it were level ground. Bashere's helmet hung from his saddle, and the man himself looked tired. Without preamble, he spoke in a flat voice. "We're finished, here. Part of fighting is knowing when to go, and it's time. I've left five hundred dead behind, near enough, and two of your Soldiers for salt. I sent three more to find Semaradrid, Gregorin and Weiramon and tell them to rally on you. I doubt they're in any better condition than I am. How does *your* butcher's bill run?"

Rand ignored the question. His own dead topped Bashere's by close to two hundred. "You had no right sending orders to the others. So long as there are half a dozen

Asha'man left—so long as there's me!—I have enough! I mean to find the rest of the Seanchan army and destroy it, Bashere. I won't let them add Altara to Tarabon and Amadicia."

Bashere knuckled his thick mustaches with a wry laugh. "You want to find them. Look out there." He swept a gauntleted hand across the hills to the west. "I can't point to a particular spot, but there are ten, maybe fifteen thousand close enough to see from here, if those trees weren't in the way. I danced with the Dark One getting through them unseen to reach you. Maybe a hundred *damane* down there. Maybe more. More coming, for sure, and more men. Seems their general has decided to concentrate on you. I suppose it isn't always cheese and ale being *ta'veren*."

"If they're out there . . ." Rand scanned the hills. The rain fell more heavily. Where had he seen movement? Light, he was tired. *Saidin* hammered at him. Unconsciously he touched the wrapped bundle beneath his stirrup leather. His hand jerked away of its own accord. Ten thousand, even fifteen . . . Once Semaradrid reached him, and Gregorin, and Weiramon . . . More important, once the rest of the Asha'man did . . . "If they're out there, that's where I'll destroy them, Bashere. I'll hit them from all sides, the way we intended in the first place."

Frowning, Bashere reined his horse closer, until his knee almost touched Rand's. Flinn moved his mount away, but Adley was too focused on staring through the rain to notice anything so near, and Dashiva, still wiping his face incessantly, stared with open interest. Bashere lowered his voice to a murmur. "You aren't thinking straight. That was a good plan, in the beginning, but their general thinks fast. He spread out to blunt our attacks before we could fall on him spread out marching. We've cost him even so, it seems, and now he's pulling everything together. You won't catch him by surprise. He *wants* us to come at him. He's out there *waiting* for it. Asha'man or no Asha'man, if we stand nose-to-nose with this fellow, I think maybe the vultures grow fat and nobody rides away."

"Nobody stands nose-to-nose with the Dragon Reborn," Rand growled. "The Forsaken could tell him that, whoever he is. Right, Flinn? Dashiva?" Flinn nodded uncertainly. Dashiva flinched. "You think I can't surprise him, Bashere?

Watch!" Pulling the long bundle loose, he stripped away the cloth covering, and Rand heard gasps as raindrops glistened on a sword seemingly made of crystal. The Sword That Is Not a Sword. "Let's see if he's surprised by *Callandor* in the hands of the Dragon Reborn, Bashere."

Cradling the translucent blade in the crook of his elbow, Rand rode Tai'daishar forward a few steps. There was no reason to. He had no clearer view from there. Except . . . Something spidered across the outer surface of the Void, a wriggling black web. He was afraid. The last time he had used *Callandor,* really used it, he had tried to bring the dead back to life. He had been sure he could do anything, then, anything at all. Like a madman thinking he could fly. But he was the Dragon Reborn. He *could* do anything. Had he not proved it time and again? He reached for the Source through the Sword That Is Not a Sword.

Saidin seemed to leap into *Callandor* before he touched the Source through it. From pommel to point, the crystal sword shone with a white light. He had only thought the Power filled him before. Now he held more than ten men could have unaided, a hundred, he did not know how many. The fires of the sun, searing through his head. The cold of all of the winters of all the Ages, eating into his heart. In that torrent, the taint was all the midden heaps in the world emptying into his soul. *Saidin* still tried to kill him, tried to scour away, burn away, freeze away, every scrap of him, but he fought, and he lived for a moment more, and another moment, another. He wanted to laugh. He *could* do anything!

Once, holding *Callandor,* he had made a weapon that searched out Shadowspawn through the Stone of Tear, struck them dead with hunting lightning wherever they stood or ran or hid. Surely there must be something like that, to use against his enemies here. But when he called to Lews Therin, only anguished whimpers answered, as if that disembodied voice feared the pain of *saidin.*

With *Callandor* blazing in his hand—he did not remember raising the blade overhead—he stared at the hills where his enemies hid. They were gray now, with thickening rain, and dense black clouds blocking the sun. What was it he had told Eagan Padros?

"I am the storm," he whispered—a shout in his ears, a roar—and he channeled.

Overhead, the clouds boiled. Where they had been the black of soot, they became midnight, the heart of midnight. He did not know what he was channeling. So often, he did not, in spite of Asmodean's teaching. Maybe Lews Therin was guiding him, in spite of the man's weeping. Flows of *saidin* spun across the sky, Wind and Water and Fire. Fire. The sky truly did rain lightning. A hundred bolts at once, hundreds, forked blue-white shafts stabbing down as far as he could see. The hills before him erupted. Some flew apart under the torrent of lightning like kicked anthills. Flames sprang up in thickets, trees turning to torches in the rain, flames racing through olive orchards.

Something struck him hard, and he realized he was picking himself up from the ground. The crown had fallen from his head. *Callandor* still blazed in his hand, though. Vaguely, he was aware of Tai'daishar scrambling to his feet, trembling. So they thought to strike back at him, did they.

Shoving *Callandor* high, he screamed at them. "Come against me, if you dare! I *am* the storm! Come if you dare, Shai'tan! I am the Dragon Reborn!" A thousand sizzling lightning bolts hailed down from the clouds.

Again something struck him down. He tried to fight up again. *Callandor*, still shining, lay a pace from his outstretched hand. The sky shattered with lightnings. Suddenly, he realized that the weight atop him was Bashere, that the man was shaking him. It must have been Bashere who had flung him down!

"Stop it!" the Saldaean shouted. Blood fanned down his face from a split across his scalp. "You're killing us, man! Stop!"

Rand turned his head, and one stunned look was enough. Lightnings flashed *all* around him, in *every* direction. A bolt stabbed down onto the reverse slope, where Denharad and the armsmen were; the screams of men and horses rose. Anaiyella and Ailil were both afoot, trying vainly to quiet mounts that reared, eyes rolling, trying to rip reins free. Flinn was bending over someone, not far from a dead horse with legs already stiff.

Rand let *saidin* go. He let it go, but for moments it still flowed into him, and lightning raged. The flow into him dwindled, tailed off and vanished. Dizziness swept through him in its place. For three more heartbeats, two of *Cal-*

landor shone where they lay on the ground, and lightning fell. Then, silence except for the rising drum of the rain. And the screams from behind the hill.

Slowly Bashere climbed off of him, and Rand rose unaided on tottering legs, blinking as his sight returned to normal. The Saldaean watched him as he might have a rabid lion, fingering his sword hilt. Anaiyella took one look at Rand on his feet and collapsed in a faint; her horse dashed away, reins dangling. Ailil, still fighting her rearing animal, spared few glances for Rand. Rand let *Callandor* lie where it was for the moment. He was not sure he dared pick it up. Not yet.

Flinn straightened, shaking his head, then stood silently as Rand went unsteadily to stand beside him. The rain fell on Jonan Adley's sightless eyes, bulging as if in horror. Jonan had been one of the first. Those screams from behind the hill seemed to slice through the rain. How many more, Rand wondered. Among the Defenders? The Companions? Among . . . ?

Rain thick as a blanket hid the hills where the Seanchan army lay. Had he hurt them at all, striking out blindly? Or were they still waiting out there with all their *damane*? Waiting to see how many more of his own he could kill for them.

"Set whatever guard you think we need," Rand told Bashere. His voice was iron. One of the first. His heart was iron. "When Gregorin and the others reach us, we'll Travel to where the carts are waiting as fast as we can." Bashere nodded without speaking, and turned away in the rain.

I've lost, Rand thought dully. *I'm the Dragon Reborn, but for the first time, I've lost.*

Suddenly, Lews Therin raged up inside him, sly digs forgotten. *I've* never *been defeated*, he snarled. *I am the Lord of the Morning!* No *one can defeat me!*

Rand sat in the rain, turning the Crown of Swords in his hands, looking at *Callandor* lying in the mud. He let Lews Therin rage.

Abaldar Yulan wept, grateful for the downpour that hid the tears on his cheeks. Someone would have to give the order. Eventually someone would have to apologize to the Empress, might she live forever, and maybe to Suroth sooner.

Those were not why he wept, though, nor even for a dead comrade. Roughly ripping a sleeve from his coat, he laid it across Miraj's staring eyes so the rain would not fall in them.

"Send out orders for retreat," Yulan ordered, and saw the men standing around him jerk. For the second time on these shores, the Ever Victorious Army had suffered a devastating defeat, and Yulan did not think he was the only one who wept.

CHAPTER
25

An Unwelcome Return

Seated behind her gilded writing table, Elaida fingered an age-dark ivory carving of a strange bird with a beak as long as its body and listened with some amusement to the six women standing on the other side on the table. Each a Sitter for her Ajah, they frowned sideways at one another, shifted velvet slippers on the brightly patterned carpet that covered most of the russet floor tiles, twitched at vine-worked shawls so the colored fringes danced, and generally looked and sounded like a gaggle of peevish serving girls wishing they had the nerve to go for each others' throats in front of their mistress. Frost coated the glassed casements fitted into the windows so that it was hardly possible to see the snow swirling outside, though sometimes the winds howled with an icy rage. Elaida felt quite warm, and not just for the thick logs blazing in the white marble fireplace. Whether these women knew it or not—well, Duhara knew, certainly, and perhaps the others did—she *was* their mistress. The elaborate gold-covered case clock that Cemaile had commissioned ticked away. Cemaile's vanished dream *would* come true; the Tower returned to its glory. And firmly in the capable hands of Elaida do Avriny a'Roihan.

"No *ter'angreal* has ever been found that can 'control' a woman's channeling," Velina was saying in a voice cool and precise but almost girlishly high-pitched, a voice at strong odds with her eagle's beak of a nose and her sharp, tilted eyes. She sat for the White, and was the very model of a White sister, in all but her fierce appearance. Her plain, snowy dress seemed stark and cold. "Very few have ever been found that perform the same function. Therefore, logically, if such a *ter'angreal* were found, or more than one, improbable as that must be, there could not be sufficient of them to control more than two or three women at most. It follows that the reports of these so-called Seanchan are exaggerated wildly. If women on 'leashes' exist, they cannot channel. Plainly not. I do not deny these people hold Ebou Dar, and Amador, and perhaps more, but clearly they are but a creation of Rand al'Thor, perhaps to frighten people into flocking to him. Like this Prophet of his. It is simple logic."

"I am very glad you don't deny Amador and Ebou Dar at least, Velina," Shevan said drily. And she could be *very* dry indeed. As tall as most men, and bonily thin with it, the Brown Sitter had an angular face and a long chin, not improved by a cap of curls. With spidery fingers she rearranged her shawl and smoothed skirts of dark golden silk, and her voice took on pointed amusement. "I'm uncomfortable saying what can and can't be. For example, not long gone, everyone 'knew' only a shield woven by a sister could stop a woman channeling. Then comes a simple herb, forkroot, and anyone at all can feed you a tea that leaves you unable as a stone to channel for hours. Useful with unruly wilders or the like, I suppose, but a nasty little surprise for those who think they knew everything, eh? Maybe next, someone will learn to make *ter'angreal* again."

Elaida's mouth tightened. She did not concern herself with impossibilities, and if no sister had managed to rediscover the making of *ter'angreal* in three thousand years, one never would and that was that. It was knowledge slipping through her fingers when she wanted it held close that curled Elaida's tongue. In spite of all her efforts, every last initiate in the Tower had learned of forkroot, now. No one liked knowing in the least. No one liked suddenly being vulnerable to anyone with a knowledge of herbs and a little hot water. That knowledge was worse than poison, as the Sitters here made clear.

At mention of the herb, Duhara's big, dark eyes grew uneasy in her coppery face, and she held herself more stiffly than usual, hands clutching skirts so red they seemed nearly black. Sedore actually swallowed, and her fingers tightened on the worked leather folder Elaida had handed her, though the round-faced Yellow usually carried herself with a frosty elegance. Andaya shivered! She actually wrapped her gray-fringed shawl around her convulsively.

Elaida wondered what they would do if they learned the Asha'man had rediscovered Traveling. As it was, they were barely able to make themselves speak of them. At least she had managed to hold that knowledge to a handful.

"I think we might better concern ourselves with what we know to be true, yes?" Andaya said firmly, back in control of herself. Her light brown hair, brushed till it gleamed, hung flowing down her back, and her silver-slashed blue dress was cut in the style of Andor, but Tarabon still rested strongly on her tongue. Though neither particularly small nor particularly slim, she somehow always reminded Elaida of a sparrow about to hop on a branch. A most unlikely-appearing negotiator, though her reputation had been earned. She smiled at the others, not very pleasantly, and that seemed sparrowlike, too. Perhaps it was how she held her head. "Idle speculation, it wastes precious time. The world hangs by a thread, and myself, I do not wish to fritter away valuable hours prattling about supposed logic or chattering over what every fool and novice knows. Does anyone have anything useful to say?" For a sparrow, she could put acid on her words. Velina's face went red, and Shevan's darkened.

Rubinde twisted her lips at the Gray. Perhaps they were meant to make a smile, but they merely seemed to writhe. With raven-black hair and eyes like sapphires, the Mayener usually looked as if she intended to walk through a stone wall, and planting her fists on her hips now, she seemed ready to walk through two. "We've dealt with what we can for the time being, Andaya. Most of it, anyway. The rebels are caught by the snows in Murandy, and we'll make winter hot enough for them that in the spring they'll come crawling back to apologize and beg penance. Tear will be taken care of as soon as we find where the High Lord Darlin has vanished to, and Cairhien once we root Caraline Damodred and Toram Riatin out of their hiding places. Al'Thor has the crown of Illian for the moment, but that's in work. So, unless you have a scheme for snaffling the man into the Tower or making these so-called 'Asha'man' vanish, I have the business of my Ajah to be about."

Andaya drew herself up, her feathers well and truly ruffled. For that matter, Duhara's eyes narrowed; mention of men who could channel always lit fires in her head. Shevan clicked her tongue as if at children squabbling—though she looked pleased to see it—and Velina frowned, for some reason sure Shevan had aimed at her. This was amusing, but getting out of hand.

"The business of the Ajahs is important, daughters." Elaida did not raise her voice, but every head swiveled toward her. She replaced the ivory carving with the rest of her collection in the large box covered with roses and golden scrolls, carefully adjusted the positions of her writing case and correspondence box so the three lacquered boxes lined up just so on the table, and once their silence was perfect she went on. "The business of the Tower is *more* important, though. I trust you will effect my decrees promptly. I see too much sloth in the Tower. I fear Silviana may find herself very busy if matters do not come right soon." She did not voice any further threat. She merely smiled.

"As you command, Mother," murmured six voices not so steady as their owners might have wished. Even Duhara's face was pasty pale as they made their curtsies. Two Sitters had been stripped of their chairs, and half a dozen had served days of Labor for penance—which was humiliating enough in their position to be Mortification of the Spirit besides; Shevan and Sedore certainly wore tight mouths as they remembered all too well scrubbing floors and working in the laundries—but none had been sent to Silviana for Mortification of the Flesh. No one wanted to be. The Mistress of Novices had two or three visits each week from sisters who had been given penance by their Ajahs or set one for themselves—a dose of the strap, however painful, was done with much more quickly than raking garden paths for a month—but Silviana possessed considerably less mercy with sisters than with the novices and Accepted in her charge. More than one sister must have spent the next few days wondering whether a month pulling a rake might not have been preferable after all.

They scurried toward the doors, eager to be away. Sitters or no, not one would have set foot this high in the Tower without Elaida's direct summons. Fingering her striped stole, Elaida let her smile become one of pleasure. Yes, she was the mistress in the White Tower. As was only proper for the Amyrlin Seat.

Before that fast-stepping knot of Sitters reached the doorway, the left-hand door opened, and Alviarin stepped in, the narrow white stole of the Keeper almost vanishing against a silk dress that made Velina's seem dingy.

Elaida felt her smile go crooked and begin sliding from her face. Alviarin had a single sheet of parchment in one slim hand. Odd, what one noticed at a time like this. The woman had been gone almost two weeks, vanished from the Tower without word or note, without anyone so much as seeing her go, and Elaida had begun to think fond thoughts of Alviarin lying in a snowbank, or swept away in a river, sliding beneath the ice.

The six Sitters skidded to a halt uncertainly when Alviarin did not move out of their way. Even a Keeper with Alviarin's influence did not impede Sitters. Though Velina, normally the most self-possessed woman in the Tower, flinched for some reason. Alviarin glanced once at Elaida, coolly, studied the Sitters for a moment, and understood everything.

"I think you should leave that with me," she said to Sedore in tones only a fraction warmer than the snow outside. "The Mother likes to consider her decrees carefully, as you know. This would not be the first time she changed her mind after signing." She held out a slim hand.

Sedore, whose arrogance was notable even among Yellows, barely hesitated before giving her the leather folder.

Elaida ground her teeth in fury. Sedore had hated her five days up to her elbows in hot water and scrub boards. Elaida would find something less comfortable for her next time. Maybe Silviana after all. Maybe cleaning the cesspits!

Alviarin stepped aside without a word, and the Sitters went, adjusting shawls, muttering to themselves, reassuming the dignity of the Hall. Briskly, Alviarin closed the door behind them and walked toward Elaida thumbing through the papers in the folder. The decrees she had signed hoping Alviarin was dead. Of course, she had not rested on hope. She had not spoken to Seaine, in case someone might see and tell Alviarin when she returned, but Seaine was certainly working away as instructed, following the path of treason that surely would lead to Alviarin Freidhen. But Elaida had hoped. Oh, how she had hoped.

Alviarin murmured to herself as she rifled through the folder. "This can go through, I suppose. But not this. Or this. And certainly not this!" She crumpled a decree, signed and sealed by the Amyrlin Seat, and tossed it to the floor contemptuously. Stopping beside Elaida's gilded chair, with the Flame of Tar Valon in moonstones atop its high back, she slapped the folder and her own parchment down on the table. And then slapped Elaida's face so hard she saw black flecks.

"I thought we had settled this, Elaida." The monstrous woman's voice made the snowstorm outside seem warm. "I know how to save the Tower from your blunders, and I won't have you making new ones behind my back. If you persist, be assured that I will see you deposed, stilled, and howling under the birch before every initiate and even the servants!"

With an effort, Elaida kept her hand away from her cheek. She did not need a mirror to tell her it was red. She had to be careful. Seaine had found nothing yet, or she would have come. Alviarin could open her mouth before the Hall and reveal the whole disastrous kidnapping of the al'Thor boy. She might see her deposed, and stilled and birched with that alone, but Alviarin had another string to her bow. Toveine Gazal was leading fifty sisters and two hundred of the Tower Guard against a Black Tower Elaida had been sure, when she gave the orders, held perhaps two or three men who could channel. Yet even with the hundreds—hundreds! with Alviarin staring coldly down at her, that thought still curdled Elaida's stomach!—even with hundreds of these Asha'man, she had hope for Toveine. The Black Tower would be rent in fire and blood, she had Foretold, and sisters would walk its grounds. Surely that meant that somehow, Toveine would triumph. More, the rest of the Foretelling had told her that the Tower would regain all its old glories under her, that al'Thor himself would quail at her anger. Alviarin had heard the words coming out of Elaida's mouth when the Foretelling took her. And she had not remembered later, when she began her blackmail, had not understood her own doom. Elaida waited in patience.

She would repay the woman three-fold! But she could be patient. For now.

Making no attempt to hide her sneer, Alviarin pushed the folder aside and moved the single parchment in front of Elaida. She flipped open the green-and-gold writing case, dipped Elaida's pen in the inkwell and thrust it at her. "Sign."

Elaida took the pen wondering what madness she would be putting her name to this time. Yet another increase in the Tower Guard, when the rebels would be done before there was any use for soldiers? Another attempt to make the Ajahs reveal publicly which sisters headed them? That had certainly fallen on its nose! Reading quickly, she felt a knot of ice grow in her belly and keep growing. Giving each Ajah final authority over any sister in its quarter no matter her own Ajah had been the worst insanity so far—how could picking apart the very fabric of the Tower save it?—but this—!

The world now knows that Rand al'Thor is the Dragon Reborn. The world knows that he is a man who can touch the One Power. Such men have lain within the authority of the White Tower since time immemorial. The Dragon Reborn is granted the protection of the Tower, but whosoever attempts to approach him save through the White Tower lies attainted of treason against the Light, and anathema is pronounced against them now and forever. The world may rest easily knowing that the White Tower will safely guide the Dragon Reborn to the Last Battle and the inevitable triumph.

Automatically, numbly, she added "of the Light" after "triumph," but then her hand froze. Publicly acknowledging al'Thor as the Dragon Reborn could be borne, since he was, and this might lead many to accept the rumors that he had knelt to her already, which would prove useful, but for the rest, she could not believe so much damage could be contained in so few words.

"The Light have mercy," she breathed fervently. "If this is proclaimed, it will be impossible to convince al'Thor that his abduction was unsanctioned." It would be hard enough without, but she had seen people convinced before that what had happened, had not, and them in the middle of it happening. "And he will be ten times on his guard against another attempt. Alviarin, at best, this will frighten away a few of his followers. At best!" Many likely had waded so deep with him they did not dare try to wade back. Certainly not if they thought anathema already hung over their heads! "I might as well set fire to the Tower with my own hand as sign this!"

Alviarin sighed impatiently. "You haven't forgotten your catechism, have you? Say it for me, as I taught you."

Elaida's lips compressed of their own accord. One pleasure in the woman's absence—not the greatest, but a very real pleasure—had been not being forced to repeat that vile litany every day. "I will do as I am told," she said at last, in a flat voice. She was the Amyrlin Seat! "I will speak the words you tell me to speak, and no more." Her Foretelling ordained her triumph, but, oh, Light, let it come soon! "I will sign what you tell me to sign, and nothing else. I am . . ." She choked over the last. "I am obedient to your will."

"You sound as if you need to be reminded of the truth of that," Alviarin said with another sigh. "I suppose I've left you alone too long." She tapped the parchment with a peremptory finger. "Sign."

Elaida signed, dragging the pen across the parchment. There was nothing else she could do.

Alviarin barely waited for the pen's nib to lift before snatching up the decree. "I will seal this myself," she said, heading for the door. "I shouldn't have left the Amyrlin's seal where you could find it. I want to talk to you later. I *have* left you to yourself too long. Be here when I return."

"Later?" Elaida said. "When? Alviarin? Alviarin?"

The door closed behind the woman, leaving Elaida to fume. Be there when Alviarin returned! Confined to her quarters like a novice in the punishment cells!

For a time she fingered her correspondence box, with its golden hawks fighting among white clouds in a blue sky, yet she could not make herself open it. With Alviarin gone, that box had begun once more to hold letters and reports of importance, not just the table scraps Alviarin let fall to her, yet with the woman's return, it might as well have been empty. Rising, she began rearranging the roses in their white vases, each atop a white marble plinth in a corner of the room. Blue roses; the most rare.

Abruptly she realized that she was staring at a broken rose stem in her hands, snapped in two. Half a dozen more littered the floor tiles. She made a vexed sound in her throat. She had been thinking of her hands around Alviarin's throat. It was not the first time she had considered killing the woman. But Alviarin would have taken precautions. Sealed documents, to be opened should anything untoward happen, had no doubt been left with the last sisters Elaida would suspect. That had been her one real worry during Alviarin's absence, that someone else might think the woman dead, and come forward with the evidence that would drag the stole from her shoulders. Sooner or later, though, one way or another, Alviarin was finished, as surely as those roses were—

"You didn't answer my knock, Mother, so I came on in," a woman said gruffly behind her.

Elaida turned, ready to flay with her tongue, but at the sight of the stocky, square-faced woman in a red-fringed shawl standing just inside the room, the blood drained from her own cheeks.

"The Keeper said you wanted to speak me," Silviana said irritably. "About a private penance." Even to the Amyrlin Seat, she made no effort to hide her disgust. Silviana believed private penance a ridiculous affectation. Penance was public; only punishment took place in private. "She also asked me to remind you of something, but she rushed off before saying what." She finished with a snort. Silviana saw anything that took time away from her novices and Accepted as needless interruption.

"I think I remember," Elaida told her dully.

When Silviana finally left—after only half an hour by the chimes of Cemaile's clock, yet an endless eternity—all that kept Elaida from calling the Hall to sit immediately so she could demand Alviarin be stripped of the Keeper's stole were the certainty of her Foretelling and the certainty that Seaine would trace that trail of treason back to Alviarin. That, and the sure fact that whether or not Alviarin fell in the confrontation, she herself definitely would. So, Elaida do Avriny a'Roihan, Watcher of the Seals, the Flame of Tar Valon, the Amyrlin Seat, surely the most powerful ruler in the world, lay facedown on her bed and blubbered into her pillows, too tender to don the shift that lay discarded on the floor, certain that when Alviarin returned, the woman would insist on her sitting through the entire interview. She blubbered, and through her tears she prayed for Alviarin's downfall to come soon.

"I did not tell you to have Elaida . . . beaten," that voice of crystal chimes said. "Do you rise above yourself?"

Alviarin flung herself from her knees onto her belly before the woman who seemed made of dark shadows and silvery light. Seizing the hem of Mesaana's dress, she rained kisses on it. The weave of Illusion—it must be that, though she could not see a single thread of *saidar* any more than she could sense the ability to channel in the woman who stood over her—did not hold completely, with her frantically shifting the skirt's edge. Flickers of bronze silk with a thin border of intricately embroidered black scrollwork showed through.

"I live to serve and obey you, Great Mistress," Alviarin panted between kisses. "I know that I am among the lowest of the low, a worm in your presence, and I pray only for your smile." She had been punished once for "rising above herself"—not for disobedience, thanks be to the Great Lord of the Dark!—and she knew that whatever howls Elaida might be raising right then, they could not be half so loud as her own had been.

Mesaana let the kissing go on for some time, and finally signaled an end by tipping Alviarin's face up with the toe of a slipper beneath the chin. "The decree has gone out." It was not a question, but Alviarin answered hastily.

"Yes, Great Mistress. Copies went to Northharbor and Southharbor even before I had Elaida sign. The first couriers have gone, and no merchant will leave the city without copies to distribute." Mesaana knew all that, of course. She knew everything. A cramp tightened the back of Alviarin's awkwardly craned neck, but she did not move. Mesaana would tell her when to move. "Great Mistress, Elaida is an empty husk. With all humility, would it not be better without the need to use her?" She held her breath. Questions could be dangerous, with the Chosen.

A shadow-nailed silvery finger tapped silver lips pursed in an amused smile. "Better if you wore the Amyrlin's stole, child?" Mesaana said at last. "An ambition small enough to fit you, but all in its time. For now, I have a tiny task for you. In spite of all the walls that have gone up between the Ajahs, the heads of the Ajahs seem to encounter one another with surprising frequency. By chance, they make it seem. All but the Red, at least; a pity Galina got herself killed, or she could tell you what they are about. Very probably it is trivial, but you will learn why they bare teeth at one another in public, then whisper together in private."

"I hear and obey, Great Mistress," Alviarin replied promptly, grateful that Mesaana considered it unimportant. The great "secret" of who headed the Ajahs was none to her—every Black sister was required to relay to the Supreme Council every whisper inside her supposed Ajah—but only Galina among them had been Black. That meant querying the Black sisters among the Sitters, which meant going through all the layers between them and her. That would take time, and without any certainty of success. Except for Ferane Neheran and Suana Dragand, who *were* the heads of their Ajahs, Sitters rarely seemed to know what their Ajah's head was thinking until they were told. "I will tell you as soon as I learn, Great Mistress."

But she did file away a tidbit for herself. Trivial matter or not, Mesaana did *not* know everything that happened in the White Tower. And Alviarin would keep her eyes open for a sister in bronze skirts bordered on the hem in black scrollwork. Mesaana was hiding herself in the Tower, and knowledge was power.

CHAPTER
26

The Extra Bit

Seaine strode the hallways of the Tower with a growing sense of being confounded at every turn. The White Tower was quite large, true, but she had been at this for hours. She very much wanted to be snug in her own rooms. Despite casements in place in every window, drafts drifted along the broad, tapestry-hung corridors and made the stand-lamps flicker. Cold drafts, and difficult to ignore when they slipped under her skirts. Her rooms were warm and comfortable, and safe.

Maids bobbed curtsies and manservants bowed in her wake, half-seen and completely ignored. Most sisters were in their own Ajahs' quarters, and those few out and about moved with wary pride, often in pairs, always of the same Ajah, shawls spread along their arms and displayed like banners. She smiled and nodded pleasantly to Talene, but the statuesque, golden-haired Sitter returned a hard stare, beauty carved from ice, then stalked away twitching her green-fringed shawl.

Too late now to approach Talene about being part of the search, even had Pevara been agreeable. Pevara counseled caution, then more caution, and truth to tell, Seaine was more than willing to listen under the circumstances. It was just that Talene was a friend. Had been a friend.

Talene was not the worst. Several ordinary sisters sniffed at her openly. At a Sitter! None White, of course, but that should have made no difference. No matter what was going on in the Tower, proprieties should be observed. Juilaine Madome, a tall, attractive woman with short-cut black hair who had held a chair for the Brown less than a year, brushed past her without so much as a murmur of apology and went off with those mannish strides of hers. Saerin Asnobar, another Brown Sitter, gave Seaine a fierce scowl and fingered that curved knife she always carried behind her belt before disappearing down a side corridor. Saerin was Altaran, slight touches of white at her dark temples emphasizing a thin age-faded white scar across one olive cheek, and only a Warder could match her for scowling.

Perhaps these things were all to be expected. There had been several unfortunate incidents recently, and no sister would forget being bundled unceremoniously from the hallways around another Ajah's quarters, much less what had sometimes gone with it. Rumor said a Sitter—a Sitter!—had had more than her dignity ruffled by the Reds, though not who. A great pity the Hall could not obstruct Elaida's mad decree, but first one Ajah, then another, had leaped on the new prerogatives, few Sitters were willing to think of giving them up now that they were in place, and the result was a Tower divided very nearly into armed camps. Once Seaine had thought the air in the Tower felt like a quivering hot jelly of suspicion and backbiting; now it was quivering hot jelly with an acid bite.

Clicking her tongue in vexation, she adjusted her own white-fringed shawl as Saerin vanished. It was illogical to flinch because an Altaran scowled—even Saerin would go no farther; surely not—and more than illogical to worry over what she could not change when she had a task.

And then, after all of her search that morning, she took a single step and saw her long-sought quarry walking toward her. Zerah Dacan was a slim, black-haired girl with a prideful air, properly self-possessed, and by all outward evidence untouched by the heated currents flowing through the Tower these days. Well, not a girl precisely, but Seaine was sure she had not worn that white-fringed shawl fifty years yet. She was inexperienced. Relatively inexperienced. That might help.

Zerah made no move to avoid a Sitter of her own Ajah, bowing her head in respect as Seaine fell in beside her. Quite a lot of intricate golden embroidery climbed the sleeves of her snowy dress and made a wide band at the bottom of her skirt. It was an unusual degree of show for the White Ajah. "Sitter," she murmured. Did her blue eyes hold a touch of worry?

"I need you for something," Seaine said more calmly than she felt. Very likely she was transplanting her own feelings into Zerah's big eyes. "Come with me." There was nothing to fear, not in the heart of the White Tower, but keeping her hands folded at her waist, unclenched, required surprising effort.

As expected—as hoped—Zerah went along with only another murmur, this of acquiescence. She glided at Seaine's side quite gracefully as they descended broad marble staircases and wide curving ramps, and gave only the slightest frown when Seaine opened a door on the ground floor, onto narrow stairs that spiraled down into darkness.

"After you, sister," Seaine said, channeling a small ball of light. By protocol, she should have preceded the other woman, but she could not bring herself to do that.

Zerah did not hesitate in going down. Logically, she had nothing to fear from a Sitter, a White Sitter. Logically, Seaine would tell her what she wanted when the time was ripe, and it would be nothing she could not do. Illogically, Seaine's stomach fluttered like a huge moth. Light, she held *saidar* and the other woman did not. Zerah was weaker in any case. There was nothing to fear. Which did nothing to quiet those fluttering wings in her middle.

Down they climbed and down, past doors letting onto basements and subbasements, until they reached the very lowest level, below even where the Accepted were tested. The dark hallway was lit only by Seaine's small light. They held their skirts high, but their slippers kicked up small clouds of dust however carefully they stepped. Plain wooden doors lined the smooth stone walls, many with great lumps of rust for hinges and locks.

"Sitter," Zerah asked, finally showing doubt, "whatever can we be after down here? I don't believe anyone has been this deep for years."

Seaine was sure her own visit, a few days earlier, had been the first to this level in at least a century. That was one of the reasons she and Pevara had chosen it. "Just in here," she said, swinging open a door that moved with only a little squealing. No amount of oil could loosen all the rust, and efforts to use the Power had been useless. Her abilities with Earth were better than Pevara's, but that was not saying very much.

Zerah stepped in, and blinked in surprise. In an otherwise empty room, Pevara sat behind a sturdy if rather worn table with three small benches around it. Getting those few pieces down unseen had been difficult—especially when servants could not be trusted. Clearing out the dust had been much simpler if no more pleasant, and smoothing the dust in the hall outside, necessary after every visit, had been simply onerous.

"I was about to give up sitting here in the dark," Pevara growled. The glow of *saidar* surrounded her as she lifted a lantern from beneath the table and channeled it alight, casting as much illumination as the rough-walled former storeroom deserved. Somewhat plump and normally pretty, the Red Sitter looked a bear with two sore teeth. "We want to ask you a few questions, Zerah." And she shielded the woman as Seaine shut the door.

Zerah's shadowed face remained utterly calm, but she swallowed audibly. "About what, Sitters?" There was the faintest tremor in the younger woman's voice, as well. It could be simply the mood of the Tower, though.

"The Black Ajah," Pevara replied curtly. "We want to know whether you're a Darkfriend."

Amazement and outrage shattered Zerah's calm. Most would have taken that for sufficient denial without her snapped "I don't have to take that from you! You Reds have been setting up false Dragons for years! If you ask me, there's no need to look further than the Red quarters to find Black sisters!"

Pevara's face darkened with fury. Her loyalty to her Ajah was strong, which went without saying, but worse, she had lost her entire family to Darkfriends. Seaine decided to step in before Pevara resorted to brute force. They had no proof. Not yet.

"Sit, Zerah," she said with as much warmth as she could muster. "Sit down, sister."

Zerah turned toward the door as though she might disobey an order from a Sitter—and of her own Ajah!—but at last she settled onto one of the benches, stiffly, sitting right at the edge.

Before Seaine had finished taking a seat that placed Zerah between them, Pevara laid the ivory-white Oath Rod on the battered tabletop. Seaine sighed. They were Sitters,

with a perfect right to use any *ter'angreal* they wished, but
she had been the one to filch it—she could not help thinking
of it as filching when she had observed none of the proper
procedures—and the whole time, in the back of her head,
she had been sure she would turn to find long-dead Sereille
Bagand standing here, ready to haul her off to the Mistress
of Novices' study by her ear. Irrational, but no less real.

"We want to make sure you tell the truth," Pevara said,
still sounding like an angry bear, "so you will swear an
oath on this, and then I'll ask again."

"I should not be subjected to this," Zerah said with an accusing look at Seaine, "but I will re-swear all of the Oaths,
if that's what it needs to satisfy you. And I will demand
an apology from you *both*, afterward." She hardly sounded
like a woman shielded and asked such a question. Almost
contemptuously, she reached for the slim, foot-long rod. It
shone in the dim light of the lantern.

"You'll swear to obey the two of us absolutely," Pevara
told her, and that hand snatched back as if from a coiled
viper. Pevara went right on, even sliding the Rod closer to
the woman with two fingers. "That way, we can tell you to
answer truthfully and know you will, and if you give the
wrong answer, we can know you'll be obedient and helpful
in helping us hunt down your Black sisters. The Rod can be
used to free you of the oath, if you give the right answer."

"To *free*—?" Zerah exclaimed. "I've never heard of anyone being *loosed* from an oath on the Oath Rod."

"That is why we are taking all these precautions," Seaine
told her. "Logically, a Black sister must be able to lie, which
means she must have been freed of at least that Oath and
likely all three. Pevara and I tested, and found the proce-
dure much the same as taking an oath." She did not mention
how painful it had been, though, leaving the pair of them
weeping. She also did not mention that Zerah would not be
freed of her oath whatever her answer, not until the search
for the Black Ajah came to a conclusion. For one thing, she
could not be allowed to run off and complain about this
questioning, which she most certainly would, with every
right, if she was not of the Black. If.

Light, but Seaine wished they had found a sister from
another Ajah who fit the criteria they had set. A Green or
a Yellow would have done quite nicely. That lot were over-

weening at the best of times, and of late . . . ! No. She was not going to fall prey to the sickness spreading through the Tower. Yet she could not help the names that flashed through her head, a dozen Greens, twice as many Yellows, and every one long past due taking down a few rungs. Sniff at a Sitter?

"You *freed* yourselves from one of the Oaths?" Zerah sounded startled, disgusted, uneasy, all at the same time. Perfectly reasonable responses.

"And took it again," Pevara muttered impatiently. Snatching up the slim rod, she channeled a little Spirit into one end while maintaining Zerah's shield. "Under the Light, I vow to speak no word that is not true. Under the Light, I vow to make no weapon for one man to kill another. Under the Light, I vow not to use the One Power as a weapon except against Darkfriends or Shadowspawn, or in the last defense of my life, the life of my Warder, or that of another sister." She did not grimace over the part about Warders; new sisters bound for the Red often did. "I am not a Darkfriend. I hope that satisfies you." She showed Zerah her teeth, but whether in smile or snarl was hard to say.

Seaine retook the Oaths in turn, each producing a slight momentary pressure everywhere from her scalp to the soles of her feet. In truth, the pressure was difficult to detect at all, with her skin still feeling too tight from retaking the Oath against speaking a lie. Claiming that Pevara had a beard or that the streets of Tar Valon were paved with cheese had been strangely exhilarating for a time—even Pevara had giggled—but hardly worth the discomfort now. Testing had not really seemed necessary, to her. Logically, it must be so. Saying that she was not of the Black twisted her tongue—a vile thing to be forced to deny—but she handed Zerah the Oath Rod with a decisive nod.

Shifting on her bench, the slender woman turned the smooth white rod in her fingers, swallowing convulsively. The pale lantern light made her appear ill. She looked from one of them to the other, wide-eyed, then her hands tightened on the Rod, and she nodded.

"Exactly as I said," Pevara growled, channeling Spirit to the Rod again, "or you'll be swearing until you have it right."

"I vow to obey the two of you absolutely," Zerah said in

a tight voice, then shuddered as the oath took hold. It was always tighter at the first. "Ask me about the Black Ajah," she demanded. Her hands shook holding the Rod. "Ask me about the Black Ajah!" Her intensity told Seaine the answer even before Pevara released the flow of Spirit and asked the question, commanding utter truth. "No!" Zerah practically shouted. "No, I am not Black Ajah! Now take this oath from me! Free me!"

Seaine slumped dejectedly, resting her elbows on the table. She certainly had not *wanted* Zerah to answer yes, but she had been sure they had found the other woman out in a lie. One lie found, or so it had seemed, after weeks of searching. How many more weeks of searching lay ahead? And of looking over her shoulder from waking to sleeping? When she managed to sleep.

Pevara stabbed an accusing finger at the woman. "You told people that you came from the north."

Zerah's eyes went wide again. "I did," she said slowly. "I rode down the bank of the Erinin to Jualdhe. Now free me of this oath!" She licked her lips.

Seaine frowned at her. "Goldenthorn seeds and a red cockleburr were found on your saddlecloth, Zerah. Goldenthorn and red cockleburr can't be found for a hundred miles *south* of Tar Valon."

Zerah leaped to her feet, and Pevara snapped, "Sit down!"

The woman dropped onto the bench with a loud smack, but she did not even wince. She was trembling. No, shaking. Her mouth was clamped shut, otherwise Seaine was sure her teeth would have been chattering. Light, the question of north or south frightened her more than an accusation of being a Darkfriend.

"From where did you start out," Seaine asked slowly, "and why—?" She meant to ask why the woman had gone roundabout—which plainly she had—just to hide which direction she came from, but answers burst from Zerah's mouth.

"From Salidar," she squealed. There was no other word for it. Still clutching the Oath Rod, she writhed on her bench. Tears spilled from her eyes, eyes as wide as they would go and fixed on Pevara. Words poured out, though her teeth truly did chatter now. "I c-came to m-make sure all the sisters here know about the R-Reds and Logain, so they'll d-depose Elaida and the T-Tower can be whole again." With a wail she collapsed into openmouthed bawling as she stared at the Red Sitter.

"Well," Pevara said. Then again, more grimly, "Well!" Her face was all composure, but the glitter in her dark eyes was far from the mischief Seaine remembered as novice and Accepted. "So you are the source of that . . . rumor. You are going to stand before the Hall and reveal it for the lie it is! Admit the lie, girl!"

If Zerah's eyes had been wide before, they bulged now. The Rod dropped from her hands to roll across the tabletop, and she clutched her throat. A choking sound came from her suddenly gaping mouth. Pevara stared at her in shock, but suddenly Seaine understood.

"Light's mercy," she breathed. "You do not have to lie, Zerah." Zerah's legs thrashed beneath the table as if she were trying to rise and could not get her feet under her. "Tell her, Pevara. She believes it's true! You've commanded her to speak the truth *and* to lie. Don't look at me that way! She believes!" A bluish tinge appeared on Zerah's lips. Her eyelids fluttered. Seaine gathered calm with both hands. "Pevara, you gave the order so apparently you must release her, or she will suffocate right in front of us."

"She's a *rebel*." Pevara's mutter invested that word with all the scorn it could hold. But then she sighed. "She hasn't been tried, yet. You don't have to . . . lie . . . girl." Zerah toppled forward and lay with her cheek pressed against the tabletop, gulping air between whimpers.

Seaine shook her head in wonder. They had not considered the possibility of *conflicting* oaths. What if the Black Ajah did not merely remove the Oath against lying, but replaced it with one of their own? What if they replaced all Three with their own oaths? She and Pevara would need to go very carefully if they did find a Black sister, or they might have her fall dead before they knew what the conflict was. Perhaps first a renunciation of *all* oaths—no way to go about it more carefully without knowing what Black sisters swore—followed by retaking the Three? Light, the pain of being loosed from everything at once would be little short of being put to the question. Maybe not short of it at all. But certainly a Darkfriend deserved that and more. If they ever found one.

Pevara glared down at the gasping woman without the slightest touch of pity on her face. "When she stands trial for rebellion, I intend to sit on her court."

"When she *is* tried, Pevara," Seaine said thoughtfully. "A pity to lose the assistance of one we know isn't a Darkfriend. And since she *is* a rebel, we need not be overly concerned about using her." There had been a number of discussions, none to a conclusion, about the second reason for leaving the new oath in place. A sister sworn to obey could be compelled—Seaine shifted uneasily; that sounded entirely too close to the forbidden vileness of Compulsion—she could be *induced* to help in the hunt, so long as you did not mind forcing her to accept the danger, whether she wished to or not. "I cannot think they would send only one," she went on. "Zerah, how many of you came to spread this tale?"

"Ten," the woman mumbled against the tabletop, then jerked erect, glaring in defiance. "I will not betray my sisters! I won't—!" Abruptly she cut off, lips twisting bitterly as she realized she had done just that.

"Names!" Pevara barked. "Give me their names, or I will have your hide here and now!"

Names spilled from Zerah's unwilling lips. At the command, certainly, more than the threat. Looking at Pevara's grim face, though, Seaine was sure she needed little provocation to stripe Zerah like a novice caught stealing. Strangely, she herself did not feel the same animosity. Revulsion, yes, but clearly not as strong. The woman was a rebel who had helped break the White Tower when a sister must accept anything to keep the Tower whole, and yet. . . . Very strange.

"You agree, Pevara?" she said when the list concluded. The stubborn woman gave her only a fierce nod for agreement. "Very well. Zerah, you will bring Bernaile to my rooms this afternoon." There were two from each Ajah excepting the Blue and the Red, it seemed, but best to begin with the other White. "You will say only that I wish to speak to her on a private matter. You will give her no warning by word, deed, or omission. Then you will stand quietly and let Pevara and me do what is necessary. You are being recruited into a worthier cause than your misguided rebellion, Zerah." Of course it was misguided. No matter how mad with power Elaida had become. "You are going to help us hunt down the Black Ajah."

Zerah's head jerked unwilling nods at each injunction, her face pained, but at mention of a hunt for the Black Ajah, she gasped. Light, her wits must have been totally unhinged by her experiences not to see that!

"And you will stop spreading these . . . stories," Pevara put in sternly. "From this moment, you'll not mention the Red Ajah and false Dragons together. Am I understood?"

Zerah's face donned a mask of sullen stubbornness. Zerah's mouth said, "I understand, Sitter." She looked ready to begin weeping again from sheer frustration.

"Then get out of my sight," Pevara told her, releasing the shield and *saidar* together. "And compose yourself! Wash your face and straighten your hair!" That last was directed at the back of the woman already darting from the table. Zerah had to pull her hands away from her hair to open the door. As the door squeaked shut behind her, Pevara snorted. "I wouldn't put it past her to have gone to this Bernaile like a sloven, hoping to warn her that way."

"A valid point," Seaine admitted. "But who will we warn if we scowl right and left at these women? At the very least, we will attract notice."

"The way matters are, Seaine, we wouldn't attract notice kicking them across the Tower grounds." Pevara sounded as if that were an attractive notion. "They are *rebels*, and I intend to hold them so hard they squeak if one of them so much as has a wrong thought!"

They went round and round about that. Seaine insisted that care in the orders they gave, leaving no loopholes, would be sufficient. Pevara pointed out that they were letting ten rebels—ten!—walk the Tower's halls unpunished. Seaine said they *would* face punishment eventually, and Pevara growled that eventually was not soon enough. Seaine had always admired the other woman's strength of will, but really, sometimes it was pure stubbornness.

A faint creak from a hinge was all the warning Seaine had to snatch the Oath Rod into her lap, hiding it in folds of her skirt as the door opened wide. She and Pevara embraced the Source almost as one.

Saerin walked into the room calmly, holding a lantern, and stood aside for Talene, who was followed by tiny

Yukiri, with a second light, and boyishly slim Doesine, tall for a Cairhienin, who closed the door quite firmly and settled her back against it as if to keep anyone from leaving. Four Sitters, representing all the remaining Ajahs in the Tower. They seemed to ignore the fact that Seaine and Pevara held *saidar*. Suddenly, to Seaine, the room felt rather crowded. Imagination, and irrational, but . . .

"Strange to see the pair of you together," Saerin said. Her face might be serene, but she slid fingers along the hilt of that curved knife behind her belt. She had held her chair forty years, longer than anyone else in the Hall, and everyone had learned to be careful of her temper.

"We might say the same of you," Pevara replied dryly. Saerin's temper never upset *her*. "Or did you come down here to help Doesine try to get some of her own back?" A sudden flush made the Yellow's face look even more that of a pretty boy despite her elegant bearing, and told Seaine which Sitter had strayed too near the Red quarters with unfortunate results. "I wouldn't have thought that would bring you together, though. Greens at Yellows' throats, Browns at Grays'. Or did you just bring them down for a quiet duel, Saerin?"

Frantically, Seaine cast around for what reason *would* have these four this deep into the bedrock of Tar Valon. What could tie them together? Their Ajahs—*all* of the Ajahs—truly were at one another's throats. All four had been handed penances by Elaida. No Sitter could enjoy Labor, especially when everyone knew exactly why she was scrubbing floors or pots, yet that was hardly a bond. What else? None were nobly born. Saerin and Yukiri were the daughters of innkeepers, Talene of farmers, while Doesine's father had been a cutler. Saerin had been trained first by the Daughters of Silence, the only one of that lot to reach the shawl. Absolutely useless drivel. Suddenly, something did strike her, and dried her throat. Saerin with her temper often barely in rein. Doesine, who had actually run away three times as a novice, though she had only once made it as far as the bridges. Talene, who might have earned more punishments than any other novice in the history of the Tower. Yukiri, always the last Gray to join her sisters' consensus when she wanted to go another way, the last to join the Hall's, for that matter. All four were considered rebels, in a way, and Elaida had humiliated every one. Could they be thinking they had made a mistake, standing to depose Siuan and raise Elaida? Could *they* have found out about Zerah and the others? And if so, what did they intend to do?

Mentally, Seaine prepared herself to weave *saidar*, though without much hope that she could escape. Pevara matched Saerin and Yukiri in strength, but she herself was weaker than any here save Doesine. She prepared herself, and Talene stepped forward and burst all of her logical deductions to flinders.

"Yukiri noticed you two sneaking about together, and we want to know why." Her surprisingly deep voice held heat despite the ice that seemed to coat her face. "Did the heads of your Ajahs set you a secret task? In public, the Ajahs' heads snarl at one another worse than anyone else, but they've been sneaking off into corners to talk, it seems. Whatever they're scheming, the Hall has a right to know."

"Oh, do give over, Talene." Yukiri's voice was always an even bigger surprise than Talene's. The woman looked a miniature queen, in dark silver silk with ivory lace, but she sounded a comfortable country woman. She claimed the contrast helped in negotiations. She smiled at Seaine and Pevara, a monarch perhaps unsure how gracious she should be. "I saw the pair of you sniffing about like ferrets at the hencoop," she said, "but I held my tongue—you might be pillow friends, for all I know, and whose business is that but yours?—I held my tongue till Talene here started yelping about who's been huddling in corners. I've seen a bit of huddling in corners myself, and I suspect some of those women might head their Ajahs as well, so. . . . Sometimes six and six make a dozen, and sometimes they make a mess. Tell us if you can, now. The Hall does have a right."

"We are not leaving until you do tell," Talene put in even more heatedly than before.

Pevara snorted and folded her arms. "If the head of my Ajah spoke two words to me, I'd see no reason to tell you what they were. As it happens, what Seaine and I were discussing has nothing to do with the Red or the White. Snoop elsewhere." But she did not release *saidar*. Neither did Seaine.

"Bloody useless and I bloody knew it," Doesine muttered from her place by the door. "Why I ever flaming let you talk

me into this. . . . Just as bloody well nobody else knows, or
we'd have sheepswallop all over faces for the whole bloody
Tower to see." At times she had a tongue like a boy, too, a
boy who needed his mouth washed out.

Seaine would have stood to leave if she had not feared
her knees would betray her. Pevara did stand, and raised an
impatient eyebrow at the women between her and the door.

Saerin fingered her knife hilt and eyed them quizzically,
not shifting a step. "A puzzle," she murmured. Suddenly she
glided forward, her free hand dipping into Seaine's lap so
quickly that Seaine gasped. She tried to keep the Oath Rod
hidden, but the only result was that she ended with Saerin
holding the Rod waist high with one hand while she held
the other end and a fistful of her skirts. "I enjoy puzzles,"
Saerin said.

Seaine let go and adjusted her dress; there seemed nothing else to do.

The appearance of the Rod produced a momentary babble as nearly everyone spoke at once.

"Blood and fire," Doesine growled. "Are you down here
raising new bloody sisters?"

"Oh, leave it with them, Saerin," Yukiri laughed right on
top of her. "Whatever they're up to, it's their own business."

Atop both, Talene barked, "Why else are they sneaking
about—together!—if it isn't to do with the Ajah heads?"

Saerin waved a hand, and after a moment gained quiet.
All present were Sitters, but she had the right to speak first
in the Hall, and her forty years counted for something, too.
"This is the key to the puzzle, I think," she said, stroking
the Rod with her thumb. "Why this, after all?" Abruptly
the glow of *saidar* surrounded her, too, and she channeled
Spirit to the Rod. "Under the Light, I will speak no word
that is not true. I am not a Darkfriend."

In the silence that followed, a mouse sneezing would
have sounded loud.

"Am I right?" Saerin said, releasing the Power. She held
the Rod out toward Seaine.

For the third time, Seaine retook the Oath against lying,
and for the second time repeated that she was not of the
Black. Pevara did the same with frozen dignity. And eyes
sharp as an eagle's.

"This is ridiculous," Talene said. "There *is* no Black Ajah."

Yukiri took the Rod from Pevara and channeled. "Under the Light, I will speak no word that is not true. I am not Black Ajah." The light of *saidar* around her winked out, and she handed the Rod to Doesine.

Talene frowned in disgust. "Stand aside, Doesine. I for one will not put up with this filthy suggestion."

"Under the Light, I will speak no word that is not true," Doesine said almost reverently, the glow around her like a halo. "I am not of the Black Ajah." When matters were serious, her tongue was as clean as any Mistress of Novices could have wished. She extended the Rod to Talene.

The golden-haired woman started back as from a poisonous snake. "Even to ask this is a slander. Worse than slander!" Something feral moved in her eyes. An irrational thought, perhaps, but that was what Seaine saw. "Now move out of my way," Talene demanded with all the authority of a Sitter in her voice. "I am leaving!"

"I think not," Pevara said quietly, and Yukiri nodded slowly in agreement. Saerin did not stroke her knife hilt; she gripped it till her knuckles went white.

Riding through the deep snows of Andor, floundering through them, Toveine Gazal cursed the day she was born. Short and slightly plump, with smooth copper skin and long glossy dark hair, she had seemed pretty to many over the years, but none had ever called her beautiful. Certainly none would now. The dark eyes that had once been direct now bored into whatever she looked at. That was when she was not angry. She was angry today. When Toveine was angry, serpents fled.

Four other Reds rode—floundered—at her back, and behind them twenty of the Tower Guard in dark coats and cloaks. None of the men liked it that their armor was stowed away on the packhorses, and they watched the forest lining both sides of the road as though expecting attack any moment. How they thought to cross three hundred miles of Andor unnoticed, wearing coats and cloaks with the Flame of Tar Valon shining bright on them, Toveine could not imagine.

The journey was almost done, though. In another day, perhaps two with roads knee-deep in snow on the horses, she would join with nine other parties exactly like hers. Not all of the sisters in them were Red, unfortunately, but that did not trouble her overmuch. Toveine Gazal, once a Sitter for the Red, would go into the histories as the woman who destroyed this *Black* Tower.

She was sure Elaida thought her grateful for the chance, called back from exile and disgrace, given the opportunity for redemption. She sneered, and if a wolf had been looking into the deep hood of her cloak, it might have quailed. What had been done twenty years ago was necessary, and the Light burn all those who muttered that the Black Ajah must have been involved. It had been necessary and right, but Toveine Gazal had been driven from her chair in the Hall, and forced to howl for mercy under the birch, with the assembled sisters watching, and even novices and Accepted witnessing that Sitters, too, lay beneath the law, though they were not told what law. And then she had been sent to work these last twenty years on the isolated Black Hills farm of Mistress Jara Doweel, a woman who considered an Aes Sedai serving penance in exile no different from any other hand laboring in sun and snow. Toveine's hands shifted on her reins; she could feel the calluses. Mistress Doweel—even now, she could not think of the woman without the honorific she had demanded—Mistress Doweel believed in hard work. And discipline as tight as any novice faced! She had no mercy on anyone who tried to shirk the backbreaking labor that she herself shared, and less than none for a woman who sneaked away to comfort herself with a pretty boy. That had been Toveine's life for fifteen years. And Elaida had slipped through the cracks uncaught, danced her way to the Amyrlin Seat that Toveine had once dreamed of for herself. No, she was not grateful. But she had learned to wait her chance.

Abruptly, a tall man in a black coat, dark hair falling to his shoulders, spurred his horse out of the forest into the road ahead of her, spraying snow. "There's no point struggling," he announced firmly, raising a gloved hand. "Surrender peacefully, and no one will be hurt."

It was neither his appearance nor his words that made Toveine rein up short, letting the other sisters gather beside her. "Take him," she said calmly. "You had better link. He has me shielded." It seemed one of these Asha'man had come to her. How convenient of him.

Abruptly she realized that nothing was happening and took her eyes from the fellow to frown at Jenare. The woman's pale, square face seemed absolutely bloodless. "Toveine," she said unsteadily, "I also am shielded."

"I am shielded, too," Lemai breathed in disbelief, and the others chimed in, increasingly frantic. All shielded.

More men in black coats appeared from among the trees, their horses stepping slowly, all around. Toveine stopped counting at fifteen. The Guards muttered angrily, waiting on a sister's command. They knew nothing yet except that a band of rogues had waylaid them. Toveine clicked her tongue in irritation. These men could not all channel, of course, but apparently every Asha'man who could do so had come against her. She did not panic. Unlike some of the sisters with her, these were not the first men who channeled that she had confronted. The tall man began riding toward her, smiling, apparently thinking they had obeyed his ridiculous order.

"At my command," she said quietly, "we will break in every direction. As soon as you are far enough away that the man loses the shield," men always thought they had to be able to see to hold their weaves, which meant that they did have to, "turn back and help the Guards. Ready yourselves." She raised her voice to a shout. "Guardsmen, fight them!"

Roaring, the Guardsmen surged forward, waving their swords and no doubt thinking to surround and protect the sisters. Pulling her mare around to the right, Toveine dug in her heels and crouched low over Sparrow's neck, dodging between startled Guardsmen, then between two very young men in black coats who gaped at her in astonishment. Then she was into the trees, urging more speed, snow spraying wildly, careless of whether the mare broke a leg. She liked the animal, but more than a horse would die today. Behind her, shouts. And one voice, roaring through all the cacophony. The tall man's voice.

"Take them alive, by order of the Dragon Reborn! Harm an Aes Sedai, and you'll answer to me!"

By order of the Dragon Reborn. For the first time, Toveine felt fear, an icicle worming into her middle. The Dragon

Reborn. She thrashed Sparrow's neck with the reins. The shield was still on her! Surely there were enough trees between them already to block the cursed men's sight of her! Oh, Light, the Dragon Reborn!

She grunted as something struck her across the middle, a branch where there was no branch, snatching her out of the saddle. She hung there watching Sparrow plow off at as much of a gallop as the snow allowed. She hung there. In the middle of the air, arms trapped at her sides, feet dangling a pace or more above the ground. She swallowed. Hard. It had to be the male part of the Power holding her up. She had never been touched by *saidin* before. She could feel the thick band of nothing snug around her middle. She thought she could feel the Dark One's taint. She quivered, fighting down screams.

The tall man reined his horse to a halt in front of her, and she floated down to sit sideways in front of his saddle. He did not seem particularly interested in the Aes Sedai he had captured, though. "Hardlin!" he shouted. "Norley! Kajima! One of you bloody young louts come here now!"

He was very tall, with shoulders an axe-handle wide. That was how Mistress Doweel would have put it. Just short of his middle years, handsome in a brooding, rugged fashion. Not at all like the pretty boys Toveine liked, eager and grateful and so easily controlled. A silver sword decorated the tall collar of his black wool coat on one side, with a peculiar creature in gold and red enamel on the other. He was a man who could channel. And he had her shielded and a prisoner.

The shriek that burst from her throat startled even her. She would have held it back if she could, but another leaped out behind it, higher still, and another even higher, another and another. Kicking wildly, she flung herself from side to side. Useless against the Power. She knew that, but only in a tiny corner of her mind. The rest of her howled at the top of her lungs, howled wordless pleas for rescue from the Shadow. Screaming, she struggled like a mad beast.

Dimly she was aware of his horse plunging and dancing as her heels drummed its shoulder. Dimly she heard the man talking. "Easy, you lump-eared sack of coal! Calm down, sister. I'm not going to— Easy, you spavined mule!

Light! My apologies, sister, but this is how we learn to do it." And then he kissed her.

She had only a heartbeat to realize his lips were touching hers, then sight vanished, and warmth flooded through her. More than warmth. She was melted honey inside, bubbling honey, rushing toward the boil. She was a harpstring, vibrating faster and faster, vibrating to invisibility and faster still. She was a thin crystal vase, quivering on the brink of shattering. The harpstring broke; the vase shattered.

"Aaaaaaaaaaaaaaaaaah!"

At first, she did not realize that sound had come from her gaping mouth. For a moment, she could not think coherently. Panting, she stared up at the male face above her, wondering who it belonged to. Yes. The tall man. The man who could—

"I could have done without the extra bit," he sighed, patting the horse's neck; the animal snorted, but it no longer leaped about, "yet I suppose it is necessary. You're hardly a wife. Be calm. Don't try to escape, don't attack anyone in a black coat, and don't touch the Source unless I give you permission. Now, what's your name?"

Unless he gave permission? The effrontery of the man!

"Toveine Gazal," she said, and blinked. Now, why had she answered him?

"There you are," another black-coated man said, splashing his horse through the snow to them. This one would be much more to her liking—if he could not actually channel, at least. She doubted this pink-cheeked lad shaved more than twice in the week. "Light, Logain!" the pretty boy exclaimed. "Did you take a *second* one? The M'Hael won't like that! I don't think he likes us taking any! Maybe it won't matter, though, you two being so close and all."

"Close, Vinchova?" Logain said wryly. "If the M'Hael had his way, I'd be hoeing turnips with the new boys. Or buried under the field," he added in a mutter she did not think he meant to be heard.

However much he heard, the pretty boy laughed with incredulous disbelief. Toveine barely heard him. She was gazing up at the man looming over her. Logain. The false Dragon. But he was dead! Stilled and dead! And holding her before his saddle with a casual hand. Why was she not

screaming, or striking at him? Even her belt knife would
do, this near. Yet she had no desire at all to reach for the
ivory haft. She could, she realized. That band around her
middle was gone. She could at least slip down off the horse
and try to— She had no desire to do that, either.

"What did you do to me?" she demanded. Calmly. At
least she had managed to hold on to that!

Turning his horse to ride back to the road, Logain told
her what he had done, and she put her head against that
wide chest, not caring at all how big he was, and wept. She
was going to make Elaida pay for this, she vowed. If Logain
ever let her, she would. That last was an especially bitter
thought.

CHAPTER

27

The Bargain

Seated cross-legged in a heavily gilded, high-backed chair, Min tried to lose herself in the leather-bound copy of Herid Fel's *Reason and Unreason* lying open on her knees. It was not easy. Oh, the book itself was mesmerizing; Master Fel's writings always swept her into worlds of thought she had not dreamed of while working in stables. She very much regretted the sweet old man's death. She hoped to find a clue in his books to why he had been killed. Her dark ringlets swung as she shook her head and tried to apply herself.

The book was fascinating, but the room was oppressive. Rand's small throne room in the Sun Palace was thick with gilt from the wide cornices to the tall mirrors on the walls replacing those Rand had smashed, from the two rows of chairs like the one she sat in to the dais at the head of the rows and the Dragon Throne atop the dais. That was a monstrosity, in the style of Tear as imagined by Cairhienin craftsmen, resting on the backs of a pair of Dragons with two more Dragons for the arms and others climbing the back, all with large sunstones for eyes, the whole glittering with gilt and red enamel. A huge golden, wavy-rayed Rising Sun set in the polished stone floor only added to the sense of heaviness. At least the fires blazing in two great fireplaces, tall enough for her to walk into, gave a pleasing warmth, especially with snow spilling down outside. And these were Rand's rooms; the comfort of that alone outweighed any amount of oppression. An irritating thought. This was Rand's room if he ever deigned to return. A very irritating thought. Being in love with a man seemed to consist largely of a great many irritating admissions to yourself!

Shifting in a vain attempt to make the hard chair comfortable, she tried to read, but her eyes kept swinging to the tall doors, each climbed by its own line of gilded Rising Suns. She hoped to see Rand walk in; she feared to see Sorilea, or Cadsuane. Unconsciously, she adjusted her pale blue coat, fingering the tiny snowflowers embroidered on the lapels. More twined around the sleeves, and the legs of breeches made as snug as she could manage to wriggle herself into. Not that great a change from what she had always worn. Not really. So far, she had avoided dresses, however much embroidery she wore, but she very much feared that Sorilea meant to stuff her into a dress if the Wise One had to peel her out of what she was wearing with her own hands.

The woman knew all about her and Rand. *All* about. She felt her cheeks heating. Sorilea seemed to be trying to decide whether Min Farshaw was a suitable . . . lover . . . for Rand al'Thor. That word made her feel foolishly giddy; she was not a fluff-brained girl! That word made her want to look over her shoulder guiltily for the aunts who had raised her. *No,* she thought wryly, *you're not fluff-brained. Fluff has its wits about it compared to you!*

Or maybe Sorilea wanted to know whether Rand was suitable for Min; it seemed that way, at times. The Wise Ones accepted Min as one of them, or very nearly, but these past weeks, Sorilea had wrung her out like a laundress's mangle. The leather-faced, white-haired Wise One wanted to know every scrap about Min, and every shred about Rand. She wanted the dust from the bottoms of his pockets! Twice Min had tried balking at the incessant interrogation, and twice Sorilea had produced a switch! That terrible old woman simply bundled her over the side of the nearest table, and afterward told her that maybe *that* would loosen another scrap in her head. None of the other Wise Ones gave the slightest commiseration, either! Light, the things you had to put up with for a man! And she could not have him for herself alone, at that!

Cadsuane was a different proposition altogether. The immensely dignified Aes Sedai, as gray-haired as Sorilea was white, did not seem to care two figs for Min or Rand either one, but she spent a great deal of time in the Sun Palace. Avoiding her entirely was impossible; she seemed to wander wherever she wanted. And when Cadsuane looked at Min, however briefly, Min could not help seeing a woman who could teach bulls to dance and bears to sing. She kept expecting the woman to point at her and announce that it was time Min Farshaw learned to balance a ball on her nose. Sooner or later, Rand had to face Cadsuane again, and the thought tied Min's stomach in knots.

She made herself bend back over her book. One of the doors swung open, and Rand strolled in with the Dragon Scepter nestled in the crook of his arm. He wore a golden crown, a broad circlet of laurel leaves—that must be this Crown of Swords everyone was talking about—snug breeches that showed his legs to advantage, and a gold-worked green silk coat that fit him beautifully. *He* was beautiful.

Marking her place with the note Master Fel had written saying she was "too pretty," she carefully closed the book and carefully set it on the floor beside her chair. Then she folded her arms and waited. Had she been standing, she would have tapped her foot, but she would not have the man thinking she was springing up just because he *finally* appeared.

For a moment he stood smiling at her, and tugging his earlobe for some reason—he seemed to be humming!—then abruptly he swung round to frown at the doors. "The Maidens out there didn't tell me you were in here. They hardly said a word at all. Light, they looked ready to veil at the sight of me."

"Maybe they are upset," she said calmly. "Maybe they wondered where you were. The way I did. Maybe *they* wondered whether you were hurt, or sick, or cold." *The way I did,* she thought bitterly. The man looked confused!

"I wrote to you," he said slowly, and she sniffed.

"Twice! With Asha'man to deliver your letters, you wrote twice, Rand al'Thor. If you call it writing!"

He staggered as if she had slapped him—no; as if she had kicked him in the belly!—and blinked. She took a firm hold on herself and settled against the chairback. Give a man sympathy at the wrong moment, and you never regained the ground lost. A part of her wanted to throw her arms around him, comfort him, draw out all his pains, soothe all his hurts. He had so many, and refused to admit a one. She was *not* going to spring up and rush to him, gushing to know what was wrong or . . . Light, he had to be all right.

Something took her gently beneath the elbows and lifted her out of the chair. Blue boots dangling, she floated toward him through the air. The Dragon Scepter floated away from him. So, he thought he could smile, did he? He thought a pretty smile could turn her around? She opened her mouth to give him a piece of her mind. A very sharp piece! Folding his arms around her, he kissed her.

When she could breathe again, she peered up at him through her lashes. "The first time . . ." She swallowed to clear her voice. "First, Jahar Narishma stalked in trying to stare inside everybody's skull the way he does, and vanished after handing me a scrap of parchment. Let me see. It said, 'I have claimed the crown of Illian. Trust no one until I return. Rand.' A little short of a proper love letter, I'd say."

He kissed her again.

This time, getting her breath back took longer. This was not going as she had expected at all. On the other hand, it was not going very badly. "The second time, Jonan Adley delivered a bit of paper that said, 'I will return when I finish here. Trust no one. Rand.' Adley walked in on me in my bath," she added, "and he wasn't shy about getting an eyeful." Rand always tried to pretend he was not jealous—as if there were a man in the world who was not—but she had noticed his scowls at men who looked at her. And his very considerable ardor was more heated afterward, too. She wondered what this kiss would be like. Maybe she should suggest retiring to the bedchamber? No, she would not be that forward no matter—

Rand set her down, his face suddenly bleak. "Adley's dead," he said. Suddenly the crown flew from his head, spinning the length of the room as though hurled. Just when she thought it would crash into the back of the Dragon Throne, perhaps smash through it, the wide ring of gold stopped short and settled slowly onto the throne's seat.

Min's breath caught as she looked up at him. Blood glistened in the dark red curls above his left ear. Pulling a lace-edged handkerchief from her sleeve, she reached for his temple, but he caught her wrist.

"I killed him," he said quietly.

She shivered at the sound of his voice. Quiet, the way the grave was quiet. Perhaps the bedchamber was a very good idea. No matter how forward it was. Making herself smile—and blushing when she realized how easy it was to smile, thinking of that huge bed—she gripped the front of his shirt, preparing to rip shirt and coat from his back right then and there.

Someone knocked at the doors.

Min's hands sprang away from Rand's shirt. She sprang away, too. Who could it be, she wondered irritably. The Maidens either announced visitors when Rand was there, or simply sent them in.

"Come," he said loudly, giving her a rueful smile. And she blushed again at that.

Dobraine put his head in at the door, then entered and shut the door behind him when he saw them standing together. The Cairhienin lord was a small man, little taller than she, with the front of his head shaved and the rest of his mostly gray hair falling to his shoulders. Stripes of blue and white decorated the front of his nearly black coat to below his waist. Even before gaining Rand's favor he had been a power in the land. Now, he ruled here, at least until Elayne could claim the Sun Throne. "My Lord Dragon," he murmured, bowing. "My Lady *Ta'veren*."

"A joke," Min muttered, when Rand quirked an eyebrow at her.

"Perhaps," Dobraine said, shrugging slightly, "yet half the noblewomen in the city now wear bright colors in imitation of the Lady Min. Breeches that display their legs, and many in coats that do not even cover their . . ." He coughed discreetly, realizing that Min's coat did not cover *her* hips completely.

She thought about telling him *he* had very pretty legs, even if they were decidedly knobby, then quickly thought better. Rand's jealousy might be a wonderful flame if they were alone, but she did not want him striking out at Dobraine. He was capable of that, she feared. Besides, she thought it really was a slip; Lord Dobraine Taborwin was not the sort to make even slightly rough jokes.

"So you're changing the world, too, Min." Grinning, Rand tapped the tip of her nose with a finger. He tapped her nose! Like a child he was amused with! Worse, she felt herself grinning back at him like a fool. "In better ways than I am, it appears," he went on, and that momentary boyish grin faded like mist.

"Is all well in Tear and Illian, my Lord Dragon?" Dobraine enquired.

"In Tear and Illian, all is well," Rand replied grimly. "What do you have for me, Dobraine? Sit, man. Sit." He motioned toward the rows of chairs, and took one for himself.

"I have acted on all of your letters," Dobraine said, seating himself across from Rand, "but there is little good to report, I fear."

"I'll get us something to drink," Min said in a tight voice. Letters? It was not easy to stalk in heeled boots—she had grown accustomed to them, but the things made you sway whatever you did—not easy, yet enough anger made anything possible. She stalked to the small gilded table beneath one of the huge mirrors where a silver pitcher and goblets sat. She busied herself with pouring spiced wine, splashing it out furiously. The servants always brought extra goblets, in case she had visitors, though she seldom did except for Sorilea or a fool lot of noblewomen. The wine was barely warm, but it was more than hot enough for the likes of that pair. She had received two letters, but she would bet Dobraine had had ten! Twenty! Banging pitcher and goblets about, she listened carefully. What had they been up to behind her back with their dozens of letters?

"Toram Riatin appears to have vanished," Dobraine said, "though rumor, at least, says he still lives, worse luck. Rumors also say that Daved Hanlon and Jeraal Mordeth—Padan Fain, as you call the man—have deserted him. By the way, I have settled Toram's sister, the Lady Ailil, in generous apartments, with servants who are . . . trustworthy." By his tone, he clearly meant trustworthy toward himself. The woman would not be able to change her dress without him knowing. "I can understand bringing her here, and Lord Bertome and the others, but why High Lord Weiramon, or High Lady Anaiyella? It goes without saying, of course, that their servants also are trustworthy."

"How do you know when a woman wants to kill you?" Rand mused.

"When she knows your name?" Dobraine did not sound as if he were joking. Rand tilted his head thoughtfully, then nodded. Nodded! She hoped he was not still hearing voices.

Rand gestured as if brushing away the women who wanted to kill him. A dangerous thing, with her about. She did not want to kill him, certainly, but she would not mind seeing Sorilea go at him with that switch! Breeches did not give much protection.

"Weiramon is a fool who makes too many mistakes," Rand told Dobraine, who nodded sober agreement. "My mistake for thinking I could use him. He seems happy enough to stay near the Dragon Reborn in any case. What else?" Min handed him a goblet, and he smiled at her despite the wine that slopped over his wrist. Maybe he thought it was an accident.

"Little else and too much," Dobraine began, then jerked back in his chair to avoid spilling wine as Min shoved the second silver goblet at him. She had not liked her brief stint as a tavernmaid. "My thanks, my Lady Min," he murmured graciously, but he eyed her askance as he took the goblet. She walked calmly back to fetch her own wine. Calmly.

"I fear that Lady Caraline and the High Lord Darlin are in Lady Arilyn's palace here in the City," the Cairhienin lord went on, "under the protection of Cadsuane Sedai. Perhaps protection is not the correct word. I have been refused entry to see them, but I hear that they have attempted to leave the City and been brought back like sacks. *In* a sack, one story claims. Having met Cadsuane, I can almost believe it."

"Cadsuane," Rand murmured, and Min felt a chill. He did not sound afraid, precisely, yet he did sound more than uneasy. "What do you think I should do about Caraline and Darlin, Min?"

Settling into a chair two away from him, Min jerked at suddenly being included. Ruefully, she stared down at the wine soaking through her best cream silk blouse, and her breeches, too. "Caraline will support Elayne for the Sun Throne," she said glumly. For warm wine, it seemed very cold, and she doubted the stain would ever come out of the blouse. "Not a viewing, but I believe her." She did not glance toward Dobraine, though he nodded sagely. Everyone knew about her viewings, now. The only result had been a stream of noblewomen who wanted to know their futures, and right sulky, too, when she said she could not tell them. Most would not have been pleased with the little she had seen; nothing dire, but not at all the bright wonders that fortune-tellers at the fair forecast. "As for Darlin, aside from the fact that he'll marry Caraline, after she's wrung him out and hung him up to dry, all I can say is that one day he'll be a king. I saw the crown on his head, a thing with a sword on the front of it, but I don't know what country it belongs to. And, oh, yes. He'll die in bed, and she will survive him."

Dobraine choked on his wine, spluttering and dabbing at his lips with a plain linen handkerchief. Most of those who *knew* did not *believe*. Quite satisfied with herself, Min drank the little that remained in her goblet. And then *she* was choking and gasping, jerking her handkerchief from her sleeve to wipe at her mouth. Light, she *would* have to give herself the dregs!

Rand simply nodded, peering into his goblet. "So they will live to trouble me," he murmured. A very soft sound, for words like stone. He was hard as a blade, her sheep-herder. "And what do I do about—"

Abruptly he twisted in his chair, toward the doors. One was opening. He had very sharp ears. Min had heard nothing.

Neither of the two Aes Sedai who entered was Cadsuane, and Min felt her shoulders loosen as she tucked her handkerchief away. While Rafela shut the door, Merana curtsied deeply to Rand, though the Gray sister's hazel eyes took in Min and Dobraine and filed them away, and then the round-faced Rafela was spreading her deep blue skirts wide, too. Neither rose until Rand gestured. They glided to him wearing cool serenity as they did their dresses. Except that the plump Blue sister fingered her shawl briefly as though to remind herself it was there. Min had seen that gesture before, from other sisters who had sworn fealty to Rand. It could not be easy for them. Only the White Tower commanded Aes Sedai, but Rand crooked a finger and they came, pointed and they went. Aes Sedai spoke with kings and queens as equals, perhaps slightly as their betters, yet the Wise Ones called them apprentices and expected them to obey twice as fast as Rand did.

None of that showed on Merana's smooth face. "My

Lord Dragon," she said respectfully. "We only just learned that you had returned, and we thought you might be eager to learn how matters went with the Atha'an Miere." She merely glanced at Dobraine, but he rose immediately. Cairhienin were used to people wanting to speak in private.

"Dobraine can stay," Rand said curtly. Had he hesitated? He did not stand. His eyes like blue ice, he was being the Dragon Reborn for all he was worth. Min had told him these women were his in truth, that all five who had accompanied him to the Sea Folk ship were his, utterly loyal to their oath and therefore obedient to his will, yet he seemed to find trusting any Aes Sedai difficult. She understood, but he was going to have to learn how.

"As you wish," Merana replied, inclining her head briefly. "Rafela and I have reached a bargain with the Sea Folk. The Bargain, they call it." The difference was clear to the ear. Hands lying still on gray-slashed green skirts, she drew a deep breath. She needed it. "Harine din Togara Two Winds, Wavemistress of Clan Shodein, speaking for Nesta din Reas Two Moons, Mistress of the Ships to the Atha'an Miere, and thus binding all the Atha'an Miere, has promised such ships as the Dragon Reborn needs, to sail when and where he needs them, for whatever purposes he requires." Merana did seem to grow a touch pontifical when there were no Wise Ones around; the Wise Ones did not allow it. "In return, Rafela and I, speaking for you, promised that the Dragon Reborn will not change any laws of the Atha'an Miere, as he has done among the . . ." For a moment, she faltered. "Forgive me. I am used to delivering agreements exactly as made. The word they used was 'shorebound,' but what they mean is what you have done in Tear and Cairhien." A question appeared in her eyes, and was gone. Perhaps she was wondering whether he had done the same in Illian. She had expressed relief that he had changed nothing in her native Andor.

"I suppose I can live with that," he muttered.

"Secondly," Rafela took up, folding plump hands at her waist, "you must give the Atha'an Miere land, a square one mile on a side, at every city on navigable water that you control now or come to control." She sounded less pompous than her companion, but only just. Nor did she sound entirely pleased with what she was saying. She was Tairen, after all, and few ports held a tighter control on their trade than Tear. "Within that area, the laws of the Atha'an Miere are to hold sway above any others. This agreement must also be made by the rulers of those ports so that . . ." It was her turn to falter, and her dark cheeks turned a trifle gray.

"So the agreement will survive me?" Rand said dryly. He barked a laugh. "I can live with that, too."

"Every city on water?" Dobraine exclaimed. "Do they mean here, too?" He leaped to his feet and began pacing, spilling more of his wine than Min had. He did not seem to notice. "A mile square? Under the Light alone knows what peculiar laws? I've traveled on a Sea Folk ship, and it *is* peculiar! Bare legs are not in it! And what of the customs duties, and docking fees, and . . ." Suddenly he rounded on Rand. He scowled at the Aes Sedai, who paid him no mind, but it was to Rand he spoke, in a tone bordering on roughness. "They will ruin Cairhien in a year, my Lord Dragon. They will ruin any port where you allow them to do this."

Min agreed, silently, but Rand merely waved a hand and laughed again. "They may think so, but I know something of this, Dobraine. They didn't say who chooses the land, so it doesn't have to be *on* the water at all. They'll have to buy their food from you, and live with your laws when they leave, so they can't be too arrogant. At worst, you can collect your customs when the goods come out of their . . . sanctuary. For the rest . . . If I can accept it, you can, too." There was no laughter in his voice now, and Dobraine bowed his head.

Min wondered where he had learned all that. He sounded a king, and one who knew what he was doing. Maybe Elayne had taught him.

"'Secondly' implies more," Rand said to the two Aes Sedai.

Merana and Rafela exchanged glances, unconsciously touched skirts and shawls, and then Merana spoke, her voice not at all pompous. In fact, it was much too light. "Thirdly, the Dragon Reborn agrees to keep an ambassador chosen by the Atha'an Miere with him at all times. Harine din Togara has named herself. She will be accompanied by her Windfinder, her Swordmaster and a retinue."

"What?" Rand roared, springing from the chair.

Rafela rushed in, rushed ahead, as though afraid he might

cut her off. "And fourthly, the Dragon Reborn agrees to go promptly to a summons from the Mistress of the Ships, but not more than twice in any three consecutive years." She finished panting a little, trying to make the last sound like extenuation.

The Dragon Scepter flew from the floor behind Rand, and he snagged it out of the air without looking. His eyes were not ice any more. They were blue fire. "A Sea Folk ambassador clinging to my heels?" he shouted. "Obey summonses?" He shook the carved spearhead at them, the green-and-white tassel flailing. "There are a people out there who want to conquer all of us, and might be able to do it! The Forsaken are out there! The Dark One is waiting! Why didn't you agree I'd caulk their hulls while you were about it!"

Normally, Min tried to soothe his temper when it flared, but this time she sat forward and glared at the Aes Sedai. She agreed with him fully. They had given away the barn to sell a horse!

Rafela actually swayed before that blast, but Merana drew herself up, her own eyes managing a good imitation of brown fire flecked with gold. "You castigate *us*?" she snapped in tones as frosty as her eyes were hot. She was Aes Sedai as the child Min had seen them, regal above queens, powerful above powers. "You were present in the beginning, *ta'veren*, and you twisted them as you wanted them. You could have had them all kneeling to you! But you left! They were not pleased to know they had been dancing for a *ta'veren*. Somewhere, they learned to weave shields, and before you were well off their ship, Rafela and I were shielded. So we could not take advantage with the Power, they said. More than once, Harine threatened to hang us in the rigging by our toes until we came to our senses, and I for one believe she meant it! Feel lucky that you have the ships you want, Rand al'Thor. Harine would have given you a handful! Feel lucky she didn't want your new boots and that ghastly throne of yours as well! Oh, by the by, she formally acknowledged you as the Coramoor, may you get a bellyache from it!"

Min stared at her. Rand and Dobraine stared at her, and the Cairhienin's jaw hung open. Rafela stared, her mouth working soundlessly. For that matter, the fire faded from

Merana's eyes, and they slowly grew wider and wider as if she were just hearing what she had said.

The Dragon Scepter trembled in Rand's fist. Min had seen his fury swell near to bursting for far less. She prayed for a way to avoid the explosion, and could not see one.

"It seems," he said finally, "that the words a *ta'veren* drags out aren't always the words he wants to hear." He sounded . . . calm; Min was not about to think, sane. "You've done well, Merana. I handed you a dog's dinner, but you and Rafela have done well."

The two Aes Sedai swayed, and for a moment, Min thought they might collapse in puddles on the floor from sheer relief.

"At least we managed to keep the details from Cadsuane," Rafela said, smoothing her skirts unsteadily. "There was no way to stop everyone learning we had made *some* sort of agreement, but we kept that much from her."

"Yes," Merana said breathlessly. "She even waylaid us on the way here. It's difficult keeping anything from her, but we did. We didn't think you'd want her to . . ." She trailed off at the stony look on Rand's face.

"Cadsuane again," he said flatly. He frowned at the carved length of spearhead in his hand, then tossed it onto a chair as if he did not trust himself with it. "She's in the Sun Palace, is she? Min, tell the Maidens outside to carry a message to Cadsuane. She is to attend the Dragon Reborn in all haste."

"Rand, I don't think," Min began uneasily, but Rand cut in. Not harshly, but quite firmly.

"Do it, please, Min. This woman is like a wolf eyeing the sheepfold. I intend to find out what she wants."

Min took her time getting up, and dragged her feet to the doors. She was not the only one to think this a bad idea. Or at least to want to be elsewhere when the Dragon Reborn faced Cadsuane Melaidhrin. Dobraine passed her on the way to the door, making a hasty bow with barely a pause, and even Merana and Rafela were out of the room before her, though they made it appear they were not hurrying. Inside the room, they did, anyway. When Min put her head into the hallway, the two sisters had caught Dobraine and were scurrying along at little short of a trot.

Strangely, the half-dozen Maidens who had been outside

when Min entered earlier had now grown in number until they lined the corridor as far as she could see in both directions, tall hard-faced women in the grays and browns and grays of the *cadin'sor*, *shoufa* wrapped around their heads with the long black veil hanging down. A good many carried their spears and bull-hide bucklers as if they expected a battle. Some were playing a finger-game called "knife, paper, stone," and the rest were watching intently.

Not so intently that they did not see her, though. When she passed Rand's message, handtalk flashed up and down the rows, then two lanky Maidens went trotting off. The others promptly returned to the game, playing or watching.

Scratching her head in puzzlement, Min went back in. The Maidens often made her nervous, yet they always had a word for her, sometimes respectful, as to a Wise One, sometimes joking, though their humor was odd, to say the least. Never had they ignored her like this.

Rand was in the bedchamber. That simple fact set her heart racing. He had his coat off, his snowy shirt unlaced at neck and cuffs and pulled out of his breeches. Sitting on the foot of the bed, she leaned back against one of the heavy blackwood bedposts and swung her feet up, crossing her ankles. She had not had a chance to watch Rand undress himself, and she intended to enjoy it.

Instead of continuing, though, he stood there looking at her. "What can Cadsuane possibly teach me?" he asked suddenly.

"You, and all the Asha'man," she replied. That had been her viewing. "I don't know what, Rand. I only know you have to learn it. All of you do." It did not seem he intended to progress beyond letting his shirt hang down. Sighing, she went on. "You need her, Rand. You can't afford to make her angry. You can't afford to chase her away." Actually, she did not think fifty Myrddraal and a thousand Trollocs could *chase* Cadsuane anywhere, but the point was the same.

A far-off look came into Rand's eyes, and after a moment, he shook his head. "Why should I listen to a madman?" he muttered almost under his breath. Light, did he really believe Lews Therin Telamon spoke in his head? "Let someone know you need them, Min, and they have a hold on you. A leash, to pull you where they want. I won't put a halter on my own neck for any Aes Sedai. Not for anyone!" Slowly his fists unclenched. "You, I need, Min," he said simply. "Not for your viewings. I just need you."

Burn her, but the man could sweep her feet out from under her with a few words!

With a smile as eager as hers, he grasped the bottom of his shirt with both hands and bent to begin hauling it over his head. Lacing her fingers over her stomach, she settled back to watch.

The three Maidens who marched into the room no longer wore the *shoufa* that had concealed their short hair in the corridor. They were empty-handed, and no longer wore those heavy-blade belt knives, either. That was all Min had time to notice.

Rand's head and arms were still inside the shirt, and Somara, flaxen-haired and tall even for an Aiel woman, seized the white linen and tangled it, trapping him. Almost in the same movement, she kicked him between the legs. With a strangled groan, he bent farther, staggering.

Nesair, fiery-haired and beautiful despite white scars on both sun-dark cheeks, planted a fist in his right side hard enough to make him stumble sideways.

With a cry, Min launched herself from the bed. She did not know what madness was happening here, could not even begin to guess. One of her knives came smoothly from each sleeve, and she threw herself at the Maidens, shouting, "Help! Oh, Rand! Somebody, help!" At least, that was what she tried to shout.

The third Maiden, Nandera, turned like a snake, and Min found a foot planted in her stomach. Breath rushed out of her in a wheeze. Her knives flew from numb hands, and she turned a somersault over the graying Maiden's foot, landing on her back with a crash that drove out what little air remained in her. Trying to move, trying to breathe—trying to understand!—all she could do was lie there and watch.

The three women were quite thorough. Nesair and Nandera pounded Rand with their fists while Somara held him bent over and caught in his own shirt. Again and again and again they drove studied blows into Rand's hard belly, into his right side. Min would have laughed hysterically, had she had any breath. They were trying to beat him to death, and they very carefully avoided hitting anywhere near the tender round scar in his left side with the half-healed slash running through it.

She knew very well how hard Rand's body was, how strong, but no one could stand up to that. Slowly, his knees folded, and when they thumped to the floor tiles, Nandera and Nesair stood back. Each nodded, and Somara released her hold on Rand's shirt. He fell forward on his face. She could hear him gasping, fighting groans that bubbled up despite his efforts. Kneeling, Somara pulled his shirt down almost tenderly. He lay there with his cheek on the floor, eyes bulging, struggling for breath.

Nesair bent to catch a fistful of his hair and jerk his head up. "We won the right for this," she growled, "but every Maiden wanted to lay her hands on you. I left my clan for you, Rand al'Thor. I will not have you spit on me!"

Somara moved a hand as if to smooth hair out of his face, then snatched it back. "This is how we treat a first-brother who dishonors us, Rand al'Thor," she said firmly. "The first time. The next, we will use straps."

Nandera stood over Rand with fist planted on her hips and a face of stone. "You carry the honor of *Far Dareis Mai*, son of a Maiden," she said grimly. "You promised to call us to dance the spears for you, and then you ran to battle and left us behind. You will not do this again."

She stepped over him to stride out, and the other two followed. Only Somara glanced back, and if sympathy touched her blue eyes, there was none in her voice when she said, "Do not make this necessary again, son of a Maiden."

Rand had pushed himself up to hands and knees by the time Min managed to crawl to him. "They must be mad," she croaked. Light, but her middle hurt! "Rhuarc will—!" She did not know what Rhuarc would do. Not enough, whatever it was. "Sorilea." Sorilea would stake them out in the sun! To start! "When we tell her—"

"We tell no one," he said. He almost sounded as if he had his breath back, although he was still slightly pop-eyed. How could he do that? "They have the right. They've *earned* the right."

Min recognized that tone much to well. When a man decided to be stubborn, he would sit bare in a nettle patch and deny to your face that they made his bottom sting! She was almost pleased to hear him groan as she helped him to his feet. Well, as they helped each other. If he was going to be a pure wool-headed idiot, he deserved a few bruises!

He eased himself onto the bed, lying back on the heaped pillows, and she snuggled in beside him. Not what she had been hoping for, but as much as was going to happen, she was sure.

"Not what I was hoping to use this bed for," he muttered. She was not sure she had been supposed to hear.

She laughed. "I enjoy you holding me just as much as . . . as the other." Strangely, he smiled at her as if he knew she was lying. Her Aunt Miren claimed that was one of the three lies any man would believe from a woman.

"If I am interrupting," a woman's cool voice said from the doorway, "I suppose I could return when it is more convenient."

Min jerked away from Rand as though burned, but when he pulled her back, she settled against him again. She recognized the Aes Sedai standing in the doorway, a plump little Cairhienin with four thin stripes of color across her full bosom and white slashes in her dark skirts. Daigian Moseneillin was one of the sisters who had come with Cadsuane. And she was almost as overbearing as Cadsuane herself, in Min's opinion.

"Who might you be when you're at home?" Rand said lazily. "Whoever you are, didn't anyone ever teach you to knock?" Min realized that every muscle in the arm holding her was hard as a rock, though.

The moonstone dangling onto Daigian's forehead on a thin silver chain swung as she slowly shook her head. Plainly, she was not pleased. "Cadsuane Sedai received your request," she said, even more coolly than before, "and asked me to convey her regrets. She very much wishes to finish the piece of needlepoint she is working on. Perhaps she might be able to see you another day. If she can find time."

"Is that what she said?" Rand asked dangerously.

Daigian sniffed disdainfully. "I will leave you to resume . . . whatever you were doing." Min wondered whether she could get away with slapping an Aes Sedai. Daigian eyed her frostily, as if hearing the thought, and turned to glide from the room.

Rand sat up with a muffled oath. "You tell Cadsuane she can go to the Pit of Doom!" he shouted after the retreating sister. "Tell her she can rot!"

"It won't do, Rand," Min sighed. This was going to be harder than she had thought. "You need Cadsuane. She doesn't need you."

"Doesn't she?" he said softly, and she shivered. She had only thought his voice was dangerous before.

Rand prepared carefully, dressing in the green coat again, sending Min with messages for the Maidens to carry. At least they would still do that. His ribs ached almost as much on his right side as the wounds did on his left, and his belly felt as if he had been beaten with a board. He had promised them. He seized hold of *saidin* alone in his bedchamber, unwilling to let even Min see him falter again. He could keep her safe, at least, somehow, but how could she feel safe if she saw him about to fall over? He had to be strong, for her sake. He had to be strong, for the world. That bundle of emotions in the back of his head that was Alanna reminded him of the cost of carelessness. Right then, Alanna was sulking. She must have pushed a Wise One too far, because if she was sitting, she was sitting gingerly.

"I still think this is lunacy, Rand al'Thor," Min said as he placed the Crown of Swords carefully on his head. He did not want those tiny blades to draw blood again now. "Are you listening to me? Well, if you intend to go through with it, I'm going with you. You admitted you need me, and you'll need me more than ever for this!" She was in full fig, fists on her hips, foot tapping, eyes all but glowing.

"You're staying here," he told her firmly. He was still not sure what he intended to do, not fully, and he did not want her to see him stumble. He was very afraid he might stumble. He expected an argument, though.

She frowned at him, and her foot stopped tapping. The angry light in her eyes faded into worry that vanished in a twinkling. "Well, I suppose you're old enough to cross the stableyard without your hand held, sheepherder. Besides, I *am* falling behind in my reading."

Dropping into one of the tall gilded chairs, she folded her legs beneath her and picked up the book she had been reading when he came in. In moments, she seemed totally engrossed in the page before her.

Rand nodded. That was what he wanted; her here, and safe. Still, she did not have to forget him so completely.

There were six Maidens squatting in the hallway outside his door. They stared at him flat-eyed, not speaking, Nandera's gaze the flattest of all. Though Somara and Nesair came close. He thought Nesair was Shaido; he would have to keep a hard eye on her.

The Asha'man were waiting, too—Lews Therin muttered darkly of killing in Rand's head—all but Narishma with the Dragon on their collars as well as the Sword. Curtly, he ordered Narishma to stand guard on his apartments, and the man saluted sharply, those dark too-big eyes seeing too much, faintly accusing. Rand did not think the Maidens would take out their displeasure on Min, but he was not taking any chances. Light, he *had* told Narishma everything about the traps he had woven in the Stone when he sent the man to fetch *Callandor*. The man was imagining things. Burn him, but that had been a mad risk to take.

Only madmen never *trust.* Lews Therin sounded amused. And quite mad. The wounds in Rand's side throbbed; they seemed to resonate with each other in distant pain.

"Show me where to find Cadsuane," he commanded. Nandera rose smoothly to her feet and started off without a backward glance. He followed, and the others fell in behind him, Dashiva and Flinn, Morr and Hopwil. He gave them hasty instructions as they walked. Flinn, of all people, tried to protest, but Rand bore him down; this was no time for quailing. The grizzled onetime Guardsman was the last Rand had expected it of. Morr or Hopwil, perhaps. If no longer exactly dewy-eyed, they were still young enough to leave their razors dry as many days as wet. But not Flinn. Nandera's soft boots made no sound; their footsteps reverberated from the high square-vaulted ceiling, chasing away everyone with the shadow of a reason for fear. His wounds pulsed.

Every last person in the Sun Palace knew the Dragon Reborn on sight by now, and they knew who the black-coated men were, too. Black-liveried servants made deep bows or curtsies, and hurried to get out of his sight. Most nobles were almost as quick to put distance between themselves and five men who could channel, going somewhere with purpose on their faces. Ailil watched them pass with an unreadable expression. Anaiyella simpered, of course, but when Rand glanced back, she was staring after him with a face to match Nandera's. Bertome smiled as he made his leg, a dark smile with neither mirth nor pleasure in it.

Nandera did not speak even when they reached their destination, merely pointed to a closed door with one of her spears, turned on her heel, and strode back the way they had come. The *Car'a'carn* without a single Maiden to guard him. Did they think four Asha'man enough to keep him safe? Or was her departure another sign of displeasure?

"Do what I told you," Rand said.

Dashiva gave a jerk as if coming back to himself, then seized the Source. The wide door, carved in vertical lines, swung open with a bang on a flow of Air. The other three took hold of *saidin* and followed Dashiva in, faces grim.

"The Dragon Reborn," Dashiva's voice sounded loud, magnified slightly by the Power, "the King of Illian, the Lord of the Morning, comes to see the woman, Cadsuane Melaidhrin."

Rand stepped in, standing tall. He did not recognize the other weave Dashiva had created, but the air seemed to hum with menace, a sense of something inexorable approaching, drawing ever nearer.

"I sent for you, Cadsuane," Rand said. He did not use weaves. His voice was hard and flat enough without aid.

The Green sister he remembered sat beside a small table with an embroidery hoop in her hands, an opened basket on the polished tabletop spilling out skeins of bright thread from some of its many compartments. She was exactly as he remembered. That strong face topped by an iron-gray bun decorated with small dangling golden fish and birds, stars and moons. Those dark eyes, seeming almost black in her fair face. Cool, considering eyes. Lews Therin gave a wail and fled at the sight of her.

"Well," she said, setting the embroidery hoop on the table, "I must say I've seen better without paying. With all I've been hearing about you, boy, the least I expected was peals of thunder, trumpets in the heavens, flashing lights in the sky." Calmly, she regarded the five stone-faced men who could channel, which should have been enough to make any

Aes Sedai flinch. Calmly, she regarded the Dragon Reborn. "I hope one of you is at least going to juggle," she said. "Or eat fire? I've always enjoyed watching gleemen eat fire."

Flinn barked a laugh before catching himself, and even then raked a hand through his fringe of hair and seemed to be struggling with amusement. Morr and Hopwil exchanged looks both puzzled and more than a little outraged. Dashiva smiled unpleasantly, and the weave he was holding grew stronger, until Rand felt as if he wanted to look over his shoulder to see what was rushing toward him.

"It is enough that you know I am who I am," Rand told her. "Dashiva, all of you, wait outside."

Dashiva opened his mouth as if to protest. That had not been part of Rand's instructions, but they were not going to overawe the woman, not this way. The man went, though, muttering to himself. Hopwil and Morr actually stepped out eagerly, with sidelong glances at Cadsuane. Flinn was the only one to make a dignified withdrawal, in spite of his limp. And he still seemed amused!

Rand channeled, and a heavy, leopard-carved chair floated into the air from its place by the wall, spinning end over end in somersaults before settling like a feather in front of Cadsuane. At the same time, a heavy silver pitcher drifted up from a long, draped table across the room, making a loud ping as it was suddenly heated; steam gushed from the top, and it tipped over, whirling round and round like a slow top, as a silver cup darted up to neatly catch the dark pouring.

"Too hot, I think," Rand said, and the glassed casements leaped from the tall, narrow windows. Snowflakes billowed in on an icy blast, and the cup soared out through one of the windows, soared back again, straight to his hand as he sat himself. Let her see how calm she could stay with a madman staring at her. The dark liquid was tea, too strong after his boiling, and bitter enough to set his teeth on edge. But the warmth was just right. His skin pebbled in the gusts howling into the room and flapping tapestries against the walls, but in the Void, that was far away, someone else's skin.

"The Laurel Crown is prettier than some," Cadsuane said with a faint smile. Her hair ornaments swayed whenever the wind rose, and small wisps flailed about her bun, but the only notice she took was to catch her embroidery hoop just before it was blown from the table. "I prefer that name. But you can't expect me to be impressed by crowns. I've paddled the bottoms of two reigning kings and three queens. Not sitting rulers, you understand, once I was done with them, not for a day or so, but it did get their attention. You can see why crowns don't impress me, though."

Rand eased his jaw. Grinding his teeth would not help. He widened his eyes, hoping he looked insane instead of simply furious. "Most Aes Sedai avoid the Sun Palace," he told her. "Except for those who have sworn fealty to me. And those I hold prisoner." Light, what was he to do with *those*? As long as the Wise Ones kept them out of his hair, all was well enough.

"The Aiel seem to think I should come and go as I please," she said absently, eyeing the hoop in her hand as if thinking of taking up her needle again. "A matter of some trifling help I gave some boy or other. Though why anyone but his mother should think him worth it, I can hardly say."

Rand made another effort not to grind his teeth. The woman *had* saved his life. Her and Darner Flinn between them, and plenty of others in the bargain, Min among them. But he still owed Cadsuane something for that. Burn her. "I want you to be my advisor. I'm King of Illian now, and kings have Aes Sedai advisors."

She gave his crown a dismissive glance. "Certainly not. An advisor has to stand and watch her charge make a muddle much too often to suit me. She also has to take orders, something I am particularly bad at. Won't someone else do? Alanna, perhaps?"

Despite himself, Rand sat up straight. Did she know about the bond? Merana had said it was hard to keep anything from her. No; he could worry later about how much his "faithful" Aes Sedai were telling Cadsuane. Light, he wished Min could be wrong for once. But he would believe himself breathing water, first. "I . . ." He could not make himself tell her that he needed her. No halter! "What if you didn't have to swear any oaths?"

"I suppose that might work," she said doubtfully, peering at her cursed stitchery. Her eyes rose to his. Considering. "You sound . . . uneasy. I don't like to tell a man he's afraid even when he has reason to be. Uneasy over a sister you haven't turned into a tame lapdog snaring you in some fashion? Let me see. I can make you a few promises; perhaps they will set your mind at rest. I expect you to listen, of course—make me waste my breath, and you'll yelp for it—but I won't make you do what I want. I won't tolerate anyone lying to me, certainly—that's another thing you'll find decidedly uncomfortable—but I don't expect you to tell me the deepest yearnings of your heart, either. Oh, yes. Whatever I do, it will be for your own good; not mine, not the good of the White Tower, yours. Now, does that ease your fears? Pardon me. Your unease."

Wondering whether he was supposed to laugh, Rand stared at her. "Do they teach you how to do that?" he demanded. "Make a promise sound a threat, I mean."

"Oh, I see. You want rules. Most boys do, whatever they say. Very well. Let me see. I cannot abide incivility. So you will be properly civil to me, to my friends, and my guests. That includes not channeling at them, in case you haven't guessed, and holding your temper, which I understand is memorable. It also takes in your . . . companions in those black coats. A pity if I had to spank you for something one of them did. Does that suffice? I can make more, if you need them."

Rand set his cup down beside the chair. The tea had gone cold as well as bitter. Snow was beginning to pile up in drifts beneath the windows. "I'm the one who's supposed to go mad, Aes Sedai, but you already are." Rising, he strode for the door.

"I do hope you haven't tried to use *Callandor*," she said complacently behind him. "I have heard it's vanished from the Stone. You managed to escape once, but you might not twice."

He stopped short, looking over his shoulder. The woman was pushing that bloody needle through the cloth stretched on her hoop! The wind gusted, swirling snow around her, and she did not even lift her head. "What do you mean, escape?"

"What?" She did not look up. "Oh. Very few even in the Tower knew what *Callandor* is before you drew it, but there are surprising things hidden in musty corners of the Tower Library. I went rummaging some years ago, when I first had the suspicion you might be suckling at your mother's breast.

Just before I decided to go back into retirement. Babes are messy things, and I could not see how to find you before you stopped dripping at one end or the other."

"What do you mean?" he demanded roughly.

Cadsuane looked up then, and with her hair flung about and snow settling on her dress, she looked a queen. "I told you I cannot abide incivility. If you ask for my help again, I expect you to ask *politely.* And I will expect an apology for your behavior today!"

"What do you mean about *Callandor*?"

"It is flawed," she replied curtly, "lacking the buffer that makes other *sa'angreal* safe to use. And it apparently magnifies the taint, inducing wildness of the mind. So long as a man is using it, anyway. The only safe way for you to use The Sword That Is Not a Sword, the only way to use it without the risk of killing yourself, or trying to do the Light alone knows what insanity, is linked with two women, and one of them guiding the flows."

Trying not to hunch his shoulders, he strode away from her. So it had been not just the wildness of *saidin* around Ebou Dar that had killed Adley. He had murdered the man the moment he sent Narishma for the thing.

Cadsuane's voice pursued him. "Remember, boy. You must ask very nicely, and apologize. I might even agree, if your apology sounds truly sincere."

Rand barely heard her. He had hoped to use *Callandor* again, hoped it would be strong enough. Now only one chance remained, and it terrified him. He seemed to hear another woman's voice, a dead woman's voice. *You could challenge the Creator.*

CHAPTER
28

Crimsonthorn

I t hardly seemed the setting for the explosion Elayne feared. Harlon Bridge was a village of moderate size, with three inns and enough houses that no one had to sleep in a hayloft. When Elayne and Birgitte went downstairs to the common room that morning, Mistress Dill, the round innkeeper, smiled warmly and offered as much of a curtsy as her size allowed. It was not just that Elayne was Aes Sedai. Mistress Dill was so pleased that her inn was full, what with the roads snow-packed, that she bobbed at nearly everyone. At their entrance, Aviendha hastily gulped the last of her breakfast bread and cheese, brushed a few crumbs from her green dress, and snatched up her dark cloak to join them.

Outside, the sun was just peeking over the horizon, a low dome of pale yellow. Only a few clouds marred a beautiful blue sky, and they were white and fluffy, not the sort to carry snow. It seemed a wonderful day for traveling.

Except that Adeleas was trampling a path up the snowy street, and the white-haired sister was dragging one of the Kin, Garenia Rosoinde, by her arm. Garenia was a slim-hipped Saldaean who had spent the last twenty years as a merchant although she looked only a few years older than Nynaeve did. Normally, her strongly hooked nose gave her a forceful appearance, a woman who would make hard trading and not back away. Now her dark tilted eyes were large in her face and her wide mouth hung open, emitting a wordless wail. A growing knot of Kinswomen followed behind, skirts held high out of the snow, whispering among themselves, with more running from every direction to join.

Reanne and the rest of the Knitting Circle were in the front, all grim-faced except for Kirstian, who seemed even paler than usual. Alise was there, too, wearing an utterly blank expression.

Adeleas stopped in front of Elayne and shoved Garenia so hard the woman fell to hands and knees in the snow. Where she stayed, still wailing. The Kinswomen gathered behind her, more of their number flocking in.

"I'm bringing this to you because Nynaeve is busy," the Brown sister told Elayne. She meant that Nynaeve was enjoying a little time alone with Lan somewhere, but for once, not so much as a hint of a smile crossed her lips. "Be quiet, child!" she snapped at Garenia. Who promptly went silent. Adeleas gave a satisfied nod. "This is not Garenia Rosoinde," she said. "I finally recognized her. Zarya Alkaese, a novice who ran away just before Vandene and I decided to retire and write our history of the world. She admitted it, when I confronted her. I'm surprised Careane didn't recognize her before this; they were novices together for two years. The law is clear, Elayne. A runaway must be put back in white as soon as possible and kept under strict discipline until she can be returned to the Tower for proper punishment. She won't think of running again after that!"

Elayne nodded slowly, trying to think of what to say. Whether or not Garenia—Zarya—thought of running again, she would not be allowed the opportunity. She was very strong in the Power; the Tower would not let her go if it took the rest of her life to earn the shawl. But Elayne was recalling something she had heard this woman say the first time she met her. The meaning had not registered then, but now it did. How would Zarya face novice white again after living as her own woman for seventy years? Worse, those whispers among the Kinswomen had begun to sound like rumbles.

She did not have long to think. Suddenly Kirstian fell to her knees, clutching at Adeleas' skirts with one hand. "I submit myself," she said calmly, her tone a wonder coming from that bloodless face. "I was enrolled in the novice book almost three hundred years ago, and ran away less than a year later. I submit myself, and . . . and beg mercy."

It was white-haired Adeleas' turn to go wide-eyed. Kirstian was claiming to have run away from the White

Tower when she herself was an infant, if not before she was born! Most of the sisters still did not really believe the ages claimed by the Kin. Indeed, Kirstian appeared just into her middle years.

Even so, Adeleas recovered herself quickly. However old the other woman was, Adeleas had been Aes Sedai about as long as anyone living. She carried an aura of age, and authority. "If that is so, child," her voice did falter just a bit at that, "I fear we must put you in white, too. You will still be punished, but surrendering as you have will gain you some mitigation."

"That is why I did it." Kirstian's steady tone was spoiled somewhat by a hard swallow. She was almost as strong as Zarya—none of the Knitting Circle were weak—and she would be held very closely. "I knew you would find me out sooner or later."

Adeleas nodded as though that were clearly obvious, though how the woman would have been found out, Elayne could not guess. She very much doubted that Kirstian Chalwin was the name the woman had been born with. Most of the Kin believed in Aes Sedai omniscience, though. They had, at least.

"Rubbish!" Sarainya Vostovan's husky voice cut through the murmured babble of the Kin. Neither strong enough to become Aes Sedai nor nearly old enough to stand very high among the Kin, she still stepped from the pack defiantly. "Why should we give them up to the White Tower? We have helped women run away, and rightly so! It is not part of the rules to give them back!"

"Control yourself!" Reanne said sharply. "Alise, take Sarainya in hand, please. It seems she forgets too many of the rules she claims to know."

Alise looked at Reanne, her face still unreadable. Alise, who enforced the Kin's rules with a firm hand. "It is not part of our rules to hand runaways back, Reanne," she said.

Reanne jerked as though struck. "And how do you suggest keeping them?" she demanded finally. "We have always held runaways apart until we were sure they were no longer hunted, and if they were found before, we let the sisters take them. That is the *rule*, Alise. What other rule do you propose violating? Do you suggest that we actually set ourselves *against* Aes Sedai?" Ridicule of such a notion larded her voice, yet Alise stood looking at her, silent.

"Yes!" a voice shouted from the crowd of Kinswomen. "We are many, and they are few!" Adeleas stared at the crowd in disbelief. Elayne embraced *saidar*, though she knew the voice was right—the Kin were too many. She felt Aviendha embracing the Power, and Birgitte setting herself.

Giving herself a shake as if coming to, Alise did something far more practical, certainly far more effective. "Sarainya," she said loudly, "you will report to me when we stop tonight, with a switch you cut yourself before we leave this morning. You, too, Asra; I recognize your voice!" And then, just as loudly, she said to Reanne, "I will report myself for your judgment when we stop tonight. I don't see anyone getting ready!"

The Kinswomen broke up quickly then, heading off to gather their things, yet Elayne saw some of them talking quietly as they went. When they rode over the bridge across the frozen stream that wound down beside the village, with Nynaeve incredulous over what she had missed and glaring about for someone to call down, Sarainya and Asra carried switches—as did Alise—and Zarya and Kirstian wore hastily found white dresses beneath their dark cloaks. The Windfinders pointed at them and laughed uproariously. But many of the Kinswomen still talked in clusters, falling silent whenever a sister or one of the Knitting Circle looked at them. And there was a darkness to their eyes when they looked at Aes Sedai.

Eight more days of floundering through the snow when it was not falling, and grinding her teeth in an inn when it was. Eight more days of brooding by the Kin, of staring bleakly at the sisters, days of strutting by the Windfinders around Kin and Aes Sedai alike. On the morning of the ninth day, Elayne began to wish everyone had simply gone for everyone else's throat.

She was just wondering whether they could cover the last ten miles to Caemlyn without a murder, when Kirstian rapped at her door and darted in without waiting for an answer. The woman's plain woolen dress was not the shade of white proper for a novice, and she had regained much of her dignity somehow, as if knowing her future had smoothed

her present, but now she made a hasty curtsy, almost tripping over her cloak, and her nearly black eyes were anxious. "Nynaeve Sedai, Elayne Sedai, Lord Lan says you
are to come at once," she said breathlessly. "He told me to
speak to no one, and you aren't to, either."

Elayne and Nynaeve exchanged looks with Aviendha
and Birgitte. Nynaeve growled something under her breath
about the man not knowing private from public, but it was
clear before she blushed that she did not believe it. Elayne
felt Birgitte focus, the drawn arrow hunting a target.

Kirstian did not know what Lan wanted, only where she
was to lead them. The small hut outside of Cullen's Crossing where Adeleas had taken Ispan the night before. Lan
stood outside, his eyes as cold as the air, and would not let
Kirstian enter. When Elayne went inside, she saw why.

Adeleas lay on her side beside an overturned stool, a cup
on the rough wooden floor not far from one outstretched
hand. Her eyes stared, and a pool of congealed blood spread
out from the deep slash across her throat. Ispan lay on a
small cot, staring at the ceiling. Lips drawn back in a rictus
bared her teeth, and her bulging eyes seemed full of horror.
As well they might have, since a wrist-thick wooden stake
stood out from between her breasts. The hammer that had
plainly been used to drive it in lay beside the cot, on the
edge of a dark stain that ran back under the cot.

Elayne forced herself to stop thinking about emptying
her stomach on the spot. "Light," she breathed. "Light!
Who could do this? *How* could anyone do this?" Aviendha
shook her head wonderingly, and Lan did not even bother
with that. He just watched nine directions at once, as though
he expected whoever, or whatever, had committed this murder to come through one of the two tiny windows if not
through the walls. Birgitte drew her belt knife, and by her
face, she dearly wished she had her bow. That drawn arrow
was stronger than ever in Elayne's head.

At first, Nynaeve simply stood in one spot, studying the
hut's interior. There was little to see, aside from the obvious. A second three-legged stool, a rough table holding a
flickering lamp, a green teapot and a second cup, a rude
stone fireplace with cold ash on the hearthstone. That was
all. The hut was so small it only took Nynaeve a step to
reach the table. Dipping her finger into the teapot, she

touched it to the tip of her tongue, then spat vigorously and emptied the whole teapot onto the table in a wash of tea and tea leaves. Elayne blinked wonderingly.

"What happened?" Vandene asked coolly from the door. Lan moved to bar her way, but she stopped him with a small gesture. Elayne started to put an arm around her, and received another raised hand to keep her back. Vandene's eyes remained on her sister, calm in a face of Aes Sedai serenity. The dead woman on the cot might as well not have existed. "When I saw all of you heading this way, I thought . . . We knew we didn't have many years remaining, but . . ." Her voice sounded serenity itself, but small wonder if that was a mask. "What have you found, Nynaeve?"

Sympathy looked odd on Nynaeve's face. Clearing her throat, she pointed to the tea leaves without touching them. To white shavings among the matted black leaves. "This is crimsonthorn root," she said, trying to sound matter-of-fact and failing. "It's sweet, so you might miss it in tea unless you know what it is, especially if you take a lot of honey."

Vandene nodded, never taking her eyes from her sister. "Adeleas developed a taste for sweet tea in Ebou Dar."

"A little kills pain," Nynaeve said. "This much . . . This much kills, but slowly. Even a few sips would be enough." Taking a deep breath, she added, "They might have remained conscious for hours. Not able to move, but aware. Either whoever did this didn't want to risk someone coming too soon with an antidote—not that I know one, for a brew this strong—or else they wanted one or the other to know who was killing them." Elayne gasped at the brutality, but Vandene simply nodded.

"Ispan, I think, since they appear to have taken the most time with her." The white-haired Green almost seemed to be thinking aloud, working out a puzzle. Cutting a throat took less time than driving a stake through someone's heart. The calm of her made Elayne's skin crawl. "Adeleas would never have accepted anything to drink from someone she didn't know, not out here with Ispan. Those two facts name her killer, in a way. A Darkfriend, and one of our party. One of us." Elayne felt two chills, her own, and Birgitte's.

"One of us," Nynaeve agreed sadly. Aviendha began testing the edge of her belt knife on her thumb, and for once, Elayne felt no objection.

Vandene asked to be left alone with her sister for a few moments, and sat on the floor to cradle Adeleas in her arms before they were out of the door. Jaem, Vandene's gnarled old Warder, was waiting outside with a shivering Kirstian.

Suddenly a wail burst out inside the hut, the full-throated cry of a woman mourning the loss of everything. Nynaeve, of all people, turned to go back, but Lan laid a hand on her arm, and Jaem planted himself before the door with eyes not much warmer than Lan's. There was nothing to do but leave them, Vandene to shriek her pain, and Jaem to guard her in it. And share it, Elayne realized, feeling that knot of emotions in her head that was Birgitte. She shivered, and Birgitte put an arm around her shoulders. Aviendha did the same from the other side, and motioned for Nynaeve to join them, which she did, after a moment. The murder Elayne had thought of so lightly had come, one of their companions was a Darkfriend, and the day suddenly felt cold enough to shatter bones, but there was a warmth in the closeness of her friends.

The last ten funereal miles to Caemlyn took two days in the snow, with even the Windfinders decently subdued. Not that they pushed Merilille any less hard. Not that Kin stopped talking, and falling silent whenever a sister or one of the Knitting Circle came near. Vandene, with her sister's silver-mounted saddle on her horse, appeared as serene as she had at Adeleas' graveside, but Jaem's eyes carried a silent promise of death that surely rode in Vandene's heart, too. Elayne could not have been happier to see the walls and towers of Caemlyn if the very sight had given her the Rose Crown and brought back Adeleas.

Even Caemlyn, one of the great cities of the world, had never seen the likes of their party before, and once inside the fifty-foot walls of gray stone they attracted notice as they crossed the New City along wide, slush-filled streets bustling with people and carts and wagons. Shopkeepers stood in their doorways and gaped. Wagon drivers reined in their teams to stare. Towering Aielmen and tall Maidens eyed them from every corner, it seemed. The people seemed to take no notice of the Aiel, but Elayne did. She loved Aviendha as she did herself, more, but she could not love an army of armed Aiel walking Caemlyn's streets.

The Inner City, ringed by towered walls of silver-streaked

white, was a remembered delight, and Elayne finally began to feel that she was coming home. The streets followed the curves of the hills, and every rise presented a new vista of snow-covered parks and monuments laid out to be seen from above as well as up close, of brightly tiled towers shining with a hundred colors in the afternoon sun. And then the Royal Palace itself was before them, a confection of pale spires and golden domes and intricate stonework traceries. The banner of Andor waved from nearly every prominence, the White Lion on red. And from the others, the Dragon Banner or the Banner of Light.

At the tall gilded gates of the Palace, Elayne rode forward alone in her travel-stained gray riding dress. Tradition and legend said women who first approached the Palace in splendor always failed. She had made clear that she had to do it alone, yet she almost wished Aviendha and Birgitte had succeeded in overruling her. Half the two dozen guards in front of the gates were Aiel Maidens, the others men in blue helmets and blue coats with a red-and-gold Dragon marching across the chest.

"I am Elayne Trakand," she announced loudly, surprised at how calm she sounded. Her voice carried, and across the great plaza people turned from staring at her companions to stare at her. The ancient formula rolled from her tongue. "In the name of House Trakand, by right of descent from Ishara, I have come to claim the Lion Throne of Andor, if the Light wills it so."

The gates opened wide.

It would not be that easy, of course. Even possession of the Palace was not enough to hold the throne of Andor by itself. Passing her companions into the care of an astonished Reene Harfor—and very pleased to see that the graying First Maid, round and as regal as any queen, still had the Palace in her capable hands—and a coterie of servants in red-and-white livery, Elayne hurried to the Grand Hall, the throne room of Andor. Alone, again. This was not part of the ritual, not yet. She should have been going to change into the red silk with the pearl-worked bodice and white lions climbing the sleeves, but she felt compelled. This time, not even Nynaeve tried to object.

White columns twenty paces high marched down the sides of the Grand Hall. The throne room was empty, still.

That would not last long. Clear afternoon light through the glassed casements in tall windows along the walls mingled with the colored light through the great windows set in the ceiling, where the White Lion of Andor alternated with scenes of Andoran victories and the faces of the land's earliest queens, beginning with Ishara herself, as dark as any of the Atha'an Miere, as full of authority as any Aes Sedai. No ruler of Andor could forget herself with the predecessors who had forged this nation staring down at her.

One thing she feared to see—the huge monstrosity of a throne, all gilded Dragons, that she had seen standing on the dais at the far end of the Hall in *Tel'aran'rhiod*. It was not there, thank the Light. The Lion Throne no longer rested on a tall plinth like some trophy, either, but kept its proper place upon the dais, a massive chair, carved and gilded, but sized for a woman. The White Lion, picked out in moonstones on a field of rubies, would stand above the head of any woman who sat there. No man could feel at his ease sitting on that throne, because, so legend said, he would know he had sealed his doom. Elayne thought it more likely the builders had simply made sure a man would not *fit* on it easily.

Climbing the white marble steps of the dais, she laid a hand on one arm of the throne. She had no right to sit on it herself, not yet. Not until she was acknowledged Queen. But taking oaths on the Lion Throne was a custom as old as Andor. She had to resist the desire to simply fall on her knees and weep into the throne's seat. Reconciled to her mother's death she might be, but this brought back all the pain. She could not break down now.

"Under the Light, I will honor your memory, Mother," she said softly. "I will honor the name of Morgase Trakand, and try to bring only honor to House Trakand."

"I ordered the guards to keep the curious and the favor-seekers away. I suspected you might want to be alone here for a time."

Elayne turned slowly to face Dyelin Taravin, as the golden-haired woman walked the length of the Grand Hall. Dyelin had been one of her mother's earliest supporters in her own quest for the throne. There was more gray in her hair than Elayne remembered, more lines at the corners of her eyes. She was still quite beautiful. A strong woman. And powerful as friend or foe.

She stopped at the foot of the dais, looking up. "I've been hearing for two days that you were alive, but I didn't really believe it until now. You've come to accept the throne from the Dragon Reborn, then?"

"I claim the throne by my own right, Dyelin, with my own hand. The Lion Throne is no bauble to be accepted from a man." Dyelin nodded, as at self-evident truth. Which it was, to any Andoran. "How do you stand, Dyelin? With Trakand, or against? I have heard your name often on my way here."

"Since you claim the throne by your own right, with." Few people could sound as dry as she. Elayne sat down on the top step, and motioned the older woman to join her. "There are a few obstacles, of course," Dyelin went on as she gathered her blue skirts to sit. "There have been several claimants already, as you may know. Naean and Elenia, I have securely locked up. On a charge of treason that most people seem willing to accept. For the time being. Elenia's husband is still active for her, though quietly, and Arymilla has announced a claim, the silly goose. She's getting support of a kind, but nothing that need worry you. Your real worries—aside from Aiel all over the city waiting for the Dragon Reborn to come back—are Aemlyn, Arathelle, and Pelivar. For the moment, Luan and Ellorien will be behind you, but they might go over to those three."

A very succinct list, delivered in a tone suitable for discussing a possible horse trade. Naean and Elenia she knew about, if not that Jarid still thought his wife had a chance at the throne. Arymilla *was* a goose to believe she would be accepted, whatever her support. The last five names were worrying, though. Each had been as strong a supporter of her mother, as had Dyelin, and each led a strong House.

"So Arathelle and Aemlyn want the throne," Elayne murmured. "I can't believe it of Ellorien, not for herself." Pelivar might be acting for one of his daughters, but Luan had only granddaughters, none near old enough. "You spoke as if they might unite, all five Houses. Behind whom?" That would be a dire threat.

Smiling, Dyelin propped her chin in her hand. "They

seem to think *I* should have the throne. Now, what do you intend about the Dragon Reborn? He hasn't been back here in some time, but he can pop out of the air, it seems."

Elayne squeezed her eyes shut for a moment, but when she opened them, she was still sitting on the steps of the dais in the Grand Hall, and Dyelin was still smiling at her. Her brother fought for Elaida, and her half-brother was a Whitecloak. She had filled the Palace with women who might turn on one another at any moment, not to mention the fact that one was a Darkfriend, maybe even Black Ajah. And the strongest threat she faced in claiming the throne, a *very* strong one, stood behind a woman who said *she* supported Elayne. The world was quite mad. She might as well add her bit.

"I mean to bond him my Warder," she said, and went on before the other woman could more than blink in astonishment. "I also hope to marry him. Those things have nothing to do with the Lion Throne, however. The very first thing I intend . . ."

As she went on, Dyelin began to laugh. Elayne wished she knew whether it was from delight over her plans or because Dyelin saw her own path to the Lion Throne being made smooth. At least she knew what she faced, now.

Riding into Caemlyn, Daved Hanlon could not help thinking what a city for the looting it was. In his years soldiering, he had seen many villages and towns looted, and once, twenty years ago, a great city, Cairhien, after the Aiel left. Strange that all these Aiel had left Caemlyn so apparently untouched, but then, if the tallest towers in Cairhien had not been burning, it might have been hard to know they had been there; plenty of gold, among other things, lying about for the picking up, and plenty of men to do the picking. He could see these broad streets full of horsemen and fleeing people, fat merchants who would give up their gold before the knife touched them in the hope their lives would be spared, slim girls and plump women so terrified when they were dragged into a corner that they could hardly manage to squeal, much less struggle. He had seen those things and done them, and he hoped to again. Not in Caemlyn, though, he admitted with a sigh. If the orders that sent him here had been the sort he could disobey, he would have gone where the pickings might not be so rich, but definitely easier to pluck.

His instructions had been clear. Stabling his horse at The Red Bull, in the New City, he walked a mile to a tall stone house on a side street, the house of a wealthy merchant discreet about her gold, marked with a tiny painted sigil on the doors, a red heart on a golden hand. The hulking fellow who let him in was no merchant's servant, with his sunken knuckles and sullen eyes. Without a word, the huge man led him deeper into the house, then down, toward the basements. Hanlon eased his sword in its scabbard. Among the things he had seen were men and women, failures, led to their own very elaborate executions. He did not think he had failed, but then again, he had hardly succeeded. He had followed orders, though. Which was not always enough.

In the rough stone basement, lit by gilded lamps set all around, his eyes went first to a pretty woman in a lace-trimmed dress of scarlet silk, with her hair caught in frothy lace net. He did not know who this Lady Shiaine was, but his orders had been to obey her. He made his best leg, smiling. She simply looked at him, as if waiting for him to notice what else the basement held.

He could hardly have missed it, since except for a few casks the room held only a large heavy table, decorated in a very strange fashion. Two ovals had been cut in the table-top, and from one stuck the head and shoulders of a man, his head wrenched back against the wooden surface and held there by means of leather straps nailed to the tabletop and fastened to a block of wood jammed between his teeth. A woman, prepared the same, provided the other decoration. Beneath the table, they knelt with wrists tied to ankles. Quite securely held for any sort of pleasure. The man had a touch of gray in his hair and the face of a lord, but unsurprisingly, his deep-set eyes rolled wildly. The woman's hair, spread out on the table, was dark and glossy, but her face was a little long for Hanlon's taste.

Suddenly he really saw her face, and his hand leaped to his sword before he could stop it. Releasing the hilt took some effort, which he took pains to hide. An Aes Sedai's face, but an Aes Sedai who let herself be fastened like that was no threat.

"So you have some brains," Shiaine said. By her accents, she was a noble, and she certainly had the commanding air, sweeping around the table to peer down into the bound man's face. "I asked the Great Master Moridin to send me a man with brains. Poor Jaichim here has very few."

Hanlon frowned, and smoothed it away immediately. His orders had come from Moghedien herself. Who in the Pit of Doom was Moridin? It did not matter. His orders had come from Moghedien; that was enough.

The hulking fellow handed Shiaine a funnel, which she fitted into a hole bored through the block of wood between this Jaichim's teeth. The man's eyes seemed ready to leap from his head. "Poor Jaichim here failed very badly," Shiaine said, smiling like a fox looking at a chicken. "Moridin wishes him punished. Poor Jaichim does like his brandy."

She stepped back, not so far that she could not see clearly, and Hanlon gave a start as the hulking man came to the table with one of the casks. Hanlon did think he could have lifted the thing unaided, but the big man tipped it easily. The bound man shrieked once, and then a stream of dark liquid was pouring from the cask into the funnel, turning his cry to gurgling. The rough smell of crude brandy filled the air. Secured as he was, the man fought, thrashing about, even managing to heave the table sideways, but the brandy kept pouring. Bubbles rose in the funnel as he tried to shout or scream, but the steady stream never faltered. And then his thrashing slowed and stopped. Wide, glazing eyes stared up the ceiling, and brandy trickled from his nostrils. The big fellow still did not stop until the last drops fell from an empty cask.

"I think poor Jaichim has finally had enough brandy," Shiaine said, and laughed in delight.

Hanlon nodded. He supposed the man had, at that. He wondered who he had been.

Shiaine was not quite finished. At a gesture from her, the hulking man ripped one of the straps holding the Aes Sedai's gag off of its nail. Hanlon thought the wooden block might have loosened a few of her teeth coming out of her mouth, but if so, she did not waste time on them. She began babbling before the fellow let go of the strap.

"I will obey you!" she howled. "I will obey, as the Great Master commanded! He set the shield on me to dissolve so I could obey! He told me so! Let me prove myself! I will crawl! I am a worm, and you are the sun! Oh, please! Please! Please!"

Shiaine stifled words if not whimpers by putting a hand over the Aes Sedai's mouth. "How do I know you won't fail again, Falion? You have failed before, and Moridin left your punishment to me. He gave me another; do I need two of you? I may give you a second chance to plead your case, Falion—perhaps—but if I do, you will have to convince me. I will expect *true* enthusiasm."

Falion began screaming pleas again, making extravagant promises, the moment Shiaine's hand moved, but soon enough she was reduced to wordless shrieks and tears as the gag was replaced, the nail driven through the strap again, and Jaichim's funnel placed above her gaping throat. The hulking man stood another cask on the table beside her head. The Aes Sedai seemed to go mad, bulging eyes rolling, flinging herself about below the table till it trembled.

Hanlon was impressed. An Aes Sedai must be harder to break than a plump merchant or his round-cheeked daughter. Still, she had had the help of one of the Chosen, it seemed. Realizing that Shiaine was looking at him, he stopped smiling down at Falion. His first rule in life was never to offend those the Chosen set above him.

"Tell me, Hanlon," Shiaine said, "how would you like to put your hands on a queen?"

He licked his lips in spite of himself. A queen? *That*, he had never done.

CHAPTER
29

A Cup of Sleep

D on't be an utter woolhead, Rand," Min said. Making herself remain seated, she crossed her legs and kicked her foot idly, but she could not keep exasperation out of her voice. "Go to her! Speak to her!"

"Why?" he snapped. "I know which letter to believe, now. It's better this way. She's safe, now. From anyone who wants to strike at me. Safe from me! It's better!" But he stalked up and down in his shirtsleeves between the two rows of chairs in front of the Dragon Throne, his fists white-knuckle hard, glaring to beat the black clouds beyond the casements that were laying a new blanket of snow on Cairhien.

Min exchanged looks with Fedwin Morr, who stood by the sun-carved doors. The Maidens now let anyone who was not an obvious threat walk in unannounced, but those Rand did not want to see this morning would be turned away by the husky boy. He wore the Dragon and Sword on his black collar, and Min knew he had already seen more battles—more horror—than most men three times his age, yet he was a boy. Today, casting uneasy glances at Rand, he seemed younger than ever. The sword on his hip still looked out of place, to her.

"The Dragon Reborn is a man, Fedwin," she said. "And like any man, he's sulking because he thinks a woman doesn't want to see him again."

Goggling, the boy jerked as if she had goosed him. Rand stopped to scowl at her sullenly. All that kept her from laughing was knowing that he was hiding pain as real as any stab wound. That, and the sure knowledge that he would be as hurt if she had done what had been done. Not that she would ever have the chance to rip down his banners, but the point applied. Rand had been stunned at first by the news Taim brought from Caemlyn at dawn, but as soon as the man left, he had stopped looking like a pole-axed bull and started . . . This!

Standing, she adjusted her pale green coat, folded her arms beneath her breasts, and confronted him directly. "What else can it be?" she asked calmly. Well, she tried for calm, and almost made it. She loved the man, but after a morning of this, she wanted to box his ears soundly. "You haven't mentioned Mat twice, and you don't know whether *he's* even alive."

"Mat's alive," Rand snarled. "I'd know if he was dead. What do you mean I'm—!" His jaw clenched as if he could not make himself say the word.

"Sulking," she provided. "Soon, you'll be pouting. Some women think men are prettier when they pout. I'm not one of them." Well, enough of that. His face had darkened, and he was not blushing. "Haven't you twisted yourself into knots to make sure she got the throne of Andor? Which is hers by right, might I add. Didn't you say you wanted her to have Andor whole, not ripped apart like Cairhien or Tear?"

"I did!" he roared. "And now it's hers, and she wants me out of it! Good enough, I say! And don't tell me again to stop shouting! I'm not—!" He realized that he was, and clamped his teeth shut. A low growl came from his throat. Morr set to studying one of his buttons, twisting it back and forth. He had been doing a lot of that this morning.

Min kept her face smooth. She was *not* going to slap him, and he was too big for her to spank. "Andor is hers, just as you wanted," she said. Calmly. Almost. "None of the Forsaken are going after her now she's torn your banners down." A dangerous light appeared in those blue-gray eyes, but she pressed on. "Just as you wanted. And you can't believe she's siding with your enemies. Andor will follow the Dragon Reborn, and you know it. So the only reason for you to be in a snit is because you think she doesn't want to see you. Go to her, you fool!" The next part was the hardest to say. "Before you can say two words, she'll be kissing you." Light, she loved Elayne almost as much as she did Rand—maybe as much, in a very different way—but how was a woman to compete with a beautiful golden-haired queen who had a powerful nation at her beck and call?

"I am not . . . angry," Rand said in a tight voice. And started pacing again. Min considered kicking him square in the bottom. Hard.

One of the doors opened to admit leathery white-haired Sorilea, who brushed Morr aside even as he was looking to see whether Rand wanted her allowed entry. Rand opened his mouth—angrily, whatever he chose to claim—and five women in thick black robes damp with melted snow followed the Wise One into the room, hands folded, eyes down, and deep hoods not quite hiding their faces. Their feet were wrapped in rags.

Min's scalp prickled. To her eyes, images and auras danced and vanished and were replaced around all six women, just as around Rand. She had been hoping he had forgotten those five were alive. What in the name of the Light was that wicked old woman doing?

Sorilea gestured once in a clatter of gold and ivory brace-lets, and the five hastily arranged themselves in a line atop the golden Rising Sun set in the stone floor. Rand strode along that row, stripping back hoods, baring faces that he stared into cold-eyed.

Every one of the black-robed women was unwashed, her hair lank and dirty with sweat. Elza Penfell, a Green sister, met his gaze eagerly, a strangely fervent look on her face. Nesune Bihara, a slender Brown, studied him as intently as he did her. Sarene Nemdahl, so beautiful even in her dirt that you thought her agelessness must be natural, appeared to be holding to her White Ajah coolness by a fingernail. Beldeine Nyram, too new to the shawl to have the ageless features, essayed an uncertain smile that melted under his stare. Erian Boroleos, pale and almost as lovely as Sarene, flinched, then visibly forced herself to look into that frigid gaze. Those last two also were Green, and all five had been among the sisters who kidnapped him on Elaida's orders. Some had been among those who tortured him while trying to carry him to Tar Valon. Sometimes Rand still woke, sweating and panting, mumbling about being confined, being beaten. Min hoped she did not see murder in his stare.

"These were named *da'tsang*, Rand al'Thor," Sorilea said. "I think they feel their shame in the bone, now. Erian Boroleos was the first to ask to be beaten as you were, sunrise and sunset, but now each has done so. That plea has been granted. Each has asked to serve you however she may. The *toh* for their betrayal cannot be met," her voice darkened for a moment; to the Aiel, the betrayal of the kidnapping was far worse than what they had done after, "yet they know their shame, and they wish to try. We have decided to leave the choice to you."

Min frowned. Leave the choice to him? Wise Ones rarely left any choice they could make to anyone else. Sorilea *never* did. The sinewy Wise One casually shifted her dark shawl on her shoulders and watched Rand as if this was of no importance at all. But she shot one blue ice glance at Min, and suddenly Min was sure that if she said the wrong thing here, that bony old woman would have her hide. It was not a viewing. She just knew Sorilea better than she wanted to, by now.

Determinedly she set to studying what was appearing and vanishing around the women. No easy task when they stood so close together she could not be certain whether a particular image belonged to one woman or the woman next to her. At least the auras were always certain. Light, let her be able to understand at least some of what she saw!

Rand took Sorilea's announcement coolly, on the surface. He rubbed his hands together slowly, then thoughtfully examined the herons branded on his palms. He examined each of those Aes Sedai faces in turn. Finally, he focused on Erian.

"Why?" he asked her in a mild voice. "I killed two of your Warders. Why?" Min winced. Rand was many things, but seldom mild. And Erian was one of the few who had beaten him more than once.

The pale Illianer sister straightened. Images danced, and auras flashed and were gone. Nothing Min could read. Dirty-faced and her long black hair matted, Erian gathered Aes Sedai authority around her and met his gaze levelly. But her answer came simply and directly. "We did be wrong in taking you. I have considered long on it. You must fight the Last Battle, and we must help you. If you will no accept me, I do understand, but I will help as you do require if you will allow."

Rand stared at her without expression.

He put that same one-word question to each, and their answers were as different as the women.

"The Green is the Battle Ajah," Beldeine told him proudly, and despite smudges on her cheeks and dark circles beneath her eyes, she did look a Queen of Battles. But then, Saldaean women seemed to find that second nature. "When you go to Tarmon Gai'don, the Green must be there. I will follow, if you will accept me." Light, she was going to bond an Asha'man as a Warder! How . . . ? No; it was not important now.

"What we did was logical at the time." Sarene's tightly held cool serenity slipped into clear worry, and she shook her head. "I say that to explain, not to exculpate. Circumstances have changed. For you, the logical course might seem to . . ." She drew a decidedly unsteady breath. Images and auras; a tempestuous love affair, of all things! The woman was ice, however beautiful. And there was nothing useful in knowing some man would melt her! "To send us back to captivity," she went on, "or even execute us. For me, logic says I must serve you."

Nesune tilted her head, and her nearly black eyes seemed to be trying to store away every scrap of him. One red-and-green aura spoke of honors, and fame. A huge building appeared above her head and vanished. A library she would found. "I want to study you," she said simply. "I can hardly do that carrying stones or digging holes. They do leave plenty of time for thought, but serving you seems a fair exchange for what I might learn." Rand blinked at the directness of that, but otherwise, his expression did not alter.

The most surprising answer came from Elza, in her manner of delivery more than the words. Sinking to her knees, she gazed up at Rand with feverish eyes. Her whole face seemed to shine with fervor. Auras flared and images cascaded around her, telling nothing. "You are the Dragon Reborn," she said breathlessly. "You must be there for the Last Battle. I must help you be there! Whatever is necessary, I will do!" And she flung herself facedown, pressing her lips to the polished stone floor in front of his boots. Even Sorilea looked taken aback, and Sarene's mouth dropped open. Morr gaped at her and hastily returned to twisting his button. Min thought he giggled nervously, almost under his breath.

Turning on his heel, Rand stalked halfway to the Dragon Throne, where his scepter and the crown of Illian rested atop his gold-embroidered red coat. His face was so bleak that Min wanted to rush to him no matter who was watching, but she continued to study the Aes Sedai. And Sorilea. She had never seen anything really useful around that white-haired harridan.

Abruptly, Rand turned back, striding toward the line of women so quickly that Beldeine and Sarene stepped back. A sharp gesture from Sorilea jerked them into place again.

"Would you accept being confined in a box?" His voice grated, stone grinding on frozen stone. "Locked in a chest all day, and beaten before you go in and when you come out?" That was what they had done to him.

"Yes!" Elza moaned against the floor. "Whatever I must do, I will!"

"If you do require it," Erian managed shakily, and, faces aghast, the others nodded slowly.

Min stared in amazement, knotting her fists in her coat pockets. That he might think of getting his own back in the same manner seemed almost natural, but she had to stop it, somehow. She knew him better than he did himself; she knew where he was hard as a knife blade, and where he was vulnerable no matter how he denied it. He would never forgive himself this. But how? Fury contorted his face, and he shook his head as he did when arguing with that voice he heard. He muttered one word aloud that she understood. *Ta'veren.* Sorilea stood there calmly examining him as closely as Nesune did. Not even the threat of the chest shook the Brown. Except for Elza, still moaning and kissing the floor, the others were hollow-eyed, as if seeing themselves doubled up and bound as he had been.

Among all of those images spilling around Rand and the women, suddenly an aura flashed, blue and yellow tinged with green, encompassing them all. And Min knew its meaning. She gasped, half in surprise, half in relief.

"They will serve you, each in her fashion, Rand," she

said hurriedly. "I saw it." *Sorilea* would serve him? Suddenly Min wondered exactly what "in her fashion" meant. The words came with the knowing, but she did not always know what the words themselves meant. But they *would* serve; that much was plain.

The fury drained from Rand's face as he silently studied the Aes Sedai. Some of them glanced at Min with raised eyebrows, obviously marveling that a few words from her carried so much weight, but for the most part, they watched Rand and hardly seemed to breathe. Even Elza lifted her head to gaze up at him. Sorilea gave Min one quick look, and the faintest nod. Approving, Min thought. So the old woman pretended not to care one way or the other, did she?

At last, Rand spoke. "You can swear to me as Kiruna and the others did. That, or go back to wherever the Wise Ones have been keeping you. I'll accept nothing less." Despite a hint of demand in his voice, he looked as if he, too, did not care, arms folded, eyes impatient. The oath he demanded of them came out in a rush.

Min did not expect quibbles, not after her viewing, yet it was still a surprise when Elza scrambled up to her knees, and the others lowered themselves to theirs. In ragged unison, five more Aes Sedai swore under the Light and by their hope of salvation to serve the Dragon Reborn faithfully until the Last Battle had come and gone. Nesune delivered the words as though examining each one, Sarene as if stating a principle of logic, Elza wearing a wide, victorious smile, but they all swore. How many Aes Sedai would he gather around him?

With the oath, Rand seemed to lose interest. "Find them clothes and put them with your other 'apprentices,'" he told Sorilea absently. He was frowning, but not at her or the Aes Sedai. "How many do you think you'll end up with?" Min almost jumped at the echo of her own thought.

"However many are necessary," Sorilea said dryly. "I think more will come." She clapped her hands once and gestured, and the five sisters sprang to their feet. Only Nesune looked surprised at the alacrity with which they had obeyed. Sorilea smiled, a very satisfied smile for an Aiel, and Min did not think it was caused by the other women's obedience.

Nodding, Rand turned away. He was already beginning

to pace again, already beginning to scowl over Elayne. Min settled into her chair once more, wishing she had one of Master Fel's books to read. Or to throw at Rand. Well, one of Master Fel's to read, and someone else's to throw.

Sorilea herded the black-clad sisters out of the room, but at the last, she paused with one hand holding a door and looked back at Rand striding away from her toward the gilded throne. Her lips pursed thoughtfully. "That woman, Cadsuane Melaidhrin, is beneath this roof again today," she said at last, to his back. "I think she believes you are afraid of her, Rand al'Thor, the way you avoid her whereabouts." With that, she left.

For a long moment, Rand stood staring at the throne. Or maybe at something beyond it. Abruptly, he gave himself a shake and strode the remaining distance to pick up the Crown of Swords. On the point of setting it on his head, though, he hesitated, then put it back. Donning the coat, he left crown and scepter where they lay.

"I mean to find out what Cadsuane wants," he announced. "She doesn't come to the palace every day because she likes a trip through the snow. Will you come with me, Min? Maybe you'll have a viewing."

She was on her feet faster than any of those Aes Sedai. A visit with Cadsuane would likely be as pleasurable as a visit with Sorilea, yet anything was better than sitting there alone. Besides, maybe she *would* have a viewing. Fedwin fell in behind her and Rand with an alert look in his eyes.

The six Maidens outside in the tall vaulted hallway rose, but they did not follow. Somara was the only one Min knew; she gave Min a brief smile, and Rand a flat, disapproving stare. The others glowered. The Maidens had accepted his explanation about why he had gone without them in the first place, so any watchers would believe for as long as possible that he was still in Cairhien, but they still demanded to know why he had not sent for them afterward, and Rand had had no answers. He muttered something under his breath, and quickened his pace so Min had to stretch her legs to keep up.

"Watch Cadsuane carefully, Min," he said. "And you, too, Morr. She's up to some Aes Sedai scheme, but burn me if I can see what. I don't know. There's—"

A stone wall seemed to strike Min from behind; she

thought she heard roaring, crashing. And then Rand was turning her over—she was lying on the floor?—looking down at her with the first fear she remembered seeing in those morning-blue eyes. It only faded when she sat up, coughing. The air was full of dust! And then she saw the corridor.

The Maidens were gone from in front of Rand's doors. The doors themselves were gone, along with most of the wall, and a jagged hole nearly as big gaped in the wall opposite. She could see into his apartments clearly despite the dust, into devastation. Massive piles of rubble lay everywhere, and above, the ceiling yawned open to the sky. Snow swirled down onto flames dancing among the rubble. One of the massive blackwood posts of his bed stuck burning out of shattered stone, and she realized she could see all the way outside to the stepped towers veiled by the snowfall. It was as if a huge hammer had smashed into the Sun Palace. And had they been in there, instead of going to see Cadsuane . . . Min shivered.

"What . . . ?" she began unsteadily, then abandoned the useless question. Any fool would see *what* had happened. "Who?" she asked instead.

Covered in dust, hair every which way, and with tears in their coats, the two men looked as if they had been rolled along the corridor, and perhaps they had. She thought they were all a good ten paces farther from the doors than she remembered. From where the doors had been. In the distance, anxious shouts rose, echoing along the halls. Neither man answered her.

"Can I trust you, Morr?" Rand asked.

Fedwin met his gaze openly. "With your life, my Lord Dragon," he said simply.

"That's what I *am* trusting you with," Rand said. His fingers brushed her cheek, and then he stood abruptly. "Guard her with *your* life, Morr." Hard as steel, his voice. Grim as death. "If they're still in the Palace, they'll feel you try to make a gateway, and strike before you can finish. Don't channel at all unless you must, but be ready. Take her down to the servants' quarters, and kill anyone or anything that tries to get to her. Anyone!"

With a last look down at her—oh, Light, any other time,

she would have thought she could die happily, seeing that look in his eyes!—he went running, away from the ruination. Away from her. Whoever had tried to kill him would be hunting for him.

Morr patted her on the arm with a dusty hand and gave her a boyish grin. "Don't worry, Min. I'll take care of you."

But who was going to take care of Rand? *Can I trust you,* he had asked this boy who had been one of the first to come asking to learn. *Light, who would make him safe?*

Rounding a corner, Rand stopped with a hand against one wall to seize the Source. A fool thing, not wanting Min to see him stagger when someone tried to kill him, but there it was. Not just any someone. A man, Demandred, or perhaps Asmodean come back at last. Maybe both; there had been an oddity, as if the weaving came from different directions. He had felt the channeling too late to do anything. He would have died, in his rooms. He was ready to die. But not Min, no, not Min. Elayne was better off, turning against him. Oh, Light, she was!

He seized the Source, and *saidin* flooded him with molten cold and freezing heat, with life and sweetness, filth and death. His stomach twisted, and the hallway in front of him doubled itself. For an instant, he thought he saw a face. Not with his eyes; in his head. A man, shimmering and unrecognizable, gone. He floated in the Void, empty, and full of the Power.

You won't win, he told Lews Therin. *If I die, I'll die* me!

I should have sent Ilyena away, Lews Therin whispered back. *She would have lived.*

Pushing the voice away as he pushed himself from the wall, Rand slipped along the Palace corridors with all the stealth he could muster, stepping lightly, gliding close to tapestry-hung walls, around gold-worked chests and gilded cabinets bearing fragile golden porcelains and ivory statuettes. His eyes searched for his attackers. They would not be satisfied short of finding his body, but they would be very careful in approaching his rooms in case he had survived by some *ta'veren* swirl of fate. They would wait, to see whether he stirred. In the Void, he was as near one with the Power as any man could live through. In the Void, as with a sword, he was one with his surroundings.

Frantic shouts and clamor rose in every direction, some screaming to know what had happened, others crying that the Dragon Reborn had gone mad. The bundle of frustration in his head that was Alanna provided one small comfort. She was out of the Palace, as she had been all morning, maybe even outside the city walls. He wished Min was, too. Sometimes he saw men and women down one hallway or another, black-liveried servants mainly, running, falling down and scrambling up to run again. They did not see him. With the Power in him, he could hear every whisper. Including the whisper of soft boots running, light-footed.

Backing against the wall beside a long table topped with porcelain, he quickly wove Fire and Air around himself and held very still wrapped in Folded Light.

Maidens appeared, a stream of them, veiled, and ran by without seeing him. Toward his apartments. He could not let them accompany him; he had promised, but to let them fight, not to lead them to slaughter. When he found Demandred and Asmodean, all the Maidens could do was die, and he already had five names to learn and add to his list. Somara of the Bent Peak Daryne was already there. A promise he had had to make, a promise he had to keep. For that promise alone, he deserved to die!

Eagles and women can only be kept safe in cages, Lews Therin said as though quoting, then abruptly began weeping as the last of the Maidens vanished.

Rand moved on, sweeping back and forth through the palace in arcs that slowly moved away from his apartments. Folded Light used very little of the Power—so little no man could have felt the use of *saidin* unless right on top of it—and he used it whenever anyone seemed about to see him. His attackers had not struck at his rooms on the chance he would be there. They had eyes-and-ears in the Palace. Maybe it had been *ta'veren* work that pulled him out of the apartments, if a *ta'veren* could work on himself, and maybe just happenstance, but perhaps his tugging at the Pattern could bring his attackers within his grasp while they thought him dead or injured. Lews Therin chuckled at the thought. Rand could almost feel the man rubbing his hands in anticipation.

Three more times he had to hide behind the Power as veiled Maidens rushed by, and once when he saw Cadsuane sweeping along the corridor ahead with no fewer than six Aes Sedai at her heels, and not one other that he recognized besides her. They seemed to be hunting. He was not afraid of the gray-haired sister, precisely. No, of course not afraid! But he waited until she and her friends were well out of sight before letting his concealing weave go. Lews Therin did not chuckle over Cadsuane. He was deathly silent until she was gone.

Rand stepped away from the wall, a door opened right beside him, and Ailil peeked out. He had not known he was near her rooms. Behind her shoulder stood a dark woman with fat golden rings in her ears and a medallion-filled golden chain running across her left cheek to her nose ring. Shalon, Windfinder to Harine din Togara, the Atha'an Miere ambassador who had moved into the Palace with her retinue almost as Merana informed him of the agreement. And meeting with a woman who might want him dead. Their eyes popped at the sight of him.

He was as gentle as he could be, but he had to be quick. A few moments after the door opened, he was tucking a somewhat rumpled Ailil beneath her bed alongside Shalon. Perhaps they were not part of what was happening. Perhaps. Safe was better than sorry. Glaring at him above mouths wadded full of Ailil's scarves, the two women writhed against the torn strips of bedsheet he had used to bind their wrists and ankles. The shield he had tied off on Shalon would hold her for a day or two before the knot unraveled, but someone would find them and cut their other bonds before too much longer.

Worrying about that shield, he opened the door enough to check the hallway, and hurried out, along the empty corridor. He could not have left the Windfinder free to channel, but shielding a woman was not a matter of dribbles of the Power. If one of his attackers had been close enough . . . But he saw no one down any of the crossing corridors, either.

Fifty paces beyond Ailil's rooms, the corridor opened into a square-railed balcony of blue marble with broad stairs at either end, fronting a square chamber with a high, vaulted ceiling and the same sort of balcony at the other side. Tapestries ten paces long hung along the walls, birds soaring to the skies in rigid patterns. Below, Dashiva stood looking about, licking his lips uncertainly. Gedwyn and Rochaid were with him! Lews Therin chittered of killing.

". . . telling you *I* felt nothing," Gedwyn was saying. "He's dead!"

And Dashiva saw Rand, at the head of the stairs.

The only warning he had was the sudden snarl that contorted Dashiva's face. Dashiva channeled, and with no time to think, Rand wove—as so often, he did not know what; something dredged from Lews Therin's memories; he was not even sure he created the weave entirely himself, or whether Lews Therin snatched at *saidin*—Air and Fire and Earth woven around himself just so. The fire that leaped from Dashiva erupted, shattering marble, flinging Rand back down the hallway, bounding and rolling in his cocoon.

That barrier would keep out anything short of balefire. Including air to breathe. Rand released it panting, scraping along the floor, with the crash of the explosions still ringing in the air, dust still hanging and bits of broken marble tumbling. As much as for breath, though, he let it go because what could keep the Power out, kept it in. Before he stopped sliding, he channeled Fire and Air, but woven much differently than for Folded Light. Thin red wires leaped from his left hand, fanning out as they sliced through the intervening stone toward where Dashiva and the others had been standing. From his left sped balls of flame, Fire woven with Air, faster than he could count, and they burned through the stone before exploding in that chamber. One continuous deafening roar made the Palace tremble. Dust that had fallen rose up again, and pieces of stone bounced.

Almost immediately, though, he was up and running, back past Ailil's apartments. The man who struck and stayed in one spot was asking to die. He was ready to die, but not yet. Snarling soundlessly, he sped down another hall, descended narrow servants' stairs, and came out on the floor below.

He took care making his way back to where he had seen Dashiva, deadly weaves ready to fling at so much as a glimpse.

I should have killed them all in the beginning, Lews Therin panted. *I should have killed them all!*

Rand let him rage.

The large chamber seemed to have been washed in fire. Only charred fragments licked by flames remained of the tapestries, and great gouges a pace across had been burned into floor and walls. The stairs Rand had been about to descend ended in a ten-foot gap halfway down. Of the three men, there was no sign. They would not have been consumed completely. Something would have remained.

A servant in a black coat cautiously poked his head from a tiny door beside the stairs on the other side of the chamber. His eyes fell on Rand, rolled up in his head, and he fell forward in a heap. Another servant peeped out of a corridor, then gathered her skirts and raced back the way she had come, shrieking at the top of her lungs that the Dragon Reborn was killing everyone in the Palace.

Rand slipped out of the chamber grimacing. He was very good at frightening people who could not harm him. Very good at destroying.

To destroy, or be destroyed, Lews Therin laughed. *When that's your choice, is there a difference?*

Somewhere in the Palace, a man channeled enough of the Power to make a gateway. Dashiva and the others fleeing? Or wanting him to think that?

He walked the corridors of the Palace, no longer bothering to hide. Everyone else seemed to be. The few servants he saw, fled screaming. Corridor after corridor, he hunted, filled near to bursting with *saidin*, full of fire and ice trying to annihilate him as surely as Dashiva had, full of the taint worming its way into his soul. He had no need of Lews Therin's ragged laughter and ravings to be filled with a desire to kill.

A glimpse of a black coat ahead, and his hand shot up, fire streaking, exploding, tearing away the corner where the two hallways met. Rand let the weave subside, but did not let it go. Had he killed him?

"My Lord Dragon," a voice shouted from beyond the torn stonework, "it's me, Narishma! And Flinn!"

"I didn't recognize you," Rand lied. "Come here."

"I think maybe your blood's hot," Flinn's voice called. "I think maybe we should wait for everybody to cool down."

"Yes," Rand said slowly. Had he really tried to kill Narishma? He did not think he could claim the excuse of Lews Therin. "Yes, that might be best. For a little while longer." There was no answer. Did he hear boots retreating? He forced his hands down and turned another way.

He searched through the Palace for hours without finding a sign of Dashiva or the others. The corridors and great halls, even the kitchens, were empty of people. He found nothing, and learned nothing. No. He realized that he had learned one thing. Trust was a knife, and the hilt was as sharp as the blade.

Then he found pain.

The small stone-walled room was deep below the Sun Palace and warm despite the lack of a fireplace, but Min felt cold. Three gilded lamps on the tiny wooden table gave more than enough light. Rand had said that from there, he could get her away even if someone tried to root the Palace out of the ground. He had not sounded as if he were joking.

Holding the crown of Illian on her lap, she watched Rand. Watched Rand watching Fedwin. Her hands tightened on the crown, and loosened immediately at the stabs of those small swords hidden among the laurel leaves. Strange, that the crown and scepter should have survived when the Dragon Throne itself was a pile of gilded splinters buried in rubble. A large leather scrip beside her chair, with Rand's sword belt and scabbarded sword resting against it, held what else he had been able to salvage. Strange choices for the most part, in her estimation.

You brainless loobie, she thought. *Not thinking about what's right in front of you won't make it go away.*

Rand sat cross-legged on the bare stone floor, still covered in dust and scratches, his coat torn. His face might have been carved. He seemed to watch Fedwin without blinking. The boy was sitting on the floor, too, his legs sprawled out. Tongue caught between his teeth, Fedwin was concentrating on making a tower out of blocks of wood. Min swallowed hard.

She could still remember the horror when she realized the boy "guarding" her now had the mind of a small child. The sadness remained, too—Light, he was only a boy! it was not right!—but she hoped Rand still had him shielded. It had not been easy, talking Fedwin into playing with those wooden blocks instead of pulling stones out of the walls with the Power to make a "big tower to keep you safe in." And then *she* had sat guarding *him* until Rand came. Oh, Light, she wanted to cry. For Rand even more than Fedwin.

"You hide yourself in the depths, it appears."

The deep voice was not finished speaking from the doorway before Rand was on his feet, facing Mazrim Taim. As usual, the hook-nosed man wore a black coat with blue-and-gold Dragons spiraling up the arms. Unlike the other Asha'man, he had neither Sword nor Dragon on his high collar. His dark face wore nearly as little expression as Rand's. Now, staring at Taim, Rand seemed to be gritting his teeth. Min surreptitiously eased a knife in her coat-sleeve. As many images and auras danced around one as the other, but it was not a viewing that made her suddenly wary. She had seen a man trying to decide whether to kill another before, and she was seeing it again.

"You come here holding *saidin*, Taim?" Rand said, much too softly. Taim spread his hands, and Rand said, "That's better." But he did not relax.

"It was just that I thought I might be stabbed by accident," Taim said, "making my way here through corridors packed with those Aiel women. They seem agitated." His eyes never left Rand, but Min was sure he had noticed her touching her knife. "Understandably, of course," he went on smoothly. "I cannot express my joy at finding you alive after seeing what I did above. I came to report deserters. Normally, I wouldn't have bothered, but these are Gedwyn, Rochaid, Torval, and Kisman. It seems they were malcontented over events in Altara, but I never thought they would go this far. I haven't seen any of the men I left with you." For an instant, his gaze flickered to Fedwin. For no more than an instant. "There were . . . other . . . casualties? I will take this one with me, if you wish."

"I told them to stay out of sight," Rand said in a harsh

voice. "And I'll take care of Fedwin. Fedwin Morr, Taim; not 'this one.'" He actually backed to the small table to pick up the silver cup sitting among the lamps. Min's breath caught.

"The Wisdom in my village could cure anything," Rand said as he knelt beside Fedwin. Somehow, he managed to smile at the boy without taking his eyes from Taim. Fedwin smiled back happily and tried to take the cup, but Rand held it for him to drink. "She knows more about herbs than anybody I've ever met. I learned a little from her, which are safe, which not." Fedwin sighed as Rand took the cup away and held the boy to his chest. "Sleep, Fedwin," Rand murmured.

It did seem that the boy was going to sleep. His eyes closed. His chest rose and fell more slowly. Slower. Until it stopped. The smile never left his lips.

"A little something in the wine," Rand said softly as he laid Fedwin down. Min's eyes burned, but she would not cry. She would not!

"You are harder than I thought," Taim muttered.

Rand smiled at him, a hard feral smile. "Add Corlan Dashiva to your list of deserters, Taim. Next time I visit the Black Tower, I expect to see his head on your Traitor's Tree."

"Dashiva?" Taim snarled, his eyes widening in surprise. "It will be as you say. When next you visit the Black Tower." That quickly, he recovered himself, all polished stone and poise once more. How she wished she could read her viewings of him.

"Return to the Black Tower, and don't come here again." Standing, Rand faced the other man over Fedwin's body. "I may be moving about for a while."

Taim's bow was minuscule. "As you command."

As the door closed behind him, Min let out a long breath.

"No point wasting time, and no time to waste," Rand muttered. Kneeling in front of her, he took the crown and slipped it into the scrip with the other things. "Min, I thought I was the whole pack of hounds, chasing down one wolf after another, but it seems I'm the wolf."

"Burn you," she breathed. Tangling both hands in his hair, she stared in his eyes. Now blue, now gray, a morning sky just at sunrise. And dry. "You can cry, Rand al'Thor. You won't melt if you cry!"

"I don't have time for tears, either, Min," he said gently. "Sometimes, the hounds catch the wolf and wish they hadn't. Sometimes, he turns on them, or waits in ambush. But first, the wolf has to run."

"When do we go?" she asked. She did not let go of his hair. She was never going to let go of him. Never.

CHAPTER

30

Beginnings

Holding his fur-lined cloak close with one hand, Perrin let Stayer walk at the bay's own pace. The midmorning sun gave no warmth, and the rutted snow on the road leading into Abila made poor footing. He and his dozen companions shared the way with only two lumbering ox-carts and a handful of farm-folk in plain dark woolens. They all trudged along with heads down, clutching at hat or cap whenever a gust rose but otherwise concentrating on the ground beneath their shoes.

Behind him, he heard Neald make a ribald joke in a low voice; Grady grunted in reply, and Balwer sniffed prissily. None of the three seemed at all affected by what they had seen and heard this past month since crossing the border into Amadicia, or by what lay ahead. Edarra was sharply berating Masuri for letting her hood slip. Edarra and Carelle both wore their shawls wrapped around their heads and shoulders in addition to cloaks, but even after admitting the necessity to ride, they had refused to change out of their bulky skirts, so their dark-stockinged legs were bared above the knee. The cold did not seem to bother them in the least; just the strangeness of snow. Carelle began quietly advising Seonid as to what would happen if she did not keep her face hidden.

Of course, if she let her face be seen too soon, a dose of the strap would be the least she had to fear, as she and the Wise One knew well. Perrin did not have to look back to know the sisters' three Warders, bringing up the rear in ordinary cloaks, were men expecting the need at any moment to out sword and carve a way clear. They had been that way since leaving the camp at dawn. He ran a gloved thumb along the axe hanging at his belt, then regathered his own cloak just before a sudden gust could make it billow. If this went badly, the Warders might be right.

Off to the left, short of where the road crossed a wooden bridge over a frozen stream that twisted along the town's edge, charred timbers thrust out of the snow atop a large square stone platform with drifts piled around the bottom. Slow to proclaim allegiance to the Dragon Reborn, the local lord had been lucky merely to be flogged and fined all that he possessed. A knot of men standing at the bridge watched the mounted party approaching. Perrin saw no sign of helmets or armor, but every man clutched spear or crossbow almost as hard as he did his cloak. They did not talk to one another. They just watched, the mist of their breath curling before their faces. There were other guards bunched all around the town, at every road leading out, at every space between two buildings. This was the Prophet's country, but the Whitecloaks and King Ailron's army still held large parts of it.

"I was right not to bring her," he muttered, "but I'll pay for it anyway."

"Of course you'll pay," Elyas snorted. For a man who had spent most of the last fifteen years afoot, he handled his mouse-colored gelding well. He had acquired a cloak lined with black fox, dicing with Gallenne. Aram, riding on Perrin's other side, eyed Elyas darkly, but the bearded man ignored him. They did not get on well. "A man always pays sooner or later, with any woman, whether he owes or not. But I was right, wasn't I?"

Perrin nodded. Grudgingly. It still did not seem right taking advice about his wife from another man, even circumspectly, obliquely, yet it did seem to be working. Of course, raising his voice to Faile was as hard as not raising it to Berelain, but he had managed the last quite often and the first several times. He had followed Elyas' advice to the letter. Well, most of it. As well as he could. That spiky scent of jealousy still flared at the sight of Berelain, yet on the other hand, the hurt smell had vanished as they made their slow way south. Still, he was uneasy. When he firmly told her she was not coming with him this morning, she had not raised a single word of protest! She even smelled . . .

pleased! Among other things, including startled. And how could she be pleased and angry at the same time? Not a scrap of it had showed on her face, but his nose never lied. Somehow, it seemed that the more he learned about women, the less he knew!

The bridge guards frowned and fingered their weapons as Stayer's hooves thudded hollowly onto the wooden planking. They were the usual odd mix that followed the Prophet, dirty-faced fellows in silk coats too big for them, scar-faced street toughs and pink-cheeked apprentices, former merchants and craftsmen who looked as if they had slept in their once fine woolens for months. Their weapons appeared well cared for, though. Some of the men had a fever in their eyes; the rest wore guarded, wooden faces. Along with unwashed, they smelled eager, anxious, fervent, afraid, all jumbled together.

They made no move to bar passage, just watched, hardly blinking. By what Perrin had heard, all sorts from ladies in silks to beggars in rags came to the Prophet hoping that submitting to him in person might gain added blessings. Or maybe added protection. That was why he had come this way, with only a handful of companions. He would frighten Masema if he had to, if Masema could be frightened, but it had seemed better to try reaching the man without fighting a battle. He could feel the guard's eyes on his back until he and the others were all across the short bridge and onto the paved streets of Abila. When that pressure left, though, it brought no sense of relief.

Abila was a goodly sized town, with several tall watchtowers and many buildings rising four stories, every last one roofed in slate. Here and there, mounded stone and timbers filled a gap between two structures where an inn or some merchant's house had been pulled down. The Prophet disapproved of wealth gained by trade as much as he did carousing or what his followers called lewd behavior. He disapproved of a great many things, and made his feelings known with sharp examples.

The streets were jammed with people, but Perrin and his companions were the only ones on horseback. The snow had long since been trampled to half-frozen ankle-deep mush. Plenty of ox-carts made their slow way through the throng, but very few wagons, and not a single carriage. Except for those wearing worn castoffs or possibly stolen clothes, everyone wore drab woolens. Most people hurried, but like the folk on the road, with heads down. Those who did not hurry were straggling groups of men carrying weapons. In the streets, the smell was mainly dirt and fear. It made Perrin's hackles rise. At least, if it came to that, getting out of a town with no wall would not prove harder than getting in.

"My Lord," Balwer murmured as they came abreast of one of those heaps of rubble. He barely waited for Perrin's nod before turning his hammer-nosed mount aside and making his way in another direction, hunched in his saddle with his brown cloak held tight around him. Perrin had no worries about the dried-up little man going off alone, even here. For a secretary, he managed to learn a surprising amount on these forays of his. He seemed to know what he was about.

Dismissing Balwer from his thoughts, Perrin set to what *he* was there about.

It took only one question, put to a lanky young man with an ecstatic light on his face, to learn where the Prophet was staying, and three more to other folk in the streets to find the merchant's house, four stories of gray stone with white marble moldings and window frames. Masema disapproved of grubbing for money, but he was willing to accept accommodations from those who did. On the other hand, Balwer said he had slept in a leaky farmhouse as often and been as satisfied. Masema drank only water, and wherever he went, he hired a poor widow and ate the food she prepared, fair or foul, without complaint. The man had made too many widows for that charity to count far with Perrin.

The throng that packed the streets elsewhere was absent in front of the tall house, yet the number of armed guards like those at the bridge almost made up for it. They stared at Perrin sullenly, those who did not sneer insolently. The two Aes Sedai kept their faces hidden in their deep hoods and their heads down, white breath rising from the cowls like steam. From the corner of his eye, Perrin saw Elyas thumbing the hilt of his long knife. It was hard not to stroke his axe.

"I've come with a message for the Prophet from the Dragon Reborn," he announced. When none of the men moved, he added, "My name is Perrin Aybara. The Prophet knows me." Balwer had cautioned him about the dangers of using Masema's name, or calling Rand anything but the Lord Dragon Reborn. He was not there to start a riot.

The claim of knowing Masema seemed to put a spark into the guards. Several exchanged wide-eyed looks, and one went running inside. The rest stared at him as if he were a gleeman. In a few moments, a woman came to the door. Handsome, with white at her temples, in a high-necked dress of blue wool that was fine if unadorned, she might have been the merchant herself. Masema did not throw those who offered him hospitality into the streets, but their servants or farmhands usually ended up with one of the bands "spreading the glories of the Lord Dragon."

"If you will come with me, Master Aybara," the woman said calmly, "you and your friends, I will take you to the Prophet of the Lord Dragon, may the Light illumine his name." Calm she might sound, but terror filled her scent.

Telling Neald and the Warders to watch the horses until they returned, Perrin followed her inside with the others. The interior was dark, with few lamps lit, and not much warmer than outside. Even the Wise Ones seemed subdued. They did not smell afraid, but almost as close to it as the Aes Sedai, and Grady and Elyas smelled of wariness, of raised hackles and ears laid back. Strangely, Aram's scent was eager. Perrin hoped the man did not try to draw that sword on his back.

The large, carpeted room the woman led them to, with fires blazing on hearths at either end, might have been a general's study, every table and half the chairs covered with maps and papers, and warm enough that Perrin tossed his cloak back and regretted wearing two shirts under his coat. But it was Masema standing in the middle of the room who drew his eyes immediately, like iron filings to a lodestone, a dark, scowling man with a shaven head and a pale triangular scar on one cheek, in a wrinkled gray coat and scuffed boots. His deep-set eyes burned with a black fire, and his scent . . . The only name Perrin could give that smell, steel-hard and blade-sharp and quivering with wild intensity, was madness. And Rand thought he could put a leash on this?

"So, it is you," Masema growled. "I did not think you would dare show your face. I know what you've been up to! Hari told me more than a week ago, and I have kept myself informed." A man shifted in a corner of the room, a narrow-eyed fellow with a thrusting nose, and Perrin upbraided himself for not noticing him before. Hari's green silk coat was much finer than what he had worn when he denied collecting ears. The fellow rubbed his hands together and grinned at Perrin viciously, but he kept silent as Masema went on. The Prophet's voice grew hotter by the word, not with anger, but as though he meant to burn every syllable deep into Perrin's flesh. "I know about you murdering men who have come to the Lord Dragon. I know about you trying to carve out your own kingdom! Yes, I know about Manetheren! About your ambition! Your greed for glory! You have turned your back on—!"

Suddenly Masema's eyes bulged, and for the first time, anger flamed in his scent. Hari made a strangled sound and tried to back through the wall. Seonid and Masuri had lowered their hoods and stood with bare faces, calm and cool, and plainly Aes Sedai to anyone who knew the look. Perrin wondered whether they held the Power. He would have wagered that the Wise Ones did. Edarra and Carelle were quietly watching every direction at once, and smooth faces or no, if he had ever seen anyone ready to fight, it was them. For that matter, Grady wore readiness like his black coat; maybe he held the Power, too. Elyas was leaning against the wall beside the open doors, outwardly as composed as the sisters, but he smelled ready to bite. And Aram stood gazing at Masema with his mouth hanging open! Light!

"So that is true, too!" Masema snapped, spittle flying from his lips. "With filthy rumors spreading against the holy name of the Lord Dragon, you dare to ride with these . . . these . . . !"

"They've sworn fealty to the Lord Dragon, Masema," Perrin cut in. "They serve him! Do you? He sent me to stop the killing. And to bring you to him." No one was offering him a chair, so he pushed a stack of papers from one and sat. He wished the rest would sit, too; shouting seemed harder when you were sitting down.

Hari goggled at him, and Masema was practically shaking. Because he had taken a chair without being asked? Oh. Yes.

"I have given up the names of men," Masema said coldly. "I am simply the Prophet of the Lord Dragon, may the

Light illumine him and the world come to kneel before
him." By his tone, the world and the Light would regret failure equally. "There is much to do here, yet Great works. All
must obey when the Lord Dragon calls, but in winter, travel
is always slow. A delay of a few weeks will make little difference."

"I can have you in Cairhien today," Perrin said. "Once
the Lord Dragon has spoken to you, you can return the
same way and be back here in a few days." If Rand let him
return.

Masema actually recoiled. Baring his teeth, he glared at
the Aes Sedai. "Some contrivance of the Power? I will not
be touched with the Power! It is blasphemy for mortals to
touch it!"

Perrin came close to gaping. "The Dragon Reborn chan-
nels, man!"

"The blessed Lord Dragon is not as other men, Aybara!"
Masema snarled. "He is the Light made flesh! I will obey
his summons, but I will not be touched by the filth these
women do!"

Slumping back in the chair, Perrin sighed. If the man
was this bad over Aes Sedai, how would he be when he
learned that Grady and Neald could channel? For a moment, he considered simply knocking Masema over the
head, and . . . Men were passing by in the corridor, pausing
to glance in before hurrying on. All it took was one of them
raising a shout, and Abila could become a slaughterhouse.
"Then we ride, Prophet," he said sourly. Light, Rand had
said to keep this secret until Masema stood in front of him!
How to manage *that* riding all the way to Cairhien? "But no
delays. The Lord Dragon is very anxious to talk with you."

"I am anxious to speak with the Lord Dragon, may his
name be blessed by the Light." His eyes flickered toward
the two Aes Sedai. He tried to hide it, actually smiling at
Perrin. But he smelled . . . grim. "I am very anxious indeed."

"Would my Lady like me to ask one of the handlers to
bring her a hawk?" Maighdin asked. One of Alliandre's
four hawk handlers, all men as lean as their birds, urged a
sleek duckhawk wearing a feathered hood onto his heavy

gauntlet from the wooden stand in front of his saddle and lifted the gray bird toward her. The falcon, with its blue-tipped wings, was on Alliandre's green-gloved wrist. That bird was reserved to her, unfortunately. Alliandre knew her place as a vassal, but Faile understood not wanting to relinquish a favorite bird.

She merely shook her head, and Maighdin bowed in her saddle and moved her roan mare away from Swallow, far enough not to intrude but close enough to be at hand without Faile raising her voice. The dignified golden-haired woman had proved to be every bit as good a lady's maid as Faile had hoped, knowledgeable, capable. At least, she had once she learned that whatever their relative positions with their former mistress, Lini was first among Faile's serving women, and willing to use her authority. Surprisingly, that had actually taken an episode with a switch, but Faile pretended not to know. Only an utter fool embarrassed her servants. There was still the matter of Maighdin and Tallanvor, of course. She was certain Maighdin had begun sharing his bed, and if she found proof, they would marry if she had to turn Lini loose on both of them. Still, that was a small matter, and could not spoil her morning.

Hawking had been Alliandre's idea, but Faile had not objected to a ride through this sparse forest, where snow made a rolling blanket over everything and lay thick and white on bare branches. The green of the trees that still held their leaves seemed sharper. The air was crisp, and it smelled new and fresh.

Bain and Chiad had insisted on accompanying her, but they squatted nearby, *shoufa* wrapped around their heads, watching her with disgruntled expressions. Sulin had wanted to come with all of the Maidens, but with a hundred stories of Aiel depredations floating everywhere, the sight of an Aiel was enough to send most people in Amadicia running or reaching for a sword. There must be some truth in those tales, or so many would *not* know an Aiel, though the Light alone knew who they were or where they had come from, yet even Sulin agreed that whoever they were, they had moved on east, perhaps into Altara.

In any case, this close to Abila, twenty of Alliandre's soldiers and as many Mayener Winged Guards provided sufficient escort. The streamers on their lances, red or green, lifted like ribbons when the breeze stirred. Berelain's presence was the only blight. Though watching the woman shiver in her fur-trimmed red cloak, thick enough for two blankets, was certainly amusing. Mayene did not have a real winter. This was like the last days of autumn. In Saldaea, the heart of winter could freeze exposed flesh hard as wood. Faile took a deep breath. She felt like laughing.

By some miracle, her husband, her beloved wolf, had begun behaving as he should. Instead of shouting at Berelain or running from her, Perrin now tolerated the jade's blandishments, plainly tolerated them the way he would a child playing around his knees. And best of all, there was no longer any need to tamp down her anger when she wanted to let it loose. When she shouted, he shouted back. She knew he was not Saldaean, but it had been so hard, thinking in her heart of hearts that he believed her too weak to stand up to him. A few nights ago at supper, she had almost pointed out to him that Berelain was going to fall out of her dress if she leaned over the table any farther. Well, she was not going to go that far, not with Berelain; the trull *still* thought she could win him. And that very morning, he had been commanding, quietly brooking no argument, the sort of man a woman knew she had to be strong to deserve, to equal. Of course, she would have to nip him over that. A commanding man was wonderful, so long as he did not come to believe he could always command. Laugh? She could have sung!

"Maighdin, I think after all I will . . ." Maighdin was there immediately with an enquiring smile, but Faile trailed off at the sight of three riders ahead of her, plowing through the snow as fast as they could push their horses.

"At least there are plenty of hares, my Lady," Alliandre said, walking her tall white gelding up beside Swallow, "but I had hoped . . . Who are they?" Her falcon shifted on her thick glove, the bells on its jesses jingling. "Why, it looks like some of your people, my Lady."

Faile nodded grimly. She recognized them, too. Parelean, Arrela and Lacile. But what were they doing here?

The three drew rein before her, their horses panting steam. Parelean looked as wide-eyed as his dapple. Lacile, her pale face nearly hidden in the deep cowl of her cloak, was swallowing anxiously, and Arrela's dark face seemed gray. "My Lady," Parelean said urgently, "dire news! The Prophet Masema has been meeting with the Seanchan!"

"The Seanchan!" Alliandre exclaimed. "Surely he cannot believe *they* will come to the Lord Dragon!"

"It might be simpler," Berelain said, heeling her too-showy white mare up on Alliandre's other side. Without Perrin about for her to try to impress, her dark blue riding dress was cut quite modestly, with a neck up under her chin. She still shivered. "Masema dislikes Aes Sedai, and the Seanchan keep women who can channel as prisoners."

Faile clicked her tongue in vexation. Dire news indeed, if true. And she could only hope Parelean and the others retained enough of their wits to at least pretend they had simply overheard talk by chance. Even so, she had to be sure, and quickly. Perrin might already have reached Masema. "What proof do you have, Parelean?"

"We talked to three farmers who saw a large flying creature land four nights ago, my Lady. It brought a woman who was taken to Masema and remained with him for three hours."

"We were able to trace her all the way to where Masema stays in Abila," Lacile added.

"The three men all thought the creature was Shadowspawn," Arrela put in, "but they seemed fairly reliable." For her to say any man not of *Cha Faile* was fairly reliable was the same as anyone else saying they thought he was honest as a bell.

"I think I must ride into Abila," Faile said, gathering Swallow's reins. "Alliandre, take Maighdin and Berelain with you." Any other time, the tightening of Berelain's lips over that would have been amusing. "Parelean, Arrela and Lacile will accompany me—" A man screamed, and everyone jerked.

Fifty paces away, one of Alliandre's green-coated soldiers was toppling from his saddle, and a moment later, a Winged Guard fell with an arrow standing out from his throat. Aiel appeared among the trees, veiled and wielding bows as they ran. More soldiers fell. Bain and Chiad were on their feet, dark veils hiding their faces to the eyes; their spears were thrust through the straps of the bow cases on their back, and they worked their bows smoothly, but they cast glances toward Faile, too. There were Aiel all around, hundreds it seemed, a great noose closing in. Mounted soldiers lowered lances, pulling back in their own circle around Faile and the others, but gaps appeared immediately as Aiel arrows struck home.

"Someone must get this news of Masema to Lord Perrin," Faile told Parelean and the two women. "One of you must reach him! Ride like fire!" Her sweeping gaze took in Alliandre and Maighdin. And Berelain, too. "All of you, ride like fire, or die here!" Barely waiting for their nods, she suited actions to words, and dug her heels into Swallow's flanks, bursting through the useless ring of soldiers. "Ride!" she shouted. Someone had to get the news to Perrin. "Ride!"

Leaning low on Swallow's neck, she urged the black mare for speed. Fleet hooves splashed snow as Swallow ran, light as her namesake. For a hundred strides, Faile thought she might break free. And then Swallow screamed and stumbled, pitching forward with the sharp snap of a breaking leg. Faile flew through air and struck hard, most of the breath driven out of her as she plunged facedown into the snow. Fighting for air, she struggled to her feet and snatched a knife from her belt. Swallow had screamed before she stumbled, before that awful crack.

A veiled Aielman loomed up before her as if out of the air, chopping at her wrist with a stiffened hand. Her knife dropped from suddenly numb fingers, and before she could try to draw another with her left hand, the man was on her.

She fought, kicking, punching, even biting, but the fellow was as wide as Perrin and a head taller. He seemed as hard as Perrin, too, for all the impression she made on him. She could have wept with frustration at the humiliating ease with which he handled her, first rooting out all of her knives and tucking them behind his belt, then using one of her own blades to cut her clothes away. Almost before she knew it, she was naked in the snow, her elbows bound together behind her back with one of her stockings, the other tied about her neck for a leash.

She had no choice except to follow him, shivering and stumbling through the snow. Her skin pebbled with the cold. Light, how she had ever thought this day anything less than icy? Light, if only someone had managed to escape with the news of Masema! To carry word of her capture to

Perrin, of course, but she could escape somehow. The other was more important.

The first body she saw was Parelean, sprawled on his back with his sword in one outflung hand and blood all over his fine coat with the satin-striped sleeves. There were plenty of corpses after, Winged Guards in their red breast-plates, Alliandre's soldiers in their dark green helmets, one of the hawkers, the hooded duckhawk flapping vainly against the jesses still gripped in the dead man's fist. She held on to hope, though.

The first other prisoners she saw, kneeling among some Aiel, men and Maidens with their veils hanging down their chests, were Bain and Chiad, each naked, unbound hands on her knees. Blood ran down across Bain's face and matted her flame-red hair. Chiad's left cheek was purple and swollen, and her gray eyes looked slightly glazed. They knelt there, straight-backed, impassive, and unashamed, but as the big Aielman pushed her roughly to her knees beside them, they roused themselves.

"This is not right, Shaido," Chiad mumbled angrily.

"She does not follow *ji'e'toh*," Bain barked. "You cannot make her *gai'shain*."

"The *gai'shain* will be quiet," a graying Maiden said absently. Bain and Chiad gave Faile regretful looks, then settled back to their calm waiting. Huddling, trying to hide her nakedness against her knees, Faile did not know whether to weep or laugh. The two women she would have chosen to help her escape from anywhere, and neither would raise a hand to try because of *ji'e'toh*.

"I say again, Efalin," the man who had captured her muttered, "this is foolishness. We travel at a crawl in this . . . snow." He said the word awkwardly. "There are too many armed men, here. We should be moving east, not taking more *gai'shain* to slow us further."

"Sevanna wants more *gai'shain*, Rolan," the graying Maiden replied. She frowned, though, and her hard gray eyes seemed disapproving for a moment.

Shivering, Faile blinked as the names sank in. Light, but the cold was making her wits slow. Sevanna. Shaido. They were in Kinslayer's Dagger, as far from here as was possible to be without crossing the Spine of the World! Clearly they were not, though. That was something Perrin should know, another reason for her to escape soon. There seemed little chance of that, crouching there in the snow and wondering which bits of her were going to freeze first. The Wheel was balancing her amusement over Berelain's shivers with a vengeance. She was actually looking forward to the thick woolen robes that *gai'shain* wore. Her captors made no move to depart, though. There were other captives to be brought in.

First was Maighdin, stripped bare and bound as Faile was, and struggling every step of the way. Until the Maiden who was pushing her along abruptly kicked her feet out from under her. Maighdin plunked down sitting in the snow, and her eyes popped so wide that Faile might have laughed if she had not felt sorry for the woman. Alliandre came next, bent nearly double in an effort to shield herself, and then Arrela, who seemed half paralyzed by her nudity and was almost being dragged by a pair of Maidens. Finally, another tall Aielman appeared with a furiously kicking Lacile tucked under one arm like a package.

"The rest are dead or escaped," the man said, dropping the small Cairhienin woman beside Faile. "Sevanna will have to be satisfied, Efalin. She puts too much store in taking people who wear silk."

Faile did not struggle at all when she was prodded to her feet and set to laboring through the snow at the head of the other prisoners. She was too stunned to fight. Parelean dead, Arrela and Lacile captive, and Alliandre, and Maighdin. Light, someone had to warn Perrin about Masema. Someone. It seemed a final blow. Here she was, shivering and gritting her teeth to keep them from chattering, trying her best to pretend that she was not stark naked and bound, on her way to an uncertain captivity. All of that, and she had to hope that that slinking cat—that pouting trull!—Berelain, had managed to escape so she could reach Perrin. Alongside everything else, that seemed the worst of all.

Egwene walked Daishar along the column of initiates, sisters on their horses among the wagons, Accepted and novices afoot despite the snow. The sun was bright in a sky with few clouds, but mist curled from her gelding's nostrils. Sheriam and Siuan rode at her back, talking quietly about information learned from Siuan's eyes-and-ears. Egwene had thought the fire-haired woman an efficient Keeper once she learned that she was not the Amyrlin, but day by day, Sheriam seemed to grow ever more assiduous about her duties. Chesa followed on her tubby mare in case the Amyrlin wanted anything, and unlike her, she was muttering again about Meri and Selame both running away, the ungrateful wretches, leaving her to do the work of three. They rode slowly, and Egwene very carefully did not look toward the column.

A month of recruiting, a month of the novice book being open to all, had brought in startling numbers, a flood anxious to become Aes Sedai, women of every age some from hundreds of miles away. There were now twice as many novices with the column as before. Almost a thousand! Most by far would never wear the shawl, yet the number of them had everyone staring. Some might cause minor problems, and one, a grandmother named Sharina with a potential above even that of Nynaeve, certainly had everyone startled, but it was not the sight of a mother and daughter squabbling because the daughter would be the stronger by far one day that she was trying to avoid, or noblewomen who were beginning to think they had made the wrong choice asking to be tested, or even Sharina's disturbingly direct looks. The gray-haired woman obeyed every rule and showed every proper respect, but she had run her large family by the sheer force of her presence, and even some of the sisters stepped warily around her. What Egwene did not want to see were the young women who had joined them two days before. The four sisters who brought them had been more than startled to find Egwene as Amyrlin, but their charges could not believe it, not Egwene al'Vere, the Mayor's daughter from Emond's Field. She did not want to order anyone else punished, but she would have to if she saw another stick her tongue out at her.

Gareth Bryne had his army in a wide column, too, cavalry and foot all arrayed and stretching out of sight through the trees. The pale sun glinted off breastplates and helmets and the points of pikes. Horses stamped their hooves in the snow impatiently.

Bryne walked his sturdy bay to meet her before she reached the Sitters waiting on their horses, in a large clearing ahead of both columns. He smiled at her through the face-bars of his helmet. A reassuring smile, she thought. "A fine morning for it, Mother," he said. "Here."

She only nodded, and he fell in behind her, beside Siuan. Who did not immediately begin spitting at him. Egwene was not certain exactly what accommodation Siuan had reached with the man, but she seldom grumbled about him anymore in Egwene's hearing, and never when he was present. Egwene was glad he was there, now. The Amyrlin Seat could not let her general know she wanted his reassurance, but she felt the need of it this morning.

The Sitters had their horses in a line at the edge of the trees, and thirteen more sisters sat their mounts a little way off, watching the Sitters carefully. Romanda and Lelaine spurred their animals forward almost together, and Egwene could hardly help sighing as they approached, cloaks flaring behind them, hooves spraying snow as if at the charge. The Hall obeyed her because it had no choice. In matters concerning the war against Elaida, they did, but Light, how they could quibble over what did or did not concern the war. When it did not, getting anything out of them was like pulling duck's teeth! Except for Sharina, they might have found a way to put a stop to accepting women of any age. Even Romanda was impressed by Sharina.

The pair reined in before her, but before they could open their mouths, she spoke. "It's time we got on with it, daughters, and no time for wasting in idle chatter. Proceed." Romanda sniffed, though softly, and Lelaine looked as though she wanted to.

They wheeled their horses as one, then glared at one another a moment. Events this past month had only heightened their dislike for each other. Lelaine tossed her head angrily in concession, and Romanda smiled, a faint curving of her lips. Egwene almost smiled, too. That mutual animosity was still her greatest strength in the Hall.

"The Amyrlin Seat commands you to proceed," Romanda announced, raising one hand grandly.

The light of *saidar* sprang up around the thirteen sisters near the Sitters, around all of them together, and a thick slash of silver appeared in the middle of the clearing, rotating into a gateway ten paces tall and a hundred wide. Falling snow drifted through from the other side. Shouted orders rose among the soldiers, and the first armored heavy calvary rode through. The swirling snow beyond the gateway was too thick to see far, yet Egwene imagined that she could make out the Shining Walls of Tar Valon, and the White Tower itself.

"It has begun, Mother," Sheriam said, sounding almost surprised.

"It has begun," Egwene agreed. And the Light willing, soon Elaida would fall. She was supposed to wait until Bryne said sufficient of his soldiers were through, but she could not stop herself. Digging her heels into Daishar's flanks, she rode through into the falling snow, onto the plain where Dragonmount reared black and smoking against a white sky.

CHAPTER
31

After

Winter winds and winter snows slowed the passage of trade across lands where they did not end it until spring, and for every three pigeons sent by merchants, two fell to hawks or weather, but where ice did not cover the rivers, ships still sailed, and rumor flew faster than lightnings. A thousand rumors, each throwing off a thousand seeds that sprouted and grew in snow and ice as in fertile soil.

At Tar Valon, some stories said, great armies had clashed, and the streets ran with blood, and rebel Aes Sedai had stuck the head of Elaida a'Roihan on a pike. No; Elaida had closed her hand, and those who survived among the rebels groveled at Elaida's feet. There had been no rebels, no division of the White Tower. It was the Black Tower that had been broken, by Aes Sedai designs and Aes Sedai power, and Asha'man hunted Asha'man across the nations. The White Tower had shattered the Sun Palace in Cairhien, and the Dragon Reborn himself was bound now to the Amyrlin Seat, her puppet and her tool. Some tales said Aes Sedai had been bound to him, bound to the Asha'man, yet few believed that, and those few were ridiculed.

Artur Hawkwing's armies had returned to reclaim his long-dead empire, and the Seanchan were sweeping all before them, even to driving the Dragon Reborn from Altara in defeat. The Seanchan had come to serve him. No; he had cast the Seanchan into the sea, destroying their army utterly. They had carried the Dragon Reborn away, to kneel before their Empress. The Dragon Reborn was dead, and there was as much celebration as mourning, as many tears as cries of joy.

Across the nations the stories spread like spiderweb laid upon spiderweb, and men and women planned the future, believing they knew truth. They planned, and the Pattern absorbed their plans, weaving toward the future foretold.

The End

of the Eighth Book of

The Wheel of Time

GLOSSARY

A Note on Dates in This Glossary. The Toman Calendar (devised by Toma dur Ahmid) was adopted approximately two centuries after the death of the last male Aes Sedai, recording years After the Breaking of the World (AB). So many records were destroyed in the Trolloc Wars that at their end there was argument about the exact year under the old system. A new calendar, proposed by Tiam of Gazar, celebrated freedom from the Trolloc threat and recorded each year as a Free Year (FY). The Gazaran Calendar gained wide acceptance within twenty years after the Wars' end. Artur Hawkwing attempted to establish a new calendar based on the founding of his empire (FF, From the Founding), but only historians now refer to it. After the death and destruction of the War of the Hundred Years, a third calendar was devised by Uren din Jubai Soaring Gull, a scholar of the Sea Folk, and promulgated by the Panarch Farede of Tarabon. The Farede Calendar, dating from the arbitrarily decided end of the War of the Hundred Years and recording years of the New Era (NE), is currently in use.

armsmen: Soldiers who owe allegiance or fealty to a particular lord or lady.

Asha'man: (1) In the Old Tongue, "Guardian" or "Guardians," but always a guardian of justice and truth. (2) The name given, both collectively and as a rank, to the men who have come to the Black Tower, near Caemlyn in Andor, in order to learn to channel. Their training concentrates on the ways in which the One Power can be used as a weapon, and in another departure from the usages of the White Tower, once they learn to seize *saidin*, the male half of the Power, they are required to perform all chores and labors with the Power. When newly enrolled, a man is termed a Soldier; he wears a plain black coat with a high collar, in the Andoran fashion. Being raised to Dedicated brings the right to wear a silver pin, called the Sword, on the collar of his coat. Promotion to Asha'man brings the right to wear a Dragon pin, in gold and red enamel, on the collar opposite the Sword. Although many women, including wives, flee when they learn that their men actually can channel, a fair number of men at the Black Tower are married, and they use a version of the Warder bond to create a link with their wives. This same bond, altered to compel obedience, has recently been used to bond captured Aes Sedai as well.

Balwer, Sebban: Formerly Pedron Niall's secretary, in public, and secretly Niall's spymaster. He aided Morgase's escape from the Seanchan in Amador for his own reasons, and now is employed as secretary to Perrin t'Bashere Aybara and Faile ni Bashere t'Aybara.

Blood, the: Term used by the Seanchan to designate the nobility. One can be raised to the Blood as well as born to it.

Cha Faile: (1) In the Old Tongue, "the Falcon's Talon." (2) Name taken by the young Cairhienin and Tairens, attempted followers of *ji'e'toh*, who have sworn fealty to Faile ni Bashere t'Aybara. In secret, they act as her personal scouts and spies.

Companions, the: The elite military formation of Illian, currently commanded by First Captain Demetre Marcolin. The Companions provide a bodyguard for the King of Illian and guard key points around the nation. Additionally, the Companions have traditionally been used in battle to assault the enemy's strongest positions, to exploit weaknesses, and, if necessary, to cover the retreat of the King. Unlike most other such elite formations, foreigners (excepting Tairens, Altarans and Murandians) are not only welcome, they can rise even to the highest rank, as can commoners, which also is unusual. The uniform of the Companions consists of a green coat, a breastplate worked with the Nine Bees of Illian, and a conical helmet with a faceguard of steel bars. The First Captain wears four rings of golden braid on the cuffs of his coat, and three thin golden plumes on his helmet. The Second Captain wears three rings of golden braid on each cuff, and three golden plumes tipped with green. Lieutenants wear two yellow rings on their cuffs, and two thin green plumes, under-lieutenants one yellow ring and a single green plume. Bannermen are designated by two broken rings of yellow on the cuffs and a single yellow plume, squadmen by a single broken ring of yellow.

Consolidation, the: When the armies sent by Artur Hawkwing under his son Luthair landed in Seanchan, they discovered a shifting quilt of nations often at war with one another, where Aes Sedai often reigned. Without any equivalent of the White Tower, Aes Sedai worked for their own individual power, using the Power. Forming small groups, they schemed against one another constantly. In large part it was this constant scheming for personal advantage and the resulting wars among the myriad nations that allowed the armies from east of the Aryth Ocean to begin the conquest of an entire continent, and for their descendants to complete it. This conquest, during which the descendants of the original armies became Seanchan as much as they conquered Seanchan, took more than nine hundred years and is called the Consolidation.

Corenne: In the Old Tongue, "the Return." The name given by the Seanchan both to the fleet of thousands of ships and to the hundreds of thousands of soldiers, craftsmen and others carried by those ships, who will come behind the Forerunners to reclaim the lands stolen from Artur Hawkwing's descendants. *See also* Forerunners.

Daughters of Silence, the: During the history of the White Tower (over three thousand years), various women who have been put out have been unwilling to accept their fates and have tried to band together. Such groups— most of them by far, at least—have been dispersed by the White Tower as soon as found and punished severely and publicly to make sure that the lesson is carried to everyone.

The last group to be dispersed called themselves the Daughters of Silence (794–798 NE). The Daughters consisted of two Accepted who had been put out of the Tower and twenty-three women they had gathered and trained. All were carried back to Tar Valon and punished, and the twenty-three were enrolled in the novice book. Only one of those managed to reach the shawl. *See also* Kin, the.

da'covale: (1) In the Old Tongue, "one who is owned," or "person who is property." (2) Among the Seanchan, the term often used, along with property, for slaves. Slavery has a long and unusual history among the Seanchan, with slaves having the ability to rise to positions of great power and open authority, including over those who are free. *See also* so'jhin.

Deathwatch Guards, the: The elite military formation of the Seanchan Empire, including both humans and Ogier. The human members of the Deathwatch Guard are all *da'covale*, born as property and chosen while young to serve the Empress, whose personal property they are. Fanatically loyal and fiercely proud, they often display the ravens tattooed on their shoulders, the mark of a *da'covale* of the Empress. The helmets and armor are lacquered in dark green and blood-red, their shields are lacquered black, and their spears and swords carry black tassels. *See also da'covale.*

Defenders of the Stone, the: The elite military formation of Tear. The current Captain of the Stone (commander of the Defenders) is Rodrivar Tihera. Only Tairens are accepted into the Defenders, and officers are usually of noble birth, though often from minor Houses or minor branches of strong Houses. The Defenders are tasked to hold the great fortress called the Stone of Tear, in the city of Tear, to defend the city, and to provide police services in place of any City Watch or the like. Except in times of war, their duties seldom take them far from the city. Then, as with other elite formations, they are the core around which the army is formed. The uniform of the Defenders consists of a black coat with padded sleeves striped black-and-gold with black cuffs, a burnished breastplate, and a rimmed helmet with a faceguard of steel bars. The Captain of the Stone wears three short white plumes on his helmet, and on the cuffs of his coat three intertwined golden braids on a white band. Captains wear two white plumes and a single line of golden braid on white cuffs, lieutenants one white plume and a single line of black braid on white cuffs and under-lieutenants one short black plume and plain white cuffs. Bannermen have gold-colored cuffs on their coats, and squadmen have cuffs striped black-and-gold.

Delving: (1) The ability to use the One Power to diagnose physical condition and illness. (2) The ability to find deposits of metal ores with the One Power. That this has long been a lost ability among Aes Sedai may account for the name becoming attached to another ability.

der'morat-: (1) In the Old Tongue, "master handler." (2) Among the Seanchan, the suffix applied to indicate a senior and highly skilled handler of one of the exotics, one who trains others, as in *der'morat'raken*. *Der'morat* can have a fairly high social status, the highest of all held by *der'sul'dam*, the trainers of *sul'dam*, who rank with fairly high military officers. *See also morat-*.

Fain, Padan: Former Darkfriend, now more and worse than a Darkfriend, and an enemy of the Forsaken as much as he is of Rand al'Thor, whom he hates with a passion. Last seen using the name Jeraal Mordeth, advising Lord Toram Riatin in his rebellion against the Dragon Reborn in Cairhien.

Fists of Heaven, the: Lightly armed and lightly armored Seanchan infantry carried into battle on the backs of the flying creatures called *to'raken*. All are small men, or women, largely because of limits as to how much weight a *to'raken* can carry for any distance. Considered to be among the toughest soldiers, they are used primarily for raids, surprise assaults on positions at an enemy's rear, and where speed in getting soldiers into place is of the essence.

Forerunners, the: *See* Hailene.

Forsaken, the: The name given to thirteen powerful Aes Sedai, men and women both, who went over to the Shadow during the Age of Legends and were trapped in the sealing of the Bore into the Dark One's prison. While it has long been believed that they alone abandoned the Light during the War of the Shadow, in fact others did as well; these thirteen were only the highest ranking among them. The Forsaken (who call themselves the Chosen) are somewhat reduced in number since their awakening in the present day. The known survivors are Demandred, Semirhage, Graendal, Mesaana, Moghedien, and two who were reincarnated in new bodies and given new names, Osan'gar and Aran'gar. Recently, a man calling himself Moridin has appeared, and may be yet another of the dead Forsaken brought back from the grave by the Dark One. The same possibility may exist regarding the woman calling herself Cyndane, but since Aran'gar was a man brought back as a woman, speculation as to the identities of Moridin and Cyndane may prove futile until more is learned.

Hailene: In the Old Tongue, "Forerunners," or "Those Who Come Before." The term applied by the Seanchan to the massive expeditionary force sent across the Aryth Ocean to scout out the lands where Artur Hawkwing once ruled. Now under the command of the High Lady Suroth, its numbers swollen by recruits from conquered lands, the Hailene has gone far beyond its original goals.

Hanlon, Daved: A Darkfriend, formerly commander of the White Lions in service to the Forsaken Rahvin while he held Caemlyn using the name Lord Gaebril. From there, Hanlon took the White Lions to Cairhien under orders to further the rebellion against the Dragon Reborn. The White Lions were destroyed by a "bubble of evil," and Hanlon has been ordered back to Caemlyn for purposes as yet unknown.

Ishara: The first Queen of Andor (circa FY 994–1020). At the death of Artur Hawkwing, Ishara convinced her husband, one of Hawkwing's foremost generals, to raise the siege of Tar Valon and accompany her to Caemlyn with as many soldiers as he could break away from the army. Where others tried to seize the whole of Hawkwing's empire and failed, Ishara took a firm hold on a small part and succeeded. Today, nearly every noble House in Andor contains some of Ishara's blood, and the right to claim the Lion Throne depends both on direct descent from her and on the number of lines of connection to her that can be established.

Kin, the: Even during the Trolloc Wars, more than two thousand years ago (circa 1000–1350 AB), the White Tower continued to maintain its standards, putting out women who failed to measure up. One group of these women, fearing to return home in the midst of the wars, fled to Barashta (near the present-day site of Ebou Dar), as far from the fighting as was possible to go at that time. Calling themselves the Kin, and Kinswomen, they kept in hiding and offered a safe haven for others who had been put out. In time, their approaches to women told to leave the Tower led to contacts with runaways, and while the exact reasons may never be known, the Kin began to accept runaways, as well. They made great efforts to keep these girls from learning anything about the Kin until they were sure that Aes Sedai would not swoop down and retake them. After all, everyone knew that runaways were always caught sooner or later, and the Kin knew that unless they held themselves secret, they themselves would be punished severely.

Unknown to the Kin, Aes Sedai in the Tower were aware of their existence almost from the very first, but prosecution of the wars left no time for dealing with them. By the end of the wars, the Tower realized that it might not be in their best interests to snuff out the Kin. Prior to that time, a majority of runaways actually had managed to escape, whatever the Tower's propaganda, but once the Kin began helping them, the Tower knew exactly where any runaway was heading, and they began retaking nine out of ten. Since Kinswomen moved in and out of Barashta (and later Ebou Dar) in an effort to hide their existence and their numbers, never staying more than ten years lest someone notice that they did not age at a normal speed, the Tower believed they were few, and they certainly were keeping themselves low. In order to use the Kin as a trap for runaways, the Tower decided to leave them alone, unlike any other similar group in history, and to keep the very existence of the Kin a secret known only to full Aes Sedai.

The Kin do not have laws, but rather rules based in part on the rules for novices and Accepted in the White Tower, and in part on the necessity of maintaining secrecy. As might be expected given the origins of the Kin, they maintain their rules very firmly on all of their members.

Recent open contacts between Aes Sedai and Kinswomen, while known only to a handful of sisters, have produced a number of shocks, including the facts that there are twice as many Kinswomen as Aes Sedai and that some are more than a hundred years older than any Aes Sedai has lived since before the Trolloc Wars. The effect of these revelations, both on Aes Sedai and on Kinswomen, is as yet a matter for speculation. *See also* Daughters of Silence, the; Knitting Circle, the.

Knitting Circle, the: The leaders of the Kin. Since no member of the Kin has ever known how Aes Sedai arrange their own hierarchy—knowledge passed on only when an Accepted has passed her test for the shawl—they put no store in strength in the Power but give great weight to age, with the older woman always standing above the younger. The Knitting Circle (a title chosen, like the Kin, because it is innocuous) thus consists of the thirteen oldest Kinswomen resident in Ebou Dar, with the oldest given the title of Eldest. By the rules, all will have to step down when it is time for them to move on, but so long as they are resident in Ebou Dar, they have supreme authority over the Kin, to a degree that any Amyrlin Seat would envy. *See also* Kin, the.

Lance-Captain: In most lands, noblewomen do not personally lead their armsmen into battle under normal circumstances. Instead, they hire a professional soldier, almost always a commoner, who is responsible both for training and leading their armsmen. Depending on the land, this man can be called a Lance-Captain, Sword-Captain, Master of the Horse, or Master of the Lances. Rumors of closer relationships than Lady and servant often spring up, perhaps inevitably. Sometimes they are true.

Legion of the Dragon, the: A large military formation, all infantry, giving allegiance to the Dragon Reborn, trained by Davram Bashere along lines worked out by himself and Mat Cauthon, lines which depart sharply from the usual employment of foot. While many men simply walk in to volunteer, large numbers of the Legion are scooped up by recruiting parties from the Black Tower, who first gather all of the men in an area who were willing to follow the Dragon Reborn, and only after taking them through gateways to near Caemlyn winnow out those who can be taught to channel. The remainder, by far the greater number, are sent to Bashere's training camps.

marath'damane: In the Old Tongue, "those who must be leashed," and also "one who must be leashed." The term applied by the Seanchan to any woman capable of channeling who has not been collared as a *damane*.

Master of the Horse: *See* Lance-Captain.

Master of the Lances: *See* Lance-Captain.

Mera'din: In the Old Tongue, "the Brotherless." The name adopted, as a society, by those Aiel who abandoned clan and sept and went to the Shaido because they could not accept Rand al'Thor, a wetlander, as the *Car'a'carn*, or because they refused to accept his revelations concerning the history and origins of the Aiel. Deserting clan and sept for any reason is anathema among the Aiel, therefore their own warrior societies among the Shaido were unwilling to take them in, and they formed this society, the Brotherless.

morat-: In the Old Tongue, "handler." Among the Seanchan, it is used for those who handle exotics, such as *morat'raken*, a *raken* handler or rider, also informally called a flier. *See also der'morat.*

Prophet, the: More formally, the Prophet of the Lord Dragon. Once known as Masema Dagar, a Shienaran soldier, he underwent a revelation and decided that he had been called to spread the word of the Dragon's Rebirth. He believes that nothing—nothing!—is more important than acknowledging the Dragon Reborn as the Light made flesh and being ready when the Dragon Reborn calls, and he and his followers will use any means to force others to sing the glories of the Dragon Reborn.

Forsaking any name but "the Prophet," he has brought chaos to much of Ghealdan and Amadicia, large parts of which he controls.

Return, the: *See Corenne.*

Sea Folk hierarchy: The Atha'an Miere, the Sea Folk, are ruled by the Mistress of the Ships to the Atha'an Miere. She is assisted by the Windfinder to the Mistress of the Ships, and by the Master of the Blades. Below this come the clan Wavemistresses, each assisted by her Windfinder and her Swordmaster. Below her are the Sailmistresses (ship captains) of her clan, each assisted by her Windfinder and her Cargomaster. The Windfinder to the Mistress of the Ships has authority over all Windfinders to clan Wavemistresses, who in turn have authority over all the Windfinders of her clan. Likewise, the Master of the Blades has authority over all Swordmasters, and they in turn over the Cargomasters of their clans. Rank is not hereditary among the Sea Folk. The Mistress of the Ships is chosen, for life, by the First Twelve of the Atha'an Miere, the twelve most senior clan Wavemistresses. A clan Wavemistress is elected by the twelve seniormost Sailmistresses of her clan, called simply the First Twelve, a term which is also used to designate the senior Sailmistresses present anywhere. She can also be removed by a vote of those same First Twelve. In fact, anyone other than the Mistress of the Ships can be demoted, even all the way down to deckhand, for malfeasance, cowardice or other crimes. Also, the Windfinder to a Wavemistress or Mistress of the Ship who dies will, of necessity, have to serve a lower ranking woman, and her own rank thus decreases. The Windfinder to the Mistress of the Ships has authority over all Windfinders, and the Windfinder to a clan Wavemistress authority over all Windfinders of her clan. Likewise, the Master of the Blades has authority over all Swordmasters and Cargomasters, and a Swordmaster over the Cargomaster of his clan.

sei'mosiev: In the Old Tongue, "lowered eyes," or "downcast eyes." Among the Seanchan, to say that one has "become *sei'mosiev*" means that one has "lost face." *See also sei'taer.*

sei'taer: In the Old Tongue, "straight eyes," or "level eyes." Among the Seanchan, it refers to honor or face, to the ability to meet someone's eyes. It is possible to "be" or "have" *sei'taer*, meaning that one has honor and face, and also to "gain" or "lose" *sei'taer*. See also *sei'mosiev*.

Shen an Calhar: In the Old Tongue, "the Band of the Red Hand." (1) A legendary group of heroes who had many exploits, finally dying in the defense of Manetheren when that land was destroyed during the Trolloc Wars. (2) A military formation put together almost by accident by Mat Cauthon and organized along the lines of military forces during what is considered the height of the military arts, the days of Artur Hawkwing and the centuries immediately preceding.

so'jhin: The closest translation from the Old Tongue would be "a height among lowness," though some translate it as meaning "both sky and valley" among several other possibilities. *So'jhin* is the term applied by the Seanchan to hereditary upper servants. They are *da'covale*, property, yet occupy positions of considerable authority and often power. Even the Blood step carefully around *so'jhin* of the Imperial family, and speak to *so'jhin* of the Empress herself as to equals. See also Blood, the; *da'covale*.

Sword-Captain: See Lance-Captain.

Wise Woman: Honorific used in Ebou Dar for women famed for their incredible abilities at healing almost any injury. A Wise Woman is traditionally marked by a red belt. While some have noted that many, indeed most, Ebou Dari Wise Women were not even from Altara, much less Ebou Dar, what was not known until recently, and still is known only to a few, is that all Wise Women are in fact Kinswomen and use various versions of Healing, giving out herbs and poultices only as a cover. With the flight of the Kin from Ebou Dar after the Seanchan took the city, no Wise Women remain there. See also Kin, the.

PROLOGUE

A preview of
Winter's Heart

Book Nine of
The Wheel of Time

Snow

Three lanterns cast a flickering light, more than enough to illuminate the small room with its stark white walls and ceiling, but Seaine kept her eyes fixed on the heavy wooden door. Illogical, she knew; foolish in a Sitter for the White. The weave of *saidar* she had pushed around the jamb brought her occasional whispers of distant footsteps in the warren of hallways outside, whispers that faded away almost as soon as heard. A simple thing learned from a friend in her long-ago novice days, but she would have warning long before anyone came near. Few people came down as deep as the second basement, anyway.

Her weave picked up the far-off chittering of rats. Light! How long since there had been rats in Tar Valon, in the Tower itself? Were any of them spies for the Dark One? She wet her lips uneasily. Logic counted for nothing in this. True. If illogical. She wanted to laugh. With an effort she crept back from the brink of hysteria. Think of something besides rats. Something besides . . . A muffled squeal rose in the room behind her, faltered into muted whimpering. She tried to stop up her ears. Concentrate!

In a way, she and her companions had been led to this

room because the heads of the Ajahs seemed to be meeting
in secret. She herself had glimpsed Ferane Neheran whispering in a secluded nook of the library with Jesse Bilal, who
stood very high among the Browns if not at the very top. She
thought she was on firmer ground concerning Suana Dragand, of the Yellows. She thought so. But why had Ferane
gone walking with Suana in a secluded part of the Tower
grounds, both swathed in plain cloaks? Sitters of different
Ajahs still talked to one another openly, if coldly. The others had seen similar things; they would not give names from
their own Ajahs, of course, but two had mentioned Ferane.
A troubling puzzle. The Tower was a seething swamp these
days, every Ajah at every other Ajah's throat, yet the heads
met in corners. No one outside an Ajah knew for certain
who within it led, but apparently the leaders knew each
other. What *could* they be up to? What? It was unfortunate
that she could not simply ask Ferane, but even had Ferane
been tolerant of anyone's questions, she did not dare. Not
now.

Concentrate as she would, Seaine could not keep her
mind on the question. She knew she was staring at the door
and worrying at puzzles she could not solve just to avoid
looking over her shoulder. Toward the source of those stifled
whimpers and snuffling groans.

As if thinking of the sounds compelled her, she looked
back slowly to her companions, her breath growing more
uneven as her head moved by inches. Snow was falling
heavily on Tar Valon, far overhead, but the room seemed
unaccountably hot. She made herself *see*!

Brown-fringed shawl looped on her elbows, Saerin stood
with her feet planted apart, fingering the hilt of the curved
Altaran dagger thrust behind her belt. Cold anger darkened her olive complexion enough to make the scar along
her jaw stand out in a pale line. Pevara appeared calmer,
at first glance, yet one hand gripped her red-embroidered
skirts tightly and the other held the smooth white cylinder
of the Oath Rod like a foot-long club she was ready to use.
She might be ready; Pevara was far tougher than her plump
exterior suggested, and determined enough to make Saerin
seem a shirker.

On the other side of the Chair of Remorse, tiny Yukiri
had her arms wrapped tightly around herself; the long

silvery-gray fringe on her shawl trembled with her shivers. Licking her lips, Yukiri cast a worried glance at the woman standing beside her. Doesine, looking more like a pretty boy than a Yellow sister of considerable repute, displayed no reaction to what they were doing. She was the one actually manipulating the weaves that stretched into the Chair, and she stared at the *ter'angreal*, focusing so hard on her work that perspiration beaded on her pale forehead. They were all Sitters, including the tall woman writhing on the Chair.

Sweat drenched Talene, matting her golden hair, soaking her linen shift till it clung to her. The rest of her clothes made a jumbled pile in a corner. Her closed eyelids fluttered, and she let out a constant stream of strangled moans and mewling, half-uttered pleas. Seaine felt ill, but could not drag her eyes away. Talene was a friend. Had been a friend.

Despite its name, the *ter'angreal* looked nothing like a chair, just a large rectangular block of marbled gray. No one knew what it was made of, but the material was hard as steel everywhere except the slanted top. The statuesque Green sank a little into that, and somehow it molded itself to her no matter how she twisted. Doesine's weavings flowed into the only break anywhere on the Chair, a palm-sized rectangular hole in one side with tiny notches spaced unevenly around it. Criminals caught in Tar Valon were brought down here to experience the Chair of Remorse, to experience carefully selected consequences of their crimes. On release, they invariably fled the island. There was very little crime in Tar Valon. Queasily, Seaine wondered whether this was anything like the use the Chair had been put to in the Age of Legends.

"What is she . . . seeing?" Her question came out a whisper in spite of herself. Talene would be more than seeing; to her, it all would seem real. Thank the Light she had no Warder, almost unheard of for a Green. She had claimed a Sitter had no need for one. Different reasons came to mind, now.

"She is bloody being flogged by bloody Trollocs," Doesine said hoarsely. Touches of her native Cairhien had appeared in her voice, something that seldom happened except under stress. "When they are done. . . . She can see the Trollocs' cook kettle boiling over a fire, and a Myrddraal watching her. She must know it will be one or the other next. Burn me, if she doesn't break this time. . . ." Doesine brushed perspiration from her forehead irritably and drew a ragged breath. "Stop joggling my elbow. It has been a long while since I did this."

"Three times under," Yukiri muttered. "The toughest strongarm is broken by his own guilt, if nothing else, after two! What if she's innocent? Light, this is like stealing sheep with the shepherd watching!" Even shaking, she managed to appear regal, but she always sounded like what she had been, a village woman. She glared around at the rest of them in a sickly fashion. "The law forbids using the Chair on initiates. We'll all be unchaired! And if being thrown out of the Hall isn't enough, we'll probably be exiled. And birched before we go, just to drop salt in our tea! Burn me, if we're wrong, we could all be stilled!"

Seaine shuddered. They would escape that last, if their suspicions proved right. No, not suspicions; certainties. They had to be right! But even if they were, Yukiri was correct about the rest. Tower law seldom allowed for necessity, or any supposed higher good. If they were right, though, the price was worth paying. Please, the Light send they were right!

"Are you blind and deaf?" Pevara snapped, shaking the Oath Rod at Yukiri. "She refused to reswear the Oath against speaking an untrue word, and it had to be more than stupid Green Ajah pride after we'd all done as much already. When I shielded her, she tried to *stab* me! Does *that* shout innocence? Does it? For all she knew, we just meant to talk at her until our tongues dried up! What reason would she have to expect more?"

"Thank you both," Saerin put in dryly, "for stating the obvious. It's too late to go back, Yukiri, so we might as well go forward. And if I were you, Pevara, I wouldn't be shouting at one of the four women in the whole Tower I knew I could trust."

Yukiri flushed and shifted her shawl, and Pevara looked a trifle abashed. A trifle. They might all be Sitters, but Saerin had most definitely taken charge. Seaine was unsure how she felt about that. A few hours ago, she and Pevara had been two old friends alone on a dangerous quest, equals reaching decisions together; now they had allies. She should be grateful for more companions. They were not in the Hall, though, and they could not claim Sitters' rights on this. Tower hierarchies had taken over, all the subtle and not-so-subtle distinctions as to who stood where with respect to whom. In truth, Saerin had been both novice and Accepted twice as long as most of them, but forty years as a Sitter, longer than anyone else in the Hall, counted for a great deal. Seaine would be lucky if Saerin asked her opinion, much less her advice, before deciding anything at all. Foolish, yet the knowledge pricked like a thorn in her foot.

"The Trollocs are dragging her toward the kettle," Doesine said suddenly, her voice grating. A thin keening escaped through Talene's clenched teeth; she shook so hard she seemed to vibrate. "I—I do not know if I can . . . can flaming make myself . . ."

"Bring her awake," Saerin commanded without so much as glancing at anyone else to see what they thought. "Stop sulking, Yukiri, and be ready."

The Gray gave her a proud, furious stare, but when Doesine let her weaves fade and Talene's blue eyes fluttered open, the glow of *saidar* surrounded Yukiri and she shielded the woman lying on the Chair without uttering a word. Saerin was in charge, and everyone knew it, and that was that. A very sharp thorn.

A shield hardly seemed necessary. Her face a mask of terror, Talene trembled and panted as though she had run ten miles at top speed. She still sank into the soft surface, but without Doesine channeling, it no longer formed itself to her. Talene stared at the ceiling with bulging eyes, then squeezed them shut, but they popped right open again. Whatever memories lay behind her eyelids were nothing she wanted to face.

Covering the two strides to the Chair, Pevara thrust the Oath Rod at the distraught woman. "Forswear all oaths that bind you and retake the Three Oaths, Talene," she said harshly. Talene recoiled from the Rod as from a poisonous serpent, then jerked the other way as Saerin bent over her.

"Next time, Talene, it's the cookpot for you. Or the Myrddraal's tender attentions." Saerin's face was implacable, but her tone made it seem soft by comparison. "No waking up before. And if that doesn't do, there'll be another time, and another, as many as it takes if we must stay down here until summer." Doesine opened her mouth in protest before giving over with a grimace. Only she among them knew how to operate the Chair, but in this group, she stood as low as Seaine.

Talene continued to stare up at Saerin. Tears filled her big eyes, and she began to weep, great shuddering, hopeless sobs. Blindly, she reached out, groping until Pevara stuck the Oath Rod into her hand. Embracing the Source, Pevara channeled a thread of Spirit into the Rod. Talene gripped the wrist-thick rod so hard that her knuckles turned white, yet she just lay there sobbing.

Saerin straightened. "I fear it's time to put her back to sleep, Doesine."

Talene's tears redoubled, but she mumbled through them. "I—forswear—all oaths—that bind me." With the last word, she began to howl.

Seaine jumped, then swallowed hard. She personally knew the pain of removing a single oath and had speculated on the agony of removing more than one at once, but now the reality was in front of her. Talene screamed till there was no breath left in her, then pulled in air only to scream again, until Seaine half expected people to come running down from the Tower itself. The tall Green convulsed, flinging her arms and legs about, then suddenly arched up till only her heels and head touched the gray surface, every muscle clenched, her whole body spasming wildly.

As abruptly as the seizure had begun, Talene collapsed bonelessly and lay there weeping like a lost child. The Oath Rod rolled from her limp hand down the sloping gray surface. Yukiri murmured something with the sound of a fervent prayer. Doesine kept whispering, "Light!" over and over in a shaken voice. "Light! Light!"

Pevara scooped up the Rod and closed Talene's fingers around it again. There was no mercy in Seaine's friend, not in this matter. "Now swear the Three Oaths," she spat.

For an instant, it seemed Talene might refuse, but slowly she repeated the oaths that made them all Aes Sedai and held them together. To speak no word that was not true. Never to make a weapon for one man to kill another. Never to use the One Power as a weapon except against Darkfriends or Shadowspawn, or in defense of her life, or that of her Warder or of another sister. At the end, she began weeping in silence, shaking without a sound. Perhaps it was the oaths tightening down on her. They were uncomfortable when fresh. Perhaps.

Then Pevara told the other oath they required of her. Talene flinched, but muttered the words in tones of hopelessness. "I vow to obey all five of you absolutely." Otherwise, she only stared straight ahead dully, tears trailing down her cheeks.

"Answer me truthfully," Saerin told her. "Are you of the Black Ajah?"

"I am." The words creaked, as if Talene's throat were rusty.

The simple words froze Seaine in a way she had never expected. She had set out to hunt the Black Ajah, after all, and believed in her quarry as many sisters did not. She had laid hands on another sister, on a Sitter, had helped bundle Talene along deserted basement hallways wrapped in flows of Air, had broken a dozen Tower laws, committed serious crimes, all to hear an answer she had been nearly certain of before the question was asked. Now she had heard. The Black Ajah really did exist. She was staring at a Black sister, a Darkfriend who wore the shawl. And believing turned out to be a pale shadow of confronting. Only her jaw clenched near to cramping kept her teeth from chattering. She struggled to compose herself, to think rationally. But nightmares were awake and walking the Tower.

Someone exhaled heavily, and Seaine realized she was not the only one who found her world turned upside down. Yukiri gave herself a shake, then fixed her eyes on Talene as though determined to hold the shield on her by willpower if need be. Doesine was licking her lips, and smoothing her dark golden skirts uncertainly. Only Saerin and Pevara appeared at ease.

"So," Saerin said softly. Perhaps "faintly" was a better word. "So. Black Ajah." She drew a deep breath, and her tone became brisk. "There's no more need for that, Yukiri. Talene, you won't try to escape, or resist in any way. You won't so much as touch the Source without permission from one of us. Though I suppose someone else will take this forward once we hand you over. Yukiri?" The shield on Talene dissipated, but the glow remained around Yukiri, as if she did not trust the effect of the Rod on a Black sister.

Pevara frowned. "Before we give her to Elaida, Saerin, I want to dig out as much as we can. Names, places, anything. Everything she knows!" Darkfriends had killed Pevara's entire family, and Seaine was sure she would go into exile ready to hunt down every last Black sister personally.

Still huddled on the Chair, Talene made a sound half bitter laugh, half weeping. "When you do that, we are all dead. Dead! Elaida is Black Ajah!"

"That's impossible!" Seaine burst out. "Elaida gave me the order herself."

"She must be," Doesine half whispered. "Talene's sworn the oaths again; she just named her!" Yukiri nodded vehemently.

"Use your heads," Pevara growled, shaking her own in disgust. "You know as well as I do if you believe a lie, you can say it for truth."

"And that *is* truth," Saerin said firmly. "What proof do you have, Talene? Have you seen Elaida at your . . . meetings?" She gripped her knife hilt so hard that her knuckles paled. Saerin had had to fight harder than most for the shawl, for the right to remain in the Tower at all. To her, the Tower was more than home, more important than her own life. If Talene gave the wrong answer, Elaida might not live to face trial.

"They don't have meetings," Talene muttered sullenly. "Except the Supreme Council, I suppose. But she must be. They know every report she receives, even the secret ones, every word spoken to her. They know every decision she makes before it's announced. Days before; sometimes weeks. How else, unless she tells them?" Sitting up with an effort, she tried to fix them each in turn with an intent stare. It only made her eyes seem to dart anxiously. "We have to run; we have to find a place to hide. I'll help you—tell you everything I know!—but they'll kill us unless we run."

Strange, Seaine thought, how quickly Talene had made her former cronies "they" and tried to identify herself with the rest of them. No. She was avoiding the real problem, and avoidance was witless. *Had* Elaida really set her to dig out the Black Ajah? She had never once actually mentioned the name. Could she have meant something else? Elaida had always jumped down the throat of anyone who even mentioned the Black. Nearly any sister would do the same, yet . . .

"Elaida's proven herself a fool," Saerin said, "and more than once I've regretted standing for her, but I'll not believe she's Black, not without more than that." Tight-lipped, Pevara jerked an agreeing nod. As a Red, she would want much more.

"That's as may be, Saerin," Yukiri said, "but we cannot hold Talene long before the Greens start asking where she is. Not to mention the . . . the Black. We'd better decide what to do fast, or we'll still be digging at the bottom of the well when the rains hit." Talene gave Saerin a feeble smile that was probably meant to be ingratiating. It faded under the Brown Sitter's frown.

"We don't dare tell Elaida anything until we can cripple the Black at one blow," Saerin said finally. "Don't argue, Pevara; it's sense." Pevara threw up her hands and put on a stubborn expression, but she closed her mouth. "If Talene is right," Saerin went on, "the Black knows about Seaine or soon will, so we must ensure her safety, as much as we can. That won't be easy, with only the five of us. We can't trust *anyone* until we are certain of them! At least we have Talene, and who knows what we'll learn before she's wrung out?" Talene attempted to look willing to be wrung out, but no one was paying her any mind. Seaine's throat had gone dry.

"We might not be entirely alone," Pevara said reluctantly. "Seaine, tell them your little scheme with Zerah and her friends."

"Scheme?" Saerin said. "Who's Zerah? Seaine? Seaine!"

Seaine gave a start. "What? Oh. Pevara and I uncovered a small nest of rebels here in the Tower," she began breathily. "Ten sisters sent to spread dissent." Saerin was going to make sure she was safe, was she? Without so much as asking. She was a Sitter herself; she had been Aes Sedai for almost a hundred and fifty years. What right had Saerin or anyone to . . . ? "Pevara and I have begun putting an end to that. We've already made one of them, Zerah Dacan, take the same extra oath Talene did, and told her to bring Bernaile Gelbarn to my rooms this afternoon without rousing her suspicions." Light, any sister outside this room might be Black. Any sister. "Then we will use those two to bring another, until they have all been made to swear obedience. Of course, we'll ask the same question we put to Zerah, the same we put to Talene." The Black Ajah might already have her name, already know she had been set hunting them. How could Saerin keep her safe? "Those who give the wrong answer can be questioned, and those who give the right can repay for a little of their treachery by hunting the Black under our direction." Light, how?

When she was done, the others discussed the matter at some length, which could only mean that Saerin was unsure what decision she would make. Yukiri insisted on giving Zerah and her confederates over to the law immediately—if it could be done without exposing their own situation with Talene. Pevara argued for using the rebels, though half-heartedly; the dissent they had been spreading centered around vile tales concerning the Red Ajah and false Dragons. Doesine seemed to be suggesting that they kidnap every sister in the Tower and force them all to take the added oath, but the other three paid little attention to her.

Seaine took no part in the discussion. Her reaction to their predicament was the only possible one, she thought. Tottering to the nearest corner, she vomited noisily.

Elayne tried not to grind her teeth. Outside, another blizzard pelted Caemlyn, darkening the midday sky enough that the lamps along the sitting room's paneled walls were all lit. Fierce gusts rattled the casements set into the tall arched windows. Flashes of lightning lit the clear glass panes, and thunder boomed hollowly overhead. Thunder snow, the worst kind of winter storm, the most violent. The room was not precisely cold, but . . . Spreading her fingers in front of the logs crackling in the broad marble fireplace, she could still feel a chill rising through the carpets layered over the floor tiles, and through her thickest velvet slippers, too. The wide black fox collar and cuffs on her red-and-white gown were pretty, but she was not sure they added any more to its warmth than the pearls on the sleeves. Refusing to let the cold touch her did not mean she was unaware.

Where *was* Nynaeve? And Vandene? Her thoughts snarled like the weather. *They should be here already! Light! I wish I could learn to go without sleep, and they take their sweet time!* No, that was unfair. Her formal claim for the Lion Throne was only a few days old, and for her, everything else had to take second place for the time being. Nynaeve and Vandene had other priorities; other responsibilities, as they saw them. Nynaeve was up to her neck planning with Reanne and the rest of the Knitting Circle how to spirit Kinswomen out of Seanchan-controlled lands before they were discovered and collared. The Kin were very good at staying low, but the Seanchan would not just pass them by for wilders the way Aes Sedai always had. Supposedly, Vandene was still shaken by her sister's murder, barely eating and hardly able to give advice of any sort. The barely eating part was true, but finding the killer consumed her. Supposedly walking the halls in grief at odd hours, she was secretly hunting the Darkfriend among them. Three days earlier, just the thought of that could make Elayne shiver; now, it was one danger among many. More intimate than most, true, but only most.

They were doing important tasks, approved and encouraged by Egwene, but she still wished they would hurry, selfish though it might be. Vandene had a wealth of good advice, the advantage of long experience and study, and Nynaeve's years dealing with the Village Council and the Women's Circle back in Emond's Field gave her a keen eye for practical politics, however much she denied it. *Burn me, I have a hundred problems, some right here in the Palace, and I* need *them!* If she had *her* way, Nynaeve al'Meara was going to be the Aes Sedai advisor to the next Queen of Andor. She needed all the help she could find—help she could trust.

Smoothing her face, she turned away from the blazing hearth. Thirteen tall armchairs, carved simply but with a fine hand, made a horseshoe arc in front of the fireplace. Paradoxically, the place of honor, where the Queen would sit if receiving here, stood farthest from the fire's heat. Such as it was. Her back began to warm immediately, and her front to cool. Outside, snow fell, thunder crashed and lightning flared. Inside her head, too. Calm. A ruler had as much need of calm as any Aes Sedai.

"It must be the mercenaries," she said, not quite managing to keep regret out of her voice. Armsmen from her estates surely would begin arriving inside a month—once they learned she was alive—but it might be spring before any significant numbers came, and the men Birgitte was recruiting would require half a year or more before they were fit to ride and handle a sword at the same time. "And Hunters for the Horn, if any will sign and swear." There were plenty of both trapped in Caemlyn by the weather. Too many of both, most people said, carousing, brawling, troubling women who wanted no part of their attentions. At least she would be putting them to good use, to stop trouble instead of beginning it. She wished she did not think she was still trying to convince herself of that. "Expensive, but the coffers will cover it." For a little while, they would. She had better start receiving revenues from her estates soon.

Wonder of wonders, the two women standing before her reacted in much the same fashion.

Dyelin gave an irritated grunt. A large, round silver pin worked with Taravin's Owl and Oak was fastened at the high neck of her dark green dress, her only jewelry. A show of pride in her House, perhaps too much pride; the High Seat of House Taravin was a proud woman altogether. Gray streaked her golden hair and fine lines webbed the corners of her eyes, yet her face was strong, her gaze level and sharp. Her mind was a razor. Or maybe a sword. A plainspoken woman, or so it seemed, who did not hide her opinions.

"Mercenaries know the work," she said dismissively, "but they are hard to control, Elayne. When you need a feather touch, they're liable to be a hammer, and when you need a hammer, they're liable to be elsewhere, and stealing to boot. They are loyal to gold, and only as long as the gold lasts. If they don't betray for more gold first. I'm sure this once Lady Birgitte will agree with me."

Arms folded tightly beneath her breasts and heeled boots planted wide, Birgitte grimaced, as always when anyone used her new title. Elayne had granted her an estate as soon as they reached Caemlyn, where it could be registered. In private, Birgitte grumbled incessantly over that, *and* the other change in her life. Her sky-blue trousers were cut the same as those she usually wore, billowing and gathered at the ankles, but her short red coat had a high white collar, and wide white cuffs banded with gold. She was the Lady Birgitte Trahelion *and* the Captain-General of the Queen's Guard, and she could mutter and whine all she wanted, so long as she kept it private.

"I do," she growled unwillingly, and gave Dyelin a not-quite-sidelong glare. The Warder bond carried what Elayne had been sensing all morning. Frustration, irritation, determination. Some of that might have been a reflection of herself, though. They mirrored each other in surprising ways since the bonding, emotionally and otherwise. Why, her courses had shifted by more than a week to match the other woman's!

Birgitte's reluctance to take the second-best argument was clearly almost as great as her reluctance to agree. "Hunters aren't much bloody better, Elayne," she muttered. "They took the Hunter's Oath to find adventure, and a place in the histories if they can. Not to settle down keeping the law. Half are supercilious prigs, looking down their flaming noses at everyone else; the rest don't just take necessary chances, they look for chances to take. And one whisper of a rumor of the Horn of Valere, and you'll be lucky if only two in three vanish overnight."

Dyelin smiled a thin smile, as though she had won a point. Oil and water were not in it compared to those two; each managed well enough with nearly anyone else, but for some reason they could argue over the color of charcoal. Could and would. "Besides, Hunters and mercenaries alike, nearly all are foreigners. That will sit poorly with high and low alike. Very poorly. The last thing you want is to start a rebellion." Lightning flared, briefly lighting the casements, and a particularly loud peal of thunder punctuated her words. In a thousand years, seven Queens of Andor had been toppled by open rebellion, and the two who survived probably wished they had not.

Elayne stifled a sigh. One of the small inlaid tables along the walls held a heavy silver ropework tray with cups and a tall pitcher of hot spiced wine. Lukewarm spiced wine, now. She channeled briefly, Fire, and a thin wisp of steam rose from the pitcher. Reheating gave the spices a slight bitterness, but the warmth of the worked-silver cup in her hands was worth it. With an effort she resisted the desire to heat the air in the room with the Power and released the Source; the warmth would not have lasted unless she maintained the weaves, anyway. She had conquered her unwillingness to let go every time she took in *saidar*—well, to some extent—yet of late, the desire to draw more grew every time. Every sister had to face that dangerous desire. A gesture brought the others to pour their own wine.

"You know the situation," she told them. "Only a fool could think it anything but dire, and you're neither of you fools." The Guards were a shell, a handful of acceptable men and a double handful of strongarms and toughs better suited to throwing drunks out of taverns, or being thrown out themselves. And with the Saldaeans gone and the Aiel leaving, crime was blooming like weeds in spring. She would have thought the snow would damp it down, but every day brought robbery, arson and worse. Every day, the situation *grew* worse. "At this rate, we'll see riots in a few weeks. Maybe sooner. If I can't keep order in Caemlyn itself, the people *will* turn against me." If she could not keep order in the capital, she might as well announce to the world that she was unfit to rule. "I don't like it, but it has to be done, so it will be." Both opened their mouths, ready to argue further, but she gave them no chance. She made her voice firm. "It will be done."

Birgitte's waist-long golden braid swung as she shook her head, yet grudging acceptance filtered through the bond. She took a decidedly odd view of their relationship as Aes Sedai and Warder, but she had learned to recognize when Elayne would not be pressed. After a fashion she had learned. There was the estate and title. And commanding the Guards. And a few other small matters.

Dyelin bent her neck a fraction, and perhaps her knees; it might have been a curtsy, yet her face was stone. It was well to remember that many who did not want Elayne Trakand on the Lion Throne wanted Dyelin Taravin instead. The woman had been nothing but helpful, but it was early days yet, and sometimes a niggling voice whispered in the back of Elayne's head. Was Dyelin simply waiting for her to bungle badly before stepping in to "save" Andor? Someone sufficiently prudent, sufficiently devious, might try that route, and might even succeed.

Elayne raised a hand to rub her temple but made it into adjusting her hair. So much suspicion, so little trust. The Game of Houses had infected Andor since she left for Tar Valon. She was grateful for her months among Aes Sedai for more than learning the Power. *Daes Dae'mar* was breath and bread, to most sisters. Grateful for Thom's teaching, too. Without both, she might not have survived her return as long as she had. The Light send Thom was safe, that he and Mat and the others had escaped the Seanchan and were on their way to Caemlyn. Every day since leaving Ebou Dar she prayed for their safety, but that brief prayer was all she had time for, now.

Taking the chair at the center of the arc, the Queen's chair, she tried to look like a queen, back straight, her free hand resting lightly on the carved chair arm. *Looking a queen is not enough,* her mother had told her often, *but a fine mind, a keen grasp of affairs, and a brave heart will go for nothing if people do not see you as a queen.* Birgitte was watching her closely, almost suspiciously. Sometimes the bond was decidedly inconvenient! Dyelin raised her winecup to her lips.

Elayne took a deep breath. She had harried this question from every direction she knew, and she could see no other way. "Birgitte, by spring, I want the Guards to be an army equal to anything *ten* Houses can put in the field." Impossible to achieve, likely, but just trying meant keeping the mercenaries who signed now and finding more, signing every man who showed the least inclination. Light, what a foul tangle!

Dyelin choked, her eyes bulging; dark wine sprayed from her mouth. Still spluttering, she plucked a lace-edged handkerchief from her sleeve and dabbed at her chin.

A wave of panic shot down the bond from Birgitte. "Oh, burn me, Elayne, you can't mean . . . ! I'm am archer, not a general! That's all I've ever been, don't you understand yet? I just did what I had to do, what circumstances forced on me! Anyway, I'm not her, anymore; I'm just me, and . . . !" She trailed off, realizing she might have said too much. Not for the first time. Her face went crimson as Dyelin eyed her curiously.

They had put it about that Birgitte was from Kandor, where country women wore something like her clothes, yet Dyelin clearly suspected the lie. And every time Birgitte let her tongue slip, she came closer to letting her secret slip, too. Elayne shot her a look that promised a talking-to, later.

She would not have thought Birgitte's cheeks could get any redder. Mortification drowned everything else in the bond, flooding through until Elayne felt her own face coloring.

Quickly she put on a stern expression, hoping her crimson cheeks would pass for something other than an intense desire to squirm in her seat with *Birgitte's* humiliation. That mirroring effect could be *more* than merely inconvenient!

Dyelin wasted only a moment on Birgitte. Tucking her handkerchief back in its place, she carefully set her cup back on the tray, then planted her hands on her hips. Her face was a thunderhead, now. "The Guards have always been the *core* of Andor's army, Elayne, but this. . . . Light's mercy, this is madness! You could turn every hand against you from the River Erinin to the Mountains of Mist!"

Elayne focused on calm. If she was wrong, Andor would become another Cairhien, another blood-soaked land filled with chaos. And she would die, of course, a price not high enough to meet the cost. Not trying was unthinkable and in any case would have the same result for Andor as failure. Cool, composed, steely calm. A queen could not show herself afraid, even when she was. Especially when she was. Her mother had always said to explain decisions as seldom as possible; the more often you explained, the more explanations were necessary, until they were all you had time for. Gareth Bryne said to explain if you could; your people did better if they knew the why as well as the what. Today, she would follow Gareth Bryne. A good many victories had been won by following him.

"I have three declared challengers." And maybe one not declared. She made herself meet Dyelin's gaze. Not angrily; just eyes meeting eyes. Or maybe Dyelin did take it for anger, with her jaw tight and her face flushed. If so, so be it. "By herself, Arymilla is negligible, but Nasin has joined House Caeren to her, and whether or not he's sane, his support means she must be considered. Naean and Elenia are imprisoned; their armsmen are not. Naean's people may dither and argue until they find a leader, but Jarid is High Seat of Sarand, and he will take chances to feed his wife's ambition. House Baryn and House Anshar flirt with both; the *best* I can hope is that one goes with Sarand and one with Arawn. Nineteen Houses in Andor are strong enough that smaller Houses will follow where they lead. Six are arrayed against me, and I have two." Six so far, and the Light send she had two! She would not mention the three great Houses that had all but declared for

Dyelin; at least Egwene had them tied down in Murandy for now.

She motioned to a chair near her, and Dyelin sat, carefully arranging her skirts. The storm clouds had left the older woman's face. She studied Elayne, giving no hint as to her questions or conclusions. "I know all that as well as you, Elayne, but Luan and Ellorien will bring their Houses to you, and Abelle will as well, I'm sure." A careful voice, too, but it gathered heat as she went on. "Other Houses will see reason, then. As long as you don't frighten them *out* of reason. Light, Elayne, this is not a Succession. Trakand succeeds Trakand, not another House. Even a Succession has seldom come to open fighting! Make the Guards into an army, and you risk everything."

Elayne threw her head back, but her laughter held no amusement. It fit right in with the peals of thunder. "I risked everything the day I came home, Dyelin. You say Norwelyn and Traemane will come to me, and Pendar? Fine; then I have five to face six. I don't think the other Houses will 'see reason,' as you put it. If any of them move before it's clear as good glass the Rose Crown is mine, it will be against me, not for." With luck, those lords and ladies would shy away from associating with cronies of Gaebril, but she did not like depending on luck. She was not Mat Cauthon. Light, most people were sure Rand had killed her mother, and few believed that "Lord Gaebril" had been one of the Forsaken. Mending the damage Rahvin had done in Andor might take her entire lifetime even if she managed to live as long as the Kinswomen! Some Houses would stand aside from supporting her because of the outrages Gaebril had perpetrated in Morgase's name, and others because Rand had said he intended to "give" her the throne. She loved the man to her toes, but *burn* him for giving voice to *that*! Even if it was what reined in Dyelin. The meanest crofter in Andor would shoulder his scythe to pull a puppet from the Lion Throne!

"I want to avoid Andoran killing Andoran if I can, Dyelin, but Succession or no Succession, Jarid is ready to fight, even with Elenia locked away. Naean is ready to fight." Best to bring both women to Caemlyn as soon as possible; too much chance of them slipping messages, and orders, out of Aringill. "*Arymilla* is ready, with Nasin's men behind her. To them, this *is* a Succession, and the only way to *stop* them from fighting is to be so strong they don't dare. If Birgitte can build the Guards into an army by spring, well and good, because if I don't have an army before then, I *will* have need of one. And if that isn't enough, remember the Seanchan. They won't be satisfied with Tanchico and Ebou Dar; they want everything. I won't let them have Andor, Dyelin, any more than I'll let Arymilla." Thunder roared overhead.

Twisting a little to look back at Birgitte, Dyelin moistened her lips. Her fingers plucked unconsciously at her skirts. Very little frightened her, but tales of the Seanchan had. What she murmured, though, as if to herself, was, "I had hoped to avoid outright civil war." And *that* might mean nothing, or a great deal! Perhaps a little probing might show which.

"Gawyn," Birgitte said suddenly. Her expression had lightened, and so had the emotions flowing though the bond. Relief stood out strong. "When he comes, he'll take command. He'll be your First Prince of the Sword."

"Mother's milk in a cup!" Elayne snapped, and lightning flared in the windows for emphasis. Why did the woman have to change the subject *now*? Dyelin gave a start, and heat flooded back into Elayne's face. By the older woman's gaping mouth, she knew exactly how coarse that curse was. Strangely embarrassing, that; it should not have counted for anything that Dyelin had been her mother's friend. Unthinking, she took a deep swallow of wine—and nearly gagged at the bitterness. Quickly she suppressed images of Lini threatening to wash out her mouth and reminded herself that she was a grown woman with a throne to win. She doubted her mother had ever found herself feeling foolish so often.

"Yes, he will, Birgitte," she went on, more calmly. "When he comes." Three couriers were on their way to Tar Valon. Even if none managed to get past Elaida, Gawyn would learn eventually that she had made her claim, and he would come. She needed him desperately. She had no illusions of herself as a general, and Birgitte was so fearful she could not live up to the legends about her that sometimes she seemed afraid to try. Face an army, yes; lead an army, never under the sun!

Birgitte was well aware of the tangle in her own mind. Right that moment her face was frozen, but her emotions were full of self-anger and embarrassment, with the first growing stronger by the moment. With a stab of irritation, Elayne opened her mouth to pursue Dyelin's mention of civil war before she began reflecting Birgitte's anger.

Before she could utter a word, though, the tall red doors opened. Her hopes for Nynaeve or Vandene were dashed by the entrance of two Sea Folk women, barefoot despite the weather.

About the Author

Robert Jordan was born in 1948 in Charleston, South Carolina. He taught himself to read when he was four with the incidental aid of a twelve-years-older brother, and was tackling Mark Twain and Jules Verne by five. He was a graduate of the Citadel, the Military College of South Carolina, with a degree in physics. He served two tours in Vietnam with the U.S. Army; among his decorations are the Distinguished Flying Cross with bronze oak leaf cluster, the Bronze Star with "V" and bronze oak leaf cluster, and two Vietnamese Gallantry Crosses with Palm. A history buff, he also wrote dance and theater criticism. He enjoyed the outdoor sports of hunting, fishing, and sailing, and the indoor sports of poker, chess, pool, and pipe collecting. He began writing in 1977 and continued until his death on September 16, 2007.